John Greenleaf Whittier

The Complete Poetical Works of John Greenleaf Whittier

John Greenleaf Whittier

The Complete Poetical Works of John Greenleaf Whittier

ISBN/EAN: 9783337398514

Printed in Europe, USA, Canada, Australia, Japan

Cover: Foto ©Andreas Hilbeck / pixelio.de

More available books at **www.hansebooks.com**

THE

COMPLETE POETICAL WORKS

OF

JOHN GREENLEAF WHITTIER.

HOUSEHOLD EDITION.

BOSTON:
HOUGHTON, OSGOOD AND COMPANY.
Cambridge: The Riverside Press.
1879.

NOTE BY THE AUTHOR

TO THE EDITION OF 1857.

IN these volumes, for the first time, a complete collection of my poetical writings has been made. While it is satisfactory to know that these scattered children of my brain have found a home, I cannot but regret that I have been unable, by reason of illness, to give that attention to their revision and arrangement, which respect for the opinions of others and my own afterthought and experience demand.

That there are pieces in this collection which I would "willingly let die," I am free to confess. But it is now too late to disown them, and I must submit to the inevitable penalty of poetical as well as other sins. There are others, intimately connected with the author's life and times, which owe their tenacity of vitality to the circumstances under which they were written, and the events by which they were suggested.

The long poem of Mogg Megone was in a great measure composed in early life ; and it is scarcely necessary to say that its subject is not such as the writer would have chosen at any subsequent period.

J. G. W.

AMESBURY, 18th 3d mo., 1857.

PROEM.

I LOVE the old melodious lays
Which softly melt the ages through,
    The songs of Spenser's golden days,
    Arcadian Sidney's silvery phrase,
Sprinkling our noon of time with freshest morning dew.

    Yet, vainly in my quiet hours
To breathe their marvellous notes I try ;
    I feel them, as the leaves and flowers
    In silence feel the dewy showers,
And drink with glad still lips the blessing of the sky.

    The rigor of a frozen clime,
The harshness of an untaught ear,
    The jarring words of one whose rhyme
    Beat often Labor's hurried time,
Or Duty's rugged march through storm and strife, are here.

    Of mystic beauty, dreamy grace,
No rounded art the lack supplies ;
    Unskilled the subtle lines to trace,
    Or softer shades of Nature's face,
I view her common forms with unanointed eyes.

    Nor mine the seer-like power to show
The secrets of the heart and mind ;
    To drop the plummet-line below
    Our common world of joy and woe,
A more intense despair or brighter hope to find.

    Yet here at least an earnest sense
Of human right and weal is shown ;
    A hate of tyranny intense,
    And hearty in its vehemence,
As if my brother's pain and sorrow were my own.

    O Freedom ! if to me belong
Nor mighty Milton's gift divine,
    Nor Marvell's wit and graceful song,
    Still with a love as deep and strong
As theirs, I lay, like them, my best gifts on thy shrine !

AMESBURY, 11th mo., 1847

CONTENTS.

MOGG MEGONE.

[The story of Mogg Megone has been considered by the author only as a framework for sketches of the scenery of New England, and of its early inhabitants. In portraying the Indian character, he has followed, as closely as his story would admit, the rough but natural delineations of Church, Mayhew, Charlevoix, and Roger Williams; and in so doing he has necessarily discarded much of the romance which poets and novelists have thrown around the ill-fated red man.]

PART I.

Who stands on that cliff, like a figure
    of stone,
  Unmoving and tall in the light of the
    sky,
  Where the spray of the cataract spar-
    kles on high,
Lonely and sternly, save Mogg Me-
    gone ?[1]
Close to the verge of the rock is he,
  While beneath him the Saco its work
    is doing,
Hurrying down to its grave, the sea,
  And slow through the rock its path-
    way hewing !
Far down, through the mist of the fall-
    ing river,
Which rises up like an incense ever,
The splintered points of the crags are
    seen,
With water howling and vexed between,
While the scooping whirl of the pool be-
    neath
Seems an open throat, with its granite
    teeth !

But Mogg Megone never trembled yet
Wherever his eye or his foot was set.
He is watchful : each form in the moon-
    light dim,
Of rock or of tree, is seen of him :
He listens ; each sound from afar is
    caught,
The faintest shiver of leaf and limb :
But he sees not the waters, which foam
    and fret,

Whose moonlit spray has his moccasin
    wet, —
And the roar of their rushing, he hears
    it not.

The moonlight, through the open bough
  Of the gnarl'd beech, whose naked
    root
  Coils like a serpent at his foot,
Falls, checkered, on the Indian's brow.
His head is bare, save only where
Waves in the wind one lock of hair,
  Reserved for him, whoe'er he be,
More mighty than Megone in strife,
  When breast to breast and knee to
    knee,
Above the fallen warrior's life
Gleams, quick and keen, the scalping-
    knife.

Megone hath his knife and hatchet and
    gun,
And his gaudy and tasselled blanket
    on :
His knife hath a handle with gold inlaid,
And magic words on its polished blade, —
'T was the gift of Castine[2] to Mogg Me-
    gone,
For a scalp or twain from the Yengees
    torn :
His gun was the gift of the Tarrantine,
  And Modocawando's wives had strung
The brass and the beads, which tinkle
    and shine
On the polished breach, and broad bright
    line
  Of beaded wampum around it hung.

What seeks Megone? His foes are
  near —
  Grey Jocelyn's eye is never sleeping,
And the garrison lights are burning
  clear,
  Where Phillips'[4] men their watch are
  keeping.
Let him hie him away through the dank
  river fog,
  Never rustling the boughs nor dis-
  placing the rocks,
For the eyes and the ears which are
  watching for Mogg
  Are keener than those of the wolf or
  the fox.

He starts, — there's a rustle among the
  leaves :
  Another, — the click of his gun is
  heard !
A footstep, — is it the step of Cleaves,
  With Indian blood on his English
  sword ?
Steals Harmon[5] down from the sands of
  York,
With hand of iron and foot of cork ?
Has Scamman, versed in Indian wile,
For vengeance left his vine-hung isle ?[6]
Hark ! at that whistle, soft and low,
  How lights the eye of Mogg Megone !
A smile gleams o'er his dusky brow, —
  "Boon welcome, Johnny Bonython !"

Out steps, with cautious foot and slow,
And quick, keen glances to and fro,
  The hunted outlaw, Bonython ![7]
A low, lean, swarthy man is he,
With blanket-garb and buskined knee,
  And naught of English fashion on ;
For he hates the race from whence he
  sprung,
And he couches his words in the Indian
  tongue.

"Hush, — let the Sachem's voice be
  weak ;
The water-rat shall hear him speak, —
The owl shall whoop in the white man's
  ear,
That Mogg Megone, with his scalps, is
  here !"
He pauses, — dark, over cheek and
  brow,
A flush, as of shame, is stealing now :
"Sachem !" he says, "let me have the
  land,
Which stretches away upon either hand,

As far about as my feet can stray
In the half of a gentle summer's day,
  From the leaping brook[8] to the Saco
  river, —
And the fair-haired girl, thou hast sought
  of me,
Shall sit in the Sachem's wigwam, and be
  The wife of Mogg Megone forever."

There's a sudden light in the Indian's
  glance,
  A moment's trace of powerful feeling,
Of love or triumph, or both perchance,
  Over his proud, calm features steal-
  ing.
"The words of my father are very good ;
He shall have the land, and water, and
  wood ;
And he who harms the Sagamore John,
Shall feel the knife of Mogg Megone ;
But the fawn of the Yengees shall sleep
  on my breast,
And the bird of the clearing shall sing
  in my nest."

"But, father !" — and the Indian's hand
  Falls gently on the white man's arm,
And with a smile as shrewdly bland
  As the deep voice is slow and calm, —
"Where is my father's singing-bird, —
  The sunny eye, and sunset hair ?
I know I have my father's word,
  And that his word is good and fair ;
But will my father tell me where
Megone shall go and look for his
  bride ? —
For he sees her not by her father's side."

The dark, stern eye of Bonython
  Flashes over the features of Mogg Me-
  gone,
  In one of those glances which search
  within ;
But the stolid calm of the Indian alone
  Remains where the trace of emotion
  has been.
"Does the Sachem doubt ? Let him
  go with me,
And the eyes of the Sachem his bride
  shall see."

Cautious and slow, with pauses oft,
And watchful eyes and whispers soft,
The twain are stealing through the wood,
Leaving the downward-rushing flood,
Whose deep and solemn roar behind
Grows fainter on the evening wind.

Hark ! — is that the angry howl
  Of the wolf, the hills among ? —
Or the hooting of the owl,
  On his leafy cradle swung ? —
Quickly glancing, to and fro,
Listening to each sound they go
Round the columns of the pine,
  Indistinct, in shadow, seeming
Like some old and pillared shrine ;
  With the soft and white moonshine,
Round the foliage-tracery shed
  Of each column's branching head,
  For its lamps of worship gleaming !
And the sounds awakened there,
  In the pine-leaves fine and small,
  Soft and sweetly musical,
By the fingers of the air,
For the anthem's dying fall
Lingering round some temple's wall !
Niche and cornice round and round
Wailing like the ghost of sound !
Is not Nature's worship thus,
  Ceaseless ever, going on ?
Hath it not a voice for us
  In the thunder, or the tone
Of the leaf-harp faint and small,
  Speaking to the unsealed ear
  Words of blended love and fear,
Of the mighty Soul of all ?

Naught had the twain of thoughts like
  these
As they wound along through the
  crowded trees,
Where never had rung the axeman's stroke
On the gnarled trunk of the rough-barked
  oak ; —
Climbing the dead tree's mossy log,
  Breaking the mesh of the bramble fine,
Turning aside the wild grapevine,
And lightly crossing the quaking bog
Whose surface shakes at the leap of the
  frog,
And out of whose pools the ghostly fog
  Creeps into the chill moonshine !
Yet, even that Indian's ear had heard
The preaching of the Holy Word :
Sanchekantacket's isle of sand
Was once his father's hunting land,
Where zealous Hiacoomes [9] stood, —
The wild apostle of the wood,
Shook from his soul the fear of harm,
And trampled on the Powwaw's charm ;
Until the wizard's curses hung
Suspended on his palsying tongue,
And the fierce warrior, grim and tall,
Trembled before the forest Paul !

A cottage hidden in the wood, —
  Red through its seams a light is glowing,
On rock and bough and tree-trunk rude,
  A narrow lustre throwing.
" Who 's there ? " a clear, firm voice
  demands ;
  " Hold, Ruth, — 't is I, the Saga-
  more ! "
Quick, at the summons, hasty hands
  Unclose the bolted door ;
And on the outlaw's daughter shine
The flashes of the kindled pine.

Tall and erect the maiden stands,
  Like some young priestess of the wood,
  The freeborn child of Solitude,
  And bearing still the wild and rude,
Yet noble trace of Nature's hands.
Her dark brown cheek has caught its stain
More from the sunshine than the rain ;
Yet, where her long fair hair is parting,
A pure white brow into light is starting ;
And, where the folds of her blanket sever,
Are a neck and bosom as white as ever
The foam-wreaths rise on the leaping river.
But in the convulsive quiver and grip
Of the muscles around her bloodless lip,
  There is something painful and sad to
  see ;
And her eye has a glance more sternly
  wild
Than even that of a forest child
  In its fearless and untamed freedom
  should be.
Yet, seldom in hall or court are seen
So queenly a form and so noble a mien,
  As freely and smiling she welcomes
  them there, —
Her outlawed sire and Mogg Megone :
  " Pray, father, how does thy hunting
  fare ?
  And, Sachem, say, — does Scamman
  wear,
In spite of thy promise, a scalp of his
  own ? "
Hurried and light is the maiden's tone ;
  But a fearful meaning lurks within
Her glance, as it questions the eye of
  Megone, —
  An awful meaning of guilt and sin ! —
The Indian hath opened his blanket, and
  there
Hangs a human scalp by its long damp
  hair !
With hand upraised, with quick-drawn
  breath,
She meets that ghastly sign of death.

In one long, glassy, spectral stare
The enlarging eye is fastened there,
As if that mesh of pale brown hair
  Had power to change at sight alone,
Even as the fearful locks which wound
Medusa's fatal forehead round,
  The gazer into stone.
With such a look Herodias read
The features of the bleeding head,
So looked the mad Moor on his dead,
Or the young Cenci as she stood,
O'er-dabbled with a father's blood !

Look !—feeling melts that frozen glance,
It moves that marble countenance,
As if at once within her strove
Pity with shame, and hate with love.
The Past recalls its joy and pain,
Old memories rise before her brain, —
The lips which love's embraces met,
The hand her tears of parting wet,
The voice whose pleading tones beguiled
The pleased ear of the forest-child, —
And tears she may no more repress
Reveal her lingering tenderness.

O, woman wronged can cherish hate
  More deep and dark than manhood may ;
But when the mockery of Fate
  Hath left Revenge its chosen way,
And the fell curse, which years have
  nursed,
Full on the spoiler's head hath burst, —
When all her wrong, and shame, and pain,
Burns fiercely on his heart and brain, —
Still lingers something of the spell
  Which bound her to the traitor's
  bosom, —
Still, midst the vengeful fires of hell,
  Some flowers of old affection blossom.

John Bonython's eyebrows together are
  drawn
With a fierce expression of wrath and
  scorn, —
He hoarsely whispers, "Ruth, beware !
  Is this the time to be playing the fool, —
Crying over a paltry lock of hair,
  Like a love-sick girl at school ? —
Curse on it !—an Indian can see and
  hear :
Away, — and prepare our evening cheer !"

How keenly the Indian is watching now
Her tearful eye and her varying brow, —
  With a serpent eye, which kindles
  and burns,

Like a fiery star in the upper air :
On sire and daughter his fierce glance
  turns : —
  " Has my old white father a scalp to
  spare ?
For his young one loves the pale
  brown hair
Of the scalp of an English dog far more
Than Mogg Megone, or his wigwam floor ;
  Go, — Mogg is wise : he will keep his
  land, —
  And Sagamore John, when he feels
  with his hand,
Shall miss his scalp where it grew before."

The moment's gust of grief is gone, —
  The lip is clenched, — the tears are
  still, —
God pity thee, Ruth Bonython !
  With what a strength of will
Are nature's feelings in thy breast,
As with an iron hand, repressed !
And how, upon that nameless woe,
Quick as the pulse can come and go,
While shakes the unsteadfast knee, and
  yet
The bosom heaves, — the eye is wet, —
Has thy dark spirit power to stay
The heart's wild current on its way ?
  And whence that baleful strength of
  guile,
Which over that still working brow
And tearful eye and cheek can throw
  The mockery of a smile ?
Warned by her father's blackening frown,
With one strong effort crushing down
Grief, hate, remorse, she meets again
  The savage murderer's sullen gaze,
  And scarcely look or tone betrays
How the heart strives beneath its chain.

"Is the Sachem angry, — angry with
  Ruth,
Because she cries with an ache in her
  tooth,[10]
Which would make a Sagamore jump
  and cry,
And look about with a woman's eye ?
No, — Ruth will sit in the Sachem's
  door
And braid the mats for his wigwam floor,
And broil his fish and tender fawn,
And weave his wampum, and grind his
  corn, —
For she loves the brave and the wise,
  and none
Are braver and wiser than Mogg Megone !"

The Indian's brow is clear once more :
  With grave, calm face, and half-shut
    eye,
He sits upon the wigwam floor,
  And watches Ruth go by,
Intent upon her household care ;
  And ever and anon, the while,
Or on the maiden, or her fare,
Which smokes in grateful promise there,
  Bestows his quiet smile.

Ah, Mogg Megone ! — what dreams are
    thine,
  But those which love's own fancies
    dress, —
    The sum of Indian happiness ! —
A wigwam, where the warm sunshine
Looks in among the groves of pine, —
A stream, where, round thy light canoe,
The trout and salmon dart in view,
And the fair girl, before thee now,
Spreading thy mat with hand of snow,
Or plying, in the dews of morn,
Her hoe amidst thy patch of corn,
Or offering up, at eve, to thee,
Thy birchen dish of hominy !

From the rude board of Bonython,
Venison and succotash have gone, —
For long these dwellers of the wood
Have felt the gnawing want of food.
But untasted of Ruth is the frugal cheer, —
With head averted, yet ready ear,
She stands by the side of her austere
    sire,
Feeding, at times, the unequal fire
With the yellow knots of the pitch-pine
    tree,
Whose flaring light, as they kindle, falls
On the cottage-roof, and its black log
    walls,
And over its inmates three.

From Sagamore Bonython's hunting flask
  The fire-water burns at the lip of Me-
    gone :
" Will the Sachem hear what his father
    shall ask ?
  Will he make his mark, that it may
    be known,
On the speaking-leaf, that he gives the
    land,
From the Sachem's own, to his father's
    hand ? "
The fire-water shines in the Indian's eyes,
  As he rises, the white man's bidding
    to do :

" Wuttamuttata — weekan ! [11] Mogg is
    wise, —
  For the water he drinks is strong and
    new, —
Mogg's heart is great ! — will he shut his
    hand,
When his father asks for a little land ?"—
With unsteady fingers, the Indian has
    drawn
  On the parchment the shape of a
    hunter's bow,
" Boon water, — boon water, — Saga-
    more John !
  Wuttamuttata, — weekan ! our hearts
    will grow ! "
He drinks yet deeper, — he mutters
    low,
He reels on his bear-skin to and fro, —
His head falls down on his naked
    breast, —
He struggles, and sinks to a drunken rest.

" Humph — drunk as a beast ! " — and
    Bonython's brow
  Is darker than ever with evil thought—
" The fool has signed his warrant ; but
    how
  And when shall the deed be wrought ?
Speak, Ruth ! why, what the devil is
    there,
To fix thy gaze in that empty air ? —
Speak, Ruth ! by my soul, if I thought
    that tear,
Which shames thyself and our purpose
    here,
Were shed for that cursed and pale-
    faced dog,
Whose green scalp hangs from the belt
    of Mogg,
  And whose beastly soul is in Satan's
    keeping, —
This — this ! " — he dashes his hand
    upon
The rattling stock of his loaded gun, —
  " Should send thee with him to do
    thy weeping ! "

" Father ! " — the eye of Bonython
Sinks at that low, sepulchral tone,
Hollow and deep, as it were spoken
  By the unmoving tongue of death, —
Or from some statue's lips had broken, —
  A sound without a breath !
" Father ! — my life I value less
Than yonder fool his gaudy dress ;
And how it ends it matters not,
By heart-break or by rifle-shot ;

But spare awhile the scoff and threat, —
Our business is not finished yet."

"True, true, my girl, — I only meant
To draw up again the bow unbent.
Harm thee, my Ruth! I only sought
To frighten off thy gloomy thought;
Come, — let's be friends!" He seeks
    to clasp
His daughter's cold, damp hand in his.
Ruth startles from her father's grasp,
As if each nerve and muscle felt,
Instinctively, the touch of guilt,
Through all their subtle sympathies.

He points her to the sleeping Mogg:
"What shall be done with yonder dog?
Scamman is dead, and revenge is thine, —
The deed is signed and the land is mine;
    And this drunken fool is of use no more,
Save as thy hopeful bridegroom, and
    sooth,
'T were Christian mercy to finish him,
    Ruth,
Now, while he lies like a beast on our
    floor, —
If not for thine, at least for his sake,
Rather than let the poor dog awake
To drain my flask, and claim as his bride
Such a forest devil to run by his side, —
Such a Wetuomanit [12] as thou wouldst
    make!"

He laughs at his jest.   Hush — what is
    there? —
    The sleeping Indian is striving to rise,
    With his knife in his hand, and glar-
        ing eyes! —
"Wagh! — Mogg will have the pale-
    face's hair,
    For his knife is sharp, and his fingers
        can help
The hair to pull and the skin to peel, —
Let him cry like a woman and twist like
    an eel,
    The great Captain Scamman must lose
        his scalp!
And Ruth, when she sees it, shall dance
    with Mogg."
His eyes are fixed, — but his lips draw
    in, —
With a low, hoarse chuckle, and fiendish
    grin, —
And he sinks again, like a senseless log.

Ruth does not speak, — she does not stir;
But she gazes down on the murderer,
Whose broken and dreamful slumbers tell
Too much for her ear of that deed of hell.
She sees the knife, with its slaughter red,
And the dark fingers clenching the bear-
    skin bed!
What thoughts of horror and madness
    whirl
Through the burning brain of that fallen
    girl!

John Bonython lifts his gun to his eye,
    Its muzzle is close to the Indian's ear, —
But he drops it again.   "Some one may
    be nigh,
    And I would not that even the wolves
        should hear."
He draws his knife from its deer-skin
    belt, —
Its edge with his fingers is slowly felt; —
Kneeling down on one knee, by the In-
    dian's side,
From his throat he opens the blanket
    wide;
And twice or thrice he feebly essays
A trembling hand with the knife to raise.

"I cannot," — he mutters, — "did he
    not save
My life from a cold and wintry grave,
When the storm came down from Agioo-
    chook,
And the north-wind howled, and the
    tree-tops shook, —
And I strove, in the drifts of the rush-
    ing snow,
Till my knees grew weak and I could
    not go,
And I felt the cold to my vitals creep,
And my heart's blood stiffen, and pulses
    sleep!
I cannot strike him — Ruth Bonython!
In the Devil's name, tell me — what's
    to be done?"

O, when the soul, once pure and high,
Is stricken down from Virtue's sky,
As, with the downcast star of morn,
Some gems of light are with it drawn, —
And, through its night of darkness, play
Some tokens of its primal day, —
Some lofty feelings linger still, —
    The strength to dare, the nerve to meet
    Whatever threatens with defeat
Its all-indomitable will! —
But lacks the mean of mind and heart,
    Though eager for the gains of crime,
    Oft, at his chosen place and time,

The strength to bear his evil part ;
And, shielded by his very Vice,
Escapes from Crime by Cowardice.

Ruth starts erect, — with bloodshot eye,
  And lips drawn tight across her teeth,
Showing their locked embrace beneath,
In the red firelight :— "Mogg must die !
Give me the knife !" — The outlaw turns,
  Shuddering in heart and limb, away, —
But, fitfully there, the hearth-fire burns,
  And he sees on the wall strange shad-
    ows play.
A lifted arm, a tremulous blade,
Are dimly pictured in light and shade,
  Plunging down in the darkness. Hark,
    that cry
Again — and again — he sees it fall, —
That shadowy arm down the lighted wall !
  He hears quick footsteps — a shape
    flits by —
  The door on its rusted hinges creaks :—
"Ruth — daughter Ruth !" the outlaw
  shrieks.
But no sound comes back, — he is stand-
  ing alone
By the mangled corse of Mogg Megone !

PART II.

'T is morning over Norridgewock, —
On tree and wigwam, wave and rock.
Bathed in the autumnal sunshine, stirred
At intervals by breeze and bird,
And wearing all the hues which glow
In heaven's own pure and perfect bow,
  That glorious picture of the air,
Which summer's light-robed angel forms
On the dark ground of fading storms,
  With pencil dipped in sunbeams
    there, —
And, stretching out, on either hand,
O'er all that wide and unshorn land,
Till, weary of its gorgeousness,
The aching and the dazzled eye
Rests, gladdened, on the calm blue sky, —
  Slumbers the mighty wilderness !
The oak, upon the windy hill,
  Its dark green burthen upward
    heaves —
The hemlock broods above its rill,
Its cone-like foliage darker still,
  Against the birch's graceful stem,
And the rough walnut-bough receives
The sun upon its crowded leaves,
  Each colored like a topaz gem ;

And the tall maple wears with them
The coronal, which autumn gives,
  The brief, bright sign of ruin near,
  The hectic of a dying year !

The hermit priest, who lingers now
On the Bald Mountain's shrubless brow,
The gray and thunder-smitten pile
Which marks afar the Desert Isle,[13]
  While gazing on the scene below,
May half forget the dreams of home,
  That nightly with his slumbers come, —
The tranquil skies of sunny France,
The peasant's harvest song and dance,
The vines around the hillsides wreathing
The soft airs midst their clusters breath-
  ing,
The wings which dipped, the stars which
  shone
Within thy bosom, blue Garonne !
And round the Abbey's shadowed wall,
At morning spring and even-fall,
  Sweet voices in the still air singing, —
The chant of many a holy hymn, —
  The solemn bell of vespers ringing, —
And hallowed torchlight falling dim
  On pictured saint and seraphim !
For here beneath him lies unrolled,
Bathed deep in morning's flood of gold,
A vision gorgeous as the dream
Of the beatified may seem,
  When, as his Church's legends say,
Borne upward in ecstatic bliss,
  The rapt enthusiast soars away
Unto a brighter world than this :
A mortal's glimpse beyond the pale, —
A moment's lifting of the veil !

Far eastward o'er the lovely bay,
Penobscot's clustered wigwams lay ;
And gently from that Indian town
The verdant hillside slopes adown,
  To where the sparkling waters play
  Upon the yellow sands below ;
And shooting round the winding shores
  Of narrow capes, and isles which lie
  Slumbering to ocean's lullaby, —
With birchen boat and glancing oars,
  The red men to their fishing go ;
While from their planting ground is borne
The treasure of the golden corn,
By laughing girls, whose dark eyes glow
Wild through the locks which o'er them
  flow.
The wrinkled squaw, whose toil is done,
Sits on her bear-skin in the sun,
Watching the huskers, with a smile

For each full ear which swells the pile ;
And the old chief, who nevermore
May bend the bow or pull the oar,
Smokes gravely in his wigwam door,
Or slowly shapes, with axe of stone,
The arrow-head from flint and bone.

Beneath the westward turning eye
A thousand wooded islands lie, —
Gems of the waters ! — with each hue
Of brightness set in ocean's blue.
Each bears aloft its tuft of trees
    Touched by the pencil of the frost,
And, with the motion of each breeze,
    A moment seen, — a moment lost, —
    Changing and blent, confused and
        tossed,
    The brighter with the darker crossed,
Their thousand tints of beauty glow
Down in the restless waves below,
    And tremble in the sunny skies,
As if, from waving bough to bough,
    Flitted the birds of paradise.
There sleep Placentia's group, — and
        there
Père Breteaux marks the hour of prayer ;
And there, beneath the sea-worn cliff,
    On which the Father's hut is seen,
The Indian stays his rocking skiff,
    And peers the hemlock-boughs be-
        tween,
Half trembling, as he seeks to look
Upon the Jesuit's Cross and Book.[14]
There, gloomily against the sky
The Dark Isles rear their summits high ;
And Desert Rock, abrupt and bare,
Lifts its gray turrets in the air, —
Seen from afar, like some stronghold
Built by the ocean kings of old ;
And, faint as smoke-wreath white and
        thin,
Swells in the north vast Katahdin :
And, wandering from its marshy feet,
The broad Penobscot comes to meet
    And mingle with his own bright bay.
Slow sweep his dark and gathering floods,
Arched over by the ancient woods,
Which Time, in those dim solitudes,
    Wielding the dull axe of Decay,
    Alone hath ever shorn away.

Not thus, within the woods which hide
The beauty of thy azure tide,
    And with their falling timbers block
Thy broken currents, Kennebec !
Gazes the white man on the wreck
    Of the down-trodden Norridgewock, —

In one lone village hemmed at length,
In battle shorn of half their strength,
Turned, like the panther in his lair,
    With his fast-flowing life-blood wet,
For one last struggle of despair,
    Wounded and faint, but tameless yet !
Unreaped, upon the planting lands,
The scant, neglected harvest stands :
    No shout is there, — no dance, — no
        song :
The aspect of the very child
Scowls with a meaning sad and wild
    Of bitterness and wrong.
The almost infant Norridgewock
Essays to lift the tomahawk ;
And plucks his father's knife away,
To mimic, in his frightful play,
    The scalping of an English foe :
Wreathes on his lip a horrid smile,
Burns, like a snake's, his small eye, while
    Some bough or sapling meets his blow.
The fisher, as he drops his line,
Starts, when he sees the hazels quiver
Along the margin of the river,
Looks up and down the rippling tide,
And grasps the firelock at his side.
For Bomazeen [15] from Tacconock
Has sent his runners to Norridgewock,
With tidings that Moulton and Harmon
    of York
Far up the river have come :
They have left their boats, — they have
    entered the wood,
And filled the depths of the solitude
    With the sound of the ranger's drum.

On the brow of a hill, which slopes to
    meet
The flowing river, and bathe its feet, —
The bare-washed rock, and the drooping
        grass,
And the creeping vine, as the waters
        pass, —
A rude and unshapely chapel stands,
Built up in that wild by unskilled hands,
Yet the traveller knows it a place of
        prayer,
For the holy sign of the cross is there :
And should he chance at that place to be,
    Of a Sabbath morn, or some hallowed
        day,
When prayers are made and masses are
        said,
Some for the living and some for the dead,
Well might that traveller start to see
    The tall dark forms, that take their way
From the birch canoe, on the river-shore,

And the forest paths, to that chapel door;
And marvel to mark the naked knees
    And the dusky foreheads bending there,
While, in coarse white vesture, over these
    In blessing or in prayer,
Stretching abroad his thin pale hands,
Like a shrouded ghost, the Jesuit[16] stands.

Two forms are now in that chapel dim,
    The Jesuit, silent and sad and pale,
    Anxiously heeding some fearful tale,
Which a stranger is telling him.
That stranger's garb is soiled and torn,
And wet with dew and loosely worn ;
Her fair neglected hair falls down
O'er cheeks with wind and sunshine
        brown ;
Yet still, in that disordered face,
The Jesuit's cautious eye can trace
Those elements of former grace
Which, half effaced, seem scarcely less,
Even now, than perfect loveliness.

With drooping head, and voice so low
    That scarce it meets the Jesuit's ears, —
While through her clasped fingers flow,
From the heart's fountain, hot and slow,
    Her penitential tears, —
She tells the story of the woe
    And evil of her years.

"O father, bear with me ; my heart
    Is sick and death-like, and my brain
Seems girdled with a fiery chain,
    Whose scorching links will never part,
    And never cool again.
Bear with me while I speak, — but turn
    Away that gentle eye, the while, —
The fires of guilt more fiercely burn
    Beneath its holy smile ;
For half I fancy I can see
My mother's sainted look in thee.

"My dear lost mother ! sad and pale,
    Mournfully sinking day by day,
And with a hold on life as frail
    As frosted leaves, that, thin and gray,
    Hang feebly on their parent spray,
And tremble in the gale ;
Yet watching o'er my childishness
    With patient fondness, — not the less
For all the agony which kept
    Her blue eye wakeful, while I slept ;
And checking every tear and groan
That haply might have waked my own,
    And bearing still, without offence,
My idle words, and petulance ;

Reproving with a tear, — and, while
The tooth of pain was keenly preying
Upon her very heart, repaying
    My brief repentance with a smile.

"O, in her meek, forgiving eye
    There was a brightness not of mirth,
A light whose clear intensity
    Was borrowed not of earth.
Along her cheek a deepening red
Told where the feverish hectic fed ;
    And yet, each fatal token gave
To the mild beauty of her face
A newer and a dearer grace,
    Unwarning of the grave.
'T was like the hue which Autumn gives
To yonder changed and dying leaves,
    Breathed over by his frosty breath ;
Scarce can the gazer feel that this
Is but the spoiler's treacherous kiss,
    The mocking-smile of Death !

"Sweet were the tales she used to tell
    When summer's eve was dear to us,
And, fading from the darkening dell,
The glory of the sunset fell
    On wooded Agamenticus, —
When, sitting by our cottage wall,
The murmur of the Saco's fall,
    And the south-wind's expiring sighs,
Came, softly blending, on my ear,
With the low tones I loved to hear :
    Tales of the pure, — the good, — the
        wise, —
The holy men and maids of old,
In the all-sacred pages told ; —
Of Rachel, stooped at Haran's fount-
    ains,
    Amid her father's thirsty flock,
Beautiful to her kinsman seeming
As the bright angels of his dreaming,
    On Padan-aran's holy rock ;
Of gentle Ruth, — and her who kept
    Her awful vigil on the mountains,
By Israel's virgin daughters wept ;
Of Miriam, with her maidens, singing
    The song for grateful Israel meet,
While every crimson wave was bringing
    The spoils of Egypt at her feet ;
Of her, — Samaria's humble daughter,
    Who paused to hear, beside her well,
Lessons of love and truth, which fell
Softly as Shiloh's flowing water ;
    And saw, beneath his pilgrim guise,
The Promised One, so long foretold
By holy seer and bard of old,
    Revealed before her wondering eyes !

"Slowly she faded. Day by day
Her step grew weaker in our hall,
And fainter, at each even-fall,
  Her sad voice died away.
Yet on her thin, pale lip, the while,
Sat Resignation's holy smile :
And even my father checked his tread,
And hushed his voice, beside her bed :
Beneath the calm and sad rebuke
Of her meek eye's imploring look,
The scowl of hate his brow forsook,
  And in his stern and gloomy eye,
At times, a few unwonted tears
Wet the dark lashes, which for years
Hatred and pride had kept so dry.

"Calm as a child to slumber soothed,
As if an angel's hand had smoothed
  The still, white features into rest,
Silent and cold, without a breath
  To stir the drapery on her breast,
Pain, with its keen and poisoned fang,
The horror of the mortal pang,
The suffering look her brow had worn,
The fear, the strife, the anguish gone, —
  She slept at last in death !

"O, tell me, father, *can* the dead
  Walk on the earth, and look on us,
And lay upon the living's head
  Their blessing or their curse ?
For, O, last night she stood by me,
As I lay beneath the woodland tree ! "

The Jesuit crosses himself in awe, —
"Jesu ! what was it my daughter saw ? "

" *She* came to me last night.
  The dried leaves did not feel her
    tread ;
She stood by me in the wan moonlight,
  In the white robes of the dead !
Pale, and very mournfully
She bent her light form over me.
I heard no sound, I felt no breath
Breathe o'er me from that face of death :
Its blue eyes rested on my own,
Rayless and cold as eyes of stone ;
Yet, in their fixed, unchanging gaze,
Something, which spoke of early days, —
A sadness in their quiet glare,
As if love's smile were frozen there, —
Came o'er me with an icy thrill ;
O God ! I feel its presence still ! "

The Jesuit makes the holy sign, —
"How passed the vision, daughter mine ? "

"All dimly in the wan moonshine,
As a wreath of mist will twist and twine,
And scatter, and melt into the light, —
So scattering, — melting on my sight,
  The pale, cold vision passed ;
But those sad eyes were fixed on mine
  Mournfully to the last."

"God help thee, daughter, tell me why
That spirit passed before thine eye ! "

"Father, I know not, save it be
  That deeds of mine have summoned her
From the unbreathing sepulchre,
To leave her last rebuke with me.
Ah, woe for me ! my mother died
Just at the moment when I stood
Close on the verge of womanhood,
A child in everything beside ;
And when my wild heart needed most
Her gentle counsels, they were lost.

"My father lived a stormy life,
Of frequent change and daily strife ;
And — God forgive him ! — left his child
To feel, like him, a freedom wild ;
To love the red man's dwelling-place,
  The birch boat on his shaded floods,
The wild excitement of the chase
  Sweeping the ancient woods,
The camp-fire, blazing on the shore
Of the still lakes, the clear stream where
  The idle fisher sets his wear,
Or angles in the shade, far more
  Than that restraining awe I felt
Beneath my gentle mother's care,
  When nightly at her knee I knelt,
With childhood's simple prayer.

"There came a change. The wild, glad
    mood
  Of unchecked freedom passed.
Amid the ancient solitude
Of unshorn grass and waving wood,
  And waters glancing bright and fast,
A softened voice was in my ear,
Sweet as those lulling sounds and fine
The hunter lifts his head to hear,
Now far and faint, now full and near —
  The murmur of the wind-swept pine.
A manly form was ever nigh,
A bold, free hunter, with an eye
  Whose dark, keen glance had power
    to wake
Both fear and love, — to awe and charm ;
  'T was as the wizard rattlesnake,
Whose evil glances lure to harm —

Whose cold and small and glittering
    eye,
And brilliant coil, and changing dye,
Draw, step by step, the gazer near,
With drooping wing and cry of fear,
Yet powerless all to turn away,
A conscious, but a willing prey !

"Fear, doubt, thought, life itself, erelong
Merged in one feeling deep and strong.
Faded the world which I had known,
    A poor vain shadow, cold and waste ;
In the warm present bliss alone
    Seemed I of actual life to taste.
Fond longings dimly understood,
The glow of passion's quickening blood,
And cherished fantasies which press
The young lip with a dream's caress, —
The heart's forecast and prophecy
Took form and life before my eye,
Seen in the glance which met my own,
Heard in the soft and pleading tone,
Felt in the arms around me cast,
And warm heart-pulses beating fast.
Ah ! scarcely yet to God above
With deeper trust, with stronger love,
Has prayerful saint his meek heart
    lent,
Or cloistered nun at twilight bent,
Than I, before a human shrine,
As mortal and as frail as mine,
With heart, and soul, and mind, and form,
Knelt madly to a fellow-worm.

"Full soon, upon that dream of sin,
An awful light came bursting in.
The shrine was cold at which I knelt,
    The idol of that shrine was gone ;
A humbled thing of shame and guilt,
    Outcast, and spurned and lone,
Wrapt in the shadows of my crime,
    With withering heart and burning
        brain,
    And tears that fell like fiery rain,
I passed a fearful time.

"There came a voice — it checked the
    tear —
    In heart and soul it wrought a change ;—
My father's voice was in my ear ;
    It whispered of revenge !
A new and fiercer feeling swept
    All lingering tenderness away ;
And tiger passions, which had slept
    In childhood's better day,
Unknown, unfelt, arose at length
In all their own demoniac strength.

"A youthful warrior of the wild,
By words deceived, by smiles beguiled,
Of crime the cheated instrument,
Upon our fatal errands went.
  Through camp and town and wilderness
He tracked his victim ; and, at last,
Just when the tide of hate had passed,
And milder thoughts came warm and fast,
Exulting, at my feet he cast
    The bloody token of success.

"O God ! with what an awful power
    I saw the buried past uprise,
And gather, in a single hour,
    Its ghost-like memories !
And then I felt — alas ! too late —
That underneath the mask of hate,
That shame and guilt and wrong had
    thrown
O'er feelings which they might not own,
    The heart's wild love had known no
        change ;
And still that deep and hidden love,
With its first fondness, wept above
    The victim of its own revenge !
There lay the fearful scalp, and there
The blood was on its pale brown hair !
I thought not of the victim's scorn,
    I thought not of his baleful guile,
My deadly wrong, my outcast name,
The characters of sin and shame
On heart and forehead drawn ;
    I only saw that victim's smile, —
The still, green places where we met, —
The moonlit branches, dewy wet ;
I only felt, I only heard
    The greeting and the parting word, —
The smile, — the embrace, — the tone,
        which made
An Eden of the forest shade.

"And oh, with what a loathing eye,
    With what a deadly hate, and deep,
I saw that Indian murderer lie
    Before me, in his drunken sleep !
What though for me the deed was done,
And words of mine had sped him on !
Yet when he murmured, as he slept,
    The horrors of that deed of blood,
The tide of utter madness swept
    O'er brain and bosom, like a flood.
And, father, with this hand of mine —"
    "Ha ! what didst thou ?" the Jesuit
        cries,
Shuddering, as smitten with sudden pain,
    And shading, with one thin hand, his
        eyes,

With the other he makes the holy sign.
"— I smote him as I would a worm ; —
With heart as steeled, with nerves as
    firm :
  He never woke again !"

"Woman of sin and blood and shame,
Speak, — I would know that victim's
    name."

"Father," she gasped, "a chieftain,
    known
As Saco's Sachem, — MOGG MEGONE !"

Pale priest ! What proud and lofty
    dreams,
What keen desires, what cherished
    schemes,
What hopes, that time may not recall,
Are darkened by that chieftain's fall !
Was he not pledged, by cross and vow,
  To lift the hatchet of his sire,
And, round his own, the Church's foe,
  To light the avenging fire ?
Who now the Tarrantine shall wake,
For thine and for the Church's sake ?
  Who summon to the scene
Of conquest and unsparing strife,
And vengeance dearer than his life,
  The fiery-souled Castine ? [17]
Three backward steps the Jesuit takes, —
His long, thin frame as ague shakes ;
  And loathing hate is in his eye,
As from his lips these words of fear
Fall hoarsely on the maiden's ear, —
  "The soul that sinneth shall surely
      die !"

She stands, as stands the stricken deer,
  Checked midway in the fearful chase,
When bursts, upon his eye and ear,
The gaunt, gray robber, baying near,
  Between him and his hiding-place ;
While still behind, with yell and blow,
Sweeps, like a storm, the coming foe.
"Save me, O holy man !" — her cry
  Fills all the void, as if a tongue,
  Unseen, from rib and rafter hung,
Thrilling with mortal agony ;
Her hands are clasping the Jesuit's
    knee,
  And her eye looks fearfully into his
      own ; —
"Off, woman of sin ! — nay, touch not
    me
  With those fingers of blood ; — be-
      gone !"

With a gesture of horror, he spurns the
    form
That writhes at his feet like a trodden
    worm.

  Ever thus the spirit must,
    Guilty in the sight of Heaven,
    With a keener woe be riven,
  For its weak and sinful trust
  In the strength of human dust ;
    And its anguish thrill afresh,
  For each vain reliance given
    To the failing arm of flesh.

PART III.

AH, weary Priest ! — with pale hands
    pressed
  On thy throbbing brow of pain,
Baffled in thy life-long quest,
  Overworn with toiling vain,
How ill thy troubled musings fit
    The holy quiet of a breast
    With the Dove of Peace at rest,
  Sweetly brooding over it.
Thoughts are thine which have no part
With the meek and pure of heart,
Undisturbed by outward things,
Resting in the heavenly shade,
By the overspreading wings
    Of the Blessed Spirit made.
Thoughts of strife and hate and wrong
Sweep thy heated brain along,
Fading hopes for whose success
  It were sin to breathe a prayer ; —
Schemes which Heaven may never
      bless, —
  Fears which darken to despair.
Hoary priest ! thy dream is done
Of a hundred red tribes won
  To the pale of Holy Church ;
And the heretic o'erthrown,
And his name no longer known,
And thy weary brethren turning,
Joyful from their years of mourning,
'Twixt the altar and the porch.
Hark ! what sudden sound is heard
  In the wood and in the sky,
Shriller than the scream of bird, —
  Than the trumpet's clang more
      high !
Every wolf-cave of the hills, —
  Forest arch and mountain gorge,
  Rock and dell, and river verge, —
With an answering echo thrills.
Well does the Jesuit know that cry,

Which summons the Norridgewock to
  die,
And tells that the foe of his flock is nigh.
He listens, and hears the rangers come,
With loud hurrah, and jar of drum,
And hurrying feet (for the chase is hot),
And the short, sharp sound of rifle shot,
And taunt and menace, — answered well
By the Indians' mocking cry and yell, —
The bark of dogs, — the squaw's mad
  scream, —
The dash of paddles along the stream, —
The whistle of shot as it cuts the leaves
Of the maples around the church's
  caves, —
And the gride of hatchets fiercely
  thrown,
On wigwam-log and tree and stone.
Black with the grime of paint and dust,
  Spotted and streaked with human
    gore,
A grim and naked head is thrust
  Within the chapel-door.
"Ha — Bomazeen! — In God's name say,
What mean these sounds of bloody fray?"
Silent, the Indian points his hand
  To where across the echoing glen
Sweep Harmon's dreaded ranger-band,
  And Moulton with his men.
"Where are thy warriors, Bomazeen?
Where are De Rouville [18] and Castine,
And where the braves of Sawga's queen?"
"Let my father find the winter snow
Which the sun drank up long moons ago!
Under the falls of Tacconock,
The wolves are eating the Norridgewock;
Castine with his wives lies closely hid
Like a fox in the woods of Pemaquid!
On Sawga's banks the man of war
Sits in his wigwam like a squaw, —
Squando has fled, and Mogg Megone,
Struck by the knife of Sagamore John,
Lies stiff and stark and cold as a stone."

Fearfully over the Jesuit's face,
Of a thousand thoughts, trace after trace,
Like swift cloud-shadows, each other
  chase.
One instant, his fingers grasp his knife,
For a last vain struggle for cherished
  life, —
The next, he hurls the blade away,
And kneels at his altar's foot to pray;
Over his beads his fingers stray,
And he kisses the cross, and calls aloud
On the Virgin and her Son;
For terrible thoughts his memory crowd

Of evil seen and done, —
Of scalps brought home by his savage
  flock
From Casco and Sawga and Sagadahock
In the Church's service won.

No shrift the gloomy savage brooks,
As scowling on the priest he looks:
"Cowesass — cowesass — tawhich wessa.
  seen?[19]
Let my father look upon Bomazeen, —
My father's heart is the heart of a squaw,
But mine is so hard that it does not thaw;
Let my father ask his God to make
  A dance and a feast for a great saga-
    more,
When he paddles across the western lake,
  With his dogs and his squaws to the
    spirit's shore.
"Cowesass — cowesass — tawhich wessa-
  seen?
Let my father die like Bomazeen!"

Through the chapel's narrow doors,
  And through each window in the walls,
Round the priest and warrior pours
  The deadly shower of English balls.
Low on his cross the Jesuit falls;
While at his side the Norridgewock,
With failing breath, essays to mock
And menace yet the hated foe, —
Shakes his scalp-trophies to and fro
Exultingly before their eyes, —
  Till, cleft and torn by shot and blow,
    Defiant still, he dies.

"So fare all eaters of the frog!
Death to the Babylonish dog!
  Down with the beast of Rome!"
With shouts like these, around the dead,
Unconscious on his bloody bed,
  The rangers crowding come.
Brave men! the dead priest cannot hear
The unfeeling taunt, — the brutal jeer; —
Spurn — for he sees ye not — in wrath,
The symbol of your Saviour's death;
  Tear from his death-grasp, in your zeal,
And trample, as a thing accursed,
The cross he cherished in the dust:
  The dead man cannot feel!

Brutal alike in deed and word,
  With callous heart and hand of strife,
How like a fiend may man be made,
Plying the foul and monstrous trade
  Whose harvest-field is human life,
  Whose sickle is the reeking sword!

Quenching, with reckless hand in blood,
Sparks kindled by the breath of God ;
Urging the deathless soul, unshriven,
 Of open guilt or secret sin,
Before the bar of that pure Heaven
 The holy only enter in !
O, by the widow's sore distress,
The orphan's wailing wretchedness,
By Virtue struggling in the accursed
Embraces of polluting Lust,
By the fell discord of the Pit,
And the pained souls that people it,
And by the blessed peace which fills
 The Paradise of God forever,
Resting on all its holy hills,
 And flowing with its crystal river, —
Let Christian hands no longer bear
 In triumph on his crimson car
 The foul and idol god of war ;
No more the purple wreaths prepare
To bind amid his snaky hair ;
Nor Christian bards his glories tell,
Nor Christian tongues his praises swell.

Through the gun-smoke wreathing white,
Glimpses on the soldiers' sight
A thing of human shape I ween,
For a moment only seen,
With its loose hair backward streaming,
And its eyeballs madly gleaming,
Shrieking, like a soul in pain,
 From the world of light and breath,
Hurrying to its place again,
 Spectre-like it vanisheth !

Wretched girl ! one eye alone
Notes the way which thou hast gone.
That great Eye, which slumbers never,
Watching o'er a lost world ever,
Tracks thee over vale and mountain,
By the gushing forest-fountain,
Plucking from the vine its fruit,
Searching for the ground-nut's root,
Peering in the she-wolf's den,
Wading through the marshy fen,
Where the sluggish water-snake
Basks beside the sunny brake,
Coiling in his slimy bed,
Smooth and cold against thy tread, —
Purposeless, thy mazy way
Threading through the lingering day.
And at night securely sleeping
Where the dogwood's dews are weeping !
Still, though earth and man discard thee,
Doth thy Heavenly Father guard thee ·
He who spared the guilty Cain,
 Even when a brother's blood,

Crying in the ear of God,
Gave the earth its primal stain, —
He whose mercy ever liveth,
Who repenting guilt forgiveth,
And the broken heart receiveth, —
Wanderer of the wilderness,
 Haunted, guilty, crazed, and wild,
He regardeth thy distress,
 And careth for his sinful child !

'T is springtime on the eastern hills !
Like torrents gush the summer rills ;
Through winter's moss and dry dead
 leaves
The bladed grass revives and lives,
Pushes the mouldering waste away,
And glimpses to the April day.
In kindly shower and sunshine bud
The branches of the dull gray wood ;
Out from its sunned and sheltered nooks
The blue eye of the violet looks ;
 The southwest wind is warmly blowing,
And odors from the springing grass,
The pine-tree and the sassafras, ·
 Are with it on its errands going.

A band is marching through the wood
Where rolls the Kennebec his flood, —
The warriors of the wilderness,
Painted, and in their battle dress ;
And with them one whose bearded cheek,
And white and wrinkled brow, bespeak
 A wanderer from the shores of France.
A few long locks of scattering snow
Beneath a battered morion flow,
And from the rivets of the vest
Which girds in steel his ample breast,
 The slanted sunbeams glance.
In the harsh outlines of his face
Passion and sin have left their trace ;
Yet, save worn brow and thin gray hair,
No signs of weary age are there.
 His step is firm, his eye is keen,
Nor years in broil and battle spent,
Nor toil, nor wounds, nor pain have bent
 The lordly frame of old Castine.

No purpose now of strife and blood
 Urges the hoary veteran on :
The fire of conquest and the mood
 Of chivalry have gone.
A mournful task is his, — to lay
Within the earth the bones of those
Who perished in that fearful day,
When Norridgewock became the prey
 Of all unsparing foes.
Sadly and still, dark thoughts between,

Of coming vengeance mused Castine,
Of the fallen chieftain Bomazeen,
Who bade for him the Norridgewocks
Dig up their buried tomahawks
    For firm defence or swift attack ;
And him whose friendship formed the tie
    Which held the stern self-exile back
From lapsing into savagery ;
Whose garb and tone and kindly glance
    Recalled a younger, happier day,
    And prompted memory's fond essay,
    To bridge the mighty waste which lay
    Between his wild home and that gray,
Tall chateau of his native France,
Whose chapel bell, with far-heard din,
Ushered his birth-hour gayly in,
And counted with its solemn toll
The masses for his father's soul.

Hark ! from the foremost of the band
    Suddenly bursts the Indian yell ;
For now on the very spot they stand
    Where the Norridgewocks fighting fell.
No wigwam smoke is curling there ;
The very earth is scorched and bare :
And they pause and listen to catch a sound
    Of breathing life, — but there comes
        not one,
Save the fox's bark and the rabbit's bound ;
But here and there, on the blackened
        ground,
    White bones are glistening in the sun.
And where the house of prayer arose,
And the holy hymn, at daylight's close,

And the aged priest stood up to bless
The children of the wilderness,
There is naught save ashes sodden and
    dank ;
    And the birchen boats of the Nor-
        ridgewock,
    Tethered to tree and stump and rock,
Rotting along the river bank !

Blessed Mary ! who is she
Leaning against that maple-tree ?
The sun upon her face burns hot,
But the fixed eyelid moveth not ;
The squirrel's chirp is shrill and clear
From the dry bough above her ear ;
Dashing from rock and root its spray,
    Close at her feet the river rushes ;
    The blackbird's wing against her
        brushes,
    And sweetly through the hazel-bushes
    The robin's mellow music gushes ; —
God save her ! will she sleep alway ?

Castine hath bent him over the sleeper :
    " Wake, daughter, — wake ! " — but
        she stirs no limb :
    The eye that looks on him is fixed and
        dim ;
And the sleep she is sleeping shall be no
        deeper,
    Until the angel's oath is said,
And the final blast of the trump goes forth
To the graves of the sea and the graves
    of earth.
    RUTH BONYTHON IS DEAD !

THE BRIDAL OF PENNACOOK.[20]

WE had been wandering for many days
Through the rough northern country.
    We had seen
The sunset, with its bars of purple cloud,
Like a new heaven, shine upward from
    the lake
Of Winnepiscogee ; and had felt
The sunrise breezes, midst the leafy isles
Which stoop their summer beauty to the
    lips
Of the bright waters. We had checked
    our steeds,

Silent with wonder, where the mountain
    wall
Is piled to heaven ; and, through the
    narrow rift
Of the vast rocks, against whose rugged
    feet
Beats the mad torrent with perpetual roar,
Where noonday is as twilight, and the
    wind
Comes burdened with the everlasting
    moan
Of forests and of far-off waterfalls,

We had looked upward where the sum-
  mer sky,
Tasselled with clouds light-woven by
  the sun,
Sprung its blue arch above the abutting
  crags
O'er-roofing the vast portal of the land
Beyond the wall of mountains. We had
  passed
The high source of the Saco; and be-
  wildered
In the dwarf spruce-belts of the Crystal
  Hills,
Had heard above us, like a voice in the
  cloud,
The horn of Fabyan sounding; and atop
Of old Agioochook had seen the mountains
Piled to the northward, shagged with
  wood, and thick
As meadow mole-hills, — the far sea of
  Casco,
A white gleam on the horizon of the east;
Fair lakes, embosomed in the woods
  and hills;
Moosehillock's mountain range, and
  Kearsarge
Lifting his Titan forehead to the sun!

And we had rested underneath the oaks
Shadowing the bank, whose grassy spires
  are shaken
By the perpetual beating of the falls
Of the wild Ammonoosuc. We had
  tracked
The winding Pemigewasset, overhung
By beechen shadows, whitening down
  its rocks,
Or lazily gliding through its intervals,
From waving rye-fields sending up the
  gleam
Of sunlit waters. We had seen the moon
Rising behind Umbagog's eastern pines,
Like a great Indian camp-fire; and its
  beams
At midnight spanning with a bridge of
  silver
The Merrimack by Uncanoonuc's falls.

There were five souls of us whom trav-
  el's chance
Had thrown together in these wild
  north hills: —
A city lawyer, for a month escaping
From his dull office, where the weary eye
Saw only hot brick walls and close
  thronged streets, —
Briefless as yet, but with an eye to see

Life's sunniest side, and with a heart to
  take
Its chances all as godsends; and his
  brother,
Pale from long pulpit studies, yet re-
  taining
The warmth and freshness of a genial
  heart,
Whose mirror of the beautiful and true,
In Man and Nature, was as yet un-
  dimmed
By dust of theologic strife, or breath
Of sect, or cobwebs of scholastic lore;
Like a clear crystal calm of water, taking
The hue and image of o'erleaning flowers,
Sweet human faces, white clouds of the
  noon,
Slant starlight glimpses through the
  dewy leaves,
And tenderest moonrise. 'T was, in
  truth, a study,
To mark his spirit, alternating between
A decent and professional gravity
And an irreverent mirthfulness, which
  often
Laughed in the face of his divinity,
Plucked off the sacred ephod, quite un-
  shrined
The oracle, and for the pattern priest
Left us the man. A shrewd, sagacious
  merchant,
To whom the soiled sheet found in
  Crawford's inn,
Giving the latest news of city stocks
And sales of cotton, had a deeper meaning
Than the great presence of the awful
  mountains
Glorified by the sunset; — and his
  daughter
A delicate flower on whom had blown
  too long
Those evil winds, which, sweeping from
  the ice
And winnowing the fogs of Labrador,
Shed their cold blight round Massachu-
  setts Bay,
With the same breath which stirs
  Spring's opening leaves
And lifts her half-formed flower-bell on
  its stem,
Poisoning our seaside atmosphere.

                It chanced
That as we turned upon our homeward way,
A drear northeastern storm came howl-
  ing up
The valley of the Saco; and that girl

Who had stood with us upon Mount
Washington,
Her brown locks ruffled by the wind
which whirled
In gusts around its sharp cold pinnacle,
Who had joined our gay trout-fishing in
the streams
Which lave that giant's feet ; whose
laugh was heard
Like a bird's carol on the sunrise breeze
Which swelled our sail amidst the lake's
green islands,
Shrank from its harsh, chill breath, and
visibly drooped
Like a flower in the frost. So, in that
quiet inn
Which looks from Conway on the moun-
tains piled
Heavily against the horizon of the north,
Like summer thunder-clouds, we made
our home :
And while the mist hung over dripping
hills,
And the cold wind-driven rain-drops all
day long
Beat their sad music upon roof and pane,
We strove to cheer our gentle invalid.

The lawyer in the pauses of the storm
Went angling down the Saco, and, re-
turning,
Recounted his adventures and mishaps ;
Gave us the history of his scaly clients,
Mingling with ludicrous yet apt citations
Of barbarous law Latin, passages
From Izaak Walton's Angler, sweet and
fresh
As the flower-skirted streams of Stafford-
shire,
Where, under aged trees, the southwest
wind
Of soft June mornings fanned the thin,
white hair
Of the sage fisher. And, if truth be told,
Our youthful candidate forsook his ser-
mons,
His commentaries, articles and creeds,
For the fair page of human loveliness, —
The missal of young hearts, whose sa-
cred text
Is music, its illumining sweet smiles.
He sang the songs she loved ; and in
his low,
Deep, earnest voice, recited many a page
Of poetry, — the holiest, tenderest lines
Of the sad bard of Olney, — the sweet
songs,

Simple and beautiful as Truth and Na-
ture,
Of him whose whitened locks on Rydal
Mount
Are lifted yet by morning breezes blowing
From the green hills, immortal in his lays.
And for myself, obedient to her wish,
I searched our landlord's proffered li-
brary, —
A well-thumbed Bunyan, with its nice
wood pictures
Of scaly fiends and angels not unlike
them, —
Watts' unmelodious psalms, — Astrol-
ogy's
Last home, a musty pile of almanacs,
And an old chronicle of border wars
And Indian history. And, as I read
A story of the marriage of the Chief
Of Saugus to the dusky Weetamoo,
Daughter of Passaconaway, who dwelt
In the old time upon the Merrimack,
Our fair one, in the playful exercise
Of her prerogative, — the right divine
Of youth and beauty, — bade us versify
The legend, and with ready pencil
sketched
Its plan and outlines, laughingly as-
signing
To each his part, and barring our excuses
With absolute will. So, like the cavaliers
Whose voices still are heard in the Ro-
mance
Of silver-tongued Boccaccio, on the banks
Of Arno, with soft tales of love beguiling
The ear of languid beauty, plague-exiled
From stately Florence, we rehearsed our
rhymes
To their fair auditor, and shared by turns
Her kind approval and her playful cen-
sure.

It may be that these fragments owe alone
To the fair setting of their circum-
stances, —
The associations of time, scene, and
audience, —
Their place amid the pictures which
fill up
The chambers of my memory. Yet I trust
That some, who sigh, while wandering
in thought,
Pilgrims of Romance o'er the olden world,
That our broad land, — our sea-like
lakes and mountains
Piled to the clouds, — our rivers over-
hung

By forests which have known no other change
For ages, than the budding and the fall
Of leaves, — our valleys lovelier than those
Which the old poets sang of, — should but figure
On the apocryphal chart of speculation
As pastures, wood-lots, mill-sites, with the privileges,
Rights, and appurtenances, which make up
A Yankee Paradise, — unsung, unknown,
To beautiful tradition; even their names,
Whose melody yet lingers like the last
Vibration of the red man's requiem,
Exchanged for syllables significant
Of cotton-mill and rail-car, will look kindly
Upon this effort to call up the ghost
Of our dim Past, and listen with pleased ear
To the responses of the questioned Shade.

I. THE MERRIMACK.

O CHILD of that white-crested mountain whose springs
Gush forth in the shade of the cliff-eagle's wings,
Down whose slopes to the lowlands thy wild waters shine,
Leaping gray walls of rock, flashing through the dwarf pine.

From that cloud-curtained cradle so cold and so lone,
From the arms of that wintry-locked mother of stone,
By hills hung with forests, through vales wide and free,
Thy mountain-born brightness glanced down to the sea!

No bridge arched thy waters save that where the trees
Stretched their long arms above thee and kissed in the breeze:
No sound save the lapse of the waves on thy shores,
The plunging of otters, the light dip of oars.

Green-tufted, oak-shaded, by Amoskeag's fall
Thy twin Uncanoonucs rose stately and tall,

Thy Nashua meadows lay green and unshorn,
And the hills of Pentucket were tasselled with corn.

But thy Pennacook valley was fairer than these,
And greener its grasses and taller its trees,
Ere the sound of an axe in the forest had rung,
Or the mower his scythe in the meadows had swung.

In their sheltered repose looking out from the wood
The bark-builded wigwams of Pennacook stood,
There glided the corn-dance, the council-fire shone,
And against the red war-post the hatchet was thrown.

There the old smoked in silence their pipes, and the young
To the pike and the white-perch their baited lines flung;
There the boy shaped his arrows, and there the shy maid
Wove her many-hued baskets and bright wampum braid.

O Stream of the Mountains! if answer of thine
Could rise from thy waters to question of mine,
Methinks through the din of thy thronged banks a moan
Of sorrow would swell for the days which have gone.

Not for thee the dull jar of the loom and the wheel,
The gliding of shuttles, the ringing of steel;
But that old voice of waters, of bird and of breeze,
The dip of the wild-fowl, the rustling of trees!

II. THE BASHABA.[21]

LIFT we the twilight curtains of the Past,
And, turning from familiar sight and sound,
Sadly and full of reverence let us cast
A glance upon Tradition's shadowy ground,

Led by the few pale lights which, glim-
    mering round
  That dim, strange land of Eld, seem
    dying fast ;
And that which history gives not to the
    eye,
The faded coloring of Time's tapestry,
Let Fancy, with her dream-dipped brush,
    supply.

Roof of bark and walls of pine,
Through whose chinks the sunbeams
    shine,
Tracing many a golden line
  On the ample floor within ;
Where, upon that earth-floor stark,
Lay the gaudy mats of bark,
With the bear's hide, rough and dark,
  And the red-deer's skin.

Window-tracery, small and slight,
Woven of the willow white,
Lent a dimly checkered light,
  And the night-stars glimmered down,
Where the lodge-fire's heavy smoke,
Slowly through an opening broke,
In the low roof, ribbed with oak,
  Sheathed with hemlock brown.

Gloomed behind the changeless shade,
By the solemn pine-wood made ;
Through the rugged palisade,
  In the open foreground planted,
Glimpses came of rowers rowing,
Stir of leaves and wild-flowers blow-
    ing,
Steel-like gleams of water flowing,
  In the sunlight slanted.

Here the mighty Bashaba
Held his long-unquestioned sway,
From the White Hills, far away,
  To the great sea's sounding shore ;
Chief of chiefs, his regal word
All the river Sachems heard,
At his call the war-dance stirred,
  Or was still once more.

There his spoils of chase and war,
Jaw of wolf and black bear's paw,
Panther's skin and eagle's claw ;
  Lay beside his axe and bow ;
And, adown the roof-pole hung,
Loosely on a snake-skin strung,
In the smoke his scalp-locks swung
  Grimly to and fro.

Nightly down the river going,
Swifter was the hunter's rowing,
When he saw that lodge-fire glowing
  O'er the waters still and red ;
And the squaw's dark eye burned brighter,
And she drew her blanket tighter,
As, with quicker step and lighter,
  From that door she fled.

For that chief had magic skill,
And a Panisee's dark will,
Over powers of good and ill,
  Powers which bless and powers which
    ban, —
Wizard lord of Pennacook,
Chiefs upon their war-path shook,
When they met the steady look
  Of that wise dark man.

Tales of him the gray squaw told,
When the winter night-wind cold
Pierced her blanket's thickest fold,
  And her fire burned low and small,
Till the very child abed,
Drew its bear-skin over head,
Shrinking from the pale lights shed
  On the trembling wall.

All the subtle spirits hiding
Under earth or wave, abiding
In the caverned rock, or riding
  Misty clouds or morning breeze ;
Every dark intelligence,
Secret soul, and influence
Of all things which outward sense
  Feels, or hears, or sees, —

These the wizard's skill confessed,
At his bidding banned or blessed,
Stormful woke or lulled to rest
  Wind and cloud, and fire and flood ;
Burned for him the drifted snow,
Bade through ice fresh lilies blow,
And the leaves of summer grow
  Over winter's wood !

Not untrue that tale of old !
Now, as then, the wise and bold
All the powers of Nature hold
  Subject to their kingly will ;
From the wondering crowds ashore,
Treading life's wild waters o'er,
As upon a marble floor,
  Moves the strong man still.

Still, to such, life's elements
With their sterner laws dispense,

And the chain of consequence
  Broken in their pathway lies ;
Time and change their vassals making,
Flowers from icy pillows waking,
Tresses of the sunrise shaking
  Over midnight skies.

Still, to earnest souls, the sun
Rests on towered Gibeon,
And the moon of Ajalon
  Lights the battle-grounds of life ;
To his aid the strong reverses
Hidden powers and giant forces,
And the high stars, in their courses,
  Mingle in his strife !

III. THE DAUGHTER.

THE soot-black brows of men, — the
  yell
Of women thronging round the bed,—
The tinkling charm of ring and shell, —
  The Powah whispering o'er the
  dead ! —
All these the Sachem's home had
  known,
  When, on her journey long and wild
To the dim World of Souls, alone,
In her young beauty passed the mother
  of his child.

Three bow-shots from the Sachem's
  dwelling
  They laid her in the walnut shade,
Where a green hillock gently swelling
  Her fitting mound of burial made.
There trailed the vine in summer hours,
  The tree-perched squirrel dropped
  his shell, —
On velvet moss and pale-hued flowers,
Woven with leaf and spray, the softened
  sunshine fell !

The Indian's heart is hard and cold, —
  It closes darkly o'er its care,
And formed in Nature's sternest mould,
  Is slow to feel, and strong to bear.
The war-paint on the Sachem's face,
  Unwet with tears, shone fierce and
  red,
And, still in battle or in chase,
Dry leaf and snow-rime crisped beneath
  His foremost tread.

Yet when her name was heard no more,
  And when the robe her mother gave,

And small, light moccasin she wore,
  Had slowly wasted on her grave,
Unmarked of him the dark maids sped
  Their sunset dance and moonlit play;
No other shared his lonely bed,
No other fair young head upon his
  bosom lay.

A lone, stern man. Yet, as sometimes
  The tempest-smitten tree receives
From one small root the sap which
  climbs
  Its topmost spray and crowning
  leaves,
So from his child the Sachem drew
  A life of Love and Hope, and felt
His cold and rugged nature through
The softness and the warmth of her
  young being melt.

A laugh which in the woodland rang
  Bemocking April's gladdest bird, —
A light and graceful form which sprang
  To meet him when his step was
  heard, —
Eyes by his lodge-fire flashing dark,
  Small fingers stringing bead and shell
Or weaving mats of bright-hued bark,—
With these the household-god [22] had
  graced his wigwam well.

Child of the forest ! — strong and free,
  Slight-robed, with loosely flowing
  hair,
She swam the lake or climbed the tree,
  Or struck the flying bird in air.
O'er the heaped drifts of winter's moon
  Her snow-shoes tracked the hunter's
  way ;
And dazzling in the summer noon
The blade of her light oar threw off its
  shower of spray !

Unknown to her the rigid rule,
  The dull restraint, the chiding frown,
The weary torture of the school,
  The taming of wild nature down.
Her only lore, the legends told
  Around the hunter's fire at night ;
Stars rose and set, and seasons rolled,
Flowers bloomed and snow-flakes fell,
  unquestioned in her sight.

Unknown to her the subtle skill
  With which the artist-eye can trace
In rock and tree and lake and hill
  The outlines of divinest grace ;

Unknown the fine soul's keen unrest,
  Which sees, admires, yet yearns
    alway ;
Too closely on her mother's breast
o note her smiles of love the child of
    Nature lay !

It is enough for such to be
  Of common, natural things a part,
To feel, with bird and stream and tree,
  The pulses of the same great heart ;
But we, from Nature long exiled
  In our cold homes of Art and
    Thought,
Grieve like the stranger-tended child,
Ihich seeks its mother's arms, and sees
    but feels them not.

The garden rose may richly bloom
  In cultured soil and genial air
To cloud the light of Fashion's room
  Or droop in Beauty's midnight hair,
In lonelier grace, to sun and dew
  The sweetbrier on the hillside shows
Its single leaf and fainter hue,
ntrained and wildly free, yet still a
    sister rose !

Thus o'er the heart of Weetamoo
  Their mingling shades of joy and ill
The instincts of her nature threw, —
  The savage was a woman still.
Midst outlines dim of maiden schemes,
  Heart-colored prophecies of life,
Rose on the ground of her young dreams
he light of a new home, — the lover
    and the wife.

IV. THE WEDDING.

OOL and dark fell the autumn night,
ut the Bashaba's wigwam glowed with
    light,
or down from its roof by green withes
    hung
laring and smoking the pine-knots
    swung.

nd along the river great wood-fires
hot into the night their long red spires,
howing behind the tall, dark wood,
lashing before on the sweeping flood.

u the changeful wind, with shimmer
    and shade,
low high, now low, that firelight played,

On tree-leaves wet with evening dews,
On gliding water and still canoes.

The trapper that night on Turee's brook,
And the weary fisher on Contoocook,
Saw over the marshes and through the
    pine,
And down on the river the dance-lights
    shine.

For the Saugus Sachem had come to woo
The Bashaba's daughter Weetamoo,
And laid at her father's feet that night
His softest furs and wampum white.

From the Crystal Hills to the far south-
    east
The river Sagamores came to the feast ;
And chiefs whose homes the sea-winds
    shook,
Sat down on the mats of Pennacook.

They came from Sunapee's shore of rock,
From the snowy sources of Snooganock,
And from rough Coös whose thick woods
    shake
Their pine-cones in Umbagog Lake.

From Ammonoosuc's mountain pass,
Wild as his home, came Chepewass ;
And the Keenomps of the hills which
    throw
Their shade on the Smile of Manito.

With pipes of peace and bows unstrung,
Glowing with paint came old and young,
In wampum and furs and feathers arrayed,
To the dance and feast the Bashaba made.

Bird of the air and beast of the field,
All which the woods and waters yield,
On dishes of birch and hemlock piled,
Garnished and graced that banquet wild.

Steaks of the brown bear fat and large
From the rocky slopes of the Kearsarge ;
Delicate trout from Babboosuck brook,
And salmon speared in the Contoocook ;

Squirrels which fed where nuts fell thick
In the gravelly bed of the Otternic ;
And small wild-hens in reed-snares caught
From the banks of Sondagardee brought ;

Pike and perch from the Suncook taken,
Nuts from the trees of the Black Hills
    shaken,

Cranberries picked in the Squamscot bog,
And grapes from the vines of Piscataquog:

And, drawn from that great stone vase
   which stands
In the river scooped by a spirit's hands,[23]
Garnished with spoons of shell and horn,
Stood the birchen dishes of smoking corn.

Thus bird of the air and beast of the field,
All which the woods and the waters yield,
Furnished in that olden day
The bridal feast of the Bashaba.

And merrily when that feast was done
On the fire-lit green the dance begun,
With squaws' shrill stave, and deeper hum
Of old men beating the Indian drum.

Painted and plumed, with scalp-locks
   flowing,
And red arms tossing and black eyes
   glowing,
Now in the light and now in the shade
Around the fires the dancers played.

The step was quicker, the song more shrill,
And the beat of the small drums louder still
Whenever within the circle drew
The Saugus Sachem and Weetamoo.

The moons of forty winters had shed
Their snow upon that chieftain's head,
And toil and care, and battle's chance
Had seamed his hard dark countenance.

A fawn beside the bison grim, —
Why turns the bride's fond eye on him,
In whose cold look is naught beside
The triumph of a sullen pride?

Ask why the graceful grape entwines
The rough oak with her arm of vines;
And why the gray rock's rugged cheek
The soft lips of the mosses seek:

Why, with wise instinct, Nature seems
To harmonize her wide extremes,
Linking the stronger with the weak,
The haughty with the soft and meek!

V. THE NEW HOME.

A WILD and broken landscape, spiked
   with firs,
  Roughening the bleak horizon's northern edge,

Steep, cavernous
   hemlock sp
And sharp, gray
   swept ledge
Pierced the thin-g
   rose,
Where the cold rin
   upon the sn

And eastward
   stretched a
Dull, dreary fla
   tree,
O'er-crossed by icy
   day
Gurgled the wat
   sea;
And faint with dis
   roar,
The melancholy la
   low shore.

No cheerful villag
   smokes,
No laugh of chi
   snow,
No camp-fire blaz
   side oaks,
No fishers kneel
Yet midst all des
   and view,
Through the long
   dark-eyed

Her heart had foun
   all
Its beautiful aff
Their rugged prop
   wall
Soft vine-leaves
   ing dew
And warm bright
   young wife
Found on a hard
   and warmtl

The steep bleak l
   shore,
The long dead l
   tween,
A coloring of unre
Through the sof
   love seen.
For o'er those hill
   plain,
Nightly she welco
   chief again.

No warmth of heart, no passionate burst
  of feeling,
  Repaid her welcoming smile and parting kiss,
No fond and playful dalliance half concealing,
  Under the guise of mirth, its tenderness ;
But, in their stead, the warrior's settled
  pride,
And vanity's pleased smile with homage
  satisfied.

Enough for Weetamoo, that she alone
  Sat on his mat and slumbered at his
  side ;
That he whose fame to her young ear
  had flown
  Now looked upon her proudly as his
  bride ;
That he whose name the Mohawk trembling heard
Vouchsafed to her at times a kindly look
  or word.

For she had learned the maxims of her
  race,
  Which teach the woman to become a
  slave
And feel herself the pardonless disgrace
  Of love's fond weakness in the wise
  and brave, —
The scandal and the shame which they
  incur,
Who give to woman all which man requires of her.

So passed the winter moons. The sun
  at last
  Broke link by link the frost chain of
  the rills,
And the warm breathings of the southwest passed
  Over the hoar rime of the Saugus hills,
The gray and desolate marsh grew green
  once more,
And the birch-tree's tremulous shade fell
  round the Sachem's door.

Then from far Pennacook swift runners
  came,
  With gift and greeting for the Saugus
  chief ;
Beseeching him in the great Sachem's
  name,
  That, with the coming of the flower
  and leaf,

The song of birds, the warm breeze and
  the rain,
Young Weetamoo might greet her lonely
  sire again.

And Winnepurkit called his chiefs to-
  gether,
  And a grave council in his wigwam
  met,
Solemn and brief in words, considering
  whether
  The rigid rules of forest etiquette
Permitted Weetamoo once more to look
Upon her father's face and green-banked
  Pennacook.

With interludes of pipe-smoke and
  strong water,
  The forest sages pondered, and at
  length,
Concluded in a body to escort her
  Up to her father's home of pride and
  strength,
Impressing thus on Pennacook a sense
Of Winnepurkit's power and regal con-
  sequence.

So through old woods which Aukeeta-
  mit's [24] hand,
  A soft and many-shaded greenness lent,
Over high breezy hills, and meadow land
  Yellow with flowers, the wild proces-
  sion went,
Till, rolling down its wooded banks be-
  tween,
A broad, clear, mountain stream, the
  Merrimack was seen.

The hunter leaning on his bow undrawn,
  The fisher lounging on the pebbled
  shores,
Squaws in the clearing dropping the
  seed-corn,
  Young children peering through the
  wigwam doors,
Saw with delight, surrounded by her
  train
Of painted Saugus braves, their Weetamoo
  again.

VI. AT PENNACOOK.

THE hills are dearest which our childish
  feet
Have climbed the earliest ; and the
  streams most sweet

Are ever those at which our young lips
   drank,
Stooped to their waters o'er the grassy
   bank :

Midst the cold dreary sea-watch, Home's
   hearth-light
Shines round the helmsman plunging
   through the night ;
And still, with inward eye, the traveller
   sees
In close, dark, stranger streets his native
   trees.

The home-sick dreamer's brow is nightly
   fanned
By breezes whispering of his native land,
And on the stranger's dim and dying
   eye
The soft, sweet pictures of his childhood lie.

Joy then for Weetamoo, to sit once more
A child upon her father's wigwam floor !
Once more with her old fondness to be-
   guile
From his cold eye the strange light of a
   smile.

The long bright days of summer swiftly
   passed,
The dry leaves whirled in autumn's rising blast,
And evening cloud and whitening sunrise rime
Told of the coming of the winter-time.

But vainly looked, the while, young
   Weetamoo,
Down the dark river for her chief's canoe ;
No dusky messenger from Saugus brought
The grateful tidings which the young
   wife sought.

At length a runner from her father sent,
To Winnepurkit's sea-cooled wigwam
   went :
" Eagle of Saugus, — in the woods the
   dove
Mourns for the shelter of thy wings of
   love."

But the dark chief of Saugus turned aside
In the grim anger of hard-hearted pride ;
"I bore her as became a chieftain's
   daughter,
Up to her home beside the gliding water.

" If now no more
Of all which line
   round,
Let Pennacook cal
And send her bac]
   again."

The baffled runner
Bearing the words
" Dog of the Mars
   " no more
Shall child of mi1
   floor.

" Go, — let him se
   to spread
The stolen bear-sk
Son of a fish-haw
   clams
For some vile dau[

"Or coward Nipm
   dry black
In Mohawk smok
   back."
He shook his clenc
   ocean wave,
While hoarse asser
   oil gave.

Alas poor bride ! -
   impart
His iron hardness
Or cold self-torturi
For love denied an
   flown ?

On Autumn's gray
   the snow
Hung its white
   voice and l(
The river crept, b]
   crossed,
Built by the hoar-l

And many a Moon
Pierced the red su
   horn,
Or, from the east,
Rolled the wide b
   orbed shield

Yet Winnepurkit c;
Of the scorned wif(
And he, the while, i
Urged the long ch
   of war.

Dry up thy tears, young daughter of a
  chief !
Waste not on him the sacredness of grief;
Be the fierce spirit of thy sire thine own,
His lips of scorning, and his heart of stone.

What heeds the warrior of a hundred
  fights,
The storm-worn watcher through long
  hunting nights,
Cold, crafty, proud of woman's weak
  distress,
Her home-bound grief and pining lone-
  liness ?

VII. THE DEPARTURE.

THE wild March rains had fallen fast and
  long
The snowy mountains of the North among,
Making each vale a watercourse, — each
  hill
Bright with the cascade of some new-
  made rill.

Gnawed by the sunbeams, softened by
  the rain,
Heaved underneath by the swollen current's strain,
The ice-bridge yielded, and the Merrimack
Bore the huge ruin crashing down its
  track.

On that strong turbid water, a small boat
Guided by one weak hand was seen to
  float ;
Evil the fate which loosed it from the
  shore,
Too early voyager with too frail an oar !

Down the vexed centre of that rushing
  tide,
The thick huge ice-blocks threatening
  either side,
The foam-white rocks of Amoskeag in
  view,
With arrowy swiftness sped that light
  canoe.

The trapper, moistening his moose's meat
On the wet bank by Uncanoonuc's feet,
Saw the swift boat flash down the trou-
  bled stream —
Slept he, or waked he ? — was it truth
  or dream ?

The straining eye bent fearfully before,
The small hand clenching on the useless
  oar,
The bead-wrought blanket trailing o'er
  the water —
He knew them all — woe for the Sachem's
  daughter !

Sick and aweary of her lonely life,
Heedless of peril the still faithful wife
Had left her mother's grave, her father's
  door,
To seek the wigwam of her chief once
  more.

Down the white rapids like a sear leaf
  whirled,
On the sharp rocks and piled-up ices
  hurled,
Empty and broken, circled the canoe
In the vexed pool below — but, where
  was Weetamoo ?

VIII. SONG OF INDIAN WOMEN.

THE Dark eye has left us,
  The Spring-bird has flown ;
On the pathway of spirits
  She wanders alone.
The song of the wood-dove has died on
  our shore, —
Mat wonck kunna-monee ! [25] — We hear
  it no more !

O dark water Spirit !
  We cast on thy wave
These furs which may never
  Hang over her grave ;
Bear down to the lost one the robes **that**
  she wore, —
Mat wonck kunna-monee ! — We see her
  no more !

Of the strange land she walks in
  No Powah has told :
It may burn with the sunshine,
  Or freeze with the cold.
Let us give to our lost one the robes that
  she wore,
Mat wonck kunna-monee ! — We see her
  no more !

The path she is treading
  Shall soon be our own ;
Each gliding in shadow
  Unseen and alone ! —

Iu vain shall we call on the souls gone
    before, —
Mat wonck kunna-monee ! — They hear
    us no more !

O mighty Sowanna ! [26]
    Thy gateways unfold,
From thy wigwam of sunset
    Lift curtains of gold !
Take home the poor Spirit whose journey
    is o'er, —
Mat wonck kunna-monee ! — We see her
    no more !

So sang the Children of the Leaves beside
The broad, dark river's coldly flowing tide,
Now low, now harsh, with sob-like
    pause and swell,
On the high wind their voices rose and fell.
Nature's wild music, — sounds of wind-
    swept trees,
The scream of birds, the wailing of the
    breeze,
The roar of waters, steady, deep, and
    strong, —
Mingled and murmured in that farewell
    song.

LEGENDARY.

THE MERRIMACK.

["The Indians speak of a beautiful river, far
to the south, which they call Merrimack." —
SIEUR DE MONTS: 1604.]

STREAM of my fathers ! sweetly still
The sunset rays thy valley fill ;
Poured slantwise down the long defile,
Wave, wood, and spire beneath them
    smile.
I see the winding Powow fold
The green hill in its belt of gold,
And following down its wavy line,
Its sparkling waters blend with thine.
There's not a tree upon thy side,
Nor rock, which thy returning tide
As yet hath left abrupt and stark
Above thy evening water-mark ;
No calm cove with its rocky hem,
No isle whose emerald swells begem
Thy broad, smooth current ; not a sail
Bowed to the freshening ocean gale ;
No small boat with its busy oars,
Nor gray wall sloping to thy shores ;
Nor farm-house with its maple shade,
Or rigid poplar colonnade,
But lies distinct and full in sight,
Beneath this gush of sunset light.
Centuries ago, that harbor-bar,
Stretching its length of foam afar,
And Salisbury's beach of shining sand,
And yonder island's wave-smoothed
    strand,
Saw the adventurer's tiny sail,

Flit, stooping from the eastern gale ; [27]
And o'er these woods and waters broke
The cheer from Britain's hearts of oak,
As brightly on the voyager's eye,
Weary of forest, sea, and sky,
Breaking the dull continuous wood,
The Merrimack rolled down his flood ;
Mingling that clear pellucid brook,
Which channels vast Agioochook
When spring-time's sun and shower un-
    lock
The frozen fountains of the rock,
And more abundant waters given
From that pure lake, "The Smile of
    Heaven," [28]
Tributes from vale and mountain-side, —
With ocean's dark, eternal tide !

On yonder rocky cape, which braves
The stormy challenge of the waves,
Midst tangled vine and dwarfish wood,
The hardy Anglo-Saxon stood,
Planting upon the topmost crag
The staff of England's battle-flag ;
And, while from out its heavy fold
Saint George's crimson cross unrolled,
Midst roll of drum and trumpet blare,
And weapons brandishing in air,
He gave to that lone promontory
The sweetest name in all his story ; [29]
Of her, the flower of Islam's daughters,
Whose harems look on Stamboul's
    waters, —
Who, when the chance of war had bound

The Moslem chain his limbs around,
Wreathed o'er with silk that iron chain,
Soothed with her smiles his hours of
    pain,
And fondly to her youthful slave
A dearer gift than freedom gave.

But look ! — the yellow light no more
Streams down on wave and verdant
    shore ;
And clearly on the calm air swells
The twilight voice of distant bells.
From Ocean's bosom, white and thin,
The mists come slowly rolling in ;
Hills, woods, the river's rocky rim,
Amidst the sea-like vapor swim,
While yonder lonely coast-light, set
Within its wave-washed minaret,
Half quenched, a beamless star and pale,
Shines dimly through its cloudy veil !

Home of my fathers ! — I have stood
Where Hudson rolled his lordly flood :
Seen sunrise rest and sunset fade
Along his frowning Palisade ;
Looked down the Apalachian peak
On Juniata's silver streak;
Have seen along his valley gleam
The Mohawk's softly winding stream ;
The level light of sunset shine
Through broad Potomac's hem of pine ;
And autumn's rainbow-tinted banner
Hang lightly o'er the Susquehanna ;
Yet wheresoe'er his step might be,
Thy wandering child looked back to
    thee !
Heard in his dreams thy river's sound
Of murmuring on its pebbly bound,
The unforgotten swell and roar
Of waves on thy familiar shore ;
And saw, amidst the curtained gloom
And quiet of his lonely room,
Thy sunset scenes before him pass ;
As, in Agrippa's magic glass,
The loved and lost arose to view,
Remembered groves in greenness grew,
Bathed still in childhood's morning
    dew,
Along whose bowers of beauty swept
Whatever Memory's mourners wept,
Sweet faces, which the charnel kept,
Young, gentle eyes, which long had
    slept ;
And while the gazer leaned to trace,
More near, some dear familiar face,
He wept to find the vision flown, —
A phantom and a dream alone !

THE NORSEMEN.[30]

Gift from the cold and silent Past !
A relic to the present cast ;
Left on the ever-changing strand
Of shifting and unstable sand,
Which wastes beneath the steady chime
And beating of the waves of Time !
Who from its bed of primal rock
First wrenched thy dark, unshapely
    block ?
Whose hand, of curious skill untaught,
Thy rude and savage outline wrought ?

The waters of my native stream
Are glancing in the sun's warm beam :
From sail-urged keel and flashing oar
The circles widen to its shore :
And cultured field and peopled town
Slope to its willowed margin down.
Yet, while this morning breeze is bringing
The home-life sound of school-bells ring-
    ing,
And rolling wheel, and rapid jar
Of the fire-winged and steedless car,
And voices from the wayside near
Come quick and blended on my ear,
A spell is in this old gray stone, —
My thoughts are with the Past alone !

A change ! — The steepled town no more
Stretches along the sail-thronged shore :
Like palace-domes in sunset's cloud,
Fade sun-gilt spire and mansion proud :
Spectrally rising where they stood,
I see the old, primeval wood ;
Dark, shadow-like, on either hand
I see its solemn waste expand :
It climbs the green and cultured hill,
It arches o'er the valley's rill ;
And leans from cliff and crag, to throw
Its wild arms o'er the stream below.
Unchanged, alone, the same bright river
Flows on, as it will flow forever !
I listen, and I hear the low
Soft ripple where its waters go ;
I hear behind the panther's cry,
The wild-bird's scream goes thrilling by,
And shyly on the river's brink
The deer is stooping down to drink.

But hark ! — from wood and rock flung
    back,
What sound comes up the Merrimack ?
What sea-worn barks are those which
    throw
The light spray from each rushing prow ?

Have they not in the North Sea's blast
Bowed to the waves the straining mast ?
Their frozen sails the low, pale sun
Of Thulé's night has shone upon ;
Flapped by the sea-wind's gusty sweep
Round icy drift, and headland steep.
Wild Jutland's wives and Lochlin's
　　daughters
Have watched them fading o'er the waters,
Lessening through driving mist and spray,
Like white-winged sea-birds on their way !

Onward they glide, — and now I view
Their iron-armed and stalwart crew ;
Joy glistens in each wild blue eye,
Turned to green earth and summer sky :
Each broad, seamed breast has cast aside
Its cumbering vest of shaggy hide ;
Bared to the sun and soft warm air,
Streams back the Norsemen's yellow hair.
I see the gleam of axe and spear,
The sound of smitten shields I hear,
Keeping a harsh and fitting time
To Saga's chant, and Runic rhyme ;
Such lays as Zetland's Scald has sung,
His gray and naked isles among ;
Or muttered low at midnight hour
Round Odin's mossy stone of power.
The wolf beneath the Arctic moon
Has answered to that startling rune ;
The Gael has heard its stormy swell,
The light Frank knows its summons well ;
Iona's sable-stoled Culdee
Has heard it sounding o'er the sea,
And swept, with hoary beard and hair,
His altar's foot in trembling prayer !

'T is past, — the 'wildering vision dies
In darkness on my dreaming eyes !
The forest vanishes in air, —
Hill-slope and vale lie starkly bare ;
I hear the common tread of men,
And hum of work-day life again :
The mystic relic seems alone
A broken mass of common stone ;
And if it be the chiselled limb
Of Berserker or idol grim,
A fragment of Valhalla's Thor,
The stormy Viking's god of War,
Or Praga of the Runic lay,
Or love-awakening Siona,
I know not, — for no graven line,
Nor Druid mark, nor Runic sign,
Is left me here, by which to trace
Its name, or origin, or place.
Yet, for this vision of the Past,
This glance upon its darkness cast,

My spirit bows in gratitude
Before the Giver of all good,
Who fashioned so the human mind,
That, from the waste of Time behind
A simple stone, or mound of earth,
Can summon the departed forth ;
Quicken the Past to life again, —
The Present lose in what hath been,
And in their primal freshness show
The buried forms of long ago.
As if a portion of that Thought
By which the Eternal will is wrought,
Whose impulse fills anew with breath
The frozen solitude of Death,
To mortal mind were sometimes lent,
To mortal musings sometimes sent,
To whisper — even when it seems
But Memory's fantasy of dreams —
Through the mind's waste of woe and
　　sin,
Of an immortal origin !

CASSANDRA SOUTHWICK.

1658.

To the God of all sure mercies let my
　　blessing rise to-day,
From the scoffer and the cruel He hath
　　plucked the spoil away, —
Yea, He who cooled the furnace around
　　the faithful three,
And tamed the Chaldean lions, hath set
　　his handmaid free !

Last night I saw the sunset melt through
　　my prison bars,
Last night across my damp earth-floor
　　fell the pale gleam of stars ;
In the coldness and the darkness all
　　through the long night-time,
My grated casement whitened with au-
　　tumn's early rime.

Alone, in that dark sorrow, hour after
　　hour crept by ;
Star after star looked palely in and sank
　　adown the sky ;
No sound amid night's stillness, save that
　　which seemed to be
The dull and heavy beating of the pulses
　　of the sea ;

All night I sat unsleeping, for I knew
　　that on the morrow
The ruler and the cruel priest would mock
　　me in my sorrow,

Dragged to their place of market, and
    bargained for and sold,
Like a lamb before the shambles, like a
    heifer from the fold !

O, the weakness of the flesh was there, —
    the shrinking and the shame ;
And the low voice of the Tempter like
    whispers to me came :
" Why sit'st thou thus forlornly !" the
    wicked murmur said,
" Damp walls thy bower of beauty, cold
    earth thy maiden bed ?

" Where be the smiling faces, and voices
    soft and sweet,
Seen in thy father's dwelling, heard in
    the pleasant street ?
Where be the youths whose glances, the
    summer Sabbath through,
Turned tenderly and timidly unto thy
    father's pew ?

" Why sit'st thou here, Cassandra ? —
    Bethink thee with what mirth
Thy happy schoolmates gather around the
    warm bright hearth ;
How the crimson shadows tremble on
    foreheads white and fair,
On eyes of merry girlhood, half hid in
    golden hair.

" Not for thee the hearth-fire brightens,
    not for thee kind words are spoken,
Not for thee the nuts of Wenham woods
    by laughing boys are broken,
No first-fruits of the orchard within thy
    lap are laid,
For thee no flowers of autumn the youth-
    ful hunters braid.

" O, weak, deluded maiden ! — by crazy
    fancies led,
With wild and raving railers an evil path
    to tread ;
To leave a wholesome worship, and teach-
    ing pure and sound ;
And mate with maniac women, loose-
    haired and sackcloth bound.

" Mad scoffers of the priesthood, who
    mock at things divine,
Who rail against the pulpit, and holy
    bread and wine ;
Sore from their cart-tail scourgings, and
    from the pillory lame,
Rejoicing in their wretchedness, and
    glorying in their shame.

" And what a fate awaits thee ?—a sadly
    toiling slave,
Dragging the slowly lengthening chain
    of bondage to the grave !
Think of thy woman's nature, subdued
    in hopeless thrall,
The easy prey of any, the scoff and scorn
    of all ! "

O, ever as the Tempter spoke, and feeble
    Nature's fears
Wrung drop by drop the scalding flow
    of unavailing tears,
I wrestled down the evil thoughts, and
    strove in silent prayer,
To feel, O Helper of the weak ! that
    Thou indeed wert there !

I thought of Paul and Silas, within
    Philippi's cell,
And how from Peter's sleeping limbs the
    prison-shackles fell,
Till I seemed to hear the trailing of an
    angel's robe of white,
And to feel a blessed presence invisible
    to sight.

Bless the Lord for all his mercies !— for
    the peace and love I felt,
Like dew of Hermon's holy hill, upon
    my spirit melt ;
When "'Get behind me, Satan !" was
    the language of my heart,
And I felt the Evil Tempter with all his
    doubts depart.

Slow broke the gray cold morning ; again
    the sunshine fell,
Flecked with the shade of bar and grate
    within my lonely cell ;
The hoar-frost melted on the wall, and
    upward from the street
Came careless laugh and idle word, and
    tread of passing feet.

At length the heavy bolts fell back, my
    door was open cast,
And slowly at the sheriff's side, up the
    long street I passed ;
I heard the murmur round me, and felt,
    but dared not see,
How, from every door and window, the
    people gazed on me.

And doubt and fear fell on me, shame
    burned upon my cheek,
Swam earth and sky around me, my
    trembling limbs grew weak :

"O Lord ! support thy handmaid ; and
    from her soul cast out
The fear of man, which brings a snare, —
    the weakness and the doubt."

Then the dreary shadows scattered, like
    a cloud in morning's breeze,
And a low deep voice within me seemed
    whispering words like these :
"Though thy earth be as the iron, and
    thy heaven a brazen wall,
Trust still His loving-kindness whose
    power is over all."

We paused at length, where at my feet
    the sunlit waters broke
On glaring reach of shining beach, and
    shingly wall of rock ;
The merchant-ships lay idly there, in
    hard clear lines on high,
Tracing with rope and slender spar their
    network on the sky.

And there were ancient citizens, cloak-
    wrapped and grave and cold,
And grim and stout sea-captains with
    faces bronzed and old,
And on his horse, with Rawson, his cruel
    clerk at hand,
Sat dark and haughty Endicott, the
    ruler of the land.

And poisoning with his evil words the
    ruler's ready ear,
The priest leaned o'er his saddle, with
    laugh and scoff and jeer ;
It stirred my soul, and from my lips the
    seal of silence broke,
As if through woman's weakness a warn-
    ing spirit spoke.

I cried, "The Lord rebuke thee, thou
    smiter of the meek,
Thou robber of the righteous, thou tram-
    pler of the weak !
Go light the dark, cold hearth-stones, —
    go turn the prison lock
Of the poor hearts thou hast hunted, thou
    wolf amid the flock !"

Dark lowered the brows of Endicott,
    and with a deeper red
O'er Rawson's wine-empurpled cheek the
    flush of anger spread ;
"Good people," quoth the white-lipped
    priest, "heed not her words so wild,
Her Master speaks within her, — the
    Devil owns his child !"

But gray heads shook, and young brows
    knit, the while the sheriff read
That law the wicked rulers against the
    poor have made,
Who to their house of Rimmon and idol
    priesthood bring
No bended knee of worship, nor gainful
    offering.

Then to the stout sea-captains the sher-
    iff, turning, said, —
"Which of ye, worthy seamen, will take
    this Quaker maid ?
In the Isle of fair Barbadoes, or on Vir-
    ginia's shore,
You may hold her at a higher price than
    Indian girl or Moor."

Grim and silent stood the captains ; and
    when again he cried,
"Speak out, my worthy seamen !" — no
    voice, no sign replied ;
But I felt a hard hand press my own,
    and kind words met my ear, —
"God bless thee, and preserve thee, my
    gentle girl and dear !"

A weight seemed lifted from my heart, —
    a pitying friend was nigh,
I felt it in his hard, rough hand, and saw
    it in his eye ;
And when again the sheriff spoke, that
    voice, so kind to me,
Growled back its stormy answer like the
    roaring of the sea, —

"Pile my ship with bars of silver, — pack
    with coins of Spanish gold,
From keel-piece up to deck-plank, the
    roomage of her hold,
By the living God who made me ! — I
    would sooner in your bay
Sink ship and crew and cargo, than bear
    this child away !"

"Well answered, worthy captain, shame
    on their cruel laws !"
Ran through the crowd in murmurs loud
    the people's just applause.
"Like the herdsman of Tekoa, in Israel
    of old,
Shall we see the poor and righteous again
    for silver sold ?"

I looked on haughty Endicott ; with
    weapon half-way drawn,
Swept round the throng his lion glare of
    bitter hate and scorn ;

Fiercely he drew his bridle-rein, and
    turned in silence back,
And sneering priest and baffled clerk rode
    murmuring in his track.

Hard after them the sheriff looked, in
    bitterness of soul ;
Thrice smote his staff upon the ground,
    and crushed his parchment roll.
" Good friends," he said, " since both
    have fled, the ruler and the priest,
Judge ye, if from their further work I
    be not well released."

Loud was the cheer which, full and
    clear, swept round the silent bay,
As, with kind words and kinder looks,
    he bade me go my way ;
For He who turns the courses of the
    streamlet of the glen,
And the river of great waters, had turned
    the hearts of men.

O, at that hour the very earth seemed
    changed beneath my eye,
A holier wonder round me rose the blue
    walls of the sky,
A lovelier light on rock and hill and stream
    and woodland lay,
And softer lapsed on sunnier sands the
    waters of the bay.

Thanksgiving to the Lord of life ! — to
    Him all praises be,
Who from the hands of evil men hath
    set his handmaid free ;
All praise to Him before whose power
    the mighty are afraid,
Who takes the crafty in the snare which
    for the poor is laid !

Sing, O my soul, rejoicingly, on even-
    ing's twilight calm
Uplift the loud thanksgiving, — pour
    forth the grateful psalm ;
Let all dear hearts with me rejoice, as
    did the saints of old,
When of the Lord's good angel the res-
    cued Peter told.

And weep and howl, ye evil priests and
    mighty men of wrong,
The Lord shall smite the proud, and lay
    his hand upon the strong.
Woe to the wicked rulers in his avenging
    hour !
Woe to the wolves who seek the flocks to
    raven and devour !

But let the humble ones arise, — the
    poor in heart be glad,
And let the mourning ones again with
    robes of praise be clad,
For He who cooled the furnace, and
    smoothed the stormy wave,
And tamed the Chaldean lions, is mighty
    still to save !

FUNERAL TREE OF THE SOKOKIS.

1756.

AROUND Sebago's lonely lake
There lingers not a breeze to break
The mirror which its waters make.

The solemn pines along its shore,
The firs which hang its gray rocks o'er,
Are painted on its glassy floor.

The sun looks o'er, with hazy eye,
The snowy mountain-tops which lie
Piled coldly up against the sky.

Dazzling and white ! save where the bleak,
Wild winds have bared some splintering
    peak,
Or snow-slide left its dusky streak.

Yet green are Saco's banks below,
And belts of spruce and cedar show,
Dark fringing round those cones of snow.

The earth hath felt the breath of spring,
Though yet on her deliverer's wing
The lingering frosts of winter cling.

Fresh grasses fringe the meadow-brooks
And mildly from its sunny nooks
The blue eye of the violet looks.

And odors from the springing grass,
The sweet birch and the sassafras,
Upon the scarce-felt breezes pass.

Her tokens of renewing care
Hath Nature scattered everywhere,
In bud and flower, and warmer air.

But in their hour of bitterness,
What reck the broken Sokokis,
Beside their slaughtered chief, of this ?

The turf's red stain is yet undried, —
Scarce have the death-shot echoes died
Along Sebago's wooded side :

And silent now the hunters stand,
Grouped darkly, where a swell of land
Slopes upward from the lake's white
   sand.

Fire and the axe have swept it bare,
Save one lone beech, unclosing there
Its light leaves in the vernal air.

With grave, cold looks, all sternly mute,
They break the damp turf at its foot,
And bare its coiled and twisted root.

They heave the stubborn trunk aside,
The firm roots from the earth divide, —
The rent beneath yawns dark and wide.

And there the fallen chief is laid,
In tasselled garbs of skins arrayed,
And girded with his wampum-braid.

The silver cross he loved is pressed
Beneath the heavy arms, which rest
Upon his scarred and naked breast.

'T is done : the roots are backward sent,
The beechen-tree stands up unbent, —
The Indian's fitting monument !

When of that sleeper's broken race
Their green and pleasant dwelling-place
Which knew them once, retains no trace ;

O, long may sunset's light be shed
As now upon that beech's head, —
A green memorial of the dead !

There shall his fitting requiem be,
In northern winds, that, cold and free,
Howl nightly in that funeral tree.

To their wild wail the waves which break
Forever round that lonely lake
A solemn undertone shall make !

And who shall deem the spot unblest,
Where Nature's younger children rest,
Lulled on their sorrowing mother's breast ?

Deem ye that mother loveth less
These bronzed forms of the wilderness
She foldeth in her long caress ?

As sweet o'er them her wild-flowers
   blow
As if with fairer hair and brow
The blue-eyed Saxon slept below.

What though the places of their rest
No priestly knee hath ever pressed, —
No funeral rite nor prayer hath blessed !

What though the bigot's ban be there,
And thoughts of wailing and despair,
And cursing in the place of prayer !

Yet Heaven hath angels watching round
The Indian's lowliest forest-mound, —
And *they* have made it holy ground.

There ceases man's frail judgment ; all
His powerless bolts of cursing fall
Unheeded on that grassy pall.

O, peeled, and hunted, and reviled,
Sleep on, dark tenant of the wild !
Great Nature owns her simple child !

And Nature's God, to whom alone
The secret of the heart is known, —
The hidden language traced thereon ;

Who from its many cumberings
Of form and creed, and outward things,
To light the naked spirit brings ;

Not with our partial eye shall scan,
Not with our pride and scorn shall
   ban,
The spirit of our brother man !

ST. JOHN.

1647.

" To the winds give our banner !
   Bear homeward again ! "
Cried the Lord of Acadia,
   Cried Charles of Estienne ;
From the prow of his shallop
   He gazed, as the sun,
From its bed in the ocean,
   Streamed up the St. John.

O'er the blue western waters
   That shallop had passed,
Where the mists of Penobscot
   Clung damp on her mast.
St. Saviour had looked
   On the heretic sail,
As the songs of the Huguenot
   Rose on the gale.

The pale, ghostly fathers
   Remembered her well,

And had cursed her while passing,
  With taper and bell,
But the men of Monhegan,
  Of Papists abhorred,
Had welcomed and feasted
  The heretic Lord.

They had loaded his shallop
  With dun-fish and ball,
With stores for his larder,
  And steel for his wall.
Pemequid, from her bastions
  And turrets of stone,
Had welcomed his coming
  With banner and gun.

And the prayers of the elders
  Had followed his way,
As homeward he glided,
  Down Pentecost Bay.
O, well sped La Tour !
  For, in peril and pain,
His lady kept watch,
  For his coming again.

O'er the Isle of the Pheasant
  The morning sun shone,
On the plane-trees which shaded
  The shores of St. John.
"Now, why from yon battlements
  Speaks not my love !
Why waves there no banner
  My fortress above ?"

Dark and wild, from his deck
  St. Estienne gazed about,
On fire-wasted dwellings,
  And silent redoubt ;
From the low, shattered walls
  Which the flame had o'errun,
There floated no banner,
  There thundered no gun !

But beneath the low arch
  Of its doorway there stood
A pale priest of Rome,
  In his cloak and his hood.
With the bound of a lion,
  La Tour sprang to land,
On the throat of the Papist
  He fastened his hand.

"Speak, son of the Woman
  Of scarlet and sin !
What wolf has been prowling
  My castle within ?"

From the grasp of the soldier
  The Jesuit broke,
Half in scorn, half in sorrow,
  He smiled as he spoke :

" No wolf, Lord of Estienne,
  Has ravaged thy hall,
But thy red-handed rival,
  With fire, steel, and ball !
On an errand of mercy
  I hitherward came,
While the walls of thy castle
  Yet spouted with flame.

" Pentagoet's dark vessels
  Were moored in the bay,
Grim sea-lions, roaring
  Aloud for their prey."
" But what of my lady ?"
  Cried Charles of Estienne :
" On the shot-crumbled turret
  Thy lady was seen :

" Half-veiled in the smoke-cloud,
  Her hand grasped thy pennon,
While her dark tresses swayed
  In the hot breath of cannon !
But woe to the heretic,
  Evermore woe !
When the son of the church
  And the cross is his foe !

" In the track of the shell,
  In the path of the ball,
Pentagoet swept over
  The breach of the wall !
Steel to steel, gun to gun,
  One moment, — and then
Alone stood the victor,
  Alone with his men !

" Of its sturdy defenders,
  Thy lady alone
Saw the cross-blazoned banner
  Float over St. John."
" Let the dastard look to it !"
  Cried fiery Estienne,
" Were D'Aulney King Louis,
  I'd free her again !"

" Alas for thy lady !
  No service from thee
Is needed by her
  Whom the Lord hath set free :
Nine days, in stern silence,
  Her thraldom she bore,

But the tenth morning came,
 And Death opened her door !"

As if suddenly smitten
 La Tour staggered back ;
His hand grasped his sword-hilt,
 His forehead grew black.
He sprang on the deck
 Of his shallop again.
" We cruise now for vengeance !
 Give way !" cried Estienne.

" Massachusetts shall hear
 Of the Huguenot's wrong,
And from island and creekside
 Her fishers shall throng !
Pentagoet shall rue
 What his Papists have done,
When his palisades echo
 The Puritan's gun !"

O, the loveliest of heavens
 Hung tenderly o'er him,
There were waves in the sunshine,
 And green isles before him :
But a pale hand was beckoning
 The Huguenot on ;
And in blackness and ashes
 Behind was St. John !

PENTUCKET.

1708.

How sweetly on the wood-girt town
The mellow light of sunset shone !
Each small, bright lake, whose waters still
Mirror the forest and the hill,
Reflected from its waveless breast
The beauty of a cloudless west,
Glorious as if a glimpse were given
Within the western gates of heaven,
Left, by the spirit of the star
Of sunset's holy hour, ajar !

Beside the river's tranquil flood
The dark and low-walled dwellings stood,
Where many a rood of open land
Stretched up and down on either hand,
With corn-leaves waving freshly green
The thick and blackened stumps between.
Behind, unbroken, deep and dread,
The wild, untravelled forest spread,
Back to those mountains, white and cold,
Of which the Indian trapper told,
Upon whose summits never yet
Was mortal foot in safety set.

Quiet and calm, without a fear
Of danger darkly lurking near,
The weary laborer left his plough, —
The milkmaid carolled by her cow, —
From cottage door and household hearth
Rose songs of praise, or tones of mirth.
At length the murmur died away,
And silence on that village lay, —
So slept Pompeii, tower and hall,
Ere the quick earthquake swallowed all,
Undreaming of the fiery fate
Which made its dwellings desolate !

Hours passed away. By moonlight sped
The Merrimack along his bed.
Bathed in the pallid lustre, stood
Dark cottage-wall and rock and wood,
Silent, beneath that tranquil beam,
As the hushed grouping of a dream.
Yet on the still air crept a sound, —
No bark of fox, nor rabbit's bound,
Nor stir of wings, nor waters flowing,
Nor leaves in midnight breezes blowing.

Was that the tread of many feet,
Which downward from the hillside beat ?
What forms were those which darkly
 stood
Just on the margin of the wood ? —
Charred tree-stumps in the moonlight
 dim,
Or paling rude, or leafless limb ?
No, — through the trees fierce eyeballs
 glowed,
Dark human forms in moonshine showed,
Wild from their native wilderness,
With painted limbs and battle-dress !

A yell the dead might wake to hear
Swelled on the night air, far and clear, —
Then smote the Indian tomahawk
On crashing door and shattering lock, --
Then rang the rifle-shot, — and then
The shrill death-scream of stricken
 men,
Sank the red axe in woman's brain,
And childhood's cry arose in vain, —
Bursting through roof and window came,
Red, fast, and fierce, the kindled flame ;
And blended fire and moonlight glared
On still dead men and weapons bared.

The morning sun looked brightly through
The river willows, wet with dew.
No sound of combat filled the air, —
No shout was heard, — nor gunshot there :
Yet still the thick and sullen smoke

From smouldering ruins slowly broke ;
And on the greensward many a stain,
And, here and there, the mangled slain,
Told how that midnight bolt had sped,
Pentucket, on thy fated head !

Even now the villager can tell
Where Rolfe beside his hearthstone fell,
Still show the door of wasting oak,
Through which the fatal death-shot broke,
And point the curious stranger where
De Rouville's corse lay grim and bare, —
Whose hideous head, in death still feared,
Bore not a trace of hair or beard, —
And still, within the churchyard ground,
Heaves darkly up the ancient mound,
Whose grass-grown surface overlies
The victims of that sacrifice.

THE FAMILIST'S HYMN. ˙

FATHER ! to thy suffering poor
  Strength and grace and faith impart,
And with thy own love restore
  Comfort to the broken heart !
O, the failing ones confirm
  With a holier strength of zeal ! —
Give thou not the feeble worm
  Helpless to the spoiler's heel !

Father ! for thy holy sake
  We are spoiled and hunted thus ;
Joyful, for thy truth we take
  Bonds and burthens unto us :
Poor, and weak, and robbed of all,
  Weary with our daily task,
That thy truth may never fall
  Through our weakness, Lord, we ask.

Round our fired and wasted homes
  Flits the forest-bird unscared,
And at noon the wild beast comes
  Where our frugal meal was shared ;
For the song of praises there
  Shrieks the crow the livelong day ;
For the sound of evening prayer
  Howls the evil beast of prey !

Sweet the songs we loved to sing
  Underneath thy holy sky, —
Words and tones that used to bring
  Tears of joy in every eye, —
Dear the wrestling hours of prayer,
  When we gathered knee to knee,
Blameless youth and hoary hair,
  Bowed. O God, alone to thee.

As thine early children, Lord,
  Shared their wealth and daily bread,
Even so, with one accord,
  We, in love, each other fed.
Not with us the miser's hoard,
  Not with us his grasping hand ;
Equal round a common board,
  Drew our meek and brother band !

Safe our quiet Eden lay
  When the war-whoop stirred the
    land
And the Indian turned away
  From our home his bloody hand.
Well that forest-ranger saw,
  That the burthen and the curse
Of the white man's cruel law
  Rested also upon us.

Torn apart, and driven forth
  To our toiling hard and long,
Father ! from the dust of earth
  Lift we still our grateful song !
Grateful, — that in bonds we share
  In thy love which maketh free ;
Joyful, — that the wrongs we bear,
  Draw us nearer, Lord, to thee !

Grateful ! — that where'er we toil, —
  By Wachuset's wooded side,
On Nantucket's sea-worn isle,
  Or by wild Neponset's tide, —
Still, in spirit, we are near,
  And our evening hymns, which rise
Separate and discordant here,
  Meet and mingle in the skies !

Let the scoffer scorn and mock,
  Let the proud and evil priest
Rob the needy of his flock,
  For his wine-cup and his feast, —
Redden not thy bolts in store
  Through the blackness of thy skies !
For the sighing of the poor
  Wilt Thou not, at length, arise !

Worn and wasted, oh ! how long
  Shall thy trodden poor complain ?
In thy name they bear the wrong,
  In thy cause the bonds of pain !
Melt oppression's heart of steel,
  Let the haughty priesthood see,
And their blinded followers feel,
  That in us they mock at Thee !

In thy time, O Lord of hosts,
  Stretch abroad that hand to save

Which of old, on Egypt's coasts,
  Smote apart the Red Sea's wave !
Lead us from this evil land,
  From the spoiler set us free,
And once more our gathered band,
  Heart to heart, shall worship thee !

THE FOUNTAIN.

TRAVELLER ! on thy journey toiling
  By the swift Powow,
With the summer sunshine falling
  On thy heated brow,
Listen, while all else is still,
To the brooklet from the hill.

Wild and sweet the flowers are blowing
  By that streamlet's side,
And a greener verdure showing
  Where its waters glide, —
Down the hill-slope murmuring on,
Over root and mossy stone.

Where yon oak his broad arms flingeth
  O'er the sloping hill,
Beautiful and freshly springeth
  That soft-flowing rill,
Through its dark roots wreathed and
      bare,
Gushing up to sun and air.

Brighter waters sparkled never
  In that magic well,
Of whose gift of life forever
  Ancient legends tell, —
In the lonely desert wasted,
And by mortal lip untasted.

Waters which the proud Castilian [31]
  Sought with longing eyes,
Underneath the bright pavilion
  Of the Indian skies ;
Where his forest pathway lay
Through the blooms of Florida.

Years ago a lonely stranger,
  With the dusky brow
Of the outcast forest-ranger,
  Crossed the swift Powow ;
And betook him to the rill
And the oak upon the hill.

O'er his face of moody sadness
  For an instant shone
Something like a gleam of gladness,
  As he stooped him down

To the fountain's grassy side,
And his eager thirst supplied.

With the oak its shadow throwing
  O'er his mossy seat,
And the cool, sweet waters flowing
  Softly at his feet,
Closely by the fountain's rim
That lone Indian seated him.

Autumn's earliest frost had given
  To the woods below
Hues of beauty, such as heaven
  Lendeth to its bow ;
And the soft breeze from the west
Scarcely broke their dreamy rest.

Far behind was Ocean striving
  With his chains of sand ;
Southward, sunny glimpses giving,
  'Twixt the swells of land,
Of its calm and silvery track,
Rolled the tranquil Merrimack.

Over village, wood, and meadow
  Gazed that stranger man,
Sadly, till the twilight shadow
  Over all things ran,
Save where spire and westward pane
Flashed the sunset back again.

Gazing thus upon the dwelling
  Of his warrior sires,
Where no lingering trace was telling
  Of their wigwam fires,
Who the gloomy thoughts might know
Of that wandering child of woe ?

Naked lay, in sunshine glowing,
  Hills that once had stood
Down their sides the shadows throw-
      ing
  Of a mighty wood,
Where the deer his covert kept,
And the eagle's pinion swept !

Where the birch canoe had glided
  Down the swift Powow,
Dark and gloomy bridges strided
  Those clear waters now ;
And where once the beaver swam,
Jarred the wheel and frowned the dam.

For the wood-bird's merry singing,
  And the hunter's cheer,
Iron clang and hammer's ringing
  Smote upon his ear ;

And the thick and sullen smoke
From the blackened forges broke.

Could it be his fathers ever
　Loved to linger here ?
These bare hills, this conquered river, —
　Could they hold them dear,
With their native loveliness
Tamed and tortured into this ?

Sadly, as the shades of even
　Gathered o'er the hill,
While the western half of heaven
　Blushed with sunset still,
From the fountain's mossy seat
Turned the Indian's weary feet.

Year on year hath flown forever,
　But he came no more
To the hillside or the river
　Where he came before.
But the villager can tell
Of that strange man's visit well.

And the merry children, laden
　With their fruits or flowers, —
Roving boy and laughing maiden,
　In their school-day hours,
Love the simple tale to tell
Of the Indian and his well.

THE EXILES.

1660.

THE goodman sat beside his door
　One sultry afternoon,
With his young wife singing at his side
　An old and goodly tune.

A glimmer of heat was in the air ;
　The dark green woods were still ;
And the skirts of a heavy thunder-cloud
　Hung over the western hill.

Black, thick, and vast arose that cloud
　Above the wilderness,
As some dark world from upper air
　Were stooping over this.

At times the solemn thunder pealed,
　And all was still again,
Save a low murmur in the air
　Of coming wind and rain.

Just as the first big rain-drop fell,
　A weary stranger came,

And stood before the farmer's door,
　With travel soiled and lame.

Sad seemed he, yet sustaining hope
　Was in his quiet glance,
And peace, like autumn's moonlight, clothed
　His tranquil countenance.

A look, like that his Master wore
　In Pilate's council-hall :
It told of wrongs, — but of a love
　Meekly forgiving all.

"Friend ! wilt thou give me shelter
　here ?"
　The stranger meekly said ;
And, leaning on his oaken staff,
　The goodman's features read.

" My life is hunted, — evil men
　Are following in my track ;
The traces of the torturer's whip
　Are on my aged back.

" And much, I fear, 't will peril thee
　Within thy doors to take
A hunted seeker of the Truth,
　Oppressed for conscience' sake."

O, kindly spoke the goodman's wife, —
　"Come in, old man !" quoth she, —
" We will not leave thee to the storm,
　Whoever thou mayst be."

Then came the aged wanderer in,
　And silent sat him down ;
While all within grew dark as night
　Beneath the storm-cloud's frown.

But while the sudden lightning's blaze
　Filled every cottage nook,
And with the jarring thunder-roll
　The loosened casements shook,

A heavy tramp of horses' feet
　Came sounding up the lane,
And half a score of horse, or more,
　Came plunging through the rain.

"Now, Goodman Macey, ope thy door, —
　We would not be house-breakers ;
A rueful deed thou 'st done this day,
　In harboring banished Quakers."

Out looked the cautious goodman then,
　With much of fear and awe,

For there, with broad wig drenched with
    rain,
  The parish priest he saw.

"Open thy door, thou wicked man,
  And let thy pastor in,
And give God thanks, if forty stripes
  Repay thy deadly sin."

"What seek ye?" quoth the goodman, —
  "The stranger is my guest:
He is worn with toil and grievous
    wrong, —
  Pray let the old man rest."

"Now, out upon thee, canting knave!"
  And strong hands shook the door.
"Believe me, Macey," quoth the
    priest, —
  "Thou 'lt rue thy conduct sore."

Then kindled Macey's eye of fire:
  "No priest who walks the earth,
Shall pluck away the stranger-guest
  Made welcome to my hearth."

Down from his cottage wall he caught
  The matchlock, hotly tried
At Preston-pans and Marston-moor,
  By fiery Ireton's side;

Where Puritan, and Cavalier,
  With shout and psalm contended;
And Rupert's oath, and Cromwell's
    prayer,
  With battle-thunder blended.

Up rose the ancient stranger then:
  "My spirit is not free
To bring the wrath and violence
  Of evil men on thee:

"And for thyself, I pray forbear, —
  Bethink thee of thy Lord,
Who healed again the smitten ear,
  And sheathed his follower's sword.

"I go, as to the slaughter led:
  Friends of the poor, farewell!"
Beneath his hand the oaken door
  Back on its hinges fell.

"Come forth, old graybeard, yea and
    nay,"
  The reckless scoffers cried,
As to a horseman's saddle-bow
  The old man's arms were tied.

And of his bondage hard and long
  In Boston's crowded jail,
Where suffering woman's prayer was
    heard,
  With sickening childhood's wail,

It suits not with our tale to tell:
  Those scenes have passed away, —
Let the dim shadows of the past
  Brood o'er that evil day.

"Ho, sheriff!" quoth the ardent
    priest, —
  "Take Goodman Macey too;
The sin of this day's heresy
  His back or purse shall rue."

"Now, goodwife, haste thee!" Macey
    cried,
  She caught his manly arm: —
Behind, the parson urged pursuit,
  With outcry and alarm.

Ho! speed the Maceys, neck or naught, —
  The river-course was near: —
The plashing on its pebbled shore
  Was music to their ear.

A gray rock, tasselled o'er with birch,
  Above the waters hung,
And at its base, with every wave,
  A small light wherry swung.

A leap — they gain the boat — and there
  The goodman wields his oar:
"Ill luck betide them all," — he cried, —
  "The laggards upon the shore."

Down through the crashing underwood,
  The burly sheriff came: —
"Stand, Goodman Macey, — yield thy-
    self;
  Yield in the King's own name."

"Now out upon thy hangman's face!"
  Bold Macey answered then, —
"Whip women, on the village green,
  But meddle not with men."

The priest came panting to the shore, —
  His grave cocked hat was gone;
Behind him, like some owl's nest, hung
  His wig upon a thorn.

"Come back, — come back!" the par-
    son cried,
  "The church's curse beware."

"Curse, an' thou wilt," said Macey, "but
  Thy blessing prithee spare."

"Vile scoffer!" cried the baffled priest, —
  "Thou 'lt yet the gallows see."
"Who 's born to be hanged, will not be
    drowned,"
Quoth Macey, merrily ;

"And so, sir sheriff and priest, good by !"
  He bent him to his oar,
And the small boat glided quietly
  From the twain upon the shore.

Now in the west, the heavy clouds
  Scattered and fell asunder,
While feebler came the rush of rain,
  And fainter growled the thunder.

And through the broken clouds, the sun
  Looked out serene and warm,
Painting its holy symbol-light
  Upon the passing storm.

O, beautiful ! that rainbow span,
  O'er dim Crane-neck was bended ; —
One bright foot touched the eastern hills,
  And one with ocean blended.

By green Pentucket's southern slope
  The small boat glided fast, —
The watchers of "the Block-house" saw
  The strangers as they passed.

That night a stalwart garrison
  Sat shaking in their shoes,
To hear the dip of Indian oars, —
  The glide of birch canoes.

The fisher-wives of Salisbury,
  (The men were all away,)
Looked out to see the stranger oar
  Upon their waters play.

Deer-Island's rocks and fir-trees threw
  Their sunset-shadows o'er them,
And Newbury's spire and weathercock
  Peered o'er the pines before them.

Around the Black Rocks, on their left,
  The marsh lay broad and green ;
And on their right, with dwarf shrubs
    crowned,
Plum Island's hills were seen.

With skilful hand and wary eye
  The harbor-bar was crossed ; —

A plaything of the restless wave,
  The boat on ocean tossed.

The glory of the sunset heaven
  On land and water lay, —
On the steep hills of Agawam,
  On cape, and bluff, and bay.

They passed the gray rocks of Cape Ann,
  And Gloucester's harbor-bar ;
The watch-fire of the garrison
  Shone like a setting star.

How brightly broke the morning
  On Massachusetts Bay !
Blue wave, and bright green island,
  Rejoicing in the day.

On passed the bark in safety
  Round isle and headland steep, —
No tempest broke above them,
  No fog-cloud veiled the deep.

Far round the bleak and stormy Cape
  The vent'rous Macey passed,
And on Nantucket's naked isle
  Drew up his boat at last.

And how, in log-built cabin,
  They braved the rough sea-weather ;
And there, in peace and quietness,
  Went down life's vale together :

How others drew around them,
  And how their fishing sped,
Until to every wind of heaven
  Nantucket's sails were spread ;

How pale Want alternated
  With Plenty's golden smile ;
Behold, is it not written
  In the annals of the isle ?

And yet that isle remaineth
  A refuge of the free,
As when true-hearted Macey
  Beheld it from the sea.

Free as the winds that winnow
  Her shrubless hills of sand, —
Free as the waves that batter
  Along her yielding land.

Than hers, at duty's summons,
  No loftier spirit stirs, —
Nor falls o'er human suffering
  A readier tear than hers.

God bless the sea-beat island! —
And grant forevermore,
That charity and freedom dwell
As now upon her shore!

THE NEW WIFE AND THE OLD.

DARK the halls, and cold the feast, —
Gone the bridemaids, gone the priest:
All is over, — all is done,
Twain of yesterday are one!
Blooming girl and manhood gray,
Autumn in the arms of May!

Hushed within and hushed without,
Dancing feet and wrestlers' shout;
Dies the bonfire on the hill;
All is dark and all is still,
Save the starlight, save the breeze
Moaning through the graveyard trees;
And the great sea-waves below,
Pulse of the midnight beating slow.

From the brief dream of a bride
She hath wakened, at his side.
With half-uttered shriek and start, —
Feels she not his beating heart?
And the pressure of his arm,
And his breathing near and warm?

Lightly from the bridal bed
Springs that fair dishevelled head,
And a feeling, new, intense,
Half of shame, half innocence,
Maiden fear and wonder speaks
Through her lips and changing cheeks.

From the oaken mantel glowing
Faintest light the lamp is throwing
On the mirror's antique mould,
High-backed chair, and wainscot old,
And, through faded curtains stealing,
His dark sleeping face revealing.

Listless lies the strong man there,
Silver-streaked his careless hair;
Lips of love have left no trace
On that hard and haughty face;
And that forehead's knitted thought
Love's soft hand hath not unwrought.

"Yet," she sighs, "he loves me well,
More than these calm lips will tell.
Stooping to my lowly state,
He hath made me rich and great,
And I bless him, though he be
Hard and stern to all save me!"

While she speaketh, falls the light
O'er her fingers small and white;
Gold and gem, and costly ring
Back the timid lustre fling, —
Love's selectest gifts, and rare,
His proud hand had fastened there.

Gratefully she marks the glow
From those tapering lines of snow;
Fondly o'er the sleeper bending
His black hair with golden blending,
In her soft and light caress,
Cheek and lip together press.

Ha! — that start of horror! — Why
That wild stare and wilder cry,
Full of terror, full of pain?
Is there madness in her brain?
Hark! that gasping, hoarse and low,
"Spare me, — spare me, — let me
    go!"

God have mercy! — Icy cold
Spectral hands her own enfold,
Drawing silently from them
Love's fair gifts of gold and gem,
"Waken! save me!" still as death
At her side he slumbereth.

Ring and bracelet all are gone,
And that ice-cold hand withdrawn;
But she hears a murmur low,
Full of sweetness, full of woe,
Half a sigh and half a moan:
"Fear not! give the dead her own!"

Ah! — the dead wife's voice she knows!
That cold hand, whose pressure froze,
Once in warmest life had borne
Gem and band her own hath worn.
"Wake thee! wake thee!" Lo, his
    eyes
Open with a dull surprise.

In his arms the strong man folds her,
Closer to his breast he holds her;
Trembling limbs his own are meeting,
And he feels her heart's quick beating:
"Nay, my dearest, why this fear?"
"Hush!" she saith, "the dead is here!"

"Nay, a dream, — an idle dream."
But before the lamp's pale gleam
Tremblingly her hand she raises, —
There no more the diamond blazes,
Clasp of pearl, or ring of gold, —
"Ah!" she sighs, "her hand was cold!"

Broken words of cheer he saith,
But his dark lip quivereth,
And as o'er the past he thinketh,
From his young wife's arms he shrinketh;
Can those soft arms round him lie,
Underneath his dead wife's eye ?

She her fair young head can rest
Soothed and childlike on his breast,
And in trustful innocence
Draw new strength and courage thence ;
He, the proud man, feels within
But the cowardice of sin !

She can murmur in her thought
Simple prayers her mother taught,
And His blessed angels call,
Whose great love is over all ;
He, alone, in prayerless pride,
Meets the dark Past at her side !

One, who living shrank with dread
From his look, or word, or tread,
Unto whom her early grave
Was as freedom to the slave,
Moves him at this midnight hour,
With the dead's unconscious power !

Ah, the dead, the unforgot !
From their solemn homes of thought,
Where the cypress shadows blend
Darkly over foe and friend,
Or in love or sad rebuke,
Back upon the living look.

And the tenderest ones and weakest,
Who their wrongs have borne the meekest,
Lifting from those dark, still places,
Sweet and sad-remembered faces,
O'er the guilty hearts behind
An unwitting triumph find.

VOICES OF FREEDOM.

TOUSSAINT L'OUVERTURE.[82]

'T was night. The tranquil moonlight smile
  With which Heaven dreams of Earth, shed down
Its beauty on the Indian isle, —
  On broad green field and white-walled town ;
And inland waste of rock and wood,
In searching sunshine, wild and rude,
Rose, mellowed through the silver gleam,
Soft as the landscape of a dream,
All motionless and dewy wet,
Tree, vine, and flower in shadow met :
The myrtle with its snowy bloom,
Crossing the nightshade's solemn gloom, —
The white cecropia's silver rind
Relieved by deeper green behind, —
The orange with its fruit of gold, —
The lithe paullinia's verdant fold, —
The passion-flower, with symbol holy,
Twining its tendrils long and lowly, —
The rhexias dark, and cassia tall,
And proudly rising over all,
The kingly palm's imperial stem,
Crowned with its leafy diadem,

Star-like, beneath whose sombre shade,
The fiery-winged cucullo played !
Yes, — lovely was thine aspect, then,
  Fair island of the Western Sea !
Lavish of beauty, even when
Thy brutes were happier than thy men,
  For they, at least, were free !
Regardless of thy glorious clime,
  Unmindful of thy soil of flowers,
The toiling negro sighed, that Time
  No faster sped his hours.
For, by the dewy moonlight still,
He fed the weary-turning mill,
Or bent him in the chill morass,
To pluck the long and tangled grass,
And hear above his scar-worn back
The heavy slave-whip's frequent crack :
While in his heart one evil thought
In solitary madness wrought,
One baleful fire surviving still
  The quenching of the immortal mind,
  One sterner passion of his kind,
Which even fetters could not kill, —
The savage hope, to deal, erelong,
A vengeance bitterer than his wrong !

Hark to that cry ! — long, loud, and shrill,
From field and forest, rock and hill,

Thrilling and horrible it rang,
  Around, beneath, above ; —
The wild beast from his cavern sprang,
  The wild bird from her grove !
Nor fear, nor joy, nor agony
Were mingled in that midnight cry ;
But like the lion's growl of wrath,
When falls that hunter in his path
Whose barbed arrow, deeply set,
Is rankling in his bosom yet.
It told of hate, full, deep, and strong,
Of vengeance kindling out of wrong ;
It was as if the crimes of years —
The unrequited toil, the tears,
The shame and hate, which liken well
Earth's garden to the nether hell —
Had found in nature's self a tongue,
On which the gathered horror hung ;
As if from cliff, and stream, and glen
Burst on the startled ears of men
That voice which rises unto God,
Solemn and stern, — the cry of blood !
It ceased, — and all was still once more,
Save ocean chafing on his shore,
The sighing of the wind between
The broad banana's leaves of green,
Or bough by restless plumage shook,
Or murmuring voice of mountain brook.

Brief was the silence. Once again
  Pealed to the skies that frantic yell,
Glowed on the heavens a fiery stain,
  And flashes rose and fell ;
And painted on the blood-red sky,
Dark, naked arms were tossed on high ;
And, round the white man's lordly hall,
  Trod, fierce and free, *the brute he made ;*
And those who crept along the wall,
And answered to his lightest call
  With more than spaniel dread, —
The creatures of his lawless beck, —
Were trampling on his very neck !
And on the night-air, wild and clear,
Rose woman's shriek of more than fear ;
For bloodied arms were round her thrown,
And dark cheeks pressed against her own !

Then, injured Afric ! — for the shame
Of thy own daughters, vengeance came
Full on the scornful hearts of those,
Who mocked thee in thy nameless woes,
And to thy hapless children gave
One choice, — pollution or the grave !
Where then was he whose fiery zeal
Had taught the trampled heart to feel,
Until despair itself grew strong,
And vengeance fed its torch from wrong ?

Now, when the thu
Now, when oppress
    ing ;
Now, when the late
  Is raining down
That curse which,
    crime,
Has gathered, drop
Why strikes he no
Where murder's ste

He stood the aged
  That shadowed o
Listening, with ha
To the wild sounds
  Toussaint l'Ouve
What marvel that
  The blow for fre
And blood had ans
  Which Earth se
What marvel that
Smiled grimly o'er
As groan and shou
Told where the mi
With blood and fir
And death behind

Yes, dark-souled cl
  Of mild Religion
Unveiled not to th
  The lowlier and
In which the Holy
  Meekly amidst t
That calm reliance
  For justice in hi
That gentleness to
Forgiveness for its
Even as the prima
For mercy on the
Let not the favore
Thy stern appeal,
Has *he* not, with t
  Broadly around
Yea, on his thousa
  And gloried in h
Kneeling amidst hi
To offer mockery u
As if the High and
Could smile on dee
As if a human sacr
Were purer in his
Though offered up
Than the foul rites

  *   *

Sternly, amidst hi
His carbine graspe

The white man stood, prepared and still,
Waiting the shock of maddened men,
Unchained, and fierce as tigers, when
　　The horn winds through their caverned
　　　hill.
And one was weeping in his sight, —
　　The sweetest flower of all the isle, —
The bride who seemed but yesternight
　　Love's fair embodied smile.
And, clinging to her trembling knee,
Looked up the form of infancy,
With tearful glance in either face
The secret of its fear to trace.

"Ha ! stand or die !" The white man's
　　eye
His steady musket gleamed along,
As a tall Negro hastened nigh,
　　With fearless step and strong.
"What, ho, Toussaint !" A moment
　　more,
His shadow crossed the lighted floor.
"Away !" he shouted; "fly with me, —
The white man's bark is on the sea ; —
Her sails must catch the seaward wind,
For sudden vengeance sweeps behind.
Our brethren from their graves have
　　spoken,
The yoke is spurned, — the chain is
　　broken ;
On all the hills our fires are glowing, —
Through all the vales red blood is flowing!
No more the mocking White shall rest
His foot upon the Negro's breast ;
No more, at morn or eve, shall drip
The warm blood from the driver's whip:
Yet, though Toussaint has vengeance
　　sworn
For all the wrongs his race have borne, —
Though for each drop of Negro blood
The white man's veins shall pour a flood ;
Not all alone the sense of ill
Around his heart is lingering still,
Nor deeper can the white man feel
The generous warmth of grateful zeal.
Friends of the Negro ! fly with me, —
The path is open to the sea :
Away, for life !" — He spoke, and pressed
The young child to his manly breast,
As, headlong, through the cracking cane,
Down swept the dark insurgent train, —
Drunken and grim, with shout and yell
Howled through the dark, like sounds
　　from hell.

Far out, in peace, the white man's sail
Swayed free before the sunrise gale.

Cloud-like that island hung afar,
　　Along the bright horizon's verge,
O'er which the curse of servile war
　　Rolled its red torrent, surge on surge ;
And he — the Negro champion — where
　　In the fierce tumult struggled he ?
Go trace him by the fiery glare
Of dwellings in the midnight air, —
The yells of triumph and despair, —
The streams that crimson to the sea !

Sleep calmly in thy dungeon-tomb,
　　Beneath Besançon's alien sky,
Dark Haytien ! — for the time shall come,
　　Yea, even now is nigh, —
When, everywhere, thy name shall be
Redeemed from *color's infamy* ;
And men shall learn to speak of thee,
As one of earth's great spirits, born
In servitude, and nursed in scorn,
Casting aside the weary weight
And fetters of its low estate,
In that strong majesty of soul
　　Which knows no color, tongue, or
　　　clime, —
Which still hath spurned the base control
　　Of tyrants through all time !
Far other hands than mine may wreathe
The laurel round thy brow of death,
And speak thy praise, as one whose word
A thousand fiery spirits stirred, —
Who crushed his foeman as a worm, —
Whose step on human hearts fell firm : — [33]
Be mine the better task to find
A tribute for thy lofty mind,
Amidst whose gloomy vengeance shone
Some milder virtues all thine own, —
Some gleams of feeling pure and warm,
Like sunshine on a sky of storm, —
Proofs that the Negro's heart retains
Some nobleness amidst its chains, —
That kindness to the wronged is never
　　Without its excellent reward, —
Holy to human-kind and ever
　　Acceptable to God.

THE SLAVE-SHIPS.[34]

" That fatal, that perfidious bark,
Built i' the eclipse, and rigged with curses dark."
Milton's Lycidas.

" All ready ?" cried the captain ;
　　" Ay, ay !" the seamen said ;
" Heave up the worthless lubbers, —
　　The dying and the dead."
Up from the slave-ship's prison
　　Fierce, bearded heads were thrust :

" Now let the sharks look to it, —
  Toss up the dead ones first ! "

Corpse after corpse came up, —
  Death had been busy there ;
Where every blow is mercy,
  Why should the spoiler spare ?
Corpse after corpse they cast
  Sullenly from the ship,
Yet bloody with the traces
  Of fetter-link and whip.

Gloomily stood the captain,
  With his arms upon his breast,
With his cold brow sternly knotted,
  And his iron lip compressed.
" Are all the dead dogs over ? "
  Growled through that matted lip, —
" The blind ones are no better,
  Let 's lighten the good ship."

Hark ! from the ship's dark bosom,
  The very sounds of hell !
The ringing clank of iron, —
  The maniac's short, sharp yell ! —
The hoarse, low curse, throat-stifled, —
  The starving infant's moan, —
The horror of a breaking heart
  Poured through a mother's groan.

Up from that loathsome prison
  The stricken blind ones came :
Below, had all been darkness, —
  Above, was still the same.
Yet the holy breath of heaven
  Was sweetly breathing there,
And the heated brow of fever
  Cooled in the soft sea air.

" Overboard with them, shipmates ! "
  Cutlass and dirk were plied ;
Fettered and blind, one after one,
  Plunged down the vessel's side.
The sabre smote above, —
  Beneath, the lean shark lay,
Waiting with wide and bloody jaw
  His quick and human prey.

God of the earth ! what cries
  Rang upward unto thee ?
Voices of agony and blood,
  From ship-deck and from sea.
The last dull plunge was heard, —
  The last wave caught its stain, —
And the unsated shark looked up
  For human hearts in vain.

* * * * *

Red glowed the western waters, —
  The setting sun was there,
Scattering alike on wave and cloud
  His fiery mesh of hair.
Amidst a group in blindness,
  A solitary eye
Gazed, from the burdened slaver's deck
  Into that burning sky.

" A storm," spoke out the gazer,
  " Is gathering and at hand, —
Curse on 't — I 'd give my other eye
  For one firm rood of land."
And then he laughed, — but only
  His echoed laugh replied, —
For the blinded and the suffering
  Alone were at his side.

Night settled on the waters,
  And on a stormy heaven,
While fiercely on that lone ship's track
  The thunder-gust was driven.
" A sail ! — thank God, a sail ! "
  And as the helmsman spoke,
Up through the stormy murmur
  A shout of gladness broke.

Down came the stranger vessel,
  Unheeding on her way,
So near that on the slaver's deck
  Fell off her driven spray.
" Ho ! for the love of mercy, —
  We 're perishing and blind ! "
A wail of utter agony
  Came back upon the wind :

" Help us ! for we are stricken
  With blindness every one ;
Ten days we 've floated fearfully,
  Unnoting star or sun.
Our ship 's the slaver Leon, —
  We 've but a score on board, —
Our slaves are all gone over, —
  Help, — for the love of God ! "

On livid brows of agony
  The broad red lightning shone, —
But the roar of wind and thunder
  Stifled the answering groan ;
Wailed from the broken waters
  A last despairing cry,
As, kindling in the stormy light,
  The stranger ship went by.

* * * * *

In the sunny Guadaloupe
  A dark-hulled vessel lay, —

With a crew who noted never
  The nightfall or the day.
The blossom of the orange
  Was white by every stream,
And tropic leaf, and flower, and bird
  Were in the warm sunbeam.

And the sky was bright as ever,
  And the moonlight slept as well,
On the palm-trees by the hillside,
  And the streamlet of the dell :
And the glances of the Creole
  Were still as archly deep,
And her smiles as full as ever
  Of passion and of sleep.

But vain were bird and blossom,
  The green earth and the sky,
And the smile of human faces,
  To the slaver's darkened eye ;
At the breaking of the morning,
  At the star-lit evening time,
O'er a world of light and beauty
  Fell the blackness of his crime.

STANZAS.

[" The despotism which our fathers could not
bear in their native country is expiring, and the
sword of justice in her reformed hands has ap-
plied its exterminating edge to slavery. Shall
the United States -- the free United States,
which could not bear the bonds of a king —
cradle the bondage which a king is abolishing?
Shall a Republic be less free than a Monarchy?
Shall we, in the vigor and buoyancy of our
manhood, be less energetic in righteousness than
a kingdom in its age?" — *Dr. Follen's Address.*

" Genius of America! — Spirit of our free in-
stitutions! — where art thou? — How art thou
fallen, O Lucifer! son of the morning, — how
art thou fallen from Heaven! Hell from beneath
is moved for thee, to meet thee at thy coming!
— The kings of the earth cry out to thee, Aha!
Aha! — ART THOU BECOME LIKE UNTO US?" —
Speech of Samuel J. May.]

OUR fellow-countrymen in chains!
  Slaves — in a land of light and law!
Slaves — crouching on the very plains
  Where rolled the storm of Freedom's
    war !
A groan from Eutaw's haunted wood, —
  A wail where Camden's martyrs fell, —
By every shrine of patriot blood,
  From Moultrie's wall and Jaspar's well!

By storied hill and hallowed grot,
  By mossy wood and marshy glen,
Whence rang of old the rifle-shot,
  And hurrying shout of Marion's men !

The groan of breaking hearts is there, —
  The falling lash, — the fetter's clank !
Slaves, — SLAVES are breathing in that
    air,
  Which old De Kalb and Sumter drank !

What, ho ! — *our* countrymen in chains !
  The whip on WOMAN's shrinking flesh !
Our soil yet reddening with the stains
  Caught from her scourging, warm and
    fresh !
What ! mothers from their children
    riven !
  What ! God's own image bought and
    sold !
AMERICANS to market driven,
  And bartered as the brute for gold !

Speak ! shall their agony of prayer
  Come thrilling to our hearts in vain ?
To us whose fathers scorned to bear
  The paltry *menace* of a chain ;
To us, whose boast is loud and long
  Of holy Liberty and Light, —
Say, shall these writhing slaves of Wrong
  Plead vainly for their plundered Right ?

What ! shall we send, with lavish breath,
  Our sympathies across the wave,
Where Manhood, on the field of death,
  Strikes for his freedom or a grave ?
Shall prayers go up, and hymns be sung
  For Greece, the Moslem fetter spurning,
And millions hail with pen and tongue
  Our light on all her altars burning ?

Shall Belgium feel, and gallant France,
  By Vendome's pile and Schoenbrun's
    wall,
And Poland, gasping on her lance,
  The impulse of our cheering call ?
And shall the SLAVE, beneath our eye,
  Clank o'er *our* fields his hateful chain ?
And toss his fettered arms on high,
  And groan for Freedom's gift, in vain !

O, say, shall Prussia's banner be
  A refuge for the stricken slave ?
And shall the Russian serf go free
  By Baikal's lake and Neva's wave ?
And shall the wintry-bosomed Dane
  Relax the iron hand of pride,
And bid his bondmen cast the chain,
  From fettered soul and limb, aside ?

Shall every flap of England's flag
  Proclaim that all around are free,

From "farthest Ind " to each blue crag
  That beetles o'er the Western Sea ?
And shall we scoff at Europe's kings,
  When Freedom's fire is dim with us,
And round our country's altar clings
  The damning shade of Slavery's curse ?

Go — let us ask of Constantine
  To loose his grasp on Poland's throat ;
And beg the lord of Mahmoud's line
  To spare the struggling Suliote, —
Will not the scorching answer come
  From :urbaned Turk, and scornful
    Russ :
" Go, loose your fettered slaves at home,
  Then turn, and ask the like of us ! "

Just God ! and shall we calmly rest,
  The Christian's scorn, — the heathen's
    mirth, —
Content to live the lingering jest
  And by-word of a mocking Earth ?
Shall our own glorious land retain
  That curse which Europe scorns to bear ?
Shall our own brethren drag the chain
  Which not even Russia's menials wear ?

Up, then, in Freedom's manly part,
  From graybeard eld to fiery youth,
And on the nation's naked heart
  Scatter the living coals of Truth !
Up, — while ye slumber, deeper yet
  The shadow of our fame is growing !
Up, — while ye pause, our sun may set
  In blood, around our altars flowing !

Oh ! rouse ye, ere the storm comes
    forth, —
  The gathered wrath of God and man, —
Like that which wasted Egypt's earth,
  When hail and fire above it ran.
Hear ye no warnings in the air ?
  Feel ye no earthquake underneath ?
Up, — up ! why will ye slumber where
  The sleeper only wakes in death ?

Up *now* for Freedom ! — not in strife
  Like that your sterner fathers saw, —
The awful waste of human life, —
  The glory and the guilt of war :
But break the chain, — the yoke remove,
  And smite to earth Oppression's rod,
With those mild arms of Truth and Love,
  Made mighty through the living God !

Down let the shrine of Moloch sink,
  And leave no traces where it stood ;

Nor longer let its i
  His daily cup of
But rear another a
  To Truth and L
And Freedom's gift,
  Shall call an
    Heaven !

THE YA?

SHE sings by her v
  tage-door,
Which the long
  stretching b
With a music as
  which seem:
Breathed softly ar
  our dreams :

How brilliant and
  her eye,
Like a star glancir
  of the sky !
And lightly and f
  play
O'er a brow and a bc

Who comes in his
  tage-door, –
The haughty and r
  poor ?
'T is the great Sou
  master who
His whip of domir
  slaves.

" Nay, Ellen, — fc
  Yankee fool:
Who would pass :
  change of th
Let them toil as t
  or the whee!
Too stupid for shar
  feel !

" But thou art too
  gem
To be bound to th
  lied by then:
For shame, Ellen,
  bondage asi(
And away to the S
  and pride.

" O, come where n(
  can wrong,

But where flowers are blossoming all the
    year long,
Where the shade of the palm-tree is
    over my home,
And the lemon and orange are white in
    their bloom !

"O, come to my home, where my ser-
    vants shall all
Depart at thy bidding and come at thy
    call ;
They shall heed thee as mistress with
    trembling and awe,
And each wish of thy heart shall be felt
    as a law."

O, could ye have seen her — that pride
    of our girl's —
Arise and cast back the dark wealth of
    her curls,
With a scorn in her eye which the gazer
    could feel,
And a glance like the sunshine that
    flashes on steel !

"Go back, haughty Southron ! thy
    treasures of gold
Are dim with the blood of the hearts thou
    hast sold ;
Thy home may be lovely, but round it
    I hear
The crack of the whip and the footsteps
    of fear !

"And the sky of thy South may be
    brighter than ours,
And greener thy landscapes, and fairer
    thy flowers ;
But dearer the blast round our moun-
    tains which raves,
Than the sweet summer zephyr which
    breathes over slaves !

"Full low at thy bidding thy negroes
    may kneel,
With the iron of bondage on spirit and
    heel ;
Yet know that the Yankee girl sooner
    would be
In fetters with them, than in freedom
    with thee !"

TO W. L. G.

CHAMPION of those who groan beneath
    Oppression's iron hand :
In view of penury, hate, and death,
    I see thee fearless stand.

Still bearing up thy lofty brow,
    In the steadfast strength of truth,
In manhood sealing well the vow
    And promise of thy youth.

Go on, — for thou hast chosen well ;
    On in the strength of God !
Long as one human heart shall swell
    Beneath the tyrant's rod.
Speak in a slumbering nation's ear,
    As thou hast ever spoken,
Until the dead in sin shall hear, —
    The fetter's link be broken !

I love thee with a brother's love,
    I feel my pulses thrill,
To mark thy spirit soar above
    The cloud of human ill.
My heart hath leaped to answer thine,
    And echo back thy words,
As leaps the warrior's at the shine
    And flash of kindred swords !

They tell me thou art rash and vain, —
    A searcher after fame ;
That thou art striving but to gain
    A long-enduring name ;
That thou hast nerved the Afric's hand
    And steeled the Afric's heart,
To shake aloft his vengeful brand,
    And rend his chain apart.

Have I not known thee well, and read
    Thy mighty purpose long ?
And watched the trials which have made
    Thy human spirit strong ?
And shall the slanderer's demon breath
    Avail with one like me,
To dim the sunshine of my faith
    And earnest trust in thee ?

Go on, — the dagger's point may glare
    Amid thy pathway's gloom, —
The fate which sternly threatens there
    Is glorious martyrdom !
Then onward with a martyr's zeal ;
    And wait thy sure reward
When man to man no more shall kneel,
    And God alone be Lord !
1833.

SONG OF THE FREE.

PRIDE of New England !
    Soul of our fathers !
Shrink we all craven-like,
    When the storm gathers ?

What though the tempest be
  Over us lowering,
Where 's the New-Englander
  Shamefully cowering ?
Graves green and holy
  Around us are lying, —
Free were the sleepers all,
  Living and dying !

Back with the Southerner's
  Padlocks and scourges !
Go, — let him fetter down
  Ocean's free surges !
Go, — let him silence
  Winds, clouds, and waters, —
Never New England's own
  Free sons and daughters !
Free as our rivers are
  Ocean-ward going, —
Free as the breezes are
  Over us blowing.

Up to our altars, then,
  Haste we, and summon
Courage and loveliness,
  Manhood and woman !
Deep let our pledges be :
  Freedom forever !
Truce with oppression,
  Never, O, never !
By our own birthright-gift,
  Granted of Heaven, —
Freedom for heart and lip,
  Be the pledge given !

If we have whispered truth,
  Whisper no longer ;
Speak as the tempest does,
  Sterner and stronger ;
Still be the tones of truth
  Louder and firmer,
Startling the haughty South
  With the deep murmur ;
God and our charter's right,
  Freedom forever !
Truce with oppression,
  Never, O, never !

1836.

THE HUNTERS OF MEN.

HAVE ye heard of our hunting, o'er
  mountain and glen,
Through cane-brake and forest, — the
  hunting of men ?
The lords of our land to this hunting
  have gone,
As the fox-hunter follows the sound of
  the horn ;
Hark ! — the cheer and the hallo ! — the
  crack of the whip,
And the yell of the hound as he fastens
  his grip !
All blithe are our hunters, and noble
  their match, —
Though hundreds are caught, there are
  millions to catch.
So speed to their hunting, o'er mountain
  and glen,
Through cane-brake and forest, — the
  hunting of men !

Gay luck to our hunters ! — how nobly
  they ride
In the glow of their zeal, and the strength
  of their pride ! —
The priest with his cassock flung back
  on the wind,
Just screening the politic statesman behind, —
The saint and the sinner, with cursing
  and prayer,
The drunk and the sober, ride merrily
  there.
And woman, — kind woman, — wife,
  widow, and maid,
For the good of the hunted, is lending
  her aid :
Her foot 's in the stirrup, her hand on
  the rein,
How blithely she rides to the hunting of
  men !

O, goodly and grand is our hunting to
  see,
In this " land of the brave and this
  home of the free."
Priest, warrior, and statesman, from
  Georgia to Maine,
All mounting the saddle, — all grasping
  the rein, —
Right merrily hunting the black man,
  whose sin
Is the curl of his hair and the hue of
  his skin !
Woe, now, to the hunted who turns him
  at bay !
Will our hunters be turned from their
  purpose and prey ?
Will their hearts fail within them ! —
  their nerves tremble, when
All roughly they ride to the hunting of
  men !

Ho! — ALMS for our hunters! all weary
and faint,
Wax the curse of the sinner and prayer
of the saint.
The horn is wound faintly, — the echoes
are still,
Over cane-brake and river, and forest
and hill.
Haste, — alms for our hunters! the
hunted once more
Have turned from their flight with their
backs to the shore:
What right have *they* here in the home
of the white,
Shadowed o'er by *our* banner of Freedom and Right?
Ho! — alms for the hunters! or never
again
Will they ride in their pomp to the
hunting of men!

ALMS, — ALMS for our hunters! why
will ye delay,
When their pride and their glory are
melting away?
The parson has turned; for, on charge
of his own,
Who goeth a warfare, or hunting, alone?
The politic statesman looks back with a
sigh, —
There is doubt in his heart, — there is
fear in his eye.
O, haste, lest that doubting and fear
shall prevail,
And the head of his steed take the place
of the tail.
O, haste, ere he leave us! for who will
ride then,
For pleasure or gain, to the hunting of
men?
1835.

CLERICAL OPPRESSORS.

[In the report of the celebrated proslavery
meeting in Charlestown, S. C., on the 4th of
the 9th month, 1835, published in the Courier
of that city, it is stated: " *The* CLERGY *of all
denominations attended in a body,* LENDING THEIR
SANCTION TO THE PROCEEDINGS, *and adding by
their presence to the impressive character of the
scene!* "]

JUST GOD! — and these are they
Who minister at thine altar, God of Right!
Men who their hands with prayer and
blessing lay
On Israel's Ark of light!

What! preach and kidnap men?
Give thanks, — and rob thy own af-
flicted poor?
Talk of thy glorious liberty, and then
Bolt hard the captive's door?

What! servants of thy own
Merciful Son, who came to seek and
save
The homeless and the outcast, — fetter-
ing down
The tasked and plundered slave!

Pilate and Herod, friends!
Chief priests and rulers, as of old, com-
bine!
Just God and holy! is that church,
which lends
Strength to the spoiler, thine?

Paid hypocrites, who turn
Judgment aside, and rob the Holy Book
Of those high words of truth which
search and burn
In warning and rebuke;

Feed fat, ye locusts, feed!
And, in your tasselled pulpits, thank
the Lord
That, from the toiling bondman's utter
need,
Ye pile your own full board.

How long, O Lord! how long
Shall such a priesthood barter truth away,
And in thy name, for robbery and wrong
At thy own altars pray?

Is not thy hand stretched forth
Visibly in the heavens, to awe and smite?
Shall not the living God of all the
earth,
And heaven above, do right?

Woe, then, to all who grind
Their brethren of a common Father
down!
To all who plunder from the immortal
mind
Its bright and glorious crown!

Woe to the priesthood! woe
To those whose hire is with the price of
blood, —
Perverting, darkening, changing, as they
go,
The searching truths of God!

4

Their glory and their might
Shall perish; and their very names
    shall be
Vile before all the people, in the light
Of a world's liberty.

O, speed the moment on
When Wrong shall cease, and Liberty
    and Love
And Truth and Right throughout the
    earth be known
As in their home above.

THE CHRISTIAN SLAVE.

[In a late publication of L. F. Tasistro —
"Random Shots and Southern Breezes" — is a
description of a slave auction at New Orleans, at
which the auctioneer recommended the woman
on the stand as " A GOOD CHRISTIAN ! "]

A CHRISTIAN ! going, gone !
Who bids for God's own image ? — for
    his grace,
Which that poor victim of the market-
    place
Hath in her suffering won ?

My God ! can such things be ?
Hast thou not said that whatsoe'er is done
Unto thy weakest and thy humblest one
Is even done to thee ?

In that sad victim, then,
Child of thy pitying love, I see thee
    stand, —
Once more the jest-word of a mocking
    band,
Bound, sold, and scourged again !

A Christian up for sale !
Wet with her blood your whips, o'er-
    task her frame,
Make her life loathsome with your wrong
    and shame,
Her patience shall not fail !

A heathen hand might deal
Back on your heads the gathered wrong
    of years :
But her low, broken prayer and nightly
    tears,
Ye neither heed nor feel.

Con well thy lesson o'er,
Thou *prudent* teacher, — tell the toiling
    slave

No dangerous tale of Him who came to
    save
The outcast and the poor.

But wisely shut the ray
Of God's free Gospel from her simple heart,
And to her darkened mind alone impart
One stern command, — OBEY !

So shalt thou deftly raise
The market price of human flesh ; and
    while
On thee, their pampered guest, the
    planters smile,
Thy church shall praise.

Grave, reverend men shall tell
From Northern pulpits how thy work
    was blest,
While in that vile South Sodom first
    and best,
Thy poor disciples sell.

O, shame ! the Moslem thrall,
Who, with his master, to the Prophet
    kneels,
While turning to the sacred Kebla feels
His fetters break and fall.

Cheers for the turbaned Bey
Of robber-peopled Tunis ! he hath torn
The dark slave-dungeons open, and hath
    borne
Their inmates into day :

But our poor slave in vain
Turns to the Christian shrine his aching
    eyes, —
Its rites will only swell his market price,
And rivet on his chain.

God of all right ! how long
Shall priestly robbers at thine altar stand,
Lifting in prayer to thee, the bloody hand
And haughty brow of wrong ?

O, from the fields of cane,
From the low rice-swamp, from the
    trader's cell, —
From the black slave-ship's foul and
    loathsome hell,
And coffle's weary chain, —

Hoarse, horrible, and strong,
Rises to Heaven that agonizing cry,
Filling the arches of the hollow sky,
HOW LONG, O GOD, HOW LONG ?

STANZAS FOR THE TIMES.

Is this the land our fathers loved,
  The freedom which they toiled to win ?
Is this the soil whereon they moved ?
  Are these the graves they slumber in ?
Are *we* the sons by whom are borne
The mantles which the dead have worn ?

And shall we crouch above these graves,
  With craven soul and fettered lip ?
Yoke in with marked and branded slaves,
  And tremble at the driver's whip ?
Bend to the earth our pliant knees,
And speak — but as our masters please ?

Shall outraged Nature cease to feel ?
  Shall Mercy's tears no longer flow ?
Shall ruffian threats of cord and steel, —
  The dungeon's gloom, — the assas-
    sin's blow,
Turn back the spirit roused to save
The Truth, our Country, and the Slave ?

Of human skulls that shrine was made,
  Round which the priests of Mexico
Before their loathsome idol prayed ; —
  Is Freedom's altar fashioned so ?
And must we yield to Freedom's God,
As offering meet, the negro's blood ?

Shall tongues be mute, when deeds are
    wrought
  Which well might shame extremest
    hell ?
Shall freemen lock the indignant thought ?
  Shall Pity's bosom cease to swell ?
Shall Honor bleed ? — shall Truth suc-
    cumb ?
Shall pen, and press, and soul be dumb ?

No ; — by each spot of haunted ground,
  Where Freedom weeps her children's
    fall, —
By Plymouth's rock, and Bunker's
    mound, —
  By Griswold's stained and shattered
    wall, —
By Warren's ghost, — by Langdon's
    shade, —
By all the memories of our dead !

By their enlarging souls, which burst
  The bands and fetters round them
    set, —
By the free Pilgrim spirit nursed
  Within our inmost bosoms, yet, —

By all above, aroun
Be ours the indign∈

No ; — guided by c
  For truth, and rig
Be ours to strive in
  As Christians *ma*
Still pouring on un
That truth oppress:

What ! shall we gu∈
  While woman sh
And while he tram
  The image of a c∈
Shall watch and w∈
Of Northern nerve

And shall we know
  The danger and :
And see our Freedc
  Which should l
    with flame ?
And, writhing, feel
A world's reproach

Is 't not enough th
  And asks our hai
Must fetters which
  Clank round the
Must he be told, b∈
What he must sp
    how ?

Must he be told hi:
  On   Slavery's
    strong, —
On breaking hearts
  On robbery, and
That all his father:
That Freedom's en

Its life, its soul, fr
  False, foul, pro:
    well
Of holy Truth fron
  Of Heaven refres
Of Virtue in the a
  Of Demons plantin

Rail   on,   then,
    South," —
  Ye shall not hear
No seal is on the Y
  No fetter on the
From our Green M
One voice shall
    FREE !

LINES,

WRITTEN ON READING THE MESSAGE OF GOVERNOR RITNER, OF PENN-SYLVANIA, 1836.

THANK God for the token! — one lip is
  still free, —
One spirit untrammelled, — unbending
  one knee!
Like the oak of the mountain, deep-
  rooted and firm,
Erect, when the multitude bends to the
  storm;
When traitors to Freedom, and Honor,
  and God,
Are bowed at an Idol polluted with
  blood;
When the recreant North has forgotten
  her trust,
And the lip of her honor is low in the
  dust, —
Thank God, that one arm from the
  shackle has broken!
Thank God, that one man as a *freeman*
  has spoken!

O'er thy crags, Alleghany, a blast has
  been blown!
Down thy tide, Susquehanna, the mur-
  mur has gone!
To the land of the South, — of the char-
  ter and chain, —
Of Liberty sweetened with Slavery's
  pain;
Where the cant of Democracy dwells on
  the lips
Of the forgers of fetters, and wielders of
  whips!
Where "chivalric" honor means really
  no more
Than scourging of women, and robbing
  the poor!
Where the Moloch of Slavery sitteth on
  high,
And the words which he utters, are —
  WORSHIP, OR DIE!

Right onward, O speed it! Wherever
  the blood
Of the wronged and the guiltless is crying to God;
Wherever a slave in his fetters is pining;
Wherever the lash of the driver is twining;
Wherever from kindred, torn rudely
  apart,

Comes the sorrowful wail of the broken
  of heart;
Wherever the shackles of tyranny bind,
In silence and darkness, the God-given
  mind;
There, God speed it onward! — its truth
  will be felt, —
The bonds shall be loosened, — the iron
  shall melt!

And O, will the land where the free soul
  of PENN
Still lingers and breathes over mountain
  and glen, —
Will the land where a BENEZET's spirit
  went forth
To the peeled and the meted, and outcast
  of Earth, —
Where the words of the Charter of Liberty first
From the soul of the sage and the patriot burst, —
Where first for the wronged and the weak
  of their kind,
The Christian and statesman their efforts
  combined, —
Will that land of the free and the good
  wear a chain?
Will the call to the rescue of Freedom
  be vain?

No, RITNER! — her "Friends" at thy
  warning shall stand
Erect for the truth, like their ancestral
  band;
Forgetting the feuds and the strife of
  past time,
Counting coldness injustice, and silence
  a crime;
Turning back from the cavil of creeds,
  to unite
Once again for the poor in defence of the
  Right;
Breasting calmly, but firmly, the full
  tide of Wrong,
Overwhelmed, but not borne on its surges
  along;
Unappalled by the danger, the shame,
  and the pain,
And counting each trial for Truth as
  their gain!

And that bold-hearted yeomanry, honest and true,
Who, haters of fraud, give to labor its due;
Whose fathers, of old, sang in concert
  with thine,

On the banks of Swetara, the songs of
   the Rhine, —
The German-born pilgrims, who first
   dared to brave
The scorn of the proud in the cause of
   the slave : —
Will the sons of such men yield the
   lords of the South
One brow for the brand, — for the pad-
   lock one mouth ?
They cater to tyrants ? — They rivet the
   chain,
Which their fathers smote off, on the
   negro again ?

No, never ! — one voice, like the sound
   in the cloud,
When the roar of the storm waxes loud
   and more loud,
Wherever the foot of the freeman hath
   pressed
From the Delaware's marge to the Lake
   of the West,
On the South-going breezes shall deepen
   and grow
Till the land it sweeps over shall tremble
   below !
The voice of a PEOPLE, — uprisen, —
   awake, —
Pennsylvania's watchword, with Free-
   dom at stake,
Thrilling up from each valley, flung
   down from each height,
" OUR COUNTRY AND LIBERTY ! — GOD
   FOR THE RIGHT ! "

THE PASTORAL LETTER.

So, this is all, — the utmost reach
   Of priestly power the mind to fetter !
When laymen think — when women
   preach —
   A war of words — a "Pastoral Let-
   ter !"
Now, shame upon ye, parish Popes !
   Was it thus with those, your prede-
   cessors,
Who sealed with racks, and fire, and
   ropes
   Their loving-kindness to transgressors?

A " Pastoral Letter," grave and dull —
   Alas ! in hoof and horns and features,
How different is your Brookfield bull,
   From him who bellows from St. Pe-
   ter's !

Your pastoral rights and powers from
   harm,
Think ye, can words alone preserve
   them ?
Your wiser fathers taught the arm
   And sword of temporal power to serve
   them.

O, glorious days, — when Church and
   State
Were wedded by your spiritual fathers !
And on submissive shoulders sat
   Your Wilsons and your Cotton Ma-
   thers.
No vile " itinerant " then could mar
   The beauty of your tranquil Zion,
But at his peril of the scar
   Of hangman's whip and branding-iron.

Then, wholesome laws relieved the Church
   Of heretic and mischief-maker,
And priest and bailiff joined in search,
   By turns, of Papist, witch, and Qua-
   ker !
The stocks were at each church's door,
   The gallows stood on Boston Common,
A Papist's ears the pillory bore, —
   The gallows-rope, a Quaker woman !

Your fathers dealt not as ye deal
   With " non-professing " frantic teach-
   ers ;
They bored the tongue with red-hot steel,
   And flayed the backs of " female
   preachers."
Old Newbury, had her fields a tongue,
   And Salem's streets could tell their
   story,
Of fainting woman dragged along,
   Gashed by the whip, accursed and
   gory!

And will ye ask me, why this taunt
   Of memories sacred from the scorner !
And why with reckless hand I plant
   A nettle on the graves ye honor ?
Not to reproach New England's dead
   This record from the past I summon,
Of manhood to the scaffold led,
   And suffering and heroic woman.

No, — for yourselves alone, I turn
   The pages of intolerance over,
That, in their spirit, dark and stern,
   Ye haply may your own discover !
For, if ye claim the " pastoral right,"
   To silence Freedom's voice of warning,

And from your precincts shut the light
  Of Freedom's day around ye dawn-
    ing ;

If when an earthquake voice of power,
  And signs in earth and heaven, are
    showing
That forth, in its appointed hour,
  The Spirit of the Lord is going !
And, with that Spirit, Freedom's light
  On kindred, tongue, and people break-
    ing,
Whose slumbering millions, at the sight,
  In glory and in strength are waking !

When for the sighing of the poor,
  And for the needy, God hath risen,
And chains are breaking, and a door
  Is opening for the souls in prison !
If then ye would, with puny hands,
  Arrest the very work of Heaven,
And bind anew the evil bands
  Which God's right arm of power hath
    riven, —

What marvel that, in many a mind,
  Those darker deeds of bigot madness
Are closely with your own combined,
  Yet "less in anger than in sadness" ?
What marvel, if the people learn
  To claim the right of free opinion ?
What marvel, if at times they spurn
  The ancient yoke of your dominion ?

A glorious remnant linger yet,
  Whose lips are wet at Freedom's foun-
    tains,
The coming of whose welcome feet
  Is beautiful upon our mountains !
Men, who the gospel tidings bring
  Of Liberty and Love forever,
Whose joy is an abiding spring,
  Whose peace is as a gentle river !

But ye, who scorn the thrilling tale
  Of Carolina's high-souled daughters,
Which echoes here the mournful wail
  Of sorrow from Edisto's waters,
Close while ye may the public ear, —
  With malice vex, with slander wound
    them, —
The pure and good shall throng to hear,
  And tried and manly hearts surround
    them.

O, ever may the power which led
  Their way to such a fiery trial,

And strengthened womanhood to tread
  The wine-press of such self-denial,
Be round them in an evil land,
  With wisdom and with strength from
    Heaven,
With Miriam's voice, and Judith's hand,
  And Deborah's song, for triumph given !

And what are ye who strive with God
  Against the ark of his salvation,
Moved by the breath of prayer abroad,
  With blessings for a dying nation ?
What, but the stubble and the hay
  To perish, even as flax consuming,
With all that bars his glorious way,
  Before the brightness of his coming ?

And thou, sad Angel, who so long
  Hast waited for the glorious token,
That Earth from all her bonds of wrong
  To liberty and light has broken, —
Angel of Freedom ! soon to thee
  The sounding trumpet shall be given,
And over Earth's full jubilee
  Shall deeper joy be felt in Heaven !

LINES,

WRITTEN FOR THE MEETING OF THE
ANTISLAVERY SOCIETY, AT CHAT-
HAM STREET CHAPEL, N. Y., HELD
ON THE 4TH OF THE 7TH MONTH,
1834.

O Thou, whose presence went before
  Our fathers in their weary way,
As with thy chosen moved of yore
  The fire by night, the cloud by day !

When from each temple of the free,
  A nation's song ascends to Heaven,
Most Holy Father ! unto thee
  May not our humble prayer be given ?

Thy children all, — though hue and form
  Are varied in thine own good will, —
With thy own holy breathings warm,
  And fashioned in thine image still.

We thank thee, Father ! — hill and plain
  Around us wave their fruits once more,
And clustered vine, and blossomed grain,
  Are bending round each cottage door.

And peace is here ; and hope and love
  Are round us as a mantle thrown,

And unto Thee, supreme above,
  The knee of prayer is bowed alone.

But O, for those this day can bring,
  As unto us, no joyful thrill, —
For those who, under Freedom's wing,
  Are bound in Slavery's fetters still :

For those to whom thy living word
  Of light and love is never given, —
For those whose ears have never heard
  The promise and the hope of Heaven !

For broken heart, and clouded mind,
  Whereon no human mercies fall, —
O, be thy gracious love inclined,
  Who, as a Father, pitiest all !

And grant, O Father ! that the time
  Of Earth's deliverance may be near,
When every land and tongue and clime
  The message of thy love shall hear, —

When, smitten as with fire from heaven,
  The captive's chain shall sink in dust,
And to his fettered soul be given
  The glorious freedom of the just !

LINES,

WRITTEN FOR THE CELEBRATION OF
THE THIRD ANNIVERSARY OF BRIT-
ISH EMANCIPATION AT THE BROAD-
WAY TABERNACLE, N. Y., "FIRST OF
AUGUST," 1837.

O HOLY FATHER ! — just and true
  Are all thy works and words and ways,
And unto thee alone are due
  Thanksgiving and eternal praise !
As children of thy gracious care,
  We veil the eye, we bend the knee,
With broken words of praise and prayer,
  Father and God, we come to thee.

For thou hast heard, O God of Right,
  The sighing of the island slave ;
And stretched for him the arm of might,
  Not shortened that it could not save.
The laborer sits beneath his vine,
  The shackled soul and hand are free, —
Thanksgiving ! — for the work is thine !
  Praise ! — for the blessing is of thee !

And O, we feel thy presence here, —
  Thy awful arm in judgment bare !

Thine eye hath seen the bondman's tear, —
  Thine ear hath heard the bondman's
    prayer.
Praise ! — for the pride of man is low,
  The counsels of the wise are naught,
The fountains of repentance flow ;
  What hath our God in mercy wrought ?

Speed on thy work, Lord God of Hosts !
  And when the bondman's chain is
    riven,
And swells from all our guilty coasts
  The anthem of the free to Heaven,
O, not to those whom thou hast led,
  As with thy cloud and fire before,
But unto thee, in fear and dread,
  Be praise and glory evermore.

LINES,

WRITTEN FOR THE ANNIVERSARY CEL-
EBRATION OF THE FIRST OF AUGUST,
AT MILTON, 1846.

A FEW brief years have passed away
  Since Britain drove her million slaves
Beneath the tropic's fiery ray :
  God willed their freedom ; and to-day
  Life blooms above those island graves !

He spoke ! across the Carib Sea,
  We heard the clash of breaking chains,
And felt the heart-throb of the free,
  The first, strong pulse of liberty
  Which thrilled along the bondman's
    veins.

Though long delayed, and far, and slow,
  The Briton's triumph shall be ours :
Wears slavery here a prouder brow
Than that which twelve short years ago
  Scowled darkly from her island bow-
    ers ?

Mighty alike for good or ill
  With mother-land, we fully share
The Saxon strength, — the nerve of
    steel, —
The tireless energy of will, —
  The power to do, the pride to dare.

What she has done can we not do ?
  Our hour and men are both at hand ;
The blast which Freedom's angel blew
O'er her green islands, echoes through
  Each valley of our forest land.

Hear it, old Europe ! we have sworn
  The death of slavery. — When it falls,
Look to your vassals in their turn,
Your poor dumb millions, crushed and
      worn,
  Your prisons and your palace walls !

O kingly mockers ! — scoffing show
  What deeds in Freedom's name we do ;
Yet know that every taunt ye throw
Across the waters, goads our slow
  Progression towards the right and
      true.

Not always shall your outraged poor,
  Appalled by democratic crime,
Grind as their fathers ground before, —
The hour which sees our prison door
  Swing wide shall be *their* triumph time.

On then, my brothers ! every blow
  Ye deal is felt the wide earth through ;
Whatever here uplifts the low
Or humbles Freedom's hateful foe,
  Blesses the Old World through the
      New.

Take heart ! The promised hour draws
      near, —
  I hear the downward beat of wings,
And Freedom's trumpet sounding clear :
" Joy to the people ! — woe and fear
  To new-world tyrants, old-world
      kings ! "

THE FAREWELL

OF A VIRGINIA SLAVE MOTHER TO HER
DAUGHTERS SOLD INTO SOUTHERN
BONDAGE.

GONE, gone, — sold and gone,
  To the rice-swamp dank and lone.
Where the slave-whip ceaseless swings,
Where the noisome insect stings,
Where the fever demon strews
Poison with the falling dews,
Where the sickly sunbeams glare
Through the hot and misty air, —
  Gone, gone, — sold and gone,
    To the rice-swamp dank and lone,
    From Virginia's hills and waters, —
    Woe is me, my stolen daughters !

  Gone, gone, — sold and gone,
    To the rice-swamp dank and lone.

There no mother's eye is near them,
There no mother's ear can hear them ;
Never, when the torturing lash
Seams their back with many a gash,
Shall a mother's kindness bless them,
Or a mother's arms caress them.
  Gone, gone, — sold and gone,
    To the rice-swamp dank and lone,
    From Virginia's hills and waters, —
    Woe is me, my stolen daughters !

  Gone, gone, — sold and gone,
    To the rice-swamp dank and lone.
O, when weary, sad, and slow,
From the fields at night they go,
Faint with toil, and racked with pain,
To their cheerless homes again,
There no brother's voice shall greet
      them, —
There no father's welcome meet them.
  Gone, gone, — sold and gone,
    To the rice-swamp dank and lone,
    From Virginia's hills and waters, —
    Woe is me, my stolen daughters !

  Gone, gone, — sold and gone,
    To the rice-swamp dank and lone.
From the tree whose shadow lay
On their childhood's place of play, —
From the cool spring where they drank, —
Rock, and hill, and rivulet bank, —
From the solemn house of prayer,
And the holy counsels there, —
  Gone, gone, — sold and gone,
    To the rice-swamp dank and lone,
    From Virginia's hills and waters, —
    Woe is me, my stolen daughters !

  Gone, gone, — sold and gone,
    To the rice-swamp dank and lone, —
Toiling through the weary day,
And at night the spoiler's prey.
O that they had earlier died,
Sleeping calmly, side by side,
Where the tyrant's power is o'er,
And the fetter galls no more !
  Gone, gone, — sold and gone,
    To the rice-swamp dank and lone,
    From Virginia's hills and waters, —
    Woe is me, my stolen daughters !

  Gone, gone, — sold and gone,
    To the rice-swamp dank and lone.
By the holy love He beareth, —
By the bruised reed He spareth, —
O, may He, to whom alone
All their cruel wrongs are known,

Still their hope and refuge prove,
With a more than mother's love.
   Gone, gone, — sold and gone,
   To the rice-swamp dank and lone,
   From Virginia's hills and waters, —
   Woe is me, my stolen daughters!

THE MORAL WARFARE.

WHEN Freedom, on her natal day,
Within her war-rocked cradle lay,
An iron race around her stood,
Baptized her infant brow in blood ;
And, through the storm which round her
   swept,
Their constant ward and watching kept.

Then, where our quiet herds repose,
The roar of baleful battle rose,
And brethren of a common tongue
To mortal strife as tigers sprung,
And every gift on Freedom's shrine
Was man for beast, and blood for wine !

Our fathers to their graves have gone ;
Their strife is past, — their triumph won ;
But sterner trials wait the race
Which rises in their honored place, —
A moral warfare with the crime
And folly of an evil time.

So let it be. In God's own might
We gird us for the coming fight,
And, strong in Him whose cause is ours
In conflict with unholy powers,
We grasp the weapons He has given, —
The Light, and Truth, and Love of
   Heaven.

THE WORLD'S CONVENTION

OF THE FRIENDS OF EMANCIPATION,
HELD IN LONDON IN 1840.

YES, let them gather ! — Summon forth
The pledged philanthropy of Earth,
From every land, whose hills have heard
   The bugle blast of Freedom waking ;
Or shrieking of her symbol-bird
   From out his cloudy eyrie breaking :
Where Justice hath one worshipper,
Or truth one altar built to her ;
Where'er a human eye is weeping
   O'er wrongs which Earth's sad chil-
     dren know, —

Where'er a single heart is keeping
   Its prayerful watch with human woe :
Thence let them come, and greet each
     other,
And know in each a friend and brother !

Yes, let them come ! from each green vale
   Where England's old baronial halls
   Still bear upon their storied walls
The grim crusader's rusted mail,
Battered by Paynim spear and brand
On Malta's rock or Syria's sand !
And mouldering pennon-staves once set
   Within the soil of Palestine,
By Jordan and Genesaret ;
   Or, borne with England's battle line,
O'er Acre's shattered turrets stooping,
Or, midst the camp their banners droop-
     ing,
   With dews from hallowed Hermon wet,
A holier summons now is given
Than that gray hermit's voice of old,
Which unto all the winds of heaven
The banners of the Cross unrolled !
Not for the long-deserted shrine, —
   Not for the dull unconscious sod,
Which tells not by one lingering sign
   That there the hope of Israel trod ; —
But for that TRUTH, for which alone
   In pilgrim eyes are sanctified
The garden moss, the mountain stone,
Whereon his holy sandals pressed, —
The fountain which his lip hath
     blessed, —
Whate'er hath touched his garment's hem
At Bethany or Bethlehem,
   Or Jordan's river-side.
For FREEDOM, in the name of Him
   Who came to raise Earth's drooping
     poor,
To break the chain from every limb,
The bolt from every prison door !
For these, o'er all the earth hath passed
An ever-deepening trumpet blast,
As if an angel's breath had lent
Its vigor to the instrument.

And Wales, from Snowden's mountain
     wall,
Shall startle at that thrilling call,
   As if she heard her bards again ;
And Erin's " harp on Tara's wall "
   Give out its ancient strain,
Mirthful and sweet, yet sad withal, —
   The melody which Erin loves,
When o'er that harp, 'mid bursts of glad-
     ness

And slogan cries and lyke-wake sadness,
  The hand of her O'Connell moves !
Scotland, from lake and tarn and rill,
And mountain hold, and heathery hill,
  Shall catch and echo back the note,
As if she heard upon her air
Once more her Cameronian's prayer
  And song of Freedom float.
And cheering echoes shall reply
From each remote dependency,
Where Britain's mighty sway is known,
In tropic sea or frozen zone ;
Where'er her sunset flag is furling,
Or morning gun-fire's smoke is curling ;
From Indian Bengal's groves of palm
And rosy fields and gales of balm.
Where Eastern pomp and power are rolled
Through regal Ava's gates of gold ;
And from the lakes and ancient woods
And dim Canadian solitudes,
Whence, sternly from her rocky throne,
Queen of the North, Quebec looks down ;
And from those bright and ransomed
    Isles
Where all unwonted Freedom smiles,
And the dark laborer still retains
The scar of slavery's broken chains !

From the hoar Alps, which sentinel
The gateways of the land of Tell,
Where morning's keen and earliest glance
  On Jura's rocky wall is thrown,
And from the olive bowers of France
  And vine groves garlanding the
    Rhone, —
" Friends of the Blacks," as true and
    tried
As those who stood by Oge's side,
And heard the Haytien's tale of wrong,
Shall gather at that summons strong, —
Broglie, Passy, and him whose song
Breathed over Syria's holy sod,
And in the paths which Jesus trod,
And murmured midst the hills which hem
Crownless and sad Jerusalem,
Hath echoes whereso'er the tone
Of Israel's prophet-lyre is known.

Still let them come, — from Quito's
    walls,
  And from the Orinoco's tide,
From Lima's Inca-haunted halls,
From Santa Fe and Yucatan, —
  Men who by swart Guerrero's side
Proclaimed the deathless RIGHTS OF MAN,
  Broke every bond and fetter off,
  And hailed in every sable serf

A free and brother
Chiefs who across t
  Have followed
    pennon,
And seen on Junin
Glare o'er the brok
  The fire-burst of
And Hayti, from h
  Shall send the so
Defiance from her
The war-gage from
  Alone against a

Nor all unmindful
Land of the dark a
  Thy Moslem me
  All tyrants of a
When in the shad
Or, where from Al
El Gerek's upper f
Or where from Mo
El Abiad bears his
Where'er thy lotu
  Within their a
    ters, —
Where'er is heard
  Or song of Nubi
The curse of SLAV
Thy bequest from
At thy dark Mehe
Forevermore shall
  And chains forsa
Of all those tribes
Have echoed back
  And victor horr

And thou whose g
To earth's remotes
In mingled tones a
The echoes of a wo
My country ! glori
A day-star flashin
  The herald-sign
O, who could drea
  And watched th
That vapors from
  Would cloud the
Or, that earth's f
    heard,
Awe-struck, the
    thy dawnin
Would rise so soc
    king,
To mock thee with
Like Hades when h
  To greet the dow
    ing !

"Aha ! and art thou fallen thus ?
Art THOU become as one of *us* ?"

Land of my fathers ! — there will stand,
Amidst that world-assembled band,
Those owning thy maternal claim
Unweakened by thy crime and shame, —
The sad reprovers of thy wrong, —
The children thou hast spurned so long.
Still with affection's fondest yearning
To their unnatural mother turning.
No traitors they ! — but tried and leal,
Whose own is but thy general weal,
Still blending with the patriot's zeal
The Christian's love for human kind,
To caste and climate unconfined.

A holy gathering ! — peaceful all :
No threat of war, — no savage call
    For vengeance on an erring brother !
But in their stead the godlike plan
To teach the brotherhood of man
    To love and reverence one another,
As sharers of a common blood,
The children of a common God ! —
Yet, even at its lightest word,
Shall Slavery's darkest depths be stirred :
Spain, watching from her Moro's keep
Her slave-ships traversing the deep,
And Rio, in her strength and pride,
Lifting, along her mountain-side,
Her snowy battlements and towers, —
Her lemon-groves and tropic bowers,
With bitter hate and sullen fear
Its freedom-giving voice shall hear ;
And where my country's flag is flow-
    ing,
On breezes from Mount Vernon blowing
Above the Nation's council halls,
Where Freedom's praise is loud and long,
    While close beneath the outward walls
The driver plies his reeking thong, —
    The hammer of the man-thief falls,
O'er hypocritic cheek and brow   ·
The crimson flush of shame shall glow :
And all who for their native land
Are pledging life and heart and hand, —
Worn watchers o'er her changing weal,
Who for her tarnished honor feel, —
Through cottage door and council-hall
Shall thunder an awakening call.
The pen along its page shall burn
With all intolerable scorn, —
An eloquent rebuke shall go
On all the winds that Southward blow, —
From priestly lips, now sealed and dumb,
Warning and dread appeal shall come,

Like those which Israel heard from him,
The Prophet of the Cherubim, —
Or those which sad Esaias hurled
Against a sin-accursed world !
Its wizard leaves the Press shall fling
Unceasing from its iron wing,
With characters inscribed thereon,
    As fearful in the despot's hall
As to the pomp of Babylon
    The fire-sign on the palace wall !
And, from her dark iniquities,
Methinks I see my country rise :
Not challenging the nations round
    To note her tardy justice done, —
Her captives from their chains unbound,
Her prisons opening to the sun : —
But tearfully her arms extending
Over the poor and unoffending ;
Her regal emblem now no longer
A bird of prey, with talons reeking,
Above the dying captive shrieking,
But, spreading out her ample wing, —
A broad, impartial covering, —
The weaker sheltered by the stron-
    ger ! —
O, then to Faith's anointed eyes
    The promised token shall be given ;
And on a nation's sacrifice,
Atoning for the sin of years,
And wet with penitential tears, —
    The fire shall fall from Heaven !
1839.

NEW HAMPSHIRE.

1845.

GOD bless New Hampshire ! — from her
    granite peaks
Once more the voice of Stark and
    Langdon speaks.
The long-bound vassal of the exulting
    South
For very shame her self-forged chain
    has broken, —
Torn the black seal of slavery from her
    mouth,
    And in the clear tones of her old time
        spoken !
O, all undreamed-of, all unhoped-for
    changes ! —
    The tyrant's ally proves his sternest
        foe ;
To all his biddings, from her mountain
    ranges,
    New Hampshire thunders an indig-
        nant No !

Who is it now despairs? O, faint of heart,
    Look upward to those Northern moun-
      tains cold,
    Flouted by Freedom's victor-flag un-
      rolled,
And gather strength to bear a manlier
      part!
All is not lost. The angel of God's
      blessing
    Encamps with Freedom on the field
      of fight;
Still to her banner, day by day, are
      pressing,
    Unlooked-for allies, striking for the
      right!
Courage, then, Northern hearts! — Be
      firm, be true:
What one brave State hath done, can ye
      not also do?

THE NEW YEAR:

ADDRESSED TO THE PATRONS OF THE
PENNSYLVANIA FREEMAN.

THE wave is breaking on the shore, —
    The echo fading from the chime, —
Again the shadow moveth o'er
    The dial-plate of time!

O, seer-seen Angel! waiting now
    With weary feet on sea and shore,
Impatient for the last dread vow
    That time shall be no more!

Once more across thy sleepless eye
    The semblance of a smile has passed:
The year departing leaves more nigh
    Time's fearfullest and last.

O, in that dying year hath been
    The sum of all since time began, —
The birth and death, the joy and pain,
    Of Nature and of Man.

Spring, with her change of sun and
      shower,
    And streams released from Winter's
      chain,
And bursting bud, and opening flower,
    And greenly growing grain;

And Summer's shade, and sunshine warm,
    And rainbows o'er her hill-tops bowed,
And voices in her rising storm, —
    God speaking from his cloud! —

And Autumn's fruits and clustering
      sheaves,
    And soft, warm days of golden light,
The glory of her forest leaves,
    And harvest-moon at night;

And Winter with her leafless grove,
    And prisoned stream, and drifting
      snow,
The brilliance of her heaven above
    And of her earth below: —

And man, — in whom an angel's mind
    With earth's low instincts finds
      abode, —
The highest of the links which bind
    Brute nature to her God;   .

His infant eye hath seen the light,
    His childhood's merriest laughter rung,
And active sports to manlier might
    The nerves of boyhood strung!

And quiet love, and passion's fires,
    Have soothed or burned in manhood's
      breast,
And lofty aims and low desires
    By turns disturbed his rest.

The wailing of the newly-born
    Has mingled with the funeral knell;
And o'er the dying's ear has gone
    The merry marriage-bell.

And Wealth has filled his halls with
      mirth,
    While Want, in many a humble shed,
Toiled, shivering by her cheerless hearth,
    The live-long night for bread.

And worse than all, — the human
      slave, —
    The sport of lust, and pride, and
      scorn!
Plucked off the crown his Maker gave, —
    His regal manhood gone!

O, still, my country! o'er thy plains,
    Blackened with slavery's blight and
      ban,
That human chattel drags his chains, —
    An uncreated man!

And still, where'er to sun and breeze,
    My country, is thy flag unrolled,
With scorn, the gazing stranger sees
    A stain on every fold.

O, tear the gorgeous emblem down !
  It gathers scorn from every eye,
And despots smile and good men frown
  Whene'er it passes by.

Shame ! shame ! its starry splendors
    glow
  Above the slaver's loathsome jail, —
Its folds are ruffling even now
  His crimson flag of sale.

Still round our country's proudest hall
  The trade in human flesh is driven,
And at each careless hammer-fall
  A human heart is riven.

And this, too, sanctioned by the men
  Vested with power to shield the right,
And throw each vile and robber den
  Wide open to the light.

Yet, shame upon them ! — there they sit,
  Men of the North, subdued and still ;
Meek, pliant poltroons, only fit
  To work a master's will.

Sold, — bargained off for Southern
    votes, —
  A passive herd of Northern mules,
Just braying through their purchased
    throats
  Whate'er their owner rules.

And he,[85] — the basest of the base,
  The vilest of the vile, — whose name,
Embalmed in infinite disgrace,
  Is deathless in its shame ! —

A tool, — to bolt the people's door
  Against the people clamoring there,
An ass, — to trample on their floor
  A people's right of prayer !

Nailed to his self-made gibbet fast,
  Self-pilloried to the public view, —
A mark for every passing blast
  Of scorn to whistle through ;

There let him hang, and hear the boast
  Of Southrons o'er their pliant tool, —
A new Stylites on his post,
  " Sacred to ridicule ! "

Look we at home ! — our noble hall,
  To Freedom's holy purpose given,
Now rears its black and ruined wall,
  Beneath the wintry heaven, —

Telling the story of its doom, —
  The fiendish mob, — the prostrate
    law, —
The fiery jet through midnight's gloom,
  Our gazing thousands saw.

Look to our State, — the poor man's right
  Torn from him : — and the sons of
    those
Whose blood in Freedom's sternest fight
  Sprinkled the Jersey snows,

Outlawed within the land of Penn,
  That Slavery's guilty fears might cease,
And those whom God created men
  Toil on as brutes in peace.

Yet o'er the blackness of the storm
  A bow of promise bends on high,
And gleams of sunshine, soft and warm,
  Break through our clouded sky.

East, West, and North, the shout is
    heard,
  Of freemen rising for the right :
Each valley hath its rallying word, —
  Each hill its signal light.

O'er Massachusetts' rocks of gray,
  The strengthening light of freedom
    shines,
Rhode Island's Narragansett Bay, —
  And Vermont's snow-hung pines !

From Hudson's frowning palisades
  To Alleghany's laurelled crest,
O'er lakes and prairies, streams and glades,
  It shines upon the West.

Speed on the light to those who dwell
  In Slavery's land of woe and sin,
And through the blackness of that hell,
  Let Heaven's own light break in.

So shall the Southern conscience quake
  Before that light poured full and
    strong,
So shall the Southern heart awake
  To all the bondman's wrong.

And from that rich and sunny land
  The song of grateful millions rise,
Like that of Israel's ransomed band
  Beneath Arabia's skies :

And all who now are bound beneath
  Our banner's shade, our eagle's wing,

From Slavery's night of moral death
  To light and life shall spring.

Broken the bondman's chain, and gone
  The master's guilt, and hate, and fear,
And unto both alike shall dawn
  A New and Happy Year.
    1839.

MASSACHUSETTS TO VIRGINIA.

[Written on reading an account of the proceedings of the citizens of Norfolk, Va., in reference to GEORGE LATIMER, the alleged fugitive
slave, the result of whose case in Massachusetts
will probably be similar to that of the negro
SOMERSET in England, in 1772.]

THE blast from Freedom's Northern
    hills, upon its Southern way,
Bears greeting to Virginia from Massa-
    chusetts Bay: —
No word of haughty challenging, nor
    battle bugle's peal,
Nor steady tread of marching files, nor
    clang of horsemen's steel.

No trains of deep-mouthed cannon along
    our highways go, —
Around our silent arsenals untrodden
    lies the snow;
And to the land-breeze of our ports, upon
    their errands far,
A thousand sails of commerce swell, but
    none are spread for war.

We hear thy threats, Virginia! thy
    stormy words and high,
Swell harshly on the Southern winds
    which melt along our sky;
Yet, not one brown, hard hand foregoes
    its honest labor here,
No hewer of our mountain oaks suspends
    his axe in fear.

Wild are the waves which lash the reefs
    along St. George's bank, —
Cold on the shore of Labrador the fog
    lies white and dank;
Through storm, and wave, and blinding
    mist, stout are the hearts which man
The fishing-smacks of Marblehead, the
    sea-boats of Cape Ann.

The cold north light and wintry sun
    glare on their icy forms,
Bent grimly o'er their straining lines or
    wrestling with the storms;

Free as the winds they drive belore,
    rough as the waves they roam,
They laugh to scorn the slaver's threat
    against their rocky home.

What means the Old Dominion? Hath
    she forgot the day
When o'er her conquered valleys swept
    the Briton's steel array?
How side by side, with sons of hers, the
    Massachusetts men
Encountered Tarleton's charge of fire,
    and stout Cornwallis, then?

Forgets she how the Bay State, in an-
    swer to the call
Of her old House of Burgesses, spoke out
    from Faneuil Hall?
When, echoing back her Henry's cry,
    came pulsing on each breath
Of Northern winds, the thrilling sounds
    of "LIBERTY OR DEATH!"

What asks the Old Dominion? If now
    her sons have proved
False to their fathers' memory, — false
    to the faith they loved,
If she can scoff at Freedom, and its great
    charter spurn,
Must we of Massachusetts from truth
    and duty turn?

We hunt your bondmen, flying from
    Slavery's hateful hell, —
Our voices, at your bidding, take up the
    bloodhound's yell, —
We gather, at your summons, above our
    fathers' graves,
From Freedom's holy altar-horns to tear
    your wretched slaves!

Thank God! not yet so vilely can Massa-
    chusetts bow;
The spirit of her early time is with her
    even now;
Dream not because her Pilgrim blood
    moves slow and calm and cool,
She thus can stoop her chainless neck,
    a sister's slave and tool!

All that a *sister* State should do, all that
    a *free* State may,
Heart, hand, and purse we proffer, as in
    our early day;
But that one dark loathsome burden ye
    must stagger with alone,
And reap the bitter harvest which ye
    yourselves have sown!

Hold, while ye may, your struggling
   slaves, and burden God's free air
With woman's shriek beneath the lash,
   and manhood's wild despair ;
Cling closer to the "cleaving curse" that
   writes upon your plains
The blasting of Almighty wrath against
   a land of chains.

Still shame your gallant ancestry, the
   cavaliers of old,
By watching round the shambles where
   human flesh is sold, —
Gloat o'er the new-born child, and count
   his market value, when
The maddened mother's cry of woe shall
   pierce the slaver's den !

Lower than plummet soundeth, sink the
   Virginia name ;
Plant, if ye will, your fathers' graves
   with rankest weeds of shame ;
Be, if ye will, the scandal of God's fair
   universe, —
We wash our hands forever of your sin
   and shame and curse.

A voice from lips whereon the coal from
   Freedom's shrine hath been,
Thrilled, as but yesterday, the hearts of
   Berkshire's mountain men:
The echoes of that solemn voice are sadly
   lingering still
In all our sunny valleys, on every wind-
   swept hill.

And when the prowling man-thief came
   hunting for his prey
Beneath the very shadow of Bunker's
   shaft of gray,
How, through the free lips of the son,
   the father's warning spoke ;
How, from its bonds of trade and sect,
   the Pilgrim city broke !

A hundred thousand right arms were
   lifted up on high, —
A hundred thousand voices sent back
   their loud reply ;
Through the thronged towns of Essex
   the startling summons rang,
And up from bench and loom and wheel
   her young mechanics sprang !

The voice of free, broad Middlesex, — of
   thousands as of one, —
The shaft of Bunker calling to that of
   Lexington, —

From Norfolk's ancient villages, from
   Plymouth's rocky bound
To where Nantucket feels the arms of
   ocean close her round ; —

From rich and rural Worcester, where
   through the calm repose
Of cultured vales and fringing woods the
   gentle Nashua flows,
To where Wachuset's wintry blasts the
   mountain larches stir,
Swelled up to Heaven the thrilling cry
   of "God save Latimer ! "

And sandy Barnstable rose up, wet with
   the salt sea spray, —
And Bristol sent her answering shout
   down Narragansett Bay !
Along the broad Connecticut old Hampden felt the thrill,
And the cheer of Hampshire's woodmen
   swept down from Holyoke Hill.

The voice of Massachusetts ! Of her free
   sons and daughters, —
Deep calling unto deep aloud, — the
   sound of many waters !
Against the burden of that voice what
   tyrant power shall stand ?
No fetters in the Bay State ! No slave
   upon her land !

Look to it well, Virginians ! In calmness we have borne,
In answer to our faith and trust, your
   insult and your scorn ;
You 've spurned our kindest counsels, —
   you 've hunted for our lives, —
And shaken round our hearths and
   homes your manacles and gyves !

We wage no war, — we lift no arm, —
   we fling no torch within
The fire-damps of the quaking mine beneath your soil of sin ;
We leave ye with your bondmen, to
   wrestle, while ye can,
With the strong upward tendencies and
   godlike soul of man !

But for us and for our children, the vow
   which we have given
For freedom and humanity is registered
   in heaven ;
No slave-hunt in our borders, — no pirate
   on our strand !
No fetters in the Bay State, — no slave
   upon our land !

THE RELIC.

[Pennsylvania Hall, dedicated to Free Discussion and the cause of human liberty, was destroyed by a mob in 1838. The following was written on receiving a cane wrought from a fragment of the wood-work which the fire had spared.]

Token of friendship true and tried,
  From one whose fiery heart of youth
With mine has beaten, side by side,
  For Liberty and Truth ;
With honest pride the gift I take,
And prize it for the giver's sake.

But not alone because it tells
  Of generous hand and heart sincere ;
Around that gift of friendship dwells
  A memory doubly dear, —
Earth's noblest aim, — man's holiest thought,
With that memorial frail inwrought !

Pure thoughts and sweet, like flowers unfold,
  And precious memories round it cling,
Even as the Prophet's rod of old
  In beauty blossoming :
And buds of feeling pure and good
Spring from its cold unconscious wood.

Relic of Freedom's shrine ! — a brand
  Plucked from its burning ! — let it be
Dear as a jewel from the hand
  Of a lost friend to me ! —
Flower of a perished garland left,
Of life and beauty unbereft !

O, if the young enthusiast bears,
  O'er weary waste and sea, the stone
Which crumbled from the Forum's stairs,
  Or round the Parthenon ;
Or olive-bough from some wild tree
Hung over old Thermopylæ :

If leaflets from some hero's tomb,
  Or moss-wreath torn from ruins hoary, —
Or faded flowers whose sisters bloom
  On fields renowned in story, —
Or fragment from the Alhambra's crest,
Or the gray rock by Druids blessed ;

Sad Erin's shamrock greenly growing
  Where Freedom led her stalwart kern,
Or Scotia's " rough bur thistle " blowing
  On Bruce's Bannockburn, —

Or Runnymede's wild English rose,
Or lichen plucked from Sempach's snows ! —

If it be true that things like these
  To heart and eye bright visions bring,
Shall not far holier memories
  To this memorial cling ?
Which needs no mellowing mist of time
To hide the crimson stains of crime !

Wreck of a temple, unprofaned, —
  Of courts where Peace with Freedom trod,
Lifting on high, with hands unstained,
  Thanksgiving unto God ;
Where Mercy's voice of love was pleading
For human hearts in bondage bleeding ! —

Where, midst the sound of rushing feet
  And curses on the night-air flung,
That pleading voice rose calm and sweet
  From woman's earnest tongue ;
And Riot turned his scowling glance,
Awed, from her tranquil countenance !

That temple now in ruin lies ! —
  The fire-stain on its shattered wall,
And open to the changing skies
  Its black and roofless hall,
It stands before a nation's sight,
A gravestone over buried Right !

But from that ruin, as of old,
  The fire-scorched stones themselves are crying,
And from their ashes white and cold
  Its timbers are replying !
A voice which slavery cannot kill
Speaks from the crumbling arches still !

And even this relic from thy shrine,
  O holy Freedom ! hath to me
A potent power, a voice and sign
  To testify of thee ;
And, grasping it, methinks I feel
A deeper faith, a stronger zeal.

And not unlike that mystic rod,
  Of old stretched o'er the Egyptian wave,
Which opened, in the strength of God,
  A pathway for the slave,
It yet may point the bondman's way,
And turn the spoiler from his prey.

THE BRANDED HAND.

1846.

WELCOME home again, brave seaman! with thy thoughtful brow and gray,
And the old heroic spirit of our earlier, better day, —
With that front of calm endurance, on whose steady nerve in vain
Pressed the iron of the prison, smote the fiery shafts of pain!

Is the tyrant's brand upon thee? Did the brutal cravens aim
To make God's truth thy falsehood, his holiest work thy shame?
When, all blood-quenched, from the torture the iron was withdrawn,
How laughed their evil angel the baffled fools to scorn!

They change to wrong the duty which God hath written out
On the great heart of humanity, too legible for doubt!
They, the loathsome moral lepers, blotched from footsole up to crown,
Give to shame what God hath given unto honor and renown!

Why, that brand is highest honor! — than its traces never yet
Upon old armorial hatchments was a prouder blazon set;
And thy unborn generations, as they tread our rocky strand,
Shall tell with pride the story of their father's BRANDED HAND!

As the Templar home was welcome, bearing back from Syrian wars
The scars of Arab lances and of Paynim scymitars,
The pallor of the prison, and the shackle's crimson span,
So we meet thee, so we greet thee, truest friend of God and man.

He suffered for the ransom of the dear Redeemer's grave,
Thou for his living presence in the bound and bleeding slave;
He for a soil no longer by the feet of angels trod,
Thou for the true Shechinah, the present home of God!

For, while the jurist, sitting with the slave-whip o'er him swung,
From the tortured truths of freedom the lie of slavery wrung,
And the solemn priest to Moloch, on each God-deserted shrine,
Broke the bondman's heart for bread, poured the bondman's blood for wine,—

While the multitude in blindness to a far-off Saviour knelt,
And spurned, the while, the temple where a present Saviour dwelt;
Thou beheld'st him in the task-field, in the prison shadows dim,
And thy mercy to the bondman, it was mercy unto him!

In thy lone and long night-watches, sky above and wave below,
Thou didst learn a higher wisdom than the babbling schoolmen know;
God's stars and silence taught thee, as his angels only can,
That the one sole sacred thing beneath the cope of heaven is Man!

That he who treads profanely on the scrolls of law and creed,
In the depth of God's great goodness may find mercy in his need;
But woe to him who crushes the soul with chain and rod,
And herds with lower natures the awful form of God!

Then lift that manly right-hand, bold ploughman of the wave!
Its branded palm shall prophesy, "SALVATION TO THE SLAVE!"
Hold up its fire-wrought language, that whoso reads may feel
His heart swell strong within him, his sinews change to steel.

Hold it up before our sunshine, up against our Northern air, —
Ho! men of Massachusetts, for the love of God, look there!
Take it henceforth for your standard, like the Bruce's heart of yore,
In the dark strife closing round ye, let that hand be seen before!

And the tyrants of the slave-land shall tremble at that sign,

When it points its finger Southward
    along the Puritan line :
Woe to the State-gorged leeches and the
    Church's locust band,
When they look from slavery's ramparts
    on the coming of that hand !

TEXAS.

VOICE OF NEW ENGLAND.

Up the hillside, down the glen,
Rouse the sleeping citizen ;
Summon out the might of men !

Like a lion growling low, —
Like a night-storm rising slow, —
Like the tread of unseen foe, —

It is coming, — it is nigh !
Stand your homes and altars by ;
On your own free thresholds die.

Clang the bells in all your spires ;
On the gray hills of your sires
Fling to heaven your signal-fires.

From Wachuset, lone and bleak,
Unto Berkshire's tallest peak,
Let the flame-tongued heralds speak.

O, for God and duty stand,
Heart to heart and hand to hand,
Round the old graves of the land.

Whoso shrinks or falters now,
Whoso to the yoke would bow,
Brand the craven on his brow !

Freedom's soil hath only place
For a free and fearless race, —
None for traitors false and base.

Perish party, — perish clan ;
Strike together while ye can,
Like the arm of one strong man.

Like that angel's voice sublime,
Heard above a world of crime,
Crying of the end of time, —

With one heart and with one mouth,
Let the North unto the South
Speak the word befitting both :

" What though Issachar be strong !
Ye may load his back with wrong
Overmuch and over long :

" Patience with h
With her weary tl
Murmurs that her

" Make our Union
Weak as tow in F1
Link by link shal

" Vainly shall yor
Bind the starry cl
Shattered over hea

" Give us bright t
Rather than etern
Clouding o'er the

" Take your land
Only leave to Free
For her plough, a1

" Take your slave1
Leave us but our
Blowing on our th

" Boldly, or with
Strike the blood-w
Break the Union's

" Work the ruin,
Pluck upon your l
Which shall grow

" With your bond
With his heart of
Stand alone, if sta

" Onward with yo
Dig the gulf and d
Fire beneath your

" Deeply, when tl
Yawns between yo
Shall ye feel your

" By the hearth,
Shaken by a look
Ye shall own a gu

" And the curse o
Downward throug
Like a fire shall bu

" Our bleak hills
Vines our rocks sh
Plenty in our valle

" And when venge
Hither shall ye tu
As the lost on Par

" We but ask our rocky strand,
Freedom's true and brother band,
Freedom's strong and honest hand, —

"Valleys by the slave untrod,
And the Pilgrim's mountain sod,
Blessed of our fathers' God ! "

TO FANEUIL HALL.

1844.

MEN ! — if manhood still ye claim,
   If the Northern pulse can thrill,
Roused by wrong or stung by shame,
   Freely, strongly still, —
Let the sounds of traffic die :
   Shut the mill-gate, — leave the stall, —
Fling the axe and hammer by, —
   Throng to Faneuil Hall !

Wrongs which freemen never brooked, —
   Dangers grim and fierce as they,
Which, like couching lions, looked
   On your fathers' way, —
These your instant zeal demand,
   Shaking with their earthquake-call
Every rood of Pilgrim land,
   Ho, to Faneuil Hall !

From your capes and sandy bars, —
   From your mountain-ridges cold,
Through whose pines the westering stars
   Stoop their crowns of gold, —
Come, and with your footsteps wake
   Echoes from that holy wall ;
Once again, for Freedom's sake,
   Rock your fathers' hall !

Up, and tread beneath your feet
   Every cord by party spun :
Let your hearts together beat
   As the heart of one.
Banks and tariffs, stocks and trade,
   Let them rise or let them fall :
Freedom asks your common aid, —
   Up, to Faneuil Hall !

Up, and let each voice that speaks
   Ring from thence to Southern plains,
Sharply as the blow which breaks
   Prison-bolts and chains !
Speak as well becomes the free :
   Dreaded more than steel or ball,
Shall your calmest utterance be,
   Heard from Faneuil Hall !

Have they wronged us ? Let us then
   Render back nor threats nor prayers ;
Have they chained our free-born men ?
   LET US UNCHAIN THEIRS !
Up, your banner leads the van,
   Blazoned, " Liberty for all ! "
Finish what your sires began !
   Up, to Faneuil Hall !

TO MASSACHUSETTS.

1844.

WHAT though around thee blazes
   No fiery rallying sign ?
From all thy own high places,
   Give heaven the light of thine !
What though unthrilled, unmoving,
   The statesman stand apart,
And comes no warm approving
   From Mammon's crowded mart ?

Still, let the land be shaken
   By a summons of thine own !
By all save truth forsaken,
   Why, stand with that alone !
Shrink not from strife unequal !
   With the best is always hope ;
And ever in the sequel
   God holds the right side up !

But when, with thine uniting,
   Come voices long and loud,
And far-off hills are writing
   Thy fire-words on the cloud ;
When from Penobscot's fountains
   A deep response is heard,
And across the Western mountains
   Rolls back thy rallying word ;

Shall thy line of battle falter,
   With its allies just in view ?
O, by hearth and holy altar,
   My fatherland, be true !
Fling abroad thy scrolls of Freedom !
   Speed them onward far and fast !
Over hill and valley speed them,
   Like the sibyl's on the blast !

Lo ! the Empire State is shaking
   The shackles from her hand ;
With the rugged North is waking
   The level sunset land !
On they come, — the free battalions !
   East and West and North they come,
And the heart-beat of the millions
   Is the beat of Freedom's drum.

" To the tyrant's plot no favor !
  No heed to place-fed knaves !
Bar and bolt the door forever
  Against the land of slaves ! "
Hear it, mother Earth, and hear it,
  The Heavens above us spread !
The land is roused, — its spirit
  Was sleeping, but not dead !

THE PINE-TREE.

1846.

LIFT again the stately emblem on the
    Bay State's rusted shield,
Give to Northern winds the Pine-Tree
    on our banner's tattered field.
Sons of men who sat in council with their
    Bibles round the board,
Answering England's royal missive with
    a firm, "THUS SAITH THE LORD !"
Rise again for home and freedom ! — set
    the battle in array ! —
What the fathers did of old time we
    their sons must do to-day.

Tell us not of banks and tariffs, — cease
    your paltry pedler cries, —
Shall the good State sink her honor that
    your gambling stocks may rise !
Would ye barter man for cotton ? — That
    your gains may sum up higher,
Must we kiss the feet of Moloch, pass
    our children through the fire ?
Is the dollar only real ? — God and truth
    and right a dream !
Weighed against your lying ledgers must
    our manhood kick the beam ?

O my God ! — for that free spirit, which
    of old in Boston town
Smote the Province House with terror,
    struck the crest of Andros down ! —
For another strong-voiced Adams in the
    city's streets to cry,
" Up for God and Massachusetts ! — Set
    your feet on Mammon's lie !
Perish banks and perish traffic, — spin
    your cotton's latest pound, —
But in Heaven's name keep your honor, —
    keep the heart o' the Bay State
    sound ! "

Where 's the MAN for Massachusetts ? —
    Where 's the voice to speak her
    free ? —

Where 's the hand
    from her mo
Beats her Pilgrim
    Sits she dun
Has she none to t
    Has she non
O my God ! for on
    up her ruste
And to plant again
    .   banner's tat

LI:

SUGGESTED BY A Y
WASHINGTON, IN
OF 1845.

WITH a cold and
  On its roofs an
Shadows weaving
  From the gray
Broadly, vaguely, a
  half-built to

Through this broa
  Ebbs and flow:
Wave on wave a
  Wealth and fa:
Toiler, idler, slave
  same quick

Underneath yon
  Springs above
Grave men in th
  For the larges:
Which the hand of
  crumbs whic

Base of heart ! '
  Honor's wealtl
Step by step on l
  Leaving footpr
For to-day's poor p
  the great ho

Yet, where festal
  Glory round th
Gold-tressed, lik
  Backward on t
And the low quick
  its measure :
  .
There to-night sh
  Star-like, welc
Fawning fools wi
  Seek to touch
With the tongue of
  which God a

From this glittering lie my vision
Takes a broader, sadder range,
Full before me have arisen
Other pictures dark and strange ;
rom the parlor to the prison must the
scene and witness change.

Hark ! the heavy gate is swinging
On its hinges, harsh and slow ;
One pale prison lamp is flinging
On a fearful group below
uch a light as leaves to terror whatso-
e'er it does not show.

Pitying God ! — Is that a WOMAN
On whose wrist the shackles clash ?
Is that shriek she utters human,
Underneath the stinging lash ?
re they MEN whose eyes of madness
from that sad procession flash ?

Still the dance goes gayly onward !
What is it to Wealth and Pride
That without the stars are looking
On a scene which earth should hide ?
hat the SLAVE-SHIP lies in waiting,
rocking on Potomac's tide !

Vainly to that mean Ambition
Which, upon a rival's fall,
Winds above its old condition,
With a reptile's slimy crawl,
hall the pleading voice of sorrow, shall
the slave in anguish call.

Vainly to the child of Fashion,
Giving to ideal woe
Graceful luxury of compassion,
Shall the stricken mourner go ;
ateful seems the earnest sorrow, beau-
tiful the hollow show !

Nay, my words are all too sweeping :
In this crowded human mart,
Feeling is not dead, but sleeping ;
Man's strong will and woman's heart,
ı the coming strife for Freedom, yet
shall bear their generous part.

And from yonder sunny valleys,
Southward in the distance lost,
Freedom yet shall summon allies
Worthier than the North can boast,
Vith the Evil by their hearth-stones
grappling at severer cost.

Now, the soul alone is willing :
Faint the heart and weak the knee ;

And as yet no lip is thrilling
With the mighty words, "BE FREE !"
Tarrieth long the land's Good Angel,
but his advent is to be !

Meanwhile, turning from the revel
To the prison-cell my sight,
For intenser hate of evil,
For a keener sense of right,
Shaking off thy dust, I thank thee, City
of the Slaves, to-night !

"To thy duty now and ever !
Dream no more of rest or stay ;
Give to Freedom's great endeavor
All thou art and hast to-day " : —
Thus, above the city's murmur, saith a
Voice, or seems to say.

Ye with heart and vision gifted
To discern and love the right,
Whose worn faces have been lifted
To the slowly-growing light,
Where from Freedom's sunrise drifted
slowly back the murk of night ! —

Ye who through long years of trial
Still have held your purpose fast,
While a lengthening shade the dial
From the westering sunshine cast,
And of hope each hour's denial seemed
an echo of the last ! —

O my brothers ! O my sisters !
Would to God that ye were near,
Gazing with me down the vistas
Of a sorrow strange and drear ;
Would to God that ye were listeners to
the Voice I seem to hear !

With the storm above us driving,
With the false earth mined below, —
Who shall marvel if thus striving
We have counted friend as foe ;
Unto one another giving in the darkness
blow for blow.

Well it may be that our natures
Have grown sterner and more hard,
And the freshness of their features
Somewhat harsh and battle-scarred,
And their harmonies of feeling over-
tasked and rudely jarred.

Be it so. It should not swerve us
From a purpose true and brave ;

Dearer Freedom's rugged service
  Than the pastime of the slave ;
Better is the storm above it than the
    quiet of the grave.

Let us then, uniting, bury
  All our idle feuds in dust,
And to future conflicts carry
  Mutual faith and common trust ;
Always he who most forgiveth in his
    brother is most just.

From the eternal shadow rounding
  All our sun and starlight here,
Voices of our lost ones sounding
  Bid us be of heart and cheer,
Through the silence, down the spaces,
    falling on the inward ear.

Know we not our dead are looking
  Downward with a sad surprise,
All our strife of words rebuking
  With their mild and loving eyes ?
Shall we grieve the holy angels ? Shall
  we cloud their blessed skies ?

Let us draw their mantles o'er us
  Which have fallen in our way ;
Let us do the work before us,
  Cheerly, bravely, while we may,
Ere the long night-silence cometh, and
  with us it is not day !

LINES,

FROM A LETTER TO A YOUNG CLERI-
CAL FRIEND.

A STRENGTH Thy service cannot tire, —
A faith which doubt can never dim, —
A heart of love, a lip of fire, —
O Freedom's God ! be thou to him !

Speak through him words of power and
  fear,
  As through thy prophet bards of old,
And let a scornful people hear
  Once more thy Sinai-thunders rolled.

For lying lips thy blessing seek,
  And hands of blood are raised to Thee,
And on thy children, crushed and weak,
  The oppressor plants his kneeling knee.

Let then, O God ! thy servant dare
  Thy truth in all its power to tell,

Unmask the priestl
  The Bible from t

From hollow rite a
  Of law and sect l
O, teach him that
  Is holier than th

Chase back the sha
  Of the dead ages,
And let his hopeful
  The dawn of thy

That day when fett
  Shall know the
    free,
And he alone who
  Shall, childlike, c

YORK

FROM Yorktown's r
Two lines stretch f
Who curbs his stee
Hark ! the low mr
Who bends his kee
Where down the go
Shine knightly sta
Thou too art victor

The earth which b
Shook with the wa
Ploughed deep wit
  wheel,
Shot-sown and bla
October's clear and
Paled in the breatl
And down night's
Like a dropped sta

Now all is hushed
Stand moveless as t
While through th
  slow,
The conquered hos
O'Hara's brow beli
Gay Tarleton's tro
Shout, from thy fl
Thy scourge, Virg

Nor thou alone : v
Let all thy sister S
Let Freedom, in w
She waits with sle
Shouting from cav
Make glad her des

While they who hunt her quail with fear ;
The New World's chain lies broken here !

But who are they, who, cowering, wait
Within the shattered fortress gate ?
Dark tillers of Virginia's soil,
Classed with the battle's common spoil,
With household stuffs, and fowl, and
   swine,
With Indian weed and planters' wine,
With stolen beeves, and foraged corn, —
Are they not men, Virginian born ?

O, veil your faces, young and brave !
Sleep, Scammel, in thy soldier grave !
Sons of the Northland, ye who set
Stout hearts against the bayonet,
And pressed with steady footfall near
The moated battery's blazing tier,
Turn your scarred faces from the sight,
Let shame do homage to the right !

Lo ! threescore years have passed ; and
  · where
The Gallic timbrel stirred the air,
With Northern drum-roll, and the clear,
Wild horn-blow of the mountaineer,
While Britain grounded on that plain
The arms she might not lift again,
As abject as in that old day
The slave still toils his life away.

O, fields still green and fresh in story,
Old days of pride, old names of glory,
Old marvels of the tongue and pen,
Old thoughts which stirred the hearts
   of men,
Ye spared the wrong ; and over all
Behold the avenging shadow fall !
Your world-wide honor stained with
   shame, —
Your freedom's self a hollow name !

Where 's now the flag of that old war ?
Where flows its stripe ? Where burns
   its star ?
Bear witness, Palo Alto's day,
Dark Vale of Palms, red Monterey,
Where Mexic Freedom, young and weak,
Fleshes the Northern eagle's beak ;
Symbol of terror and despair,
Of chains and slaves, go seek it there !

Laugh, Prussia, midst thy iron ranks !
Laugh, Russia, from thy Neva's banks !
Brave sport to see the fledgling born
Of Freedom by its parent torn !

Safe now is Speilberg's dungeon cell,
Safe drear Siberia's frozen hell :
With Slavery's flag o'er both unrolled,
What of the New World fears the Old ?

LINES,

WRITTEN IN THE BOOK OF A FRIEND.

ON page of thine I cannot trace
The cold and heartless commonplace, —
A statue's fixed and marble grace.

For ever as these lines I penned,
Still with the thought of thee will blend
That of some loved and common friend, —

Who in life's desert track has made
His pilgrim tent with mine, or strayed
Beneath the same remembered shade.

And hence my pen unfettered moves
In freedom which the heart approves, —
The negligence which friendship loves.

And wilt thou prize my poor gift less
For simple air and rustic dress,
And sign of haste and carelessness ? —

O, more than specious counterfeit
Of sentiment or studied wit,
A heart like thine should value it.

Yet half I fear my gift will be
Unto thy book, if not to thee,
Of more than doubtful courtesy.

A banished name from fashion's sphere,
A lay unheard of Beauty's ear,
Forbid, disowned, — what do they
   here ? —

Upon my ear not all in vain
Came the sad captive's clanking chain, —
The groaning from his bed of pain.

And sadder still, I saw the woe
Which only wounded spirits know
When Pride's strong footsteps o'er them
   go.

Spurned not alone in walks abroad,
But from the "temples of the Lord"
Thrust out apart, like things abhorred.

Deep as I felt, and stern and strong,
In words which Prudence smothered long,
My soul spoke out against the wrong ;

Not mine alone the task to speak
Of comfort to the poor and weak,
And dry the tear on Sorrow's cheek ;

But, mingled in the conflict warm,
To pour the fiery breath of storm
Through the harsh trumpet of Reform ;

To brave Opinion's settled frown,
From ermined robe and saintly gown,
While wrestling reverenced Error down.

Founts gushed beside my pilgrim way,
Cool shadows on the greensward lay,
Flowers swung upon the bending spray.

And, broad and bright, on either hand,
Stretched the green slopes of Fairy-land,
With Hope's eternal sunbow spanned ;

Whence voices called me like the flow,
Which on the listener's ear will grow,
Of forest streamlets soft and low.

And gentle eyes, which still retain
Their picture on the heart and brain,
Smiled, beckoning from that path of
     pain.

In vain !— nor dream, nor rest, nor
     pause
Remain for him who round him draws
The battered mail of Freedom's cause.

From youthful hopes, — from each green
     spot
Of young Romance, and gentle Thought,
Where storm and tumult enter not, —

From each fair altar, where belong
The offerings Love requires of Song
In homage to her bright-eyed throng, —

With soul and strength, with heart and
     hand,
I turned to Freedom's struggling band, —
To the sad Helots of our land.

What marvel then that Fame should
     turn
Her notes of praise to those of scorn, —
Her gifts reclaimed, — her smiles with-
     drawn ?

What matters it ! — a few years more,
Life's surge so restless heretofore
Shall break upon the unknown shore !

In that far land shall disappear
The shadows which we follow here, —
The mist-wreaths of our atmosphere !

Before no work of mortal hand,
Of human will or strength expand
The pearl gates of the Better Land ;

Alone in that great love which gave
Life to the sleeper of the grave,
Resteth the power to "seek and save."

Yet, if the spirit gazing through
The vista of the past can view
One deed to Heaven and virtue true, —

If through the wreck of wasted powers,
Of garlands wreathed from Folly's
     bowers,
Of idle aims and misspent hours, —

The eye can note one sacred spot
By Pride and Self profaned not, —
A green place in the waste of thought, —

Where deed or word hath rendered less
"The sum of human wretchedness,"
And Gratitude looks forth to bless, —

The simple burst of tenderest feeling
From sad hearts worn by evil-dealing,
For blessing on the hand of healing, —

Better than Glory's pomp will be
That green and blessed spot to me,
A palm-shade in Eternity ! —

Something of Time which may invite
The purified and spiritual sight
To rest on with a calm delight.

And when the summer winds shall
     sweep
With their light wings my place of sleep,
And mosses round my headstone creep, —

If still, as Freedom's rallying sign,
Upon the young heart's altars shine
The very fires they caught from mine, —

If words my lips once uttered still,
In the calm faith and steadfast will
Of other hearts, their work fulfil, —

Perchance with joy the soul may learn
These tokens, and its eye discern
The fires which on those altars burn, —

A marvellous joy that even then,
The spirit hath its life again,
In the strong hearts of mortal men.

Take, lady, then, the gift I bring,
No gay and graceful offering, —
No flower-smile of the laughing spring.

Midst the green buds of Youth's fresh
    May,
With Fancy's leaf-enwoven bay,
My sad and sombre gift I lay.

And if it deepens in thy mind
A sense of suffering human-kind, —
The outcast and the spirit-blind :

Oppressed and spoiled on every side,
By Prejudice, and Scorn, and Pride,
Life's common courtesies denied ;

Sad mothers mourning o'er their trust,
Children by want and misery nursed,
Tasting life's bitter cup at first ;

If to their strong appeals which come
From fireless hearth, and crowded room,
And the close alley's noisome gloom, —

Though dark the hands upraised to thee
In mute beseeching agony,
Thou lend'st thy woman's sympathy, —

Not vainly on thy gentle shrine,
Where Love, and Mirth, and Friendship
    twine
Their varied gifts, I offer mine.

PÆAN.

1848.

Now, joy and thanks forevermore !
    The dreary night has wellnigh passed,
The slumbers of the North are o'er,
    The Giant stands erect at last !

More than we hoped in that dark time
    When, faint with watching, few and
        worn,
We saw no welcome day-star climb
    The cold gray pathway of the morn !

O weary hours ! O night of years !
    What storms our darkling pathway
        swept,
Where, beating back our thronging fears,
    By Faith alone our march we kept.

How jeered the scoffing crowd behind,
    How mocked before the tyrant train,
As, one by one, the true and kind
    Fell fainting in our path of pain !

They died, — their brave hearts breaking
        slow, —
    But, self-forgetful to the last,
In words of cheer and bugle blow
    Their breath upon the darkness passed.

A mighty host, on either hand,
    Stood waiting for the dawn of day
To crush like reeds our feeble band ;
    The morn has come, — and where are
        they ?

Troop after troop their line forsakes ;
    With peace-white banners waving
        free,
And from our own the glad shout breaks,
    Of Freedom and Fraternity !

Like mist before the growing light,
    The hostile cohorts melt away ;
Our frowning foemen of the night
    Are brothers at the dawn of day !

As unto these repentant ones
    We open wide our toil-worn ranks,
Along our line a murmur runs
    Of song, and praise, and grateful
        thanks.

Sound for the onset ! — Blast on blast !
    Till Slavery's minions cower and
        quail ;
One charge of fire shall drive them fast
    Like chaff before our Northern gale !

O prisoners in your house of pain,
    Dumb, toiling millions, bound and
        sold,
Look ! stretched o'er Southern vale and
        plain,
    The Lord's delivering hand behold !

Above the tyrant's pride of power,
    His iron gates and guarded wall,
The bolts which shattered Shinar's
        tower
    Hang, smoking, for a fiercer fall.

Awake ! awake ! my Fatherland !
    It is thy Northern light that shines ;
This stirring march of Freedom's band
    The storm-song of thy mountain pines.

Wake, dwellers where the day expires !
  And hear, in winds that sweep your
    lakes
And fan your prairies' roaring fires,
  The signal-call that Freedom makes !

TO THE MEMORY OF THOMAS SHIPLEY.

GONE to thy Heavenly Father's rest !
  The flowers of Eden round thee blow-
    ing,
And on thine ear the murmurs blest
  Of Siloa's waters softly flowing !
Beneath that Tree of Life which gives
To all the earth its healing leaves
In the white robe of angels clad,
  And wandering by that sacred river,
Whose streams of holiness make glad
  The city of our God forever !

Gentlest of spirits ! — not for thee
  Our tears are shed, our sighs are given ;
Why mourn to know thou art a free
  Partaker of the joys of Heaven ?
Finished thy work, and kept thy faith
In Christian firmness unto death ;
And beautiful as sky and earth,
  When autumn's sun is downward go-
    ing,
The blessed memory of thy worth
  Around thy place of slumber glowing !

But woe for us ! who linger still
  With feebler strength and hearts less
    lowly,
And minds less steadfast to the will
  Of Him whose every work is holy.
For not like thine, is crucified
The spirit of our human pride :
And at the bondman's tale of woe,
  And for the outcast and forsaken,
Not warm like thine, but cold and slow,
  Our weaker sympathies awaken.

Darkly upon our struggling way
  The storm of human hate is sweeping ;
Hunted and branded, and a prey,
  Our watch amidst the darkness keep-
    ing,
O for that hidden strength which can
Nerve unto death the inner man !
O for thy spirit, tried and true,
  And constant in the hour of trial,
Prepared to suffer, or to do,
  In meekness and in self-denial.

O for that spirit, meek and mild,
  Derided, spurned, yet uncomplain-
    ing, —
By man deserted and reviled,
  Yet faithful to its trust remaining.
Still prompt and resolute to save
From scourge and chain the hunted
    slave ;
Unwavering in the Truth's defence,
  Even where the fires of Hate were
    burning,
The unquailing eye of innocence
  Alone upon the oppressor turning !

O loved of thousands ! to thy grave,
  Sorrowing of heart, thy brethren bore
    thee.
The poor man and the rescued slave
  Wept as the broken earth closed o'er
    thee ;
And grateful tears, like summer rain,
Quickened its dying grass again !
And there, as to some pilgrim-shrine,
  Shall come the outcast and the lowly,
Of gentle deeds and words of thine
  Recalling memories sweet and holy !

O for the death the righteous die !
  An end, like autumn's day declining,
On human hearts, as on the sky,
  With holier, tenderer beauty shining ;
As to the parting soul were given
The radiance of an opening Heaven !
As if that pure and blessed light,
  From off the Eternal altar flowing,
Were bathing, in its upward flight,
  The spirit to its worship going !

TO A SOUTHERN STATESMAN.

1846.

Is this thy voice, whose treble notes of
    fear
Wail in the wind ? And dost thou shake
    to hear,
Actæon-like, the bay of thine own
    hounds,
Spurning the leash, and leaping o'er
    their bounds ?
Sore-baffled statesman ! when thy eager
    hand,
With game afoot, unslipped the hungry
    pack,
To hunt down Freedom in her chosen
    land,

Hadst thou no fear, that, erelong,
    doubling back,
These dogs of thine might snuff on
    Slavery's track ?
Where 's now the boast, which even thy
    guarded tongue,
Cold, calm, and proud, in the teeth o'
    the Senate flung,
O'er the fulfilment of thy baleful plan,
Like Satan's triumph at the fall of man ?
How stood'st thou then, thy feet on
    Freedom planting,
And pointing to the lurid heaven afar,
Whence all could see, through the south
    windows slanting,
Crimson as blood, the beams of that
    Lone Star !
The Fates are just ; they give us but our
    own ;
Nemesis ripens what our hands have
    sown.
There is an Eastern story, not unknown,
Doubtless, to thee, of one whose magic
    skill
Called demons up his water-jars to fill ;
Deftly and silently, they did his will,
But, when the task was done, kept
    pouring still.
In vain with spell and charm the wizard
    wrought,
Faster and faster were the buckets
    brought,
Higher and higher rose the flood around,
Till the fiends clapped their hands above
    their master drowned !
So, Carolinian, it may prove with thee,
For God still overrules man's schemes,
    and takes
Craftiness in its self-set snare, and
    makes
The wrath of man to praise Him. It
    may be,
That the roused spirits of Democracy
May leave to freer States the same wide
    door
Through which thy slave-cursed T xas
    entered in,
From out the blood and fire, the wrong
    and sin,
Of the stormed city and the ghastly
    plain,
Beat by hot hail, and wet with bloody
    rain,
A myriad-handed Aztec host may pour,
And swarthy South with pallid North
    combine
Back on thyself to turn thy dark design.

LI

WRITTEN ON THE
NEY'S RESOLUTI
OF REPRESENTA'
SAGE OF CALHO
CLUDING PAPER
ED, TOUCHING
SLAVERY, FROM
OFFICE," IN TI
UNITED STATES.

MEN of the Nort
    manly spiri
Of the true-heart
    gone ?
Sons of old freemer
    Th

Is the old Pilgrim
    in us,
Stoops the stro
    souls so low
That Mammon's lu
    win us
    To

Now, when our la
    verging,
In God's name,
    there is time
Now, when the p
    are forging,
    Sil

What ! shall we he
    as favors
Rights all our
    shall we bar
For treacherous
    Nature gave
    Go

Here shall the sta
    man fetters
Here the false
    deny,
And, in the chur
    skilled abett
    Ma

Torture the pages o
    To sanction crin
    blood ?
And, in Oppressic
    libel
    Bo

Shall our New England stand erect no
    longer,
But stoop in chains upon her down-
    ward way,
Thicker to gather on her limbs and
    stronger
                Day after day !

O no ; methinks from all her wild, green
    mountains, —
From valleys where her slumbering
    fathers lie, —
From her blue rivers and her welling
    fountains,
            And clear, cold sky, —

From her rough coast, and isles, which
    hungry Ocean
    Gnaws with his surges, — from the
    fisher's skiff,
With white sail swaying to the billows'
    motion
            Round rock and cliff, —

From the free fireside of her unbought
    farmer, —
    From her free laborer at his loom and
    wheel, —
From the brown smith-shop, where, be-
    neath the hammer,
            Rings the red steel, —

From each and all, if God hath not
    forsaken
Our land, and left us to an evil choice,
Loud as the summer thunderbolt shall
    waken
            A People's voice.

Startling and stern ! the Northern winds
    shall bear it
Over Potomac's to St. Mary's wave ;
And buried Freedom shall awake to
    hear it
            Within her grave.

O, let that voice go forth ! The bond-
    man sighing
By Santee's wave, in Mississippi's
    cane,
Shall feel the hope, within his bosom
    dying,
            Revive again.

Let it go forth ! The millions who are
    gazing
Sadly upon us from afar, shall smile,

And unto God devout thanksgiving
    raising,
            Bless us the while.

O for your ancient freedom, pure and
    holy,
    For the deliverance of a groaning earth,
For the wronged captive, bleeding,
    crushed, and lowly,
            Let it go forth !

Sons of the best of fathers ! will ye falter
    With all they left ye perilled and at
    stake ?
Ho ! once again on Freedom's holy altar
            The fire awake !

Prayer-strengthened for the trial, come
    together,
    Put on the harness for the moral fight,
And, with the blessing of your Heav-
    enly Father,
            MAINTAIN THE RIGHT !

THE CURSE OF THE CHARTER-BREAKERS.[37]

IN Westminster's royal halls,
Robed in their pontificals,
England's ancient prelates stood
For the people's right and good.

Closed around the waiting crowd,
Dark and still, like winter's cloud ;
King and council, lord and knight,
Squire and yeoman, stood in sight, —

Stood to hear the priest rehearse,
In God's name, the Church's curse,
By the tapers round them lit,
Slowly, sternly uttering it.

" Right of voice in framing laws,
Right of peers to try each cause ;
Peasant homestead, mean and small,
Sacred as the monarch's hall, —

" Whoso lays his hand on these,
England's ancient liberties, —
Whoso breaks, by word or deed,
England's vow at Runnymede, —

" Be he Prince or belted knight,
Whatsoe'er his rank or might,
If the highest, then the worst,
Let him live and die accursed.

"Thou, who to thy Church hast given
Keys alike, of hell and heaven,
Make our word and witness sure,
Let the curse we speak endure ! "

Silent, while that curse was said,
Every bare and listening head
Bowed in reverent awe, and then
All the people said, Amen !

Seven times the bells have tolled,
For the centuries gray and old,
Since that stoled and mitred band
Cursed the tyrants of their land.

Since the priesthood, like a tower,
Stood between the poor and power ;
And the wronged and trodden down
Blessed the abbot's shaven crown.

Gone, thank God, their wizard spell,
Lost, their keys of heaven and hell ;
Yet I sigh for men as bold
As those bearded priests of old.

Now, too oft the priesthood wait
At the threshold of the state, —
Waiting for the beck and nod
Of its power as law and God.

Fraud exults, while solemn words
Sanctify his stolen hoards ;
Slavery laughs, while ghostly lips
Bless his manacles and whips.

Not on them the poor rely,
Not to them looks liberty,
Who with fawning falsehood cower
To the wrong, when clothed with power.

O, to see them meanly cling,
Round the master, round the king,
Sported with, and sold and bought, —
Pitifuller sight is not !

Tell me not that this must be :
God's true priest is always free ;
Free, the needed truth to speak,
Right the wronged, and raise the weak.

Not to fawn on wealth and state,
Leaving Lazarus at the gate, —
Not to peddle creeds like wares, —
Not to mutter hireling prayers, —

Nor to paint the new life's bliss
On the sable ground of this, —

Golden streets for idle knave,
Sabbath rest for weary slave !

Not for words and works like these,
Priest of God, thy mission is ;
But to make earth's desert glad,
In its Eden greenness clad ;

And to level manhood bring
Lord and peasant, serf and king ;
And the Christ of God to find
In the humblest of thy kind !

Thine to work as well as pray,
Clearing thorny wrongs away ;
Plucking up the weeds of sin,
Letting heaven's warm sunshine in, —

Watching on the hills of Faith ;
Listening what the spirit saith,
Of the dim-seen light afar,
Growing like a nearing star.

God's interpreter art thou,
To the waiting ones below ;
'Twixt them and its light midway
Heralding the better day, —

Catching gleams of temple spires,
Hearing notes of angel choirs,
Where, as yet unseen of them,
Comes the New Jerusalem !

Like the seer of Patmos gazing,
On the glory downward blazing ;
Till upon Earth's grateful sod
Rests the City of our God !

THE SLAVES OF MARTINIQUE.

SUGGESTED BY A DAGUERREOTYPE FROM
A FRENCH ENGRAVING.

BEAMS of noon, like burning lances,
  through the tree-tops flash and
  glisten,
As she stands before her lover, with raised
  face to look and listen.

Dark, but comely, like the maiden in the
  ancient Jewish song :
Scarcely has the toil of task-fields done
  her graceful beauty wrong.

He, the strong one and the manly, with
  the vassal's garb and hue,

Holding still his spirit's birthright, to
   his higher nature true ;

Hiding deep the strengthening purpose
   of a freeman in his heart,
As the greegree holds his Fetich from
   the white man's gaze apart.

Ever foremost of his comrades, when the
   driver's morning horn
Calls away to stifling mill-house, to the
   fields of cane and corn :

Fall the keen and burning lashes never
   on his back or limb ;
Scarce with look or word of censure, turns
   the driver unto him.

Yet, his brow is always thoughtful, and
   his eye is hard and stern ;
Slavery's last and humblest lesson he has
   never deigned to learn.

And, at evening, when his comrades
   dance before their master's door,
Folding arms and knitting forehead,
   stands he silent evermore.

God be praised for every instinct which
   rebels against a lot
Where the brute survives the human, and
   man's upright form is not !

As the serpent-like bejuco winds his
   spiral fold on fold
Round the tall and stately ceiba, till it
   withers in his hold ; —

Slow decays the forest monarch, closer
   girds the fell embrace,
Till the tree is seen no longer, and the
   vine is in its place, —

So a base and bestial nature round the
   vassal's manhood twines,
And the spirit wastes beneath it, like the
   ceiba choked with vines.

God is Love, saith the Evangel ; and our
   world of woe and sin
Is made light and happy only when a
   Love is shining in.

Ye whose lives are free as sunshine, finding, wheresoe'er ye roam,
Smiles of welcome, looks of kindness,
   making all the world like home ;

In the veins of whose affections kindred
   blood is but a part,
Of one kindly current throbbing from the
   universal heart ;

Can ye know the deeper meaning of a
   love in Slavery nursed,
Last flower of a lost Eden, blooming in
   that Soil accursed ?

Love of Home, and Love of Woman ! —
   dear to all, but doubly dear
To the heart whose pulses elsewhere
   measure only hate and fear.

All around the desert circles, underneath
   a brazen sky,
Only one green spot remaining where the
   dew is never dry !

From the horror of that desert, from its
   atmosphere of hell,
Turns the fainting spirit thither, as the
   diver seeks his bell.

'T is the fervid tropic noontime ; faint
   and low the sea-waves beat ;
Hazy rise the inland mountains through
   the glimmer of the heat, —

Where, through mingled leaves and blossoms, arrowy sunbeams flash and
   glisten,
Speaks her lover to the slave-girl, and she
   lifts her head to listen : —

"We shall live as slaves no longer !
   Freedom's hour is close at hand !
Rocks her bark upon the waters, rests the
   boat upon the strand !

"I have seen the Haytien Captain ; I
   have seen his swarthy crew,
Haters of the pallid faces, to their race
   and color true.

"They have sworn to wait our coming
   till the night has passed its noon,
And the gray and darkening waters roll
   above the sunken moon ! "

O the blessed hope of freedom ! how with
   joy and glad surprise,
For an instant throbs her bosom, for an
   instant beam her eyes !

But she looks across the valley, where
    her mother's hut is seen,
Through the snowy bloom of coffee, and
    the lemon-leaves so green.

And she answers, sad and earnest : "It
    were wrong for thee to stay ;
God hath heard thy prayer for freedom,
    and his finger points the way.

"Well I know with what endurance, for
    the sake of me and mine,
Thou hast borne too long a burden never
    meant for souls like thine.

"Go ; and at the hour of midnight, when
    our last farewell is o'er,
Kneeling on our place of parting, I will
    bless thee from the shore.

"But for me, my mother, lying on her
    sick-bed all the day,
Lifts her weary head to watch me, coming
    through the twilight gray.

"Should I leave her sick and helpless, even
    freedom, shared with thee,
Would be sadder far than bondage, lonely
    toil, and stripes to me.

"For my heart would die within me, and
    my brain would soon be wild ;
I should hear my mother calling through
    the twilight for her child !"

Blazing upward from the ocean, shines
    the sun of morning-time,
Through the coffee-trees in blossom, and
    green hedges of the lime.

Side by side, amidst the slave-gang, toil
    the lover and the maid ;
Wherefore looks he o'er the waters, lean-
    ing forward on his spade ?

Sadly looks he, deeply sighs he : 't is the
    Haytien's sail he sees,
Like a white cloud of the mountains,
    driven seaward by the breeze !

But his arm a light hand presses, and he
    hears a low voice call :
Hate of Slavery, hope of Freedom, Love
    is mightier than all.

THE

WRITTEN ON LEAR
THE TREATY

ACROSS the Stony
    desert's dro
The circles of our e
    e'n Ocean's
From slumberous
    wild and fr
Flowing down from
    fornia's sea
And from the mou
    Santa Rosa'
The eagles of Mex
    no more.

O Vale of Rio Bra
    children we
Close watch about t
    of Pecos ke
Let Taos send her cr
    pines,
And Algodones tol
    corn and vi
For lo ! the pale la
    eager eyes
Wide scattering, li
    broad Salad

Let Sacramento's
    sound the
Of footsteps on th
    cold Nevad
Full hot and fast
    rein of trav
And, bending o'er
    sunrise at h
By many a lonely
    and pine,
On many a wintr
    camp-fires

O countrymen and
    of lake and
Of salt wastes alt
    fat with gr
Of mountains whit
    downward,
On their feet with
    and lapped
Swift through who
    o'er many a
Wind-like the Ar
    son's dusty

Great spaces yet untravelled, great lakes
  whose mystic shores
The Saxon rifle never heard, nor dip of
  Saxon oars ;
Great herds that wander all unwatched,
  wild steeds that none have tamed,
Strange fish in unknown streams, and
  birds the Saxon never named ;
Deep mines, dark mountain crucibles,
  where Nature's chemic powers
Work out the Great Designer's will ; —
  all these ye say are ours !

Forever ours ! for good or ill, on us the
  burden lies ;
God's balance, watched by angels, is hung
  across the skies.
Shall Justice, Truth, and Freedom turn
  the poised and trembling scale ?
Or shall the Evil triumph, and robber
  Wrong prevail ?
Shall the broad land o'er which our flag
  in starry splendor waves,
Forego through us its freedom, and bear
  the tread of slaves ?

The day is breaking in the East of which
  the prophets told,
And brightens up the sky of Time the
  Christian Age of Gold ;
Old Might to Right is yielding, battle
  blade to clerkly pen,
Earth's monarchs are her peoples, and
  her serfs stand up as men ;
The isles rejoice together, in a day are
  nations born,
And the slave walks free in Tunis, and
  by Stamboul's Golden Horn !

Is this, O countrymen of mine ! a day for
  us to sow
The soil of new-gained empire with
  slavery's seeds of woe ?
To feed with our fresh life-blood the Old
  World's cast-off crime,
Dropped, like some monstrous early birth,
  from the tired lap of Time ?
To run anew the evil race the old lost
  nations ran,
And die like them of unbelief of God, and
  wrong of man ?

Great Heaven ! Is this our mission ?
  End in this the prayers and tears,
The toil, the strife, the watchings of our
  younger, better years ?
Still as the Old World rolls in light, shall
  ours in shadow turn,
A beamless Chaos, cursed of God, through
  outer darkness borne ?
Where the far nations looked for light, a
  blackness in the air ?
Where for words of hope they listened,
  the long wail of despair ?

The Crisis presses on us ; face to face
  with us it stands,
With solemn lips of question, like the
  Sphinx in Egypt's sands !
This day we fashion Destiny, our web
  of Fate we spin ;
This day for all hereafter choose we
  holiness or sin ;
Even now from starry Gerizim, or Ebal's
  cloudy crown,
We call the dews of blessing or the bolts
  of cursing down !

By all for which the martyrs bore their
  agony and shame ;
By all the warning words of truth with
  which the prophets came ;
By the Future which awaits us ; by all
  the hopes which cast
Their faint and trembling beams across
  the blackness of the Past ;
And by the blessed thought of Him who
  for Earth's freedom died,
O my people ! O my brothers ! let us
  choose the righteous side.

So shall the Northern pioneer go joyful
  on his way ;
To wed Penobscot's waters to San Fran-
  cisco's bay ;
To make the rugged places smooth, and
  sow the vales with grain ;
And bear, with Liberty and Law, the
  Bible in his train :
The mighty West shall bless the East,
  and sea shall answer sea,
And mountain unto mountain call,
  PRAISE GOD, FOR WE ARE FREE !

MISCELLANEOUS.

THE KNIGHT OF ST. JOHN.

Ere down yon blue Carpathian hills
  The sun shall sink again,
Farewell to life and all its ills,
  Farewell to cell and chain.

These prison shades are dark and cold, —
  But, darker far than they,
The shadow of a sorrow old
  Is on my heart alway.

For since the day when Warkworth wood
  Closed o'er my steed and I,
An alien from my name and blood,
  A weed cast out to die, —

When, looking back in sunset light,
  I saw her turret gleam,
And from its casement, far and white,
  Her sign of farewell stream,

Like one who, from some desert shore,
  Doth home's green isles descry,
And, vainly longing, gazes o'er
  The waste of wave and sky ;

So from the desert of my fate
  I gaze across the past ;
Forever on life's dial-plate
  The shade is backward cast !

I 've wandered wide from shore to shore,
  I 've knelt at many a shrine ;
And bowed me to the rocky floor
  Where Bethlehem's tapers shine ;

And by the Holy Sepulchre
  I 've pledged my knightly sword
To Christ, his blessed Church, and her,
  The Mother of our Lord.

O, vain the vow, and vain the strife !
  How vain do all things seem !
My soul is in the past, and life
  To-day is but a dream !

In vain the penance strange and long,
  And hard for flesh to bear ;
The prayer, the fasting, and the thong
  And sackcloth shirt of hair.

The eyes of memory will not sleep,-
  Its ears are open still ;
And vigils with the past they keep
  Against my feeble will.

And still the loves and joys of old
  Do evermore uprise ;
I see the flow of locks of gold,
  The shine of loving eyes !

Ah me ! upon another's breast
  Those golden locks recline ;
I see upon another rest
  The glance that once was mine.

"O faithless priest ! O perjured knight!"
  I hear the Master cry ;
"Shut out the vision from thy sight,
  Let Earth and Nature die.

"The Church of God is now thy spouse,
  And thou the bridegroom art ;
Then let the burden of thy vows
  Crush down thy human heart !"

In vain ! This heart its grief must
    know,
  Till life itself hath ceased,
And falls beneath the self-same blow
  The lover and the priest !

O pitying Mother ! souls of light,
  And saints, and martyrs old !
Pray for a weak and sinful knight,
  A suffering man uphold.

Then let the Paynim work his will,
  And death unbind my chain,
Ere down yon blue Carpathian hill
  The sun shall fall again.

THE HOLY LAND.

FROM LAMARTINE.

I have not felt, o'er seas of sand,
  The rocking of the desert bark ;
Nor laved at Hebron's fount my hand,
  By Hebron's palm-trees cool and
    dark ;

Nor pitched my tent at even-fall,
 On dust where Job of old has lain,
Nor dreamed beneath its canvas wall,
 The dream of Jacob o'er again.

One vast world-page remains unread ;
 How shine the stars in Chaldea's
  sky,
How sounds the reverent pilgrim's tread,
 How beats the heart with God so
  nigh ! —
How round gray arch and column lone
 The spirit of the old time broods,
And sighs in all the winds that moan
 Along the sandy solitudes !

In thy tall cedars, Lebanon,
 I have not heard the nations' cries,
Nor seen thy eagles stooping down
 Where buried Tyre in ruin lies.
The Christian's prayer I have not said
 In Tadmor's temples of decay,
Nor startled, with my dreary tread,
 The waste where Memnon's empire lay.

Nor have I, from thy hallowed tide,
 O Jordan ! heard the low lament,
Like that sad wail along thy side
 Which Israel's mournful prophet sent !
Nor thrilled within that grotto lone
 Where, deep in night, the Bard of
  Kings
Felt hands of fire direct his own,
 And sweep for God the conscious
  strings.

I have not climbed to Olivet,
 Nor laid me where my Saviour lay,
And left his trace of tears as yet
 By angel eyes unwept away ;
Nor watched, at midnight's solemn time,
 The garden where his prayer and
  groan,
Wrung by his sorrow and our crime,
 Rose to One listening ear alone.

I have not kissed the rock-hewn grot
 Where in his Mother's arms he lay,
Nor knelt upon the sacred spot
 Where last his footsteps pressed the
  clay ;
Nor looked on that sad mountain head,
 Nor smote my sinful breast, where
  wide
His arms to fold the world he spread,
 And bowed his head to bless — and
  died !

PALESTINE.

BLEST land of Judæa ! thrice hallowed
  of song,
Where the holiest of memories pilgrim-
  like throng ;
In the shade of thy palms, by the shores
  of thy sea,
On the hills of thy beauty, my heart is
  with thee.

With the eye of a spirit I look on that
  shore,
Where pilgrim and prophet have lingered before ;
With the glide of a spirit I traverse the
  sod
Made bright by the steps of the angels
  of God.

Blue sea of the hills ! — in my spirit I
  hear
Thy waters, Genesaret, chime on my ear ;
Where the Lowly and Just with the people sat down,
And thy spray on the dust of his sandals was thrown.

Beyond are Bethulia's mountains of
  green,
And the desolate hills of the wild Gad-
  arene ;
And I pause on the goat-crags of Tabor
  to see
The gleam of thy waters, O dark Galilee !

Hark, a sound in the valley ! where,
  swollen and strong,
Thy river, O Kishon, is sweeping along ;
Where the Canaanite strove with Jehovah in vain,
And thy torrent grew dark with the
  blood of the slain.

There down from his mountains stern
  Zebulon came,
And Naphtali's stag, with his eyeballs
  of flame,
And the chariots of Jabin rolled harm-
  lessly on,
For the arm of the Lord was Abinoam's
  son !

There sleep the still rocks and the caverns which rang
To the song which the beautiful proph-
  etess sang,

When the princes of Issachar stood by
  her side,
And the shout of a host in its triumph
  replied.

Lo, Bethlehem's hill-site before me is
  seen,
With the mountains around, and the
  valleys between ;
There rested the shepherds of Judah,
  and there
The song of the angels rose sweet on
  the air.

And Bethany's palm-trees in beauty still
  throw
Their shadows at noon on the ruins
  below ;
But where are the sisters who hastened
  to greet
The lowly Redeemer, and sit at his feet ?

I tread where the TWELVE in their way-
  faring trod ;
I stand where they stood with the
  CHOSEN OF GOD, —
Where his blessing was heard and his
  lessons were taught,
Where the blind were restored and the
  healing was wrought.

O, here with his flock the sad Wanderer
  came, —
These hills he toiled over in grief are
  the same, —
The founts where he drank by the wayside still flow,
And the same airs are blowing which
  breathed on his brow !

And throned on her hills sits Jerusalem
  yet,
But with dust on her forehead, and
  chains on her feet ;
For the crown of her pride to the mocker
  hath gone,
And the holy Shechinah is dark where
  it shone.

But wherefore this dream of the earthly
  abode
Of Humanity clothed in the brightness
  of God ?
Were my spirit but turned from the
  outward and dim,
It could gaze, even now, on the presence
  of Him !

Not in clouds and in terrors, but gentle
  as when,
In love and in meekness, He moved
  among men ;
And the voice which breathed peace to
  the waves of the sea
In the hush of my spirit would whisper
  to me !

And what if my feet may not tread
  where He stood,
Nor my ears hear the dashing of Galilee's flood,
Nor my eyes see the cross which He
  bowed him to bear,
Nor my knees press Gethsemane's garden of prayer.

Yet, Loved of the Father, thy Spirit is
  near
To the meek, and the lowly, and penitent here ;
And the voice of thy love is the same
  even now
As at Bethany's tomb or on Olivet's
  brow.

O, the outward hath gone ! — but in
  glory and power,
The SPIRIT surviveth the things of an
  hour ;
Unchanged, undecaying, its Pentecost
  flame
On the heart's secret altar is burning
  the same !

EZEKIEL.

CHAPTER XXXIII. 30 – 33.

THEY hear thee not, O God ! nor see ;
Beneath thy rod they mock at thee ;
The princes of our ancient line
Lie drunken with Assyrian wine ;
The priests around thy altar speak
The false words which their hearers seek ;
And hymns which Chaldea's wanton
  maids
Have sung in Dura's idol-shades
Are with the Levites' chant ascending,
With Zion's holiest anthems blending !

On Israel's bleeding bosom set,
The heathen heel is crushing yet ;
The towers upon our holy hill
Echo Chaldean footsteps still.

Our wasted shrines, — who weeps for
    them ?
Who mourneth for Jerusalem ?
Who turneth from his gains away ?
Whose knee with mine is bowed to pray ?
Who, leaving feast and purpling cup,
Takes Zion's lamentation up ?

A sad and thoughtful youth, I went
With Israel's early banishment ;
And where the sullen Chebar crept,
The ritual of my fathers kept.
The water for the trench I drew,
The firstling of the flock I slew,
And, standing at the altar's side,
I shared the Levites' lingering pride,
That still, amidst her mocking foes,
The smoke of Zion's offering rose.

In sudden whirlwind, cloud and flame,
The Spirit of the Highest came !
Before mine eyes a vision passed,
A glory terrible and vast ;
With dreadful eyes of living things,
And sounding sweep of angel wings,
With circling light and sapphire throne,
And flame-like form of One thereon,
And voice of that dread Likeness sent
Down from the crystal firmament !

The burden of a prophet's power
Fell on me in that fearful hour ;
From off unutterable woes
The curtain of the future rose ;
I saw far down the coming time
The fiery chastisement of crime ;
With noise of mingling hosts, and jar
Of falling towers and shouts of war,
I saw the nations rise and fall,
Like fire-gleams on my tent's white
    wall.

In dream and trance, I saw the slain
Of Egypt heaped like harvest grain.
I saw the walls of sea-born Tyre
Swept over by the spoiler's fire ;
And heard the low, expiring moan
Of Edom on his rocky throne ;
And, woe is me ! the wild lament
From Zion's desolation sent ;
And felt within my heart each blow
Which laid her holy places low.

In bonds and sorrow, day by day,
Before the pictured tile I lay ;
And there, as in a mirror, saw
The coming of Assyria's war, —

Her swarthy lines of spearmen pass
Like locusts through Bethhoron's grass ;
I saw them draw their stormy hem
Of battle round Jerusalem ;
And, listening, heard the Hebrew wail
Blend with the victor-trump of Baal !

Who trembled at my warning word ?
Who owned the prophet of the Lord ?
How mocked the rude, — how scoffed
    the vile, —
How stung the Levites' scornful smile,
As o'er my spirit, dark and slow,
The shadow crept of Israel's woe
As if the angel's mournful roll
Had left its record on my soul,
And traced in lines of darkness there
The picture of its great despair !

Yet ever at the hour I feel
My lips in prophecy unseal.
Prince, priest, and Levite gather near,
And Salem's daughters haste to hear,
On Chebar's waste and alien shore,
The harp of Judah swept once more.
They listen, as in Babel's throng
The Chaldeans to the dancer's song,
Or wild sabbeka's nightly play,
As careless and as vain as they.

———

And thus, O Prophet-bard of old,
Hast thou thy tale of sorrow told !
The same which earth's unwelcome seers
Have felt in all succeeding years.
Sport of the changeful multitude,
Nor calmly heard nor understood,
Their song has seemed a trick of art,
Their warnings but the actor's part.
With bonds, and scorn, and evil will,
The world requites its prophets still.

So was it when the Holy One
The garments of the flesh put on !
Men followed where the Highest led
For common gifts of daily bread,
And gross of ear, of vision dim,
Owned not the godlike power of him.
Vain as a dreamer's words to them
His wail above Jerusalem,
And meaningless the watch he kept
Through which his weak disciples slept

Yet shrink not thou, whoe'er thou art,
For God's great purpose set apart,
Before whose far-discerning eyes,
The Future as the Present lies !

Beyond a narrow-bounded age
Stretches thy prophet-heritage,
Through Heaven's dim spaces angel-trod,
Through arches round the throne of
God !
Thy audience, worlds !— all Time to be
The witness of the Truth in thee !

THE WIFE OF MANOAH TO HER HUSBAND.

AGAINST the sunset's glowing wall
The city towers rise black and tall,
Where Zorah, on its rocky height,
Stands like an armed man in the light.

Down Eshtaol's vales of ripened grain
Falls like a cloud the night amain,
And up the hillsides climbing slow
The barley reapers homeward go.

Look, dearest ! how our fair child's head
The sunset light hath hallowed,
Where at this olive's foot he lies,
Uplooking to the tranquil skies.

O, while beneath the fervent heat
Thy sickle swept the bearded wheat,
I've watched, with mingled joy and
dread,
Our child upon his grassy bed.

Joy, which the mother feels alone
Whose morning hope like mine had
flown,
When to her bosom, over-blessed,
A dearer life than hers is pressed.

Dread, for the future dark and still,
Which shapes our dear one to its will ;
Forever in his large calm eyes,
I read a tale of sacrifice. —

The same foreboding awe I felt
When at the altar's side we knelt,
And he, who as a pilgrim came,
Rose, winged and glorious, through the
flame.

I slept not, though the wild bees made
A dreamlike murmuring in the shade,
And on me the warm-fingered hours
Pressed with the drowsy smell of flowers.

Before me, in a vision, rose
The hosts of Israel's scornful foes, —

Rank over rank, helm, shield, and spear,
Glittered in noon's hot atmosphere.

I heard their boast, and bitter word,
Their mockery of the Hebrew's Lord,
I saw their hands his ark assail,
Their feet profane his holy veil.

No angel down the blue space spoke,
No thunder from the still sky broke ;
But in their midst, in power and awe,
Like God's waked wrath, OUR CHILD I
saw !

A child no more !— harsh-browed and
strong,
He towered a giant in the throng,
And down his shoulders, broad and bare,
Swept the black terror of his hair.

He raised his arm ; he smote amain ;
As round the reaper falls the grain,
So the dark host around him fell,
So sank the foes of Israel !

Again I looked. In sunlight shone
The towers and domes of Askelon.
Priest, warrior, slave, a mighty crowd,
Within her idol temple bowed.

Yet one knelt not ; stark, gaunt, and
blind,
His arms the massive pillars twined, —
An eyeless captive, strong with hate,
He stood there like an evil Fate.

The red shrines smoked, — the trumpets
pealed :
He stooped, — the giant columns
reeled, —
Reeled tower and fane, sank arch and
wall,
And the thick dust-cloud closed o'er
all !

Above the shriek, the crash, the groan
Of the fallen pride of Askelon,
I heard, sheer down the echoing sky,
A voice as of an angel cry, —

The voice of him, who at our side
Sat through the golden eventide, —
Of him who, on thy altar's blaze,
Rose fire-winged, with his song of praise.

" Rejoice o'er Israel's broken chain,
Gray mother of the mighty slain !

Rejoice !" it cried, "he vanquisheth !
The strong in life is strong in death !

"To him shall Zorah's daughters raise
Through coming years their hymns of
    praise,
And gray old men at evening tell
Of all he wrought for Israel.

"And they who sing and they who
    hear
Alike shall hold thy memory dear,
And pour their blessings on thy head,
O mother of the mighty dead !"

It ceased ; and though a sound I heard
As if great wings the still air stirred,
I only saw the barley sheaves
And hills half hid by olive leaves.

I bowed my face, in awe and fear,
On the dear child who slumbered near.
"With me, as with my only son,
O God," I said, "THY WILL BE DONE !"

THE CITIES OF THE PLAIN.

"GET ye up from the wrath of God's
    terrible day !
Ungirded, unsandalled, arise and away !
'T is the vintage of blood, 't is the ful-
    ness of time,
And vengeance shall gather the harvest
    of crime !"

The warning was spoken ; the righteous
    had gone,
And the proud ones of Sodom were
    feasting alone ;
All gay was the banquet ; the revel was
    long,
With the pouring of wine and the
    breathing of song.

'T was an evening of beauty ; the air was
    perfume,
The earth was all greenness, the trees
    were all bloom ;
And softly the delicate viol was heard,
Like the murmur of love or the notes of
    a bird.

And beautiful maidens moved down in
    the dance,
With the magic of motion and sunshine
    of glance ;

And white arms wreathed lightly, and
    tresses fell free
As the plumage of birds in some tropical
    tree.

Where the shrines of foul idols were
    lighted on high,
And wantonness tempted the lust of the
    eye ;
Midst rites of obsceneness, strange,
    loathsome, abhorred,
The blasphemer scoffed at the name of
    the Lord.

Hark ! the growl of the thunder, — the
    quaking of earth !
Woe, woe to the worship, and woe to
    the mirth !
The black sky has opened, — there 's
    flame in the air, —
The red arm of vengeance is lifted and
    bare !

Then the shriek of the dying rose wild
    where the song
And the low tone of love had been whis-
    pered along ;
For the fierce flames went lightly o'er
    palace and bower,
Like the red tongues of demons, to blast
    and devour !

Down, — down on the fallen the red
    ruin rained,
And the reveller sank with his wine-cup
    undrained ;
The foot of the dancer, the music's loved
    thrill,
And the shout and the laughter grew
    suddenly still.

The last throb of anguish was fearfully
    given ;
The last eye glared forth in its madness
    on Heaven !
The last groan of horror rose wildly and
    vain,
And death brooded over the pride of the
    Plain !

THE CRUCIFIXION.

SUNLIGHT upon Judæa's hills !
    And on the waves of Galilee, —
On Jordan's stream, and on the rills
    That feed the dead and sleeping sea !

Most freshly from the green wood springs
The light breeze on its scented wings ;
And gayly quiver in the sun
The cedar tops of Lebanon !

A few more hours, — a change hath
  come !
The sky is dark without a cloud !
The shouts of wrath and joy arc dumb,
  And proud knees unto earth arc
  bowed.
A change is on the hill of Death,
The helmed watchers pant for breath,
And turn with wild and maniac eyes
From the dark scene of sacrifice !

That Sacrifice ! — the death of Him, —
  The High and ever Holy One !
Well may the conscious Heaven grow
  dim,
And blacken the beholding Sun.
The wonted light hath fled away,
Night settles on the middle day,
And earthquake from his caverned bed
Is waking with a thrill of dread !

The dead are waking underneath !
  Their prison door is rent away !
And, ghastly with the seal of death,
  They wander in the eye of day !
The temple of the Cherubim,
The House of God is cold and dim ;
A curse is on its trembling walls,
Its mighty veil asunder falls !

Well may the cavern-depths of Earth
  Be shaken, and her mountains nod ;
Well may the sheeted dead come forth
  To gaze upon a suffering God !
Well may the temple-shrine grow dim,
And shadows veil the Cherubim,
When He, the chosen one of Heaven,
A sacrifice for guilt is given !

And shall the sinful heart, alone,
  Behold unmoved the atoning hour,
When Nature trembles on her throne,
  And Death resigns his iron power ?
O, shall the heart — whose sinfulness
Gave keenness to his sore distress,
And added to his tears of blood —
Refuse its trembling gratitude !

THE STAR OF BETHLEHEM.

WHERE Time the measure of his hours
  By changeful bud and blossom keeps,
And, like a young bride crowned with
  flowers,
  Fair Shiraz in her garden sleeps ;

Where, to her poet's turban stone,
  The Spring her gift of flowers imparts,
Less sweet than those his thoughts have
  sown
  In the warm soil of Persian hearts :

There sat the stranger, where the shade
  Of scattered date-trees thinly lay,
While in the hot clear heaven delayed
  The long and still and weary day.

Strange trees and fruits above him hung,
  Strange odors filled the sultry air,
Strange birds upon the branches swung,
  Strange insect voices murmured there.

And strange bright blossoms shone
  around,
  Turned sunward from the shadowy
  bowers,
As if the Gheber's soul had found
  A fitting home in Iran's flowers.

Whate'er he saw, whate'er he heard,
  Awakened feelings new and sad, —
No Christian garb, nor Christian word,
  Nor church with Sabbath-bell chimes
  glad,

But Moslem graves, with turban stones,
  And mosque-spires gleaming white, in
  view,
And graybeard Mollahs in low tones
  Chanting their Koran service through.

The flowers which smiled on either
  hand,
  Like tempting fiends, were such as
  they
Which once, o'er all that Eastern land,
  As gifts on demon altars lay.

As if the burning eye of Baal
  The servant of his Conqueror knew,
From skies which knew no cloudy veil,
  The Sun's hot glances smote him
  through.

"Ah me !" the lonely stranger said,
  "The hope which led my footsteps on,
And light from heaven around them
  shed,
  O'er weary wave and waste, is gone !

"Where are the harvest fields all
    white,
For Truth to thrust her sickle in ?
Where flock the souls, like doves in
    flight,
From the dark hiding-place of sin ?

"A silent horror broods o'er all, —
    The burden of a hateful spell, —
The very flowers around recall
    The hoary magi's rites of hell !

"And what am I, o'er such a land
    The banner of the Cross to bear ?
Dear Lord, uphold me with thy hand,
    Thy strength with human weakness
        share !"

He ceased ; for at his very feet
    In mild rebuke a floweret smiled, —
How thrilled his sinking heart to greet
    The Star-flower of the Virgin's child !

Sown by some wandering Frank, it
    drew
    Its life from alien air and earth,
And told to Paynim sun and dew
    The story of the Saviour's birth.

From scorching beams, in kindly mood,
    The Persian plants its beauty screened,
And on its pagan sisterhood,
    In love, the Christian floweret leaned.

With tears of joy the wanderer felt
    The darkness of his long despair
Before that hallowed symbol melt,
    Which God's dear love had nurtured
        there.

From Nature's face, that simple flower
    The lines of sin and sadness swept ;
And Magian pile and Paynim bower
    In peace like that of Eden slept.

Each Moslem tomb, and cypress old,
    Looked holy through the sunset air ;
And, angel-like, the Muezzin told
    From tower and mosque the hour of
        prayer.

With cheerful steps, the morrow's dawn
From Shiraz saw the stranger part ;
The Star-flower of the Virgin-Born
    Still blooming in his hopeful heart !

HYMNS.

FROM THE FRENCH OF LAMARTINE.

ONE hymn more, O my lyre !
    Praise to the God above,
    Of joy and life and love,
Sweeping its strings of fire !

O, who the speed of bird and wind
    And sunbeam's glance will lend to me,
That, soaring upward, I may find
    My resting-place and home in Thee ?—
Thou, whom my soul, midst doubt and
        gloom,
    Adoreth with a fervent flame, —
Mysterious spirit ! unto whom
    Pertain nor sign nor name !

Swiftly my lyre's soft murmurs go,
    Up from the cold and joyless earth,
Back to the God who bade them flow,
    Whose moving spirit sent them forth.
But as for me, O God ! for me,
    The lowly creature of thy will,
Lingering and sad, I sigh to thee,
    An earth-bound pilgrim still !

Was not my spirit born to shine
    Where yonder stars and suns are glow-
        ing ?
To breathe with them the light divine
    From God's own holy altar flowing ?
To be, indeed, whate'er the soul
    In dreams hath thirsted for so long, —
A portion of Heaven's glorious whole
    Of loveliness and song ?

O, watchers of the stars at night,
    Who breathe their fire, as we the air, —
Suns, thunders, stars, and rays of light,
    O, say, is He, the Eternal, there !
Bend there around his awful throne
    The seraph's glance, the angel's knee ?
Or are thy inmost depths his own,
    O wild and mighty sea ?

Thoughts of my soul, how swift ye go !
    Swift as the eagle's glance of fire,
Or arrows from the archer's bow,
    To the far aim of your desire !
Thought after thought, ye thronging
        rise,
    Like spring-doves from the startled
        wood,
Bearing like them your sacrifice
    Of music unto God !

And shall these thoughts of joy and love
  Come back again no more to me ? —
Returning like the Patriarch's dove
  Wing-weary from the eternal sea,
To bear within my longing arms
  The promise-bough of kindlier skies,
Plucked from the green, immortal palms
  Which shadow Paradise ?

All-moving spirit ! — freely forth
  At thy command the strong wind
    goes :
Its errand to the passive earth,
  Nor art can stay, nor strength oppose,
Until it folds its weary wing
  Once more within the hand divine ;
So, weary from its wandering,
  My spirit turns to thine !

Child of the sea, the mountain stream,
  From its dark caverns, hurries on,
Ceaseless, by night and morning's beam,
By evening's star and noontide's sun,
Until at last it sinks to rest,
  O'erwearied, in the waiting sea,
And moans upon its mother's breast, —
  So turns my soul to Thee !

O Thou who bidd'st the torrent flow,
  Who lendest wings unto the wind, —
Mover of all things ! where art thou ?
  O, whither shall I go to find
The secret of thy resting-place ?
  Is there no holy wing for me,
That, soaring, I may search the space
  Of highest heaven for Thee ?

O, would I were as free to rise
  As leaves on autumn's whirlwind
    borne, —
The arrowy light of sunset skies,
  Or sound, or ray, or star of morn,
Which melts in heaven at twilight's
    close,
  Or aught which soars unchecked and
    free
Through Earth and Heaven ; that I
    might lose
    Myself in finding Thee !

———

When the breath divine is flowing,
Zephyr-like o'er all things going,
And, as the touch of viewless fingers,
Softly on my soul it lingers,
Open to a breath the lightest,

Conscious of a touch the slightest, —
As some calm, still lake, whereon
Sinks the snowy-bosomed swan,
And the glistening water-rings
Circle round her moving wings :
When my upward gaze is turning
Where the stars of heaven are burning
Through the deep and dark abyss, —
Flowers of midnight's wilderness,
Blowing with the evening's breath
Sweetly in their Maker's path :

When the breaking day is flushing
All the east, and light is gushing
Upward through the horizon's haze,
Sheaf-like, with its thousand rays,
Spreading, until all above
Overflows with joy and love,
And below, on earth's green bosom,
All is changed to light and blossom :

When my waking fancies over
Forms of brightness flit and hover,
Holy as the seraphs are,
Who by Zion's fountains wear
On their foreheads, white and broad,
" Holiness unto the Lord ! "
When, inspired with rapture high,
It would seem a single sigh
Could a world of love create, —
That my life could know no date,
And my eager thoughts could fill
Heaven and Earth, o'erflowing still ! —

Then, O Father ! thou alone,
From the shadow of thy throne,
To the sighing of my breast
And its rapture answerest.
All my thoughts, which, upward wing-
    ing,
Bathe where thy own light is spring-
    ing, —
All my yearnings to be free
Are as echoes answering thee !

Seldom upon lips of mine,
Father ! rests that name of thine, —
Deep within my inmost breast,
  In the secret place of mind,
  Like an awful presence shrined,
Doth the dread idea rest !
Hushed and holy dwells it there, —
Prompter of the silent prayer,
Lifting up my spirit's eye
And its faint, but earnest cry,
From its dark and cold abode,
Unto thee, my Guide and God !

THE FEMALE MARTYR.

[MARY G——, aged 18, a " SISTER OF CHARITY," died in one of our Atlantic cities, during the prevalence of the Indian cholera, while in voluntary attendance upon the sick.]

"BRING out your dead !" The mid-
  night street
Heard and gave back the hoarse, low
  call ;
Harsh fell the tread of hasty feet, —
Glanced through the dark the coarse
  white sheet, —
  Her coffin and her pall.
" What — only one !" the brutal hack-
  man said,
As, with an oath, he spurned away the
  dead.

How sunk the inmost hearts of all,
  As rolled that dead-cart slowly by,
With creaking wheel and harsh hoof-
  fall !
The dying turned him to the wall,
  To hear it and to die ! —
Onward it rolled ; while oft its driver
  stayed,
And hoarsely clamored, " Ho ! — bring
  out your dead."

It paused beside the burial-place ;
  "Toss in your load !" — and it was
  done. —
With quick hand and averted face,
Hastily to the grave's embrace
  They cast them, one by one, —
Stranger and friend, — the evil and the
  just,
Together trodden in the churchyard dust !

And thou, young martyr ! — thou wast
  there, —
  No white-robed sisters round thee
  trod, —
Nor holy hymn, nor funeral prayer
Rose through the damp and noisome air,
  Giving thee to thy God ;
Nor flower, nor cross, nor hallowed taper
  gave
Grace to the dead, and beauty to the
  grave !

Yet, gentle sufferer ! there shall be,
  In every heart of kindly feeling,
A rite as holy paid to thee
As if beneath the convent-tree
  Thy sisterhood were kneeling,

At vesper hours, like sorrowing angels,
  keeping
Their tearful watch around thy place of
  sleeping.

For thou wast one in whom the light
  Of Heaven's own love was kindled
  well.
Enduring with a martyr's might,
Through weary day and wakeful night
  Far more than words may tell :
Gentle, and meek, and lowly, and un-
  known, —
Thy mercies measured by thy God alone !

Where manly hearts were failing, —
  where
  The throngful street grew foul with
  death,
O high-souled martyr ! — thou wast
  there,
Inhaling, from the loathsome air,
  Poison with every breath.
Yet shrinking not from offices of dread
For the wrung dying, and the uncon-
  scious dead.

And, where the sickly taper shed
  Its light through vapors, damp, con-
  fined,
Hushed as a seraph's fell thy tread, —
A new Electra by the bed
  Of suffering human-kind !
Pointing the spirit, in its dark dismay,
To that pure hope which fadeth not away.

Innocent teacher of the high
  And holy mysteries of Heaven !
How turned to thee each glazing eye,
In mute and awful sympathy,
  As thy low prayers were given ;
And the o'er-hovering Spoiler wore, the
  while,
An angel's features, — a deliverer's
  smile !

A blessed task ! — and worthy one
  Who, turning from the world, as thou,
Before life's pathway had begun
To leave its spring-time flower and sun,
  Had sealed her early vow ;
Giving to God her beauty and her youth,
Her pure affections and her guileless
  truth.

Earth may not claim thee. Nothing here
  Could be for thee a meet reward ;

Thine is a treasure far more dear, —
Eye hath not seen it, nor the ear
  Of living mortal heard, —
The joys prepared, — the promised bliss
    above, —
The holy presence of Eternal Love !

Sleep on in peace. The earth has not
  A nobler name than thine shall be.
The deeds by martial manhood wrought,
The lofty energies of thought,
  The fire of poesy, —
These have but frail and fading hon-
    ors ; — thine
Shall Time unto Eternity consign.

Yea, and when thrones shall crumble
    down,
  And human pride and grandeur fall, —
The herald's line of long renown, —
The mitre and the kingly crown, —
  Perishing glories all !
The pure devotion of thy generous heart
Shall live in Heaven, of which it was a
    part.

THE FROST SPIRIT.

HE comes, — he comes, — the Frost Spirit
  comes ! You may trace his foot-
    steps now
On the naked woods and the blasted fields
  and the brown hill's withered brow.
He has smitten the leaves of the gray
  old trees where their pleasant
  green came forth,
And the winds, which follow wherever
  he goes, have shaken them down
  to earth.

He comes, — he comes, — the Frost
  Spirit comes ! — from the frozen
  Labrador, —
From the icy bridge of the Northern
  seas, which the white bear wan-
  ders o'er, —
Where the fisherman's sail is stiff with
  ice, and the luckless forms below
In the sunless cold of the lingering night
  into marble statues grow !

He comes, — he comes, — the Frost
  Spirit comes ! — on the rushing
  Northern blast,
And the dark Norwegian pines have
  bowed as his fearful breath went
  past.

With an unscorched wing he has hurried on, where the fires of Hecla
    glow
On the darkly beautiful sky above and
    the ancient ice below.

He comes, — he comes, — the Frost
  Spirit comes ! — and the quiet
  lake shall feel
The torpid touch of his glazing breath,
  and ring to the skater's heel ;
And the streams which danced on the
  broken rocks, or sang to the leaning grass,
Shall bow again to their winter chain,
  and in mournful silence pass.

He comes, — he comes, — the Frost
  Spirit comes ! — let us meet him
  as we may,
And turn with the light of the parlor-
  fire his evil power away ;
And gather closer the circle round, when
  that firelight dances high,
And laugh at the shriek of the baffled
  Fiend as his sounding wing goes
    by !

THE VAUDOIS TEACHER.[38]

" O LADY fair, these silks of mine are
  beautiful and rare, —
The richest web of the Indian loom,
  which beauty's queen might wear ;
And my pearls are pure as thy own fair
  neck, with whose radiant light
  they vie ;
I have brought them with me a weary
  way, — will my gentle lady buy ?"

And the lady smiled on the worn old man
  through the dark and clustering
  curls
Which veiled her brow as she bent to
  view his silks and glittering pearls ;
And she placed their price in the old
  man's hand, and lightly turned
  away,
But she paused at the wanderer's earnest
  call, — " My gentle lady, stay ! "

" O lady fair, I have yet a gem which a
  purer lustre flings,
Than the diamond flash of the jewelled
  crown on the lofty brow of
  kings, —

A wonderful pearl of exceeding price,
  whose virtue shall not decay,
Whose light shall be as a spell to thee
  and a blessing on thy way ! "

The lady glanced at the mirroring steel
  where her form of grace was seen,
Where her eye shone clear, and her dark
  locks waved their clasping pearls
  between ;
" Bring forth thy pearl of exceeding
  worth, thou traveller gray and
  old, —
And name the price of thy precious gem,
  and my page shall count thy gold."

The cloud went off from the pilgrim's
  brow, as a small and meagre book,
Unchased with gold or gem of cost, from
  his folding robe he took !
" Here, lady fair, is the pearl of price,
  may it prove as such to thee !
Nay — keep thy gold — I ask it not, for
  the word of God is free ! "

The hoary traveller went his way, but
  the gift he left behind
Hath had its pure and perfect work on
  that high-born maiden's mind,
And she hath turned from the pride of
  sin to the lowliness of truth,
And given her human heart to God in
  its beautiful hour of youth !

And she hath left the gray old halls,
  where an evil faith had power,
The courtly knights of her father's train,
  and the maidens of her bower ;
And she hath gone to the Vaudois vales
  by lordly feet untrod,
Where the poor and needy of earth are
  rich in the perfect love of God !

THE CALL OF THE CHRISTIAN.

Not always as the whirlwind's rush
  On Horeb's mount of fear,
Not always as the burning bush
  To Midian's shepherd seer,
Nor as the awful voice which came
  To Israel's prophet bards,
Nor as the tongues of cloven flame,
  Nor gift of fearful words, —

Not always thus, with outward sign
  Of fire or voice from Heaven,

The message of a truth divine,
  The call of God is given !
Awaking in the human heart
  Love for the true and right, —
Zeal for the Christian's better part,
  Strength for the Christian's fight.

Nor unto manhood's heart alone
  The holy influence steals :
Warm with a rapture not its own,
  The heart of woman feels !
As she who by Samaria's wall
  The Saviour's errand sought, —
As those who with the fervent Paul
  And meek Aquila wrought :

Or those meek ones whose martyrdom
  Rome's gathered grandeur saw :
Or those who in their Alpine home
  Braved the Crusader's war,
When the green Vaudois, trembling,
  heard,
  Through all its vales of death,
The martyr's song of triumph poured
  From woman's failing breath.

And gently, by a thousand things
  Which o'er our spirits pass,
Like breezes o'er the harp's fine strings,
  Or vapors o'er a glass,
Leaving their token strange and new
  Of music or of shade,
The summons to the right and true
  And merciful is made.

O, then, if gleams of truth and light
  Flash o'er thy waiting mind,
Unfolding to thy mental sight
  The wants of human-kind ;
If, brooding over human grief,
  The earnest wish is known
To soothe and gladden with relief
  An anguish not thine own ;

Though heralded with naught of fear,
  Or outward sign or show ;
Though only to the inward ear
  It whispers soft and low ;
Though dropping, as the manna fell,
  Unseen, yet from above,
Noiseless as dew-fall, heed it well, —
  Thy Father's call of love !

MY SOUL AND I.

Stand still, my soul, in the silent dark
  I would question thee,

Alone in the shadow drear and stark
   With God and me !

What, my soul, was thy errand here ?
   Was it mirth or ease,
Or heaping up dust from year to year ?
   " Nay, none of these ! "

Speak, soul, aright in His holy sight
   Whose eye looks still
And steadily on thee through the night :
   " To do his will ! "

What hast thou done, O soul of mine,
   That thou tremblest so ? —
Hast thou wrought his task, and kept
     the line
   He bade thee go ?

What, silent all ! — art sad of cheer ?
   Art fearful now ?
When God seemed far and men were near,
   How brave wert thou !

Aha ! thou tremblest ! — well I see
   Thou 'rt craven grown.
Is it so hard with God and me
   To stand alone ? —

Summon thy sunshine bravery back,
   O wretched sprite !
Let me hear thy voice through this deep
     and black
   Abysmal night.

What hast thou wrought for Right and
     Truth,
   For God and Man,
From the golden hours of bright-eyed
     youth
   To life's mid span ?

Ah, soul of mine, thy tones I hear,
   But weak and low,
Like far sad murmurs on my ear
   They come and go.

" I have wrestled stoutly with the
     Wrong,
   And borne the Right
From beneath the footfall of the throng
   To life and light.

" Wherever Freedom shivered a chain,
   God speed, quoth I ;
To Error amidst her shouting train
   I gave the lie."

Ah, soul of mine ! ah, soul of mine !
   Thy deeds are well :
Were they wrought for Truth's sake or
     for thine ?
   My soul, pray tell.

" Of all the work my hand hath wrought
   Beneath the sky,
Save a place in kindly human thought,
   No gain have I."

Go to, go to ! — for thy very self
   Thy deeds were done :
Thou for fame, the miser for pelf,
   Your end is one !

And where art thou going, soul of mine ?
   Canst see the end ?
And whither this troubled life of thine
   Evermore doth tend ?

What daunts thee now ? — what shakes
     thee so ?
   My sad soul say.
" I see a cloud like a curtain low
   Hang o'er my way.

" Whither I go I cannot tell :
   That cloud hangs black,
High as the heaven and deep as hell
   Across my track.

" I see its shadow coldly enwrap
   The souls before.
Sadly they enter it, step by step,
   To return no more.

" They shrink, they shudder, dear God!
     they kneel
   To thee in prayer.
They shut their eyes on the cloud, but
     feel
   That it still is there.

" In vain they turn from the dread Before
   To the Known and Gone ;
For while gazing behind them evermore
   Their feet glide on.

" Yet, at times, I see upon sweet pale
     faces
   A light begin
To tremble, as if from holy places
   And shrines within.

" And at times methinks their cold lips
     move
   With hymn and prayer,

As if somewhat of awe, but more of love
  And hope were there.

" I call on the souls who have left the
      light
  To reveal their lot ;
I bend mine ear to that wall of night,
  And they answer not.

" But I hear around me sighs of pain
  And the cry of fear,
And a sound like the slow sad dropping
      of rain,
  Each drop a tear !

" Ah, the cloud is dark, and day by day
  I am moving thither :
I must pass beneath it on my way —
  God pity me ! — WHITHER ? "

Ah, soul of mine ! so brave and wise
  In the life-storm loud,
Fronting so calmly all human eyes
  In the sunlit crowd !

Now standing apart with God and me
  Thou art weakness all,
Gazing vainly after the things to be
  Through Death's dread wall.

But never for this, never for this
  Was thy being lent ;
For the craven's fear is but selfishness,
  Like his merriment.

Folly and Fear are sisters twain :
  One closing her eyes,
The other peopling the dark inane
  With spectral lies.

Know well, my soul, God's hand controls
  Whate'er thou fearest ;
Round him in calmest music rolls
  Whate'er thou hearest.

What to thee is shadow, to him is day,
  And the end he knoweth,
And not on a blind and aimless way
  The spirit goeth.

Man sees no future, — a phantom show
  Is alone before him :
Past Time is dead, and the grasses grow,
  And flowers bloom o'er him.

Nothing before, nothing behind ;
  The steps of Faith

Fall on the seeming void, and find
  The rock beneath.

The Present, the Present is all thou ha:
  For thy sure possessing ;
Like the patriarch's angel hold it fast
  Till it gives its blessing.

Why fear the night ? why shrink fro:
      Death,
  • That phantom wan ?
There is nothing in heaven or earth b
      neath
  Save God and man.

Peopling the shadows we turn from Hi:
  And from one another ;
All is spectral and vague and dim
  Save God and our brother !

Like warp and woof all destinies
  Are woven fast,
Linked in sympathy like the keys
  Of an organ vast.

Pluck one thread, and the web ye mar
  Break but one
Of a thousand keys, and the paining je
  Through all will run.

O restless spirit ! wherefore strain
  Beyond thy sphere ?
Heaven and hell, with their joy and pai:
  Are now and here.

Back to thyself is measured well
  All thou hast given ;
Thy neighbor's wrong is thy present hel
  His bliss, thy heaven.

And in life, in death, in dark and ligh
  All are in God's care :
Sound the black abyss, pierce the dee
      of night,
  And he is there !

All which is real now remaineth,
  And fadeth never :
The hand which upholds it now sustainet
  The soul forever.

Leaning on him, make with reveren
      meekness
  His own thy will,
And with strength from Him shall th
      utter weakness
  Life's task fulfil :

And that cloud itself, which now before
    thee
    Lies dark in view,
Shall with beams of light from the inner
    glory
    Be stricken through.

And like meadow mist through autumn's
    dawn
    Uprolling thin,
Its thickest folds when about thee drawn
    Let sunlight in.

Then of what is to be, and of what is done,
    Why queriest thou ? —
The past and the time to be are one,
    And both are NOW !

TO A FRIEND,

ON HER RETURN FROM EUROPE.

How smiled the land of France
Under thy blue eye's glance,
    Light-hearted rover !
Old walls of chateaux gray,
Towers of an early day,
Which the Three Colors play
    Flauntingly over.

Now midst the brilliant train
Thronging the banks of Seine :
    Now midst the splendor
Of the wild Alpine range,
Waking with change on change
Thoughts in thy young heart strange,
    Lovely, and tender.

Vales, soft Elysian,
Like those in the vision
    Of Mirza, when, dreaming,
He saw the long hollow dell,
Touched by the prophet's spell,
Into an ocean swell
    With its isles teeming.

Cliffs wrapped in snows of years,
Splintering with icy spears
    Autumn's blue heaven :
Loose rock and frozen slide,
Hung on the mountain-side,
Waiting their hour to glide
    Downward, storm-driven !

Rhine-stream, by castle old,
Baron's and robber's hold,

Peacefully flowing ;
Sweeping through vineyards green,
Or where the cliffs are seen
O'er the broad wave between
    Grim shadows throwing.

Or, where St. Peter's dome
Swells o'er eternal Rome,
    Vast, dim, and solemn, —
Hymns ever chanting low, —
Censers swung to and fro, —
Sable stoles sweeping slow
    Cornice and column !

O, as from each and all
Will there not voices call
    Evermore back again ?
In the mind's gallery
Wilt thou not always see
Dim phantoms beckon thee
    O'er that old track again ?

New forms thy presence haunt, —
New voices softly chant, —
    New faces greet thee ! —
Pilgrims from many a shrine
Hallowed by poet's line,
At memory's magic sign,
    Rising to meet thee.

And when such visions come
Unto thy olden home,
    Will they not waken
Deep thoughts of Him whose hand
Led thee o'er sea and land
Back to the household band
    Whence thou wast taken ?

While, at the sunset time,
Swells the cathedral's chime,
    Yet, in thy dreaming,
While to thy spirit's eye
Yet the vast mountains lie
Piled in the Switzer's sky,
    Icy and gleaming :

Prompter of silent prayer,
Be the wild picture there
    In the mind's chamber,
And, through each coming day
Him who, as staff and stay,
Watched o'er thy wandering way,
    Freshly remember.

So, when the call shall be
Soon or late unto thee,
    As to all given,

Still may that picture live,
All its fair forms survive,
And to thy spirit give
    Gladness in Heaven !

THE ANGEL OF PATIENCE.

A FREE PARAPHRASE OF THE GERMAN.

To weary hearts, to mourning homes,
God's meekest Angel gently comes :
No power has he to banish pain,
Or give us back our lost again ;
And yet in tenderest love, our dear
And Heavenly Father sends him here.

There 's quiet in that Angel's glance,
There 's rest in his still countenance !
He mocks no grief with idle cheer,
Nor wounds with words the mourner's ear ;
But ills and woes he may not cure
He kindly trains us to endure.

Angel of Patience ! sent to calm
Our feverish brows with cooling palm ;
To lay the storms of hope and fear,
And reconcile life's smile and tear ;
The throbs of wounded pride to still,
And make our own our Father's will !

O thou who mournest on thy way,
With longings for the close of day ;
He walks with thee, that Angel kind,
And gently whispers, " Be resigned :
Bear up, bear on, the end shall tell
The dear Lord ordereth all things well ! "

FOLLEN.

ON READING HIS ESSAY ON THE " FU-
TURE STATE."

FRIEND of my soul ! — as with moist eye
    I look up from this page of thine,
Is it a dream that thou art nigh,
    Thy mild face gazing into mine ?

That presence seems before me now,
    A placid heaven of sweet moonrise,
When, dew-like, on the earth below
    Descends the quiet of the skies.

The calm brow through the parted hair,
    The gentle lips which knew no guile,
Softening the blue eye's thoughtful care
    With the bland beauty of their smile.

Ah me ! — at times that last dread scene
    Of Frost and Fire and moaning Sea,
Will cast its shade of doubt between
    The failing eyes of Faith and thee.

Yet, lingering o'er thy charmed page,
    Where through the twilight air of earth,
Alike enthusiast and sage,
    Prophet and bard, thou gazest forth ;

Lifting the Future's solemn veil ;
    The reaching of a mortal hand
To put aside the cold and pale
    Cloud-curtains of the Unseen Land ;

In thoughts which answer to my own,
    In words which reach my inward ear,
Like whispers from the void Unknown,
    I feel thy living presence here.

The waves which lull thy body's rest,
    The dust thy pilgrim footsteps trod,
Unwasted, through each change, attest
    The fixed economy of God.

Shall these poor elements outlive
    The mind whose kingly will they
        wrought ?
Their gross unconsciousness survive
    Thy godlike energy of thought ?

THOU LIVEST, FOLLEN ! — not in vain
    Hath thy fine spirit meekly borne
The burthen of Life's cross of pain,
    And the thorned crown of suffering
        worn.

O, while Life's solemn mystery glooms
    Around us like a dungeon's wall, —
Silent earth's pale and crowded tombs,
    Silent the heaven which bends o'er
        all ! —

While day by day our loved ones glide
    In spectral silence, hushed and lone,
To the cold shadows which divide
    The living from the dread Unknown ;

While even on the closing eye,
    And on the lip which moves in vain,
The seals of that stern mystery
    Their undiscovered trust retain ; —

And only midst the gloom of death,
    Its mournful doubts and haunting
        fears,
Two pale, sweet angels, Hope and Faith,
    Smile dimly on us through their tears ;

'T is something to a heart like mine
　To think of thee as living yet ;
To feel that such a light as thine
　Could not in utter darkness set.

Less dreary seems the untried way
　Since thou hast left thy footprints there,
And beams of mournful beauty play
　Round the sad Angel's sable hair.

Oh ! — at this hour when half the sky
　Is glorious with its evening light,
And fair broad fields of summer lie
　Hung o'er with greenness in my sight ;

While through these elm-boughs wet with
　　rain
The sunset's golden walls are seen,
With clover-bloom and yellow grain
　And wood-draped hill and stream be-
　　tween ;

I long to know if scenes like this
　Are hidden from an angel's eyes ;
If earth's familiar loveliness
　Haunts not thy heaven's serener skies.

For sweetly here upon thee grew
　The lesson which that beauty gave,
The ideal of the Pure and True
　In earth and sky and gliding wave.

And it may be that all which lends
　The soul an upward impulse here,
With a diviner beauty blends,
　And greets us in a holier sphere.

Through groves where blighting never fell
　The humbler flowers of earth may
　　twine ;
And simple draughts from childhood's
　　well
　Blend with the angel-tasted wine.

But be the prying vision veiled,
　And let the seeking lips be dumb, —
Where even seraph eyes have failed
　Shall mortal blindness seek to come ?

We only know that thou hast gone,
　And that the same returnless tide
Which bore thee from us still glides on,
　And we who mourn thee with it glide.

On all thou lookest we shall look,
　And to our gaze erelong shall turn
That page of God's mysterious book
　We so much wish, yet dread to learn.

With Him, before whose awful power
　Thy spirit bent its trembling knee ; —
Who, in the silent greeting flower,
　And forest leaf, looked out on thee, —

We leave thee, with a trust serene,
　Which Time, nor Change, nor Death
　　can move,
While with thy childlike faith we lean
　On Him whose dearest name is Love !

TO THE REFORMERS OF ENG-LAND.

God bless ye, brothers ! — in the fight
　Ye 're waging now, ye cannot fail,
For better is your sense of right
　Than king-craft's triple mail.

Than tyrant's law, or bigot's ban,
　More mighty is your simplest word ;
The free heart of an honest man
　Than crosier or the sword.

Go, — let your bloated Church rehearse
　The lesson it has learned so well ;
It moves not with its prayer or curse
　The gates of heaven or hell.

Let the State scaffold rise again, —
　Did Freedom die when Russell died ?
Forget ye how the blood of Vane
　From earth's green bosom cried ?

The great hearts of your olden time
　Are beating with you, full and strong
All holy memories and sublime
　And glorious round ye throng.

The bluff, bold men of Runnymede
　Are with ye still in times like these
The shades of England's mighty dead,
　Your cloud of witnesses !

The truths ye urge are borne abroad
　By every wind and every tide ;
The voice of Nature and of God
　Speaks out upon your side.

The weapons which your hands have
　　found
　Are those which Heaven itself has
　　wrought,
Light, Truth, and Love ; — your battle-
　　ground
　The free, broad field of Thought.

7

No partial, selfish purpose breaks
   The simple beauty of your plan,
Nor lie from throne or altar shakes
   Your steady faith in man.

The languid pulse of England starts
   And bounds beneath your words of
      power,
The beating of her million hearts
   Is with you at this hour !

O ye who, with undoubting eyes,
   Through present cloud and gathering
      storm,
Behold the span of Freedom's skies,
   And sunshine soft and warm, —

Press bravely onward ! — not in vain
   Your generous trust in human-kind ;
The good which bloodshed could not gain
   Your peaceful zeal shall find.

Press on ! — the triumph shall be won
   Of common rights and equal laws,
The glorious dream of Harrington,
   And Sidney's good old cause.

Blessing the cotter and the crown,
   Sweetening worn Labor's bitter cup ;
And, plucking not the highest down,
   Lifting the lowest up.

Press on ! — and we who may not share
   The toil or glory of your fight
May ask, at least, in earnest prayer,
   God's blessing on the right !

THE QUAKER OF THE OLDEN TIME.

The Quaker of the olden time ! —
   How calm and firm and true,
Unspotted by its wrong and crime,
   He walked the dark earth through.
The lust of power, the love of gain,
   The thousand lures of sin
Around him, had no power to stain
   The purity within.

With that deep insight which detects
   All great things in the small,
And knows how each man's life affects
   The spiritual life of all,
He walked by faith and not by sight,
   By love and not by law ;
The presence of the wrong or right
   He rather felt than saw.

He felt that wrong with wrong partakes,
   That nothing stands alone,
That whoso gives the motive, makes
   His brother's sin his own.
And, pausing not for doubtful choice
   Of evils great or small,
He listened to that inward voice
   Which called away from all.

O Spirit of that early day,
   So pure and strong and true,
Be with us in the narrow way
   Our faithful fathers knew.
Give strength the evil to forsake,
   The cross of Truth to bear,
And love and reverent fear to make
   Our daily lives a prayer !

THE REFORMER.

All grim and soiled and brown with
      tan,
   I saw a Strong One, in his wrath,
Smiting the godless shrines of man
      Along his path.

The Church, beneath her trembling dome,
   Essayed in vain her ghostly charm :
Wealth shook within his gilded home
      With strange alarm.

Fraud from his secret chambers fled
   Before the sunlight bursting in :
Sloth drew her pillow o'er her head
      To drown the din.

"Spare," Art implored, "yon holy pile
   That grand, old, time-worn turret
      spare " ;
Meek Reverence, kneeling in the aisle,
      Cried out, " Forbear ! "

Gray-bearded Use, who, deaf and blind
   Groped for his old accustomed stone,
Leaned on his staff, and wept to find
      His seat o'erthrown.

Young Romance raised his dreamy eyes
   O'erhung with paly locks of gold, —
"Why smite," he asked in sad surprise
      "The fair, the old ?"

Yet louder rang the Strong One's stroke
   Yet nearer flashed his axe's gleam :
Shuddering and sick of heart I woke,
      As from a dream.

I looked : aside the dust-cloud rolled, —
   The Waster seemed the Builder too ;
Up springing from the ruined Old
      I saw the New.

'T was but the ruin of the bad, —
   The wasting of the wrong and ill ;
Whate'er of good the old time had
      Was living still.

Calm grew the brows of him I feared ;
   The frown which awed me passed away,
And left behind a smile which cheered
      Like breaking day.

The grain grew green on battle-plains,
   O'er swarded war-mounds grazed the
      cow ;
The slave stood forging from his chains
      The spade and plough.

Where frowned the fort, pavilions gay
   And cottage windows, flower-entwined,
Looked out upon the peaceful bay
      And hills behind.

Through vine-wreathed cups with wine
      once red,
   The lights on brimming crystal fell,
Drawn, sparkling, from the rivulet head
      And mossy well.

Through prison walls, like Heaven-sent
      hope,
   Fresh breezes blew, and sunbeams
      strayed,
And with the idle gallows-rope
      The young child played.

Where the doomed victim in his cell
   Had counted o'er the weary hours,
Glad school-girls, answering to the bell,
      Came crowned with flowers.

Grown wiser for the lesson given,
   I fear no longer, for I know
That, where the share is deepest driven,
      The best fruits grow.

The outworn rite, the old abuse,
   The pious fraud transparent grown,
The good held captive in the use
      Of wrong alone, —

These wait their doom, from that great law
   Which makes the past time serve to-
      day ;

And fresher life the world shall draw
      From their decay.

O, backward-looking son of time !
   The new is old, the old is new,
The cycle of a change sublime
      Still sweeping through.

So wisely taught the Indian seer ;
   Destroying Seva, forming Brahm,
Who wake by turns Earth's love and
      fear,
   Are one, the same.

Idly as thou, in that old day
   Thou mournest, did thy sire repine :
So, in his time, thy child grown gray
      Shall sigh for thine.

But life shall on and upward go ;
   Th' eternal step of Progress beats
To that great anthem, calm and slow,
      Which God repeats.

Take heart ! — the Waster builds again, —
   A charmed life old Goodness hath ;
The tares may perish, — but the grain
      Is not for death.

God works in all things ; all obey
   His first propulsion from the night :
Wake thou and watch ! — the world is
      gray
   With morning light !

THE PRISONER FOR DEBT.

Look on him ! — through his dungeon
      grate
   Feebly and cold, the morning light
Comes stealing round him, dim and
      late,
   As if it loathed the sight.
Reclining on his strawy bed,
His hand upholds his drooping head, —
His bloodless cheek is seamed and hard,
Unshorn his gray, neglected beard ;
And o'er his bony fingers flow
His long, dishevelled locks of snow.

No grateful fire before him glows,
   And yet the winter's breath is chill ;
And o'er his half-clad person goes
   The frequent ague thrill !
Silent, save ever and anon,
A sound, half murmur and half groan,

Forces apart the painful grip
Of the old sufferer's bearded lip ;
O sad and crushing is the fate
Of old age chained and desolate !

Just God ! why lies that old man there ?
  A murderer shares his prison bed,
Whose eyeballs, through his horrid hair,
  Gleam on him, fierce and red ;
And the rude oath and heartless jeer
Fall ever on his loathing ear,
And, or in wakefulness or sleep,
Nerve, flesh, and pulses thrill and creep
Whene'er that ruffian's tossing limb,
Crimson with murder, touches him !

What has the gray-haired prisoner done ?
  Has murder stained his hands with
    gore ?
Not so ; his crime's a fouler one ;
GOD MADE THE OLD MAN POOR !
For this he shares a felon's cell, —
The fittest earthly type of hell !
For this, the boon for which he poured
His young blood on the invader's sword,
And counted light the fearful cost, —
His blood-gained liberty is lost !

And so, for such a place of rest,
  Old prisoner, dropped thy blood as
  rain
On Concord's field, and Bunker's crest,
  And Saratoga's plain ?
Look forth, thou man of many scars,
Through thy dim dungeon's iron bars ;
It must be joy, in sooth, to see
Yon monument upreared to thee, —
Piled granite and a prison cell, —
The land repays thy service well !

Go, ring the bells and fire the guns,
  And fling the starry banner out ;
Shout "Freedom !" till your lisping
  ones
  Give back their cradle-shout ;
Let boastful eloquence declaim
Of honor, liberty, and fame ;
Still let the poet's strain be heard,
With glory for each second word,
And everything with breath agree
To praise "our glorious liberty !"

But when the patron cannon jars
  That prison's cold and gloomy wall,
And through its grates the stripes and
  stars
  Rise on the wind, and fall, —

Think ye that prisoner's aged ear
Rejoices in the general cheer ?
Think ye his dim and failing eye
Is kindled at your pageantry ?
Sorrowing of soul, and chained of limb,
What is your carnival to him ?

Down with the LAW that binds him
  thus !
  Unworthy freemen, let it find
No refuge from the withering curse
  Of God and human kind !
Open the prison's living tomb,
And usher from its brooding gloom
The victims of your savage code
To the free sun and air of God ;
No longer dare as crime to brand
The chastening of the Almighty's hand.

LINES,

WRITTEN ON READING PAMPHLETS
PUBLISHED BY CLERGYMEN AGAINST
THE ABOLITION OF THE GALLOWS.

I.

THE suns of eighteen centuries have
  shone
  Since the Redeemer walked with man,
    and made
The fisher's boat, the cavern's floor of
  stone,
  And mountain moss, a pillow for his
    head ;
And He, who wandered with the peas-
  ant Jew,
  And broke with publicans the bread
    of shame,
  And drank, with blessings in his Fa-
    ther's name,
The water which Samaria's outcast drew,
  Hath now his temples upon every shore,
  Altar and shrine and priest, — and in-
    cense dim
Evermore rising, with low prayer and
  hymn,
From lips which press the temple's mar-
  ble floor,
Or kiss the gilded sign of the dread
  Cross He bore.

II.

Yet as of old, when, meekly "doing
  good,"
He fed a blind and selfish multitude,

And even the poor companions of his lot
With their dim earthly vision knew him
    not,
  How ill are his high teachings under-
    stood !
Where He hath spoken Liberty, the
    priest
  At his own altar binds the chain
    anew ;
Where He hath bidden to Life's equal
    feast,
  The starving many wait upon the few ;
Where He hath spoken Peace, his name
    hath been
The loudest war-cry of contending men ;
Priests, pale with vigils, in his name
    have blessed
The unsheathed sword, and laid the
    spear in rest,
Wet the war-banner with their sacred
    wine,
And crossed its blazon with the holy
    sign ;
Yea, in his name who bade the erring
    live,
And daily taught his lesson, — to for-
    give ! —
  Twisted the cord and edged the mur-
    derous steel ;
And, with his words of mercy on their
    lips,
Hung gloating o'er the pincer's burning
    grips,
  And the grim horror of the straining
    wheel ;
Fed the slow flame which gnawed the
    victim's limb,
Who saw before his searing eyeballs
    swim
  The image of *their* Christ in cruel
    zeal,
Through the black torment-smoke, held
    mockingly to him !

III.

The blood which mingled with the des-
    ert sand,
  And beaded with its red and ghastly
    dew
The vines and olives of the Holy Land, —
  The shrieking curses of the hunted
    Jew, —
The white-sown bones of heretics,
    where'er
They sank beneath the Crusade's holy
    spear, —

Goa's dark dungeons, — Malta's sea-
    washed cell,
  Where with the hymns the ghostly
    fathers sung
Mingled the groans by subtle torture
    wrung,
Heaven's anthem blending with the
    shriek of hell !
The midnight of Bartholomew, — the
    stake
  Of Smithfield, and that thrice-ac-
    cursed flame
Which Calvin kindled by Geneva's
    lake, —
New England's scaffold, and the priestly
    sneer
Which mocked its victims in that hour
    of fear,
  When guilt itself a human tear might
    claim, —
Bear witness, O thou wronged and mer-
    ciful One !
That Earth's most hateful crimes have
    in thy name been done !

IV.

Thank God ! that I have lived to see
    the time
When the great truth begins at last to
    find
An utterance from the deep heart of
    mankind,
Earnest and clear, that ALL REVENGE IS
    CRIME !
That man is holier than a creed, — that
    all
Restraint upon him must consult his
    good,
Hope's sunshine linger on his prison
    wall, .
  And Love look in upon his soli-
    tude.
The beautiful lesson which our Saviour
    taught
Through long, dark centuries its way
    hath wrought
Into the common mind and popular
    thought ;
And words, to which by Galilee's lake
    shore
The humble fishers listened with hushed
    oar,
Have found an echo in the general
    heart,
And of the public faith become a living
    part.

Who shall arrest this tendency ? — Bring
    back
The cells of Venice and the bigot's rack ?
Harden the softening human heart again
To cold indifference to a brother's pain ?
Ye most unhappy men ! — who, turned
    away
From the mild sunshine of the Gospel
    day,
  Grope in the shadows of Man's twi-
    light time,
What mean ye, that with ghoul-like
    zest ye brood,
O'er those foul altars streaming with
    . warm blood,
  Permitted in another age and clime ?
Why cite that law with which the bigot
    Jew
Rebuked the Pagan's mercy, when he
    knew
No evil in the Just One ? — Wherefore
    turn
To the dark cruel past ? — Can ye not
    learn
From the pure Teacher's life, how mildly
    free
Is the great Gospel of Humanity ?
The Flamen's knife is bloodless, and no
    more
Mexitli's altars soak with human gore,
No more the ghastly sacrifices smoke .
Through the green arches of the Druid's
    oak ;   .
And ye of milder faith, with your high
    claim
Of prophet-utterance in the Holiest
    name,
Will ye become the Druids of *our* time !
Set up your scaffold-altars in *our* land,
And, consecrators of Law's darkest
    crime,
  Urge to its loathsome work the hang-
    man's hand ?
Beware, — lest human nature, roused at
    last,
From its peeled shoulder your encum-
    brance cast,
  And, sick to loathing of your cry for
    blood,
Rank ye with those who led their vic-
    tims round
The Celt's red altar and the Indian's
    mound,
  Abhorred of Earth and Heaven, — a
    pagan brotherhood !

THE HUMAN SACRIFICE.

I.

Far from his close and noisome cell,
  By grassy lane and sunny stream,
Blown clover field and strawberry dell,
And green and meadow freshness, fell
  The footsteps of his dream.
Again from careless feet the dew
  Of summer's misty morn he shook ;
Again with merry heart he threw
  His light line in the rippling brook.
Back crowded all his school-day joys,
  He urged the ball and quoit again,
And heard the shout of laughing boys
  Come ringing down the walnut glen.
Again he felt the western breeze,
  With scent of flowers and crisping
    hay ;
And down again through wind-stirred
    trees
  He saw the quivering sunlight play.
An angel in home's vine-hung door,
  He saw his sister smile once more ;
Once more the truant's brown-locked
    head
  Upon his mother's knees was laid,
And sweetly lulled to slumber there,
  With evening's holy hymn and prayer !

II.

He woke.   At once on heart and brain
  The present Terror rushed again, —
Clanked on his limbs the felon's chain !
He woke, to hear the church-tower tell
Time's footfall on the conscious bell,
And, shuddering, feel that clanging din
His life's LAST HOUR had ushered in ;
To see within his prison-yard,
  Through the small window, iron barred,
The gallows shadow rising dim
Between the sunrise heaven and him, —
  A horror in God's blessed air, —
  A blackness in his morning light, —
Like some foul devil-altar there
  Built up by demon hands at night.
And, maddened by that evil sight,
Dark, horrible, confused, and strange,
A chaos of wild, weltering change,
All power of check and guidance gone,
Dizzy and blind, his mind swept on.
In vain he strove to breathe a prayer,
  In vain he turned the Holy Book,
He only heard the gallows-stair
  Creak as the wind its timbers shook.
No dream for him of sin forgiven,
  While still that baleful spectre stood,

With its hoarse murmur, "*Blood for
Blood!*"
Between him and the pitying Heaven!

III.

Low on his dungeon floor he knelt,
  And smote his breast, and on his
    chain,
Whose iron clasp he always felt,
  His hot tears fell like rain;
And near him, with the cold, calm look
  And tone of one whose formal part,
  Unwarmed, unsoftened of the heart,
Is measured out by rule and book,
With placid lip and tranquil blood,
The hangman's ghostly ally stood,
Blessing with solemn text and word
The gallows-drop and strangling cord;
Lending the sacred Gospel's awe
And sanction to the crime of Law.

IV.

He saw the victim's tortured brow, —
  The sweat of anguish starting there, —
The record of a nameless woe
  In the dim eye's imploring stare,
  Seen hideous through the long, damp
    hair, —
Fingers of ghastly skin and bone
Working and writhing on the stone! —
And heard, by mortal terror wrung
From heaving breast and stiffened tongue,
  The choking sob and low hoarse prayer;
As o'er his half-crazed fancy came
A vision of the eternal flame, —
Its smoking cloud of agonies, —
Its demon-worm that never dies, —
The everlasting rise and fall
Of fire-waves round the infernal wall;
While high above that dark red flood,
Black, giant-like, the gallows stood;
Two busy fiends attending there:
One with cold mocking rite and prayer,
The other with impatient grasp,
Tightening the death-rope's strangling
    clasp.

V.

The unfelt rite at length was done, —
  The prayer unheard at length was
    said, —
An hour had passed: — the noonday sun
  Smote on the features of the dead!
And he who stood the doomed beside,
Calm gauger of the swelling tide
Of mortal agony and fear,
Heeding with curious eye and ear

Whate'er revealed the keen excess
Of man's extremest wretchedness:
And who in that dark anguish saw
  An earnest of the victim's fate,
The vengeful terrors of God's law,
  The kindlings of Eternal hate, —
The first drops of that fiery rain
Which beats the dark red realm of pain,
Did he uplift his earnest cries
  Against the crime of Law, which gave
His brother to that fearful grave,
Whereon Hope's moonlight never lies,
  And Faith's white blossoms never wave
To the soft breath of Memory's sighs; —
Which sent a spirit marred and stained,
By fiends of sin possessed, profaned,
In madness and in blindness stark,
Into the silent, unknown dark?
No, — from the wild and shrinking dread
With which he saw the victim led
Beneath the dark veil which divides
Ever the living from the dead,
  And Nature's solemn secret hides,
The man of prayer can only draw
New reasons for his bloody law;
New faith in staying Murder's hand
By murder at that Law's command;
New reverence for the gallows-rope,
  As human nature's latest hope;
Last relic of the good old time,
When Power found license for its crime,
And held a writhing world in check
By that fell cord about its neck;
Stifled Sedition's rising shout,
Choked the young breath of Freedom out,
  And timely checked the words which
    sprung
From Heresy's forbidden tongue;
While in its noose of terror bound,
The Church its cherished union found,
Conforming, on the Moslem plan,
The motley-colored mind of man,
Not by the Koran and the Sword,
But by the Bible and the Cord!

VI.

O Thou! at whose rebuke the grave
Back to warm life its sleeper gave,
Beneath whose sad and tearful glance
The cold and changed countenance
Broke the still horror of its trance,
And, waking, saw with joy above,
A brother's face of tenderest love;
Thou, unto whom the blind and lame,
The sorrowing and the sin-sick came,
And from thy very garment's hem
Drew life and healing unto them,

The burden of thy holy faith
Was love and life, not hate and death,
Man's demon ministers of pain,
  The fiends of his revenge were sent
  From thy pure Gospel's element
To their dark home again.
Thy name is Love ! What, then, is he,
  Who in that name the gallows rears,
An awful altar built to thee,
  With sacrifice of blood and tears ?
O, once again thy healing lay
  On the blind eyes which knew thee not,
And let the light of thy pure day
  Melt in upon his darkened thought.
Soften his hard, cold heart, and show
  The power which in forbearance lies,
And let him feel that mercy now
  Is better than old sacrifice !

              VII.

As on the White Sea's charmed shore,
  The Parsee sees his holy hill
With dunnest smoke-clouds curtained
      o'er,
Yet knows beneath them, evermore,
  The low, pale fire is quivering still ;
So, underneath its clouds of sin,
  The heart of man retaineth yet
Gleams of its holy origin ;
  And half-quenched stars that never set,
Dim colors of its faded bow,
  And early beauty, linger there,
And o'er its wasted desert blow
  Faint breathings of its morning air,
O, never yet upon the scroll
Of the sin-stained, but priceless soul,
  Hath Heaven inscribed " DESPAIR !"
Cast not the clouded gem away,
Quench not the dim but living ray, —
  My brother man, Beware !
With that deep voice which from the
      skies
Forbade the Patriarch's sacrifice,
God's angel cries, FORBEAR !

        RANDOLPH OF ROANOKE.

O MOTHER EARTH ! upon thy lap
  Thy weary ones receiving,
And o'er them, silent as a dream,
  Thy grassy mantle weaving,
Fold softly in thy long embrace
  That heart so worn and broken,
And cool its pulse of fire beneath
  Thy shadows old and oaken.

Shut out from him the bitter word
  And serpent hiss of scorning ;
Nor let the storms of yesterday
  Disturb his quiet morning.
Breathe over him forgetfulness
  Of all save deeds of kindness,
And, save to smiles of grateful eyes,
  Press down his lids in blindness.

There, where with living ear and eye
  He heard Potomac's flowing,
And, through his tall ancestral trees,
  Saw autumn's sunset glowing,
He sleeps, — still looking to the west,
  Beneath the dark wood shadow,
As if he still would see the sun
  Sink down on wave and meadow.

Bard, Sage, and Tribune ! — in himself
  All moods of mind contrasting, —
The tenderest wail of human woe,
  The scorn-like lightning blasting ;
The pathos which from rival eyes
  Unwilling tears could summon,
The stinging taunt, the fiery burst
  Of hatred scarcely human !

Mirth, sparkling like a diamond shower,
  From lips of life-long sadness ;
Clear picturings of majestic thought
  Upon a ground of madness ;
And over all Romance and Song
  A classic beauty throwing,
And laurelled Clio at his side
  Her storied pages showing.

All parties feared him : each in turn
  Beheld its schemes disjointed,
As right or left his fatal glance
  And spectral finger pointed.
Sworn foe of Cant, he smote it down
  With trenchant wit unsparing,
And, mocking, rent with ruthless hand
  The robe Pretence was wearing.

Too honest or too proud to feign
  A love he never cherished,
Beyond Virginia's border line
  His patriotism perished.
While others hailed in distant skies
  Our eagle's dusky pinion,
He only saw the mountain bird
  Stoop o'er his Old Dominion !

Still through each change of fortune
      strange,
  Racked nerve, and brain all burning,

His loving faith in Mother-land
  Knew never shade of turning ;
By Britain's lakes, by Neva's wave,
  Whatever sky was o'er him,
He heard her rivers' rushing sound,
  Her blue peaks rose before him.

He held his slaves, yet made withal
  No false and vain pretences,
Nor paid a lying priest to seek
  For Scriptural defences.
His harshest words of proud rebuke,
  His bitterest taunt and scorning,
Fell fire-like on the Northern brow
  That bent to him in fawning.

He held his slaves ; yet kept the while
  His reverence for the Human ;
In the dark vassals of his will
  He saw but Man and Woman !
No hunter of God's outraged poor
  His Roanoke valley entered ;
No trader in the souls of men
  Across his threshold ventured.

And when the old and wearied man
  Lay down for his last sleeping,
And at his side, a slave no more,
  His brother-man stood weeping,
His latest thought, his latest breath,
  To Freedom's duty giving,
With failing tongue and trembling hand
  The dying blest the living.

O, never bore his ancient State
  A truer son or braver !
None trampling with a calmer scorn
  On foreign hate or favor.
He knew her faults, yet never stooped
  His proud and manly feeling
To poor excuses of the wrong
  Or meanness of concealing.

But none beheld with clearer eye
  The plague-spot o'er her spreading,
None heard more sure the steps of
    Doom
  Along her future treading.
For her as for himself he spake,
  When, his gaunt frame upbracing,
He traced with dying hand "REMORSE !"
  And perished in the tracing.

As from the grave where Henry sleeps,
  From Vernon's weeping willow,
And from the grassy pall which hides
  The Sage of Monticello,

So from the leaf-strewn burial-stone
  Of Randolph's lowly dwelling,
Virginia ! o'er thy land of slaves
  A warning voice is swelling !

And hark ! from thy deserted fields
  Are sadder warnings spoken,
From quenched hearths, where thy ex-
    iled sons
  Their household gods have broken.
The curse is on thee, — wolves for men,
  And briers for corn-sheaves giving !
O, more than all thy dead renown
  Were now one hero living !

DEMOCRACY.

*All things whatsoever ye would that men
should do to you, do ye even so to them. —
Matthew vii. 12.*

BEARER of Freedom's holy light,
  Breaker of Slavery's chain and rod,
The foe of all which pains the sight,
  Or wounds the generous ear of God !

Beautiful yet thy temples rise,
  Though there profaning gifts are
    thrown ;
And fires unkindled of the skies
  Are glaring round thy altar-stone.

Still sacred, — though thy name be
    breathed
  By those whose hearts thy truth de-
    ride ;
And garlands, plucked from thee, are
    wreathed
  Around the haughty brows of Pride.

O, ideal of my boyhood's time !
  The faith in which my father stood,
Even when the sons of Lust and Crime
  Had stained thy peaceful courts with
    blood !

Still to those courts my footsteps turn,
  For through the mists which darken
    there,
I see the flame of Freedom burn, —
  The Kebla of the patriot's prayer !

The generous feeling, pure and warm,
  Which owns the rights of *all* divine, —
The pitying heart, — the helping arm, —
  The prompt self-sacrifice, — are thine.

Beneath thy broad, impartial eye,
How fade the lines of caste and birth !
How equal in their suffering lie
The groaning multitudes of earth !

Still to a stricken brother true,
Whatever clime hath nurtured him ;
As stooped to heal the wounded Jew
The worshipper of Gerizim.

By misery unrepelled, unawed
By pomp or power, thou seest a MAN
In prince or peasant, — slave or lord, —
Pale priest, or swarthy artisan.

Through all disguise, form, place, or name,
Beneath the flaunting robes of sin,
Through poverty and squalid shame,
Thou lookest on *the man* within.

On man, as man, retaining yet,
Howe'er debased, and soiled, and dim,
The crown upon his forehead set, —
The immortal gift of God to him.

And there is reverence in thy look ;
For that frail form which mortals wear
The Spirit of the Holiest took,
And veiled his perfect brightness there.

Not from the shallow babbling fount
Of vain philosophy thou art ;
He who of old on Syria's mount
Thrilled, warmed, by turns, the listener's heart,

In holy words which cannot die,
In thoughts which angels leaned to know,
Proclaimed thy message from on high, —
Thy mission to a world of woe.

That voice's echo hath not died !
From the blue lake of Galilee,
And Tabor's lonely mountain-side,
It calls a struggling world to thee.

Thy name and watchword o'er this land
I hear in every breeze that stirs,
And round a thousand altars stand
Thy banded party worshippers.

Not to these altars of a day,
At party's call, my gift I bring ;
But on thy olden shrine I lay
A freeman's dearest offering :

The voiceless utterance of his will, —
His pledge to Freedom and to Truth,
That manhood's heart remembers still
The homage of his generous youth.

Election Day, 1843.

TO RONGE.

STRIKE home, strong - hearted man !
Down to the root
Of old oppression sink the Saxon steel.
Thy work is to hew down. In God's name then
Put nerve into thy task. Let other men
Plant, as they may, that better tree whose fruit
The wounded bosom of the Church shall heal.
Be thou the image-breaker. Let thy blows
Fall heavy as the Suabian's iron hand,
On crown or crosier, which shall interpose
Between thee and the weal of Fatherland.
Leave creeds to closet idlers. First of all,
Shake thou all German dream-land with the fall
Of that accursed tree, whose evil trunk
Was spared of old by Erfurt's stalwart monk.
Fight not with ghosts and shadows. Let us hear
The snap of chain-links. Let our gladdened ear
Catch the pale prisoner's welcome, as the light
Follows thy axe-stroke, through his cell of night.
Be faithful to both worlds ; nor think to feed
Earth's starving millions with the husks of creed.
Servant of Him whose mission high and holy
Was to the wronged, the sorrowing, and the lowly,
Thrust not his Eden promise from our sphere,
Distant and dim beyond the blue sky's span ;
Like him of Patmos, see it, now and here, —
The New Jerusalem comes down to man !

Be warned by Luther's error. Nor like
    him,
When the roused Teuton dashes from his
    limb
The rusted chain of ages, help to bind
His hands for whom thou claim'st the
    freedom of the mind !

CHALKLEY HALL.[39]

How bland and sweet the greeting of
    this breeze
    To him who flies   .
From crowded street and red wall's
    weary gleam,
Till far behind him like a hideous dream
    The close dark city lies !

Here, while the market murmurs, while
    men throng
    The marble floor
Of Mammon's altar, from the crush and
    din
Of the world's madness let me gather in
    My better thoughts once more.

O, once again revive, while on my ear
    The cry of Gain
And low hoarse hum of Traffic die away,
Ye blessed memories of my early day
    Like sere grass wet with rain ! —

Once more let God's green earth and
    sunset air
    Old feelings waken ;
Through weary years of toil and strife
    and ill,
O, let me feel that my good angel still
    Hath not his trust forsaken.

And well do time and place befit my
    mood :
    Beneath the arms
Of this embracing wood, a good man
    made
His home, like Abraham resting in the
    shade
    Of Mamre's lonely palms.

Here, rich with autumn gifts of count-
    less years,
    The virgin soil
Turned from the share he guided, and
    in rain
And summer sunshine throve the fruits
    and grain
    Which blessed his honest toil.

Here, from his voyages on the stormy
    seas,
    Weary and worn,
He came to meet his children and to
    bless
The Giver of all good in thankfulness
    And praise for his return.

And here his neighbors gathered in to
    greet
    Their friend again,
Safe from the wave and the destroying
    gales,
Which reap untimely green Bermuda's
    vales,
    And vex the Carib main.

To hear the good man tell of simple truth,
    Sown in an hour
Of weakness in some far-off Indian isle,
From the parched bosom of a barren
    soil,
    Raised up in life and power :

How at those gatherings in Barbadian
    vales,
    A tendering love
Came o'er him, like the gentle rain from
    heaven,
And words of fitness to his lips were
    given,
    And strength as from above :

How the sad captive listened to the
    Word,
    Until his chain
Grew lighter, and his wounded spirit
    felt
The healing balm of consolation melt
    Upon its life-long pain :

How the armed warrior sat him down to
    hear
    Of Peace and Truth,
And the proud ruler and his Creole
    dame,
Jewelled and gorgeous in her beauty
    came,
    And fair and bright-eyed youth.

O, far away beneath New England's
    sky,
    Even when a boy,
Following my plough by Merrimack's
    green shore,
His simple record I have pondered o'er
    With deep and quiet joy.

And hence this scene, in sunset glory
    warm, —
      Its woods around,
Its still stream winding on in light and
    shade,
Its soft, green meadows and its upland
    glade, —
      To me is holy ground.

And dearer far than haunts where
    Genius keeps
      His vigils still ;
Than that where Avon's son of song is
    laid,
Of Vaucluse hallowed by its Petrarch's
    shade,
      Or Virgil's laurelled hill.

To the gray walls of fallen Paraclete,
      To Juliet's urn,
Fair Arno and Sorrento's orange-grove,
Where Tasso sang, let young Romance
    and Love
      Like brother pilgrims turn.

But here a deeper and serener charm
      To all is given ;
And blessed memories of the faithful
    dead
O'er wood and vale and meadow-stream
    have shed
      The holy hues of Heaven !

TO J. P.

Not as a poor requital of the joy
    With which my childhood heard that
    lay of thine,
    Which, like an echo of the song divine
At Bethlehem breathed above the Holy
    Boy,
Bore to my ear the Airs of Palestine, —
Not to the poet, but the man I bring
In friendship's fearless trust my offering :
How much it lacks I feel, and thou wilt
    see,
Yet well I know that thou hast deemed
    with me
Life all too earnest, and its time too
    short
For dreamy ease and Fancy's graceful
    sport ;
    And girded for thy constant strife with
    wrong,
Like Nehemiah fighting while he
    wrought

The broken walls of Zion, even thy
    song
Hath a rude martial tone, a blow in
    every thought !

THE CYPRESS–TREE OF CEYLON.

[Ibn Batuta, the celebrated Mussulman traveller of the fourteenth century, speaks of a cypress-tree in Ceylon, universally held sacred by the natives, the leaves of which were said to fall only at certain intervals, and he who had the happiness to find and eat one of them was restored, at once, to youth and vigor. The traveller saw several venerable Jogees, or saints, sitting silent and motionless under the tree, patiently awaiting the falling of a leaf.]

They sat in silent watchfulness
    The sacred cypress-tree about,
And, from beneath old wrinkled brows,
    Their failing eyes looked out.

Gray Age and Sickness waiting there
    Through weary night and lingering
    day, —
Grim as the idols at their side,
    And motionless as they.

Unheeded in the boughs above
    The song of Ceylon's birds was sweet ;
Unseen of them the island flowers
    Bloomed brightly at their feet.

O'er them the tropic night-storm swept,
    The thunder crashed on rock and hill ;
The cloud-fire on their eyeballs blazed,
    Yet there they waited still !

What was the world without to them ?
    The Moslem's sunset-call, — the dance
Of Ceylon's maids, — the passing gleam
    Of battle-flag and lance ?

They waited for that falling leaf
    Of which the wandering Jogees sing :
Which lends once more to wintry age
    The greenness of its spring.

O, if these poor and blinded ones
    In trustful patience wait to feel
O'er torpid pulse and failing limb
    A youthful freshness steal ;

Shall we, who sit beneath that Tree
    Whose healing leaves of life are shed,
In answer to the breath of prayer,
    Upon the waiting head ;

Not to restore our failing forms,
  And build the spirit's broken shrine,
But on the fainting SOUL to shed
  A light and life divine ;

Shall we grow weary in our watch,
  And murmur at the long delay ?
Impatient of our Father's time
  And his appointed way ?

Or shall the stir of outward things
  Allure and claim the Christian's eye,
When on the heathen watcher's ear
  Their powerless murmurs die ?

Alas ! a deeper test of faith
  Than prison cell or martyr's stake,
The self-abasing watchfulness
  Of silent prayer may make.

We gird us bravely to rebuke
  Our erring brother in the wrong, —
And in the ear of Pride and Power
  Our warning voice is strong.

Easier to smite with Peter's sword
  Than "watch one hour " in humbling
     prayer.
Life's "great things," like the Syrian
     lord,
  Our hearts can do and dare.

But oh ! we shrink from Jordan's side,
  From waters which alone can save ;
And murmur for Abana's banks
  And Pharpar's brighter wave.

O Thou, who in the garden's shade
  Didst wake thy weary ones again,
Who slumbered at that fearful hour
  Forgetful of thy pain ;

Bend o'er us now, as over them,
  And set our sleep-bound spirits free,
Nor leave us slumbering in the watch
  Our souls should keep with Thee !

A DREAM OF SUMMER.

BLAND as the morning breath of June
  The southwest breezes play ;
And, through its haze, the winter noon
  Seems warm as summer's day.
The snow-plumed Angel of the North
  Has dropped his icy spear ;
Again the mossy earth looks forth,
  Again the streams gush clear.

The fox his hillside cell forsakes,
  The muskrat leaves his nook,
The bluebird in the meadow brakes
  Is singing with the brook.
"Bear up, O Mother Nature ! " cry
  Bird, breeze, and streamlet free ;
"Our winter voices prophesy
  Of summer days to thee ! "

So, in those winters of the soul,
  By bitter blasts and drear
O'erswept from Memory's frozen pole,
  Will sunny days appear.
Reviving Hope and Faith, they show
  The soul its living powers,
And how beneath the winter's snow
  Lie germs of summer flowers !

The Night is mother of the Day,
  The Winter of the Spring,
And ever upon old Decay
  The greenest mosses cling.
Behind the cloud the starlight lurks,
  Through showers the sunbeams fall ;
For God, who loveth all his works,
  Has left his Hope with all !

4th 1st month, 1847.

TO ———,

WITH A COPY OF WOOLMAN'S JOURNAL.

  "Get the writings of John Woolman by
heart." — *Essays of Elia.*

MAIDEN ! with the fair brown tresses
  Shading o'er thy dreamy eye,
Floating on thy thoughtful forehead
  Cloud wreaths of its sky.

Youthful years and maiden beauty,
  Joy with them should still abide, —
Instinct take the place of Duty,
  Love, not Reason, guide.

Ever in the New rejoicing,
  Kindly beckoning back the Old,
Turning, with the gift of Midas,
  All things into gold.

And the passing shades of sadness
  Wearing even a welcome guise,
As, when some bright lake lies open
  To the sunny skies,

Every wing of bird above it,
  Every light cloud floating on,

Glitters like that flashing mirror
  In the self-same sun.

But upon thy youthful forehead
  Something like a shadow lies ;
And a serious soul is looking
  From thy earnest eyes.

With an early introversion,
  Through the forms of outward things,
Seeking for the subtle essence,
  And the hidden springs.

Deeper than the gilded surface
  Hath thy wakeful vision seen,
Farther than the narrow present
  Have thy journeyings been.

Thou hast midst Life's empty noises
  Heard the solemn steps of Time,
And the low mysterious voices
  Of another clime.

All the mystery of Being
  Hath upon thy spirit pressed, —
Thoughts which, like the Deluge wanderer,
  Find no place of rest :

That which mystic Plato pondered,
  That which Zeno heard with awe,
And the star-rapt Zoroaster
  In his night-watch saw.

From the doubt and darkness springing
  Of the dim, uncertain Past,
Moving to the dark still shadows
  O'er the Future cast,

Early hath Life's mighty question
  Thrilled within thy heart of youth,
With a deep and strong beseeching :
  WHAT and WHERE IS TRUTH ?

Hollow creed and ceremonial,
  Whence the ancient life hath fled,
Idle faith unknown to action,
  Dull and cold and dead.

Oracles, whose wire-worked meanings
  Only wake a quiet scorn, —
Not from these thy seeking spirit
  Hath its answer drawn.

But, like some tired child at even,
  On thy mother Nature's breast,
Thou, methinks, art vainly seeking
  Truth, and peace, and rest.

O'er that mother's rugged features
  Thou art throwing Fancy's veil,
Light and soft as woven moonbeams,
  Beautiful and frail !

O'er the rough chart of Existence,
  Rocks of sin and wastes of woe,
Soft airs breathe, and green leaves tremble,
  And cool fountains flow.

And to thee an answer cometh
  From the earth and from the sky,
And to thee the hills and waters
  And the stars reply.

But a soul-sufficing answer
  Hath no outward origin ;
More than Nature's many voices
  May be heard within.

Even as the great Augustine
  Questioned earth and sea and sky,[40]
And the dusty tomes of learning
  And old poesy.

But his earnest spirit needed
  More than outward Nature taught, —
More than blest the poet's vision
  Or the sage's thought.

Only in the gathered silence
  Of a calm and waiting frame
Light and wisdom as from Heaven
  To the seeker came.

Not to ease and aimless quiet
  Doth that inward answer tend,
But to works of love and duty
  As our being's end, —

Not to idle dreams and trances,
  Length of face, and solemn tone,
But to Faith, in daily striving
  And performance shown.

Earnest toil and strong endeavor
  Of a spirit which within
Wrestles with familiar evil
  And besetting sin ;

And without, with tireless vigor,
  Steady heart, and weapon strong,
In the power of truth assailing
  Every form of wrong.

Guided thus, how passing lovely
  Is the track of WOOLMAN's feet !

And his brief and simple record
  How serenely sweet !

O'er life's humblest duties throwing
  Light the earthling never knew,
Freshening all its dark waste places
  As with Hermon's dew.

All which glows in Pascal's pages, —
  All which sainted Guion sought,
Or the blue-eyed German Rahel
  Half-unconscious taught : —

Beauty, such as Goethe pictured,
  Such as Shelley dreamed of, shed
Living warmth and starry brightness
  Round that poor man's head.

Not a vain and cold ideal,
  Not a poet's dream alone,
But a presence warm and real,
  Seen and felt and known.

When the red right-hand of slaughter
  Moulders with the steel it swung,
When the name of seer and poet
  Dies on Memory's tongue,

All bright thoughts and pure shall gather
  Round that meek and suffering one, —
Glorious, like the seer-seen angel
  Standing in the sun !

Take the good man's book and ponder
  What its pages say to thee, —
Blessed as the hand of healing
  May its lesson be.

If it only serves to strengthen
  Yearnings for a higher good,
For the fount of living waters
  And diviner food ;

If the pride of human reason
  Feels its meek and still rebuke,

* Quailing like the eye of Peter
  From the Just One's look ! —

If with readier ear thou heedest
  What the Inward Teacher saith,
Listening with a willing spirit
  And a childlike faith, —

Thou mayst live to bless the giver,
  Who, himself but frail and weak,
Would at least the highest welfare
  Of another seek ;

And his gift, though poor and lowly
  It may seem to other eyes,
Yet may prove an angel holy
  In a pilgrim's guise.

LEGGETT'S MONUMENT.

" Ye build the tombs of the prophets."
  Holy Writ

YES, — pile the marble o'er him !   It is
    well
That ye who mocked him in his long
    stern strife,
And planted in the pathway of his life
The ploughshares of your hatred hot
    from hell,
Who clamored down the bold reformer
    when
He pleaded for his captive fellow-men,
Who spurned him in the market-place,
    and sought
Within thy walls, St. Tammany, to
    bind
In party chains the free and honest
    thought,
The angel utterance of an upright mind,
Well is it now that o'er his grave ye raise
The stony tribute of your tardy praise,
For not alone that pile shall tell to Fame
Of the brave heart beneath, but of the
    builders' shame !

SONGS OF LABOR,

AND OTHER POEMS.

DEDICATION.

I WOULD the gift I offer here
  Might graces from thy favor take,
And, seen through Friendship's at-
    mosphere,
On softened lines and coloring, wear
The unaccustomed light of beauty, for
  thy sake.

Few leaves of Fancy's spring remain :
  But what I have I give to thee, —
The o'er-sunned bloom of summer's
    plain,
And paler flowers, the latter rain
Calls from the westering slope of life's
  autumnal lea.

Above the fallen groves of green,
  Where youth's enchanted forest
    stood,
Dry root and mosséd trunk between,
A sober after-growth is seen,
As springs the pine where falls the gay-
  leafed maple wood !

Yet birds will sing, and breezes play
  Their leaf-harps in the sombre tree ;
And through the bleak and wintry day
It keeps its steady green alway, —
So, even my after-thoughts may have a
  charm for thee.

Art's perfect forms no moral need,
  And beauty is its own excuse ; [41]
But for the dull and flowerless weed
Some healing virtue still must plead,
And the rough ore must find its honors
  in its use.

So haply these, my simple lays
  Of homely toil, may serve to show
The orchard bloom and tasselled maize
That skirt and gladden duty's ways,
The unsung beauty hid life's common
  things below.

Haply from them the toiler, bent
  Above his forge or plough, may gain,

A manlier spirit of content,
And feel that life is wisest spent
Where the strong working hand makes
  strong the working brain.

The doom which to the guilty pair
  Without the walls of Eden came,
Transforming sinless ease to care
And rugged toil, no more shall bear
The burden of old crime, or mark of
  primal shame.

A blessing now, — a curse no more ;
  Since He, whose name we breathe
    with awe,
The coarse mechanic vesture wore, —
A poor man toiling with the poor,
In labor, as in prayer, fulfilling the same
  law.

THE SHIP-BUILDERS.

THE sky is ruddy in the east,
  The earth is gray below,
And, spectral in the river-mist,
  The ship's white timbers show.
Then let the sounds of measured stroke
  And grating saw begin ;
The broad-axe to the gnarléd oak,
  The mallet to the pin !

Hark ! — roars the bellows, blast on blast,
  The sooty smithy jars,
And fire-sparks, rising far and fast,
  Are fading with the stars.
All day for us the smith shall stand
  Beside that flashing forge ;
All day for us his heavy hand
  The groaning anvil scourge.

From far-off hills, the panting team
  For us is toiling near ;
For us the raftsmen down the stream
  Their island barges steer.
Rings out for us the axe-man's stroke
  In forests old and still, —
For us the century-circled oak
  Falls crashing down his hill.

Up ! — up ! — in nobler toil than ours
  No craftsmen bear a part :
We make of Nature's giant powers
  The slaves of human Art.
Lay rib to rib and beam to beam,
  And drive the treenails free ;
Nor faithless joint nor yawning seam
  Shall tempt the searching sea !

Where'er the keel of our good ship
  The sea's rough field shall plough, —
Where'er her tossing spars shall drip
  With salt-spray caught below, —
That ship must heed her master's beck,
  Her helm obey his hand,
And seamen tread her reeling deck
  As if they trod the land.

Her oaken ribs the vulture-beak
  Of Northern ice may peel ;
The sunken rock and coral peak
  May grate along her keel ;
And know we well the painted shell
  We give to wind and wave,
Must float, the sailor's citadel,
  Or sink, the sailor's grave !

Ho ! — strike away the bars and blocks,
  And set the good ship free !
Why lingers on these dusty rocks
  The young bride of the sea ?
Look ! how she moves adown the grooves,
  In graceful beauty now !
How lowly on the breast she loves
  Sinks down her virgin prow !

God bless her ! wheresoe'er the breeze
  Her snowy wing shall fan,
Aside the frozen Hebrides,
  Or sultry Hindostan !
Where'er, in mart or on the main,
  With peaceful flag unfurled,
She helps to wind the silken chain
  Of commerce round the world !

Speed on the ship ! — But let her bear
  No merchandise of sin,
No groaning cargo of despair
  Her roomy hold within ;
No Lethean drug for Eastern lands,
  Nor poison-draught for ours ;
But honest fruits of toiling hands
  And Nature's sun and showers.

Be hers the Prairie's golden grain,
  The Desert's golden sand,
The clustered fruits of sunny Spain,
  The spice of Morning-land !

8

Her pathway on the open main
  May blessings follow free,
And glad hearts welcome back again
  Her white sails from the sea !

THE SHOEMAKERS.

Ho ! workers of the old time styled
  The Gentle Craft of Leather !
Young brothers of the ancient guild,
  Stand forth once more together !
Call out again your long array,
  In the olden merry manner !
Once more, on gay St. Crispin's day,
  Fling out your blazoned banner !

Rap, rap ! upon the well-worn stone
  How falls the polished hammer !
Rap, rap ! the measured sound has grown
  A quick and merry clamor !
Now shape the sole ! now deftly curl
  The glossy vamp around it,
And bless the while the bright-eyed girl
  Whose gentle fingers bound it !

For you, along the Spanish main
  A hundred keels are ploughing ;
For you, the Indian on the plain
  His lasso-coil is throwing ;
For you, deep glens with hemlock dark
  The woodman's fire is lighting ;
For you, upon the oak's gray bark,
  The woodman's axe is smiting.

For you, from Carolina's pine
  The rosin-gum is stealing ;
For you, the dark-eyed Florentine
  Her silken skein is reeling ;
For you, the dizzy goatherd roams
  His rugged Alpine ledges;
For you, round all her shepherd homes,
  Bloom England's thorny hedges.

The foremost still, by day or night,
  On moated mound or heather,
Where'er the need of trampled right
  Brought toiling men together ;
Where the free burghers from the wall
  Defied the mail-clad master,
Than yours, at Freedom's trumpet-call,
  No craftsmen rallied faster.

Let foplings sneer, let fools deride, —
  Ye heed no idle scorner ;
Free hands and hearts are still your pride,
  And duty done, your honor.

Ye dare to trust, for honest fame,
  The jury Time empanels,
And leave to truth each noble name
  Which glorifies your annals.

Thy songs, Han Sachs, are living yet,
  In strong and hearty German ;
And Bloomfield's lay, and Gifford's wit,
  And patriot fame of Sherman ;
Still from his book, a mystic seer,
  The soul of Behmen teaches,
And England's priestcraft shakes to hear
  Of Fox's leathern breeches.

The foot is yours ; where'er it falls,
  It treads your well-wrought leather,
On earthen floor, in marble halls,
  On carpet, or on heather.
Still there the sweetest charm is found
  Of matron grace or vestal's,
As Hebe's foot bore nectar round
  Among the old celestials !

Rap, rap !—your stout and bluff brogan,
  With footsteps slow and weary,
May wander where the sky's blue span
  Shuts down upon the prairie.
On Beauty's foot your slippers glance,
  By Saratoga's fountains,
Or twinkle down the summer dance
  Beneath the Crystal Mountains !

The red brick to the mason's hand,
  The brown earth to the tiller's,
The shoe in yours shall wealth command,
  Like fairy Cinderella's !
As they who shunned the household maid
  Beheld the crown upon her,
So all shall see your toil repaid
  With hearth and home and honor.

Then let the toast be freely quaffed,
  In water cool and brimming, —
" All honor to the good old Craft,
  Its merry men and women ! "
Call out again your long array,
  In the old time's pleasant manner :
Once more, on gay St. Crispin's day,
  Fling out his blazoned banner !

THE DROVERS.

THROUGH heat and cold, and shower
    and sun,
  Still onward cheerly driving !
There 's life alone in duty done,
  And rest alone in striving.

But see ! the day is closing cool,
  The woods are dim before us ;
The white fog of the wayside pool
  Is creeping slowly o'er us.

The night is falling, comrades mine,
  Our footsore beasts are weary,
And through yon elms the tavern sign
  Looks out upon us cheery.
The landlord beckons from his door,
  His beechen fire is glowing ;
These ample barns, with feed in store,
  Are filled to overflowing.

From many a valley frowned across
  By brows of rugged mountains ;
From hillsides where, through spongy
    moss,
  Gush out the river fountains ;
From quiet farm-fields, green and low,
  And bright with blooming clover ;
From vales of corn the wandering crow
  No richer hovers over ;

Day after day our way has been,
  O'er many a hill and hollow ;
By lake and stream, by wood and glen,
  Our stately drove we follow.
Through dust-clouds rising thick and dun,
  As smoke of battle o'er us,
Their white horns glisten in the sun,
  Like plumes and crests before us.

We see them slowly climb the hill,
  As slow behind it sinking ;
Or, thronging close, from roadside rill,
  Or sunny lakelet, drinking.
Now crowding in the narrow road,
  In thick and struggling masses,
They glare upon the teamster's load,
  Or rattling coach that passes.

Anon, with toss of horn and tail,
  And paw of hoof, and bellow,
They leap some farmer's broken pale,
  O'er meadow-close or fallow.
Forth comes the startled goodman ; forth
  Wife, children, house-dog, sally,
Till once more on their dusty path
  The baffled truants rally.

We drive no starvelings, scraggy grown,
  Loose-legged, and ribbed and bony,
Like those who grind their noses down
  On pastures bare and stony, —
Lank oxen, rough as Indian dogs,
  And cows too lean for shadows,

Disputing feebly with the frogs
  The crop of saw-grass meadows !

In our good drove, so sleek and fair,
  No bones of leanness rattle ;
No tottering hide-bound ghosts are there,
  Or Pharaoh's evil cattle.
Each stately beeve bespeaks the hand
  That fed him unrepining ;
The fatness of a goodly land
  In each dun hide is shining.

We 've sought them where, in warmest
    nooks,
  The freshest feed is growing,
By sweetest springs and clearest brooks
  Through honeysuckle flowing ;
Wherever hillsides, sloping south,
  Are bright with early grasses,
Or, tracking green the lowland's drouth,
  The mountain streamlet passes.

But now the day is closing cool,
  The woods are dim before us,
The white fog of the wayside pool
  Is creeping slowly o'er us.
The cricket to the frog's bassoon
  His shrillest time is keeping ;
The sickle of yon setting moon
  The meadow-mist is reaping.

The night is falling, comrades mine,
  Our footsore beasts are weary,
And through yon elms the tavern sign
  Looks out upon us cheery.
To-morrow, eastward with our charge
  We 'll go to meet the dawning,
Ere yet the pines of Kéarsarge
  Have seen the sun of morning.

When snow-flakes o'er the frozen earth,
  Instead of birds, are flitting ;
When children throng the glowing
    hearth,
  And quiet wives are knitting ;
While in the fire-light strong and clear
  Young eyes of pleasure glisten,
To tales of all we see and hear
  The ears of home shall listen.

By many a Northern lake and hill,
  From many a mountain pasture,
Shall Fancy play the Drover still,
  And speed the long night faster.
Then let us on, through shower and sun,
  And heat and cold, be driving ;
There 's life alone in duty done,
  And rest alone in striving.

THE FISHERMEN.

HURRAH ! the seaward breezes
  Sweep down the bay amain ;
Heave up, my lads, the anchor !
  Run up the sail again !
Leave to the lubber landsmen
  The rail-car and the steed ;
The stars of heaven shall guide us,
  The breath of heaven shall speed.

From the hill-top looks the steeple,
  And the lighthouse from the sand ;
And the scattered pines are waving
  Their farewell from the land.
One glance, my lads, behind us,
  For the homes we leave one sigh,
Ere we take the change and chances
  Of the ocean and the sky.

Now, brothers, for the icebergs
  Of frozen Labrador,
Floating spectral in the moonshine,
  Along the low, black shore !
Where like snow the gannet's feathers
  On Brador's rocks are shed,
And the noisy murr are flying,
  Like black scuds, overhead ;

Where in mist the rock is hiding,
  And the sharp reef lurks below,
And the white squall smites in sum-
    mer,
  And the autumn tempests blow ;
Where, through gray and rolling vapor,
  From evening unto morn,
A thousand boats are hailing,
  Horn answering unto horn.

Hurrah ! for the Red Island,
  With the white cross on its crown !
Hurrah ! for Meccatina,
  And its mountains bare and brown !
Where the Caribou's tall antlers
  O'er the dwarf-wood freely toss,
And the footstep of the Mickmack
  Has no sound upon the moss.

There we 'll drop our lines, and gather
  Old Ocean's treasures in,
Where'er the mottled mackerel
  Turns up a steel-dark fin.
The sea 's our field of harvest,
  Its scaly tribes our grain ;
We 'll reap the teeming waters
  As at home they reap the plain !

Our wet hands spread the carpet,
  And light the hearth of home ;
From our fish, as in the old time,
  The silver coin shall come.
As the demon fled the chamber
  Where the fish of Tobit lay,
So ours from all our dwellings
  Shall frighten Want away.

Though the mist upon our jackets
  In the bitter air congeals,
And our lines wind stiff and slowly
  From off the frozen reels ;
Though the fog be dark around us,
  And the storm blow high and loud,
We will whistle down the wild wind,
  And laugh beneath the cloud !

In the darkness as in daylight,
  On the water as on land,
God's eye is looking on us,
  And beneath us is his hand !
Death will find us soon or later,
  On the deck or in the cot ;
And we cannot meet him better
  Than in working out our lot.

Hurrah ! — hurrah ! — the west-wind
  Comes freshening down the bay,
The rising sails are filling, —
  Give way, my lads, give way !
Leave the coward landsman clinging
  To the dull earth, like a weed, —
The stars of heaven shall guide us,
  The breath of heaven shall speed !

THE HUSKERS.

It was late in mild October, and the
    long autumnal rain
Had left the summer harvest-fields all
    green with grass again ;
The first sharp frosts had fallen, leaving
    all the woodlands gay
With the hues of summer's rainbow, or
    the meadow-flowers of May.

Through a thin, dry mist, that morning,
    the sun rose broad and red,
At first a rayless disk of fire, he bright-
    ened as he sped ;
Yet, even his noontide glory fell chas-
    tened and subdued,
On the cornfields and the orchards, and
    softly pictured wood.

And all that quiet afternoon, slow slop-
    ing to the night,
He wove with golden shuttle the haze
    with yellow light ;
Slanting through the painted beeches,
    he glorified the hill ;
And, beneath it, pond and meadow lay
    brighter, greener still.

And shouting boys in woodland haunts
    caught glimpses of that sky,
Flecked by the many-tinted leaves, and
    laughed, they knew not why ;
And school-girls, gay with aster-flowers,
    beside the meadow brooks,
Mingled the glow of autumn with the
    sunshine of sweet looks.

From spire and barn looked westerly the
    patient weathercocks ;
But even the birches on the hill stood
    motionless as rocks.
No sound was in the woodlands, save the
    squirrel's dropping shell,
And the yellow leaves among the boughs,
    low rustling as they fell.

The summer grains were harvested ; the
    stubble-fields lay dry,
Where June winds rolled, in light and
    shade, the pale green waves of rye ;
But still, on gentle hill-slopes, in valleys
    fringed with wood,
Ungathered, bleaching in the sun, the
    heavy corn crop stood.

Bent low, by autumn's wind and rain,
    through husks that, dry and sere,
Unfolded from their ripened charge, shone
    out the yellow ear ;
Beneath, the turnip lay concealed, in
    many a verdant fold,
And glistened in the slanting light the
    pumpkin's sphere of gold.

There wrought the busy harvesters ; and
    many a creaking wain
Bore slowly to the long barn-floor its load
    of husk and grain ;
Till broad and red, as when he rose, the
    sun sank down, at last,
And like a merry guest's farewell, the
    day in brightness passed.

And lo ! as through the western pines, on
    meadow, stream, and pond,
Flamed the red radiance of a sky, set all
    afire beyond,

Slowly o'er the eastern sea-bluffs a milder
    glory shone,
And the sunset and the moonrise were
    mingled into one !

As thus into the quiet night the twilight
    lapsed away,
And deeper in the brightening moon the
    tranquil shadows lay ;
From many a brown old farm-house, and
    hamlet without name,
Their milking and their home-tasks done,
    the merry huskers came.

Swung o'er the heaped-up harvest, from
    pitchforks in the mow,
Shone dimly down the lanterns on the
    pleasant scene below ;
The growing pile of husks behind, the
    golden ears before,
And laughing eyes and busy hands and
    brown cheeks glimmering o'er.

Half hidden in a quiet nook, serene of
    look and heart,
Talking their old times over, the old men
    sat apart ;
While, up and down the unhusked pile,
    or nestling in its shade,
At hide-and-seek, with laugh and shout,
    the happy children played.

Urged by the good host's daughter, a
    maiden young and fair,
Lifting to light her sweet blue eyes and
    pride of soft brown hair,
The master of the village school, sleek of
    hair and smooth of tongue,
To the quaint tune of some old psalm, a
    husking-ballad sung.

THE CORN-SONG.

HEAP high the farmer's wintry hoard !
  Heap high the golden corn !
No richer gift has Autumn poured
  From out her lavish horn !

Let other lands, exulting, glean
  The apple from the pine,
The orange from its glossy green,
  The cluster from the vine ;

We better love the hardy gift
  Our rugged vales bestow,

To cheer us when the storm shall drift
  Our harvest-fields with snow.

Through vales of grass and meads of
    flowers, .
  Our ploughs their furrows made,
While on the hills the sun and show-
    ers
  Of changeful April played.

We dropped the seed o'er hill and
    plain,
  Beneath the sun of May,
And frightened from our sprouting
    grain
  The robber crows away.

All through the long, bright days of
    June
  Its leaves grew green and fair,
And waved in hot midsummer's noon
  Its soft and yellow hair.

And now, with autumn's moonlit eves,
  Its harvest-time has come,
We pluck away the frosted leaves,
  And bear the treasure home.

There, richer than the fabled gift
  Apollo showered of old,
Fair hands the broken grain shall sift,
  And knead its meal of gold.

Let vapid idlers loll in silk
  Around their costly board ;
Give us the bowl of samp and milk,
  By homespun beauty poured !

Where'er the wide old kitchen hearth
  Sends up its smoky curls,
Who will not thank the kindly earth,
  And bless our farmer girls !

Then shame on all the proud and vain,
  Whose folly laughs to scorn
The blessing of our hardy grain,
  Our wealth of golden corn !

Let earth withhold her goodly root,
  Let mildew blight the rye,
Give to the worm the orchard's fruit,
  The wheat-field to the fly : .

But let the good old crop adorn
  The hills our fathers trod ;
Still let us, for his golden corn,
  Send up our thanks to God !

THE LUMBERMEN.

WILDLY round our woodland quarters,
  Sad-voiced Autumn grieves ;
Thickly down these swelling waters
  Float his fallen leaves.
Through the tall and naked timber,
  Column-like and old,
Gleam the sunsets of November,
  From their skies of gold.

O'er us, to the southland heading,
  Screams the gray wild-goose ;
On the night-frost sounds the treading
  Of the brindled moose.
Noiseless creeping, while we 're sleeping,
  Frost his task-work plies ;
Soon, his icy bridges heaping,
  Shall our log-piles rise.

When, with sounds of smothered thun-
    der,
  On some night of rain,
Lake and river break asunder
  Winter's weakened chain,
Down the wild March flood shall bear
    them
  To the saw-mill's wheel,
Or where Steam, the slave, shall tear
    them
  With his teeth of steel.

Be it starlight, be it moonlight,
  In these vales below,
When the earliest beams of sunlight
  Streak the mountain's snow,
Crisps the hoar-frost, keen and early,
  To our hurrying feet,
And the forest echoes clearly
  All our blows repeat.

Where the crystal Ambijejis
  Stretches broad and clear,
And Millnoket's pine-black ridges
  Hide the browsing deer :
Where, through lakes and wide morasses,
  Or through rocky walls,
Swift and strong, Penobscot passes
  White with foamy falls ;

Where, through clouds, are glimpses
    given
  Of Katahdin's sides, —
Rock and forest piled to heaven,
  Torn and ploughed by slides !
Far below, the Indian trapping,
  In the sunshine warm ;

Far above, the snow-cloud wrapping
  Half the peak in storm !

Where are mossy carpets better
  Than the Persian weaves,
And than Eastern perfumes sweeter
  Seem the fading leaves ;
And a music wild and solemn,
  From the pine-tree's height,
Rolls its vast and sea-like volume
  On the wind of night ;

Make we here our camp of winter ;
  And, through sleet and snow,
Pitchy knot and beechen splinter
  On our hearth shall glow.
Here, with mirth to lighten duty,
  We shall lack alone
Woman's smile and girlhood's beauty,
  Childhood's lisping tone.

But their hearth is brighter burning
  For our toil to-day ;
And the welcome of returning
  Shall our loss repay,
When, like seamen from the waters,
  From the woods we come,
Greeting sisters, wives, and daughters,
  Angels of our home !

Not for us the measured ringing
  From the village spire,
Not for us the Sabbath singing
  Of the sweet-voiced choir :
Ours the old, majestic temple,
  Where God's brightness shines
Down the dome so grand and ample,
  Propped by lofty pines !

Through each branch-enwoven skylight,
  Speaks He in the breeze,
As of old beneath the twilight
  Of lost Eden's trees !
For his ear, the inward feeling
  Needs no outward tongue ;
He can see the spirit kneeling
  While the axe is swung.

Heeding truth alone, and turning
  From the false and dim,
Lamp of toil or altar burning
  Are alike to Him.   ·
Strike, then, comrades ! — Trade is
    waiting
  On our rugged toil ;
Far ships waiting for the freighting
  Of our woodland spoil !

Ships, whose traffic links these highlands,
　Bleak and cold, of ours,
With the citron-planted islands
　Of a clime of flowers ;
To our frosts the tribute bringing
　Of eternal heats ;
In our lap of winter flinging
　Tropic fruits and sweets.

Cheerly, on the axe of labor,
　Let the sunbeams dance,
Better than the flash of sabre
　Or the gleam of lance !
Strike ! —With every blow is given
　Freer sun and sky,
And the long-hid earth to heaven
　Looks, with wondering eye !

Loud behind us grow the murmurs
　Of the age to come ;
Clang of smiths, and tread of farmers,
　Bearing harvest home !
Here her virgin lap with treasures
　Shall the green earth fill ;
Waving wheat and golden maize-ears
　Crown each beechen hill.

Keep who will the city's alleys,
　Take the smooth-shorn plain, —
Give to us the cedar valleys,
　Rocks and hills of Maine !
In our North-land, wild and woody,
　Let us still have part :
Rugged nurse and mother sturdy,
　Hold us to thy heart !

O, our free hearts beat the warmer
　For thy breath of snow ;
And our tread is all the firmer
　For thy rocks below.
Freedom, hand in hand with labor,
　Walketh strong and brave ;
On the forehead of his neighbor
　No man writeth Slave !

Lo, the day breaks ! old Katahdin's
　Pine-trees show its fires,
While from these dim forest gardens
　Rise their blackened spires.
Up, my comrades ! up and doing !
　Manhood's rugged play
Still renewing, bravely hewing
　Through the world our way !

MISCELLANEOUS.

THE ANGELS OF BUENA VISTA.

SPEAK and tell us, our Ximena, looking
　northward far away,
O'er the camp of the invaders, o'er the
　Mexican array,
Who is losing ? who is winning ? are they
　far or come they near ?
Look abroad, and tell us, sister, whither
　rolls the storm we hear.

"Down the hills of Angostura still the
　storm of battle rolls ;
Blood is flowing, men are dying ; God
　have mercy on their souls !"
Who is losing ? who is winning ?—
　"Over hill and over plain,
I see but smoke of cannon clouding
　through the mountain rain."

Holy Mother ! keep our brothers ! Look,
　Ximena, look once more.
"Still I see the fearful whirlwind rolling
　darkly as before,

Bearing on, in strange confusion, friend
　and foeman, foot and horse,
Like some wild and troubled torrent
　sweeping down its mountain
　course."

Look forth once more, Ximena ! "Ah !
　the smoke has rolled away ;
And I see the Northern rifles gleaming
　down the ranks of gray.
Hark ! that sudden blast of bugles ! there
　the troop of Minon wheels ;
There the Northern horses thunder, with
　the cannon at their heels.

"Jesu, pity ! how it thickens ! now re-
　treat and now advance !
Right against the blazing cannon shivers
　Puebla's charging lance !
Down they go, the brave young riders ;
　horse and foot together fall ;
Like a ploughshare in the fallow, through
　them ploughs the Northern ball."

Nearer came the storm and nearer, rolling fast and frightful on !
Speak, Ximena, speak and tell us, who
  has lost, and who has won ?
" Alas ! alas ! I know not ; friend and foe
  together fall,
O'er the dying rush the living : pray, my
  sisters, for them all !

" Lo ! the wind the smoke is lifting :
  Blessed Mother, save my brain !
I can see the wounded crawling slowly
  out from heaps of slain.
Now they stagger, blind and bleeding ;
  now they fall, and strive to rise ;
Hasten, sisters, haste and save them, lest
  they die before our eyes !

" O my heart's love ! O my dear one !
  lay thy poor head on my knee ;
Dost thou know the lips that kiss thee ?
  Canst thou hear me ? canst thou
  see ?
O my husband, brave and gentle ! O my
  Bernal, look once more
On the blessed cross before thee ! Mercy !
  mercy ! all is o'er ! "

Dry thy tears, my poor Ximena ; lay thy
  dear one down to rest ;
Let his hands be meekly folded, lay the
  cross upon his breast ;
Let his dirge be sung hereafter, and his
  funeral masses said :
To-day, thou poor bereaved one, the
  living ask thy aid.

Close beside her, faintly moaning, fair
  and young, a soldier lay,
Torn with shot and pierced with lances,
  bleeding slow his life away ;
But, as tenderly before him the lorn
  Ximena knelt,
She saw the Northern eagle shining on
  his pistol-belt.

With a stifled cry of horror straight she
  turned away her head ;
With a sad and bitter feeling looked she
  back upon her dead ;
But she heard the youth's low moaning,
  and his struggling breath of pain,
And she raised the cooling water to his
  parching lips again.

Whispered low the dying soldier, pressed
  her hand and faintly smiled :
Was that pitying face his mother's ? did
  she watch beside her child ?
All his stranger words with meaning her
  woman's heart supplied ;
With her kiss upon his forehead,
  " Mother ! " murmured he, and
  died !

" A bitter curse upon them, poor boy,
  who led thee forth,
From some gentle, sad-eyed mother,
  weeping, lonely, in the North ! "
Spake the mournful Mexic woman, as
  she laid him with her dead,
And turned to soothe the living, and
  bind the wounds which bled.

Look forth once more, Ximena ! " Like
  a cloud before the wind
Rolls the battle down the mountains,
  leaving blood and death behind ;
Ah ! they plead in vain for mercy ; in
  the dust the wounded strive ;
Hide your faces, holy angels ! O thou
  Christ of God, forgive ! "

Sink, O Night, among thy mountains ;
  let the cool, gray shadows fall ;
Dying brothers, fighting demons, drop
  thy curtain over all !
Through the thickening winter twilight,
  wide apart the battle rolled,
In its sheath the sabre rested, and the
  cannon's lips grew cold.

But the noble Mexic women still their
  holy task pursued,
Through that long, dark night of sorrow,
  worn and faint and lacking food.
Over weak and suffering brothers, with
  a tender care they hung,
And the dying foeman blessed them in
  a strange and Northern tongue.

Not wholly lost, O Father ! is this evil
  world of ours ;
Upward, through its blood and ashes,
  spring afresh the Eden flowers ;
From its smoking hell of battle, Love
  and Pity send their prayer,
And still thy white-winged angels hover
  dimly in our air !

FORGIVENESS.

My heart was heavy, for its trust had been
  Abused, its kindness answered with
    foul wrong ;
So, turning gloomily from my fellow-
    men,
  One summer Sabbath day I strolled
    among
The green mounds of the village burial-
    place ;
  Where, pondering how all human love
    and hate
  Find one sad level ; and how, soon or
    late,
Wronged and wrongdoer, each with
    meekened face,
  And cold hands folded over a still heart,
Pass the green threshold of our common
    grave,
  Whither all footsteps tend, whence
    none depart,
Awed for myself, and pitying my race,
Our common sorrow, like a mighty wave,
  Swept all my pride away, and trembling
    I forgave !

BARCLAY OF URY.[42]

Up the streets of Aberdeen,
By the kirk and college green,
    Rode the Laird of Ury ;
Close behind him, close beside,
Foul of mouth and evil-eyed,
    Pressed the mob in fury.

Flouted him the drunken churl,
Jeered at him the serving-girl,
    Prompt to please her master ;
And the begging carlin, late
Fed and clothed at Ury's gate,
    Cursed him as he passed her.

Yet, with calm and stately mien,
Up the streets of Aberdeen
    Came he slowly riding :
And, to all he saw and heard,
Answering not with bitter word,
    Turning not for chiding.

Came a troop with broadswords swinging,
Bits and bridles sharply ringing,
    Loose and free and froward ;
Quoth the foremost, " Ride him down !
Push him ! prick him ! through the town
    Drive the Quaker coward ! "

But from out the thickening crowd
Cried a sudden voice and loud :
    " Barclay ! Ho ! a Barclay ! "
And the old man at his side
Saw a comrade, battle tried,
    Scarred and sunburned darkly ;

Who with ready weapon bare,
Fronting to the troopers there,
    Cried aloud : " God save us,
Call ye coward him who stood
Ankle deep in Lutzen's blood,
    With the brave Gustavus ? "

" Nay, I do not need thy sword,
Comrade mine," said Ury's lord ;
    " Put it up, I pray thee :
Passive to his holy will,
Trust I in my Master still,
    Even though he slay me.

" Pledges of thy love and faith,
Proved on many a field of death,
    Not by me are needed."
Marvelled much that henchman bold,
That his laird, so stout of old,
    Now so meekly pleaded.

" Woe 's the day ! " he sadly said,
With a slowly shaking head,
    And a look of pity ;
" Ury's honest lord reviled,
Mock of knave and sport of child,
    In his own good city !

" Speak the word, and, master mine,
As we charged on Tilly's line,
    And his Walloon lancers,
Smiting through their midst we 'll teach
Civil look and decent speech
    To these boyish prancers ! "

" Marvel not, mine ancient friend,
Like beginning, like the end " :
    Quoth the Laird of Ury,
" Is the sinful servant more
Than his gracious Lord who bore
    Bonds and stripes in Jewry ?

" Give me joy that in his name
I can bear, with patient frame,
    All these vain ones offer ;
While for them He suffereth long,
Shall I answer wrong with wrong,
    Scoffing with the scoffer ?

" Happier I, with loss of all,
Hunted, outlawed, held in thrall,
    With few friends to greet me,
Than when reeve and squire were seen,
Riding out from Aberdeen,
    With bared heads to meet me.

" When each goodwife, o'er and o'er,
Blessed me as I passed her door ;
    And the snooded daughter,
Through her casement glancing down,
Smiled on him who bore renown
    From red fields of slaughter.

" Hard to feel the stranger's scoff,
Hard the old friend's falling off,
    Hard to learn forgiving :
But the Lord his own rewards,
And his love with theirs accords,
    Warm and fresh and living.

" Through this dark and stormy night
Faith beholds a feeble light
    Up the blackness streaking ;
Knowing God's own time is best,
In a patient hope I rest
    For the full day-breaking ! "

So the Laird of Ury said,
Turning slow his horse's head
    Towards the Tolbooth prison,
Where, through iron grates, he heard
Poor disciples of the Word
    Preach of Christ arisen !

Not in vain, Confessor old,
Unto us the tale is told
    Of thy day of trial ;
Every age on him, who strays
From its broad and beaten ways,
    Pours its sevenfold vial.

Happy he whose inward ear
Angel comfortings can hear,
    O'er the rabble's laughter ;
And while Hatred's fagots burn,
Glimpses through the smoke discern
    Of the good hereafter.

Knowing this, that never yet
Share of Truth was vainly set
    In the world's wide fallow ;
After hands shall sow the seed,
After hands from hill and mead
    Reap the harvests yellow.

Thus, with somewhat of the Seer,
Must the moral pioneer

From the Future borrow ;
Clothe the waste with dreams of grain,
And, on midnight's sky of rain,
    Paint the golden morrow !

WHAT THE VOICE SAID.

MADDENED by Earth's wrong and evil,
    " Lord ! " I cried in sudden ire,
" From thy right hand, clothed wit
        thunder,
    Shake the bolted fire !

" Love is lost, and Faith is dying ;
    With the brute the man is sold ;
And the dropping blood of labor
    Hardens into gold.

" Here the dying wail of Famine,
    There the battle's groan of pain ;
And, in silence, smooth-faced Mammo[n]
    Reaping men like grain.

" ' Where is God, that we should fe[ar]
        Him ?'
    Thus the earth-born Titans say ;
' God ! if thou art living, hear us !'
    Thus the weak ones pray."

"Thou, the patient Heaven upbrai[d]
        ing,"
    Spake a solemn Voice within ;
" Weary of our Lord's forbearance,
    Art thou free from sin ?

" Fearless brow to Him uplifting,
    Canst thou for his thunders call,
Knowing that to guilt's attraction
    Evermore they fall ?

" Know'st thou not all germs of evil
    In thy heart await their time ?
Not thyself, but God's restraining,
    Stays their growth of crime.

" Couldst thou boast, O child of weak
        ness !
    O'er the sons of wrong and strife,
Were their strong temptations planted
    In thy path of life ?

" Thou hast seen two streamlets gush
        ing
    From one fountain, clear and free,
But by widely varying channels
    Searching for the sea.

" Glideth one through greenest valleys,
　Kissing them with lips still sweet ;
One, mad roaring down the mountains,
　Stagnates at their feet.

" Is it choice whereby the Parsee
　Kneels before his mother's fire ?
In his black tent did the Tartar
　Choose his wandering sire ?

" He alone, whose hand is bounding
　Human power and human will,
Looking through each soul's surrounding,
　Knows its good or ill.

" For thyself, while wrong and sorrow
　Make to thee their strong appeal,
Coward wert thou not to utter
　What the heart must feel.

" Earnest words must needs be spoken
　When the warm heart bleeds or burns
With its scorn of wrong, or pity
　For the wronged, by turns.

" But, by all thy nature's weakness,
　Hidden faults and follies known,
Be thou, in rebuking evil,
　Conscious of thine own.

" Not the less shall stern-eyed Duty
　To thy lips her trumpet set,
But with harsher blasts shall mingle
　Wailings of regret."

Cease not, Voice of holy speaking,
　Teacher sent of God, be near,
Whispering through the day's cool silence,
　Let my spirit hear !

So, when thoughts of evil-doers
　Waken scorn, or hatred move,
Shall a mournful fellow-feeling
　Temper all with love.

TO DELAWARE.

[Written during the discussion in the Legisla-
ture of that State, in the winter of 1846-47, of a
bill for the abolition of slavery.]

THRICE welcome to thy sisters of the East,
　To the strong tillers of a rugged home,
With spray-wet locks to Northern winds
　released,
　And hardy feet o'erswept by ocean's
　foam ;

And to the young nymphs of the golden
　West,
　Whose harvest mantles, fringed with
　prairie bloom,
Trail in the sunset, — O redeemed and
　blest,
　To the warm welcome of thy sisters
　come !
Broad Pennsylvania, down her sail-white
　bay
Shall give thee joy, and Jersey from
　her plains,
And the great lakes, where echo, free
　alway,
Moaned never shoreward with the
　clank of chains,
Shall weave new sun-bows in their toss-
　ing spray,
And all their waves keep grateful holiday.
And, smiling on thee through her moun-
　tain rains,
　Vermont shall bless thee ; and the
　Granite peaks,
And vast Katahdin o'er his woods, shall
　wear
Their snow-crowns brighter in the cold
　keen air ;
　And Massachusetts, with her rugged
　cheeks
O'errun with grateful tears, shall turn
　to thee,
　When, at thy bidding, the electric wire
　Shall tremble northward with its words
　of fire ;
Glory and praise to God ! another State
　is free !

WORSHIP.

" Pure religion, and undefiled, before God and
the Father is this: To visit the widows and the
fatherless in their affliction, and to keep himself
unspotted from the world."— James i. 27.

THE Pagan's myths through marble lips
　are spoken,
　And ghosts of old Beliefs still flit and
　moan
Round fane and altar overthrown and
　broken,
　O'er tree-grown barrow and gray ring
　of stone.

Blind Faith had martyrs in those old
　high places,
　The Syrian hill grove and the Druid's
　wood,

With mother's offering, to the Fiend's
    embraces,
Bone of their bone, and blood of their
    own blood.

Red altars, kindling through that night
    of error,
Smoked with warm blood beneath the
    cruel eye
Of lawless Power and sanguinary Terror,
Throned on the circle of a pitiless sky;

Beneath whose baleful shadow, overcast-
    ing
All heaven above, and blighting earth
    below,
The scourge grew red, the lip grew pale
    with fasting,
And man's oblation was his fear and
    woe !

Then through great temples swelled the
    dismal moaning
Of dirge-like music and sepulchral
    prayer ;
Pale wizard priests, o'er occult symbols
    droning,
Swung their white censers in the bur-
    dened air :

As if the pomp of rituals, and the savor
Of gums and spices could the Unseen
    One please ;
As if his ear could bend, with childish
    favor,
To the poor flattery of the organ keys !

Feet red from war-fields trod the church
    aisles holy,
With trembling reverence : and the
    oppressor there,
Kneeling before his priest, abased and
    lowly,
Crushed human hearts beneath his
    knee of prayer.

Not such the service the benignant Father
Requireth at his earthly children's
    hands :
Not the poor offering of vain rites, but
    rather
The simple duty man from man de-
    mands.

For Earth he asks it : the full joy of
    Heaven
Knoweth no change of waning or in-
    crease ;

The great heart of the Infinite beats even,
Untroubled flows the river of his peace.

He asks no taper lights, on high sur-
    rounding
The priestly altar and the saintly grave,
No dolorous chant nor organ music sound-
    ing,
Nor incense clouding up the twilight
    nave.

For he whom Jesus loved hath truly
    spoken :
The holier worship which he deigns to
    bless
Restores the lost, and binds the spirit
    broken,
And feeds the widow and the fatherless !

Types of our human weakness and our
    sorrow !
Who lives unhaunted by his loved ones
    dead ?
Who, with vain longing, seeketh not to
    borrow
From stranger eyes the home lights
    which have fled ?

O brother man ! fold to thy heart thy
    brother ;
Where pity dwells, the peace of God
    is there ;
To worship rightly is to love each other,
Each smile a hymn, each kindly deed
    a prayer.

Follow with reverent steps the great ex-
    ample
Of Him whose holy work was " doing
    good " ;
So shall the wide earth seem our Father's
    temple,
Each loving life a psalm of gratitude.

Then shall all shackles fall ; the stormy
    clangor
Of wild war music o'er the earth shall
    cease ;
Love shall tread out the baleful fire of
    anger,
And in its ashes plant the tree of peace !

THE DEMON OF THE STUDY.

THE Brownie sits in the Scotchman's
    room,
And eats his meat and drinks his ale,

And beats the maid with her unused
  broom,
And the lazy lout with his idle flail,
But he sweeps the floor and threshes the
  corn,
And hies him away ere the break of
  dawn.

The shade of Denmark fled from the sun,
  And the Cocklane ghost from the barn-
  loft cheer,
The fiend of Faust was a faithful one,
  Agrippa's demon wrought in fear,
And the devil of Martin Luther sat
By the stout monk's side in social chat.

The Old Man of the Sea, on the neck of
  him
Who seven times crossed the deep,
Twined closely each lean and withered
  limb,
  Like the nightmare in one's sleep.
But he drank of the wine, and Sindbad cast
The evil weight from his back at last.

But the demon that cometh day by day
  To my quiet room and fireside nook,
Where the casement light falls dim and
  gray
On faded painting and ancient book,
Is a sorrier one than any whose names
Are chronicled well by good King James.

No bearer of burdens like Caliban,
  No runner of errands like Ariel,
He comes in the shape of a fat old man,
  Without rap of knuckle or pull of bell ;
And whence he comes, or whither he goes,
I know as I do of the wind which blows.

A stout old man with a greasy hat
  Slouched heavily down to his dark,
  red nose,
And two gray eyes enveloped in fat,
  Looking through glasses with iron
  bows.
Read ye, and heed ye, and ye who can,
Guard well your doors from that old
  man !

He comes with a careless "How d' ye do ?"
  And seats himself in my elbow-chair ;
And my morning paper and pamphlet new
  Fall forthwith under his special care,
And he wipes his glasses and clears his
  throat,
And, button by button, unfolds his coat.

And then he reads from paper and book,
  In a low and husky asthmatic tone,
With the stolid sameness of posture and
  look
Of one who reads to himself alone ;
And hour after hour on my senses come
That husky wheeze and that dolorous
  hum.

The price of stocks, the auction sales,
  The poet's song and the lover's glee,
The horrible murders, the seaboard gales,
  The marriage list, and the *jeu d'esprit*,
All reach my ear in the self-same tone, —
I shudder at each, but the fiend reads on !

O, sweet as the lapse of water at noon
  O'er the mossy roots of some forest tree,
The sigh of the wind in the woods of June,
  Or sound of flutes o'er a moonlight sea,
Or the low soft music, perchance, which
  seems
To float through the slumbering singer's
  dreams, —

So sweet, so dear is the silvery tone,
  Of her in whose features I sometimes
  look,
As I sit at eve by her side alone,
  And we read by turns from the self-
  same book, —
Some tale perhaps of the olden time,
Some lover's romance or quaint old rhyme.

Then when the story is one of woe, —
  Some prisoner's plaint through his dun-
  geon-bar,
Her blue eye glistens with tears, and low
  Her voice sinks down like a moan afar ;
And I seem to hear that prisoner's wail,
And his face looks on me worn and pale.

And when she reads some merrier song,
  Her voice is glad as an April bird's,
And when the tale is of war and wrong,
  A trumpet's summons is in her words,
And the rush of the hosts I seem to hear,
And see the tossing of plume and spear ! —

O, pity me then, when, day by day,
  The stout fiend darkens my parlor door ;
And reads me perchance the self-same lay
  Which melted in music, the night be-
  fore,
From lips as the lips of Hylas sweet,
And moved like twin roses which zephyrs
  meet !

I cross my floor with a nervous tread,
    I whistle and laugh and sing and shout,
I flourish my cane above his head,
    And stir up the fire to roast him out ;
I topple the chairs, and drum on the pane,
And press my hands on my ears, in vain !

I 've studied Glanville and James the wise,
    And wizard black-letter tomes which
        treat
Of demons of every name and size,
    Which a Christian man is presumed to
        meet,
But never a hint and never a line
Can I find of a reading fiend like mine.

I 've crossed the Psalter with Brady and
    Tate,
    And laid the Primer above them all,
I 've nailed a horseshoe over the grate,
    And hung a wig to my parlor wall
Once worn by a learned Judge, they
    say,
At Salem court in the witchcraft day !

" *Conjuro te, sceleratissime,*
    Abire ad tuum locum ! " — still
Like a visible nightmare he sits by me, —
    The exorcism has lost its skill ;
And I hear again in my haunted room
The husky wheeze and the dolorous hum !

Ah ! — commend me to Mary Magdalen
    With her sevenfold plagues, — to the
        wandering Jew,
To the terrors which haunted Orestes
    when
    The furies his midnight curtains drew,
But charm him off, ye who charm him
    can,
That reading demon, that fat old man !

THE PUMPKIN.

O, GREENLY and fair in the lands of the
    sun,
The vines of the gourd and the rich
    melon run,
And the rock and the tree and the cot-
    tage enfold,
With broad leaves all greenness and
    blossoms all gold,
Like that which o'er Nineveh's prophet
    once grew,
While he waited to know that his warn-
    ing was true,

And longed for the storm-cloud, and
    listened in vain
For the rush of the whirlwind and red
    fire-rain.

On the banks of the Xenil the dark
    Spanish maiden
Comes up with the fruit of the tangled
    vine laden ;
And the Creole of Cuba laughs out to
    behold
Through orange-leaves shining the broad
    spheres of gold ;
Yet with dearer delight from his home
    in the North,
On the fields of his harvest the Yankee
    looks forth,
Where crook-necks are coiling and yel-
    low fruit shines,
And the sun of September melts down
    on his vines.

Ah ! on Thanksgiving day, when from
    East and from West,
From North and from South come the
    pilgrim and guest,
When the gray-haired New-Englander
    sees round his board
The old broken links of affection re-
    stored,
When the care-wearied man seeks his
    mother once more,
And the worn matron smiles where the
    girl smiled before,
What moistens the lip and what bright-
    ens the eye ?
What calls back the past, like the rich
    Pumpkin pie ?

O, — fruit loved of boyhood ! — the old
    days recalling,
When wood-grapes were purpling and
    brown nuts were falling !
When wild, ugly faces we carved in its
    skin,
Glaring out through the dark with a
    candle within !
When we laughed round the corn-heap,
    with hearts all in tune,
Our chair a broad pumpkin, — our lan-
    tern the moon,
Telling tales of the fairy who travelled
    like steam,
In a pumpkin-shell coach, with two rats
    for her team !

Then thanks for thy present ! — none
    sweeter or better
E'er smoked from an oven or circled a
    platter !
Fairer hands never wrought at a pastry
    more fine,
Brighter eyes never watched o'er its
    baking, than thine !
And the prayer, which my mouth is too
    full to express,
Swells my heart that thy shadow may
    never be less,
That the days of thy lot may be length-
    ened below,
And the fame of thy worth like a pump-
    kin-vine grow,
And thy life be as sweet, and its last
    sunset sky
Golden-tinted and fair as thy own
    Pumpkin pie !

EXTRACT FROM "A NEW ENG-LAND LEGEND."

How has New England's romance fled,
    Even as a vision of the morning !
Its rites foredone, — its guardians dead, —
    Its priestesses, bereft of dread,
Waking the veriest urchin's scorning !
Gone like the Indian wizard's yell
    And fire-dance round the magic rock,
Forgotten like the Druid's spell
    At moonrise by his holy oak !
No more along the shadowy glen,
Glide the dim ghosts of murdered men ;
No more the unquiet churchyard dead
Glimpse upward from their turfy bed,
    Startling the traveller, late and lone ;
As, on some night of starless weather,
They silently commune together,
    Each sitting on his own head-stone !
The roofless house, decayed, deserted,
Its living tenants all departed,
No longer rings with midnight revel
Of witch, or ghost, or goblin evil ;
No pale blue flame sends out its flashes
Through creviced roof and shattered
    sashes ! —
The witch-grass round the hazel spring
May sharply to the night-air sing,
But there no more shall withered hags
Refresh at ease their broomstick nags,
Or taste those hazel-shadowed waters
As beverage meet for Satan's daughters ;
No more their mimic tones be heard, —
The mew of cat, — the chirp of bird, —

Shrill blending with the hoarser laughter
Of the fell demon following after !
The cautious goodman nails no more
A horseshoe on his outer door,
Lest some unseemly hag should fit
To his own mouth her bridle-bit, —
The goodwife's churn no more refuses
Its wonted culinary uses
Until, with heated needle burned,
The witch has to her place returned !
Our witches are no longer old
And wrinkled beldames, Satan-sold,
But young and gay and laughing crea-
    tures,
With the heart's sunshine on their fea-
    tures, —
Their sorcery — the light which dances
Where the raised lid unveils its glances;
Or that low-breathed and gentle tone,
    The music of Love's twilight hours,
Soft, dream-like, as a fairy's moan
    Above her nightly closing flowers,
Sweeter than that which sighed of yore
Along the charmed Ausonian shore !
Even she, our own weird heroine,
Sole Pythoness of ancient Lynn,
Sleeps calmly where the living laid her
And the wide realm of sorcery,
Left by its latest mistress free,
    Hath found no gray and skilled in-
    vader :
So perished Albion's "glammarye,"
    With him in Melrose Abbey sleeping,
His charmed torch beside his knee,
That even the dead himself might see
    The magic scroll within his keeping.
And now our modern Yankee sees
Nor omens, spells, nor mysteries ;
And naught above, below, around,
Of life or death, of sight or sound,
    Whate'er its nature, form, or look,
Excites his terror or surprise, —
All seeming to his knowing eyes
Familiar as his "catechize,"
Or "Webster's Spelling-Book."

HAMPTON BEACH.

THE sunlight glitters keen and bright,
    Where, miles away,
Lies stretching to my dazzled sight
A luminous belt, a misty light,
Beyond the dark pine bluffs and wastes
    of sandy gray.

The tremulous shadow of the Sea !
    Against its ground

Of silvery light, rock, hill, and tree,
Still as a picture, clear and free,
With varying outline mark the coast for
    miles around.

On — on — we tread with loose-flung
    rein
    Our seaward way,
Through dark-green fields and blos-
    soming grain,
Where the wild brier-rose skirts the
    lane,
And bends above our heads the flowering
    locust spray.

Ha ! like a kind hand on my brow
    Comes this fresh breeze,
Cooling its dull and feverish glow,
While through my being seems to flow
The breath of a new life, — the healing
    of the seas !

Now rest we, where this grassy mound
    His feet hath set
In the great waters, which have bound
His granite ankles greenly round
With long and tangled moss, and weeds
    with cool spray wet.

Good by to pain and care ! I take
    Mine ease to-day :
Here where these sunny waters break,
And ripples this keen breeze, I shake
All burdens from the heart, all weary
    thoughts away.

I draw a freer breath — I seem
    Like all I see —
Waves in the sun — the white-winged
    gleam
Of sea-birds in the slanting beam —
And far-off sails which flit before the
    south-wind free.

So when Time's veil shall fall asunder,
    The soul may know
No fearful change, nor sudden wonder,
Nor sink the weight of mystery under,
But with the upward rise, and with the
    vastness grow.

And all we shrink from now may seem
    No new revealing ;
Familiar as our childhood's stream,
Or pleasant memory of a dream
The loved and cherished Past upon the
    new life stealing.

Serene and mild the untried light
    May have its dawning ;
And, as in summer's northern night
The evening and the dawn unite,
The sunset hues of Time blend with the
    soul's new morning.

I sit alone ; in foam and spray
    Wave after wave
Breaks on the rocks which, stern and
    gray,
Shoulder the broken tide away,
Or murmurs hoarse and strong through
    mossy cleft and cave.

What heed I of the dusty land
    And noisy town ?
I see the mighty deep expand
From its white line of glimmering sand
To where the blue of heaven on bluer
    waves shuts down !

In listless quietude of mind,
    I yield to all
The change of cloud and wave and
    wind
And passive on the flood reclined,
I wander with the waves, and with them
    rise and fall.

But look, thou dreamer !— wave and
    shore
    In shadow lie ;
The night-wind warns me back once
    more
To where, my native hill-tops o'er,
Bends like an arch of fire the glowing
    sunset sky.

So then, beach, bluff, and wave, fare-
    well !
    I bear with me
No token stone nor glittering shell,
But long and oft shall Memory tell
Of this brief thoughtful hour of musing
    by the Sea.

LINES,

WRITTEN ON HEARING OF THE DEATH
OF SILAS WRIGHT OF NEW YORK.

As they who, tossing midst the storm at
    night,
    While turning shoreward, where a
    beacon shone,

Meet the walled blackness of the
heaven alone,
So, on the turbulent waves of party tossed,
In gloom and tempest, men have seen
thy light
Quenched in the darkness. At thy
hour of noon,
While life was pleasant to thy undimmed
sight,
And, day by day, within thy spirit grew
A holier hope than young Ambition knew,
As through thy rural quiet, not in vain,
Pierced the sharp thrill of Freedom's cry
of pain,
Man of the millions, thou art lost too
soon !
Portents at which the bravest stand
aghast, —
The birth-throes of a Future, strange
and vast,
Alarm the land ; yet thou, so wise
and strong,
Suddenly summoned to the burial bed,
Lapped in its slumbers deep and ever
long,
Hear'st not the tumult surging overhead.
Who now shall rally Freedom's scatter-
ing host ?
Who wear the mantle of the leader lost ?
Who stay the march of slavery ? He
whose voice
Hath called thee from thy task-field
shall not lack
Yet bolder champions, to beat bravely
back
The wrong which, through his poor ones,
reaches Him :
Yet firmer hands shall Freedom's torch-
lights trim,
And wave them high across the abys-
mal black,
Till bound, dumb millions there shall
see them and rejoice.

10th mo., 1847.

LINES,

ACCOMPANYING MANUSCRIPTS PRESENT-
ED TO A FRIEND.

'T is said that in the Holy Land
The angels of the place have blessed
The pilgrim's bed of desert sand,
Like Jacob's stone of rest.

That down the hush of Syrian skies
Some sweet-voiced saint at twilight
sings

The song whose holy symphonies
Are beat by unseen wings ;

Till starting from his sandy bed,
The wayworn wanderer looks to see
The halo of an angel's head
Shine through the tamarisk-tree.

So through the shadows of my way
Thy smile hath fallen soft and clear,
So at the weary close of day
Hath seemed thy voice of cheer.

That pilgrim pressing to his goal
May pause not for the vision's sake,
Yet all fair things within his soul
The thought of it shall wake :

The graceful palm-tree by the well,
Seen on the far horizon's rim ;
The dark eyes of the fleet gazelle,
Bent timidly on him ;

Each pictured saint, whose golden hair
Streams sunlike through the convent's
gloom ;
Pale shrines of martyrs young and fair,
And loving Mary's tomb ;

And thus each tint or shade which falls,
From sunset cloud or waving tree,
Along my pilgrim path, recalls
The pleasant thought of thee.

Of one in sun and shade the same,
In weal and woe my steady friend,
Whatever by that holy name
The angels comprehend.

Not blind to faults and follies, thou
Hast never failed the good to see,
Nor judged by one unseemly bough
The upward-struggling tree.

These light leaves at thy feet I lay, —
Poor common thoughts on common
things,
Which time is shaking, day by day,
Like feathers from his wings, —

Chance shootings from a frail life-tree,
To nurturing care but little known,
Their good was partly learned of thee,
Their folly is my own.

That tree still clasps the kindly mould,
Its leaves still drink the twilight dew,

And weaving its pale green with gold,
  Still shines the sunlight through.

There still the morning zephyrs play,
  And there at times the spring bird
    sings,
And mossy trunk and fading spray
  Are flowered with glossy wings.

Yet, even in genial sun and rain,
  Root, branch, and leaflet fail and fade ;
The wanderer on its lonely plain
  Erelong shall miss its shade.

O friend beloved, whose curious skill
  Keeps bright the last year's leaves
    and flowers,
With warm, glad summer thoughts to
    fill
  The cold, dark, winter hours !

Pressed on thy heart, the leaves I bring
  May well defy the wintry cold,
Until, in Heaven's eternal spring,
  Life's fairer ones unfold.

THE REWARD.

Who, looking backward from his man-
    hood's prime,
Sees not the spectre of his misspent time ?
    And, through the shade
Of funeral cypress planted thick behind,
Hears no reproachful whisper on the
    wind
    From his loved dead ?

Who bears no trace of passion's evil
    force ?
Who shuns thy sting, O terrible Re-
    morse ? —
    Who does not cast
On the thronged pages of his memory's
    book,
At times, a sad and half-reluctant look,
    Regretful of the past ?

Alas ! — the evil which we fain would
    shun
We do, and leave the wished-for good
    undone :
    Our strength to-day
Is but to-morrow's weakness, prone to
    fall ;
Poor, blind, unprofitable servants all
    Are we alway.

Yet who, thus looking backward o'er
    his years,
Feels not his eyelids wet with grateful
    tears,
    If he hath been
Permitted, weak and sinful as he was,
To cheer and aid, in some ennobling
    cause,
    His fellow-men ?

If he hath hidden the outcast, or let in
A ray of sunshine to the cell of sin, —
    If he hath lent
Strength to the weak, and, in an hour of
    need,
Over the suffering, mindless of his creed
    Or home, hath bent,

He has not lived in vain, and while he
    gives
The praise to Him, in whom he moves
    and lives,
    With thankful heart ;
He gazes backward, and with hope
    before,
Knowing that from his works he never-
    more
    Can henceforth part.

RAPHAEL.

I shall not soon forget that sight :
  The glow of autumn's westering day,
A hazy warmth, a dreamy light,
  On Raphael's picture lay.

It was a simple print I saw,
  The fair face of a musing boy ;
Yet, while I gazed, a sense of awe
  Seemed blending with my joy.

A simple print : — the graceful flow
  Of boyhood's soft and wavy hair,
And fresh young lip and cheek, and
    brow
  Unmarked and clear, were there.

Yet through its sweet and calm repose
  I saw the inward spirit shine ;
It was as if before me rose
  The white veil of a shrine.

As if, as Gothland's sage has told,
  The hidden life, the man within,
Dissevered from its frame and mould,
  By mortal eye were seen.

Was it the lifting of that eye,
  The waving of that pictured hand ?
Loose as a cloud-wreath on the sky,
  I saw the walls expand.

The narrow room had vanished, — space,
  Broad, luminous, remained alone,
Through which all hues and shapes of
      grace
  And beauty looked or shone.

Around the mighty master came
  The marvels which his pencil wrought,
Those miracles of power whose fame
  Is wide as human thought.

There drooped thy more than mortal
      face,
  O Mother, beautiful and mild !
Enfolding in one dear embrace
  Thy Saviour and thy Child !

The rapt brow of the Desert John ;
  The awful glory of that day
When all the Father's brightness shone
  Through manhood's veil of clay

And, midst gray prophet forms, and
      wild
  Dark visions of the days of old,
How sweetly woman's beauty smiled
  Through locks of brown and gold !

There Fornarina's fair young face
  Once more upon her lover shone,
Whose model of an angel's grace
  He borrowed from her own.

Slow passed that vision from my view,
  But not the lesson which it taught ;
The soft, calm shadows which it threw
  Still rested on my thought :

The truth, that painter, bard, and sage,
  Even in Earth's cold and changeful
      clime,
Plant for their deathless heritage
  The fruits and flowers of time.

We shape ourselves the joy or fear
  Of which the coming life is made,
And fill our Future's atmosphere
  With sunshine or with shade.

The tissue of the Life to be
  We weave with colors all our own,

And in the field of Destiny
  We reap as we have sown.

Still shall the soul around it call
  The shadows which it gathered here,
And, painted on the eternal wall,
  The Past shall reappear.

Think ye the notes of holy song
  On Milton's tuneful ear have died ?
Think ye that Raphael's angel throng
  Has vanished from his side ?

O no ! — We live our life again ;
  Or warmly touched, or coldly dim,
The pictures of the Past remain, —
  Man's works shall follow him !

LUCY HOOPER.[48]

THEY tell me, Lucy, thou art dead, —
    That all of thee we loved and cher
      ished
      Has with thy summer roses per·
      ished ;
And left, as its young beauty fled,
  An ashen memory in its stead, —
The twilight of a parted day
    Whose fading light is cold and vain;
    The heart's faint echo of a strain
Of low, sweet music passed away.
That true and loving heart, — that gift
  Of a mind, earnest, clear, profound,
Bestowing, with a glad unthrift,
  Its sunny light on all around,
Affinities which only could
Cleave to the pure, the true, and good ;
    And sympathies which found no rest,
    Save with the loveliest and best.
Of them — of thee — remains there
      naught
    But sorrow in the mourner's breast ?—
A shadow in the land of thought ?
No ! — Even *my* weak and trembling
      faith
    Can lift for thee the veil which doubt
    And human fear have drawn about
The all-awaiting scene of death.

Even as thou wast I see thee still ;
And, save the absence of all ill
And pain and weariness, which here
Summoned the sigh or wrung the tear,
The same as when, two summers back,
Beside our childhood's Merrimack,
I saw thy dark eye wander o'er

Stream, sunny upland, rocky shore,
And heard thy low, soft voice alone
Midst lapse of waters, and the tone
Of pine-leaves by the west-wind blown,
There 's not a charm of soul or brow, —
　Of all we knew and loved in thee, —
But lives in holier beauty now,
　Baptized in immortality !
Not mine the sad and freezing dream
　Of souls that, with their earthly mould,
　Cast off the loves and joys of old, —
Unbodied, — like a pale moonbeam,
　As pure, as passionless, and cold ;
Nor mine the hope of Indra's son,
　Of slumbering in oblivion's rest,
Life's myriads blending into one, —
　In blank annihilation blest ;
Dust-atoms of the infinite, —
Sparks scattered from the central light,
And winning back through mortal pain
Their old unconsciousness again.
No ! — I have FRIENDS in Spirit Land, —
Not shadows in a shadowy band,
　Not *others*, but *themselves* are they.
And still I think of them the same
As when the Master's summons came ;
Their change, — the holy. morn-light
　breaking
Upon the dream-worn sleeper, waking,—
　A change from twilight into day.

They 've laid thee midst the household
　graves,
　Where father, brother, sister lie ;
Below thee sweep the dark blue waves,
　Above thee bends the summer sky.
Thy own loved church in sadness read
Her solemn ritual o'er thy head,
And blessed and hallowed with her
　prayer
The turf laid lightly o'er thee there.
That church, whose rites and liturgy,
Sublime and old, were truth to thee,
Undoubted to thy bosom taken,
As symbols of a faith unshaken.
Even I, of simpler views, could feel
The beauty of thy trust and zeal ;
And, owning not thy creed, could see
How deep a truth it seemed to thee,
And how thy fervent heart had thrown
O er all, a coloring of its own,
And kindled up, intense and warm,
A life in every rite and form,
As, when on Chebar's banks of old,
The Hebrew's gorgeous vision rolled,
A spirit filled the vast machine, —
A life " within the wheels " was seen.

Farewell ! A little time, and we
　Who knew thee well, and loved thee
　　here,
One after one shall follow thee
　As pilgrims through the gate of fear,
Which opens on eternity.
Yet shall we cherish not the less
　All that is left our hearts meanwhile ;
The memory of thy loveliness
　Shall round our weary pathway smile,
Like moonlight when the sun has set, —
A sweet and tender radiance yet.
Thoughts of thy clear-eyed sense of
　duty,
　Thy generous scorn of all things
　　wrong, —
The truth, the strength, the graceful
　beauty
　Which blended in thy song.
All lovely things, by thee beloved,
　Shall whisper to our hearts of thee ;
These green hills, where thy childhood
　roved, —
　Yon river winding to the sea, —
The sunset light of autumn eves
　Reflecting on the deep, still floods,
Cloud, crimson sky, and trembling
　leaves
　Of rainbow-tinted woods, —
These, in our view, shall henceforth take
A tenderer meaning for thy sake ;
And all thou lovedst of earth and sky,
Seem sacred to thy memory.

CHANNING.[44]

Not vainly did old poets tell,
　Nor vainly did old genius paint
God's great and crowning miracle, --
　The hero and the saint !

For even in a faithless day
　Can we our sainted ones discern ;
And feel, while with them on the way,
　Our hearts within us burn.

And thus the common tongue and pen
　Which, world-wide, echo CHANNING's
　　fame,
As one of Heaven's anointed men,
　Have sanctified his name.

In vain shall Rome her portals bar,
　And shut from him her saintly prize,
Whom, in the world's great calendar.
　All men shall canonize.

By Narragansett's sunny bay,
  Beneath his green embowering wood,
To me it seems but yesterday
  Since at his side I stood.

The slopes lay green with summer rains,
  The western wind blew fresh and
    free,
And glimmered down the orchard lanes
  The white surf of the sea.

With us was one, who, calm and true,
  Life's highest purpose understood,
And, like his blessed Master, knew
  The joy of doing good.

Unlearned, unknown to lettered fame,
  Yet on the lips of England's poor
And toiling millions dwelt his name,
  With blessings evermore.

Unknown to power or place, yet where
  The sun looks o'er the Carib sea,
It blended with the freeman's prayer
  And song of jubilee.

He told of England's sin and wrong, —
  The ills her suffering children know, —
The squalor of the city's throng, —
  The green field's want and woe.

O'er Channing's face the tenderness
  Of sympathetic sorrow stole,
Like a still shadow, passionless, —
  The sorrow of the soul.

But when the generous Briton told
  How hearts were answering to his
    own,
And Freedom's rising murmur rolled
  Up to the dull-eared throne,

I saw, methought, a glad surprise
  Thrill through that frail and pain-
    worn frame,
And, kindling in those deep, calm eyes,
  A still and earnest flame.

His few, brief words were such as move
  The human heart, — the Faith-sown
    seeds
Which ripen in the soil of love
  To high heroic deeds.

No bars of sect or clime were felt, —
  The Babel strife of tongues had
    ceased, —

And at one common altar knelt
  The Quaker and the priest.

And not in vain : with strength renewed,
  And zeal refreshed, and hope less dim,
For that brief meeting, each pursued
  The path allotted him.

How echoes yet each Western hill
  And vale with Channing's dying
    word !
How are the hearts of freemen still
  By that great warning stirred !

The stranger treads his native soil,
  And pleads, with zeal unfelt before
The honest right of British toil,
  The claim of England's poor.

Before him time-wrought barriers fall,
  Old fears subside, old hatreds melt,
And, stretching o'er the sea's blue wall,
  The Saxon greets the Celt.

The yeoman on the Scottish lines,
  The Sheffield grinder, worn and grim,
The delver in the Cornwall mines,
  Look up with hope to him.

Swart smiters of the glowing steel,
  Dark feeders of the forge's flame,
Pale watchers at the loom and wheel,
  Repeat his honored name.

And thus the influence of that hour
  Of converse on Rhode Island's strand,
Lives in the calm, resistless power
  Which moves our father-land.

God blesses still the generous thought,
  And still the fitting word He speeds,
And Truth, at his requiring taught,
  He quickens into deeds.

Where is the victory of the grave ?
  What dust upon the spirit lies ?
God keeps the sacred life he gave, —
  The prophet never dies !

TO THE MEMORY OF

CHARLES B. STORRS,

LATE PRESIDENT OF WESTERN RESERVE
COLLEGE.

THOU hast fallen in thine armor,
  Thou martyr of the Lord !

With thy last breath crying, — "On-
    ward !"
And thy hand upon the sword.
The haughty heart derideth,
    And the sinful lip reviles,
But the blessing of the perishing
    Around thy pillow smiles !

When to our cup of trembling
    The added drop is given,
And the long-suspended thunder
    Falls terribly from Heaven, —
When a new and fearful freedom
    Is proffered of the Lord
To the slow-consuming Famine, —
    The Pestilence and Sword ! —

When the refuges of Falsehood
    Shall be swept away in wrath,
And the temple shall be shaken,
    With its idol, to the earth, —
Shall not thy words of warning
    Be all remembered then ?
And thy now unheeded message
    Burn in the hearts of men ?

Oppression's hand may scatter
    Its nettles on thy tomb,
And even Christian bosoms
    Deny thy memory room ;
For lying lips shall torture
    Thy mercy into crime,
And the slanderer shall flourish
    As the bay-tree for a time.

But where the south-wind lingers
    On Carolina's pines,
Or falls the careless sunbeam
    Down Georgia's golden mines, —
Where now beneath his burthen
    The toiling slave is driven, —
Where now a tyrant's mockery
    Is offered unto Heaven, —

Where Mammon hath its altars
    Wet o'er with human blood,
And pride and lust debases
    The workmanship of God, —
There shall thy praise be spoken,
    Redeemed from Falsehood's ban,
When the fetters shall be broken,
    And the *slave* shall be a *man !*

Joy to thy spirit, brother !
    A thousand hearts are warm, —
A thousand kindred bosoms
    Are baring to the storm.

What though red-handed Violence
    With secret Fraud combine ?
The wall of fire is round us, —
    Our Present Help was thine.

Lo, — the waking up of nations,
    From Slavery's fatal sleep, —
The murmur of a Universe, —
    Deep calling unto Deep !
Joy to thy spirit, brother !
    On every wind of heaven
The onward cheer and summons
    Of FREEDOM'S VOICE is given !

Glory to God forever !
    Beyond the despot's will
The soul of Freedom liveth
    Imperishable still.
The words which thou hast uttered
    Are of that soul a part,
And the good seed thou hast scattered
    Is springing from the heart.

In the evil days before us,
    And the trials yet to come, —
In the shadow of the prison,
    Or the cruel martyrdom, —
We will think of thee, O brother !
    And thy sainted name shall be
In the blessing of the captive,
    And the anthem of the free.
1834.

LINES,

ON THE DEATH OF S. O. TORREY.

Gone before us, O our brother,
    To the spirit-land !
Vainly look we for another
    In thy place to stand.
Who shall offer youth and beauty
    On the wasting shrine
Of a stern and lofty duty,
    With a faith like thine !

O, thy gentle smile of greeting
    Who again shall see ?
Who amidst the solemn meeting
    Gaze again on thee ? —
Who, when peril gathers o'er us,
    Wear so calm a brow ?
Who, with evil men before us,
    So serene as thou ?

Early hath the spoiler found thee,
    Brother of our love !

Autumn's faded earth around thee,
  And its storms above !
Evermore that turf lie lightly,
  And, with future showers,
O'er thy slumbers fresh and brightly
  Blow the summer flowers !

In the locks thy forehead gracing,
  Not a silvery streak ;
Nor a line of sorrow's tracing
  On thy fair young cheek ;
Eyes of light and lips of roses,
  Such as Hylas wore, —
Over all that curtain closes,
  Which shall rise no more !

Will the vigil Love is keeping
  Round that grave of thine,
Mournfully, like Jazer weeping
  Over Sibmah's vine,[45] —
Will the pleasant memories, swelling
  Gentle hearts, of thee,
In the spirit's distant dwelling
  All unheeded be ?

If the spirit ever gazes,
  From its journeyings, back ;
If the immortal ever traces
  O'er its mortal track ;
Wilt thou not, O brother, meet us
  Sometimes on our way,
And, in hours of sadness, greet us
  As a spirit may ?

Peace be with thee, O our brother,
  In the spirit-land !
Vainly look we for another
  In thy place to stand.
Unto Truth and Freedom giving
  All thy early powers,
Be thy virtues with the living,
  And thy spirit ours !

A LAMENT.

"The parted spirit,
Knoweth it not our sorrow? Answereth not
Its blessing to our tears?"

The circle is broken, — one seat is forsaken, —
One bud from the tree of our friendship
  is shaken, —
One heart from among us no longer
  shall thrill
With joy in our gladness, or grief in our
  ill.

Weep ! — lonely and lowly are slumbe[r]
  ing now
The light of her glances, the pride of he[r]
  brow,
Weep ! — sadly and long shall we liste[n]
  in vain
To hear the soft tones of her welcom[e]
  again.

Give our tears to the dead ! For humar[n]
  ity's claim
From its silence and darkness is ever th[e]
  same ;
The hope of that World whose existenc[e]
  is bliss
May not stifle the tears of the mourne[r]
  of this.

For, oh ! if one glance the freed spir[it]
  can throw
On the scene of its troubled probatio[n]
  below,
Than the pride of the marble, the pom[p]
  of the dead,
To that glance will be dearer the tea[r]
  which we shed.

O, who can forget the mild light of he[r]
  smile,
Over lips moved with music and feelin[g]
  the while —
The eye's deep enchantment, dark[,]
  dream-like, and clear,
In the glow of its gladness, the shade o[f]
  its tear.

And the charm of her features, whil[e]
  over the whole
Played the hues of the heart and th[e]
  sunshine of soul, —
And the tones of her voice, like the mu[-]
  sic which seems
Murmured low in our ears by the Ange[l]
  of dreams !

But holier and dearer our memories hol[d]
Those treasures of feeling, more precion[s]
  than gold, —
The love and the kindness and pit[y]
  which gave
Fresh flowers for the bridal, gree[n]
  wreaths for the grave !

The heart ever open to Charity's claim,
Unmoved from its purpose by censur[e]
  and blame,

her eye and her

eartless, the jest-

i was that beauti-

joyful, with tears
—

, whether mourn-

re to the passing

herself, she could

the spirit's pure

uld the erring re-

oof was still tem-

iset, slow melting

when the daylight

slumber, which

the world of the

IEELER.

ister of the Society of
ed in the cause of his
tain, Russia, and the
in New York in the
religious visit to this

l !

3 ! — No more
se before
ig worshipper,
erance giving
resh and living,
rd sense,
d evidence
ger !
ilver hair
of prayer, —
: and sense, shut

a's holy trance
intenance,
:loud of doubt, —
s resting here

In Time's unluminous atmosphere, —
  Were lifted by an angel's hand,
And through them on thy spiritual eye
Shone down the blessedness on high,
  The glory of the Better Land !

  The oak has fallen !
While, meet for no good work, the vine
May yet its worthless branches twine.
Who knoweth not that with thee fell
A great man in our Israel ?
Fallen, while thy loins were girded still,
Thy feet with Zion's dews still wet,
  And in thy hand retaining yet
The pilgrim's staff and scallop-shell !
Unharmed and safe, where, wild and
  free,
  Across the Neva's cold morass
The breezes from the Frozen Sea
  With winter's arrowy keenness pass ;
Or where the unwarning tropic gale
Smote to the waves thy tattered sail,
Or where the noon-hour's fervid heat
Against Tahiti's mountains beat ;
  The same mysterious Hand which
    gave
  Deliverance upon land and wave,
Tempered for thee the blasts which
    blew
  Ladaga's frozen surface o'er,
And blessed for thee the baleful dew
  Of evening upon Eimeo's shore,
Beneath this sunny heaven of ours,
Midst our soft airs and opening flowers
  Hath given thee a grave !

  His will be done,
Who seeth not as man, whose way
  Is not as ours ! — 'T is well with
    thee !
Nor anxious doubt nor dark dismay
Disquieted thy closing day,
But, evermore, thy soul could say,
  " My Father careth still for me !"
Called from thy hearth and home, —
    from her,
  The last bud on thy household tree,
The last dear one to minister
  In duty and in love to thee,
From all which nature holdeth dear,
  Feeble with years and worn with
    pain,
  To seek our distant land again,
Bound in the spirit, yet unknowing
  The things which should befall thee
    here,
Whether for labor or for death,

In childlike trust serenely going
  To that last trial of thy faith !

      O, far away,
Where never shines our Northern star
  On that dark waste which Balboa saw
From Darien's mountains stretching far,
So strange, heaven-broad, and lone, that
    there,
With forehead to its damp wind bare,
  He bent his mailed knee in awe ;
In many an isle whose coral feet
The surges of that ocean beat,
In thy palm shadows, Oahu,
  And Honolulu's silver bay,
Amidst Owyhee's hills of blue,
  And taro-plains of Tooboonai,
Are gentle hearts, which long shall be
Sad as our own at thought of thee, —
Worn sowers of Truth's holy seed,
Whose souls in weariness and need
  Were strengthened and refreshed by
    thine.
For blessed by our Father's hand
  Was thy deep love and tender care,
  Thy ministry and fervent prayer, —
Grateful as Eschol's clustered vine
To Israel in a weary land !

      And they who drew
By thousands round thee, in the hour
  Of prayerful waiting, hushed and
    deep,
  That He who bade the islands keep
Silence before him, might renew
  Their strength with his unslumbering
    power,
They too shall mourn that thou art gone,
  That nevermore thy aged lip
Shall soothe the weak, the erring warn,
Of those who first, rejoicing, heard
Through thee the Gospel's glorious
    word, —
  Seals of thy true apostleship.
And, if the brightest diadem,
  Whose gems of glory purely burn
  Around the ransomed ones in bliss,
Be evermore reserved for them
  Who here, through toil and sorrow,
    turn
  Many to righteousness, —
May we not think of thee as wearing
That star-like crown of light, and bear-
    ing,
Amidst Heaven's white and blissful
    band,
The fadeless palm-branch in thy hand ;

And joining with a seraph's tongue
In that new song the elders sung,
Ascribing to its blessed Giver
Thanksgiving, love, and praise forever !

      Farewell !
And though the ways of Zion mourn
When her strong ones are called away,
Who like thyself have calmly borne
The heat and burden of the day,
Yet He who slumbereth not nor sleep-
    eth
His ancient watch around us keepeth ;
Still, sent from his creating hand,
New witnesses for Truth shall stand, —
New instruments to sound abroad
The Gospel of a risen Lord ;
  To gather to the fold once more
The desolate and gone astray,
The scattered of a cloudy day,
  And Zion's broken walls restore ;
And, through the travail and the toil
Of true obedience, minister
Beauty for ashes, and the oil
  Of joy for mourning, unto her !
So shall her holy bounds increase
With walls of praise and gates of peace :
So shall the Vine, which martyr tears
And blood sustained in other years,
  With fresher life be clothed upon ;
And to the world in beauty show
Like the rose-plant of Jericho,
  And glorious as Lebanon !

            DANIEL NEALL.

                  I.

FRIEND of the Slave, and yet the friend
    of all ;
  Lover of peace, yet ever foremost when
  The need of battling Freedom called
    for men
To plant the banner on the outer wall ;
Gentle and kindly, ever at distress
Melted to more than woman's tender-
    ness,
Yet firm and steadfast, at his duty's post
Fronting the violence of a maddened
    host,
Like some gray rock from which the
    waves are tossed !
Knowing his deeds of love, men ques-
    tioned not
  The faith of one whose walk and word
    were right, —

Who tranquilly in Life's great task-
    field wrought,
And, side by side with evil, scarcely
    caught
    A stain upon his pilgrim garb of white :
Prompt to redress another's wrong, his
    own
Leaving to Time and Truth and Peni-
    tence alone.

II.

Such was our friend. Formed on the
    good old plan,
A true and brave and downright honest
    man ! —
He blew no trumpet in the market-place,
Nor in the church with hypocritic face
Supplied with cant the lack of Christian
    grace ;
Loathing pretence, he did with cheerful
    will
What others talked of while their hands
    were still ;
And, while " Lord, Lord ! " the pious
    tyrants cried,
Who, in the poor, their Master crucified,
His daily prayer, far better understood
In acts than words, was simply DOING
    GOOD.
So calm, so constant was his rectitude,
That by his loss alone we know its
    worth,
And feel how true a man has walked with
    us on earth.

6th 6th month, 1846.

TO MY FRIEND ON THE DEATH OF HIS SISTER.[46]

THINE is a grief, the depth of which
    another
      May never know ;
Yet, o'er the waters, O my stricken
    brother !
      To thee I go.

I lean my heart unto thee, sadly folding
    Thy hand in mine ;
With even the weakness of my soul up-
    holding
      The strength of thine.

I never knew, like thee, the dear de-
    parted ;
      I stood not by

When, in calm trust, the pure and tran-
    quil-hearted
      Lay down to die.

And on thy ears my words of weak con-
    doling
      Must vainly fall :
The funeral bell which in thy heart is
    tolling,
      Sounds over all !

I will not mock thee with the poor
    world's common
      And heartless phrase,
Nor wrong the memory of a sainted
    woman
      With idle praise.

With silence only as their benediction,
    God's angels come
Where, in the shadow of a great afflic-
    tion,
      The soul sits dumb !

Yet, would I say what thy own heart
    approveth :
      Our Father's will,
Calling to Him the dear one whom He
    loveth,
      Is mercy still.

Not upon thee or thine the solemn an-
    gel
      Hath evil wrought :
Her funeral anthem is a glad evangel, —
      The good die not !

God calls our loved ones, but we lose
    not wholly
      What He hath given ;
They live on earth, in thought and
    deed, as truly
      As in his heaven.

And she is with thee ; in thy path of
    trial
      She walketh yet ;
Still with the baptism of thy self-denial
      Her locks are wet.

Up, then, my brother ! Lo, the fields
    of harvest
      Lie white in view !
She lives and loves thee, and the God
    thou servest
      To both is true.

Thrust in thy sickle ! — England's toil-
worn peasants
Thy call abide ;
And she thou mourn'st, a pure and holy
presence,
Shall glean beside !

GONE.

ANOTHER hand is beckoning us,
Another call is given ;
And glows once more with Angel-steps
The path which reaches Heaven.

Our young and gentle friend, whose
smile
Made brighter summer hours,
Amid the frosts of autumn time
Has left us with the flowers.

No paling of the check of bloom
Forewarned us of decay ;
No shadow from the Silent Land
Fell round our sister's way.

The light of her young life went down,
As sinks behind the hill
The glory of a setting star, —
Clear, suddenly, and still.

As pure and sweet, her fair brow seemed
Eternal as the sky ;
And like the brook's low song, her
voice, —
A sound which could not die.

And half we deemed she needed not
The changing of her sphere,
To give to Heaven a Shining One,
Who walked an Angel here.

The blessing of her quiet life
Fell on us like the dew ;
And good thoughts, where her footsteps
pressed
Like fairy blossoms grew.

Sweet promptings unto kindest deeds
Were in her very look ;
We read her face, as one who reads
A true and holy book:

The measure of a blessed hymn,
To which our hearts could move ;
The breathing of an inward psalm ;
A canticle of love.

We miss her in the place of prayer,
And by the hearth-fire's light ;
We pause beside her door to hear
Once more her sweet " Good-night ! "

There seems a shadow on the day,
Her smile no longer cheers ;
A dimness on the stars of night,
Like eyes that look through tears.

Alone unto our Father's will
One thought hath reconciled ;
That He whose love exceedeth ours
Hath taken home his child.

Fold her, O Father ! in thine arms,
And let her henceforth be
A messenger of love between
Our human hearts and thee.

Still let her mild rebuking stand
Between us and the wrong,
And her dear memory serve to make
Our faith in Goodness strong.

And grant that she who, trembling, hurt
Distrusted all her powers,
May welcome to her holier home
The well-beloved of ours.

THE LAKE-SIDE.

THE shadows round the inland sea
Are deepening into night ;
Slow up the slopes of Ossipee
They chase the lessening light.
Tired of the long day's blinding heat,
I rest my languid eye,
Lake of the Hills ! where, cool and
sweet,
Thy sunset waters lie !

Along the sky, in wavy lines,
O'er isle and reach and bay,
Green-belted with eternal pines,
The mountains stretch away.
Below, the maple masses sleep
Where shore with water blends,
While midway on the tranquil deep
The evening light descends.

So seemed it when yon hill's red crown,
Of old, the Indian trod,
And, through the sunset air, looked
down
Upon the Smile of God.[47]

To him of light and shade the laws
  No forest sceptic taught ;
Their living and eternal Cause
  His truer instinct sought.

He saw these mountains in the light
  Which now across them shines ;
This lake, in summer sunset bright,
  Walled round with sombering pines.
God near him seemed ; from earth and
    skies
  His loving voice he heard,
As, face to face, in Paradise,
  Man stood before the Lord.

Thanks, O our Father ! that, like him,
  Thy tender love I see,
In radiant hill and woodland dim,
  And tinted sunset sea.
For not in mockery dost thou fill
  Our earth with light and grace ;
Thou hid'st no dark and cruel will
  Behind thy smiling face !

THE HILL-TOP.

The burly driver at my side,
  We slowly climbed the hill,
Whose summit, in the hot noontide,
  Seemed rising, rising still.
At last, our short noon-shadows hid
  The top-stone, bare and brown,
From whence, like Gizeh's pyramid,
  The rough mass slanted down.

I felt the cool breath of the North ;
  Between me and the sun,
O'er deep, still lake, and ridgy earth,
  I saw the cloud-shades run.
Before me, stretched for glistening miles,
  Lay mountain-girdled Squam ;
Like green-winged birds, the leafy isles
  Upon its bosom swam.

And, glimmering through the sun-haze
    warm,
  Far as the eye could roam,
Dark billows of an earthquake storm
  Beflecked with clouds like foam,
Their vales in misty shadow deep,
  Their rugged peaks in shine,
I saw the mountain ranges sweep
  The horizon's northern line.

There towered Chocorua's peak ; and
   west,
  Mooschillock's woods were seen,

With many a nameless slide-scarred
   crest
  And pine-dark gorge between.
Beyond them, like a sun-rimmed cloud,
  The great Notch mountains shone,
Watched over by the solemn-browed
  And awful face of stone !

" A good look-off ! " the driver spake :
  " About this time, last year,
I drove a party to the Lake,
  And stopped, at evening, here.
'T was duskish down below ; but all
  These hills stood in the sun,
Till, dipped behind yon purple wall,
  He left them, one by one.

" A lady, who, from Thornton hill,
  Had held her place outside,
And, as a pleasant woman will,
  Had cheered the long, dull ride,
Besought me, with so sweet a smile,
  That — though I hate delay —
I could not choose but rest awhile, —
  (These women have such ways !)

" On yonder mossy ledge she sat,
  Her sketch upon her knees,
A stray brown lock beneath her hat
  Unrolling in the breeze ;
Her sweet face, in the sunset light
  Upraised and glorified, —
I never saw a prettier sight
  In all my mountain ride.

" As good as fair ; it seemed her joy
  To comfort and to give ;
My poor, sick wife, and cripple boy,
  Will bless her while they live ! "
The tremor in the driver's tone
  His manhood did not shame :
"I dare say, sir, you may have known—"
  He named a well-known name.

Then sank the pyramidal mounds,
  The blue lake fled away ;
For mountain-scope a parlor's bounds,
  A lighted hearth for day !
From lonely years and weary miles
  The shadows fell apart ;
Kind voices cheered, sweet human
    smiles
  Shone warm into my heart.

We journeyed on ; but earth and sky
  Had power to charm no more ;
Still dreamed my inward-turning eye
  The dream of memory o'er.

Ah ! human kindness, human love, —
  To few who seek denied, —
Too late we learn to prize above
  The whole round world beside !

ON RECEIVING AN EAGLE'S QUILL FROM LAKE SUPERIOR.

ALL day the darkness and the cold
  Upon my heart have lain,
Like shadows on the winter sky,
  Like frost upon the pane ;

But now my torpid fancy wakes,
  And, on thy Eagle's plume,
Rides forth, like Sindbad on his bird,
  Or witch upon her broom !

Below me roar the rocking pines,
  Before me spreads the lake
Whose long and solemn-sounding waves
  Against the sunset break.

I hear the wild Rice-Eater thresh
  The grain he has not sown ;
I see, with flashing scythe of fire,
  The prairie harvest mown !

I hear the far-off voyager's horn ;
  I see the Yankee's trail, —
His foot on every mountain-pass,
  On every stream his sail.

By forest, lake, and waterfall,
  I see his pedler show ;
The mighty mingling with the mean,
  The lofty with the low.

He 's whittling by St. Mary's Falls,
  Upon his loaded wain ;
He 's measuring o'er the Pictured Rocks,
  With eager eyes of gain.

I hear the mattock in the mine,
  The axe-stroke in the dell,
The clamor from the Indian lodge,
  The Jesuit chapel bell !

I see the swarthy trappers come
  From Mississippi's springs ;
And war-chiefs with their painted brows,
  And crests of eagle wings.

Behind the scared squaw's birch canoe,
  The steamer smokes and raves ;
And city lots are staked for sale
  Above old Indian graves.

I hear the tread of pioneers
  Of nations yet to be ;
The first low wash of waves, where soon
  Shall roll a human sea.

The rudiments of empire here
  Are plastic yet and warm ;
The chaos of a mighty world
  Is rounding into form !

Each rude and jostling fragment soon
  Its fitting place shall find, —
The raw material of a State,
  Its muscle and its mind !

And, westering still, the star which leads
  The New World in its train
Has tipped with fire the icy spears
  Of many a mountain chain.

The snowy cones of Oregon
  Are kindling on its way ;
And California's golden sands
  Gleam brighter in its ray !

Then blessings on thy eagle quill,
  As, wandering far and wide,
I thank thee for this twilight dream
  And Fancy's airy ride !

Yet, welcomer than regal plumes,
  Which Western trappers find,
Thy free and pleasant thoughts, chance
    sown,
  Like feathers on the wind.

Thy symbol be the mountain-bird,
  Whose glistening quill I hold ;
Thy home the ample air of hope,
  And memory's sunset gold !

In thee, let joy with duty join,
  And strength unite with love,
The eagle's pinions folding round
  The warm heart of the dove !

So, when in darkness sleeps the vale
  Where still the blind bird clings,
The sunshine of the upper sky
  Shall glitter on thy wings !

MEMORIES.

A BEAUTIFUL and happy girl,
  With step as light as summer air,
Eyes glad with smiles, and brow of pearl,
Shadowed by many a careless curl
  Of unconfined and flowing hair ;

A seeming child in everything,
  Save thoughtful brow and ripening
    charms,
As Nature wears the smile of Spring
  When sinking into Summer's arms.

A mind rejoicing in the light
  Which melted through its graceful
    bower,
Leaf after leaf, dew-moist and bright,
And stainless in its holy white,
  Unfolding like a morning flower :
A heart, which, like a fine-toned lute,
  With every breath of feeling woke,
And, even when the tongue was mute,
  From eye and lip in music spoke.

How thrills once more the lengthening
    chain
  Of memory, at the thought of thee !
Old hopes which long in dust have lain
Old dreams, come thronging back again,
  And boyhood lives again in me ;
I feel its glow upon my cheek,
  Its fulness of the heart is mine,
As when I leaned to hear thee speak,
  Or raised my doubtful eye to thine.

I hear again thy low replies,
  I feel thy arm within my own,
And timidly again uprise
The fringéd lids of hazel eyes,
  With soft brown tresses overblown.
Ah ! memories of sweet summer eves,
  Of moonlit wave and willowy way,
Of stars and flowers, and dewy leaves,
  And smiles and tones more dear than
    they !

Ere this, thy quiet eye hath smiled
  My picture of thy youth to see,
When, half a woman, half a child,
Thy very artlessness beguiled,
  And folly's self seemed wise in thee ;
I too can smile, when o'er that hour
  The lights of memory backward stream,
Yet feel the while that manhood's power
  Is vainer than my boyhood's dream.

Years have passed on, and left their trace,
  Of graver care and deeper thought ;
And unto me the calm, cold face
Of manhood, and to thee the grace
  Of woman's pensive beauty brought.
More wide, perchance, for blame than
    praise,
  The school-boy's humble name has
    flown ;

Thine, in the gree
  Of unobtrusive

And wider yet in
  Diverge our pat
Thine the Geneva
  While answers to
  The Derby dale
For thee, the prie
  And holy day,
For me, the silent
  My brethren ga

Yet hath thy spir
  An impress Tim
And something of
  A shadow from th
  Lingering, even
Not wholly can th
  That lesson of i
Not yet has Time'
  To common dus

Thus, while at tin
  The shadows m
And, smiling thr
    lies
The warm light of
  The Indian Sun
In secret sympath
  In founts of feel
Their pure, fresl
    find
  Our early dream

THE LEGEND

THE day is closing
  With roaring bl
And through the
  The bloom of su

I turn me from th
  To ponder o'er a
A legend of the ag
  By dreaming m

On Tintoretto's ca
  That fancy of a
In graceful lines a
  And hues immo

In Provence (so th
  There lived a lo
A peasant-boy of t
  The chance of t

Forth-looking from the castle tower,
  Beyond the hills with almonds dark,
The straining eye could scarce discern
  The chapel of the good St. Mark.

And there, when bitter word or fare
  The service of the youth repaid,
By stealth, before that holy shrine,
  For grace to bear his wrong, he prayed.

The steed stamped at the castle gate,
  The boar-hunt sounded on the hill;
Why stayed the Baron from the chase,
  With looks so stern, and words so
    ill?

" Go, bind yon slave! and let him learn,
  By scath of fire and strain of cord,
How ill they speed who give dead saints
  The homage due their living lord!"

They bound him on the fearful rack,
  When, through the dungeon's vaulted
    dark,
He saw the light of shining robes,
  And knew the face of good St. Mark.

Then sank the iron rack apart,
  The cords released their cruel clasp,
The pincers, with their teeth of fire,
  Fell broken from the torturer's grasp.

And lo! before the Youth and Saint,
  Barred door and wall of stone gave way;
And up from bondage and the night
  They passed to freedom and the
    day!

O dreaming monk! thy tale is true; —
  O painter! true thy pencil's art;
In tones of hope and prophecy,
  Ye whisper to my listening heart!

Unheard no burdened heart's appeal
  Moans up to God's inclining ear;
Unheeded by his tender eye,
  Falls to the earth no sufferer's tear.

For still the Lord alone is God!
  The pomp and power of tyrant man
Are scattered at his lightest breath,
  Like chaff before the winnower's fan.

Not always shall the slave uplift
  His heavy hands to Heaven in vain.
God's angel, like the good St. Mark,
  Comes shining down to break his chain!

O weary ones! ye may not see
  Your helpers in their downward flight;
Nor hear the sound of silver wings
  Slow beating through the hush of night!

But not the less gray Dothan shone,
  With sunbright watchers bending low,
That Fear's dim eye beheld alone
  The spear-heads of the Syrian foe.

There are, who, like the Seer of old,
  Can see the helpers God has sent,
And how life's rugged mountain-side
  Is white with many an angel tent!

They hear the heralds whom our Lord
  Sends down his pathway to prepare;
And light, from others hidden, shines
  On their high place of faith and prayer.

Let such, for earth's despairing ones,
  Hopeless, yet longing to be free,
Breathe once again the Prophet's prayer:
  " Lord, ope their eyes, that they may
    see!"

THE WELL OF LOCH MAREE.[49]

CALM on the breast of Loch Maree
  A little isle reposes;
A shadow woven of the oak
  And willow o'er it closes.

Within, a Druid's mound is seen,
  Set round with stony warders;
A fountain, gushing through the turf,
  Flows o'er its grassy borders.

And whoso bathes therein his brow,
  With care or madness burning,
Feels once again his healthful thought
  And sense of peace returning.

O restless heart and fevered brain,
  Unquiet and unstable,
That holy well of Loch Maree
  Is more than idle fable!

Life's changes vex, its discords stun,
  Its glaring sunshine blindeth,
And blest is he who on his way
  That fount of healing findeth!

The shadows of a humbled will
  And contrite heart are o'er it;
Go read its legend — " TRUST IN GOD "
  On Faith's white stones before it.

TO MY SISTER;

WITH A COPY OF " SUPERNATURALISM
OF NEW ENGLAND."

DEAR SISTER ! — while the wise and sage
Turn coldly from my playful page,
And count it strange that ripened age
   Should stoop to boyhood's folly ;
I know that thou wilt judge aright
Of all which makes the heart more light,
Or lends one star-gleam to the night
   Of clouded Melancholy.

Away with weary cares and themes ! —
Swing wide the moonlit gate of dreams !
Leave free once more the land which teems
   With wonders and romances !
Where thou, with clear discerning eyes,
Shalt rightly read the truth which lies
Beneath the quaintly masking guise
   Of wild and wizard fancies.

Lo ! once again our feet we set
On still green wood-paths, twilight wet,
By lonely brooks, whose waters fret
   The roots of spectral beeches ;
Again the hearth-fire glimmers o'er
Home's whitewashed wall and painted
   floor,
And young eyes widening to the lore
   Of faery-folks and witches.

Dear heart ! — the legend is not vain
Which lights that holy hearth again,
And calling back from care and pain,
   And death's funereal sadness,
Draws round its old familiar blaze
The clustering groups of happier days,
And lends to sober manhood's gaze
   A glimpse of childish gladness.

And, knowing how my life hath been
A weary work of tongue and pen,
A long, harsh strife with strong-willed
   men,
   Thou wilt not chide my turning
To con, at times, an idle rhyme,
To pluck a flower from childhood's clime,
Or listen, at Life's noonday chime,
   For the sweet bells of Morning !

AUTUMN THOUGHTS.

FROM " MARGARET SMITH'S JOURNAL."

GONE hath the Spring, with all its flowers,
   And gone the Summer's pomp and show,

And Autumn, in his leafless bowers,
   Is waiting for the Winter's snow.

I said to Earth, so cold and gray,
   " An emblem of myself thou art " ;
" Not so," the Earth did seem to say,
   " For Spring shall warm my frozen
     heart."

I soothe my wintry sleep with dreams
   Of warmer sun and softer rain,
And wait to hear the sound of streams
   And songs of merry birds again.

But thou, from whom the Spring hath
   gone,
   For whom the flowers no longer blow,
Who standest blighted and forlorn,
   Like Autumn waiting for the snow :

No hope is thine of sunnier hours,
   Thy Winter shall no more depart ;
No Spring revive thy wasted flowers,
   Nor Summer warm thy frozen heart.

CALEF IN BOSTON.

1692.

IN the solemn days of old,
   Two men met in Boston town,
One a tradesman frank and bold,
   One a preacher of renown.

Cried the last, in bitter tone, —
   " Poisoner of the wells of truth !
Satan's hireling, thou hast sown
   With his tares the heart of youth ! "

Spake the simple tradesman then, —
   " God be judge 'twixt thou and I ;
All thou knowest of truth hath been
   Unto men like thee a lie.

" Falsehoods which we spurn to-day
   Were the truths of long ago ;
Let the dead boughs fall away,
   Fresher shall the living grow.

" God is good and God is light,
   In this faith I rest secure ;
Evil can but serve the right,
   Over all shall love endure.

" Of your spectral puppet play
   I have traced the cunning wires ;

Come what will, I needs must say,
  God is true, and ye are liars."

When the thought of man is free,
  Error fears its lightest tones ;
So the priest cried, " Sadducee ! "
  And the people took up stones.

In the ancient burying-ground,
  Side by side the twain now lie, —
One with humble grassy mound,
  One with marbles pale and high.

But the Lord hath blest the seed
  Which that tradesman scattered then,
And the preacher's spectral creed
  Chills no more the blood of men.

Let us trust, to one is known
  Perfect love which casts out fear,
While the other's joys atone
  For the wrong he suffered here.

TO PIUS IX.[50]

THE cannon's brazen lips are cold ;
  No red shell blazes down the air ;
And street and tower, and temple old,
  Are silent as despair.

The Lombard stands no more at bay, —
  Rome's fresh young life has bled in
    vain ;
The ravens scattered by the day
  Come back with night again.

Now, while the fratricides of France
  Are treading on the neck of Rome,
Hider at Gaeta, — seize thy chance !
  Coward and cruel, come !

Creep now from Naples' bloody skirt ;
  Thy mummer's part was acted well,
While Rome, with steel and fire begirt,
  Before thy crusade fell !

Her death-groans answered to thy prayer ;
  Thy chant, the drum and bugle-
    call :
Thy lights, the burning villa's glare ;
  Thy beads, the shell and ball !

Let Austria clear thy way, with hands
  Foul from Ancona's cruel sack,
And Naples, with his dastard bands
  Of murderers, lead thee back !

Rome's lips are dumb ; the orphan's wail,
  The mother's shriek, thou mayst not
    hear
Above the faithless Frenchman's hail,
  The unsexed shaveling's cheer !

Go, bind on Rome her cast-off weight,
  The double curse of crook and crown,
Though woman's scorn and manhood's
    hate
From wall and roof flash down !

Nor heed those blood-stains on the wall,
  Not Tiber's flood can wash away,
Where, in thy stately Quirinal,
  Thy mangled victims lay !

Let the world murmur ; let its cry
  Of horror and disgust be heard ; —
Truth stands alone ; thy coward lie
  Is backed by lance and sword !

The cannon of St. Angelo,
  And chanting priest and clanging bell,
And beat of drum and bugle blow,
  Shall greet thy coming well !

Let lips of iron and tongues of slaves
  Fit welcome give thee ; — for her part,
Rome, frowning o'er her new-made
    graves,
  Shall curse thee from her heart !

No wreaths of sad Campagna's flowers
  Shall childhood in thy pathway fling ;
No garlands from their ravaged bowers
  Shall Terni's maidens bring ;

But, hateful as that tyrant old,
  The mocking witness of his crime,
In thee shall loathing eyes behold
  The Nero of our time !

Stand where Rome's blood was freest shed,
  Mock Heaven with impious thanks,
    and call
Its curses on the patriot dead,
  Its blessings on the Gaul !

Or sit upon thy throne of lies,
  A poor, mean idol, blood-besmeared,
Whom even its worshippers despise, —
  Unhonored, unrevered !

Yet, Scandal of the World ! from thee
  One needful truth mankind shall
    learn, —

10

That kings and priests to Liberty
And God are false in turn.

Earth wearies of them ; and the long
  Meek sufferance of the Heavens doth
    fail ;
Woe for weak tyrants, when the strong
  Wake, struggle, and prevail !

Not vainly Roman hearts have bled
  To feed the Crozier and the Crown,
If, roused thereby, the world shall tread
  The twin-born vampires down !

ELLIOTT.[51]

HANDS off ! thou tithe-fat plunderer ! play
  No trick of priestcraft here !
Back, puny lordling ! darest thou lay
  A hand on Elliott's bier ?
Alive, your rank and pomp, as dust,
  Beneath his feet he trod :
He knew the locust swarm that cursed
  The harvest-fields of God.

On these pale lips, the smothered
  thought
  Which England's millions feel,
A fierce and fearful splendor caught,
  As from his forge the steel.
Strong-armed as Thor, — a shower of fire
  His smitten anvil flung ;
God's curse, Earth's wrong, dumb Hun-
    ger's ire, —
  He gave them all a tongue !

Then let the poor man's horny hands
  Bear up the mighty dead,
And labor's swart and stalwart bands
  Behind as mourners tread.
Leave cant and craft their baptized
    bounds,
  Leave rank its minster floor ;
Give England's green and daisied
    grounds
  The poet of the poor !

Lay down upon his Sheaf's green verge
  That brave old heart of oak,
With fitting dirge from sounding forge,
  And pall of furnace smoke !
Where whirls the stone its dizzy rounds,
  And axe and sledge are swung,
And, timing to their stormy sounds,
  His stormy lays are sung.

There let the peasant's step be heard,
  The grinder chant his rhyme ;
Nor patron's praise nor dainty word
  Befits the man or time.
No soft lament nor dreamer's sigh
  For him whose words were bread, —
The Runic rhyme and spell whereby
  The foodless poor were fed !

Pile up thy tombs of rank and pride,
  O England, as thou wilt !
With pomp to nameless worth denied,
  Emblazon titled guilt !
No part or lot in these we claim ;
  But, o'er the sounding wave,
A common right to Elliott's name,
  A freehold in his grave !

ICHABOD !

So fallen ! so lost ! the light with-
    drawn
  Which once he wore !
The glory from his gray hairs gone
  Forevermore !

Revile him not, — the Tempter hath
  A snare for all ;
And pitying tears, not scorn and wrath,
  Befit his fall !

O, dumb be passion's stormy rage,
  When he who might
Have lighted up and led his age,
  Falls back in night.

Scorn ! would the angels laugh, to
    mark
  A bright soul driven,
Fiend-goaded, down the endless dark,
  From hope and heaven !

Let not the land once proud of him
  Insult him now,
Nor brand with deeper shame his dim,
  Dishonored brow.

But let its humbled sons, instead,
  From sea to lake;
A long lament, as for the dead,
  In sadness make.

Of all we loved and honored, naught
  Save power remains, —
A fallen angel's pride of thought,
  Still strong in chains.

All else is gone ; from those great eyes
    The soul has fled :
When faith is lost, when honor dies,
    The man is dead !

Then, pay the reverence of old days
    To his dead fame ;
Walk backward, with averted gaze,
    And hide the shame !

THE CHRISTIAN TOURISTS.

No aimless wanderers, by the fiend
    Unrest
    Goaded from shore to shore ;
No schoolmen, turning, in their classic
    quest,
    The leaves of empire o'er.
Simple of faith, and bearing in their
    hearts
    The love of man and God,
Isles of old song, the Moslem's ancient
    marts,
    And Scythia's steppes, they trod.

Where the long shadows of the fir and pine
    In the night sun are cast,
And the deep heart of many a Norland
    mine
    Quakes at each riving blast ;
Where, in barbaric grandeur, Moskwa
    stands,
    A baptized Scythian queen,
With Europe's arts and Asia's jewelled
    hands,
    The North and East between !

Where still, through vales of Grecian
    fable, stray
    The classic forms of yore, .
And beauty smiles, new risen from the
    spray,
    And Dian weeps once more ;
Where every tongue in Smyrna's mart
    resounds ;
    And Stamboul from the sea •
Lifts her tall minarets over burial-
    grounds
    Black with the cypress-tree !

From Malta's temples to the gates of
    Rome,
    Following the track of Paul,
And where the Alps gird round the
    Switzer's home
    Their vast, eternal wall ;

They paused not by the ruins of old
    time,
    They scanned no pictures rare,
Nor lingered where the snow-locked
    mountains climb
    The cold abyss of air !

But unto prisons, where men lay in
    chains,
    To haunts where Hunger pined,
To kings and courts forgetful of the
    pains
    And wants of human-kind,
Scattering sweet words, and quiet deeds
    of good,
    Along their way, like flowers,
Or pleading, as Christ's freemen only
    could,
    With princes and with powers ;

Their single aim the purpose to ful-
    fil
    Of Truth, from day to day,
Simply obedient to its guiding will,
    They held their pilgrim way.
Yet dream not, hence, the beautiful and
    old
    Were wasted on their sight,
Who in the school of Christ had learned
    to hold
    All outward things aright.

Not less to them the breath of vineyards
    blown
    From off the Cyprian shore,
Not less for them the Alps in sunset
    shone,
    That man they valued more.
A life of beauty lends to all it sees
    The beauty of its thought ;
And fairest forms and sweetest harmo-
    nies
    Make glad its way, unsought.

In sweet accordancy of praise and
    love,
    The singing waters run ;
And sunset mountains wear in light
    above
    The smile of duty done ;
Sure stands the promise, — ever to the
    meek
    A heritage is given ;
Nor lose they Earth who, single-hearted,
    seek
    The righteousness of Heaven !

THE MEN OF OLD.

WELL speed thy mission, bold Icono-
  clast !
Yet all unworthy of its trust thou
  art,
If, with dry eye, and cold, unloving
  heart,
Thou tread'st the solemn Pantheon of
  the Past,
By the great Future's dazzling hope
  made blind
To all the beauty, power, and truth
  behind.
Not without reverent awe shouldst thou
  put by
  The cypress branches and the ama-
    ranth blooms,
  Where, with clasped hands of prayer,
    upon their tombs
The effigies of old confessors lie,
God's witnesses ; the voices of his will,
Heard in the slow march of the cen-
  turies still !
Such were the men at whose rebuking
  frown,
Dark with God's wrath, the tyrant's
  knee went down ;
Such from the terrors of the guilty drew
The vassal's freedom and the poor man's
  due.

St. Anselm (may he rest forevermore
  In Heaven's sweet peace !) forbade,
  of old, the sale
Of men as slaves, and from the sacred
  pale
Hurled the Northumbrian buyers of the
  poor.
To ransom souls from bonds and evil
  fate
St. Ambrose melted down the sacred
  plate, —
Image of saint, the chalice, and the pix,
Crosses of gold, and silver candlesticks.
"MAN IS WORTH MORE THAN TEM-
  PLES !" he replied
To such as came his holy work to chide.
And brave Cesarius, stripping altars bare,
  And coining from the Abbey's golden
    hoard
The captive's freedom, answered to the
  prayer
  Or threat of those whose fierce zeal for
    the Lord
Stifled their love of man, — "An earth-
  en dish

The last sad supper of the Master bore :
Most miserable sinners ! do ye wish
  More than your Lord, and grudge his
    dying poor
What your own pride and not his need
  requires ?
  Souls, than these shining gauds, He
    values more ;
Mercy, not sacrifice, his heart desires !"
O faithful worthies ! resting far behind
In your dark ages, since ye fell asleep,
Much has been done for truth and hu-
  man-kind, —
Shadows are scattered wherein ye groped
  blind ;
Man claims his birthright, freer pulses
  leap
Through peoples driven in your day like
  sheep ;
Yet, like your own, our age's sphere of
  light,
Though widening still, is walled around
  by night ;
With slow, reluctant eye, the Church has
  read,
Sceptic at heart, the lessons of its Head ;
Counting, too oft, its living members
  less
Than the wall's garnish and the pulpit's
  dress ;
World-moving zeal, with power to bless
  and feed
Life's fainting pilgrims, to their utter
  need,
Instead of bread, holds out the stone of
  creed ;
Sect builds and worships where its
  wealth and pride
And vanity stand shrined and deified,
Careless that in the shadow of its walls
God's living temple into ruin falls.
We need, methinks, the prophet-hero
  still,
Saints true of life, and martyrs strong of
  will,
To tread the land, even now, as Xavier
  trod
  The streets of Goa, barefoot, with his
    bell,
Proclaiming freedom in the name of God,
  And startling tyrants with the fear of
    hell !
  Soft words, smooth prophecies, are
    doubtless well ;
But to rebuke the age's popular crime,
We need the souls of fire, the hearts of
  that old time !

THE PEACE CONVENTION AT BRUSSELS.

STILL in thy streets, O Paris ! doth the
stain
Of blood defy the cleansing autumn rain;
Still breaks the smoke Messina's ruins
through,
And Naples mourns that new Bartholo-
mew,
When squalid beggary, for a dole of bread,
At a crowned murderer's beck of license,
fed
The yawning trenches with her noble
dead ;
Still, doomed Vienna, through thy stately
halls
The shell goes crashing and the red shot
falls,
And, leagued to crush thee, on the Dan-
ube's side,
The bearded Croat and Bosniak spear-
man ride ;
Still in that vale where Himalaya's snow
Melts round the cornfields and the vines
below,
The Sikh's hot cannon, answering ball
for ball,
Flames in the breach of Moultan's shat-
tered wall ;
On Chenab's side the vulture seeks the
slain,
And Sutlej paints with blood its banks
again.
"What folly, then," the faithless critic
cries,
With sneering lip, and wise world-know-
ing eyes,
"While fort to fort, and post to post,
repeat
The ceaseless challenge of the war-drum's
beat,
And round the green earth, to the church-
bell's chime,
The morning drum-roll of the camp
keeps time,
To dream of peace amidst a world in arms,
Of swords to ploughshares changed by
Scriptural charms,
Of nations, drunken with the wine of
blood,
Staggering to take the Pledge of Broth-
erhood,
Like tipplers answering Father Mathew's
call, —
The sullen Spaniard, and the mad-cap
Gaul,

The bull-dog Briton, yielding but with
life,
The Yankee swaggering with his bowie-
knife,
The Russ, from banquets with the vul-
ture shared,
The blood still dripping from his amber
beard,
Quitting their mad Berserker dance to
hear
The dull, meek droning of a drab-coat
seer ;
Leaving the sport of Presidents and
Kings,
Where men for dice each titled gambler
flings,
To meet alternate on the Seine and
Thames, \
For tea and gossip, like old country
dames !
No ! let the cravens plead the weakling's
cant,
Let Cobden cipher, and let Vincent rant,
Let Sturge preach peace to democratic
throngs,
And Burritt, stammering through his
hundred tongues,
Repeat, in all, his ghostly lessons o'er,
Timed to the pauses of the battery's roar;
Check Ban or Kaiser with the barricade
Of "Olive-leaves" and Resolutions made,
Spike guns with pointed Scripture-texts,
and hope
To capsize navies with a windy trope ;
Still shall the glory and the pomp of War
Along their train the shouting millions
draw ;
Still dusty Labor to the passing Brave
His cap shall doff, and Beauty's kerchief
wave ;
Still shall the bard to Valor tune his song,
Still Hero-worship kneel before the
Strong ;
Rosy and sleek, the sable-gowned divine,
O'er his third bottle of suggestive wine.
To plumed and sworded auditors, shall
prove
Their trade accordant with the Law of
Love ;
And Church for State, and State for
Church, shall fight,
And both agree, that Might alone is
Right ! "
Despite of sneers like these, O faithful
few,
Who dare to hold God's word and wit-
ness true,

Whose clear-eyed faith transcends our
    evil time,
And o'er the present wilderness of crime
Sees the calm future, with its robes of
    green,
Its fleece-flecked mountains, and soft
    streams between, —
Still keep the path which duty bids ye
    tread,
Though worldly wisdom shake the cau-
    tious head ;
No truth from Heaven descends upon
    our sphere,
Without the greeting of the sceptic's
    sneer ;
Denied and mocked at, till its blessings
    fall,
Common as dew and sunshine, over all.

Then, o'er Earth's war-field, till the
    strife shall cease,
Like Morven's harpers, sing your song
    of peace ;
As in old fable rang the Thracian's lyre,
Midst howl of fiends and roar of penal fire,
Till the fierce din to pleasing murmurs
    fell,
And love subdued the maddened heart
    of hell.
Lend, once again, that holy song a
    tongue,
Which the glad angels of the Advent
    sung,
Their cradle-anthem for the Saviour's
    birth,
Glory to God, and peace unto the earth !
Through the mad discord send that
    calming word
Which wind and wave on wild Genesa-
    reth heard,
Lift in Christ's name his Cross against
    the Sword !
Not vain the vision which the prophets
    saw,
Skirting with green the fiery waste of war,
Through the hot sand-gleam, looming
    soft and calm
On the sky's rim, the fountain-shading
    palm.
Still lives for Earth, which fiends so long
    have trod,
The great hope resting on the truth of
    God, —
Evil shall cease and Violence pass away,
And the tired world breathe free through
    a long Sabbath day.

    11th mo., 1845.

THE WISH OF TO-DAY.

I ASK not now for gold to gild
  With mocking shine a weary frame ;
The yearning of the mind is stilled, —
  I ask not now for Fame.

A rose-cloud, dimly seen above,
  Melting in heaven's blue depths
    away, —
O, sweet, fond dream of human Love !
  For thee I may not pray.

But, bowed in lowliness of mind,
  I make my humble wishes known, —
I only ask a will resigned,
  O Father, to thine own !

To-day, beneath thy chastening eye
  I crave alone for peace and rest,
Submissive in thy hand to lie,
  And feel that it is best.

A marvel seems the Universe,
  A miracle our Life and Death ;
A mystery which I cannot pierce,
  Around, above, beneath.

In vain I task my aching brain,
  In vain the sage's thought I scan,
I only feel how weak and vain,
  How poor and blind, is man.

And now my spirit sighs for home,
  And longs for light whereby to see,
And, like a weary child, would come,
  O Father, unto thee !

Though oft, like letters traced on sand,
  My weak resolves have passed away,
In mercy lend thy helping hand
  Unto my prayer to-day !

OUR STATE.

THE South-land boasts its teeming cane,
The prairied West its heavy grain,
And sunset's radiant gates unfold
On rising marts and sands of gold !

Rough, bleak, and hard, our little State
Is scant of soil, of limits strait ;
Her yellow sands are sands alone,
Her only mines are ice and stone !

From Autumn frost to April rain,
Too long her winter woods complain ;
From budding flower to falling leaf,
Her summer time is all too brief.

Yet, on her rocks, and on her sands,
And wintry hills, the school-house stands,
And what her rugged soil denies,
The harvest of the mind supplies.

The riches of the Commonwealth
Are free, strong minds, and hearts of
  health ;
And more to her than gold or grain,
The cunning hand and cultured brain.

For well she keeps her ancient stock,
The stubborn strength of Pilgrim Rock ;
And still maintains, with milder laws,
And clearer light, the Good Old Cause !

Nor heeds the sceptic's puny hands,
While near her school the church-spire
  stands ;
Nor fears the blinded bigot's rule,
While near her church-spire stands the
  school.

ALL'S WELL.

THE clouds, which rise with thunder,
    slake
  Our thirsty souls with rain ;
The blow most dreaded falls to break
  From off our limbs a chain ;
And wrongs of man to man but make
  The love of God more plain.
As through the shadowy lens of even
The eye looks farthest into heaven
On gleams of star and depths of blue
The glaring sunshine never knew !

SEED-TIME AND HARVEST.

As o'er his furrowed fields which lie
Beneath a coldly-dropping sky,
Yet chill with winter's melted snow,
The husbandman goes forth to sow,

Thus, Freedom, on the bitter blast
The ventures of thy seed we cast,
And trust to warmer sun and rain
To swell the germs and fill the grain.

Who calls thy glorious service hard ?
Who deems it not its own reward ?

Who, for its trials, counts it less
A cause of praise and thankfulness ?

It may not be our lot to wield
The sickle in the ripened field ;
Nor ours to hear, on summer eves,
The reaper's song among the sheaves.

Yet where our duty's task is wrought
In unison with God's great thought,
The near and future blend in one,
And whatsoe'er is willed, is done !

And ours the grateful service whence
Comes, day by day, the recompense ;
The hope, the trust, the purpose stayed,
The fountain and the noonday shade.

And were this life the utmost span,
The only end and aim of man,
Better the toil of fields like these
Than waking dream and slothful ease.

But life, though falling like our grain,
Like that revives and springs again ;
And, early called, how blest are they
Who wait in heaven their harvest-day !

TO A. K.

ON RECEIVING A BASKET OF SEA-MOSSES.

THANKS for thy gift
    Of ocean flowers,
  Born where the golden drift
  Of the slant sunshine falls
  Down the green, tremulous walls
Of water, to the cool still coral bowers,
Where, under rainbows of perpetual
    showers,
    God's gardens of the deep
    His patient angels keep ;
Gladdening the dim, strange solitude
  With fairest forms and hues, and
    thus
    Forever teaching us
The lesson which the many-colored skies,
The flowers, and leaves, and painted
    butterflies,
The deer's branched antlers, the gay
    bird that flings
The tropic sunshine from its golden
    wings,
The brightness of the human counte-
    nance,
Its play of smiles, the magic of a glance,

Forevermore repeat,
In varied tones and sweet,
That beauty, in and of itself, is good.

O kind and generous friend, o'er whom
The sunset hues of Time are cast,
Painting, upon the overpast
And scattered clouds of noonday
    sorrow
The promise of a fairer morrow,
An earnest of the better life to come ;
The binding of the spirit broken,
The warning to the erring spoken,
The comfort of the sad,
The eye to see, the hand to cull
Of common things the beautiful,
The absent heart made glad
By simple gift or graceful token
Of love it needs as daily food,
All own one Source, and all are good !
Hence, tracking sunny cove and
    reach,
Where spent waves glimmer up the
    beach,
And toss their gifts of weed and shell
From foamy curve and combing swell,
No unbefitting task was thine
    To weave these flowers so soft and
    fair
In unison with His design
    Who loveth beauty everywhere ;
And makes in every zone and clime,
    In ocean and in upper air,
" All things beautiful in their time."

For not alone in tones of awe and
    power
He speaks to man ;
The cloudy horror of the thunder-
    shower
His rainbows span ;

And where the caravan
Winds o'er the desert, leaving, as in
    air
The crane-flock leaves, no trace of pas-
    sage there,
He gives the weary eye
The palm-leaf shadow for the hot noon
    hours,
And on its branches dry
Calls out the acacia's flowers ;
And where the dark shaft pierces
    down
Beneath the mountain roots,
Seen by the miner's lamp alone,
The star-like crystal shoots ;
So, where, the winds and waves
    below,
The coral-branchéd gardens grow,
His climbing weeds and mosses
    show,
Like foliage, on each stony bough,
Of varied hues more strangely gay
Than forest leaves in autumn's
    day ; —
Thus evermore,
On sky, and wave, and shore,
An all-pervading beauty seems to
    say :
God's love and power are one ; and
    they,
Who, like the thunder of a sultry
    day,
Smite to restore,
And they, who, like the gentle wind,
    uplift
The petals of the dew-wet flowers, and
    drift
Their perfume on the air,
Alike may serve Him, each, with their
    own gift,
Making their lives a prayer !

THE CHAPEL OF THE HERMITS,

AND OTHER POEMS.

THE CHAPEL OF THE HERMITS.

'I do believe, and yet, in grief,
  pray for help to unbelief;
'or needful strength aside to lay
he daily cumberings of my way.

' I 'm sick at heart of craft and cant,
ick of the crazed enthusiast's rant,
'rofession's smooth hypocrisies,
ind creeds of iron, and lives of ease.

' I ponder o'er the sacred word,
  read the record of our Lord ;
ind, weak and troubled, envy them
Who touched his seamless garment's
    hem ; —

' Who saw the tears of love he wept
ibove the grave where Lazarus slept ; .
ind heard, amidst the shadows dim
)f Olivet, his evening hymn.

' How blessed the swineherd's low
    estate,
he beggar crouching at the gate,
he leper loathly and abhorred,   .
Vhose eyes of flesh beheld the Lord !

' O sacred soil his sandals pressed !
iweet fountains of his noonday rest !
) light and air of Palestine,
mpregnate with his life divine !

' O, bear me thither ! Let me look
)n Siloa's pool, and Kedron's brook, —
Ineel at Gethsemane, and by
iennesaret walk, before I die !

' Methinks this cold and northern night
Vould melt before that Orient light ;
ind, wet by Hermon's dew and rain,
Aly childhood's faith revive again !"

io spake my friend, one autumn day,
Where the still river slid away
Ieneath us, and above the brown
Red curtains of the woods shut down.

Then said I, — for I could not brook
The mute appealing of his look, —
" I, too, am weak, and faith is small,
And blindness happeneth unto all.

" Yet, sometimes glimpses on my sight.
Through present wrong, the eternal
    right ;
And, step by step, since time began,
I see the steady gain of man ;

" That all of good the past hath had
Remains to make our own time glad, —
Our common daily life divine,
And every land a Palestine.

" Thou weariest of thy present state ;
What gain to thee time's holiest date ?
The doubter now perchance had been
As High Priest or as Pilate then !

" What thought Chorazin's scribes!
    What faith
In Him had Nain and Nazareth ?
Of the few followers whom He led
One sold him, — all forsook and fled.

" O friend ! we need nor rock nor sand,
Nor storied stream of Morning-Land ;
The heavens are glassed in Merri-
    mack, —
What more could Jordan render back ?

" We lack but open eye and ear
To find the Orient's marvels here ; —
The still small voice in autumn's hush,
Yon maple wood the burning bush.

" For still the new transcends the old,
In signs and tokens manifold ; —
Slaves rise up men ; the olive waves,
With roots deep set in battle graves !

" Through the harsh noises of our day
A low, sweet prelude finds its way ;
Through clouds of doubt, and creeds of
    fear,
A light is breaking, calm and clear.

"That song of Love, now low and far,
Erelong shall swell from star to star !
That light, the breaking day, which tips
The golden-spired Apocalypse !"

Then, when my good friend shook his
    head,
And, sighing, sadly smiled, I said :
"Thou mind'st me of a story told
In rare Bernardin's leaves of gold." [53]

And while the slanted sunbeams wove
The shadows of the frost-stained grove,
And, picturing all, the river ran
O'er cloud and wood, I thus began :

In Mount Valerien's chestnut wood
The Chapel of the Hermits stood ;
And thither, at the close of day,
Came two old pilgrims, worn and gray.

One, whose impetuous youth defied
The storms of Baikal's wintry side,
And mused and dreamed where tropic
    day
Flamed o'er his lost Virginia's bay.

His simple tale of love and woe
All hearts had melted, high or low ; —
A blissful pain, a sweet distress,
Immortal in its tenderness.

Yet, while above his charméd page
Beat quick the young heart of his age,
He walked amidst the crowd unknown,
A sorrowing old man, strange and lone.

A homeless, troubled age, — the gray
Pale setting of a weary day ;
Too dull his ear for voice of praise,
Too sadly worn his brow for bays.

Pride, lust of power and glory, slept ;
Yet still his heart its young dream kept,
And, wandering like the deluge-dove,
Still sought the resting-place of love.

And, mateless, childless, envied more
The peasant's welcome from his door
By smiling eyes at eventide,
Than kingly gifts or lettered pride.

Until, in place of wife and child,
All-pitying Nature on him smiled,
And gave to him the golden keys
To all her inmost sanctities.

Mild Druid of her wood-paths dim !
She laid her great heart bare to him,
Its loves and sweet accords ; — he saw
The beauty of her perfect law.

The language of her signs he knew,
What notes her cloudy clarion blew ;
The rhythm of autumn's forest dyes,
The hymn of sunset's painted skies.

And thus he seemed to hear the song
Which swept, of old, the stars along ;
And to his eyes the earth once more
Its fresh and primal beauty wore.

Who sought with him, from summe
    air,
And field and wood, a balm for care ;
And bathed in light of sunset skies
His tortured nerves and weary eyes ?

His fame on all the winds had flown ;
His words had shaken crypt and throne
Like fire, on camp and court and cell
They dropped, and kindled as they
    fell.

Beneath the pomps of state, below
The mitred juggler's masque and show,
A prophecy — a vague hope — ran
His burning thought from man to man.

For peace or rest too well he saw
The fraud of priests, the wrong of law,
And felt how hard, between the two,
Their breath of pain the millions drew.

A prophet-utterance, strong and wild,
The weakness of an unweaned child,
A sun-bright hope for human-kind,
And self-despair, in him combined.

He loathed the false, yet lived no
    true
To half the glorious truths he knew ;
The doubt, the discord, and the sin,
He mourned without, he felt within.

Untrod by him the path he showed,
Sweet pictures on his easel glowed
Of simple faith, and loves of home,
And virtue's golden days to come.

But weakness, shame, and folly made
The foil to all his pen portrayed ;
Still, where his dreamy splendors shone,
The shadow of himself was thrown.

Lord, what is man, whose thought, at
    times,
Up to thy sevenfold brightness climbs,
While still his grosser instinct clings
To earth, like other creeping things !

So rich in words, in acts so mean ;
So high, so low ; chance-swung between
The foulness of the penal pit
And Truth's clear sky, millennium-
    lit !

Vain pride of star-lent genius ! — vain
Quick fancy and creative brain,
Unblest by prayerful sacrifice,
Absurdly great, or weakly wise !

Midst yearnings for a truer life,
Without were fears, within was strife ;
And still his wayward act denied
The perfect good for which he sighed.

The love he sent forth void returned ;
The fame that crowned him scorched
    and burned,
Burning, yet cold and drear and lone, —
A fire-mount in a frozen zone !

Like that the gray-haired sea-king
    passed,[54]
Seen southward from his sleety mast,
About whose brows of changeless frost
A wreath of flame the wild winds tossed.

Far round the mournful beauty played
Of lambent light and purple shade,
Lost on the fixed and dumb despair
Of frozen earth and sea and air !

A man apart, unknown, unloved
By those whose wrongs his soul had
    moved,
He bore the ban of Church and State,
The good man's fear, the bigot's hate !

Forth from the city's noise and throng,
Its pomp and shame, its sin and wrong,
The twain that summer day had strayed
To Mount Valerien's chestnut shade.

To them the green fields and the wood
Lent something of their quietude,
And golden-tinted sunset seemed
Prophetical of all they dreamed.

The hermits from their simple cares
The bell was calling home to prayers,

And, listening to its sound, the twain
Seemed lapped in childhood's trust
    again.

Wide open stood the chapel door ;
A sweet old music, swelling o'er
Low prayerful murmurs, issued thence, —
The Litanies of Providence !

Then Rousseau spake : "Where two or
    three
In His name meet, He there will be ! "
And then, in silence, on their knees
They sank beneath the chestnut-trees.

As to the blind returning light,
As daybreak to the Arctic night,
Old faith revived : the doubts of years
Dissolved in reverential tears.

That gush of feeling overpast,
" Ah me ! " Bernardin sighed at last,
" I would thy bitterest foes could see
Thy heart as it is seen of me !

" No church of God hast thou denied ;
Thou hast but spurned in scorn aside
A base and hollow counterfeit,
Profaning the pure name of it !

" With dry dead moss and marish weeds
His fire the western herdsman feeds,
And greener from the ashen plain
The sweet spring grasses rise again.

" Nor thunder-peal nor mighty wind
Disturb the solid sky behind ;
And through the cloud the red bolt rends
The calm, still smile of Heaven descends !

" Thus through the world, like bolt and
    blast,
And scourging fire, thy words have
    passed.
Clouds break, — the steadfast heavens
    remain ;
Weeds burn, — the ashes feed the grain !

" But whoso strives with wrong may find
Its touch pollute, its darkness blind ;
And learn, as latent fraud is shown
In others' faith, to doubt his own.

" With dream and falsehood, simple trust
And pious hope we tread in dust ;
Lost the calm faith in goodness, — lost
The baptism of the Pentecost !

"Alas ! — the blows for error meant
Too oft on truth itself are spent,
As through the false and vile and base
Looks forth her sad, rebuking face.

"Not ours the Theban's charméd life ;
We come not scathless from the strife !
The Python's coil about us clings,
The trampled Hydra bites and stings !

"Meanwhile, the sport of seeming
        chance,
The plastic shapes of circumstance,
What might have been we fondly guess,
If earlier born, or tempted less.

"And thou, in these wild, troubled
        days,
Misjudged alike in blame and praise,
Unsought and undeserved the same
The sceptic's praise, the bigot's blame ; —

"I cannot doubt, if thou hadst been
Among the highly favored men
Who walked on earth with Fenelon,
He would have owned thee as his son ;

"And, bright with wings of cherubim
Visibly waving over him,
Seen through his life, the Church had
        seemed
All that its old confessors dreamed.

"I would have been," Jean Jaques re-
        plied,
"The humblest servant at his side,
Obscure, unknown, content to see
How beautiful man's life may be !

"O, more than thrice-blest relic, more
Than solemn rite or sacred lore,
The holy life of one who trod
The foot-marks of the Christ of God !

"Amidst a blinded world he saw
The oneness of the Dual law ;
That Heaven's sweet peace on Earth
        began,   .
And God was loved through love of
        man.
                        .
"He lived the Truth which reconciled
The strong man Reason, Faith the child :
In him belief and act were one,
The homilies of duty done !"

So speaking, through the twilight gray
The two old pilgrims went their way.

What seeds of life that day were sown,
The heavenly watchers knew alone.

Time passed, and Autumn came to fold
Green Summer in her brown and gold ;
Time passed, and Winter's tears of snow
Dropped on the grave-mound of Rous-
‹   seau.

"The tree remaineth where it fell,
The pained on earth is pained in hell !"
So priestcraft from its altars cursed
The mournful doubts its falsehood
        nursed.

Ah ! well of old the Psalmist prayed,
"Thy hand, not man's, on me be laid !"
Earth frowns below, Heaven weeps above,
And man is hate, but God is love !

No Hermits now the wanderer sees,
Nor chapel with its chestnut-trees ;
A morning dream, a tale that 's told,
The wave of change o'er all has rolled.

Yet lives the lesson of that day ;
And from its twilight cool and gray
Comes up a low, sad whisper, " Make
The truth thine own, for truth's own
        sake. ·

"Why wait to see in thy brief span
Its perfect flower and fruit in man ?
No saintly touch can save ; no balm
Of healing hath the martyr's palm.

"Midst soulless forms, and false pre-
        tence
Of spiritual pride and pampered sense,
A voice saith, ' What is that to thee !
Be true thyself, and follow Me ! '

"In days when throne and altar heard
The wanton's wish, the bigot's word,
And pomp of state and ritual show
Scarce hid the loathsome death be-
        low, —

"Midst fawning priests and courtiers
        foul,
The losel swarm of crown and cowl,
White-robed walked François Fenelon,
Stainless as Uriel in the sun !   ·

"Yet in his time the stake blazed red,
The poor were eaten up like bread :
Men knew him not : his garment's hem
No healing virtue had for them.

" Alas ! no present saint we find ;
The white cymar gleams far behind,
Revealed in outline vague, sublime,
Through telescopic mists of time !

" Trust not in man with passing breath,
But in the Lord, old Scripture saith ;
The truth which saves thou mayst not
        blend
With false professor, faithless friend.

" Search thine own heart. What pain-
        eth thee
In others in thyself may be ;
All dust is frail, all flesh is weak ;
Be thou the true man thou dost seek !

" Where now with pain thou treadest, trod
The whitest of the saints of God !
To show thee where their feet were set,
The light which led them shineth yet.

" The footprints of the life divine,
Which marked their path, remain in
        thine ;
And that great Life, transfused in theirs,
Awaits thy faith, thy love, thy prayers !"

A lesson which I well may heed,
A word of fitness to my need ;
So from that twilight cool and gray
Still saith a voice, or seems to say.

We rose, and slowly homeward turned,
While down the west the sunset burned;
And, in its light, hill, wood, and tide,
And human forms seemed glorified.

The village homes transfigured stood,
And purple bluffs, whose belting wood
Across the waters leaned to hold
The yellow leaves like lamps of gold.

Then spake my friend : " Thy words are
        true ;
Forever old, forever new,
These home-seen splendors are the same
Which over Eden's sunsets came.

" To these bowed heavens let wood and
        hill
Lift voiceless praise and anthem still ;
Fall, warm with blessing, over them,
Light of the New Jerusalem !

" Flow on, sweet river, like the stream
Of John's Apocalyptic dream !
This mapled ridge shall Horeb be,
Yon green-banked lake our Galilee !

" Henceforth my heart shall sigh no
        more
For olden time and holier shore ;
God's love and blessing, then and there,
Are now and here and everywhere."

MISCELLANEOUS.

QUESTIONS OF LIFE.

And the angel that was sent unto me, whose
name was Uriel, gave me an answer and said,
" Thy heart hath gone too far in this world,
and thinkest thou to comprehend the way of the
Most High? "
    Then said I, " Yea, my Lord."
    Then said he unto me, " Go thy way, weigh me
the weight of the fire or measure me the blast
of the wind, or call me again the day that is
past." — 2 *Esdras*, chap. iv.

A BENDING staff I would not break,
A feeble faith I would not shake,
Nor even rashly pluck away
The error which some truth may stay,
Whose loss might leave the soul without
A shield against the shafts of doubt.

And yet, at times, when over all
A darker mystery seems to fall,
(May God forgive the child of dust,
Who seeks to *know*, where Faith should
        trust !)
I raise the questions, old and dark,
Of Uzdom's tempted patriarch,
And, speech-confounded, build again
The baffled tower of Shinar's plain.

I am : how little more I know !
Whence came I ? Whither do I go ?
A centred self, which feels and is ;
A cry between the silences ;
A shadow-birth of clouds at strife
With sunshine on the hills of life ;

A shaft from Nature's quiver cast
Into the Future from the Past ;
Between the cradle and the shroud,
A meteor's flight from cloud to cloud.

Thorough the vastness, arching all,
I see the great stars rise and fall,
The rounding seasons come and go,
The tided oceans ebb and flow ;
The tokens of a central force,
Whose circles, in their widening course,
O'erlap and move the universe ;
The workings of the law whence springs
The rhythmic harmony of things,
Which shapes in earth the darkling
    spar,
And orbs in heaven the morning star.
Of all I see, in earth and sky, —
Star, flower, beast, bird, — what part
    have I ?
This conscious life, — is it the same
Which thrills the universal frame,
Whereby the cavernal crystal shoots,
And mounts the sap from forest roots,
Whereby the exiled wood-bird tells
When Spring makes green her native
    dells ?
How feels the stone the pang of birth,
Which brings its sparkling prism forth ?
The forest-tree the throb which gives
The life-blood to its new-born leaves ?
Do bird and blossom feel, like me,
Life's many-folded mystery, —
The wonder which it is TO BE ?
Or stand I severed and distinct,
From Nature's chain of life unlinked ?
Allied to all, yet not the less
Prisoned in separate consciousness,
Alone o'erburdened with a sense
Of life, and cause, and consequence ?

In vain to me the Sphinx propounds
The riddle of her sights and sounds ;
Back still the vaulted mystery gives
The echoed question it receives.
What sings the brook ? What oracle
Is in the pine-tree's organ swell ?
What may the wind's low burden
    be ?
The meaning of the moaning sea ?
The hieroglyphics of the stars ?
Or clouded sunset's crimson bars ?
I vainly ask, for mocks my skill
The trick of Nature's cipher still.

I turn from Nature unto men,
I ask the stylus and the pen ;

What sang the bards of old ? What
    meant
The prophets of the Orient ?
The rolls of buried Egypt, hid
In painted tomb and pyramid ?
What mean Idúmea's arrowy lines,
Or dusk Elora's monstrous signs ?
How speaks the primal thought of man
From the grim carvings of Copan ?
Where rests the secret ? Where the keys
Of the old death-bolted mysteries ?
Alas ! the dead retain their trust ;
Dust hath no answer from the dust.

The great enigma still unguessed,
Unanswered the eternal quest ;
I gather up the scattered rays
Of wisdom in the early days,
Faint gleams and broken, like the light
Of meteors in a northern night,
Betraying to the darkling earth
The unseen sun which gave them birth ;
I listen to the sibyl's chant,
The voice of priest and hierophant ;
I know what Indian Kreeshna saith,
And what of life and what of death
The demon taught to Socrates ;
And what, beneath his garden-trees
Slow pacing, with a dream-like tread,
The solemn-thoughted Plato said ;
Nor lack I tokens, great or small,
Of God's clear light in each and all,
While holding with more dear regard
The scroll of Hebrew seer and bard,
The starry pages promise-lit
With Christ's Evangel over-writ,
Thy miracle of life and death,
O holy one of Nazareth !

On Aztec ruins, gray and lone,
The circling serpent coils in stone, —
Type of the endless and unknown ;
Whereof we seek the clew to find,
With groping fingers of the blind !
Forever sought, and never found,
We trace that serpent-symbol round
Our resting-place, our starting bound !
O thriftlessness of dream and guess !
O wisdom which is foolishness !
Why idly seek from outward things
The answer inward silence brings ;
Why stretch beyond our proper sphere
And age, for that which lies so near ?
Why climb the far-off hills with pain,
A nearer view of heaven to gain ?
In lowliest depths of bosky dells
The hermit Contemplation dwells.

A fountain's pine-hung slope his seat,
And lotus-twined his silent feet,
Whence, piercing heaven, with screenéd
  sight,
He sees at noon the stars, whose light
Shall glorify the coming night.

Here let me pause, my quest forego ;
Enough for me to feel and know
That He in whom the cause and end,
The past and future, meet and blend, —
Who, girt with his immensities,
Our vast and star-hung system sees,
Small as the clustered Pleiades, —
Moves not alone the heavenly quires,
But waves the spring-time's grassy
  spires,
Guards not archangel feet alone,
But deigns to guide and keep my own ;
Speaks not alone the words of fate
Which worlds destroy, and worlds
  create,
But whispers in my spirit's ear,
In tones of love, or warning fear,
A language none beside may hear.

To Him, from wanderings long and
  wild,
I come, an over-wearied child,
In cool and shade his peace to find,
Like dew-fall settling on my mind.
Assured that all I know is best,
And humbly trusting for the rest,
I turn from Fancy's cloud-built scheme,
Dark creed, and mournful eastern dream
Of power, impersonal and cold,
Controlling all, itself controlled,
Maker and slave of iron laws,
Alike the subject and the cause ;
From vain philosophies, that try
The sevenfold gates of mystery,
And, baffled ever, babble still,
Word-prodigal of fate and will ;
From Nature, and her mockery, Art,
And book and speech of men apart,
To the still witness in my heart ;
With reverence waiting to behold
His Avatár of love untold,
The Eternal Beauty new and old !

THE PRISONERS OF NAPLES.

I HAVE been thinking of the victims
  bound
In Naples, dying for the lack of air
And sunshine, in their close, damp
  cells of pain,
Where hope is not, and innocence in
  vain
Appeals against the torture and the
  chain !
Unfortunates ! whose crime it was to
  share
Our common love of freedom, and to
  dare,*
In its behalf, Rome's harlot triple-
  crowned,
And her base pander, the most hateful
  thing
Who upon Christian or on Pagan
  ground
Makes vile the old heroic name of king.
O God most merciful ! Father just and
  kind !
Whom man hath bound let thy right
  hand unbind.
Or, if thy purposes of good behind
Their ills lie hidden, let the sufferers
  find
Strong consolations ; leave them not to
  doubt
Thy providential care, nor yet without
The hope which all thy attributes in-
  spire,
That not in vain the martyr's robe of
  fire
Is worn, nor the sad prisoner's fretting
  chain ;
Since all who suffer for thy truth send
  forth,
Electrical, with every throb of pain,
Unquenchable sparks, thy own bap-
  tismal rain
Of fire and spirit over all the earth,
Making the dead in slavery live again.
Let this great hope be with them, as
  they lie
Shut from the light, the greenness, and
  the sky, —
From the cool waters and the pleasant
  breeze,
The smell of flowers, and shade of sum-
  mer trees ;
Bound with the felon lepers, whom
  disease
And sins abhorred make loathsome ;
  let them share
Pellico's faith, Foresti's strength to bear
Years of unutterable torment, stern and
  still,
As the chained Titan victor through his
  will !

Comfort them with thy future ; let them
see
The day-dawn of Italian liberty ;
For that, with all good things, is hid
with Thee,
And, perfect in thy thought, awaits its
time to be !

I, who have spoken for freedom at the cost
Of some weak friendships, ôr some pal-
try prize
Of name or place, and more than I have
lost
Have gained in wider reach of sym-
pathies,
And free communion with the good and
wise, —
May God forbid that I should ever
boast
Such easy self-denial, or repine
That the strong pulse of health no more
is mine ;
That, overworn at noonday, I must
yield
To other hands the gleaning of the
field, —
A tired on-looker through the day's
decline.
For blest beyond deserving still, and
knowing
That kindly Providence its care is
showing
In the withdrawal as in the bestowing,
Scarcely I dare for more or less to pray.
Beautiful yet for me this autumn day
Melts on its sunset hills ; and, far away,
For me the Ocean lifts its solemn psalm,
To me the pine-woods whisper ; and
for me
Yon river, winding through its vales of
calm,
By greenest banks, with asters purple-
starred,
And gentian bloom and golden-rod
made gay,
Flows down in silent gladness to the sea,
Like a pure spirit to its great reward !

Nor lack I friends, long-tried and near
and dear,
Whose love is round me like this atmos-
phere,
Warm, soft, and golden.   For such gifts
to me
What shall I render, O my God, to thee ?
Let me not dwell upon my lighter share
Of pain and ill that human life must bear ;

Save me from selfish pining ; let my heart,
Drawn from itself in sympathy, forget
The bitter longings of a vain regret,
The anguish of its own peculiar smart.
Remembering others, as I have to-day,
In their great sorrows, let me live alway
Not for myself alone, but have a part,
Such as a frail and erring spirit may,
In love which is of Thee, and which in-
deed Thou art !

MOLOCH IN STATE STREET.

THE moon has set : while yet the dawn
    Breaks cold and gray,
Between the midnight and the morn
    Bear off your prey !

On, swift and still !— the conscious street
    Is panged and stirred ;
Tread light ! — that fall of serried feet
    The dead have heard !

The first drawn blood of Freedom's veins
    Gushed where ye tread ;
Lo ! through the dusk the martyr-stains
    Blush darkly red !

Beneath the slowly waning stars
    And whitening day,
What stern and awful presence bars
    That sacred way ?

What faces frown upon ye, dark
    With shame and pain ?
Come these from Plymouth's Pilgrim
    bark ?
    Is that young Vane ?

Who, dimly beckoning, speed ye on
    With mocking cheer ?
Lo ! spectral Andros, Hutchinson,
    And Gage are here !

For ready mart or favoring blast
    Through Moloch's fire
Flesh of his flesh, unsparing, passed
    The Tyrian sire.

Ye make that ancient sacrifice
    Of Man to Gain,
Your traffic thrives, where Freedom dies,
    Beneath the chain.

Ye sow to-day, your harvest, scorn
    And hate, is near ;

How think ye freemen, mountain-born,
    The tale will hear ?

Thank God ! our mother State can yet
    Her fame retrieve ;
To you and to your children let
    The scandal cleave.

Chain Hall and Pulpit, Court and Press,
    Make gods of gold ;
Let honor, truth, and manliness
    Like wares be sold.

Your hoards are great, your walls are
    strong,
    But God is just ;
The gilded chambers built by wrong
    Invite the rust.

What ! know ye not the gains of Crime
    Are dust and dross ;
Its ventures on the waves of time
    Foredoomed to loss !

And still the Pilgrim State remains
    What she hath been ;
Her inland hills, her seaward plains,
    Still nurture men !

Nor wholly lost the fallen mart, —
    Her olden blood
Through many a free and generous heart
    Still pours its flood.

That brave old blood, quick-flowing yet,
    Shall know no check,
Till a free people's foot is set
    On Slavery's neck.

Even now, the peal of bell and gun,
    And hills aflame,
Tell of the first great triumph won
    In Freedom's name.[66]

The long night dies : the welcome gray
    Of dawn we see ;
Speed up the heavens thy perfect day,
    God of the free !
1851.

THE PEACE OF EUROPE.

1852.

"Great peace in Europe ! Order reigns
From Tiber's hills to Danube's plains !"
So say her kings and priests ; so say
The lying prophets of our day.

Go lay to earth a listening ear ;
The tramp of measured marches hear, —
The rolling of the cannon's wheel,
The shotted musket's murderous peal,
The night alarm, the sentry's call,
The quick-eared spy in hut and
    hall !
From Polar sea and tropic fen
The dying-groans of exiled men !
The bolted cell, the galley's chains,
The scaffold smoking with its stains !
Order, — the hush of brooding slaves !
Peace, — in the dungeon-vaults and
    graves !

O Fisher ! of the world-wide net,
With meshes in all waters set,
Whose fabled keys of heaven and
    hell
Bolt hard the patriot's prison-cell,
And open wide the banquet-hall,
Where kings and priests hold carni-
    val !
Weak vassal tricked in royal guise,
Boy Kaiser with thy lip of lies ;
Base gambler for Napoleon's crown,
Barnacle on his dead renown !
Thou, Bourbon Neapolitan,
Crowned scandal, loathed of God and
    man ;
And thou, fell Spider of the North !
Stretching thy giant feelers forth,
Within whose web the freedom dies
Of nations eaten up like flies !
Speak, Prince and Kaiser, Priest and
    Czar !
If this be Peace, pray what is War ?

White Angel of the Lord ! unmeet
That soil accursed for thy pure feet.
Never in Slavery's desert flows
The fountain of thy charmed repose ;
No tyrant's hand thy chaplet weaves
Of lilies and of olive-leaves ;
Not with the wicked shalt thou dwell,
Thus saith the Eternal Oracle ;
Thy home is with the pure and free !
Stern herald of thy better day,
Before thee, to prepare thy way,
The Baptist Shade of Liberty,
Gray, scarred and hairy-robed, must
    press
With bleeding feet the wilderness !
O that its voice might pierce the ear
Of princes, trembling while they hear
A cry as of the Hebrew seer :
Repent ! God's kingdom draweth near !

WORDSWORTH.

WRITTEN ON A BLANK LEAF OF HIS
MEMOIRS.

DEAR friends, who read the world aright,
And in its common forms discern
A beauty and a harmony
The many never learn !

Kindred in soul of him who found
In simple flower and leaf and stone
The impulse of the sweetest lays
Our Saxon tongue has known, —

Accept this record of a life
As sweet and pure, as calm and good,
As a long day of blandest June
In green field and in wood.

How welcome to our ears, long pained
By strife of sect and party noise,
The brook-like murmur of his song
Of nature's simple joys ! •

The violet by its mossy stone,
The primrose by the river's brim,
And chance-sown daffodil, have found
Immortal life through him.

The sunrise on his breezy lake,
The rosy tints his sunset brought,
World-seen, are gladdening all the vales
And mountain-peaks of thought.

Art builds on sand ; the works of pride
And human passion change and fall ;
But that which shares the life of God
With him surviveth all.

TO ——.

LINES WRITTEN AFTER A SUMMER
DAY'S EXCURSION.

FAIR Nature's priestesses ! to whom,
In hieroglyph of bud and bloom,
Her mysteries are told ;
Who, wise in lore of wood and mead,
The seasons' pictured scrolls can read,
In lessons manifold !

Thanks for the courtesy, and gay
Good-humor, which on Washing Day
Our ill-timed visit bore ;
Thanks for your graceful oars, which broke
The morning dreams of Artichoke,
Along his wooded shore !

Varied as varying Nature's ways,
Sprites of the river, woodland fays,
Or mountain nymphs, ye seem ;
Free-limbed Dianas on the green,
Loch Katrine's Ellen, or Undine,
Upon your favorite stream.

The forms of which the poets told,
The fair benignities of old,
Were doubtless such as you ;
What more than Artichoke the rill
Of Helicon ? Than Pipe-stave hill
Arcadia's mountain-view ?

No sweeter bowers the bee delayed,
In wild Hymettus' scented shade,
Than those you dwell among ;
Snow-flowered azalias, intertwined
With roses, over banks inclined
With trembling harebells hung !

A charméd life unknown to death,
Immortal freshness Nature hath ;
Her fabled fount and glen
Are now and here : Dodona's shrine
Still murmurs in the wind-swept pine,
All is that e'er hath been.

The Beauty which old Greece or Rome
Sung, painted, wrought, lies close
    home ;
We need but eye and ear
In all our daily walks to trace
The outlines of incarnate grace,
The hymns of gods to hear !

IN PEACE.

A TRACK of moonlight on a quiet lake
    Whose small waves on a silver-sand
        shore
Whisper of peace, and with the low wind
    make
Such harmonies as keep the woods awak
And listening all night long for their swe
    sake ;
    A green-waved slope of meadow, ho
        ered o'er
By angel-troops of lilies, swaying light
On viewless stems, with folded wings c
    white ;
A slumberous stretch of mountain-lan
    far seen
Where the low westering day, with gol
    and green,
Purple and amber, softly blended, fills

The wooded vales, and melts among the
   hills ;
A vine-fringed river, winding to its rest
   On the calm bosom of a stormless sea,
Bearing alike upon its placid breast,
With earthly flowers and heavenly stars
   impressed,
The hues of time and of eternity :
Such are the pictures which the thought
   of thee,
O friend, awakeneth, — charming the
   keen pain
Of thy departure, and our sense of loss
Requiting with the fulness of thy gain.
   Lo ! on the quiet grave thy life-borne
     cross,
Dropped only at its side, methinks doth
   shine,
Of thy beatitude the radiant sign !
   No sob of grief, no wild lament be there,
   To break the Sabbath of the holy air ;
But, in their stead, the silent-breathing
   prayer
Of hearts still waiting for a rest like thine.
O spirit redeemed ! Forgive us, if hence-
   forth,
With sweet and pure similitudes of earth,
   We keep thy pleasant memory freshly
     green,
Of love's inheritance a priceless part,
   Which Fancy's self, in reverent awe, is
     seen
To paint, forgetful of the tricks of art,
   With pencil dipped alone in colors of
     the heart.

BENEDICITE.

God's love and peace be with thee, where
Soe'er this soft autumnal air
Lifts the dark tresses of thy hair !

Whether through city casements comes
Its kiss to thee, in crowded rooms,
Or, out among the woodland blooms,

It freshens o'er thy thoughtful face,
Imparting, in its glad embrace,
Beauty to beauty, grace to grace !

Fair Nature's book together read,
The old wood-paths that knew our tread,
The maple shadows overhead, —

The hills we climbed, the river seen
By gleams along its deep ravine, —
All keep thy memory fresh and green.

Where'er I look, where'er I stray,
Thy thought goes with me on my way,
And hence the prayer I breathe to-day ;

O'er lapse of time and change of scene,
The weary waste which lies between
Thyself and me, my heart I lean.

Thou lack'st not Friendship's spell-word,
   nor
The half-unconscious power to draw
All hearts to thine by Love's sweet law.

With these good gifts of God is cast
Thy lot, and many a charm thou hast
To hold the blessed angels fast.

If, then, a fervent wish for thee
The gracious heavens will heed from me,
What should, dear heart, its burden be ?

The sighing of a shaken reed, —
What can I more than meekly plead
The greatness of our common need ?

God's love, — unchanging, pure, and
   true, —
The Paraclete white-shining through
His peace, — the fall of Hermon's dew !

With such a prayer, on this sweet day,
As thou mayst hear and I may say,
I greet thee, dearest, far away !

PICTURES.

I.

Light, warmth, and sprouting greenness,
   and o'er all
   Blue, stainless, steel-bright ether, rain-
     ing down
   Tranquillity upon the deep-hushed
     town,
   The freshening meadows, and the hill-
     sides brown ;
    Voice of the west-wind from the hills
     of pine,
And the brimmed river from its distant
   fall,
   Low hum of bees, and joyous interlude
   Of bird-songs in the streamlet-skirting
     wood, —
   Heralds and prophecies of sound and
     sight,
   Blessed forerunners of the warmth and
     light,

Attendant angels to the house of prayer,
  With reverent footsteps keeping pace
    with mine, —
Once more, through God's great love, with
    you I share
A morn of resurrection sweet and fair
  As that which saw, of old, in Pales-
    tine,
Immortal Love uprising in fresh bloom
From the dark night and winter of
    the tomb !

5th mo., 2d, 1852.

II.

White with its sun-bleached dust, the
  pathway winds
Before me ; dust is on the shrunken
    grass,
And on the trees beneath whose
    boughs I pass ;
Frail screen against the Hunter of the
    sky,
Who, glaring on me with his lidless eye,
  While mounting with his dog-star
    high and higher
Ambushed in light intolerable, unbinds
  The burnished quiver of his shafts
    of fire.
Between me and the hot fields of his
    South
A tremulous glow, as from a furnace-
    mouth,
Glimmers and swims before my daz-
    zled sight,
  As if the burning arrows of his ire
Broke as they fell, and shattered into
    light ;
Yet on my cheek I feel the western wind,
  And hear it telling to the orchard
    trees,
  And to the faint and flower-forsaken
    bees,
Tales of fair meadows, green with con-
    stant streams,
And mountains rising blue and cool
    behind,
  Where in moist dells the purple or-
    chis gleams,
And starred with white the virgin's
    bower is twined.
So the o'erwearied pilgrim, as he fares
  Along life's summer waste, at times is
    fanned,
Even at noontide, by the cool, sweet airs
  Of a serener and a holier land,
    Fresh as the morn, and as the dew-
    fall bland.

Breath of the blessed Heaven for which
    we pray,
  Blow from the eternal hills ! — make
    glad our earthly way !

8th mo., 1852.

DERNE.[56]

Night on the city of the Moor !
  On mosque and tomb, and white-walled
    shore,
On sea-waves, to whose ceaseless knock
The narrow harbor-gates unlock,
  On corsair's galley, carack tall,
  And plundered Christian caraval !
The sounds of Moslem life are still ;
No mule-bell tinkles down the hill ;
Stretched in the broad court of the
    khan,
  The dusty Bornou caravan
Lies heaped in slumber, beast and man ;
  The Sheik is dreaming in his tent,
  His noisy Arab tongue o'erspent ;
The kiosk's glimmering lights are gone,
The merchant with his wares with-
    drawn ;
Rough pillowed on some pirate breast,
  The dancing-girl has sunk to rest ;
And, save where measured footsteps
    fall
Along the Bashaw's guarded wall,
  Or where, like some bad dream, the
    Jew
Creeps stealthily his quarter through,
  Or counts with fear his golden heaps,
  The City of the Corsair sleeps !

But where yon prison long and low
  Stands black against the pale star-glow,
Chafed by the ceaseless wash of waves,
  There watch and pine the Christian
    slaves ; —
Rough-bearded men, whose far-off wives
  Wear out with grief their lonely lives ;
  And youth, still flashing from his eyes
The clear blue of New England skies,
A treasured lock of whose soft hair
Now wakes some sorrowing mother's
    prayer ;
  Or, worn upon some maiden breast,
Stirs with the loving heart's unrest !

A bitter cup each life must drain,
The groaning earth is cursed with pain,
And, like the scroll the angel bore
The shuddering Hebrew seer before,

O'erwrit alike, without, within,
With all the woes which follow sin ;
But, bitterest of the ills beneath
Whose load man totters down to death,
Is that which plucks the regal crown
Of Freedom from his forehead down,
And snatches from his powerless hand
The sceptred sign of self-command,
Effacing with the chain and rod
The image and the seal of God ;
Till from his nature, day by day,
The manly virtues fall away,
And leave him naked, blind and mute,
The godlike merging in the brute !

Why mourn the quiet ones who die
Beneath affection's tender eye,
Unto their household and their kin
Like ripened corn-sheaves gathered in ?
O weeper, from that tranquil sod,
That holy harvest-home of God,
Turn to the quick and suffering, — shed
Thy tears upon the living dead !
Thank God above thy dear ones' graves,
They sleep with Him, — they are not
    slaves.

What dark mass, down the mountain-
    sides
Swift-pouring, like a stream divides ? —
A long, loose, straggling caravan,
Camel and horse and arméd man.
The moon's low crescent, glimmering
    o'er
Its grave of waters to the shore,
Lights up that mountain cavalcade,
And glints from gun and spear and
    blade
Near and more near ! — now o'er them
    falls
The shadow of the city walls.
Hark to the sentry's challenge, drowned
In the fierce trumpet's charging
    sound ! —
The rush of men, the musket's peal,
The short, sharp clang of meeting steel !

Vain, Moslem, vain thy lifeblood poured
So freely on thy foeman's sword !
Not to the swift nor to the strong
The battles of the right belong ;
For he who strikes for Freedom wears
The armor of the captive's prayers,
And Nature proffers to his cause
The strength of her eternal laws ;
While he whose arm essays to bind
And herd with common brutes his kind

Strives evermore at fearful odds
With Nature and the jealous gods,
And dares the dread recoil which late
Or soon their right shall vindicate.

'T is done, — the hornéd crescent falls !
The star-flag flouts the broken walls !
Joy to the captive husband ! joy
To thy sick heart, O brown-locked boy !
In sullen wrath the conquered Moor
Wide open flings your dungeon-door,
And leaves ye free from cell and chain,
The owners of yourselves again.
Dark as his allies desert-born,
Soiled with the battle's stain, and worn
With the long marches of his band
Through hottest wastes of rock and
    sand, —
Scorched by the sun and furnace-breath
Of the red desert's wind of death,
With welcome words and grasping
    hands,
The victor and deliverer stands !

The tale is one of distant skies ;
The dust of half a century lies
Upon it ; yet its hero's name
Still lingers on the lips of Fame.
Men speak the praise of him who gave
Deliverance to the Moorman's slave,
Yet dare to brand with shame and crime
The heroes of our land and time, —
The self-forgetful ones, who stake
Home, name, and life for Freedom's
    sake.
God mend his heart who cannot feel
The impulse of a holy zeal,
And sees not, with his sordid eyes,
The beauty of self-sacrifice !
Though in the sacred place he stands,
Uplifting consecrated hands,
Unworthy are his lips to tell
Of Jesus' martyr-miracle,
Or name aright that dread embrace
Of suffering for a fallen race !

ASTRÆA.

" Jove means to settle
Astræa in her seat again,
And let down from his golden chain
An age of better metal."
                    BEN JONSON, 1615

O POET rare and old !
    Thy words are prophecies ;
Forward the age of gold,
    The new Saturnian lies.

The universal prayer
And hope are not in vain ;
Rise, brothers ! and prepare
The way for Saturn's reign.

Perish shall all which takes
From labor's board and can ;
Perish shall all which makes
A spaniel of the man !

Free from its bonds the mind,
The body from the rod ;
Broken all chains that bind
The image of our God.

Just men no longer pine
Behind their prison-bars ;
Through the rent dungeon shine
The free sun and the stars.

Earth own, at last, untrod
By sect, or caste, or clan,
The fatherhood of God,
The brotherhood of man !

Fraud fail, craft perish, forth
The money-changers driven,
And God's will done on earth,
As now in heaven !

INVOCATION.

Through thy clear spaces, Lord, of
    old,
Formless and void the dead earth rolled ;
Deaf to thy heaven's sweet music, blind
To the great lights which o'er it shined ;
No sound, no ray, no warmth, no
    breath, —
A dumb despair, a wandering death.

To that dark, weltering horror came
Thy spirit, like a subtle flame, —
A breath of life electrical,
Awakening and transforming all,
Till beat and thrilled in every part
The pulses of a living heart.

Then knew their bounds the land and
    sea ;
Then smiled the bloom of mead and
    tree ;
From flower to moth, from beast to man,
The quick creative impulse ran ;
And earth, with life from thee renewed,
Was in thy holy eyesight good.

As lost and void, as dark and cold
And formless as that earth of old, —
A wandering waste of storm and night,
Midst spheres of song and realms o
    light, —
A blot upon thy holy sky,
Untouched, unwarned of thee, am I.

O thou who movest on the deep
Of spirits, wake my own from sleep !
Its darkness melt, its coldness warm,
The lost restore, the ill transform,
That flower and fruit henceforth may b
Its grateful offering, worthy thee.

THE CROSS.

ON THE DEATH OF RICHARD DILLING HAM, IN THE NASHVILLE PENITENTIARY.

" The cross, if rightly borne, shall be
No burden, but support to thee " ; *
So, moved of old time for our sake,
The holy monk of Kempen spake.

Thou brave and true one ! upon whom
Was laid the cross of martyrdom,
How didst thou, in thy generous youth
Bear witness to this blessed truth !

Thy cross of suffering and of shame
A staff within thy hands became,
In paths where faith alone could see
The Master's steps supporting thee.

Thine was the seed-time ; God alone
Beholds the end of what is sown ;
Beyond our vision, weak and dim,
The harvest-time is hid with Him.

Yet, unforgotten where it lies,
That seed of generous sacrifice,
Though seeming on the desert cast,
Shall rise with bloom and fruit at last.

EVA.

Dry the tears for holy Eva,
With the blessed angels leave her ;
Of the form so soft and fair
Give to earth the tender care.

For the golden locks of Eva
Let the sunny south-land give her

* Thomas à Kempis. Imit. Christ.

Flowery pillow of repose,—
Orange-bloom and budding rose.

In the better home of Eva
Let the shining ones receive her,
With the welcome-voicéd psalm,
Harp of gold and waving palm !

All is light and peace with Eva ;
There the darkness cometh never ;
Tears are wiped, and fetters fall,
And the Lord is all in all.

Weep no more for happy Eva,
Wrong and sin no more shall grieve
    her ;
Care and pain and weariness
Lost in love so measureless.

Gentle Eva, loving Eva,
Child confessor, true believer,
Listener at the Master's knee,
" Suffer such to come to me."

O, for faith like thine, sweet Eva,
Lighting all the solemn river,
And the blessings of the poor
Wafting to the heavenly shore !

TO FREDRIKA BREMER.[57]

SEERESS of the misty Norland,
    Daughter of the Vikings bold,
Welcome to the sunny Vineland,
    Which thy fathers sought of old !

Soft as flow of Silja's waters,
    When the moon of summer shines,
Strong as Winter from his mountains
    Roaring through the sleeted pines.

Heart and ear, we long have listened
    To thy saga, rune, and song,
As a household joy and presence
    We have known and loved thee long.

By the mansion's marble mantel,
    Round the log-walled cabin's hearth,
Thy sweet thoughts and northern fan-
    cies
Meet and mingle with our mirth.

And o'er weary spirits keeping
    Sorrow's night-watch, long and chill,
Shine they like thy sun of summer
    Over midnight vale and hill.

We alone to thee are strangers,
    Thou our friend and teacher art ;
Come, and know us as we know thee ;
    Let us meet thee heart to heart !

To our homes and household altars
    We, in turn, thy steps would lead,
As thy loving hand has led us
    O'er the threshold of the Swede.

APRIL.

" The spring comes slowly up this way."
                        Christabel.

'T IS the noon of the spring-time, yet
    never a bird
In the wind-shaken elm or the maple is
    heard ;
For green meadow-grasses wide levels of
    snow,
And blowing of drifts where the crocus
    should blow ;
Where wind-flower and violet, amber
    and white,
On south - sloping brooksides should
    smile in the light,
O'er the cold winter-beds of their late-
    waking roots
The frosty flake eddies, the ice-crystal
    shoots ;
And, longing for light, under wind-
    driven heaps,
Round the boles of the pine-wood the
    ground-laurel creeps,
Unkissed of the sunshine, unbaptized of
    showers,
With buds scarcely swelled, which
    should burst into flowers !
We wait for thy coming, sweet wind of
    the south !
For the touch of thy light wings, the
    kiss of thy mouth ;
For the yearly evangel thou bearest from
    God,
Resurrection and life to the graves of the
    sod !
Up our long river-valley, for days, have
    not ceased
The wail and the shriek of the bitter
    northeast, —
Raw and chill, as if winnowed through
    ices and snow,
All the way from the land of the wild
    Esquimau, —
Until all our dreams of the land of the
    blest,

Like that red hunter's, turn to the sunny
    southwest.
O soul of the spring-time, its light and
    its breath,
Bring warmth to this coldness, bring
    life to this death ;
Renew the great miracle ; let us behold
The stone from the mouth of the sepul-
    chre rolled,
And Nature, like Lazarus, rise, as of
    old !
Let our faith, which in darkness and
    coldness has lain,
Revive with the warmth and the bright-
    ness again,
And in blooming of flower and budding
    of tree
The symbols and types of our destiny
    see ;
The life of the spring-time, the life of
    the whole,
And, as sun to the sleeping earth, love
    to the soul !

STANZAS FOR THE TIMES.

1850.

THE evil days have come, — the poor
    Are made a prey ;
Bar up the hospitable door,
Put out the fire-lights, point no more
    The wanderer's way.

For Pity now is crime ; the chain
Which binds our States
Is melted at her hearth in twain,
Is rusted by her tears' soft rain :
    Close up her gates.

Our Union, like a glacier stirred
    By voice below,
Or bell of kine, or wing of bird,
A beggar's crust, a kindly word
    May overthrow !

Poor, whispering tremblers ! — yet we
    boast
    Our blood and name ;
Bursting its century-bolted frost,
Each gray cairn on the Northman's
    coast
    Cries out for shame !

O for the open firmament,
    The prairie free,

The desert hillside, cavern-rent,
The Pawnee's lodge, the Arab's tent,
    The Bushman's tree !

Than web of Persian loom most rare,
    Or soft divan,
Better the rough rock, bleak and bare,
Or hollow tree, which man may share
    With suffering man.

I hear a voice : "Thus saith the Law,
    Let Love be dumb ;
Clasping her liberal hands in awe,
Let sweet-lipped Charity withdraw
    From hearth and home."

I hear another voice : "The poor
    Are thine to feed ;
Turn not the outcast from thy door,
Nor give to bonds and wrong once more
    Whom God hath freed."

Dear Lord ! between that law and thee
    No choice remains ;
Yet not untrue to man's decree,
Though spurning its rewards, is he
    Who bears its pains.

Not mine Sedition's trumpet-blast
    And threatening word ;
I read the lesson of the Past,
That firm endurance wins at last
    More than the sword.

O clear-eyed Faith, and Patience, thou
    So calm and strong !
Lend strength to weakness, teach us how
The sleepless eyes of God look through
    This night of wrong !

A SABBATH SCENE.

SCARCE had the solemn Sabbath-bell
    Ceased quivering in the steeple,
Scarce had the parson to his desk
    Walked stately through his people,

When down the summer-shaded street
    A wasted female figure,
With dusky brow and naked feet,
    Came rushing wild and eager.

She saw the white spire through the
    trees,
    She heard the sweet hymn swelling :
O pitying Christ ! a refuge give
    That poor one in thy dwelling !

Like a scared fawn before the hounds,
  Right up the aisle she glided,
While close behind her, whip in hand,
  A lank-haired hunter strided.

She raised a keen and bitter cry,
  To Heaven and Earth appealing; —
Were manhood's generous pulses dead?
  Had woman's heart no feeling?

A score of stout hands rose between
  The hunter and the flying:
Age clenched his staff, and maiden eyes
  Flashed tearful, yet defying.

"Who dares profane this house and
    day?"
  Cried out the angry pastor.
"Why, bless your soul, the wench's a
    slave,
  And I'm her lord and master!

"I've law and gospel on my side,
  And who shall dare refuse me?"
Down came the parson, bowing low,
  "My good sir, pray excuse me!

"Of course I know your right divine
  To own and work and whip her;
Quick, deacon, throw that Polyglott
  Before the wench, and trip her!"

Plump dropped the holy tome, and
    o'er
  Its sacred pages stumbling,
Bound hand and foot, a slave once more,
  The hapless wretch lay trembling.

I saw the parson tie the knots,
  The while his flock addressing,
The Scriptural claims of slavery
  With text on text impressing.

"Although," said he, "on Sabbath day
  All secular occupations
Are deadly sins, we must fulfil
  Our moral obligations:

"And this commends itself as one
  To every conscience tender;
As Paul sent back Onesimus,
  My Christian friends, we send her!"

Shriek rose on shriek, — the Sabbath air
  Her wild cries tore asunder;
I listened, with hushed breath, to hear
  God answering with his thunder!

All still! — the very altar's cloth
  Had smothered down her shrieking,
And, dumb, she turned from face to
    face,
  For human pity seeking!

I saw her dragged along the aisle,
  Her shackles harshly clanking;
I heard the parson, over all,
  The Lord devoutly thanking!

My brain took fire: "Is this," I cried,
  "The end of prayer and preach-
    ing?
Then down with pulpit, down with
    priest,
  And give us Nature's teaching!

"Foul shame and scorn be on ye all
  Who turn the good to evil,
And steal the Bible from the Lord,
  To give it to the Devil!

"Than garbled text or parchment law
  I own a statute higher;
And God is true, though every book
  And every man's a liar!"

Just then I felt the deacon's hand
  In wrath my coat-tail seize on;
I heard the priest cry, "Infidel!"
  The lawyer mutter, "Treason!"

I started up, — where now were church,
  Slave, master, priest, and people?
I only heard the supper-bell,
  Instead of clanging steeple.

But, on the open window's sill,
  O'er which the white blooms drifted,
The pages of a good old Book
  The wind of summer lifted,

And flower and vine, like angel wings
  Around the Holy Mother,
Waved softly there, as if God's truth
  And Mercy kissed each other.

And freely from the cherry-bough
  Above the casement swinging,
With golden bosom to the sun,
  The oriole was singing.

As bird and flower made plain of old
  The lesson of the Teacher,
So now I heard the written Word
  Interpreted by Nature!

For to my ear methought the breeze
　　Bore Freedom's blessed word on ;
Thus saith the Lord : Break every
　　　　yoke,
Undo the heavy burden !

REMEMBRANCE.

WITH COPIES OF THE AUTHOR'S WRIT-
INGS.

Friend of mine ! whose lot was cast
With me in the distant past, —
Where, like shadows flitting fast,

Fact and fancy, thought and theme,
Word and work, begin to seem
Like a half-remembered dream !

Touched by change have all things
　　been,
Yet I think of thee as when
We had speech of lip and pen.

For the calm thy kindness lent
To a path of discontent,
Rough with trial and dissent ;

Gentle words where such were few,
Softening　blame　where　blame　was
　　true,
Praising where small praise was due ;

For a waking dream made good,
For an ideal understood,
For thy Christian womanhood ;

For thy marvellous gift to cull
From our common life and dull
Whatsoe'er is beautiful ;

Thoughts and fancies, Hybla's bees
Dropping sweetness ; true heart's-ease
Of congenial sympathies ; —

Still for these I own my debt ;
Memory, with her eyelids wet,
Fain would thank thee even yet !

And as one who scatters flowers
Where the Queen of May's sweet hours
Sits, o'ertwined with blossomed bowers,

In superfluous zeal bestowing
Gifts where gifts are overflowing,
So I pay the debt I'm owing.

To thy full thoughts, gay or sad,
Sunny-hued or sober clad,
Something of my own I add ;

Well assured that thou wilt take
Even the offering which I make
Kindly for the giver's sake.

THE POOR VOTER ON ELEC TION DAY.

The proudest now is but my peer,
　　The highest not more high ;
To-day, of all the weary year,
　　A king of men am I.
To-day, alike are great and small,
　　The nameless and the known ;
My palace is the people's hall,
　　The ballot-box my throne !

Who serves to-day upon the list
　　Beside the served shall stand ;
Alike the brown and wrinkled fist,
　　The gloved and dainty hand !
The rich is level with the poor,
　　The weak is strong to-day ;
And sleekest broadcloth counts no mor
　　Than homespun frock of gray.

To-day let pomp and vain pretence
　　My stubborn right abide ;
I set a plain man's common sense
　　Against the pedant's pride.
To-day shall simple manhood try
　　The strength of gold and land ;
The wide world has not wealth to buy
　　The power in my right hand !

While there 's a grief to seek redress,
　　Or balance to adjust,
Where weighs our living manhood less
　　Than Mammon's vilest dust, —
While there 's a right to need my vote,
　　A wrong to sweep away,
Up ! clouted knee and ragged coat !
　　A man 's a man to-day !

TRUST.

The same old baffling questions ! O my
　　friend,
I cannot answer them.　In vain I send
My soul into the dark, where never burn
　　The lamps of science, nor the natura
　　light

Of Reason's sun and stars ! I cannot
    learn
Their great and solemn meanings, nor
    discern
The awful secrets of the eyes which turn
    Evermore on us through the day and
    night
With silent challenge and a dumb
    demand,
Proffering the riddles of the dread un-
    known,
Like the calm Sphinxes, with their eyes
    of stone,
    Questioning the centuries from their
    veils of sand !
I have no answer for myself or thee,
Save that I learned beside my mother's
    knee ;
" All is of God that is, and is to be ;
    And God is good." Let this suffice
    us still,
    Resting in childlike trust upon his
    will
Who moves to his great ends unthwarted
    by the ill.

KATHLEEN.[53]

O NORAH, lay your basket down,
    And rest your weary hand,
And come and hear me sing a song
    Of our old Ireland.

There was a lord of Galaway,
    A mighty lord was he ;
And he did wed a second wife,
    A maid of low degree.

But he was old, and she was young,
    And so, in evil spite,
She baked the black bread for his kin,
    And fed her own with white.

She whipped the maids and starved the
    kern,
    And drove away the poor ;
" Ah, woe is me ! " the old lord said,
    " I rue my bargain sore ! "

This lord he had a daughter fair,
    Beloved of old and young,
And nightly round the shealing-fires
    Of her the gleeman sung.

" As sweet and good is young Kathleen
    As Eve before her fall " ;

So sang the harper at the fair,
    So harped he in the hall.

" O come to me, my daughter dear !
    Come sit upon my knee,
For looking in your face, Kathleen,
    Your mother's own I see ! "

He smoothed and smoothed her hair away,
    He kissed her forehead fair ;
" It is my darling Mary's brow,
    It is my darling's hair ! "

O, then spake up the angry dame,
    " Get up, get up," quoth she,
" I 'll sell ye over Ireland,
    I 'll sell ye o'er the sea ! "

She clipped her glossy hair away,
    That none her rank might know,
She took away her gown of silk,
    And gave her one of tow,

And sent her down to Limerick town,
    And to a seaman sold
This daughter of an Irish lord
    For ten good pounds in gold.

The lord he smote upon his breast,
    And tore his beard so gray ;
But he was old, and she was young,
    And so she had her way.

Sure that same night the Banshee howled
    To fright the evil dame,
And fairy folks, who loved Kathleen,
    With funeral torches came.

She watched them glancing through the
    trees,
    And glimmering down the hill ;
They crept before the dead-vault door,
    And there they all stood still !

" Get up, old man ! the wake-lights
    shine ! "
    " Ye murthering witch," quoth he,
" So I 'm rid of your tongue, I little care
    If they shine for you or me."

" O, whoso brings my daughter back,
    My gold and land shall have ! "
O, then spake up his handsome page,
    " No gold nor land I crave !

" But give to me your daughter dear,
    Give sweet Kathleen to me,

Be she on sea or be she on land,
  I 'll bring her back to thee."

"My daughter is a lady born,
  And you of low degree,
But she shall be your bride the day
  You bring her back to me."

He sailed east, he sailed west,
  And far and long sailed he,
Until he came to Boston town,
  Across the great salt sea.

"O, have ye seen the young Kathleen,
  The flower of Ireland ?
Ye 'll know her by her eyes so blue,
  And by her snow-white hand !"

Out spake an ancient man, "I know
  The maiden whom ye mean ;
I bought her of a Limerick man,
  And she is called Kathleen.

"No skill hath she in household work,
  Her hands are soft and white,
Yet well by loving looks and ways
  She doth her cost requite."

So up they walked through Boston town,
  And met a maiden fair,
A little basket on her arm
  So snowy-white and bare.

"Come hither, child, and say hast thou
  This young man ever seen ?"
They wept within each other's arms,
  The page and young Kathleen.

"O give to me this darling child,
  And take my purse of gold."
"Nay, not by me," her master said,
  "Shall sweet Kathleen be sold.

"We loved her in the place of one
  The Lord hath early ta'en ;
But, since her heart 's in Ireland,
  We give her back again !"

O, for that same the saints in heaven
  For his poor soul shall pray,
And Mary Mother wash with tears
  His heresies away.

Sure now they dwell in Ireland,
  As you go up Claremore
Ye 'll see their castle looking down
  The pleasant Galway shore.

And the old lord's
  And a happy ma
For he sits beside
  With her darling

FIRST-DAY

In calm and cool a
  I find my 1 ac
My brethren, v
    human tong
Shall utter word
    is sung,
Nor deep-toned
    ser swung,
Nor dim light fall
    tured pane
There, syllabled b
The still small voi
    prophet's ca
Read in my heart
Than Israel's leade
There let me striv
    sin,
Recall my wand
    strain
The sore disquie
And, as the path
May grace be giv
    therein,
Not like the hi
    gain,
With backward
    tread,
Making a merit of
But, cheerful, in
    thrown,
Walking as on
    led ;
Doing God's wil
Yet trusting not
    strength al

KOS

Type of two might
  bining
The strength
  warmth and
Of Asian song and
  ing
Of Orient spler
  snow !
Who shall receive
  ing, speak

Welcome to him, who, while he strove
  to break
The Austrian yoke from Magyar necks,
  smote off
At the same blow the fetters of the
  serf, —
Rearing the altar of his Father-land
  On the firm base of freedom, and
    thereby
Lifting to Heaven a patriot's stainless
  hand,
    Mocked not the God of Justice with a
      lie !
Who shall be Freedom's mouth-piece ?
  Who shall give
Her welcoming cheer to the great fugi-
  tive ?
Not he who, all her sacred trusts betray-
  ing,
  Is scourging back to slavery's hell of
    pain
The swarthy Kossuths of our land
  again !
Not he whose utterance now from lips
  designed
The bugle-march of Liberty to wind,
And call her hosts beneath the breaking
  light, —
The keen reveille of her morn of fight,—
  Is but the hoarse note of the blood-
    hound's baying,
The wolf's long howl behind the bond-
  man's flight !
O for the tongue of him who lies at rest
  In Quincy's shade of patrimonial
    trees, —
Last of the Puritan tribunes and the
  best, —
  To lend a voice to Freedom's sympa-
    thies,
And hail the coming of the noblest guest
The Old World's wrong has given the
  New World of the West !

TO MY OLD SCHOOLMASTER.

AN EPISTLE NOT AFTER THE MANNER
OF HORACE.

OLD friend, kind friend ! lightly down
Drop time's snow-flakes on thy crown !
Never be thy shadow less,
Never fail thy cheerfulness ;
Care, that kills the cat, may plough
Wrinkles in the miser's brow,
Deepen envy's spiteful frown,

Draw the mouths of bigots down,
Plague ambition's dream, and sit
Heavy on the hypocrite,
Haunt the rich man's door, and ride
In the gilded coach of pride ; —
Let the fiend pass ! — what can he
Find to do with such as thee ?
Seldom comes that evil guest
Where the conscience lies at rest,
And brown health and quiet wit
Smiling on the threshold sit.

I, the urchin unto whom,
In that smoked and dingy room,
Where the district gave thee rule
O'er its ragged winter school,
Thou didst teach the mysteries
Of those weary A B C's, —
Where, to fill the every pause
Of thy wise and learned saws,
Through the cracked and crazy wall
Came the cradle-rock and squall,
And the goodman's voice, at strife
With his shrill and tipsy wife, —
Luring us by stories old,
With a comic unction told,
More than by the eloquence
Of terse birchen arguments
(Doubtful gain, I fear), to look
With complacence on a book ! —
Where the genial pedagogue
Half forgot his rogues to flog,
Citing tale or apologue,
Wise and merry in its drift
As old Phædrus' twofold gift,
Had the little rebels known it,
Risum et prudentiam monet !
I, — the man of middle years,
In whose sable locks appears
Many a warning fleck of gray, —
Looking back to that far day,
And thy primal lessons, feel
Grateful smiles my lips unseal,
As, remembering thee, I blend
Olden teacher, present friend,
Wise with antiquarian search,
In the scrolls of State and Church :
Named on history's title-page,
Parish-clerk and justice sage ;
For the ferule's wholesome awe
Wielding now the sword of law.

Threshing Time's neglected sheaves,
Gathering up the scattered leaves
Which the wrinkled sibyl cast
Careless from her as she passed, —
Twofold citizen art thou,

Freeman of the past and now.
He who bore thy name of old
Midway in the heavens did hold
Over Gibeon moon and sun ;
Thou hast bidden them backward run ;
Of to-day the present ray
Flinging over yesterday !

Let the busy ones deride
What I deem of right thy pride :
Let the fools their tread-mills grind,
Look not forward nor behind,
Shuffle in and wriggle out,
Veer with every breeze about,
Turning like a windmill sail,
Or a dog that seeks his tail ;
Let them laugh to see thee fast
Tabernacled in the Past,
Working out with eye and lip,
Riddles of old penmanship,
Patient as Belzoni there
Sorting out, with loving care,
Mummies of dead questions stripped
From their sevenfold manuscript !

Dabbling, in their noisy way,
In the puddles of to-day,
Little know they of that vast
Solemn ocean of the past,
On whose margin, wreck-bespread,
Thou art walking with the dead,
Questioning the stranded years,
Waking smiles, by turns, and tears,
As thou callest up again
Shapes the dust has long o'erlain, —
Fair-haired woman, bearded man,·
Cavalier and Puritan ;
In an age whose eager view
Seeks but present things, and new,
Mad for party, sect and gold,
Teaching reverence for the old.

On that shore, with fowler's tact,
Coolly bagging fact on fact,
Naught amiss to thee can float,
Tale, or song, or anecdote ;
Village gossip, centuries old.
Scandals by our grandams told,
What the pilgrim's table spread,
Where he lived, and whom he wed,
Long-drawn bill of wine and beer
For his ordination cheer,
Or the flip that wellnigh made
Glad his funeral cavalcade ;
Weary prose, and poet's lines,
Flavored by their age, like wines,
Eulogistic of some quaint,

Doubtful, puritanic saint ;
Lays that quickened husking jigs,
Jests that shook grave periwigs,
When the parson had his jokes
And his glass, like other folks ;
Sermons that, for mortal hours,
Taxed our fathers' vital powers,
As the long nineteenthlics poured
Downward from the sounding-board,
And, for fire of Pentecost,
Touched their beards December's frost.

Time is hastening on, and we
What our father's are shall be, —
Shadow-shapes of memory !
Joined to that vast multitude
Where the great are but the good,
And the mind of strength shall prove
Weaker than the heart of love ;
Pride of graybeard wisdom less
Than the infant's guilelessness,
And his song of sorrow more
Than the crown the Psalmist wore !
Who shall then, with pious zeal,
At our moss-grown thresholds kneel,
From a stained and stony page
Reading to a careless age,
With a patient eye like thine,
Prosing tale and limping line,
Names and words the hoary rime
Of the Past has made sublime ?
Who shall work for us as well
The antiquarian's miracle ?
Who to seeming life recall
Teacher grave and pupil small ?
Who shall give to thee and me
Freeholds in futurity ?

Well, whatever lot be mine,
Long and happy days be thine,
Ere thy full and honored age
Dates of time its latest page !
Squire for master, State for school,
Wisely lenient, live and rule ;
Over grown-up knave and rogue
Play the watchful pedagogue ;
Or, while pleasure smiles on duty,
At the call of youth and beauty,
Speak for them the spell of law
Which shall bar and bolt withdraw,
And the flaming sword remove
From the Paradise of Love.
Still, with undimmed eyesight, pore
Ancient tome and record o'er ;
Still thy week-day lyrics croon,
Pitch in church the Sunday tune,
Showing something, in thy part,

Of the old Puritanic art,
Singer after Sternhold's heart !
In thy pew, for many a year,
Homilies from Oldbug hear,[6]
Who to wit like that of South,
And the Syrian's golden mouth,
Doth the homely pathos add
Which the pilgrim preachers had ;
Breaking, like a child at play,
Gilded idols of the day,
Cant of knave and pomp of fool
Tossing with his ridicule,

Yet, in earnest or in jest,
Ever keeping truth abreast.
And, when thou art called, at last,
To thy townsmen of the past,
Not as stranger shalt thou come ;
Thou shalt find thyself at home !
With the little and the big,
Woollen cap and periwig,
Madam in her high-laced ruff,
Goody in her home-made stuff, —
Wise and simple, rich and poor,
Thou hast known them all before !

THE PANORAMA,

AND OTHER POEMS.

THE PANORAMA.

" A ! fredome is a nobill thing !
Fredome mayse man to haif liking.
Fredome all solace to man giffis ;
He levys at ese that frely levys !
A nobil hart may haif nane ese
Na ellys nocht that may him plese
Gyff Fredome fallythe."
ARCHDEACON BARBOUR.

THROUGH the long hall the shuttered
  windows shed
A dubious light on every upturned
  head, —
On locks like those of Absalom the fair,
On the bald apex ringed with scanty
  hair,
On blank indifference and on curious
  stare ;
On the pale Showman reading from his
  stage
The hieroglyphics of that facial page ;
Half sad, half scornful, listening to the
  bruit
Of restless cane-tap and impatient foot,
And the shrill call, across the general
  din,
" Roll up your curtain ! Let the show
  begin ! "

At length a murmur like the winds
  that break
Into green waves the prairie's grassy
  lake,

Deepened and swelled to music clear
  and loud,
And, as the west-wind lifts a summer
  cloud,
The curtain rose, disclosing wide and far
A green land stretching to the evening star,
Fair rivers, skirted by primeval trees
And flowers hummed over by the desert
  bees,
Marked by tall bluffs whose slopes of
  greenness show
Fantastic outcrops of the rock below, —
The slow result of patient Nature's pains,
And plastic fingering of her sun and
  rains, —
Arch, tower, and gate, grotesquely win-
  dowed hall,
And long escarpment of half-crumbled
  wall,
Huger than those which, from steep
  hills of vine,
Stare through their loopholes on the
  travelled Rhine ;
Suggesting vaguely to the gazer's mind
A fancy, idle as the prairie wind,
Of the land's dwellers in an age un-
  guessed, —
The unsung Jotuns of the mystic West.

Beyond, the prairie's sea-like swells
  surpass
The Tartar's marvels of his Land of
  Grass,

Vast as the sky against whose sunset
shores
Wave after wave the billowy greenness
pours ;
And, onward still, like islands in that
main
Loom the rough peaks of many a moun-
tain chain,
Whence east and west a thousand waters
run
From winter lingering under summer's
sun.
And, still beyond, long lines of foam
and sand
Tell where Pacific rolls his waves a-
land,
From many a wide-lapped port and
land-locked bay,
Opening with thunderous pomp the
world's highway
To Indian isles of spice, and marts of far
Cathay.

"Such," said the Showman, as the
curtain fell,
"Is the new Canaan of our Israel, —
The land of promise to the swarming
North,
Which, hive-like, sends its annual sur-
plus forth,
To the poor Southron on his worn-out
soil,
Scathed by the curses of unnatural toil ;
To Europe's exiles seeking home and
rest,
And the lank nomads of the wandering
West,
Who, asking neither, in their love of
change
And the free bison's amplitude of range,
Rear the log-hut, for present shelter
meant,
Not future comfort, like an Arab's tent."

Then spake a shrewd on-looker, "Sir,"
said he,
"I like your picture, but I fain would
see
A sketch of what your promised land
will be
When, with electric nerve, and fiery-
brained,
With Nature's forces to its chariot
chained,
The future grasping, by the past obeyed,
The twentieth century rounds a new
decade."

Then said the Showman, sadly: "He
who grieves
Over the scattering of the sibyl's leaves
Unwisely mourns. Suffice it, that we
know
What needs must ripen from the seed
we sow ;
That present time is but the mould
wherein
We cast the shapes of holiness and sin.
A painful watcher of the passing hour,
Its lust of gold, its strife for place and
power ;
Its lack of manhood, honor, reverence,
truth,
Wise-thoughted age, and generous-
hearted youth ;
Nor yet unmindful of each better sign, —
The low, far lights, which on th' horizon
shine,
Like those which sometimes tremble on
the rim
Of clouded skies when day is closing
dim,
Flashing athwart the purple spears of
rain
The hope of sunshine on the hills
again : —
I need no prophet's word, nor shapes
that pass
Like clouding shadows o'er a magic
glass ;
For now, as ever, passionless and cold,
Doth the dread angel of the future hold
Evil and good before us, with no voice
Or warning look to guide us in our
choice ;
With spectral hands outreaching through
the gloom
The shadowy contrasts of the coming
doom.
Transferred from these, it now remains
to give
The sun and shade of Fate's alternative."

Then, with a burst of music, touching
all
The keys of thrifty life, — the mill-
stream's fall,
The engine's pant along its quivering
rails,
The anvil's ring, the measured beat of
flails,
The sweep of scythes, the reaper's
whistled tune,
Answering the summons of the bells of
noon.

The woodman's hail along the river
  shores,
The steamboat's signal, and the dip of
  oars, —
Slowly the curtain rose from off a land
Fair as God's garden. Broad on either
  hand
The golden wheat-fields glimmered in
  the sun,
And the tall maize its yellow tassels
  spun.
Smooth highways set with hedge-rows
  living green,
With steepled towns through shaded
  vistas seen,
The school-house murmuring with its
  hive-like swarm,
The brook-bank whitening in the grist-
  mill's storm,
The painted farm-house shining through
  the leaves
Of fruited orchards bending at its eaves,
Where live again, around the Western
  hearth,
The homely old-time virtues of the
  North ;
Where the blithe housewife rises with
  the day,
And well-paid labor counts his task a
  play.
And, grateful tokens of a Bible free,
And the free Gospel of Humanity,
Of diverse sects and differing names the
  shrines,
One in their faith, whate'er their out-
  ward signs,
Like varying strophes of the same sweet
  hymn
From many a prairie's swell and river's
  brim,
A thousand church-spires sanctify the
  air
Of the calm Sabbath, with their sign of
  prayer.   .

  Like sudden nightfall over bloom and
    green
The curtain dropped : and, momently,
  between
The clank of fetter and the crack of
  thong,
Half sob, half laughter, music swept
  along, —
A strange refrain, whose idle words and
  low,
Like drunken mourners, kept the time
  of woe ;

As if the revellers at a masquerade
Heard in the distance funeral marches
  played.
Such music, dashing all his smiles with
  tears,
The thoughtful voyager on Ponchartrain
  hears,
Where, through the noonday dusk of
  wooded shores
The negro boatman, singing to his oars,
With a wild pathos borrowed of his
  wrong
Redeems the jargon of his senseless song.
"Look," said the Showman, sternly,
  as he rolled
His curtain upward ; "Fate's reverse
  behold !"

  A village straggling in loose disarray
Of vulgar newness, premature decay ;
A tavern, crazy with its whiskey brawls,
With "*Slaves at Auction !*" garnishing
  its walls.
Without, surrounded by a motley crowd,
The shrewd-eyed salesman, garrulous
  and loud,
A squire or colonel in his pride of place,
Known at free fights, the caucus, and
  the race,
Prompt to proclaim his honor without
  blot,
And silence doubters with a ten-pace
  shot,
Mingling the negro-driving bully's rant
With pious phrase and democratic cant,
Yet never scrupling, with a filthy jest,
To sell the infant from its mother's
  breast,
Break through all ties of wedlock, home,
  and kin,
Yield shrinking girlhood up to gray-
  beard sin ;
Sell all the virtues with his human stock,
The Christian graces on his auction-
  block,
And coolly count on shrewdest bargains
  driven
In hearts regenerate, and in souls for-
  given !

  Look once again ! The moving can-
    vas shows
A slave plantation's slovenly repose,
Where, in rude cabins rotting midst
  their weeds,
The human chattel eats, and sleeps, and
  breeds ;

15

And, held a brute, in practice, as in law,
Becomes in fact the thing he 's taken for.
There, early summoned to the hemp and
  corn,
The nursing mother leaves her child
  new-born ;
There haggard sickness, weak and
  deathly faint,
Crawls to his task, and fears to make
  complaint ;
And sad-eyed Rachels, childless in de-
  cay,
Weep for their lost ones sold and torn
  away !
Of ampler size the master's dwelling
  stands,
In shabby keeping with his half-tilled
  lands, —
The gates unhinged, the yard with weeds
  unclean,
The cracked veranda with a tipsy lean.
Without, loose-scattered like a wreck
  adrift,
Signs of misrule and tokens of unthrift ;
Within, profusion to discomfort joined,
The listless body and the vacant mind ;
The fear, the hate, the theft and false-
  hood, born
In menial hearts of toil, and stripes, and
  scorn !
There, all the vices, which, like birds
  obscene,
Batten on slavery loathsome and un-
  clean,
From the foul kitchen to the parlor rise,
Pollute the nursery where the child-heir
  lies,
Taint infant lips beyond all after cure,
With the fell poison of a breast impure ;
Touch boyhood's passions with the
  breath of flame,
From girlhood's instincts steal the blush
  of shame.
So swells, from low to high, from weak
  to strong,
The tragic chorus of the baleful wrong ;
Guilty or guiltless, all within its range
Feel the blind justice of its sure revenge.

  Still scenes like these the moving
    chart reveals.
Up the long western steppes the blight-
  ing steals ;
Down the Pacific slope the evil Fate
Glides like a shadow to the Golden Gate :
From sea to sea the drear eclipse is
  thrown,

From sea to sea the *Mauvaises Terres*
  have grown,
A belt of curses on the New World's
  zone !

  The curtain fell. All drew a freer
    breath,
As men are wont to do when mournful
  death
Is covered from their sight. The Show-
  man stood
With drooping brow in sorrow's attitude
One moment, then with sudden gesture
  shook
His loose hair back, and with the air
  and look
Of one who felt, beyond the narrow stage
And listening group, the presence of the
  age,
And heard the footsteps of the things to
  be,
Poured out his soul in earnest words and
  free.

  "O friends !" he said, "in this poor
    trick of paint
You see the semblance, incomplete and
  faint,
Of the two-fronted Future, which, to-
  day,
Stands dim and silent, waiting in your
  way.
To-day, your servant, subject to your
  will ;
To-morrow, master, or for good or ill.
If the dark face of Slavery on you turns,
If the mad curse its paper barrier spurns,
If the world granary of the West is made
The last foul market of the slaver's trade,
Why rail at fate ?   The mischief is your
  own.
Why hate your neighbor ?   Blame your-
  selves alone !

  "Men of the North !   The South you
    charge with wrong
Is weak and poor, while you are rich
  and strong.
If questions, — idle and absurd as those
The old-time monks and Paduan doctors
  chose, —
Mere ghosts of questions, tariffs, and
  dead banks,
And scarecrow pontiffs, never broke
  your ranks,
Your thews united could, at once, roll
  back

The jostled nation to its primal track.
Nay, were you simply steadfast, manly,
    just,
True to the faith your fathers left in trust,
If stainless honor outweighed in your
    scale
A codfish quintal or a factory bale,
Full many a noble heart, (and such remain
In all the South, like Lot in Siddim's
    plain,
Who watch and wait, and from the
    wrong's control
Keep white and pure their chastity of
    soul,)
Now sick to loathing of your weak com-
    plaints,
Your tricks as sinners, and your prayers
    as saints,
Would half-way meet the frankness of
    your tone,
And feel their pulses beating with your
    own.

"The North! the South! no geo-
    graphic line
Can fix the boundary or the point define,
Since each with each so closely inter-
  . blends,
Where Slavery rises, and where Freedom
    ends.
Beneath your rocks the roots, far-reach-
    ing, hide
Of the fell Upas on the Southern side ;
The tree whose branches in your north-
    winds wave
Dropped its young blossoms on Mount
    Vernon's grave ;
The nursling growth of Monticello's crest
Is now the glory of the free Northwest ;
To the wise maxims of her olden school
Virginia listened from thy lips, Rantoul ;
Seward's words of power, and Sumner's
    fresh renown,
Flow from the pen that Jefferson laid
    down !
And when, at length, her years of mad-
    ness o'er,
Like the crowned grazer on Euphrates'
    shore,
From her long lapse to savagery, her
    mouth
Bitter with baneful herbage, turns the
    South,
Resumes her old attire, and seeks to
    smooth
Her unkempt tresses at the glass of truth,
Her early faith shall find a tongue again,

New Wythes and Pinckneys swell that
    old refrain,
Her sons with yours renew the ancient
    pact,
The myth of Union prove at last a fact !
Then, if one murmur mars the wide con-
    tent,
Some Northern lip will drawl the last
    dissent,
Some Union-saving patriot of your own
Lament to find his occupation gone.

"Grant that the North's insulted,
    scorned, betrayed,
O'erreached in bargains with her neigh-
    bor made,
When selfish thrift and party held the
    scales
For peddling dicker, not for honest
    sales, —
Whom shall we strike ? Who most de-
    serves our blame ?
The braggart Southron, open in his
    aim,
And bold as wicked, crashing straight
    through all
That bars his purpose, like a cannon-ball ?
Or the mean traitor, breathing northern
    air,
With nasal speech and puritanic hair,
Whose cant the loss of principle survives,
As the mud-turtle e'en its head outlives ;
Who, caught, chin-buried in some foul
    offence,
Puts on a look of injured innocence,
And consecrates his baseness to the cause
Of constitution, union, and the laws ?

"Praise to the place-man who can hold
    aloof
His still unpurchased manhood, office-
    proof ;
Who on his round of duty walks erect,
And leaves it only rich in self-respect, —
As More maintained his virtue's lofty
    port
In the Eighth Henry's base and bloody
    court.
But, if exceptions here and there are
    found,
Who tread thus safely on enchanted
    ground,
The normal type, the fitting symbol still
Of those who fatten at the public mill,
Is the chained dog beside his master's
    door,
Or Circe's victim, feeding on all four !

" Give me the heroes who, at tuck of
    drum,
Salute thy staff, immortal Quattlebum !
Or they who, doubly armed with vote
    and gun,
Following thy lead, illustrious Atchison,
Their drunken franchise shift from scene
    to scene.
As tile-beard Jourdan did his guillo-
    tine ! —
Rather than him who, born beneath our
    skies,
To Slavery's hand its supplest tool sup-
    plies, —
The party felon whose unblushing face
Looks from the pillory of his bribe of
    place,
And coolly makes a merit of disgrace, —
Points to the footmarks of indignant
    scorn,
Shows the deep scars of satire's tossing
    horn ;
And passes to his credit side the sum
Of all that makes a scoundrel's martyr-
    dom !

" Bane of the North, its canker and
    its moth ! —
These modern Esaus, bartering rights for
    broth !
Taxing our justice, with their double
    claim,
As fools for pity, and as knaves for
    blame ;
Who, urged by party, sect, or trade,
    within
The fell embrace of Slavery's sphere of
    sin,
Part at the outset with their moral sense,
The watchful angel set for Truth's de-
    fence ;
Confound all contrasts, good and ill ;
    reverse
The poles of life, its blessing and its
    curse ;
And lose thenceforth from their perverted
    sight
The eternal difference 'twixt the wrong
    and right ;
To them the Law is but the iron span
That girds the ankles of imbruted man ;
To them the Gospel has no higher aim
Than simple sanction of the master's
    claim,
Dragged in the slime of Slavery's loath-
    some trail,
Like Chalier's Bible at his ass's tail !

" Such are the men who, with instinc-
    tive dread,
Whenever Freedom lifts her drooping
    head,
Make prophet-tripods of their office-
    stools,
And scare the nurseries and the village
    schools
With dire presage of ruin grim and great,
A broken Union and a foundered State !
Such are the patriots, self-bound to the
    stake
Of office, martyrs for their country's sake :
Who fill themselves the hungry jaws of
    Fate,
And by their loss of manhood save the
    State.
In the wide gulf themselves like Curtius
    throw,
And test the virtues of cohesive dough ;
As tropic monkeys, linking heads and
    tails,
Bridge o'er some torrent of Ecuador's
    vales !

"Such are the men who in your church-
    es rave
To swearing-point, at mention of the
    slave !
When some poor parson, haply unawares,
Stammers of freedom in his timid prayers ;
Who, if some foot-sore negro through the
    town
Steals northward, volunteer to hunt him
    down.
Or, if some neighbor, flying from disease,
Courts the mild balsam of the Southern
    breeze,
With hue and cry pursue him on his
    track,
And write Free-soiler on the poor man's
    back.
Such are the men who leave the pedler's
    cart,
While faring South, to learn the driver's
    art,
Or, in white neckcloth, soothe with pious
    aim
The graceful sorrows of some languid
    dame,
Who, from the wreck of her bereavement,
    saves
The double charm of widowhood and
    slaves ! —
Pliant and apt, they lose no chance to
    show
To what base depths apostasy can go ;

Outdo the natives in their readiness
To roast a negro, or to mob a press ;
Poise a tarred schoolmate on the lynch-
  er's rail,
Or make a bonfire of their birthplace
  mail !

" So some poor wretch, whose lips no
  longer bear
The sacred burden of his mother's prayer,
By fear impelled, or lust of gold enticed,
Turns to the Crescent from the Cross of
  Christ,
And, over-acting in superfluous zeal,
Crawls prostrate where the faithful only
  kneel,
Out-howls the Dervish, hugs his rags to
  court
The squalid Santon's sanctity of dirt ;
And, when beneath the city gateway's
  span
Files slow and long the Meccan caravan,
And through its midst, pursued by Islam's
  prayers,
The prophet's Word some favored camel
  bears,
The marked apostate has his place as-
  signed
The Koran-bearer's sacred rump behind,
With brush and pitcher following, grave
  and mute,
In meek attendance on the holy brute !

" Men of the North ! beneath your
  very eyes,
By hearth and home, your real danger
  lies.
Still day by day some hold of freedom
  falls,
Through home-bred traitors fed within
  its walls. —
Men whom yourselves with vote and
  purse sustain,
At posts of honor, influence, and gain ;
The right of Slavery to your sons to
  teach,
And " South-side " Gospels in your pul-
  pits preach,
Transfix the Law to ancient freedom dear
On the sharp point of her subverted spear,
And imitate upon her cushion plump
The mad Missourian lynching from his
  stump ;
Or, in your name, upon the Senate's floor
Yield up to Slavery all it asks, and more ;
And, ere your dull eyes open to the
  cheat,

Sell your old homestead underneath your
  feet !
While such as these your loftiest outlooks
  hold,
While truth and conscience with your
  wares are sold,
While grave-browed merchants band
  themselves to aid
An annual man-hunt for their Southern
  trade,
What moral power within your grasp
  remains
To stay the mischief on Nebraska's
  plains ? —
High as the tides of generous impulse
  flow,
As far rolls back the selfish undertow ;
And all your brave resolves, though
  aimed as true
As the horse-pistol Balmawhapple drew,
To Slavery's bastions lend as slight a
  shock
As the poor trooper's shot to Stirling
  rock !

" Yet, while the need of Freedom's
  cause demands
The earnest efforts of your hearts and
  hands,
Urged by all motives that can prompt
  the heart
To prayer and toil and manhood's man-
  liest part ;
Though to the soul's deep tocsin Nature
  joins
The warning whisper of her Orphic pines,
The north-wind's anger, and the south-
  wind's sigh,
The midnight sword-dance of the north-
  ern sky,
And, to the ear that bends above the
  sod
Of the green grave-mounds in the Fields
  of God,
In low, deep murmurs of rebuke or cheer,
The land's dead fathers speak their hope
  or fear,
Yet let not Passion wrest from Reason's
  hand
The guiding rein and symbol of com-
  mand.
Blame not the caution proffering to your
  zeal
A well-meant drag upon its hurrying
  wheel ;
Nor chide the man whose honest doubt
  extends

To the means only, not the righteous
    ends ;
Nor fail to weigh the scruples and the
    fears
Of milder natures and serener years.
In the long strife with evil which began
With the first lapse of new-created man,
Wisely and well has Providence assigned
To each his part, — some forward, some
    behind ;
And they, too, serve who temper and
    restrain
The o'erwarm heart that sets on fire the
    brain.
True to yourselves, feed Freedom's altar-
    flame
With what you have ; let others do the
    same.
Spare timid doubters ; set like flint your
    face
Against the self-sold knaves of gain and
    place :
Pity the weak ; but with unsparing hand
Cast out the traitors who infest the
    land, —
From bar, press, pulpit, cast them every-
    where,
By dint of fasting, if you fail by prayer.
And in their place bring men of antique
    mould,
Like the grave fathers of your Age of
    Gold, —
Statesmen like those who sought the
    primal fount
Of righteous law, the Sermon on the
    Mount ;
Lawyers who prize, like Quincy, (to our
    day
Still spared, Heaven bless him !) honor
    more than pay,
And Christian jurists, starry-pure, like
    Jay ;
Preachers like Woolman, or like them
    who bore
The faith of Wesley to our Western shore,
And held no convert genuine till he broke
Alike his servants' and the Devil's yoke ;
And priests like him who Newport's mar-
    ket trod,
And o'er its slave-ships shook the bolts
    of God !
So shall your power, with a wise prudence
    used,
Strong but forbearing, firm but not
    abused,
In kindly keeping with the good of all,
The nobler maxims of the past recall,

Her natural home-born right to Freedom
    give,
And leave her foe his robber-right, — to
    live.
Live, as the snake does in his noisome
    fen !
Live, as the wolf does in his bone-strewn
    den !
Live, clothed with cursing like a robe of
    flame,
The focal point of million-fingered
    shame !
Live, till the Southron, who, with all his
    faults,
Has manly instincts, in his pride re-
    volts,
Dashes from off him, midst the glad
    world's cheers,
The hideous nightmare of his dream of
    years,
And lifts, self-prompted, with his own
    right hand,
The vile encumbrance from his glorious
    land !

" So, wheresoe'er our destiny sends
    forth
Its widening circles to the South or
    North,
Where'er our banner flaunts beneath
    the stars
Its mimic splendors and its cloudlike
    bars,
There shall Free Labor's hardy children
    stand
The equal sovereigns of a slaveless land.
And when at last the hunted bison tires,
And dies o'ertaken by the squatter's
    fires ;
And westward, wave on wave, the living
    flood
Breaks on the snow-line of majestic
    Hood ;
And lonely Shasta listening hears the
    tread
Of Europe's fair-haired children, Hes-
    per-led ;
And, gazing downward through his
    hoar-locks, sees
The tawny Asian climb his giant knees,
The Eastern sea shall hush his waves to
    hear
Pacific's surf-beat answer Freedom's
    cheer,
And one long rolling fire of triumph
    run
Between the sunrise and the sunset gun !"

My task is done. The Showman and his show,
Themselves but shadows, into shadows go ;
And, if no song of idlesse I have sung,
Nor tints of beauty on the canvas flung, —
If the harsh numbers grate on tender ears,
And the rough picture overwrought appears, —
With deeper coloring, with a sterner blast,
Before my soul a voice and vision passed,
Such as might Milton's jarring trump require,
Or glooms of Dante fringed with lurid fire.
O, not of choice, for themes of public wrong
I leave the green and pleasant paths of song, —
The mild, sweet words which soften and adorn,
For griding taunt and bitter laugh of scorn.
More dear to me some song of private worth,
Some homely idyl of my native North,
Some summer pastoral of her inland vales
Or, grim and weird, her winter fireside tales
Haunted by ghosts of unreturning sails, —
Lost barks at parting hung from stem to helm
With prayers of love like dreams on Virgil's elm.
Nor private grief nor malice holds my pen ;
I owe but kindness to my fellow-men ;
And, South or North, wherever hearts of prayer
Their woes and weakness to our Father bear,
Wherever fruits of Christian love are found
In holy lives, to me is holy ground.
But the time passes. It were vain to crave
A late indulgence. What I had I gave.
Forget the poet, but his warning heed,
And shame his poor word with your nobler deed.

MISCELLANEOUS.

SUMMER BY THE LAKESIDE.

I. NOON.

WHITE clouds, whose shadows haunt the deep,
Light mists, whose soft embraces keep
The sunshine on the hills asleep !

O isles of calm ! — O dark, still wood !
And stiller skies that overbrood
Your rest with deeper quietude !

O shapes and hues, dim beckoning, through
Yon mountain gaps, my longing view
Beyond the purple and the blue,

To stiller sea and greener land,
And softer lights and airs more bland,
And skies, — the hollow of God's hand !

Transfused through you, O mountain friends !
With mine your solemn spirit blends,
And life no more hath separate ends.

I read each misty mountain sign,
I know the voice of wave and pine,
And I am yours, and ye are mine.

Life's burdens fall, its discords cease,
I lapse into the glad release
Of Nature's own exceeding peace.

O, welcome calm of heart and mind !
As falls yon fir-tree's loosened rind
To leave a tenderer growth behind,

So fall the weary years away ;
A child again, my head I lay
Upon the lap of this sweet day.

This western wind hath Lethean powers,
Yon noonday cloud nepenthe showers,
The lake is white with lotus-flowers !

Even Duty's voice is faint and low,
And slumberous Conscience, waking
    slow,
Forgets her blotted scroll to show.

The Shadow which pursues us all,
Whose ever-nearing steps appall,
Whose voice we hear behind us call, —

That Shadow blends with mountain
    gray,
It speaks but what the light waves say, —
Death walks apart from Fear to-day !

Rocked on her breast, these pines and I
Alike on Nature's love rely ;
And equal seems to live or die.

Assured that He whose presence fills
With light the spaces of these hills
No evil to his creatures wills,

The simple faith remains, that He
Will do, whatever that may be,
The best alike for man and tree.

What mosses over one shall grow,
What light and life the other know,
Unanxious, leaving Him to show.

II. EVENING.

Yon mountain's side is black with night,
    While, broad-orbed, o'er its gleaming
        crown
The moon, slow-rounding into sight,
    On the hushed inland sea looks down.

How start to light the clustering isles,
    Each silver-hemmed ! How sharply
        show
The shadows of their rocky piles,
    And tree-tops in the wave below !

How far and strange the mountains
        seem,
    Dim-looming through the pale, still
        light !
The vague, vast grouping of a dream,
    They stretch into the solemn night.

Beneath, lake, wood, and peopled vale,
    Hushed by that presence grand and
        grave,

Are silent, save the cricket's wail,
    And low response of leaf and wave.

Fair scenes ! whereto the Day and Night
    Make rival love, I leave ye soon,
What time before the eastern light
    The pale ghost of the setting moon

Shall hide behind yon rocky spines,
    And the young archer, Morn, shall
        break
His arrows on the mountain pines,
    And, golden-sandalled, walk the lake !

Farewell ! around this smiling bay
    Gay-hearted Health, and Life in
        bloom,
With lighter steps than mine, may stray
    In radiant summers yet to come.

But none shall more regretful leave
    These waters and these hills than I :
Or, distant, fonder dream how eve
    Or dawn is painting wave and sky ;

How rising moons shine sad and mild
    On wooded isle and silvering bay ;
Or setting suns beyond the piled
    And purple mountains lead the day ;

Nor laughing girl, nor bearding boy,
    Nor full-pulsed manhood, lingering
        here,
Shall add, to life's abounding joy,
    The charmed repose to suffering dear.

Still waits kind Nature to impart
    Her choicest gifts to such as gain
An entrance to her loving heart
    Through the sharp discipline of pain.

Forever from the Hand that takes
    One blessing from us others fall ;
And, soon or late, our Father makes
    His perfect recompense to all !

O, watched by Silence and the Night,
    And folded in the strong embrace
Of the great mountains, with the light
    Of the sweet heavens upon thy face,

Lake of the Northland ! keep thy dower
    Of beauty still, and while above
Thy solemn mountains speak of power,
    Be thou the mirror of God's love.

THE HERMIT OF THE THEBAID.

O STRONG, upwelling prayers of faith,
  From inmost founts of life ye start, —
The spirit's pulse, the vital breath
  Of soul and heart !

From pastoral toil, from traffic's din,
  Alone, in crowds, at home, abroad,
Unheard of man, ye enter in
  The ear of God.

Ye brook no forced and measured tasks,
  Nor weary rote, nor formal chains ;
The simple heart, that freely asks
  In love, obtains.

For man the living temple is :
  The mercy-seat and cherubim,
And all the holy mysteries,
  He bears with him.

And most avails the prayer of love,
  Which, wordless, shapes itself in
    deeds,
And wearies Heaven for naught above
  Our common needs.

Which brings to God's all-perfect will
  That trust of his undoubting child
Whereby all seeming good and ill
  Are reconciled.

And, seeking not for special signs
  Of favor, is content to fall
Within the providence which shines
  And rains on all.

Alone, the Thebaid hermit leaned
  At noontime o'er the sacred word.
Was it an angel or a fiend
  Whose voice he heard ?

It broke the desert's hush of awe,
  A human utterance, sweet and mild ;
And, looking up, the hermit saw
  A little child.

A child, with wonder-widened eyes,
  O'erawed and troubled by the sight
Of hot, red sands, and brazen skies,
  And anchorite.

"What dost thou here, poor man ? No
    shade
  Of cool, green doums, nor grass, nor
    well,

Nor corn, nor vines." The hermit
    said :
  "With God I dwell.

"Alone with Him in this great calm,
  I live not by the outward sense ;
My Nile his love, my sheltering palm
  His providence."

The child gazed round him. "Does
    God live
  Here only ? — where the desert's rim
Is green with corn, at morn and eve,
  We pray to Him.

"My brother tills beside the Nile
  His little field : beneath the leaves
My sisters sit and spin the while,
  My mother weaves.

"And when the millet's ripe heads fall,
  And all the bean-field hangs in pod,
My mother smiles, and says that all
  Are gifts from God.

"And when to share our evening meal,
  She calls the stranger at the door,
She says God fills the hands that deal
  Food to the poor."

Adown the hermit's wasted cheeks
  Glistened the flow of human tears ;
"Dear Lord !" he said, "thy angel
    speaks,
  Thy servant hears."

Within his arms the child he took,
  And thought of home and life with
    men ;
And all his pilgrim feet forsook
  Returned again.

The palmy shadows cool and long,
  The eyes that smiled through lavish
    locks,
Home's cradle-hymn and harvest-song,
  And bleat of flocks.

"O child !" he said, "thou teachest me
  There is no place where God is not ;
That love will make, where'er it be,
  A holy spot."

He rose from off the desert sand,
  And, leaning on his staff of thorn,
Went, with the young child, hand-in-
    hand,
  Like night with morn.

They crossed the desert's burning line,
  And heard the palm-tree's rustling
    fan,
The Nile-bird's cry, the low of kine,
  And voice of man.

Unquestioning, his childish guide
  He followed as the small hand led
To where a woman, gentle-eyed,
  Her distaff fed.

She rose, she clasped her truant boy,
  She thanked the stranger with her
    eyes.
The hermit gazed in doubt and joy
  And dumb surprise.

And lo ! — with sudden warmth and
    light
A tender memory thrilled his frame ;
New-born, the world-lost anchorite
  A man became.

" O sister of El Zara's race,
  Behold me ! — had we not one moth-
    er ? "
She gazed into the stranger's face ; —
  " Thou art my brother ? "

" O kin of blood ! — Thy life of use
  And patient trust is more than mine ;
And wiser than the gray recluse
  This child of thine.

" For, taught of him whom God hath
    sent,
  That toil is praise, and love is prayer,
I come, life's cares and pains content
  With thee to share."

Even as his foot the threshold crossed,
  The hermit's better life began ;
Its holiest saint the Thebaid lost,
  And found a man !

BURNS.

ON RECEIVING A SPRIG OF HEATHER
IN BLOSSOM.

No more these simple flowers belong
  To Scottish maid and lover ;
Sown in the common soil of song,
  They bloom the wide world over.

In smiles and tears, in sun and showers,
  The minstrel and the heather,
The deathless singer and the flowers
  He sang of live together.

Wild heather-bells and Robert Burns !
  The moorland flower and peasant !
How, at their mention, memory turns
  Her pages old and pleasant !

The gray sky wears again its gold
  And purple of adorning,
And manhood's noonday shadows hold
  The dews of boyhood's morning.

The dews that washed the dust and
    soil
From off the wings of pleasure,
The sky, that flecked the ground of
    toil
With golden threads of leisure.

I call to mind the summer day,
  The early harvest mowing,
The sky with sun and clouds at play,
  And flowers with breezes blowing.

I hear the blackbird in the corn,
  The locust in the haying ;
And, like the fabled hunter's horn,
  Old tunes my heart is playing.

How oft that day, with fond delay,
  I sought the maple's shadow,
And sang with Burns the hours away,
  Forgetful of the meadow !

Bees hummed, birds twittered, over-
    head
I heard the squirrels leaping,
The good dog listened while I read,
  And wagged his tail in keeping.

I watched him while in sportive mood
  I read " *The Twa Dogs* " story,
And half believed he understood
  The poet's allegory.

Sweet day, sweet songs ! — The golden
    hours
Grew brighter for that singing,
From brook and bird and meadow
    flowers
A dearer welcome bringing.

New light on home-seen Nature beamed,
  New glory over Woman ;
And daily life and duty seemed
  No longer poor and common.

I woke to find the simple truth
Of fact and feeling better
Than all the dreams that held my youth
A still repining debtor :

That Nature gives her handmaid, Art,
The themes of sweet discoursing ;
The tender idyls of the heart
In every tongue rehearsing.

Why dream of lands of gold and pearl,
Of loving knight and lady,
When farmer boy and barefoot girl
Were wandering there already ?

I saw through all familiar things
The romance underlying ;
The joys and griefs that plume the wings
Of Fancy skyward flying.

I saw the same blithe day return,
The same sweet fall of even,
That rose on wooded Craigie-burn,
And sank on crystal Devon.

I matched with Scotland's heathery hills
The sweetbrier and the clover ;
With Ayr and Doon, my native rills,
Their wood-hymns chanting over.

O'er rank and pomp, as he had seen,
I saw the Man uprising ;
No longer common or unclean,
The child of God's baptizing !

With clearer eyes I saw the worth
Of life among the lowly ;
The Bible at his Cotter's hearth
Had made my own more holy.

And if at times an evil strain,
To lawless love appealing,
Broke in upon the sweet refrain
Of pure and healthful feeling,

It died upon the eye and ear,
No inward answer gaining ;
No heart had I to see or hear
The discord and the staining.

Let those who never erred forget
His worth, in vain bewailings ;
Sweet Soul of Song ! — I own my debt
Uncancelled by his failings !

Lament who will the ribald line
Which tells his lapse from duty,

How kissed the maddening lips of wine
Or wanton ones of beauty ;

But think, while falls that shade be-
tween
The erring one and Heaven,
That he who loved like Magdalen,
Like her may be forgiven.

Not his the song whose thunderous
chime
Eternal echoes render, —
The mournful Tuscan's haunted rhyme,
And Milton's starry splendor !

But who his human heart has laid
To Nature's bosom nearer ?
Who sweetened toil like him, or paid
To love a tribute dearer ?

Through all his tuneful art, how strong
The human feeling gushes !
The very moonlight of his song
Is warm with smiles and blushes !

Give lettered pomp to teeth of Time,
So " Bonnie Doon " but tarry ;
Blot out the Epic's stately rhyme,
But spare his Highland Mary !

WILLIAM FORSTER.[61]

THE years are many since his hand
Was laid upon my head,
Too weak and young to understand
The serious words he said.

Yet often now the good man's look
Before me seems to swim,
As if some inward feeling took
The outward guise of him.

As if, in passion's heated war,
Or near temptation's charm,
Through him the low-voiced monitor
Forewarned me of the harm.

Stranger and pilgrim ! — from that day
Of meeting, first and last,
Wherever Duty's pathway lay,
His reverent steps have passed.

The poor to feed, the lost to seek,
To proffer life to death,
Hope to the erring, — to the weak
The strength of his own faith.

To plead the captive's right ; remove
  The sting of hate from Law ;
And soften in the fire of love
  The hardened steel of War.

He walked the dark world, in the mild,
  Still guidance of the Light ;
In tearful tenderness a child,
  A strong man in the right.

From what great perils, on his way,
  He found, in prayer, release ;
Through what abysmal shadows lay
  His pathway unto peace,

God knoweth : we could only see
  The tranquil strength he gained ;
The bondage lost in liberty,
  The fear in love unfeigned.

And I, — my youthful fancies grown
  The habit of the man,
Whose field of life by angels sown
  The wilding vines o'erran, —

Low bowed in silent gratitude,
  My manhood's heart enjoys
That reverence for the pure and good
  Which blessed the dreaming boy's.

Still shines the light of holy lives'
  Like star-beams over doubt ;
Each sainted memory, Christlike, drives
  Some dark possession out.

O friend ! O brother ! not in vain
  Thy life so calm and true,
The silver dropping of the rain,
  The fall of summer dew !

How many burdened hearts have prayed
  Their lives like thine might be !
But more shall pray henceforth for aid
  To lay them down like thee.

With weary hand, yet steadfast will,
  In old age as in youth,
Thy Master found thee sowing still
  The good seed of his truth.

As on thy task-field closed the day
  In golden-skied decline,
His angel met thee on the way,
  And lent his arm to thine.

Thy latest care for man, — thy last
  Of earthly thought a prayer, —

O, who thy mantle, backward cast,
  Is worthy now to wear ?

Methinks the mound which marks thy
    bed
  Might bless our land and save,
As rose, of old, to life the dead
  Who touched the prophet's grave !

RANTOUL.[62]

ONE day, along the electric wire
  His manly word for Freedom sped ;
We came next morn : that tongue of fire
  Said only, " He who spake is dead ! "

Dead ! while his voice was living yet,
  In echoes round the pillared dome !
Dead ! while his blotted page lay wet
  With themes of state and loves of
    home !

Dead ! in that crowning grace of time,
  That triumph of life's zenith hour !
Dead ! while we watched his manhood's
    prime
  Break from the slow bud into flower !

Dead ! he so great, and strong, and wise,
  While the mean thousands yet drew
    breath ;
How deepened, through that dread sur-
    prise,
  The mystery and the awe of death !

From the high place whereon our votes
  Had borne him, clear, calm, earnest,
    fell
His first words, like the prelude notes
  Of some great anthem yet to swell.

We seemed to see our flag unfurled,
  Our champion waiting in his place
For the last battle of the world, —
  The Armageddon of the race.

Through him we hoped to speak the
    word
  Which wins the freedom of a land ;
And lift, for human right, the sword
  Which dropped from Hampden's dy-
    ing hand.

For he had sat at Sidney's feet,
  And walked with Pym and Vane
    apart ;

And, through the centuries, felt the beat
　Of Freedom's march in Cromwell's
　　heart.

He knew the paths the worthies held,
　Where England's best and wisest trod ;
And, lingering, drank the springs that
　welled
Beneath the touch of Milton's rod.

No wild enthusiast of the right,
　Self-poised and clear, he showed alway
The coolness of his northern night,
　The ripe repose of autumn's day.

His steps were slow, yet forward still
　He pressed where others paused or
　failed ;
The calm star clomb with constant will, —
　The restless meteor flashed and paled !

Skilled in its subtlest wile, he knew
　And owned the higher ends of Law ;
Still rose majestic on his view
　The awful Shape the schoolman saw.

Her home the heart of God ; her voice
The choral harmonies whereby
The stars, through all their spheres, re-
　joice,
　The rhythmic rule of earth and sky !

We saw his great powers misapplied
　To poor ambitions ; yet, through all,
We saw him take the weaker side,
　And right the wronged, and free the
　　thrall.

Now, looking o'er the frozen North,
　For one like him in word and act,
To call her old, free spirit forth,
　And give her faith the life of
　fact, —

To break her party bonds of shame,
　And labor with the zeal of him
To make the Democratic name
　Of Liberty the synonyme, —

We sweep the land from hill to strand,
　We seek the strong, the wise, the
　brave,
And, sad of heart, return to stand
　In silence by a new-made grave !

There, where his breezy hills of home
　Look out upon his sail-white seas,

The sounds of winds and waters come,
　And shape themselves to words like
　　these :

"Why, murmuring, mourn that he,
　whose power
Was lent to Party over-long,
Heard the still whisper at the hour
He set his foot on Party wrong ?

"The human life that closed so well
No lapse of folly now can stain :
The lips whence Freedom's protest fell
No meaner thought can now profane.

"Mightier than living voice his grave
That lofty protest utters o'er ;
Through roaring wind and smiting wave
It speaks his hate of wrong once
　more.

"Men of the North ! your weak regret
Is wasted here ; arise and pay
To freedom and to him your debt,
By following where he led the way !"

THE DREAM OF PIO NONO.

. It chanced, that while the pious
　troops of France
Fought in the crusade Pio Nono
　preached,
What time the holy Bourbons stayed
　his hands
(The Hur and Aaron meet for such a
　Moses),
Stretched forth from Naples towards
　rebellious Rome
To bless the ministry of Oudinot,
And sanctify his iron homilies
And sharp persuasions of the bayonet,
That the great pontiff fell asleep, and
　dreamed.

He stood by Lake Tiberias, in the
　sun
Of the bright Orient ; and beheld the
　lame,
The sick, and blind, kneel at the Mas-
　ter's feet,
And rise up whole. And, sweetly over
　all,
Dropping the ladder of their hymn of
　praise
From heaven to earth, in silver rounds
　of song,

He heard the blessed angels sing of peace,
Good-will to man, and glory to the Lord.

Then one, with feet unshod, and leathern face
Hardened and darkened by fierce summer suns
And hot winds of the desert, closer drew
His fisher's haick, and girded up his loins,
And spake, as one who had authority :
"Come thou with me."

                    Lakeside and eastern sky
And the sweet song of angels passed away,
And, with a dream's alacrity of change,
The priest, and the swart fisher by his side,
Beheld the Eternal City lift its domes
And solemn fanes and monumental pomp
Above the waste Campagna. On the hills
The blaze of burning villas rose and fell,
And momently the mortar's iron throat
Roared from the trenches ; and, within the walls,
Sharp crash of shells, low groans of human pain,
Shout, drum beat, and the clanging larum-bell,
And tramp of hosts, sent up a mingled sound,
Half wail and half defiance. As they passed
The gate of San Pancrazio, human blood
Flowed ankle-high about them, and dead men
Choked the long street with gashed and gory piles, —
A ghastly barricade of mangled flesh,
From which, at times, quivered a living hand,
And white lips moved and moaned. A father tore
His gray hairs, by the body of his son,
In frenzy ; and his fair young daughter wept
On his old bosom. Suddenly a flash
Clove the thick sulphurous air, and man and maid
Sank, crushed and mangled by the shattering shell.

Then spake the G
seen
The blessed Maste
love ;
Look now on thine
angels sing
Above this open
high-priest !
Thou the Vicegerei
Peace !
Thou the successor
I, Peter, fisherman
In the dear Master'
love
Of his true Church,
christ,
Alien and separate
Wide as the differ
and life,
The hate of man ar
God !   .
Hence, and repent

                    Ther
Trembling, and mı
ful dream.
"What means he ?
    "Nothing n
Than that your 1
well
Catered for your pe
in sooth,
The Holy Father'
him,"
Said Cardinal Anto

                    TAU

TAULER, the pr
autumn day
Without the walls
Rhine,
Pondering the sole1
As one who, wan
night,
Feels, momently,
waves,
And hears the thu1
sea,
Breaking along an

And as he walke
the same
Old prayer with wl
of years,

Morning, and noon, and evening, lip
and heart
Had groaned : " Have pity upon me,
Lord !
Thou seest, while teaching others, I am
blind.
Send me a man who can direct my
steps ! "

Then, as he mused, he heard along
his path
A sound as of an old man's staff among
The dry, dead linden-leaves ; and, looking up,
He saw a stranger, weak, and poor, and
old.

" Peace be unto thee, father ! " Tauler said,
" God give thee a good day ! " The old
man raised .
Slowly his calm blue eyes. " I thank
thee, son ;
But *all* my days are good, and none are
ill."

Wondering thereat, the preacher spake
again,
" God give thee happy life." The old
man smiled,
" I never am unhappy."

Tauler laid
His hand upon the stranger's coarse gray
sleeve :
" Tell me, O father, what thy strange
words mean.
Surely man's days are evil, and his
life
Sad as the grave it leads to." " Nay,
my son,
Our times are in God's hands, and all
our days
Are as our needs : for shadow as for
sun,
For cold as heat, for want as wealth,
alike
Our thanks are due, since that is best
which is ;
And that which is not, sharing not his
life,
Is evil only as devoid of good.
And for the happiness of which I spake,
I find it in submission to his will,
And calm trust in the holy Trinity
Of Knowledge, Goodness, and Al-
mighty Power."

Silently wondering, for a little space,
Stood the great preacher ; then he spake
as one
Who, suddenly grappling with a haunting thought
Which long has followed, whispering
through the dark
Strange terrors, drags it, shrieking, into
light :
" What if God's will consign thee hence
to Hell ? "

" Then," said the stranger, cheerily,
" be it so.
What Hell may be I know not ; this I
know, —
I cannot lose the presence of the Lord :
One arm, Humility, takes hold upon
His dear Humanity ; the other, Love,
Clasps his Divinity. So where I go
He goes ; and better fire-walled Hell
with Him
Than golden-gated Paradise without."

Tears sprang in Tauler's eyes. A
sudden light,
Like the first ray which fell on chaos,
clove
Apart the shadow wherein he had walked
Darkly at noon. And, as the strange
old man
Went his slow way, until his silver
hair
Set like the white moon where the hills
of vine
Slope to the Rhine, he bowed his head
and said :
" My prayer is answered. God hath
sent the man
Long sought, to teach me, by his simple
trust,
Wisdom the weary schoolmen never
knew."

So, entering with a changed and
cheerful step
The city gates, he saw, far down the
street,
A mighty shadow break the light of
noon,
Which tracing backward till its airy
lines
Hardened to stony plinths, he raised his
eyes
O'er broad façade and lofty pediment,
O'er architrave and frieze and sainted
niche,

Up the stone lace-work chiselled by the
  wise
Erwin of Steinbach, dizzily up to where
In the noon-brightness the great Min-
  ster's tower,
Jewelled with sunbeams on its mural
  crown,
Rose like a visible prayer.   "Behold!"
  he said,
"The stranger's faith made plain be-
  fore mine eyes.
As yonder tower outstretches to the
  earth
The dark triangle of its shade alone
When the clear day is shining on its
  top,
So, darkness in the pathway of Man's
  life
Is but the shadow of God's providence,
By the great Sun of Wisdom cast there-
  on ;
And what is dark below is light in
  Heaven."

LINES,

SUGGESTED BY READING A STATE PA-
PER, WHEREIN THE HIGHER LAW IS
INVOKED TO SUSTAIN THE LOWER
ONE.

A PIOUS magistrate ! sound his praise
  throughout
The wondering churches.   Who shall
  henceforth doubt
    That the long-wished millennium
    draweth nigh ?
Sin in high places has become devout,
  Tithes mint, goes painful-faced, and
    prays its lie
    Straight up to Heaven, and calls it
    piety !

The pirate, watching from his bloody
  deck
  The weltering galleon, heavy with the
    gold
Of Acapulco, holding death in check
  While prayers are said, brows crossed,
    and beads are told, —
The robber, kneeling where the wayside
  cross
On dark Abruzzo tells of life's dread loss
From his own carbine, glancing still
  abroad
For some new victim, offering thanks to
  God ! —

Rome, listening at her altars to the
  cry
Of midnight Murder, while her hounds
  of hell
Scour France, from baptized cannon and
  holy bell
  And thousand-throated priesthood,
    loud and high,
  Pealing Te Deums to the shuddering
    sky,
  "Thanks to the Lord, who giveth
    victory !"
What prove these, but that crime was
  ne'er so black
As ghostly cheer and pious thanks to
  lack ?
Satan is modest.   At Heaven's door he
  lays
His evil offspring, and, in Scriptural
  phrase
And saintly posture, gives to God the
  praise
And honor of the monstrous progeny.
What marvel, then, in our own time to
  see
His old devices, smoothly acted o'er, —
Official piety, locking fast the door
Of Hope against three million souls of
  men, —
Brothers, God's children, Christ's re-
  deemed, — and then,
With uprolled eyeballs and on bended
  knee,
Whining a prayer for help to hide the
  key !

THE VOICES.

"WHY urge the long, unequal fight,
  Since Truth has fallen in the street,
Or lift anew the trampled light,
  Quenched by the heedless million's
    feet ?

"Give o'er the thankless task ; forsake
  The fools who know not ill from good ;
Eat, drink, enjoy thy own, and take
  Thine ease among the multitude.

"Live out thyself ; with others share
  Thy proper life no more ; assume
The unconcern of sun and air,
  For life or death, or blight or bloom.

"The mountain pine looks calmly on
  The fires that scourge the plains below,

Nor heeds the eagle in the sun
The small birds piping in the snow !

"The world is God's, not thine ; let him
Work out a change, if change must be :
The hand that planted best can trim
And nurse the old unfruitful tree."

So spake the Tempter, when the light
Of sun and stars had left the sky,
I listened, through the cloud and night,
And heard, methought, a voice reply :

"Thy task may well seem over-hard,
Who scatterest in a thankless soil
Thy life as seed, with no reward
Save that which Duty gives to Toil.

"Not wholly is thy heart resigned
To Heaven's benign and just decree,
Which, linking thee with all thy kind,
Transmits their joys and griefs to
thee.

"Break off that sacred chain, and turn
Back on thyself thy love and care;
Be thou thine own mean idol, burn
Faith, Hope, and Trust, thy children,
there.

"Released from that fraternal law
Which shares the common bale and
bliss,
No sadder lot could Folly draw,
Or Sin provoke from Fate, than this.

"The meal unshared is food unblest :
Thou hoard'st in vain what love
should spend ;
Self-ease is pain ; thy only rest
Is labor for a worthy end.

"A toil that gains with what it yields,
And scatters to its own increase,
And hears, while sowing outward fields,
The harvest-song of inward peace.

"Free-lipped the liberal streamlets run,
Free shines for all the healthful ray ;
The still pool stagnates in the sun,
The lurid earth-fire haunts decay !

"What is it that the crowd requite
Thy love with hate, thy truth with
lies ?
And but to faith, and not to sight,
The walls of Freedom's temple rise !

"Yet do thy work ; it shall succeed
In thine or in another's day ;
And, if denied the victor's meed,
Thou shalt not lack the toiler's pay.

"Faith shares the future's promise ;
Love's
Self-offering is a triumph won ;
And each good thought or action moves
The dark world nearer to the sun.

"Then faint not, falter not, nor plead
Thy weakness ; truth itself is strong ;
The lion's strength, the eagle's speed,
Are not alone vouchsafed to wrong.

"Thy nature, which, through fire and
flood,
To place or gain finds out its way,
Hath power to seek the highest good,
And duty's holiest call obey !

"Strivest thou in darkness ? — Foes
without
In league with traitor thoughts with-
in ;
Thy night-watch kept with trembling
Doubt
And pale Remorse the ghost of
Sin ? —

"Hast thou not, on some week of storm,
Seen the sweet Sabbath breaking fair,
And cloud and shadow, sunlit, form
The curtains of its tent of prayer ?

"So, haply, when thy task shall end,
The wrong shall lose itself in right,
And all thy week-day darkness blend
With the long Sabbath of the light !"

THE HERO.

"O for a knight like Bayard,
Without reproach or fear ;
My light glove on his casque of steel,
My love-knot on his spear !

"O for the white plume floating
Sad Zutphen's field above, —
The lion heart in battle,
The woman's heart in love !

"O that man once more were manly,
Woman's pride, and not her scorn :
That once more the pale young mother
Dared to boast ' a man is born ' !

" But, now life's slumberous current
    No sun-bowed cascade wakes ;
No tall, heroic manhood
    The level dulness breaks.

" O for a knight like Bayard,
    Without reproach or fear !
My light glove on his casque of steel,
    My love-knot on his spear ! "

Then I said, my own heart throbbing
    To the time her proud pulse beat,
" Life hath its regal natures yet, —
    True, tender, brave, and sweet !

" Smile not, fair unbeliever !
    One man, at least, I know,
Who might wear the crest of Bayard
    Or Sidney's plume of snow.

" Once, when over purple mountains
    Died away the Grecian sun,
And the far Cyllenian ranges
    Paled and darkened, one by one, —

" Fell the Turk, a bolt of thunder,
    Cleaving all the quiet sky,
And against his sharp steel lightnings
    Stood the Suliote but to die.

" Woe for the weak and halting !
    The crescent blazed behind
A curving line of sabres,
    Like fire before the wind !

" Last to fly, and first to rally,
    Rode he of whom I speak,
When, groaning in his bridle-path,
    Sank down a wounded Greek.

" With the rich Albanian costume
    Wet with many a ghastly stain,
Gazing on earth and sky as one
    Who might not gaze again !

" He looked forward to the mountains,
    Back on foes that never spare,
Then flung him from his saddle,
    And placed the stranger there.

" ' Allah ! hu ! ' Through flashing sa-
        bres,
    Through a stormy hail of lead,
The good Thessalian charger
    Up the slopes of olives sped.

" Hot spurred the turbaned riders ,
    He almost felt their breath,
Where a mountain stream rolled dark
        down
    Between the hills and death.

" One brave and manful struggle, —
    He gained the solid land,
And the cover of the mountains,
    And the carbines of his band ! "

" It was very great and noble,"
    Said the moist-eyed listener then,
" But one brave deed makes no hero ;
    Tell me what he since hath been ! "

" Still a brave and generous manhood,
    Still an honor without stain,
In the prison of the Kaiser,
    By the barricades of Seine.

" But dream not helm and harness
    The sign of valor true ;
Peace hath higher tests of manhood
    Than battle ever knew.

" Wouldst know him now ?   Behold
        him,
    The Cadmus of the blind,
Giving the dumb lip language,
    The idiot clay a mind.

" Walking his round of duty
    Serenely day by day,
With the strong man's hand of labor
    And childhood's heart of play.

" True as the knights of story,
    Sir Lancelot and his peers,
Brave in his calm endurance
    As they in tilt of spears.

" As waves in stillest waters,
    As stars in noonday skies,
All that wakes to noble action
    In his noon of calmness lies.

' Wherever outraged Nature
    Asks word or action brave,
Wherever struggles labor,
    Wherever groans a slave, —

" Wherever rise the peoples,
    Wherever sinks a throne,
The throbbing heart of Freedom finds
    An answer in his own

"Knight of a better era,
  Without reproach or fear !
Said I not well that Bayards
  And Sidneys still are here ?"

MY DREAM.

In my dream, methought I trod,
Yesternight, a mountain road ;
Narrow as Al Sirat's span,
High as eagle's flight, it ran.

Overhead, a roof of cloud
With its weight of thunder bowed ;
Underneath, to left and right,
Blankness and abysmal night.

Here and there a wild-flower blushed,
Now and then a bird-song gushed ;
Now and then, through rifts of shade,
Stars shone out, and sunbeams played.

But the goodly company,
Walking in that path with me,
One by one the brink o'erslid,
One by one the darkness hid.

Some with wailing and lament,
Some with cheerful courage went ;
But, of all who smiled or mourned,
Never one to us returned.

Anxiously, with eye and ear,
Questioning that shadow drear,
Never hand in token stirred,
Never answering voice I heard !

Steeper, darker ! — lo ! I felt
From my feet the pathway melt.
Swallowed by the black despair,
And the hungry jaws of air,

Past the stony-throated caves,
Strangled by the wash of waves,
Past the splintered crags, I sank
On a green and flowery bank, —

Soft as fall of thistle-down,
Lightly as a cloud is blown,
Soothingly as childhood pressed
To the bosom of its rest.

Of the sharp-horned rocks instead,
Green the grassy meadows spread,
Bright with waters singing by
Trees that propped a golden sky.

Painless, trustful, sorrow-free,
Old lost faces welcomed me,
With whose sweetness of content
Still expectant hope was blent.

Waking while the dawning gray
Slowly brightened into day,
Pondering that vision fled,
Thus unto myself I said : —

"Steep, and hung with clouds of strife,
Is our narrow path of life ;
And our death the dreaded fall
Through the dark, awaiting all.

"So, with painful steps we climb
Up the dizzy ways of time,
Ever in the shadow shed
By the forecast of our dread.

"Dread of mystery solved alone,
Of the untried and unknown ;
Yet the end thereof may seem
Like the falling of my dream.

"And this heart-consuming care,
All our fears of here or there,
Change and absence, loss and death,
Prove but simple lack of faith."

Thou, O Most Compassionate !
Who didst stoop to our estate,
Drinking of the cup we drain,
Treading in our path of pain, —

Through the doubt and mystery,
Grant to us thy steps to see,
And the grace to draw from thence
Larger hope and confidence.

Show thy vacant tomb, and let,
As of old, the angels sit,
Whispering, by its open door :
"Fear not ! He hath gone before !"

THE BAREFOOT BOY.

Blessings on thee, little man,
Barefoot boy, with cheek of tan !
With thy turned-up pantaloons,
And thy merry whistled tunes ;
With thy red lip, redder still
Kissed by strawberries on the hill ;
With the sunshine on thy face,
Through thy torn brim's jaunty grace :
From my heart I give thee joy, —

I was once a barefoot boy !
Prince thou art, — the grown-up man
Only is republican.
Let the million-dollared ride !
Barefoot, trudging at his side,
Thou hast more than he can buy
In the reach of ear and eye, —
Outward sunshine, inward joy :
Blessings on thee, barefoot boy !

O for boyhood's painless play,
Sleep that wakes in laughing day,
Health that mocks the doctor's rules,
Knowledge never learned of schools,
Of the wild bee's morning chase,
Of the wild-flower's time and place,
Flight of fowl and habitude
Of the tenants of the wood ;
How the tortoise bears his shell,
How the woodchuck digs his cell,
And the ground-mole sinks his well ;
How the robin feeds her young,
How the oriole's nest is hung ;
Where the whitest lilies blow,
Where the freshest berries grow,
Where the groundnut trails its vine,
Where the wood-grape's clusters shine ;
Of the black wasp's cunning way,
Mason of his walls of clay,
And the architectural plans
Of gray hornet artisans ! —
For, eschewing books and tasks,
Nature answers all he asks ;
Hand in hand with her he walks,
Face to face with her he talks,
Part and parcel of her joy, —
Blessings on the barefoot boy !

O for boyhood's time of June,
Crowding years in one brief moon,
When all things I heard or saw,
Me, their master, waited for.
I was rich in flowers and trees,
Humming-birds and honey-bees ;
For my sport the squirrel played,
Plied the snouted mole his spade ;
For my taste the blackberry cone
Purpled over hedge and stone ;
Laughed the brook for my delight
Through the day and through the night,
Whispering at the garden wall,
Talked with me from fall to fall ;
Mine the sand-rimmed pickerel pond,
Mine the walnut slopes beyond,
Mine, on bending orchard trees,
Apples of Hesperides !
Still as my horizon grew,

Larger grew my riches too ;
All the world I saw or knew
Seemed a complex Chinese toy,
Fashioned for a barefoot boy !

O for festal dainties spread,
Like my bowl of milk and bread, —
Pewter spoon and bowl of wood,
On the door-stone, gray and rude !
O'er me, like a regal tent,
Cloudy-ribbed, the sunset bent,
Purple-curtained, fringed with gold,
Looped in many a wind-swung fold ;
While for music came the play
Of the pied frogs' orchestra ;
And, to light the noisy choir,
Lit the fly his lamp of fire.
I was monarch : pomp and joy
Waited on the barefoot boy !

Cheerily, then, my little man,
Live and laugh, as boyhood can !
Though the flinty slopes be hard,
Stubble-speared the new-mown sward,
Every morn shall lead thee through
Fresh baptisms of the dew ;
Every evening from thy feet
Shall the cool wind kiss the heat :
All too soon these feet must hide
In the prison cells of pride,
Lose the freedom of the sod,
Like a colt's for work be shod,
Made to tread the mills of toil,
Up and down in ceaseless moil :
Happy if their track be found
Never on forbidden ground ;
Happy if they sink not in
Quick and treacherous sands of sin.
Ah ! that thou couldst know thy joy,
Ere it passes, barefoot boy !

FLOWERS IN WINTER.

PAINTED UPON A PORTE LIVRE.

How strange to greet, this frosty morn,
In graceful counterfeit of flowers,
These children of the meadows, born
Of sunshine and of showers !

How well the conscious wood retains
The pictures of its flower - sown
home, —
The lights and shades, the purple
stains,
And golden hues of bloom !

It was a happy thought to bring
  To the dark season's frost and rime
This painted memory of spring,
  This dream of summer-time.

Our hearts are lighter for its sake,
Our fancy's age renews its youth,
And dim-remembered fictions take
  The guise of present truth.

A wizard of the Merrimack, —
  So old ancestral legends say, —
Could call green leaf and blossom back
  To frosted stem and spray.

The dry logs of the cottage wall,
  Beneath his touch, put out their
    leaves ;
The clay-bound swallow, at his call,
  Played round the icy caves.

The settler saw his oaken flail
  Take bud, and bloom before his eyes ;
From frozen pools he saw the pale,
  Sweet summer lilies rise.

To their old homes, by man profaned,
  Came the sad dryads, exiled long,
And through their leafy tongues com-
    plained
  Of household use and wrong.

The beechen platter sprouted wild,
  The pipkin wore its old-time green ;
The cradle o'er the sleeping child
  Became a leafy screen.

Haply our gentle friend hath met,
  While wandering in her sylvan quest,
Haunting his native woodlands yet,
  That Druid of the West ; —

And, while the dew on leaf and flower
  Glistened in moonlight clear and
    still,
Learned the dusk wizard's spell of
    power,
  And caught his trick of skill.

But welcome, be it new or old,
  The gift which makes the day more
    bright,
And paints, upon the ground of cold
  And darkness, warmth and light !

Without is neither gold nor green ;
  Within, for birds, the birch-logs sing ;

Yet, summer-like, we sit between
  The autumn and the spring.

The one, with bridal blush of rose,
  And sweetest breath of woodland
    balm,
And one whose matron lips unclose
  In smiles of saintly calm.

Fill soft and deep, O winter snow !
  The sweet azalia's oaken dells,
And hide the bank where roses blow,
  And swing the azure bells !

O'erlay the amber violet's leaves,
  The purple aster's brookside home,
Guard all the flowers her pencil gives
  A life beyond their bloom.

And she, when spring comes round again,
  By greening slope and singing flood
Shall wander, seeking, not in vain,
  Her darlings of the wood.

THE RENDITION.

I HEARD the train's shrill whistle call,
  I saw an earnest look beseech,
  And rather by that look than speech
My neighbor told me all.

And, as I thought of Liberty
  Marched   handcuffed   down   that
    sworded street,
  The solid earth beneath my feet
Reeled fluid as the sea.

I felt a sense of bitter loss, —
  Shame, tearless grief, and stifling
    wrath,
  And loathing fear, as if my path
A serpent stretched across.

All love of home, all pride of place,
  All generous confidence and trust,
  Sank smothering in that deep disgust
And anguish of disgrace.

Down on my native hills of June,
  And home's green quiet, hiding all,
  Fell sudden darkness like the fall
Of midnight upon noon !

And Law, an unloosed maniac, strong,
  Blood-drunken, through the blackness
    trod,

Hoarse-shouting in the ear of God
The blasphemy of wrong.

"O Mother, from thy memories proud,
Thy old renown, dear Commonwealth,
Lend this dead air a breeze of health,
And smite with stars this cloud.

"Mother of Freedom, wise and brave,
Rise awful in thy strength," I said ;
Ah me ! I spake but to the dead ;
I stood upon her grave !

6th mo., 1854.

LINES,

ON THE PASSAGE OF THE BILL TO PRO-
TECT THE RIGHTS AND LIBERTIES OF
THE PEOPLE OF THE STATE AGAINST
THE FUGITIVE SLAVE ACT.

I SAID I stood upon thy grave,
My Mother State, when last the moon
Of blossoms clomb the skies of June.

And, scattering ashes on my head,
I wore, undreaming of relief,
The sackcloth of thy shame and grief.

Again that moon of blossoms shines
On leaf and flower and folded wing,
And thou hast risen with the spring !

Once more thy strong maternal arms
Are round about thy children flung,—
A lioness that guards her young !

No threat is on thy closéd lips,
But in thine eye a power to smite
The mad wolf backward from its light.

Southward the baffled robber's track
Henceforth runs only ; hereaway,
The fell lycanthrope finds no prey.

Henceforth, within thy sacred gates,
His first low howl shall downward draw
The thunder of thy righteous law.

Not mindless of thy trade and gain,
But, acting on the wiser plan,
Thou 'rt grown conservative of man.

So shalt thou clothe with life the hope,
Dream-painted on the sightless eyes
Of him who sang of Paradise, —

The vision of a Christian man,
In virtue as in stature great,
Embodied in a Christian State.

And thou, amidst thy sisterhood
Forbearing long, yet standing fast,
Shalt win their grateful thanks at last ;

When North and South shall strive no
more,
And all their feuds and fears be lost
In Freedom's holy Pentecost.

6th mo., 1855.

THE FRUIT-GIFT.

LAST night, just as the tints of autumn's
sky
Of sunset faded from our hills and
streams,
I sat, vague listening, lapped in twi-
light dreams,
To the leaf's rustle, and the cricket's cry.
Then, like that basket, flush with sum-
mer fruit,
Dropped by the angels at the Prophet's
foot,
Came, unannounced, a gift of clustered
sweetness,
Full-orbed, and glowing with the
prisoned beams
Of summery suns, and rounded to com-
pleteness
By kisses of the south-wind and the
dew.
Thrilled with a glad surprise, methought
I knew
The pleasure of the homeward-turning
Jew,
When Eschol's clusters on his shoulders
lay,
Dropping their sweetness on his desert
way.

I said, "This fruit beseems no world of
sin.
Its parent vine, rooted in Paradise,
O'ercrept the wall, and never paid the
price
Of the great mischief, — an ambrosial
tree,
Eden's exotic, somehow smuggled in,
To keep the thorns and thistles com-
pany."
Perchance our frail, sad mother plucked
in haste

A single vine-slip as she passed the
gate,
Where the dread sword alternate paled
and burned,
And the stern angel, pitying her fate,
Forgave the lovely trespasser, and turned
Aside his face of fire ; and thus the waste
And fallen world hath yet its annual
taste
Of primal good, to prove of sin the cost,
And show by one gleaned ear the
mighty harvest lost.

A MEMORY.

HERE, while the loom of Winter weaves
The shroud of flowers and fountains,
I think of thee and summer eves
Among the Northern mountains.

When thunder tolled the twilight's close,
And winds the lake were rude on,
And thou wert singing, Ca' the Yowes,
The bonny yowes of Cluden !

When, close and closer, hushing breath,
Our circle narrowed round thee,
And smiles and tears made up the wreath
Wherewith our silence crowned thee ;

And, strangers all, we felt the ties
Of sisters and of brothers ;
Ah ! whose of all those kindly eyes
Now smile upon another's ?

The sport of Time, who still apart
The waifs of life is flinging ;
O, nevermore shall heart to heart
Draw nearer for that singing !

Yet when the panes are frosty-starred,
And twilight's fire is gleaming,
I hear the songs of Scotland's bard
Sound softly through my dreaming !

A song that lends to winter snows
The glow of summer weather, —
Again I hear thee ca' the yowes
To Cluden's hills of heather !

TO C. S.

IF I have seemed more prompt to censure wrong
Than praise the right ; if seldom to
thine ear

My voice hath mingled with the ex-
ultant cheer
Borne upon all our Northern winds
along ;
If I have failed to join the fickle throng
In wide-eyed wonder, that thou standest
strong
In victory, surprised in thee to find
Brougham's scathing power with Can-
ning's grace combined ;
That he, for whom the ninefold Muses
sang,
From their twined arms a giant athlete
sprang,
Barbing the arrows of his native tongue
With the spent shafts Latona's archer
flung,
To smite the Python of our land and
time,
Fell as the monster born of Crissa's slime,
Like the blind bard who in Castalian
springs
Tempered the steel that clove the crest
of kings,
And on the shrine of England's freedom
laid
The gifts of Cumæ and of Delphi's
shade, —
Small need hast thou of words of praise
from me.
Thou knowest my heart, dear friend,
and well canst guess
That, even though silent, I have not
the less
Rejoiced to see thy actual life agree
With the large future which I shaped for
thee,
When, years ago, beside the summer sea,
White in the moon, we saw the long
waves fall
Baffled and broken from the rocky wall,
That, to the menace of the brawling flood,
Opposed alone its massive quietude,
Calm as a fate ; with not a leaf nor
vine
Nor birch-spray trembling in the still
moonshine,
Crowning it like God's peace. I some-
times think
That night-scene by the sea prophet-
ical, —
(For Nature speaks in symbols and in
signs,
And through her pictures human fate
divines), —
That rock, wherefrom we saw the billows
sink

In murmuring rout, uprising clear and
  tall
In the white light of heaven, the type
  of one
Who, momently by Error's host assailed,
Stands strong as Truth, in greaves of
  granite mailed ;
  And, tranquil-fronted, listening over
    all
The tumult, hears the angels say, Well
  done !

THE KANSAS EMIGRANTS.

WE cross the prairie as of old
  The pilgrims crossed the sea,
To make the West, as they the East,
  The homestead of the free !

We go to rear a wall of men
  On Freedom's southern line,
And plant beside the cotton-tree
  The rugged Northern pine !

We 're flowing from our native hills
  As our free rivers flow ;
The blessing of our Mother-land
  Is on us as we go.

We go to plant her common schools
  On distant prairie swells,
And give the Sabbaths of the wild
  The music of her bells.

Upbearing, like the Ark of old,
  The Bible in our van,
We go to test the truth of God
  Against the fraud of man.

No pause, nor rest, save where the
  streams
That feed the Kansas run,
Save where our Pilgrim gonfalon
  Shall flout the setting sun !

We 'll tread the prairie as of old
  Our fathers sailed the sea,
And make the West, as they the East,
  The homestead of the free !

SONG OF SLAVES IN THE DESERT.[63]

WHERE are we going ? where are we going,
  Where are we going, Rubee ?

Lord of peoples, lord of lands,
Look across these shining sands,
Through the furnace of the noon,
Through the white light of the moon.
Strong the Ghiblee wind is blowing,
Strange and large the world is growing !
Speak and tell us where we are going,
  Where are we going, Rubee ?

Bornou land was rich and good,
Wells of water, fields of food,
Dourra fields, and bloom of bean,
And the palm-tree cool and green :
Bornou land we see no longer,
Here we thirst and here we hunger,
Here the Moor-man smites in anger :
  Where are we going, Rubee ?

When we went from Bornou land,
We were like the leaves and sand,
We were many, we are few ;
Life has one, and death has two :
Whitened bones our path are showing,
Thou All-seeing, thou All-knowing !
Hear us, tell us, where are we going,
  Where are we going, Rubee ?

Moons of marches from our eyes   ·
Bornou land behind us lies ;
Stranger round us day by day
Bends the desert circle gray ;
Wild the waves of sand are flowing,
Hot the winds above them blowing, —
Lord of all things ! — where are we go-
    ing ?
  Where are we going, Rubee ?

We are weak, but Thou art strong ;
Short our lives, but Thine is long ;
We are blind, but Thou hast eyes ;
We are fools, but Thou art wise !

Thou, our morrow's pathway knowing
Through the strange world round us
    growing,
Hear us, tell us where are we going,
  Where are we going, Rubee ?

LINES,

INSCRIBED TO FRIENDS UNDER ARREST
FOR TREASON AGAINST THE SLAVE
POWER.

THE age is dull and mean.   Men creep,
  Not walk ; with blood too pale and
    tame

To pay the debt they owe to shame ;
Buy cheap, sell dear ; eat, drink, and
    sleep
Down-pillowed, deaf to moaning want;
Pay tithes for soul-insurance ; keep
    Six days to Mammon, one to Cant.

In such a time, give thanks to God,
    That somewhat of the holy rage
    With which the prophets in their
    age
On all its decent seemings trod,
    Has set your feet upon the lie,
That man and ox and soul and clod
    Are market stock to sell and buy !

The hot words from your lips, my own,
    To caution trained, might not repeat ;
    But if some tares among the wheat
Of generous thought and deed were
    sown,
    No common wrong provoked your
    zeal ;
The silken gauntlet that is thrown
    In such a quarrel rings like steel.

The brave old strife the fathers saw
    For Freedom calls for men again
Like those who battled not in vain
For England's Charter, Alfred's law ;
    And right of speech and trial just
Wage in your name their ancient war
    With venal courts and perjured trust.

God's ways seem dark, but, soon or late,
    They touch the shining hills of day ;
    The evil cannot brook delay,
The good can well afford to wait.
    Give ermined knaves their hour of
    crime ;
Ye have the future grand and great,
    The safe appeal of Truth to Time !

THE NEW EXODUS.[64]

By fire and cloud, across the desert
    sand,
    And through the parted waves,
From their long bondage, with an out-
    stretched hand,
    God led the Hebrew slaves !

Dead as the letter of the Pentateuch,
    As Egypt's statues cold,
In the adytum of the sacred book
    Now stands that marvel old.

"Lo, God *is* great !" the simple Mos-
    lem says.
    We seek the ancient date,
Turn the dry scroll, and make that liv-
    ing phrase
    A dead one : " God *was* great ! "

And, like the Coptic monks by Mousa's
    wells,
    We dream of wonders past,
Vague as the tales the wandering Arab
    tells,
    Each drowsier than the last.

O fools and blind ! Above the Pyramids
    Stretches once more that hand,
And tranced Egypt, from her stony lids,
    Flings back her veil of sand.

And morning-smitten Memnon, singing,
    wakes ;
    And, listening by his Nile,
O'er Ammon's grave and awful visage
    breaks
    A sweet and human smile.

Not, as before, with hail and fire, and
    call
Of death for midnight graves,
But in the stillness of the noonday,
    fall
    The fetters of the slaves.

No longer through the Red Sea, as of
    old,
    The bondmen walk dry shod ;
Through human hearts, by love of Him
    controlled,
    Runs now that path of God !

THE HASCHISH.

Of all that Orient lands can vaunt
    Of marvels with our own competing,
The strangest is the Haschish plant,
    And what will follow on its eating.

What pictures to the taster rise,
    Of Dervish or of Almeh dances !
Of Eblis, or of Paradise,
    Set all aglow with Houri glances !

The poppy visions of Cathay,
    The heavy beer-trance of the Suabian ;
The wizard lights and demon play
    Of nights Walpurgis and Arabian !

The Mollah and the Christian dog
  Change place in mad metempsycho-
    sis ;
The Muezzin climbs the synagogue,
  The Rabbi shakes his beard at Moses !

The Arab by his desert well
  Sits choosing from some Caliph's
    daughters,
And hears his single camel's bell
  Sound welcome to his regal quarters.

The Koran's reader makes complaint
  Of Shitan dancing on and off it ;
The robber offers alms, the saint
  Drinks Tokay and blasphemes the
    Prophet.

Such scenes that Eastern plant awakes ;
  But we have one ordained to beat it,
The Haschish of the West, which makes
  Or fools or knaves of all who eat it.

The preacher eats, and straight appears
  His Bible in a new translation ;

Its angels negro overseers,
  And Heaven itself a snug planta-
    tion !

The man of peace, about whose dreams
  The sweet millennial angels cluster,
Tastes the mad weed, and plots and
    schemes,
  A raving Cuban filibuster !

The noisiest Democrat, with ease,
  It turns to Slavery's parish beadle ;
The shrewdest statesman eats and sees
  Due southward point the polar needle.

The Judge partakes, and sits erelong
  Upon his bench a railing blackguard ;
Decides off-hand that right is wrong,
  And reads the ten commandments
    backward.

O potent plant ! so rare a taste
  Has never Turk or Gentoo gotten ;
The hempen Haschish of the East
  Is powerless to our Western Cotton !

BALLADS.

MARY GARVIN.

FROM the heart of Waumbek Methna,
  from the lake that never fails,
Falls the Saco in the green lap of Conway's intervales ;
There, in wild and virgin freshness, its
  waters foam and flow,
As when Darby Field first saw them,
  two hundred years ago.

But, vexed in all its seaward course with
  bridges, dams, and mills,
How changed is Saco's stream, how lost
  its freedom of the hills,
Since travelled Jocelyn, factor Vines,
  and stately Champernoon
Heard on its banks the gray wolf's howl,
  the trumpet of the loon !

With smoking axle hot with speed, with
  steeds of fire and steam,
Wide-waked To-day leaves Yesterday
  behind him like a dream.

Still, from the hurrying train of Life,
  fly backward far and fast
The milestones of the fathers, the land-
  marks of the past.

But human hearts remain unchanged :
  the sorrow and the sin,
The loves and hopes and fears of old, are
  to our own akin ;
And if, in tales our fathers told, the
  songs our mothers sung,
Tradition wears a snowy beard, Romance
  is always young.

O sharp-lined man of traffic, on Saco's
  banks to-day !
O mill-girl watching late and long the
  shuttle's restless play !
Let, for the once, a listening ear the
  working hand beguile,
And lend my old Provincial tale, as
  suits, a tear or smile !

The evening gun had sounded from gray
    Fort Mary's walls ;
Through the forest, like a wild beast,
    roared and plunged the Saco's falls.

And westward on the sea-wind, that
    damp and gusty grew,
Over cedars darkening inland the smokes
    of Spurwink blew.

On the hearth of Farmer Garvin blazed
    the crackling walnut log ;
Right and left sat dame and goodman,
    and between them lay the dog,

Head on paws, and tail slow wagging,
    and beside him on her mat,
Sitting drowsy in the fire-light, winked
    and purred the mottled cat.

"Twenty years !" said Goodman Gar-
    vin, speaking sadly, under breath,
And his gray head slowly shaking, as
    one who speaks of death.

The goodwife dropped her needles : "It
    is twenty years to-day,
Since the Indians fell on Saco, and stole
    our child away "

Then they sank into the silence, for
    each knew the other's thought,
Of a great and common sorrow, and
    words were needed not.

"Who knocks?" cried Goodman Garvin.
    The door was open thrown ;
On two strangers, man and maiden, cloaked
    and furred, the fire-light shone.

One with courteous gesture lifted the
    bear-skin from his head ;
"Lives here Elkanah Garvin ?" "I
    am he," the goodman said.

"Sit ye down, and dry and warm ye,
    for the night is chill with rain."
And the goodwife drew the settle, and
    stirred the fire amain.

The maid unclasped her cloak-hood, the
    fire-light glistened fair
In her large, moist eyes, and over soft
    folds of dark brown hair.

Dame Garvin looked upon her : "It is
    Mary's self I see !

Dear heart ! " she cried, "now tell me,
    has my child come back to me ?"

"My name indeed is Mary," said the
    stranger, sobbing wild ;
"Will you be to me a mother ? I am
    Mary Garvin's child !

"She sleeps by wooded Simcoe, but on
    her dying day
She bade my father take me to her kins-
    folk far away.

"And when the priest besought her to
    do me no such wrong,
She said, 'May God forgive me ! I have
    closed my heart too long.

"'When I hid me from my father, and
    shut out my mother's call,
I sinned against those dear ones, and
    the Father of us all.

"'Christ's love rebukes no home-love,
    breaks no tie of kin apart ;
Better heresy in doctrine, than heresy
    of heart.

"'Tell me not the Church must censure :
    she who wept the Cross beside
Never made her own flesh strangers, nor
    the claims of blood denied ;

"'And if she who wronged her parents,
    with her child atones to them,
Earthly daughter, Heavenly mother !
    thou at least wilt not condemn !'

"So, upon her death-bed lying, my
    blessed mother spake ;
As we come to do her bidding, so receive
    us for her sake."

"God be praised !" said Goodwife Gar-
    vin, "He taketh, and he gives ;
He woundeth, but he healeth ; in her
    child our daughter lives !"

"Amen !" the old man answered, as he
    brushed a tear away,
And, kneeling by his hearthstone, said,
    with reverence, "Let us pray."

All its Oriental symbols, and its Hebrew
    paraphrase,
Warm with earnest life and feeling, rose
    his prayer of love and praise.

But he started at beholding, as he rose
    from off his knee,
The stranger cross his forehead with the
    sign of Papistrie.

"What is this?" cried Farmer Garvin.
    "Is an English Christian's home
A chapel or a mass-house, that you make
    the sign of Rome?"

Then the young girl knelt beside him,
    kissed his trembling hand, and
    cried :
"O, forbear to chide my father ; in that
    faith my mother died !

"On her wooden cross at Simcoe the
    dews and sunshine fall,
As they fall on Spurwink's graveyard ;
    and the dear God watches all !"

The old man stroked the fair head that
    rested on his knee ;
"Your words, dear child," he answered,
    "are God's rebuke to me.

"Creed and rite perchance may differ,
    yet our faith and hope be one.
Let me be your father's father, let him
    be to me a son."

When the horn, on Sabbath morning,
    through the still and frosty air,
From Spurwink, Pool, and Black Point,
    called to sermon and to prayer,

To the goodly house of worship, where,
    in order due and fit,
As by public vote directed, classed and
    ranked the people sit ;

Mistress first and goodwife after, clerkly
    squire before the clown,
From the brave coat, lace-embroidered,
    to the gray frock, shading down ;

From the pulpit read the preacher, —
    "Goodman Garvin and his wife
Fain would thank the Lord, whose kind-
    ness has followed them through
    life,

"For the great and crowning mercy,
    that their daughter, from the
    wild,
Where she rests (they hope in God's
    peace), has sent to them her child ;

"And the prayers of all God's people
    they ask, that they may prove
Not unworthy, through their weakness,
    of such special proof of love."

As the preacher prayed, uprising, the
    aged couple stood,
And the fair Canadian also, in her mod-
    est maidenhood.

Thought the elders, grave and doubting,
    "She is Papist born and bred " ;
Thought the young men, "'T is an
    angel in Mary Garvin's stead ! "

MAUD MULLER.

MAUD MULLER, on a summer's day,
Raked the meadow sweet with hay.

Beneath her torn hat glowed the wealth
Of simple beauty and rustic health.

Singing, she wrought, and her merry glee
The mock-bird echoed from his tree.

But when she glanced to the far-off
    town,
White from its hill-slope looking down,

The sweet song died, and a vague unrest
And a nameless longing filled her
    breast, —

A wish, that she hardly dared to own,
For something better than she had
    known.

The Judge rode slowly down the lane,
Smoothing his horse's chestnut mane.

He drew his bridle in the shade
Of the apple-trees, to greet the maid,

And asked a draught from the spring that
    flowed
Through the meadow across the road.

She stooped where the cool spring bub-
    bled up,
And filled for him her small tin cup,

And blushed as she gave it, looking
    down
On her feet so bare, and her tattered
    gown.

"Thanks!" said the Judge; "a sweeter draught
From a fairer hand was never quaffed."

He spoke of the grass and flowers and trees,
Of the singing birds and the humming bees;

Then talked of the haying, and wondered whether
The cloud in the west would bring foul weather.

And Maud forgot her brier-torn gown,
And her graceful ankles bare and brown;

And listened, while a pleased surprise
Looked from her long-lashed hazel eyes.

At last, like one who for delay
Seeks a vain excuse, he rode away.

Maud Muller looked and sighed: "Ah me!
That I the Judge's bride might be!

"He would dress me up in silks so fine,
And praise and toast me at his wine.

"My father should wear a broadcloth coat;
My brother should sail a painted boat.

"I'd dress my mother so grand and gay,
And the baby should have a new toy each day.

"And I'd feed the hungry and clothe the poor,
And all should bless me who left our door."

The Judge looked back as he climbed the hill,
And saw Maud Muller standing still.

"A form more fair, a face more sweet,
Ne'er hath it been my lot to meet.

"And her modest answer and graceful air
Show her wise and good as she is fair.

"Would she were mine, and I to-day,
Like her, a harvester of hay:

"No doubtful balance of rights and wrongs,
Nor weary lawyers with endless tongues,

"But low of cattle and song of birds,
And health and quiet and loving words."

But he thought of his sisters proud and cold,
And his mother vain of her rank and gold.

So, closing his heart, the Judge rode on,
And Maud was left in the field alone.

But the lawyers smiled that afternoon,
When he hummed in court an old love-tune;

And the young girl mused beside the well
Till the rain on the unraked clover fell.

He wedded a wife of richest dower,
Who lived for fashion, as he for power.

Yet oft, in his marble hearth's bright glow,
He watched a picture come and go;

And sweet Maud Muller's hazel eyes
Looked out in their innocent surprise.

Oft, when the wine in his glass was red,
He longed for the wayside well instead;

And closed his eyes on his garnished rooms
To dream of meadows and clover-blooms.

And the proud man sighed, with a secret pain,
"Ah, that I were free again!

"Free as when I rode that day,
Where the barefoot maiden raked her hay."

She wedded a man unlearned and poor,
And many children played round her door.

But care and sorrow, and childbirth pain,
Left their traces on heart and brain.

And oft, when the summer sun shone hot
On the new-mown hay in the meadow
lot,

And she heard the little spring brook fall
Over the roadside, through the wall,

In the shade of the apple-tree again
She saw a rider draw his rein.

And, gazing down with timid grace,
She felt his pleased eyes read her face.

Sometimes her narrow kitchen walls
Stretched away into stately halls;

The weary wheel to a spinnet turned,
The tallow candle an astral burned,

And for him who sat by the chimney-
lug,
Dozing and grumbling o'er pipe and
mug,

A manly form at her side she saw,
And joy was duty and love was law.

Then she took up her burden of life
again,
Saying only, "It might have been."

Alas for maiden, alas for Judge,
For rich repiner and household drudge!

God pity them both! and pity us all,
Who vainly the dreams of youth recall.

For of all sad words of tongue or pen,
The saddest are these: "It might have
been!"

Ah, well! for us all some sweet hope
lies
Deeply buried from human eyes;

And, in the hereafter, angels may
Roll the stone from its grave away!

THE RANGER.

ROBERT RAWLIN! — Frosts were falling
When the ranger's horn was calling
    Through the woods to Canada.
Gone the winter's sleet and snowing,
Gone the spring-time's bud and blowing,
Gone the summer's harvest mowing,

And again the fields are gray.
    Yet away, he 's away!
Faint and fainter hope is growing
    In the hearts that mourn his stay.

Where the lion, crouching high on
Abraham's rock with teeth of iron,
    Glares o'er wood and wave away,
Faintly thence, as pines far sighing,
Or as thunder spent and dying,
Come the challenge and replying,
    Come the sounds of flight and fray.
    Well-a-day! Hope and pray!
Some are living, some are lying
    In their red graves far away.

Straggling rangers, worn with dangers,
Homeward faring, weary strangers
    Pass the farm-gate on their way;
Tidings of the dead and living,
Forest march and ambush, giving,
Till the maidens leave their weaving,
    And the lads forget their play.
    "Still away, still away!"
Sighs a sad one, sick with grieving,
    "Why does Robert still delay!"

Nowhere fairer, sweeter, rarer,
Does the golden-locked fruit-bearer
    Through his painted woodlands stray,
Than where hillside oaks and beeches
Overlook the long, blue reaches,
Silver coves and pebbled beaches,
    And green isles of Casco Bay;
    Nowhere day, for delay,
With a tenderer look beseeches,
    "Let me with my charmed earth
      stay."

On the grain-lands of the mainlands
Stands the serried corn like train-bands,
    Plume and pennon rustling gay;
Out at sea, the islands wooded,
Silver birches, golden-hooded,
Set with maples, crimson-blooded,
    White sea-foam and sand-hills gray,
Stretch away, far away.
Dim and dreamy, over-brooded
    By the hazy autumn day.

Gayly chattering to the clattering
Of the brown nuts downward pattering,
    Leap the squirrels, red and gray.
On the grass-land, on the fallow,
Drop the apples, red and yellow;
Drop the russet pears and mellow,
    Drop the red leaves all the day.
    And away, swift away,

Sun and cloud, o'er hill and hollow
  Chasing, weave their web of play.

"Martha Mason, Martha Mason,
Prithee tell us of the reason
  Why you mope at home to-day:
Surely smiling is not sinning;
Leave your quilling, leave your spinning;
What is all your store of linen,
  If your heart is never gay?
  Come away, come away!
Never yet did sad beginning
  Make the task of life a play."

Overbending, till she's blending
With the flaxen skein she's tending
  Pale brown tresses smoothed away
From her face of patient sorrow,
Sits she, seeking but to borrow,
From the trembling hope of morrow,
 ' Solace for the weary day.
  "Go your way, laugh and play;
Unto Him who heeds the sparrow
  And the lily, let me pray."

"With our rally, rings the valley, —
Join us!" cried the blue-eyed Nelly;
  "Join us!" cried the laughing
    May,
"To the beach we all are going,
And, to save the task of rowing,
West by north the wind is blowing,
  Blowing briskly down the bay!
  Come away, come away!
Time and tide are swiftly flowing,
  Let us take them while we may!

"Never tell us that you'll fail us,
Where the purple beach-plum mellows
  On the bluffs so wild and gray.
Hasten, for the oars are falling;
Hark, our merry mates are calling:
Time it is that we were all in,
  Singing tideward down the bay!"
    "Nay, nay, let me stay;
Sore and sad for Robert Rawlin
  Is my heart," she said, "to-day."

"Vain your calling for Rob Rawlin!
Some red squaw his moose-meat's broil-
    ing,
 Or some French lass, singing gay;
Just forget as he's forgetting;
What avails a life of fretting?
If some stars must needs be setting,
  Others rise as good as they."
  "Cease, I pray; go your way!"

Martha cries, her eyelids wetting;
  "Foul and false the words you say!"

"Martha Mason, hear to reason!
Prithee, put a kinder face on!"
  "Cease to vex me," did she say;
"Better at his side be lying,
With the mournful pine-trees sighing,
And the wild birds o'er us crying,
  Than to doubt like mine a prey;
  While away, far away,
Turns my heart, forever trying
  Some new hope for each new day.

"When the shadows veil the meadows,
And the sunset's golden ladders
  Sink from twilight's walls of gray, —
From the window of my dreaming,
I can see his sickle gleaming,
Cheery-voiced, can hear him teaming
  Down the locust-shaded way;
  But away, swift away,
Fades the fond, delusive seeming,
  And I kneel again to pray.

"When the growing dawn is showing,
And the barn-yard cock is crowing,
  And the horned moon pales away:
From a dream of him awaking,
Every sound my heart is making
Seems a footstep of his taking;
  Then I hush the thought, and say,
  'Nay, nay, he's away!'
Ah! my heart, my heart is breaking
  For the dear one far away."

Look up, Martha! worn and swarthy,
Glows a face of manhood worthy:
  "Robert!" "Martha!" all they say.
O'er went wheel and reel together,
Little cared the owner whither;
Heart of lead is heart of feather,
  Noon of night is noon of day!
  Come away, come away!
When such lovers meet each other,
  Why should prying idlers stay?

Quench the timber's fallen embers,
Quench the red leaves in December's
  Hoary rime and chilly spray.
But the hearth shall kindle clearer,
Household welcomes sound sincerer,
Heart to loving heart draw nearer,
  When the bridal bells shall say:
  "Hope and pray, trust alway;
Life is sweeter, love is dearer,
  For the trial and delay!"

LATER POEMS.

THE LAST WALK IN AUTUMN.

I.

O'ER the bare woods, whose out-
stretched hands
  Plead with the leaden heavens in
    vain,
I see, beyond the valley lands,
  The sea's long level dim with rain.
Around me all things, stark and dumb,
Seem praying for the snows to come,
And, for the summer bloom and green-
    ness gone,
With winter's sunset lights and dazzling
    morn atone.

II.

Along the river's summer walk,
  The withered tufts of asters nod ;
And trembles on its arid stalk
  The hoar plume of the golden-rod.
And on a ground of sombre fir,
And azure-studded juniper,
The silver birch its buds of purple shows,
And scarlet berries tell where bloomed
    the sweet wild-rose !

III.

With mingled sound of horns and bells,
  A far-heard clang, the wild geese
    fly,
Storm-sent, from Arctic moors and
    fells,
  Like a great arrow through the sky,
Two dusky lines converged in one,
Chasing the southward-flying sun ;
While the brave snow-bird and the hardy
    jay
Call to them from the pines, as if to bid
    them stay.

IV.

I passed this way a year ago :
  The wind blew south ; the noon of
    day
Was warm as June's ; and save that
    snow
  Flecked the low mountains far away,
And that the vernal-seeming breeze
Mocked faded grass and leafless trees,
I might have dreamed of summer as I lay,
Watching the fallen leaves with the soft
    wind at play.

V.

Since then, the winter blasts have piled
  The white pagodas of the snow
On these rough slopes, and, strong and
    wild,
  Yon river, in its overflow
Of spring-time rain and sun, set free,
Crashed with its ices to the sea ;
And over these gray fields, then green
    and gold,
The summer corn has waved, the thun-
    der's organ rolled.

VI.

Rich gift of God ! A year of time !
  What pomp of rise and shut of day,
What hues wherewith our Northern
    clime
  Makes autumn's dropping woodlands
    gay,
What airs outblown from ferny dells,
And clover - bloom and sweetbrier
    smells,
What songs of brooks and birds, what
    fruits and flowers,
Green woods and moonlit snows, have in
    its round been ours !

VII.

I know not how, in other lands,
  The changing seasons come and go ;
What splendors fall on Syrian sands,
  What purple lights on Alpine snow !
Nor how the pomp of sunrise waits
On Venice at her watery gates ;
A dream alone to me is Arno's vale,
And the Alhambra's halls are but a trav-
    eller's tale.

VIII.

Yet, on life's current, he who drifts
  Is one with him who rows or sails ;

And he who wanders widest lifts
  No more of beauty's jealous veils
Than he who from his doorway sees
  The miracle of flowers and trees,
Feels the warm Orient in the noonday air,
And from cloud minarets hears the sun-
    set call to prayer !

IX.

The eye may well be glad, that looks
  Where Pharpar's fountains rise and
    fall ;
But he who sees his native brooks
  Laugh in the sun, has seen them all.
The marble palaces of Ind
  Rise round him in the snow and wind ;
From his lone sweetbrier Persian Hafiz
    smiles,
And Rome's cathedral awe is in his
    woodland aisles.

X.

And thus it is my fancy blends
  The near at hand and far and rare ;
And while the same horizon bends
  Above the silver-sprinkled hair
Which flashed the light of morning
    skies
On childhood's wonder-lifted eyes,
Within its round of sea and sky and field,
Earth wheels with all her zones, the
    Kosmos stands revealed.

XI.

And thus the sick man on his bed,
  The toiler to his task-work bound,
Behold their prison-walls outspread,
  Their clipped horizon widen round !
While freedom-giving fancy waits,
Like Peter's angel at the gates,
The power is theirs to baffle care and pain,
To bring the lost world back, and make
    it theirs again !

XII.

What lack of goodly company,
  When masters of the ancient lyre
Obey my call, and trace for me
  Their words of mingled tears and
    fire !
I talk with Bacon, grave and wise,
I read the world with Pascal's eyes ;
And priest and sage, with solemn brows
    austere,
And poets, garland-bound, the Lords of
    Thought, draw near.

XIII.

Methinks, O friend, I hear thee say,
  " In vain the human heart we mock ;
Bring living guests who love the day,
  Not ghosts who fly at crow of cock !
The herbs we share with flesh and blood,
Are better than ambrosial food,
With laurelled shades." I grant it,
    nothing loath,
But doubly blest is he who can partake
  of both.

XIV.

He who might Plato's banquet grace,
  Have I not seen before me sit,
And watched his puritanic face,
  With more than Eastern wisdom lit ?
Shrewd mystic ! who, upon the back
Of his Poor Richard's Almanack,
Writing the Sufi's song, the Gentoo's
    dream,
Links Menu's age of thought to Fulton's
  age of steam !

XV.

Here too, of answering love secure,
  Have I not welcomed to my hearth
The gentle pilgrim troubadour,
  Whose songs have girdled half the
    earth ;
Whose pages, like the magic mat
Whereon the Eastern lover sat,
Have borne me over Rhine-land's purple
    vines,
And Nubia's tawny sands, and Phrygia's
  mountain pines !

XVI.

And he, who to the lettered wealth
  Of ages adds the lore unpriced,
The wisdom and the moral health,
  The ethics of the school of Christ ;
The statesman to his holy trust,
As the Athenian archon, just,
Struck down, exiled like him for truth
    alone,
Has he not graced my home with beauty
  all his own ?

XVII.

What greetings smile, what farewells
    wave,
  What loved ones enter and depart !
The good, the beautiful, the brave,
  The Heaven-lent treasures of the
    heart !

14

How conscious seems the frozen sod
And beechen slope whereon they trod !
The oak-leaves rustle, and the dry grass bends
Beneath the shadowy feet of lost or absent friends.

XVIII.

Then ask not why to these bleak hills
I cling, as clings the tufted moss,
To bear the winter's lingering chills,
The mocking spring's perpetual loss.
I dream of lands where summer smiles,
And soft winds blow from spicy isles,
But scarce would Ceylon's breath of flowers be sweet,
Could I not feel thy soil, New England, at my feet !

XIX.

At times I long for gentler skies,
And bathe in dreams of softer air,
But homesick tears would fill the eyes
That saw the Cross without the Bear.
The pine must whisper to the palm,
The north-wind break the tropic calm ;
And with the dreamy languor of the Line,
The North's keen virtue blend, and strength to beauty join.

XX.

Better to stem with heart and hand
The roaring tide of life, than lie,
Unmindful, on its flowery strand, ·
Of God's occasions drifting by !
Better with naked nerve to bear
The needles of this goading air,
Than, in the lap of sensual ease, forego
The godlike power to do, the godlike aim to know.

XXI.

Home of my heart ! to me more fair
Than gay Versailles or Windsor's halls,
The painted, shingly town-house where
The freeman's vote for Freedom falls !
The simple roof where prayer is made,
Than Gothic groin and colonnade ;
The living temple of the heart of man,
Than Rome's sky-mocking vault, or many-spired Milan !

XXII.

More dear thy equal village schools,
Where rich and poor the Bible read,
Than classic halls where Priestcraft rules,
And Learning wears the chains of Creed ;
Thy glad Thanksgiving, gathering in
The scattered sheaves of home and kin,
Than the mad license following Lenten pains,
Or holidays of slaves who laugh and dance in chains.

XXIII.

And sweet homes nestle in these dales,
And perch along these wooded swells ;
And, blest beyond Arcadian vales,
They hear the sound of Sabbath bells !
Here dwells no perfect man sublime,
Nor woman winged before her time,
But with the faults and follies of the race,
Old home-bred virtues hold their not unhonored place.

XXIV.

Here manhood struggles for the sake
Of mother, sister, daughter, wife,
The graces and the loves which make
The music of the march of life ;
And woman, in her daily round
Of duty, walks on holy ground.
No unpaid menial tills the soil, nor here
Is the bad lesson learned at human rights to sneer.

XXV.

Then let the icy north-wind blow
The trumpets of the coming storm,
To arrowy sleet and blinding snow
You slanting lines of rain transform.
Young hearts shall hail the drifted cold,
As gayly as I did of old ;
And I, who watch them through the frosty pane,
Unenvious, live in them my boyhood o'er again.

XXVI.

And I will trust that He who heeds
The life that hides in mead and wold,
Who hangs yon alder's crimson beads,
And stains these mosses green and gold,

Will still, as He hath done, incline
  His gracious care to me and mine ;
Grant what we ask aright, from wrong
    debar,
And, as the earth grows dark, make
    brighter every star !

XXVII.

I have not seen, I may not see,
  My hopes for man take form in
    fact,
But God will give the victory
  In due time ; in that faith I act.
And he who sees the future sure,
The baffling present may endure,
And bless, meanwhile, the unseen Hand
    that leads
The heart's desires beyond the halting
    step of deeds.

XXVIII.

And thou, my song, I send thee forth,
  Where harsher songs of mine have
    flown ;
Go, find a place at home and hearth
  Where'er thy singer's name is known ;
Revive for him the kindly thought
Of friends ; and they who love him
    not,
Touched by some strain of thine, per-
    chance may take
The hand he proffers all, and thank him
    for thy sake.

THE MAYFLOWERS.

**The trailing arbutus, or mayflower, grows
abundantly in the vicinity of Plymouth, and
was the first flower that greeted the Pilgrims
after their fearful winter.**

SAD Mayflower ! watched by winter stars,
  And nursed by winter gales,
With petals of the sleeted spars,
  And leaves of frozen sails !

What had she in those dreary hours,
  Within her ice-rimmed bay,
In common with the wild-wood flowers,
  The first sweet smiles of May ?

Yet, "God be praised !" the Pilgrim
    said,
  Who saw the blossoms peer
Above the brown leaves, dry and dead,
  "Behold our Mayflower here !"

"God wills it : here our rest shall be,
  Our years of wandering o'er,
For us the Mayflower of the sea
  Shall spread her sails no more."

O sacred flowers of faith and hope,
  As sweetly now as then
Ye bloom on many a birchen slope,
  In many a pine-dark glen.

Behind the sea-wall's rugged length,
  Unchanged, your leaves unfold,
Like love behind the manly strength
  Of the brave hearts of old.

So live the fathers in their sons,
  Their sturdy faith be ours,
And ours the love that overruns
  Its rocky strength with flowers.

The Pilgrim's wild and wintry day
  Its shadow round us draws ;
The Mayflower of his stormy bay,
  Our Freedom's struggling cause.

But warmer suns erelong shall bring
  To life the frozen sod ;
And, through dead leaves of hope, shall
    spring
  Afresh the flowers of God !

BURIAL OF BARBOUR.

BEAR him, comrades, to his grave ;
  Never over one more brave
    Shall the prairie grasses weep,
  In the ages yet to come,
  When the millions in our room,
    What we sow in tears, shall reap.

Bear him up the icy hill,
  With the Kansas, frozen still
    As his noble heart, below,
  And the land he came to till
  With a freeman's thews and will,
    And his poor hut roofed with snow !

One more look of that dead face,
  Of his murder's ghastly trace !
    One more kiss, O widowed one !
  Lay your left hands on his brow,
  Lift your right hands up, and vow
    That his work shall yet be done.

Patience, friends ! The eye of God
Every path by Murder trod

Watches, lidless, day and night;
And the dead man in his shroud,
And his widow weeping loud,
  And our hearts, are in his sight.

Every deadly threat that swells
With the roar of gambling hells,
  Every brutal jest and jeer,
Every wicked thought and plan
Of the cruel heart of man,
  Though but whispered, He can hear!

We in suffering, they in crime,
Wait the just award of time,
  Wait the vengeance that is due;
Not in vain a heart shall break,
Not a tear for Freedom's sake
  Fall unheeded : God is true.

While the flag with stars bedecked
Threatens where it should protect,
  And the Law shakes hands with
    Crime,
What is left us but to wait,
Match our patience to our fate,
  And abide the better time?

Patience, friends! The human heart
Everywhere shall take our part,
  Everywhere for us shall pray;
On our side are nature's laws,
And God's life is in the cause
  That we suffer for to-day.

Well to suffer is divine;
Pass the watchword down the line,
  Pass the countersign : "ENDURE."
Not to him who rashly dares,
But to him who nobly bears,
  Is the victor's garland sure.

Frozen earth to frozen breast,
Lay our slain one down to rest;
  Lay him down in hope and faith,
And above the broken sod,
Once again, to Freedom's God,
  Pledge ourselves for life or death,

That the State whose walls we lay,
In our blood and tears, to-day,
  Shall be free from bonds of shame
And our goodly land untrod
By the feet of Slavery, shod
  With cursing as with flame!

Plant the Buckeye on his grave,
For the hunter of the slave

In its shadow cannot rest;
And let martyr mound and tree
Be our pledge and guaranty
  Of the freedom of the West !

TO PENNSYLVANIA.

O STATE prayer-founded ! never hung
Such choice upon a people's tongue,
  Such power to bless or ban,
As that which makes thy whisper Fate,
For which on thee the centuries wait,
  And destinies of man !

Across thy Alleghanian chain,
With groanings from a land in pain,
  The west-wind finds its way :
Wild-wailing from Missouri's flood
The crying of thy children's blood
  Is in thy ears to-day !

And unto thee in Freedom's hour
Of sorest need God gives the power
  To ruin or to save;
To wound or heal, to blight or bless
With fertile field or wilderness,
  A free home or a grave !

Then let thy virtue match the crime,
Rise to a level with the time;
  And, if a son of thine
Betray or tempt thee, Brutus-like
For Fatherland and Freedom strike
  As Justice gives the sign.

Wake, sleeper, from thy dream of ease,
The great occasion's forelock seize;
  And, let the north-wind strong,
And golden leaves of autumn, be
Thy coronal of Victory
  And thy triumphal song.

10th mo., 1856.

THE PASS OF THE SIERRA.

ALL night above their rocky bed
  They saw the stars march slow;
The wild Sierra overhead,
  The desert's death below.

The Indian from his lodge of bark,
  The gray bear from his den,
Beyond their camp-fire's wall of dark,
  Glared on the mountain men.

Still upward turned, with anxious strain,
  Their leader's sleepless eye,
Where splinters of the mountain chain
  Stood black against the sky.

The night waned slow : at last, a glow,
  A gleam of sudden fire,
Shot up behind the walls of snow,
  And tipped each icy spire.

"Up, men !" he cried, " yon rocky
    cone,
  To-day, please God, we 'll pass,
And look from Winter's frozen throne
  On Summer's flowers and grass !"

They set their faces to the blast,
  They trod the eternal snow,
And faint, worn, bleeding, hailed at last
  The promised land below.

Behind, they saw the snow-cloud tossed
  By many an icy horn ;
Before, warm valleys, wood-embossed,
  And green with vines and corn.

They left the Winter at their backs
  To flap his baffled wing,
And downward, with the cataracts,
  Leaped to the lap of Spring.

Strong leader of that mountain band,
  Another task remains,
To break from Slavery's desert land
  A path to Freedom's plains.

The winds are wild, the way is drear,
  Yet, flashing through the night,
Lo ! icy ridge and rocky spear
  Blaze out in morning light !

Rise up, FREMONT ! and go before ;
  The Hour must have its Man ;
Put on the hunting-shirt once more,
  And lead in Freedom's van !
8th mo., 1856.

THE CONQUEST OF FINLAND.[65]

Across the frozen marshes
  The winds of autumn blow,
And the fen-lands of the Wetter
  Are white with early snow.

But where the low, gray headlands
  Look o'er the Baltic brine,

A bark is sailing in the track
  Of England's battle-line.

No wares hath she to barter
  For Bothnia's fish and grain ;
She saileth not for pleasure,
  She saileth not for gain.

But still by isle or mainland
  She drops her anchor down,
Where'er the British cannon
  Rained fire on tower and town.

Outspake the ancient Amtman,
  At the gate of Helsingfors :
" Why comes this ship a-spying
  In the track of England's wars ?"

"God bless her," said the coast-guard,—
  " God bless the ship, I say.
The holy angels trim the sails
  That speed her on her way !

" Where'er she drops her anchor,
  The peasant's heart is glad ;
Where'er she spreads her parting sail,
  The peasant's heart is sad.

" Each wasted town and hamlet
  She visits to restore ;
To roof the shattered cabin,
  And feed the starving poor.

" The sunken boats of fishers,
  The foraged beeves and grain,
The spoil of flake and storehouse,
  The good ship brings again.

" And so to Finland's sorrow
  The sweet amend is made,
As if the healing hand of Christ
  Upon her wounds were laid !"

Then said the gray old Amtman,
  " The will of God be done !
The battle lost by England's hate,
  By England's love is won !

" We braved the iron tempest
  That thundered on our shore ;
But when did kindness fail to find
  The key to Finland's door ? ·

" No more from Aland's ramparts
  Shall warning signal come,
Nor startled Sweaborg hear again
  The roll of midnight drum.

"Beside our fierce Black Eagle
  The Dove of Peace shall rest ;
And in the mouths of cannon
  The sea-bird make her nest.

"For Finland, looking seaward,
  No coming foe shall scan ;
And the holy bells of Abo
  Shall ring, ' Good-will to man ! '

"Then row thy boat, O fisher !
  In peace on lake and bay ;
And thou, young maiden, dance again
  Around the poles of May !

"Sit down, old men, together,
  Old wives, in quiet spin ;
Henceforth the Anglo-Saxon
  Is the brother of the Finn ! "

A LAY OF OLD TIME.

WRITTEN FOR THE ESSEX COUNTY
AGRICULTURAL FAIR.

ONE morning of the first sad Fall,
  Poor Adam and his bride
Sat in the shade of Eden's wall —
  But on the outer side.

She, blushing in her fig-leaf suit
  For the chaste garb of old ;
He, sighing o'er his bitter fruit
  For Eden's drupes of gold.

Behind them, smiling in the morn,
  Their forfeit garden lay,
Before them, wild with rock and thorn,
  The desert stretched away.

They heard the air above them fanned,
  A light step on the sward,
And lo ! they saw before them stand
  The angel of the Lord !

"Arise," he said, "why look behind,
  When hope is all before,
And patient hand and willing mind,
  Your loss may yet restore ?

"I leave with you a spell whose power
  Can make the desert glad,
And call around you fruit and flower
  As fair as Eden had.

"I clothe your hands with power to lift
  The curse from off your soil ;

Your very doom sh
  Your loss a gain

"Go, cheerful as y
  To labor as to pla
White glimmering (
  The angel passed

The pilgrims of the
  Obedient to the v
And found where'er
  A garden of the I

The thorn-tree cast
  And blushed with
And seeded grass an
  Grew sweet benea

We share our prima
  And in our turn
Look back on Eden
  As sad and lost a

But still for us his
  The pitying Ange
And leads through
  New Adams and

WHAT OF

A SOUND of tumult
  Like the low thu
Far-rolling ere the
    glare ;
The hills blaze
    foes draw nig
Treading the dar
    reply.
Behold the burde
    vision, —
The gathering hos
    Decision,
Dusk with the w
    ing o'er.
Day of the Lord, (
    light !
It breaks in thu
    wind's roar !
Even so, Father !
    done, —
Turn and o'erturn,
    begun
In judgment or in r
  If but the least and
Evermore numbered
  Who find thy servic

I fain would thank Thee that my mor-
tal life
Has reached the hour (albeit through
care and pain)
When Good and Evil, as for final strife,
Close dim and vast on Armageddon's
plain ;
And Michael and his angels once again
Drive howling back the Spirits of the
Night.
O for the faith to read the signs aright
And, from the angle of thy perfect sight,
See Truth's white banner floating on
before ;
And the Good Cause, despite of venal
friends,
And base expedients, move to noble
ends ;
See Peace with Freedom make to Time
amends,
And, through its cloud of dust, the
threshing-floor,
Flailed by the thunder, heaped with
chaffless grain !
1857.

THE FIRST FLOWERS.

For ages on our river borders,
These tassels in their tawny bloom,
And willowy studs of downy silver,
Have prophesied of Spring to come.

For ages have the unbound waters
Smiled on them from their pebbly hem,
And the clear carol of the robin
And song of bluebird welcomed them.

But never yet from smiling river,
Or song of early bird, have they
Been greeted with a gladder welcome
Than whispers from my heart to-day.

They break the spell of cold and dark-
ness,
The weary watch of sleepless pain ;
And from my heart, as from the river,
The ice of winter melts again.

Thanks, Mary ! for this wild-wood token
Of Freya's footsteps drawing near ;
Almost, as in the rune of Asgard,
The growing of the grass I hear.

It is as if the pine-trees called me
From ceiled room and silent books,

To see the dance of woodland shadows,
And hear the song of April brooks !

As in the old Teutonic ballad
Live singing bird and flowering tree,
Together live in bloom and music,
I blend in song thy flowers and thee.

Earth's rocky tablets bear forever
The dint of rain and small bird's track :
Who knows but that my idle verses
May leave some trace by Merrimack !

The bird that trod the mellow layers
Of the young earth is sought in vain ;
The cloud is gone that wove the sand-
stone,
From God's design, with threads of
rain !

So, when this fluid age we live in
Shall stiffen round my careless rhyme,
Who made the vagrant tracks may puzzle
The savans of the coming time :

And, following out their dim suggestions,
Some idly-curious hand may draw
My doubtful portraiture, as Cuvier
Drew fish and bird from fin and claw.

And maidens in the far-off twilights,
Singing my words to breeze and stream,
Shall wonder if the old-time Mary
Were real, or the rhymer's dream !
1st 3d mo., 1857.

MY NAMESAKE.

You scarcely need my tardy thanks,
Who, self-rewarded, nurse and tend —
A green leaf on your own Green Banks —
The memory of your friend.

For me, no wreath, bloom-woven, hides
The sobered brow and lessening hair :
For aught I know, the myrtled sides
Of Helicon are bare.

Their scallop-shells so many bring
The fabled founts of song to try,
They 've drained, for aught I know, the
spring
Of Aganippe dry.

Ah well ! — The wreath the Muses braid
Proves often Folly's cap and bell ;

Methinks, my ample beaver's shade
   May serve my turn as well.

Let Love's and Friendship's tender debt
   Be paid by those I love in life.
Why should the unborn critic whet
   For me his scalping-knife ?

Why should the stranger peer and pry
   One's vacant house of life about,
And drag for curious ear and eye
   His faults and follies out ? —

Why stuff, for fools to gaze upon,
   With chaff of words, the garb he wore,
As corn-husks when the ear is gone
   Are rustled all the more ?

Let kindly Silence close again,
   The picture vanish from the eye,
And on the dim and misty main
   Let the small ripple die.

Yet not the less I own your claim
   To grateful thanks, dear friends of
     mine.
Hang, if it please you so, my name
   Upon your household line.

Let Fame from brazen lips blow wide
   Her chosen names, I envy none :
A mother's love, a father's pride,
   Shall keep alive my own !

Still shall that name as now recall
   The young leaf wet with morning
     dew,
The glory where the sunbeams fall
   The breezy woodlands through.

That name shall be a household word,
   A spell to waken smile or sigh ;
In many an evening prayer be heard
   And cradle lullaby.

And thou, dear child, in riper days
   When asked the reason of thy name,
Shalt answer : " One 't were vain to
     praise
Or censure bore the same.

" Some blamed him, some believed him
     good, —
   The truth lay doubtless 'twixt the
     two, —
He reconciled as best he could
   Old faith and fancies new.

" In him the grave and playful mixed,
   And wisdom held with folly truce,
And Nature compromised betwixt
   Good fellow and recluse.

" He loved his friends, forgave his foes ;
   And, if his words were harsh at times,
He spared his fellow-men, — his blows
   Fell only on their crimes.

" He loved the good and wise, but found
   His human heart to all akin
Who met him on the common ground
   Of suffering and of sin.

" Whate'er his neighbors might endure
   Of pain or grief his own became ;
For all the ills he could not cure
   He held himself to blame.

" His good was mainly an intent,
   His evil not of forethought done ;
The work he wrought was rarely meant
   Or finished as begun.

" Ill served his tides of feeling strong
   To turn the common mills of use ;
And, over restless wings of song,
   His birthright garb hung loose !

" His eye was beauty's powerless slave,
   And his the ear which discord pains :
Few guessed beneath his aspect grave
   What passions strove in chains.

" He had his share of care and pain,
   No holiday was life to him ;
Still in the heirloom cup we drain
   The bitter drop will swim.

" Yet Heaven was kind, and here a bird
   And there a flower beguiled his way ;
And, cool, in summer noons, he heard
   The fountains plash and play.

" On all his sad or restless moods
   The patient peace of Nature stole ;
The quiet of the fields and woods
   Sank deep into his soul.

" He worshipped as his fathers did,
   And kept the faith of childish days,
And, howsoe'er he strayed or slid,
   He loved the good old ways.

" The simple tastes, the kindly traits,
   The tranquil air, and gentle speech,

The silence of the soul that waits
For more than man to teach.

"The cant of party, school, and sect,
Provoked at times his honest scorn,
And Folly, in its gray respect,
He tossed on satire's horn.

"But still his heart was full of awe
And reverence for all sacred things ;
And, brooding over form and law,
He saw the Spirit's wings !

"Life's mystery wrapt him like a cloud ;
He heard far voices mock his own,
The sweep of wings unseen, the loud,
Long roll of waves unknown.

"The arrows of his straining sight
Fell quenched in darkness ; priest and sage,
Like lost guides calling left and right,
Perplexed his doubtful age.

"Like childhood, listening for the sound
Of its dropped pebbles in the well,
All vainly down the dark profound
His brief-lined plummet fell.

"So, scattering flowers with pious pains
On old beliefs, of later creeds,
Which claimed a place in Truth's domains,
He asked the title-deeds.

"He saw the old-time's groves and shrines
In the long distance fair and dim ;
And heard, like sound of far-off pines,
The century-mellowed hymn !

"He dared not mock the Dervish whirl,
The Brahmin's rite, the Lama's spell ;
God knew the heart ; Devotion's pearl
Might sanctify the shell.

"While others trod the altar stairs
He faltered like the publican ;
And, while they praised as saints, his prayers
Were those of sinful man.

"For, awed by Sinai's Mount of Law,
The trembling faith alone sufficed,
That, through its cloud and flame, he
  . saw
The sweet, sad face of Christ ! —

"And listening, with his forehead bowed,
Heard the Divine compassion fill
The pauses of the trump and cloud
With whispers small and still.

"The words he spake, the thoughts he penned,
Are mortal as his hand and brain,
But, if they served the Master's end,
He has not lived in vain ! "

Heaven make thee better than thy name,
Child of my friends ! — For thee I crave
What riches never bought, nor fame
To mortal longing gave.

I pray the prayer of Plato old :
God make thee beautiful within,
And let thine eyes the good behold
In everything save sin !

Imagination held in check
To serve, not rule, thy poiséd mind ;
Thy Reason, at the frown or beck
Of Conscience, loose or bind.

No dreamer thou, but real all, —
Strong manhood crowning vigorous youth ;
Life made by duty epical
And rhythmic with the truth.

So shall that life the fruitage yield
Which trees of healing only give,
And green-leafed in the Eternal field
Of God, forever live !

HOME BALLADS.

I CALL the old time back : I bring these lays
To thee, in memory of the summer days
When, by our native streams and forest ways,

We dreamed them over ; while the rivulets made
Songs of their own, and the great pine-trees laid
On warm noon-lights the masses of their shade.

And *she* was with us, living o'er again
Her life in ours, despite of years and pain, —
The autumn's brightness after latter rain.

Beautiful in her holy peace as one
Who stands, at evening, when the work is done,
Glorified in the setting of the sun !

Her memory makes our common landscape seem
Fairer than any of which painters dream,
Lights the brown hills and sings in every stream ;

For she whose speech was always truth's pure gold
Heard, not unpleased, its simple legends told,
And loved with us the beautiful and old.

THE WITCH'S DAUGHTER.

IT was the pleasant harvest time,
  When cellar-bins are closely stowed,
  And garrets bend beneath their load,

And the old swallow-haunted barns —
  Brown-gabled, long, and full of seams
  Through which the moted sunlight streams,

And winds blow freshly in, to shake
  The red plumes of the roosted cocks,
  And the loose hay-mow's scented locks —

Are filled with summer's ripened stores,
  Its odorous grass and barley sheaves,
  From their low scaffolds to their eaves

On Esek Harden's oaken floor,
  With many an autumn threshing worn,
  Lay the heaped ears of unhusked corn

And thither came young men and maids
  Beneath a moon that, large and low,
  Lit that sweet eve of long ago.

They took their places ; some by chance
  And others by a merry voice
  Or sweet smile guided to their choice

How pleasantly the rising moon,
  Between the shadow of the mows,
  Looked on them through the grea elm-boughs ! —

On sturdy boyhood sun-embrowned,
  On girlhood with its solid curves
  Of healthful strength and painles nerves !

And jests went round, and laughs tha made
  The house-dog answer with his howl,
  And kept astir the barn-yard fowl ;

And quaint old songs their father sung,
  In Derby dales and Yorkshire moors,
  Ere Norman William trod thei shores ;

And tales, whose merry license shook
  The fat sides of the Saxon thane,
  Forgetful of the hovering Dane !

But still the sweetest voice was mute
  That river-valley ever heard
  From lip of maid or throat of bird ;

For Mabel Martin sat apart,
And let the hay-mow's shadow fall
Upon the loveliest face of all.

She sat apart, as one forbid,
Who knew that none would conde-
scend
To own the Witch-wife's child a
friend.

The seasons scarce had gone their round,
Since curious thousands thronged to
see
Her mother on the gallows-tree ;

And mocked the palsied limbs of age,
That faltered on the fatal stairs,
And wan lip trembling with its
prayers !

Few questioned of the sorrowing child,
Or, when they saw the mother die,
Dreamed of the daughter's agony.

They went up to their homes that day,
As men and Christians justified :
God willed it, and the wretch had
died !

Dear God and Father of us all,
Forgive our faith in cruel lies, —
Forgive the blindness that denies !

Forgive thy creature when he takes,
For the all-perfect love thou art,
Some grim creation of his heart.

Cast down our idols, overturn
Our bloody altars ; let us see
Thyself in thy humanity !

Poor Mabel from her mother's grave
Crept to her desolate hearth-stone,
And wrestled with her fate alone ;

With love, and anger, and despair,
The phantoms of disordered sense,
The awful doubts of Providence !

The school-boys jeered her as they
passed,
And, when she sought the house of
prayer,
Her mother's curse pursued her there.

And still o'er many a neighboring door
She saw the horseshoe's curvéd charm,
To guard against her mother's harm ;—

That mother, poor, and sick, and
lame,
Who daily, by the old arm-chair,
Folded her withered hands in prayer ; —

Who turned, in Salem's dreary jail,
Her worn old Bible o'er and o'er,
When her dim eyes could read no
more !

Sore tried and pained, the poor girl
kept
Her faith, and trusted that her
way,
So dark, would somewhere meet the
day.

And still her weary wheel went round
Day after day, with no relief ;
Small leisure have the poor for grief.

So in the shadow Mabel sits ;
Untouched by mirth she sees and
hears,
Her smile is sadder than her tears.

But cruel eyes have found her out,
And cruel lips repeat her name,
And taunt her with her mother's
shame.

She answered not with railing words,
But drew her apron o'er her face,
And, sobbing, glided from the place.

And only pausing at the door,
Her sad eyes met the troubled gaze
Of one who, in her better days,

Had been her warm and steady friend,
Ere yet her mother's doom had made
Even Esek Harden half afraid.

He felt that mute appeal of tears,
And, starting, with an angry frown
Hushed all the wicked murmurs
down.

"Good neighbors mine," he sternly
said,
"This passes harmless mirth or jest ;
I brook no insult to my guest.

"She is indeed her mother's child ;
But God's sweet pity ministers
Unto no whiter soul than hers.

"Let Goody Martin rest in peace ;
  I never knew her harm a fly,
And witch or not, God knows, — not I.

"I know who swore her life away ;
  And, as God lives, I 'd not condemn
An Indian dog on word of them."

The broadest lands in all the town,
  The skill to guide, the power to awe,
Were Harden's ; and his word was
    law.

None dared withstand him to his face,
  But one sly maiden spake aside :
"The little witch is evil-eyed !

"Her mother only killed a cow,
  Or witched a churn or dairy-pan ;
But she, forsooth, must charm a
    man !"

Poor Mabel, in her lonely home,
  Sat by the window's narrow pane,
White in the moonlight's silver rain.

The river, on its pebbled rim,
  Made music such as childhood knew ;
The door-yard tree was whispered
    through

By voices such as childhood's ear
  Had heard in moonlights long ago ;
And through the willow-boughs below

She saw the rippled waters shine ;
  Beyond, in waves of shade and light
The hills rolled off into the night.

Sweet sounds and pictures mocking so
  The sadness of her human lot,
She saw and heard, but heeded not.

She strove to drown her sense of wrong,
  And, in her old and simple way,
To teach her bitter heart to pray.

Poor child ! the prayer, begun in faith,
  Grew to a low, despairing cry
Of utter misery : "Let me die !

"Oh ! take me from the scornful eyes,
  And hide me where the cruel speech
And mocking finger may not reach !

"I dare not breathe my mother's name :
  A daughter's right I dare not crave
To weep above her unblest grave !

"Let me not live until my heart,
  With few to pity, and with none
To love me, hardens into stone.

'O God ! have mercy on thy child,
  Whose faith in thee grows weak and
    small,
And take me ere I lose it all !"

A shadow on the moonlight fell,
  And murmuring wind and wave be-
    came
A voice whose burden was her name.

Had then God heard her ? Had he
    sent
  His angel down ? In flesh and blood,
Before her Esek Harden stood !

He laid his hand upon her arm :
  "Dear Mabel, this no more shall
    be ;
Who scoffs at you, must scoff at
    me.

"You know rough Esek Harden well ;
  And if he seems no suitor gay,
And if his hair is touched with gray,

"The maiden grown shall never find
  His heart less warm than when she
    smiled,
Upon his knees, a little child !"

Her tears of grief were tears of joy,
  As, folded in his strong embrace,
She looked in Esek Harden's face.

"O truest friend of all !" she said,
  "God bless you for your kindly
    thought,
And make me worthy of my lot !"

He led her through his dewy fields,
  To where the swinging lanterns
    glowed,
And through the doors the huskers
    showed.

"Good friends and neighbors !" Esek
    said,
  "I 'm weary of this lonely life ;
In Mabel see my chosen wife !

"She greets you kindly, one and all ;
  The past is past, and all offence
Falls harmless from her innocence.

"Henceforth she stands no more alone ;
  You know what Esek Harden is : —
He brooks no wrong to him or his."

Now let the merriest tales be told,
  And let the sweetest songs be sung
That ever made the old heart young !

For now the lost has found a home ;
  And a lone hearth shall brighter burn,
As all the household joys return !

O, pleasantly the harvest-moon,
  Between the shadow of the mows,
Looked on them through the great
  elm-boughs !

On Mabel's curls of golden hair,
  On Esek's shaggy strength it fell ;
And the wind whispered, "It is
  well !"

THE GARRISON OF CAPE ANN.

FROM the hills of home forth looking,
  far beneath the tent-like span
Of the sky, I see the white gleam of the
  headland of Cape Ann.
Well I know its coves and beaches to the
  ebb-tide glimmering down,
And the white-walled hamlet children of
  its ancient fishing-town.

Long has passed the summer morning,
  and its memory waxes old,
When along yon breezy headlands with
  a pleasant friend I strolled.
Ah ! the autumn sun is shining, and the
  ocean wind blows cool,
And the golden-rod and aster bloom
  around thy grave, Rantoul !

With the memory of that morning by the
  summer sea I blend
A wild and wondrous story, by the
  younger Mather penned,
In that quaint *Magnalia Christi*, with
  all strange and marvellous things,
Heaped up huge and undigested, like
  the chaos Ovid sings.

Dear to me these far, faint glimpses of
  the dual life of old,
Inward, grand with awe and reverence ;
  outward, mean and coarse and
  cold ;

Gleams of mystic beauty playing over
  dull and vulgar clay,
Golden-threaded fancies weaving in a
  web of hodden gray.

The great eventful Present hides the
  Past ; but through the din
Of its loud life hints and echoes from
  the life behind steal in ;
And the lore of home and fireside, and
  the legendary rhyme,
Make the task of duty lighter which the
  true man owes his time.

So, with something of the feeling which
  the Covenanter knew,
When with pious chisel wandering Scotland's moorland graveyards
  through,
From the graves of old traditions I part
  the blackberry-vines,
Wipe the moss from off the headstones,
  and retouch the faded lines.

———

Where the sea-waves back and forward,
  hoarse with rolling pebbles, ran,
The garrison-house stood watching on
  the gray rocks of Cape Ann ;
On its windy site uplifting gabled roof
  and palisade,
And rough walls of unhewn timber with
  the moonlight overlaid.

On his slow round walked the sentry,
  south and eastward looking forth
O'er a rude and broken coast-line, white
  with breakers stretching north, —
Wood and rock and gleaming sand-drift,
  jagged capes, with bush and tree,
Leaning inland from the smiting of the
  wild and gusty sea.

Before the deep-mouthed chimney, dimly lit by dying brands,
Twenty soldiers sat and waited, with
  their muskets in their hands ;
On the rough-hewn oaken table the venison haunch was shared,
And the pewter tankard circled slowly
  round from beard to beard.

Long they sat and talked together, —
  talked of wizards Satan-sold ;
Of all ghostly sights and noises, — signs
  and wonders manifold ;

Of the spectre-ship of Salem, with the
　dead men in her shrouds,
Sailing sheer above the water, in the
　loom of morning clouds ;

Of the marvellous valley hidden in the
　depths of Gloucester woods,
Full of plants that love the summer, —
　blooms of warmer latitudes ;
Where the Arctic birch is braided by
　the tropic's flowery vines,
And the white magnolia-blossoms star
　the twilight of the pines !

But their voices sank yet lower, sank to
　husky tones of fear,
As they spake of present tokens of the
　powers of evil near ;
Of a spectral host, defying stroke of steel
　and aim of gun ;
Never yet was ball to slay them in the
　mould of mortals run !

Thrice, with plumes and flowing scalp-
　locks, from the midnight wood
　they came, —
Thrice around the block-house marching,
　met, unharmed, its volleyed flame ;
Then, with mocking laugh and gesture,
　sunk in earth or lost in air,
All the ghostly wonder vanished, and
　the moonlit sands lay bare.

Midnight came ; from out the forest
　moved a dusky mass that soon
Grew to warriors, plumed and painted,
　grimly marching in the moon.
"Ghosts or witches," said the captain,
　"thus I foil the Evil One !"
And he rammed a silver button, from
　his doublet, down his gun.

Once again the spectral horror moved
　the guarded wall about ;
Once again the levelled muskets through
　the palisades flashed out,
With that deadly aim the squirrel on his
　tree-top might not shun,
Nor the beach-bird seaward flying with
　his slant wing to the sun.

Like the idle rain of summer sped the
　harmless shower of lead.
With a laugh of fierce derision, once
　again the phantoms fled ;

Once again, without a shadow on the
　sands the moonlight lay,
And the white smoke curling through it
　drifted slowly down the bay !

"God preserve us !" said the captain ;
　" never mortal foes were there ;
They have vanished with their leader,
　Prince and Power of the air !
Lay aside your useless weapons ; skill
　and prowess naught avail ;
They who do the Devil's service wear
　their master's coat of mail !"

So the night grew near to cock-crow,
　when again a warning call
Roused the score of weary soldiers watch-
　ing round the dusky hall :
And they looked to flint and priming,
　and they longed for break of day ;
But the captain closed his Bible : "Let
　us cease from man, and pray !"

To the men who went before us, all the
　unseen powers seemed near,
And their steadfast strength of courage
　struck its roots in holy fear.
Every hand forsook the musket, every
　head was bowed and bare,
Every stout knee pressed the flag-stones,
　as the captain led in prayer.

Ceased thereat the mystic marching of
　the spectres round the wall,
But a sound abhorred, unearthly, smote
　the ears and hearts of all, —
Howls of rage and shrieks of anguish !
　Never after mortal man
Saw the ghostly leaguers marching round
　the block-house of Cape Ann.

So to us who walk in summer through
　the cool and sea-blown town,
From the childhood of its people comes
　the solemn legend down.
Not in vain the ancient fiction, in whose
　moral lives the youth
And the fitness and the freshness of an
　undecaying truth.

Soon or late to all our dwellings come
　the spectres of the mind,
Doubts and fears and dread forebodings,
　In the darkness undefined ;
Round us throng the grim projections
　of the heart and of the brain,
And our pride of strength is weakness,
　and the cunning hand is vain.

In the dark we cry like children ; and
no answer from on high
Breaks the crystal spheres of silence, and
no white wings downward fly ;
But the heavenly help we pray for comes
to faith, and not to sight,
And our prayers themselves drive backward all the spirits of the night !

THE PROPHECY OF SAMUEL SEWALL.

1697.

Up and down the village streets
Strange are the forms my fancy meets,
For the thoughts and things of to-day
are hid,
And through the veil of a closéd lid
The ancient worthies I see again :
I hear the tap of the elder's cane,
And his awful periwig I see,
And the silver buckles of shoe and knee.
Stately and slow, with thoughtful air,
His black cap hiding his whitened hair,
Walks the Judge of the great Assize,
Samuel Sewall the good and wise.
His face with lines of firmness wrought,
He wears the look of a man unbought,
Who swears to his hurt and changes
not ;
Yet, touched and softened nevertheless
With the grace of Christian gentleness,
The face that a child would climb to
kiss !
True and tender and brave and just,
That man might honor and woman trust.

Touching and sad, a tale is told,
Like a penitent hymn of the Psalmist
old,
Of the fast which the good man lifelong
kept
With a haunting sorrow that never slept,
As the circling year brought round the
time
Of an error that left the sting of crime,
When he sat on the bench of the witch-
craft courts,
With the laws of Moses and Hale's Re-
ports,
And spake, in the name of both, the
word
That gave the witch's neck to the
cord,
And piled the oaken planks that pressed
The feeble life from the warlock's breast !

All the day long, from dawn to dawn,
His door was bolted, his curtain drawn ;
No foot on his silent threshold trod,
No eye looked on him save that of God,
As he baffled the ghosts of the dead with
charms
Of penitent tears, and prayers, and
psalms,
And, with precious proofs from the sacred
word
Of the boundless pity and love of the
Lord,
His faith confirmed and his trust re-
newed
That the sin of his ignorance, sorely
rued,
Might be washed away in the mingled
flood
Of his human sorrow and Christ's dear
blood !

Green forever the memory be
Of the Judge of the old Theocracy,
Whom even his errors glorified,
Like a far-seen, sunlit mountain-side
By the cloudy shadows which o'er it
glide !
Honor and praise to the Puritan
Who the halting step of his age outran,
And, seeing the infinite worth of man
In the priceless gift the Father gave,
In the infinite love that stooped to save,
Dared not brand his brother a slave !
" Who doth such wrong," he was wont
to say,
In his own quaint, picture-loving way,
" Flings up to Heaven a hand-grenade
Which God shall cast down upon his
head ! "

Widely as heaven and hell, contrast
That brave old jurist of the past
And the cunning trickster and knave of
courts
Who the holy features of Truth dis-
torts, —
Ruling as right the will of the strong,
Poverty, crime, and weakness wrong ;
Wide-eared to power, to the wronged
and weak
Deaf as Egypt's gods of leek ;
Scoffing aside at party's nod
Order of nature and law of God ;
For whose dabbled ermine respect were
waste,
Reverence folly, and awe misplaced ;
Justice of whom 't were vain to seek

As from Koordish robber or Syrian
    Sheik !
O, leave the wretch to his bribes and
    sins ;
Let him rot in the web of lies he spins !
To the saintly soul of the early day,
To the Christian judge, let us turn and
    say :
" Praise and thanks for an honest
    man ! :—
Glory to God for the Puritan ! "

I see, far southward, this quiet day,
The hills of Newbury rolling away,
With the many tints of the season gay,
Dreamily blending in autumn mist
Crimson, and gold, and amethyst.
Long and low, with dwarf trees crowned,
Plum Island lies, like a whale aground,
A stone's toss over the narrow sound.
Inland, as far as the eye can go,
The hills curve round like a bended
    bow ;
A silver arrow from out them sprung,
I see the shine of the Quasycung ;
And, round and round, over valley and
    hill,
Old roads winding, as old roads will,
Here to a ferry, and there to a mill ;
And glimpses of chimneys and gabled
    eaves,
Through green elm arches and maple
    leaves, —
Old homesteads sacred to all that can
Gladden or sadden the heart of man, —
Over whose thresholds of oak and stone
Life and Death have come and gone !
There pictured tiles in the fireplace
    show,
Great beams sag from the ceiling low,
The dresser glitters with polished wares,
The long clock ticks on the foot-worn
    stairs,
And the low, broad chimney shows the
    crack
By the earthquake made a century
    back.
Up from their midst springs the village
    spire
With the crest of its cock in the sun
    afire ;
Beyond are orchards and planting lands,
And great salt marshes and glimmering
    sands,
And, where north and south the coast-
    lines run,
The blink of the sea in breeze and sun !

I see it all like a chart unrolled,
But my thoughts are full of the past
    and old,
I hear the tales of my boyhood told ;
And the shadows and shapes of early
    days
Flit dimly by in the veiling haze,
With measured movement and rhythmic
    chime
Weaving like shuttles my web of rhyme.
I think of the old man wise and good
Who once on yon misty hillsides stood,
(A poet who never measured rhyme,
A seer unknown to his dull-eared time,)
And, propped on his staff of age, looked
    down,
With his boyhood's love, on his native
    town,
Where, written, as if on its hills and
    plains,
His burden of prophecy yet remains,
For the voices of wood, and wave, and
    wind
To read in the ear of the musing mind : —

" As long as Plum Island, to guard
    the coast
As God appointed, shall keep its post ;
As long as a salmon shall haunt the deep
Of Merrimack River, or sturgeon leap ;
As long as pickerel swift and slim,
Or red-backed perch, in Crane Pond swim ;
As long as the annual sea-fowl know
Their time to come and their time to go ;
As long as cattle shall roam at will
The green, grass meadows by Turkey Hill ;
As long as sheep shall look from the side
Of Oldtown Hill on marishes wide,
And Parker River, and salt-sea tide ;
As long as a wandering pigeon shall search
The fields below from his white-oak perch,
When the barley-harvest is ripe and
    shorn,
And the dry husks fall from the stand-
    ing corn ;
As long as Nature shall not grow old,
Nor drop her work from her doting hold,
And her care for the Indian corn forget,
And the yellow rows in pairs to set ; —
So long shall Christians here be born,
Grow up and ripen as God's sweet corn !
By the beak of bird, by the breath of
    frost,
Shall never a holy ear be lost,
But, husked by Death in the Planter's
    sight,
Be sown again in the fields of light ! "

The Island still is purple with plums,
Up the river the salmon comes,
The sturgeon leaps, and the wild-fowl
  feeds
On hillside berries and marish seeds, —
All the beautiful signs remain,
From spring-time sowing to autumn rain
The good man's vision returns again!
And let us hope, as well we can,
That the Silent Angel who garners man
May find some grain as of old he found
In the human cornfield ripe and sound,
And the Lord of the Harvest deign to
  own
The precious seed by the fathers sown !

SKIPPER IRESON'S RIDE.

Of all the rides since the birth of time,
Told in story or sung in rhyme, —
On Apuleius's Golden Ass,
Or one-eyed Calendar's horse of brass,
Witch astride of a human back,
Islam's prophet on Al-Borák, —
The strangest ride that ever was sped
Was Ireson's, out from Marblehead !
  Old Floyd Ireson, for his hard heart,
  Tarred and feathered and carried in a
    cart
  By the women of Marblehead !

Body of turkey, head of owl,
Wings a-droop like a rained-on fowl,
Feathered and ruffled in every part,
Skipper Ireson stood in the cart.
Scores of women, old and young,
Strong of muscle, and glib of tongue,
Pushed and pulled up the rocky lane,
Shouting and singing the shrill refrain :
  "Here's Flud Oirson, fur his horrd
    horrt,
  Torr'd an' futherr'd an' corr'd in a
    corrt
  By the women o' Morble'ead ! "

Wrinkled scolds with hands on hips,
Girls in bloom of cheek and lips,
Wild-eyed, free-limbed, such as chase
Bacchus round some antique vase,
Brief of skirt, with ankles bare,
Loose of kerchief and loose of hair,
With conch-shells blowing and fish-
  horns' twang,
Over and over the Mænads sang :
  "Here's Flud Oirson, fur his horrd
    horrt,

  Torr'd an' futherr'd an' corr'd in a
    corrt
  By the women o' Morble'ead ! "

Small pity for him ! — He sailed away
From a leaking ship, in Chaleur Bay, —
Sailed away from a sinking wreck,
With his own town's-people on her deck !
"Lay by ! lay by ! " they called to him.
Back he answered, "Sink or swim !
Brag of your catch of fish again ! "
And off he sailed through the fog and
  rain !
  Old Floyd Ireson, for his hard heart,
  Tarred and feathered and carried in a
    cart
  By the women of Marblehead !

Fathoms deep in dark Chaleur
That wreck shall lie forevermore.
Mother and sister, wife and maid,
Looked from the rocks of Marblehead
Over the moaning and rainy sea, —
Looked for the coming that might not
  be !
What did the winds and the sea-birds
  say
Of the cruel captain who sailed away ? —
  Old Floyd Ireson, for his hard heart,
  Tarred and feathered and carried in a
    cart
  By the women of Marblehead !

Through the street, on either side,
Up flew windows, doors swung wide ;
Sharp-tongued spinsters, old wives gray,
Treble lent the fish-horn's bray.
Sea-worn grandsires, cripple-bound,
Hulks of old sailors run aground,
Shook head, and fist, and hat, and cane,
And cracked with curses the hoarse re-
  frain :
  "Here's Flud Oirson, fur his horrd
    horrt,
  Torr'd an' futherr'd an' corr'd in a
    corrt
  By the women o' Morble'ead ! "

Sweetly along the Salem road
Bloom of orchard and lilac showed.
Little the wicked skipper knew
Of the fields so green and the sky so
  blue.
Riding there in his sorry trim,
Like an Indian idol glum and grim,
Scarcely he seemed the sound to hear
Of voices shouting, far and near :

"Here's Flud Oirson, fur his horrd
  horrt,
Torr'd an' futherr'd an' corr'd in a
  corrt
  By the women o' Morble'ead!"

"Hear me, neighbors!" at last he
  cried, —
"What to me is this noisy ride?
What is the shame that clothes the skin
To the nameless horror that lives within?
Waking or sleeping, I see a wreck,
And hear a cry from a reeling deck!
Hate me and curse me, — I only dread
The hand of God and the face of the
  dead!"
  Said old Floyd Ireson, for his hard
    heart,
  Tarred and feathered and carried in a
    cart
    By the women of Marblehead!

Then the wife of the skipper lost at sea
Said, "God has touched him! — why
  should we?"
Said an old wife mourning her only son,
"Cut the rogue's tether and let him
  run!"
So with soft relentings and rude excuse,
Half scorn, half pity, they cut him loose,
And gave him a cloak to hide him in,
And left him alone with his shame and
  sin.
  Poor Floyd Ireson, for his hard heart,
  Tarred and feathered and carried in a
    cart
    By the women of Marblehead!

TELLING THE BEES.[66]

HERE is the place; right over the hill
Runs the path I took;
You can see the gap in the old wall still,
  And the stepping-stones in the shal-
    low brook.

There is the house, with the gate red-
  barred,
  And the poplars tall;
And the barn's brown length, and the
  cattle-yard,
  And the white horns tossing above the
    wall.

There are the beehives ranged in the sun;
  And down by the brink

Of the brook are her poor flowers, weed-
  o'errun,
  Pansy and daffodil, rose and pink.

A year has gone, as the tortoise goes,
  Heavy and slow;
And the same rose blows, and the same
  sun glows,
  And the same brook sings of a year
    ago.

There's the same sweet clover-smell in
  the breeze;
  And the June sun warm
Tangles his wings of fire in the trees,
  Setting, as then, over Fernside farm.

I mind me how with a lover's care
  From my Sunday coat
I brushed off the burrs, and smoothed
  my hair,
  And cooled at the brookside my brow
    and throat.

Since we parted, a month had passed, —
  To love, a year;
Down through the beeches I looked at
  last
  On the little red gate and the well-
    sweep near.

I can see it all now, — the slantwise rain
  Of light through the leaves,
The sundown's blaze on her window-
  pane,
  The bloom of her roses under the eaves.

Just the same as a month before, —
  The house and the trees,
The barn's brown gable, the vine by the
  door, —
  Nothing changed but the hives of bees.

Before them, under the garden wall,
  Forward and back,
Went drearily singing the chore-girl
  small,
  Draping each hive with a shred of
    black.

Trembling, I listened: the summer sun
  Had the chill of snow;
For I knew she was telling the bees of
  one
  Gone on the journey we all must go!

Then I said to myself, "My Mary weeps
  For the dead to-day:

Haply her blind old grandsire sleeps
  The fret and the pain of his age away."

But her dog whined low ; on the door-
    way sill,
  With his cane to his chin,
The old man sat ; and the chore-girl still
  Sung to the bees stealing out and in.

And the song she was singing ever since
  In my ear sounds on : —
" Stay at home, pretty bees, fly not
    hence !
  Mistress Mary is dead and góne ! "

THE SYCAMORES.

IN the outskirts of the village,
  On the river's winding shores,
Stand the Occidental plane-trees,
  Stand the ancient sycamores.

One long century hath been numbered,
  And another half-way told,
Since the rustic Irish gleeman
  Broke for them the virgin mould.

Deftly set to Celtic music,
  At his violin's sound they grew,
Through the moonlit eves of summer,
  Making Amphion's fable true.

Rise again, thou poor Hugh Tallant !
  Pass in jerkin green along,
With thy eyes brimful of laughter,
  And thy mouth as full of song.

Pioneer of Erin's outcasts,
  With his fiddle and his pack ;
Little dreamed the village Saxons
  Of the myriads at his back.

How he wrought with spade and fiddle,
  Delved by day and sang by night,
With a hand that never wearied,
  And a heart forever light, —

Still the gay tradition mingles
  With a record grave and drear,
Like the rolic air of Cluny,
  With the solemn march of Mear.

When the box-tree, white with blossoms,
  Made the sweet May woodlands glad,
And the Aronia by the river
  Lighted up the swarming shad,

And the bulging nets swept shoreward,
  With their silver-sided haul,
Midst the shouts of dripping fishers,
  He was merriest of them all.

When, among the jovial huskers,
  Love stole in at Labor's side
With the lusty airs of England,
  Soft his Celtic measures vied.

Songs of love and wailing lyke-wake,
  And the merry fair's carouse ;
Of the wild Red Fox of Erin
  And the Woman of Three Cows,

By the blazing hearths of winter,
  Pleasant seemed his simple tales,
Midst the grimmer Yorkshire legends
  And the mountain myths of Wales.

How the souls in Purgatory
  Scrambled up from fate forlorn,
On St. Keven's sackcloth ladder,
  Slyly hitched to Satan's horn.

Of the fiddler who at Tara
  Played all night to ghosts of kings ;
Of the brown dwarfs, and the fairies
  Dancing in their moorland rings !

Jolliest of our birds of singing,
  Best he loved the Bob-o-link.
" Hush ! " he 'd say, " the tipsy fairies !
  Hear the little folks in drink ! "

Merry-faced, with spade and fiddle,
  Singing through the ancient town,
Only this, of poor Hugh Tallant,
  Hath Tradition handed down.

Not a stone his grave discloses ;
  But if yet his spirit walks,
'T is beneath the trees he planted,
  And when Bob-o-Lincoln talks ;

Green memorials of the gleeman !
  Linking still the river-shores,
With their shadows cast by sunset,
  Stand Hugh Tallant's sycamores !

When the Father of his Country
  Through the north-land riding came,
And the roofs were starred with banners,
  And the steeples rang acclaim, —

When each war-scarred Continental,
  Leaving smithy, mill, and farm,

Waved his rusted sword in welcome,
  And shot off his old king's arm, —

Slowly passed that august Presence
  Down the thronged and shouting street;
Village girls as white as angels,
  Scattering flowers around his feet.

Midway, where the plane-tree's shadow
  Deepest fell, his rein he drew:
On his stately head, uncovered,
  Cool and soft the west-wind blew.

And he stood up in his stirrups,
  Looking up and looking down
On the hills of Gold and Silver
  Rimming round the little town, —

On the river, full of sunshine,
  To the lap of greenest vales
Winding down from wooded headlands,
  Willow-skirted, white with sails.

And he said, the landscape sweeping
  Slowly with his ungloved hand,
" I have seen no prospect fairer
  In this goodly Eastern land."

Then the bugles of his escort
  Stirred to life the cavalcade:
And that head, so bare and stately,
  Vanished down the depths of shade.

Ever since, in town and farm-house,
  Life has had its ebb and flow;
Thrice hath passed the human har-
    vest
  To its garner green and low.

But the trees the gleeman planted,
  Through the changes, changeless
    stand;
As the marble calm of Tadmor
  Marks the desert's shifting sand.

Still the level moon at rising
  Silvers o'er each stately shaft;
Still beneath them, half in shadow,
  Singing, glides the pleasure craft.

Still beneath them, arm-enfolded,
  Love and Youth together stray;
While, as heart to heart beats faster,
  More and more their feet delay.

Where the ancient cobbler, Keezar,
  On the open hillside wrought,

Singing, as he drew his stitches,
  Songs his German masters taught, —

Singing, with his gray hair floating
  Round his rosy ample face, —
Now a thousand Saxon craftsmen
  Stitch and hammer in his place.

All the pastoral lanes so grassy
  Now are Traffic's dusty streets;
From the village, grown a city,
  Fast the rural grace retreats.

But, still green, and tall, and stately,
  On the river's winding shores,
Stand the Occidental plane-trees,
  Stand Hugh Tallant's sycamores.

THE DOUBLE-HEADED SNAKE OF NEWBURY.

" Concerning yᵉ Amphisbæna, as soon as I received your commands, I made diligent inquiry:
. . . . he assures me yᵗ it had really two heads,
one at each end; two mouths, two stings or
tongues." — REV. CHRISTOPHER TOPPAN to COT-
TON MATHER.

FAR away in the twilight time
Of every people, in every clime,
Dragons and griffins and monsters dire,
Born of water, and air, and fire,
Or nursed, like the Python, in the mud
And ooze of the old Deucalion flood,
Crawl and wriggle and foam with rage,
Through dusk tradition and ballad age.
So from the childhood of Newbury town
And its time of fable the tale comes
    down
Of a terror which haunted bush and
    brake,
The Amphisbæna, the Double Snake !

Thou who makest the tale thy mirth,
Consider that strip of Christian earth
On the desolate shore of a sailless sea,
Full of terror and mystery,
Half redeemed from the evil hold
Of the wood so dreary, and dark, and old,
Which drank with its lips of leaves the
    dew
When Time was young, and the world
    was new,
And wove its shadows with sun and
    moon,
Ere the stones of Cheops were squared
    and hewn.
Think of the sea's dread monotone,

Of the mournful wail from the pine-wood blown,
Of the strange, vast splendors that lit the North,
Of the troubled throes of the quaking earth,
And the dismal tales the Indian told,
Till the settler's heart at his hearth grew cold,
And he shrank from the tawny wizard's boasts,
And the hovering shadows seemed full of ghosts,
And above, below, and on every side,
The fear of his creed seemed verified ; —
And think, if his lot were now thine own,
To grope with terrors nor named nor known,
How laxer muscle and weaker nerve
And a feebler faith thy need might serve ;
And own to thyself the wonder more
That the snake had two heads, and not a score !

Whether he lurked in the Oldtown fen
Or the gray earth-flax of the Devil's Den,
Or swam in the wooded Artichoke,
Or coiled by the Northman's Written Rock,
Nothing on record is left to show ;
Only the fact that he lived, we know,
And left the cast of a double head
In the scaly mask which he yearly shed.
For he carried a head where his tail should be,
And the two, of course, could never agree,
But wriggled about with main and might,
Now to the left and now to the right ;
Pulling and twisting this way and that,
Neither knew what the other was at.

A snake with two heads, lurking so near ! —
Judge of the wonder, guess at the fear !
Think what ancient gossips might say,
Shaking their heads in their dreary way,
Between the meetings on Sabbath-day !
How urchins, searching at day's decline
The Common Pasture for sheep or kine,
The terrible double-ganger heard
In leafy rustle or whir of bird !
Think what a zest it gave to the sport,
In berry-time, of the younger sort,
As over pastures blackberry-twined,

Reuben and Dorothy lagged behind,
And closer and closer, for fear of harm,
The maiden clung to her lover's arm ;
And how the spark, who was forced to stay,
By his sweetheart's fears, till the break of day,
Thanked the snake for the fond delay !

Far and wide the tale was told,
Like a snowball growing while it rolled.
The nurse hushed with it the baby's cry ;
And it served, in the worthy minister's eye,
To paint the primitive serpent by.
Cotton Mather came galloping down
All the way to Newbury town,
With his eyes agog and his ears set wide,
And his marvellous inkhorn at his side ;
Stirring the while in the shallow pool
Of his brains for the lore he learned at school,
To garnish the story, with here a streak
Of Latin, and there another of Greek :
And the tales he heard and the notes he took,
Behold ! are they not in his Wonder-Book ?

Stories, like dragons, are hard to kill.
If the snake does not, the tale runs still
In Byfield Meadows, on Pipestave Hill.
And still, whenever husband and wife
Publish the shame of their daily strife,
And, with mad cross-purpose, tug and strain
At either end of the marriage-chain,
The gossips say, with a knowing shake
Of their gray heads, "Look at the Double Snake !
One in body and two in will,
The Amphisbæna is living still ! "

THE SWAN SONG OF PARSON AVERY.

WHEN the reaper's task was ended, and the summer wearing late,
Parson Avery sailed from Newbury, with his wife and children eight,
Dropping down the river-harbor in the shallop "Watch and Wait."

Pleasantly lay the clearings in the mellow summer-morn,
With the newly planted orchards dropping their fruits first-born,
And the homesteads like green islands
   amid a sea of corn.

Broad meadows reached out seaward the
   tided creeks between,
And hills rolled wave-like inland, with
   oaks and walnuts green ; —
A fairer home, a goodlier land, his eyes
   had never seen.

Yet away sailed Parson Avery, away
   where duty led,
And the voice of God seemed calling,
   to break the living bread
To the souls of fishers starving on the
   rocks of Marblehead.

All day they sailed : at nightfall the
   pleasant land-breeze died,
The blackening sky, at midnight, its
   starry lights denied,
And far and low the thunder of tempest
   prophesied !

Blotted out were all the coast-lines, gone
   were rock, and wood, and sand ;
Grimly anxious stood the skipper with
   the rudder in his hand,
And questioned of the darkness what
   was sea and what was land.

And the preacher heard his dear ones,
   nestled round him, weeping sore :
"Never heed, my little children ! Christ
   is walking on before
To the pleasant land of heaven, where
   the sea shall be no more."

All at once the great cloud parted, like
   a curtain drawn aside,
To let down the torch of lightning on
   the terror far and wide ;
And the thunder and the whirlwind
   together smote the tide.

There was wailing in the shallop, wo-
   man's wail and man's despair,
A crash of breaking timbers on the rocks
   so sharp and bare,
And, through it all, the murmur of
   Father Avery's prayer.

From his struggle in the darkness with
   the wild waves and the blast,
On a rock, where every billow broke
   above him as it passed,
Alone, of all his household, the man of
   God was cast.

There a comrade heard him praying, in
   the pause of wave and wind :
"All my own have gone before me, and
   I linger just behind ;
Not for life I ask, but only for the rest
   thy ransomed find !

"In this night of death I challenge the
   promise of thy word ! —
Let me see the great salvation of which
   mine ears have heard ! —
Let me pass from hence forgiven, through
   the grace of Christ, our Lord !

"In the baptism of these waters wash
   white my every sin,
And let me follow up to thee my household and my kin !
Open the sea-gate of thy heaven, and
   let me enter in !"

When the Christian sings his death-
   song, all the listening heavens
   draw near,
And the angels, leaning over the walls
   of crystal, hear
How the notes so faint and broken swell
   to music in God's ear.

The ear of God was open to his servant's
   last request ;
As the strong wave swept him downward
   the sweet hymn upward pressed,
And the soul of Father Avery went,
   singing, to its rest.

There was wailing on the mainland,
   from the rocks of Marblehead ;
In the stricken church of Newbury the
   notes of prayer were read ;
And long, by board and hearthstone, the
   living mourned the dead.

And still the fishers outbound, or scud-
   ding from the squall,
With grave and reverent faces, the ancient tale recall,
When they see the white waves breaking on the Rock of Avery's
   Fall !

THE TRUCE OF PISCATAQUA.

1675.

RAZE these long blocks of brick and
    stone,
These huge mill-monsters overgrown ;
Blot out the humbler piles as well,
Where, moved like living shuttles,
    dwell
The weaving genii of the bell ;
Tear from the wild Cocheco's track
The dams that hold its torrents back ;
And let the loud-rejoicing fall
Plunge, roaring, down its rocky wall ;
And let the Indian's paddle play
On the unbridged Piscataqua !
Wide over hill and valley spread
Once more the forest, dusk and dread,
With here and there a clearing cut
From the walled shadows round it shut ;
Each with its farm-house builded rude,
By English yeoman squared and hewed,
And the grim, flankered block-house
    bound
With bristling palisades around.
So, haply shall before thine eyes
The dusty veil of centuries rise,
The old, strange scenery overlay
The tamer pictures of to-day,
While, like the actors in a play,
Pass in their ancient guise along
The figures of my border song :
What time beside Cocheco's flood
The white man and the red man stood,
With words of peace and brotherhood ;
When passed the sacred calumet
From lip to lip with fire-draught wet,
And, puffed in scorn, the peace-pipe's
    smoke
Through the gray beard of Waldron broke,
And Squando's voice, in suppliant plea
For mercy, struck the haughty key
Of one who held, in any fate,
His native pride inviolate !

" Let your ears be opened wide !
He who speaks has never lied.
Waldron of Piscataqua,
Hear what Squando has to say !

" Squando shuts his eyes and sees,
Far off, Saco's hemlock-trees.
In his wigwam, still as stone,
Sits a woman all alone,

" Wampum beads and birchen strands
Dropping from her careless hands,

Listening ever for the fleet
Patter of a dead child's feet !

" When the moon a year ago
Told the flowers the time to blow,
In that lonely wigwam smiled
Menewee, our little child.

" Ere that moon grew thin and old,
He was lying still and cold ;
Sent before us, weak and small,
When the Master did not call !

" On his little grave I lay ;
Three times went and came the day ;
Thrice above me blazed the noon,
Thrice upon me wept the moon.

" In the third night-watch I heard,
Far and low, a spirit-bird ;
Very mournful, very wild,
Sang the totem of my child.

" ' Menewee, poor Menewee,
Walks a path he cannot see :
Let the white man's wigwam light
With its blaze his steps aright.

" ' All-uncalled, he dares not show
Empty hands to Manito :
Better gifts he cannot bear
Than the scalps his slayers wear.'

" All the while the totem sang,
Lightning blazed and thunder rang ;
And a black cloud, reaching high,
Pulled the white moon from the sky.

" I, the medicine-man, whose ear
All that spirits hear can hear, —
I, whose eyes are wide to see
All the things that are to be, —

" Well I knew the dreadful signs
In the whispers of the pines,
In the river roaring loud,
In the mutter of the cloud.

" At the breaking of the day,
From the grave I passed away ;
Flowers bloomed round me, birds san
    glad,
But my heart was hot and mad.

" There is rust on Squando's knife,
From the warm, red springs of life ;

On the funeral hemlock-trees
Many a scalp the totem sees.

"Blood for blood! But evermore
Squando's heart is sad and sore ;
And his poor squaw waits at home
For the feet that never come !

"Waldron of Cocheco, hear !
Squando speaks, who laughs at fear ;
Take the captives he has ta'en ;
Let the land have peace again !"

As the words died on his tongue,
Wide apart his warriors swung ;
Parted, at the sign he gave,
Right and left, like Egypt's wave.

And, like Israel passing free
Through the prophet-charméd sea,
Captive mother, wife, and child
Through the dusky terror filed.

One alone, a little maid,
Middleway her steps delayed,
Glancing, with quick, troubled sight,
Round about from red to white.

Then his hand the Indian laid
On the little maiden's head,
Lightly from her forehead fair
Smoothing back her yellow hair.

"Gift or favor ask I none ;
What I have is all my own :
Never yet the birds have sung,
'Squando hath a beggar's tongue.'

"Yet for her who waits at home,
For the dead who cannot come,
Let the little Gold-hair be
In the place of Menewee !

"Mishanock, my little star !
Come to Saco's pines afar ;
Where the sad one waits at home,
Wequashim, my moonlight, come !"

"What !" quoth Waldron, "leave a child
Christian-born to heathens wild ?
As God lives, from Satan's hand
I will pluck her as a brand !"

"Hear me, white man !" Squando cried ;
"Let the little one decide.

"Wequashim, my moonlight, say,
Wilt thou go with me, or stay ?"

Slowly, sadly, half afraid,
Half regretfully, the maid
Owned the ties of blood and race, —
Turned from Squando's pleading face.

Not a word the Indian spoke,
But his wampum chain he broke,
And the beaded wonder hung
On that neck so fair and young.

Silence-shod, as phantoms seem
In the marches of a dream,
Single-filed, the grim array
Through the pine-trees wound away.

Doubting, trembling, sore amazed,
Through her tears the young child gazed.
"God preserve her !" Waldron said ;
"Satan hath bewitched the maid !"

Years went and came.   At close of day
Singing came a child from play,
Tossing from her loose-locked head
Gold in sunshine, brown in shade.

Pride was in the mother's look,
But her head she gravely shook,
And with lips that fondly smiled
Feigned to chide her truant child.

Unabashed, the maid began :
"Up and down the brook I ran,
Where, beneath the bank so steep,
Lie the spotted trout asleep.

"'Chip !' went squirrel on the wall,
After me I heard him call,
And the cat-bird on the tree
Tried his best to mimic me.

"Where the hemlocks grew so dark
That I stopped to look and hark,
On a log, with feather-hat,
By the path, an Indian sat.

"Then I cried, and ran away ;
But he called, and bade me stay ;
And his voice was good and mild
As my mother's to her child.

"And he took my wampum chain,
Looked and looked it o'er again ;
Gave me berries, and, beside,
On my neck a plaything tied."

Straight the mother stooped to see
What the Indian's gift might be.
On the braid of wampum hung,
Lo ! a cross of silver swung.

Well she knew its graven sign,
Squando's bird and totem pine ;
And, a mirage of the brain,
Flowed her childhood back again.

Flashed the roof the sunshine through,
Into space the walls outgrew ;
On the Indian's wigwam-mat,
Blossom-crowned, again she sat.

Cool she felt the west-wind blow,
In her ear the pines sang low,
And, like links from out a chain,
Dropped the years of care and pain.

From the outward toil and din,
From the griefs that gnaw within,
To the freedom of the woods
Called the birds, and winds, and floods.

Well, O painful minister !
Watch thy flock, but blame not her,
If her ear grew sharp to hear
All their voices whispering near.

Blame her not, as to her soul
All the desert's glamour stole,
That a tear for childhood's loss
Dropped upon the Indian's cross.

When, that night, the Book was read,
And she bowed her widowed head,
And a prayer for each loved name
Rose like incense from a flame,

To the listening ear of Heaven,
Lo ! another name was given :
" Father, give the Indian rest !
Bless him ! for his love has blest ! "

MY PLAYMATE.

THE pines were dark on Ramoth hill,
　Their song was soft and low ;
The blossoms in the sweet May wind
　Were falling like the snow.

The blossoms drifted at our feet,
　The orchard birds sang clear ;
The sweetest and the saddest day
　It seemed of all the year.

For, more to me than birds or flowers,
　My playmate left her home,
And took with her the laughing spring,
　The music and the bloom.

She kissed the lips of kith and kin,
　She laid her hand in mine :
What more could ask the bashful boy
　Who fed her father's kine ?

She left us in the bloom of May :
　The constant years told o'er
Their seasons with as sweet May morns,
　But she came back no more.

I walk, with noiseless feet, the round
　Of uneventful years ;
Still o'er and o'er I sow the spring
　And reap the autumn ears.

She lives where all the golden year
　Her summer roses blow ;
The dusky children of the sun
　Before her come and go.

There haply with her jewelled hands
　She smooths her silken gown, —
No more the homespun lap wherein
　I shook the walnuts down.

The wild grapes wait us by the brook,
　The brown nuts on the hill,
And still the May-day flowers make sweet
　The woods of Follymill.

The lilies blossom in the pond,
　The bird builds in the tree,
The dark pines sing on Ramoth hill
　The slow song of the sea.

I wonder if she thinks of them,
　And how the old time seems, —
If ever the pines of Ramoth wood
　Are sounding in her dreams.

I see her face, I hear her voice :
　Does she remember mine ?
And what to her is now the boy
　Who fed her father's kine ?

What cares she that the orioles build
　For other eyes than ours, —
That other hands with nuts are filled,
　And other laps with flowers ?

O playmate in the golden time !
  Our mossy seat is green,
Its fringing violets blossom yet,
  The old trees o'er it lean.

The winds so sweet with birch and fern
  A sweeter memory blow ;

And there in spring the veeries sing
  The song of long ago.

And still the pines of Ramoth wood
  Are moaning like the sea, —
The moaning of the sea of change
  Between myself and thee !

POEMS AND LYRICS.

THE SHADOW AND THE LIGHT.

"And I sought, whence is Evil: I set before the eye of my spirit the whole creation; whatsoever we see therein, — sea, earth, air, stars, trees, moral creatures, — yea, whatsoever there is we do not see, — angels and spiritual powers. Where is evil, and whence comes it, since God the Good hath created all things? Why made He anything at all of evil, and not rather by His Almightiness cause it not to be? These thoughts I turned in my miserable heart, overcharged with most gnawing cares." "And, admonished to return to myself, I entered even into my inmost soul, Thou being my guide, and beheld even beyond my soul and mind the Light unchangeable. He who knows the Truth knows what that Light is, and he that knows it knows Eternity! O Truth, who art Eternity! Love, who art Truth! Eternity, who art Love! And I beheld that Thou madest all things good, and to Thee is nothing whatsoever evil. From the angel to the worm, from the first motion to the last, Thou settest each in its place, and everything is good in its kind. Woe is me! — how high art Thou in the highest, how deep in the deepest! and Thou never departest from us and we scarcely return to Thee." —Augustine's Soliloquies, Book VII.

The fourteen centuries fall away
  Between us and the Afric saint,
And at his side we urge, to-day,
The immemorial quest and old complaint.

No outward sign to us is given, —
  From sea or earth comes no reply ;
Hushed as the warm Numidian heaven
He vainly questioned bends our frozen
    sky.

No victory comes of all our strife, —
  From all we grasp the meaning slips ;
The Sphinx sits at the gate of life,
With the old question on her awful lips.

In paths unknown we hear the feet
  Of fear before, and guilt behind ;
We pluck the wayside fruit, and eat
Ashes and dust beneath its golden rind.

From age to age descends unchecked
  The sad bequest of sire to son,
  The body's taint, the mind's defect, —
Through every web of life the dark
    threads run.

O, why and whither ? — God knows
    all ;
  I only know that he is good,
And that whatever may befall
Or here or there, must be the best that
    could.

Between the dreadful cherubim
  A Father's face I still discern,
As Moses looked of old on him,
And saw his glory into goodness turn !

For he is merciful as just;
  And so, by faith correcting sight,
I bow before his will, and trust
Howe'er they seem he doeth all things
    right.

And dare to hope that he will
    make
  The rugged smooth, the doubtful
    plain ;
His mercy never quite forsake ;
His healing visit every realm of pain ;

That suffering is not his revenge
  Upon his creatures weak and frail,
Sent on a pathway new and strange
With feet that wander and with eyes
    that fail ;

That, o'er the crucible of pain,
  Watches the tender eye of Love
The slow transmuting of the chain
Whose links are iron below to gold
    above !

Ah me ! we doubt the shining skies,
  Seen through our shadows of offence,
And drown with our poor childish
    cries
The cradle-hymn of kindly Providence.

And still we love the evil cause,
  And of the just effect complain:
We tread upon life's broken laws,
And murmur at our self-inflicted pain ;

We turn us from the light, and find
  Our spectral shapes before us
    thrown,
As they who leave the sun behind
Walk in the shadows of themselves
    alone.

And scarce by will or strength of ours
  We set our faces to the day ;
Weak, wavering, blind, the Eternal
    Powers
Alone can turn us from ourselves away.

Our weakness is the strength of sin,
  But love must needs be stronger far,
Outreaching all and gathering in
The erring spirit and the wandering star.

A Voice grows with the growing years ;
  Earth, hushing down her bitter cry,
Looks upward from her graves, and
    hears,
" The Resurrection and the Life am I."

O Love Divine ! — whose constant
    beam
Shines on the eyes that will not see,
And waits to bless us, while we dream
Thou leavest us because we turn from
    thee !

All souls that struggle and aspire,
  All hearts of prayer by thee are lit ;
And, dim or clear, thy tongues of fire
On dusky tribes and twilight centuries
    sit.

Nor bounds, nor clime, nor creed thou
    know'st,
  Wide as our need thy favors fall ;
The white wings of the Holy Ghost
Stoop, seen or unseen, o'er the heads of
    all.

O Beauty, old yet ever new ! [67]
  Eternal Voice, and Inward Word,

The Logos of the Greek and Jew,
The old sphere-music which the Samian
    heard !

Truth which the sage and prophet
    saw,
Long sought without, but found
    within,
The Law of Love beyond all law,
The Life o'erflooding mortal death and
    sin !

Shine on us with the light which
    glowed
Upon the trance-bound shepherd's
    way,
Who saw the Darkness overflowed
And drowned by tides of everlasting
    Day. [68]

Shine, light of God ! — make broad
    thy scope
To all who sin and suffer ; more
And better than we dare to hope
With Heaven's compassion make our
    longings poor !

THE GIFT OF TRITEMIUS.

Tritemius of Herbipolis, one day,
While kneeling at the altar's foot to
    pray,
Alone with God, as was his pious choice,
Heard from without a miserable voice,
A sound which seemed of all sad things
    to tell,
As of a lost soul crying out of hell.

Thereat the Abbot paused ; the chain
    whereby
His thoughts went upward broken by
    that cry ;
And, looking from the casement, saw
    below
A wretched woman, with gray hair a-flow,
And withered hands held up to him,
    who cried
For alms as one who might not be
    denied.

She cried, " For the dear love of Him
    who gave
His life for ours, my child from bondage
    save, —
My beautiful, brave first-born, chained
    with slaves

In the Moor's galley, where the sun-smit
   waves
Lap the white walls of Tunis ! " —
   " What I can
I give," Tritemius said : " my prayers."
   —" O man
Of God ! " she cried, for grief had made
   her bold,
" Mock me not thus ; I ask not prayers,
   but gold.
Words will not serve me, alms alone
   suffice ;
Even while I speak perchance my first-
   born dies."

" Woman ! " Tritemius answered, " from
   our door
None go unfed ; hence are we always
   poor,
A single soldo is our only store.
Thou hast our prayers ; — what can we
   give thee more ? "—

" Give me," she said, " the silver can-
   dlesticks
On either side of the great crucifix.
God well may spare them on his errands
   sped,
Or he can give you golden ones instead."

Then spake Tritemius, " Even as thy
   word,
Woman, so be it ! (Our most gracious
   Lord,
Who loveth mercy more than sacrifice,
Pardon me if a human soul I prize
Above the gifts upon his altar piled !)
Take what thou askest, and redeem thy
   child."

But his hand trembled as the holy
   alms
He placed within the beggar's eager
   palms ;
And as she vanished down the linden
   shade,
He bowed his head and for forgiveness
   prayed.

So the day passed, and when the twi-
   light came
He woke to find the chapel all aflame,
And, dumb with grateful wonder, to be-
   hold
Upon the altar candlesticks of gold !

THE EVE OF ELECTION.

FROM gold to gray
Our mild sweet day
Of Indian Summer fades too soon ;
   But tenderly
   Above the sea
Hangs, white and calm, the hunter's
   moon.

   In its pale fire,
   The village spire
Shows like the zodiac's spectral lance ;
   The painted walls
   Whereon it falls
Transfigured stand in marble trance !

   O'er fallen leaves
   The west-wind grieves,
Yet comes a seed-time round again ;
   And morn shall see
   The State sown free
With baleful tares or healthful grain.

   Along the street
   The shadows meet
Of Destiny, whose hands conceal
   The moulds of fate
   That shape the State,
And make or mar the common weal.

   Around I see
   The powers that be ;
I stand by Empire's primal springs ;
   And princes meet,
   In every street,
And hear the tread of uncrowned kings !

   Hark ! through the crowd
   The laugh runs loud,
Beneath the sad, rebuking moon.
   God save the land
   A careless hand
May shake or swerve ere morrow's noon !

   No jest is this ;
   One cast amiss
May blast the hope of Freedom's year.
   O, take me where
   Are hearts of prayer,
And foreheads bowed in reverent fear !

   Not lightly fall
   Beyond recall
The written scrolls a breath can float ;
   The crowning fact
   The kingliest act
Of Freedom is the freeman's vote !

For pearls that gem
A diadem
The diver in the deep sea dies ;
The regal right
We boast to-night
Is ours through costlier sacrifice ;

The blood of Vane,
His prison pain
Who traced the path the Pilgrim trod,
And hers whose faith
Drew strength from death,
And prayed her Russell up to God !

Our hearts grow cold,
We lightly hold
A right which brave men died to gain ;
The stake, the cord,
The axe, the sword,
Grim nurses at its birth of pain.

The shadow rend,
And o'er us bend,
O martyrs, with your crowns and
palms, —
Breathe through these throngs
Your battle songs,
Your scaffold prayers, and dungeon
psalms !

Look from the sky,
Like God's great eye,
Thou solemn noon, with searching beam,
Till in the sight
Of thy pure light
Our mean self-seekings meaner seem.

Shame from our hearts
Unworthy arts,
The fraud designed, the purpose dark ;
And smite away
The hands we lay
Profanely on the sacred ark.

To party claims
And private aims,
Reveal that august face of Truth,
Whereto are given
The age of heaven,
The beauty of immortal youth.

So shall our voice
Of sovereign choice
Swell the deep bass of duty done,
And strike the key
Of time to be,
When God and man shall speak as one !

THE OVER-HEART.

" For of Him, and through Him, and to Him
are all things, to whom be glory forever ! " — Paul.

Above, below, in sky and sod,
In leaf and spar, in star and man,
Well might the wise Athenian scan
The geometric signs of God,
The measured order of his plan.

And India's mystics sang aright
Of the One Life pervading all,—
One Being's tidal rise and fall
In soul and form, in sound and sight, —
Eternal outflow and recall.

God is : and man in guilt and fear
The central fact of Nature owns ; —
Kneels, trembling, by his altar-stones,
And darkly dreams the ghastly smear
Of blood appeases and atones.

Guilt shapes the Terror : deep within
The human heart the secret lies
Of all the hideous deities ;
And, painted on a ground of sin,
The fabled gods of torment rise !

And what is He ? — The ripe grain nods,
The sweet dews fall, the sweet flowers
blow ;
But darker signs his presence show :
The earthquake and the storm are God's,
And good and evil interflow.

O hearts of love ! O souls that turn
Like sunflowers to the pure and best !
To you the truth is manifest :
For they the mind of Christ discern
Who lean like John upon his breast !

In him of whom the sibyl told,
For whom the prophet's harp was
toned,
Whose need the sage and magian
owned,
The loving heart of God behold,
The hope for which the ages groaned !

Fade, pomp of dreadful imagery
Wherewith mankind have deified
Their hate, and selfishness, and pride !
Let the scared dreamer wake to see
The Christ of Nazareth at his side !

What doth that holy Guide require ? —
No rite of pain, nor gift of blood,
But man a kindly brotherhood,

Looking, where duty is desire,
  To him, the beautiful and good.

Gone be the faithlessness of fear,
  And let the pitying heaven's sweet
    rain
Wash out the altar's bloody stain ;
The law of Hatred disappear,
  The law of Love alone remain.

How fall the idols false and grim ! —
  And lo ! their hideous wreck above
The emblems of the Lamb and Dove!
Man turns from God, not God from
    him ;
  And guilt, in suffering, whispers
    Love !

The world sits at the feet of Christ,
  Unknowing, blind, and unconsoled ;
  It yet shall touch his garment's fold,
And feel the heavenly Alchemist
  Transform its very dust to gold.

The theme befitting angel tongues
  Beyond a mortal's scope has grown.
O heart of mine ! with reverence own
The fulness which to it belongs,
  And trust the unknown for the known.

IN REMEMBRANCE OF JOSEPH
STURGE.

In the fair land o'erwatched by Ischia's
    mountains,
  Across the charméd bay
Whose blue waves keep with Capri's sil-
    ver fountains
  Perpetual holiday,

A king lies dead, his wafer duly eaten,
  His gold-bought masses given ;
And Rome's great altar smokes with
    gums to sweeten
  Her foulest gift to Heaven.

And while all Naples thrills with mute
    thanksgiving,
  The court of England's queen
For the dead monster so abhorred while
    living
  In mourning garb is seen.

With a true sorrow God rebukes that
    feigning ;
  By lone Edgbaston's side

Stands a great city in the sky's sad
    raining,
  Bareheaded and wet-eyed !

Silent for once the restless hive of labor,
  Save the low funeral tread,
Or voice of craftsman whispering to his
    neighbor
  The good deeds of the dead.

For him no minster's chant of the im-
    mortals
  Rose from the lips of sin ;
No mitred priest swung back the heav-
    enly portals
  To let the white soul in.

But Age and Sickness framed their tear-
    ful faces
  In the low hovel's door,
And prayers went up from all the dark
    by-places
  And Ghettos of the poor.

The pallid toiler and the negro chattel,
  The vagrant of the street,
The human dice wherewith in games of
    battle
  The lords of earth compete,

Touched with a grief that needs no out-
    ward draping,
  All swelled the long lament,
Of grateful hearts, instead of marble,
    shaping
  His viewless monument !

For never yet, with ritual pomp and
    splendor,
  In the long heretofore,
A heart more loyal, warm, and true,
    and tender,
  Has England's turf closed o'er.

And if there fell from out her grand old
    steeples
  No crash of brazen wail,
The murmurous woe of kindreds,
    tongues, and peoples
  Swept in on every gale.

It came from Holstein's birchen-belted
    meadows,
  And from the tropic calms
Of Indian islands in the sun-smit shad-
    ows
  Of Occidental palms ;

From the locked roadsteads of the
    Bothnian peasants,
  And harbors of the Finn,
Where war's worn victims saw his gentle
    presence
  Come sailing, Christ-like, in,

To seek the lost, to build the old waste
    places,
  To link the hostile shores
Of severing seas, and sow with Eng-
    land's daisies
  The moss of Finland's moors.

Thanks for the good man's beautiful
    example,
  Who in the vilest saw
Some sacred crypt or altar of a temple
  Still vocal with God's law ;

And heard with tender ear the spirit
    sighing
  As from its prison cell,
Praying for pity, like the mournful cry-
    ing
  Of Jonah out of hell.

Not his the golden pen's or lip's per-
    suasion,
  But a fine sense of right,
And Truth's directness, meeting each
    occasion
  Straight as a line of light.

His faith and works, like streams that
    intermingle,
  In the same channel ran :
The crystal clearness of an eye kept
    single
  Shamed all the frauds of man.

The very gentlest of all human natures
  He joined to courage strong,
And love outreaching unto all God's
    creatures
  With sturdy hate of wrong.

Tender as woman ; manliness and
    meekness
  In him were so allied
That they who judged him by his
    strength or weakness
  Saw but a single side.

Men failed, betrayed him, but his zeal
    seemed nourished
  By failure and by fall ;

Still a large faith in human-kind he
    cherished,
  And in God's love for all.

And now he rests : his greatness and his
    sweetness
  No more shall seem at strife ;
And death has moulded into calm com-
    pleteness
  The statue of his life.

Where the dews glisten and the song-
    birds warble,
  His dust to dust is laid,
In Nature's keeping, with no pomp of
    marble
  To shame his modest shade.

The forges glow, the hammers all are
    ringing ;
  Beneath its smoky vale,
Hard by, the city of his love is swing-
    ing
  Its clamorous iron flail.

But round his grave are quietude and
    beauty,
  And the sweet heaven above, —
The fitting symbols of a life of duty
  Transfigured into love !

TRINITAS.

At morn I prayed, " I fain would see
How Three are One, and One is Three ;
Read the dark riddle unto me."

I wandered forth, the sun and air
I saw bestowed with equal care
On good and evil, foul and fair.

No partial favor dropped the rain ; —
Alike the righteous and profane
Rejoiced above their heading grain.

And my heart murmured, " Is it meet
That blindfold Nature thus should treat
With equal hand the tares and wheat ? "

A presence melted through my mood, —
A warmth, a light, a sense of good,
Like sunshine through a winter wood.

I saw that presence, mailed complete
In her white innocence, pause to greet
A fallen sister of the street.

Upon her bosom snowy pure
The lost one clung, as if secure
From inward guilt or outward lure.

"Beware !" I said ; "in this I see
No gain to her, but loss to thee :
Who touches pitch defiled must be."

I passed the haunts of shame and sin,
And a voice whispered, "Who therein
Shall these lost souls to Heaven's peace
    win ?

"Who there shall hope and health dis-
    pense,
And lift the ladder up from thence
Whose rounds are prayers of penitence ?"

I said, "No higher life they know ;
These earth-worms love to have it so.
Who stoops to raise them sinks as low."

That night with painful care I read
What Hippo's saint and Calvin said, —
The living seeking to the dead !

In vain I turned, in weary quest,
Old pages, where (God give them rest !)
The poor creed-mongers dreamed and
    guessed.

And still I prayed, "Lord, let me see
How Three are One, and One is Three ;
Read the dark riddle unto me !"

Then something whispered, "Dost thou
    pray
For what thou hast ? This very day
The Holy Three have crossed thy way.

"Did not the gifts of sun and air
To good and ill alike declare
The all-compassionate Father's care ?

"In the white soul that stooped to
    raise
The lost one from her evil ways,
Thou saw'st the Christ, whom angels
    praise !

"A bodiless Divinity,
The still small Voice that spake to thee
Was the Holy Spirit's mystery !

"O blind of sight, of faith how small !
Father, and Son, and Holy Call ; —
This day thou hast denied them all !

"Revealed in love and sacrifice,
The Holiest passed before thine eyes,
One and the same, in threefold guise.

"The equal Father in rain and sun,
His Christ in the good to evil done,
His Voice in thy soul ; — and the Three
    are One !"

I shut my grave Aquinas fast ;
The monkish gloss of ages past,
The schoolman's creed aside I cast.

And my heart answered, "Lord, I see
How Three are One, and One is Three ;
Thy riddle hath been read to me !"

THE OLD BURYING-GROUND.

OUR vales are sweet with fern and
    rose,
    Our hills are maple-crowned ;
But not from them our fathers chose
    The village burying-ground.

The dreariest spot in all the land
    To Death they set apart ;
With scanty grace from Nature's hand,
    And none from that of Art.

A winding wall of mossy stone,
    Frost-flung and broken, lines
A lonesome acre thinly grown
    With grass and wandering vines.

Without the wall a birch-tree shows
    Its drooped and tasselled head ;
Within, a stag-horned sumach grows,
    Fern-leafed, with spikes of red.

There, sheep that graze the neighboring
    plain
    Like white ghosts come and go,
The farm-horse drags his fetlock chain,
    The cow-bell tinkles slow.

Low moans the river from its bed,
    The distant pines reply ;
Like mourners shrinking from the dead,
    They stand apart and sigh.

Unshaded smites the summer sun,
    Unchecked the winter blast ;
The school-girl learns the place to
    shun,
    With glances backward cast.

For thus our fathers testified, —
  That he might read who ran, —
The emptiness of human pride,
  The nothingness of man.

They dared not plant the grave with
    flowers,
  Nor dress the funeral sod,
Where, with a love as deep as ours,
  They left their dead with God.

The hard and thorny path they kept
  From beauty turned aside ;
Nor missed they over those who slept
  The grace to life denied.

Yet still the wilding flowers would
    blow,
  The golden leaves would fall,
The seasons come, the seasons go,
  And God be good to all.

Above the graves the blackberry hung
  In bloom and green its wreath,
And harebells swung as if they rung
  The chimes of peace beneath.

The beauty Nature loves to share,
  The gifts she hath for all,
The common light, the common air,
  O'ercrept the graveyard's wall.

It knew the glow of eventide,
  The sunrise and the noon,
And glorified and sanctified
  It slept beneath the moon.

With flowers or snow-flakes for its sod,
  Around the seasons ran,
And evermore the love of God
  Rebuked the fear of man.

We dwell with fears on either hand,
  Within a daily strife,
And spectral problems waiting stand
  Before the gates of life.

The doubts we vainly seek to solve,
  The truths we know, are one ;
The known and nameless stars revolve
  Around the Central Sun.

And if we reap as we have sown,
  And take the dole we deal,
The law of pain is love alone,
  The wounding is to heal.

Unharmed from change to change we
    glide,
  We fall as in our dreams ;
The far-off terror at our side
  A smiling angel seems.

Secure on God's all-tender heart
  Alike rest great and small ;
Why fear to lose our little part,
  When he is pledged for all ?

O fearful heart and troubled brain !
  Take hope and strength from this, —
That Nature never hints in vain,
  Nor prophesies amiss.

Her wild birds sing the same sweet stave,
  Her lights and airs are given
Alike to playground and the grave ;
  And over both is Heaven.

THE PIPES AT LUCKNOW.

PIPES of the misty moorlands,
  Voice of the glens and hills ;
The droning of the torrents,
  The treble of the rills !
Not the braes of broom and heather,
  Nor the mountains dark with rain,
Nor maiden bower, nor border tower,
  Have heard your sweetest strain !

Dear to the Lowland reaper,
  And plaided mountaineer, —
To the cottage and the castle
  The Scottish pipes are dear ; —
Sweet sounds the ancient pibroch
  O'er mountain, loch, and glade ;
But the sweetest of all music
  The pipes at Lucknow played.

Day by day the Indian tiger
  Louder yelled, and nearer crept ;
Round and round the jungle-serpent
  Near and nearer circles swept.
" Pray for rescue, wives and mothers, —
  Pray to-day !" the soldier said ;
" To-morrow, death 's between us
  And the wrong and shame we dread.'

O, they listened, looked, and waited,
  Till their hope became despair ;
And the sobs of low bewailing
  Filled the pauses of their prayer.
Then up spake a Scottish maiden,
  With her ear unto the ground :

" Dinna ye hear it ? — dinna ye hear it ?
  The pipes o' Havelock sound ! "

Hushed the wounded man his groaning ;
  Hushed the wife her little ones ;
Alone they heard the drum-roll
  And the roar of Sepoy guns.
But to sounds of home and childhood
  The Highland ear was true ; —
As her mother's cradle-crooning
  The mountain pipes she knew.

Like the march of soundless music
  Through the vision of the seer,
More of feeling than of hearing,
  Of the heart than of the ear,
She knew the droning pibroch,
  She knew the Campbell's call :
" Hark ! hear ye no' MacGregor's, —
  The grandest o' them all ! "

O, they listened, dumb and breathless,
  And they caught the sound at last ;
Faint and far beyond the Goomtee
  Rose and fell the piper's blast !
Then a burst of wild thanksgiving
  Mingled woman's voice and man's ;
" God be praised ! — the march of Have-
    lock !
  The piping of the clans ! "

Louder, nearer, fierce as vengeance,
  Sharp and shrill as swords at strife,
Came the wild MacGregor's clan-call,
  Stinging all the air to life.
But when the far-off dust-cloud
  To plaided legions grew,
Full tenderly and blithesomely
  The pipes of rescue blew !

Round the silver domes of Lucknow,
  Moslem mosque and Pagan shrine,
Breathed the air to Britons dearest,
  The air of Auld Lang Syne.
O'er the cruel roll of war-drums
  Rose that sweet and homelike strain ;
And the tartan clove the turban,
  As the Goomtee cleaves the plain.

MY

I MOURN no more
  Beneath a ten
An April rain of s
  My heart is y

The west-winds bl
  I hear the gla
The windows of m
  Wide open to

No longer forward
  I look in hop
But, grateful, tak
  The best of n

I plough no more
  To harvest we
The manna droppi
  Rebukes my

I break my pilgri
  Aside the toil
The angel sought
  I welcome at

The airs of spring
  Among the ri
Nor freshness of t
  Blow through

Yet shall the blue
  Through fring
And the pale aster
  Shall see its i

The woods shall
  praise,
  The south-wi
And sweet, calm d
  Melt down th

Not less shall man
  Rebuke an ag
The graven flowe
  sword

And knoweth more of all my needs
   Than all my prayers have told !

Enough that blessings undeserved
   Have marked my erring track ; —
That wheresoe'er my feet have swerved,
   His chastening turned me back ; —

That more and more a Providence
   Of love is understood,
Making the springs of time and sense
   Sweet with eternal good ; —

That death seems but a covered way
   Which opens into light,
Wherein no blinded child can stray
   Beyond the Father's sight ; —

That care and trial seem at last,
   Through Memory's sunset air,
Like mountain-ranges overpast,
   In purple distance fair ; —

That all the jarring notes of life
   Seem blending in a psalm,
And all the angles of its strife
   Slow rounding into calm.

And so the shadows fall apart,
   And so the west-winds play ;
And all the windows of my heart
   I open to the day.

LE MARAIS DU CYGNE.[69]

A BLUSH as of roses
   Where rose never grew !
Great drops on the bunch-grass,
   But not of the dew !
A taint in the sweet air
   For wild bees to shun !
A stain that shall never
   Bleach out in the sun !

Back, steed of the prairies !
   Sweet song-bird, fly back !
Wheel hither, bald vulture !
   Gray wolf, call thy pack !
The foul human vultures
   Have feasted and fled ;
The wolves of the Border
   Have crept from the dead.

From the hearths of their cabins,
   The fields of their corn,

Unwarned and unweaponed,
   The victims were torn, —
By the whirlwind of murder
   Swooped up and swept on
To the low, reedy fen-lands,
   The Marsh of the Swan.

With a vain plea for mercy
   No stout knee was crooked ;
In the mouths of the rifles
   Right manly they looked.
How paled the May sunshine,
   O Marais du Cygne !
On death for the strong life,
   On red grass for green !

In the homes of their rearing,
   Yet warm with their lives,
Ye wait the dead only,
   Poor children and wives !
Put out the red forge-fire,
   The smith shall not come ;
Unyoke the brown oxen,
   The ploughman lies dumb.

Wind slow from the Swan's Marsh,
   O dreary death-train,
With pressed lips as bloodless
   As lips of the slain !
Kiss down the young eyelids,
   Smooth down the gray hairs ;
Let tears quench the curses
   That burn through your prayers.

Strong man of the prairies,
   Mourn bitter and wild !
Wail, desolate woman !
   Weep, fatherless child !
But the grain of God springs up
   From ashes beneath,
And the crown of his harvest
   Is life out of death.

Not in vain on the dial
   The shade moves along,
To point the great contrasts
   Of right and of wrong :
Free homes and free altars,
   Free prairie and flood, —
The reeds of the Swan's Marsh,
   Whose bloom is of blood !

On the lintels of Kansas
   That blood shall not dry ;
Henceforth the Bad Angel
   Shall harmless go by ;

Henceforth to the sunset,
　Unchecked on her way,
Shall Liberty follow
　The march of the day.

"THE ROCK" IN EL GHOR.

DEAD Petra in her hill-tomb sleeps,
　Her stones of emptiness remain ;
Around her sculptured mystery sweeps
　The lonely waste of Edom's plain.

From the doomed dwellers in the cleft
　The bow of vengeance turns not back ;
Of all her myriads none are left
　Along the Wady Mousa's track.

Clear in the hot Arabian day
　Her arches spring, her statues climb ;
Unchanged, the graven wonders pay
　No tribute to the spoiler, Time !

Unchanged the awful lithograph
　Of power and glory undertrod, —
Of nations scattered like the chaff
　Blown from the threshing-floor of God.

Yet shall the thoughtful stranger turn
　From Petra's gates, with deeper awe
To mark afar the burial urn
　Of Aaron on the cliffs of Hor ;

And where upon its ancient guard
　Thy Rock, El Ghor, is standing yet,—
Looks from its turrets desertward,
　And keeps the watch that God has
　　set.

The same as when in thunders loud
　It heard the voice of God to man, —
As when it saw in fire and cloud
　The angels walk in Israel's van !

Or when from Ezion-Geber's way
　It saw the long procession file,
And heard the Hebrew timbrels play
　The music of the lordly Nile ;

Or saw the tabernacle pause,
　Cloud-bound, by Kadesh Barnea's
　　wells,
While Moses graved the sacred laws,
　And Aaron swung his golden bells.

Rock of the desert, prophet-sung !
　How grew its shadowing pile at length,

A symbol, in the Hebrew tongue,
　Of God's eternal love and strength.

On lip of bard and scroll of seer,
　From age to age went down the name,
Until the Shiloh's promised year,
　And Christ, the Rock of Ages, came !

The path of life we walk to-day
　Is strange as that the Hebrews trod ;
We need the shadowing rock, as they,—
　We need, like them, the guides of God.

God send his angels, Cloud and Fire,
　To lead us o'er the desert sand !
God give our hearts their long desire,
　His shadow in a weary land !

ON A PRAYER–BOOK,

WITH ITS FRONTISPIECE, ARY SCHEF-
FER'S "CHRISTUS CONSOLATOR,"
AMERICANIZED BY THE OMISSION OF
THE BLACK MAN.

O ARY SCHEFFER ! when beneath thine
　eye,
　Touched with the light that cometh
　　from above,
　Grew the sweet picture of the dear
　　Lord's love,
No dream hadst thou that Christian
　hands would tear
Therefrom the token of his equal care,
　And make thy symbol of his truth a
　　lie !
The poor, dumb slave whose shackles
　　fall away
　In his compassionate gaze, grubbed
　　smoothly out,
　To mar no more the exercise devout
Of sleek oppression kneeling down to
　pray
Where the great oriel stains the Sabbath
　day !
Let whoso can before such praying-books
　Kneel on his velvet cushion ; I, for
　　one,
　Would sooner bow, a Parsee, to the
　　sun,
　Or tend a prayer-wheel in Thibetar
　　brooks,
　Or beat a drum on Yedo's temple-
　　floor.
No falser idol man has bowed before,
　In Indian groves or islands of the sea,

Than that which through the quaint-
carved Gothic door
Looks forth, — a Church without hu-
manity !
Patron of pride, and prejudice, and
wrong, —
The rich man's charm and fetish of
the strong,
The Eternal Fulness meted, clipped, and
shorn,
The seamless robe of equal mercy torn,
The dear Christ hidden from his kindred
flesh,
And, in his poor ones, crucified afresh !
Better the simple Lama scattering wide,
Where sweeps the storm Alcchan's
steppes along,
His paper horses for the lost to ride,
And wearying Buddha with his prayers
to make
The figures living for the traveller's sake,
Than he who hopes with cheap praise to
beguile
The ear of God, dishonoring man the
while ;
Who dreams the pearl gate's hinges,
rusty grown,
Are moved by flattery's oil of tongue
alone ;
That in the scale Eternal Justice bears
The generous deed weighs less than self-
ish prayers,
And words intoned with graceful unction
move
The Eternal Goodness more than lives
of truth and love.
Alas, the Church ! — The reverend head
of Jay,
Enhaloed with its saintly silvered hair,
Adorns no more the places of her
prayer ;
And brave young Tyng, too early called
away,
Troubles the Haman of her courts no
more
Like the just Hebrew at the Assyrian's
door ;
And her sweet ritual, beautiful but
dead
As the dry husk from which the grain
is shed,
And holy hymns from which the life
devout
Of saints and martyrs has wellnigh
gone out,
Like candles dying in exhausted
air,

For Sabbath use in measured grists are
ground ;
And, ever while the spiritual mill goes
round,
Between the upper and the nether
stones,
Unseen, unheard, the wretched bondman groans,
And urges his vain plea, prayer-smoth-
ered, anthem-drowned !

O heart of mine, keep patience ! — Look-
ing forth,
As from the Mount of Vision, I behold,
Pure, just, and free, the Church of Christ
on earth, —
The martyr's dream, the golden age
foretold !
And found, at last, the mystic Graal I
see,
Brimmed with His blessing, pass from
lip to lip
In sacred pledge of human fellowship ;
And over all the songs of angels hear, —
Songs of the love that casteth out all
fear, —
Songs of the Gospel of Humanity !
Lo ! in the midst, with the same look
he wore,
Healing and blessing on Genesaret's
shore,
Folding together, with the all-tender
might
Of his great love, the dark hands and
the white,
Stands the Consoler, soothing every
pain,
Making all burdens light, and breaking
every chain.

TO J. T. F.

ON A BLANK LEAF OF "POEMS PRINT-
ED, NOT PUBLISHED."

WELL thought ! who would not rather
hear
The songs to Love and Friendship sung
Than those which move the stranger's
tongue,
And feed his unselected ear ?

Our social joys are more than fame.
Life withers in the public look.
Why mount the pillory of a book,
Or barter comfort for a name ?

Who in a house of glass would dwell,
With curious eyes at every pane ?
To ring him in and out again,
Who wants the public crier's bell ?

To see the angel in one's way,
Who waits to play the ass's part, —
Bear on his back the wizard Art,
And in his service speak or bray ?

And who his manly locks would shave,
And quench the eyes of common sense,
To share the noisy recompense
That mocked the shorn and blinded
    slave ?

The heart has needs beyond the head,
And, starving in the plenitude
Of strange gifts, craves its common
    food, —
Our human nature's daily bread.

We are but men : no gods are we,
To sit in mid-heaven, cold and bleak,
Each separate, on his painful peak,
Thin-cloaked in self-complacency !

Better his lot whose axe is swung
In Wartburg woods, or that poor girl's
Who by the Ilm her spindle whirls
And sings the songs that Luther sung,

Than his who, old, and cold, and vain,
At Weimar sat, a demigod,
And bowed with Jove's imperial nod
His votaries in and out again !

Ply, Vanity, thy wingéd feet !
Ambition, hew thy rocky stair !
Who envies him who feeds on air
The icy splendor of his seat ?

I see your Alps, above me, cut
The dark, cold sky ; and dim and lone
I see ye sitting, — stone on stone, —
With human senses dulled and shut.

I could not reach you, if I would,
Nor sit among your cloudy shapes ;
And (spare the fable of the grapes
And fox) I would not if I could.

Keep to your lofty pedestals !
The safer plain below I choose :
Who never wins can rarely lose,
Who never climbs as rarely falls.

Let such as love th
Divide with him hi
For me shall gentl
The valley-song of

The pastoral bleat,
The flail-beat chim
The cattle-low, at
The voice of God i

Then lend thy han
And help me to th
(In truth, I have n
Where sweet with
    tend.

THE PA

Is it the palm, the
On the Indian Sea,
Or is it a ship in tl

A ship whose keel
Whose ribs of pal
    sheath,
And a rudder of pa

Branches of palm a
Fibres of palm are
And the rope is of

What does the goo
The cocoa-nut with
And the milky sap

What are its jars, a
But hollowed nuts
    wine,
And the cabbage t
    Line ?

Who smokes his na
The master, whose
    could charm
Cargo and ship from

In the cabin he sits
From a beaker of
    quaffed,
And a palm-thatch
    aloft !

His dress is woven
And he holds a pa
    hands,
Traced with the l
    mands !

The turban folded about his head
Was daintily wrought of the palm-leaf
    braid,
And the fan that cools him of palm was
    made.

Of threads of palm was the carpet spun
Whereon he kneels when the day is done,
And the foreheads of Islam are bowed as
    one !

To him the palm is a gift divine,
Wherein all uses of man combine, —
House, and raiment, and food, and wine !

And, in the hour of his great release,
His need of the palm shall only cease
With the shroud wherein he lieth in
    peace.

" Allah il Allah ! " he sings his psalm,
On the Indian Sea, by the isles of balm ;
" Thanks to Allah who gives the palm ! "

LINES,

READ AT THE BOSTON CELEBRATION OF
THE HUNDREDTH ANNIVERSARY OF
THE BIRTH OF ROBERT BURNS, 25TH
1ST MO., 1859.

How sweetly come the holy psalms
    From saints and martyrs down,
The waving of triumphal palms
    Above the thorny crown !
The choral praise, the chanted prayers
    From harps by angels strung,
The hunted Cameron's mountain airs,
    The hymns that Luther sung !

Yet, jarring not the heavenly notes,
    The sounds of earth are heard,
As through the open minster floats
    The song of breeze and bird !
Not less the wonder of the sky
    That daisies bloom below ;
The brook sings on, though loud and
    high
    The cloudy organs blow !

And, if the tender ear be jarred
    That, haply, hears by turns
The saintly harp of Olney's bard,
    The pastoral pipe of Burns,
No discord mars His perfect plan
    Who gave them both a tongue ;

For he who sings the love of man
    The love of God hath sung !

To-day be every fault forgiven
    Of him in whom we joy !
We take, with thanks, the gold of Heaven
    And leave the earth's alloy.
Be ours his music as of spring,
    His sweetness as of flowers,
The songs the bard himself might sing
    In holier ears than ours.

Sweet airs of love and home, the hum
    Of household melodies,
Come singing, as the robins come
    To sing in door-yard trees.
And, heart to heart, two nations lean,
    No rival wreaths to twine,
But blending in eternal green
    The holly and the pine !

THE RED RIVER VOYAGEUR.

Out and in the river is winding
    The links of its long, red chain
Through belts of dusky pine-land
    And gusty leagues of plain.

Only, at times, a smoke-wreath
    With the drifting cloud-rack joins, —
The smoke of the hunting-lodges
    Of the wild Assiniboins !

Drearily blows the north-wind
    From the land of ice and snow ;
The eyes that look are weary,
    And heavy the hands that row.

And with one foot on the water,
    And one upon the shore,
The Angel of Shadow gives warning
    That day shall be no more.

Is it the clang of wild-geese ?
    Is it the Indian's yell,
That lends to the voice of the north
    wind
    The tones of a far-off bell ?

The voyageur smiles as he listens
    To the sound that grows apace ;
Well he knows the vesper ringing
    Of the bells of St. Boniface.

The bells of the Roman Mission,
    That call from their turrets twain,

To the boatman on the river,
  To the hunter on the plain!

Even so in our mortal journey
  The bitter north-winds blow,
And thus upon life's Red River
  Our hearts, as oarsmen, row.

And when the Angel of Shadow
  Rests his feet on wave and shore,
And our eyes grow dim with watching
  And our hearts faint at the oar,

Happy is he who heareth
  The signal of his release
In the bells of the Holy City,
  The chimes of eternal peace!

KENOZA LAKE.

As Adam did in Paradise,
  To-day the primal right we claim:
Fair mirror of the woods and skies,
  We give to thee a name.

Lake of the pickerel! — let no more
  The echoes answer back, "Great Pond,"
But sweet Kenoza, from thy shore
  And watching hills beyond,

Let Indian ghosts, if such there be
  Who ply unseen their shadowy lines,
Call back the ancient name to thee,
  As with the voice of pines.

The shores we trod as barefoot boys,
  The nutted woods we wandered
    through,
To friendship, love, and social joys
  We consecrate anew.

Here shall the tender song be sung,
  And memory's dirges soft and low,
And wit shall sparkle on the tongue,
  And mirth shall overflow,

Harmless as summer lightning plays
  From a low, hidden cloud by night,
A light to set the hills ablaze,
  But not a bolt to smite.

In sunny South and prairied West
  Are exiled hearts remembering still,

As bees their hive, as birds their nest,
  The homes of Haverhill.

They join us in our rites to-day;
  And, listening, we may hear, ere-
    long,
From inland lake and ocean bay,
  The echoes of our song.

Kenoza! o'er no sweeter lake
  Shall morning break or noon-cloud
    sail, —
No fairer face than thine shall take
  The sunset's golden veil.

Long be it ere the tide of trade
  Shall break with harsh-resounding
    din
The quiet of thy banks of shade,
  And hills that fold thee in.

Still let thy woodlands hide the hare,
  The shy loon sound his trumpet-note,
Wing-weary from his fields of air,
  The wild-goose on thee float.

Thy peace rebuke our feverish stir,
  Thy beauty our deforming strife;
Thy woods and waters minister
  The healing of their life.

And sinless Mirth, from care released,
  Behold, unawed, thy mirrored sky,
Smiling as smiled on Cana's feast
  The Master's loving eye.

And when the summer day grows dim,
  And light mists walk thy mimic sea,
Revive in us the thought of Him
  Who walked on Galilee!

TO G. B. C.

So spake Esaias: so, in words of flame,
Tekoa's prophet-herdsman smote with
    blame
The traffickers in men, and put to shame,
  All earth and heaven before,
The sacerdotal robbers of the poor.

All the dread Scripture lives for thee
    again,
To smite like lightning on the hinds
    profane
Lifted to bless the slave-whip and the
    chain.

Once more the old Hebrew tongue
Bends with the shafts of God a bow
   new-strung !

Take up the mantle which the prophets
   wore ;
Warn with their warnings, — show the
 • Christ once more
Bound, scourged, and crucified in his
   blameless poor ;
And shake above our land
The unquenched bolts that blazed in
   Hosea's hand !

Not vainly shalt thou cast upon our
   years
The solemn burdens of the Orient seers,
And smite with truth a guilty nation's
   ears.
   Mightier was Luther's word
Than Seckingen's mailed arm or Hut-
   ton's sword !

THE SISTERS.

A PICTURE BY BARRY.

The shade for me, but over thee
  The lingering sunshine still ;
As, smiling, to the silent stream
  Comes down the singing rill.

So come to me, my little one, —
  My years with thee I share,
And mingle with a sister's love
  A mother's tender care.

But keep the smile upon thy lip,
  The trust upon thy brow ;
Since for the dear one God hath called
  We have an angel now.

Our mother from the fields of heaven
  Shall still her ear incline ;
Nor need we fear her human love
  Is less for love divine.

The songs are sweet they sing beneath
  The trees of life so fair,
But sweetest of the songs of heaven
  Shall be her children's prayer.

Then, darling, rest upon my breast,
  And teach my heart to lean
With thy sweet trust upon the arm
  Which folds us both unseen !

LINES,

FOR THE AGRICULTURAL AND HORTI-CULTURAL EXHIBITION AT AMESBURY AND SALISBURY, SEPT. 28, 1858.

This day, two hundred years ago,
  The wild grape by the river's side,
And tasteless groundnut trailing low,
  The table of the woods supplied.

Unknown the apple's red and gold,
  The blushing tint of peach and pear ;
The mirror of the Powow told
  No tale of orchards ripe and rare.

Wild as the fruits he scorned to till,
  These vales the idle Indian trod ;
Nor knew the glad, creative skill, —
  The joy of him who toils with God.

O Painter of the fruits and flowers !
  We thank thee for thy wise design
Whereby these human hands of ours
  In Nature's garden work with thine.

And thanks that from our daily need
  The joy of simple faith is born ;
That he who smites the summer weed,
  May trust thee for the autumn corn.

Give fools their gold, and knaves their
   power ;
  Let fortune's bubbles rise and fall ;
Who sows a field, or trains a flower,
  Or plants a tree, is more than all.

For he who blesses most is blest ;
  And God and man shall own his worth
Who toils to leave as his bequest
  An added beauty to the earth.

And, soon or late, to all that sow,
  The time of harvest shall be given :
The flower shall bloom, the fruit shall
   grow,
  If not on earth, at last in heaven

THE PREACHER.

Its windows flashing to the sky,
  Beneath a thousand roofs of brown,
Far down the vale, my friend and I
  Beheld the old and quiet town ;
The ghostly sails that out at sea
Flapped their white wings of mystery

The beaches glimmering in the sun,
And the low wooded capes that run
Into the sea-mist north and south ;
The sand-bluffs at the river's mouth ;
The swinging chain-bridge, and, afar,
The foam-line of the harbor-bar.

Over the woods and meadow-lands
  A crimson-tinted shadow lay
  Of clouds through which the setting
    day
  Flung a slant glory far away.
It glittered on the wet sea-sands,
It flamed upon the city's panes,
Smote the white sails of ships that wore
Outward or in, and glided o'er
  The steeples with their veering vanes !

Awhile my friend with rapid search
  O'erran the landscape. "Yonder spire
  Over gray roofs, a shaft of fire ;
What is it, pray ?" — "The Whitefield
    Church !
Walled about by its basement stones,
There rest the marvellous prophet's
    bones."
Then as our homeward way we walked,
Of the great preacher's life we talked ;
And through the mystery of our theme
  The outward glory seemed to stream,
  And Nature's self interpreted
  The doubtful record of the dead ;
And every level beam that smote
The sails upon the dark afloat
  A symbol of the light became
  Which touched the shadows of our
    blame
  With tongues of Pentecostal flame.

Over the roofs of the pioneers
Gathers the moss of a hundred years ;
On man and his works has passed the
    change
Which needs must be in a century's
    range.
The land lies open and warm in the sun,
Anvils clamor and mill-wheels run, —
Flocks on the hillsides, herds on the
    plain,
The wilderness gladdened with fruit and
    grain !
But the living faith of the settlers old
A dead profession their children hold ;
To the lust of office and greed of trade
A stepping-stone is the altar made.
The Church, to place and power the
    door,

Rebukes the sin of the world no more,
Nor sees its Lord in the homeless poor.
Everywhere is the grasping hand,
And eager adding of land to land ;
And earth, which seemed to the fathers
    meant
But as a pilgrim's wayside tent, —
A nightly shelter to fold away
When the Lord should call at the break
    of day, —
Solid and steadfast seems to be,
And Time has forgotten Eternity !

But fresh and green from the rotting
    roots
Of primal forests the young growth
    shoots ;
From the death of the old the new pro-
    ceeds,
And the life of truth from the rot of
    creeds :
On the ladder of God, which upward leads,
The steps of progress are human needs.
For his judgments still are a mighty
    deep,
And the eyes of his providence never
    sleep :
When the night is darkest he gives the
    morn ;
When the famine is sorest, the wine
    and corn !

In the church of the wilderness Edwards
    wrought,
Shaping his creed at the forge of
    thought ;
And with Thor's own hammer welded
    and bent
The iron links of his argument,
Which strove to grasp in its mighty span
The purpose of God and the fate of man !
Yet faithful still, in his daily round
To the weak, and the poor, and sin-sick
    found,
The schoolman's lore and the casuist's art
Drew warmth and life from his fervent
    heart.
Had he not seen in the solitudes
Of his deep and dark Northampton
    woods
A vision of love about him fall !
Not the blinding splendor which fell on
    Saul,
But the tenderer glory that rests on them
Who walk in the New Jerusalem,
Where never the sun nor moon are
    known,

But the Lord and his love are the light
  alone !
And watching the sweet, still countenance
Of the wife of his bosom rapt in trance,
Had he not treasured each broken word
Of the mystical wonder seen and heard ;
And loved the beautiful dreamer more
That thus to the desert of earth she bore
Clusters of Eschol from Canaan's shore ?

As the barley-winnower, holding with
  pain
Aloft in waiting his chaff and grain,
Joyfully welcomes the far-off breeze
Sounding the pine-tree's slender keys,
So he who had waited long to hear
The sound of the Spirit drawing near,
Like that which the son of Iddo heard
When the feet of angels the myrtles
  stirred,
Felt the answer of prayer, at last,
As over his church the afflatus passed,
Breaking its sleep as breezes break
To sun-bright ripples a stagnant lake.

At first a tremor of silent fear,
The creep of the flesh at danger near,
A vague foreboding and discontent,
Over the hearts of the people went.
All nature warned in sounds and signs :
The wind in the tops of the forest pines
In the name of the Highest called to
  prayer,
As the muezzin calls from the minaret
  stair.
Through ceiléd chambers of secret sin
Sudden and strong the light shone in ;
A guilty sense of his neighbor's needs
Startled the man of title-deeds ;
The trembling hand of the worldling
  shook
The dust of years from the Holy Book ;
And the psalms of David, forgotten long,
Took the place of the scoffer's song.

The impulse spread like the outward
  course
Of waters moved by a central force :
The tide of spiritual life rolled down
From inland mountains to seaboard
  town.

Prepared and ready the altar stands
Waiting the prophet's outstretched
  hands
And prayer availing, to downward call
The fiery answer in view of all.

Hearts are like wax in the furnace, who
Shall mould, and shape, and cast them
  anew ?
Lo ! by the Merrimack WHITEFIELD
  stands
In the temple that never was made by
  hands, —
Curtains of azure, and crystal wall,
And dome of the sunshine over all ! —
A homeless pilgrim, with dubious name
Blown about on the winds of fame ;
Now as an angel of blessing classed,
And now as a mad enthusiast.
Called in his youth to sound and gauge
The moral lapse of his race and age,
And, sharp as truth, the contrast draw
Of human frailty and perfect law ;
Possessed by the one dread thought that
  lent
Its goad to his fiery temperament,
Up and down the world he went,
A John the Baptist crying, — Repent !

No perfect whole can our nature make ;
Here or there the circle will break ;
The orb of life as it takes the light
On one side leaves the other in night.
Never was saint so good and great
As to give no chance at St. Peter's gate
For the plea of the Devil's advocate.
So, incomplete by his being's law,
The marvellous preacher had his flaw :
With step unequal, and lame with faults,
His shade on the path of History halts.

Wisely and well said the Eastern bard :
Fear is easy, but love is hard, —
Easy to glow with the Santon's rage,
And walk on the Meccan pilgrimage ;
But he is greatest and best who can
Worship Allah by loving man.

Thus he, — to whom, in the painful
  stress
Of zeal on fire from its own excess,
Heaven seemed so vast and earth so small
That man was nothing, since God was
  all, —
Forgot, as the best at times have done,
That the love of the Lord and of man
  are one.

Little to him whose feet unshod
The thorny path of the desert trod,
Careless of pain, so it led to God,
Seemed the hunger-pang and the poor
  man's wrong,

The weak ones trodden beneath the strong.
Should the worm be chooser ? — the clay withstand
The shaping will of the potter's hand ?

In the Indian fable Arjoon hears
The scorn of a god rebuke his fears :
" Spare thy pity ! " Krishna saith ;
" Not in thy sword is the power of death !
All is illusion, — loss but seems ;
Pleasure and pain are only dreams ;
Who deems he slayeth doth not kill ;
Who counts as slain is living still.
Strike, nor fear thy blow is crime ;
Nothing dies but the cheats of time ;
Slain or slayer, small the odds   ·
To each, immortal as Indra's gods ! "

So by Savannah's banks of shade,
The stones of his mission the preacher laid
On the heart of the negro crushed and rent,
And made of his blood the wall's cement ;
Bade the slave-ship speed from coast to coast
Fanned by the wings of the Holy Ghost ;
And begged, for the love of Christ, the gold
Coined from the hearts in its groaning hold.
What could it matter, more or less
Of stripes, and hunger, and weariness ?
Living or dying, bond or free,   ·
What was time to eternity ?

Alas for the preacher's cherished schemes !
Mission and church are now but dreams ;
Nor prayer nor fasting availed the plan
To honor God through the wrong of man.
Of all his labors no trace remains
Save the bondman lifting his hands in chains.
The woof he wove in the righteous warp
Of freedom-loving Oglethorpe,
Clothes with curses the goodly land,
Changes its greenness and bloom to sand ;
And a century's lapse reveals once more
The slave-ship stealing to Georgia's shore.
Father of Light ! how blind is he
Who sprinkles the altar he rears to Thee
With the blood and tears of humanity !

He erred : Shall we count his gifts as naught ?
Was the work of God in him unwrought ?
The servant may through his deafness err,
And blind may be God's messenger ;
But the errand is sure they go upon, —
The word is spoken, the deed is done.
Was the Hebrew temple less fair and good
That Solomon bowed to gods of wood ?
For his tempted heart and wandering feet,
Were the songs of David less pure and sweet ?
So in light and shadow the preacher went,
God's erring and human instrument ;
And the hearts of the people where he passed   ·
Swayed as the reeds sway in the blast,
Under the spell of a voice which took
In its compass the flow of Siloa's brook,
And the mystical chime of the bells of gold
On the ephod's hem of the priest of old, —
Now the roll of thunder, and now the awe
Of the trumpet heard in the Mount of Law.

A solemn fear on the listening crowd
Fell like the shadow of a cloud.
The sailor reeling from out the ships
Whose masts stood thick in the river-slips
Felt the jest and the curse die on his lips.
Listened the fisherman rude and hard,
The calker rough from the builder's yard,
The man of the market left his load,
The teamster leaned on his bending goad,
The maiden, and youth beside her, felt
Their hearts in a closer union melt,
And saw the flowers of their love in bloom
Down the endless vistas of life to come.
Old age sat feebly brushing away
From his ears the scanty locks of gray ;
And careless boyhood, living the free
Unconscious life of bird and tree,
Suddenly wakened to a sense
Of sin and its guilty consequence.
It was as if an angel's voice   ·
Called the listeners up for their final choice ;
As if a strong hand rent apart

The veils of sense from soul and heart,
Showing in light ineffable
The joys of heaven and woes of hell !
All about in the misty air
The hills seemed kneeling in silent
    prayer ;
The rustle of leaves, the moaning sedge,
The water's lap on its gravelled edge,
The wailing pines, and, far and faint,
The wood-dove's note of sad com-
    plaint, —
To the solemn voice of the preacher
    lent
An undertone as of low lament ;
And the rote of the sea from its sandy
    coast,
On the easterly wind, now heard, now
    lost,
Seemed the murmurous sound of the
    judgment host.

Yet wise men doubted, and good men
    wept,
As that storm of passion above them
    swept,
And, comet-like, adding flame to flame,
The priests of the new Evangel came, —
Davenport, flashing upon the crowd,
Charged like summer's electric cloud,
Now holding the listener still as death
With terrible warnings under breath,
Now shouting for joy, as if he viewed
The vision of Heaven's beatitude !
And Celtic Tennant, his long coat
    bound
Like a monk's with leathern girdle
    round,
Wild with the toss of unshorn hair,
And wringing of hands, and eyes aglare,
Groaning under the world's despair !
Grave pastors, grieving their flocks to
    lose,
Prophesied to the empty pews
That gourds would wither, and mush-
    rooms die,
And noisiest fountains run soonest dry,
Like the spring that gushed in New-
    bury Street,
Under the tramp of the earthquake's
    feet,
A silver shaft in the air and light,
For a single day, then lost in night,
Leaving only, its place to tell,
Sandy fissure and sulphurous smell.
With zeal wing-clipped and white-heat
    cool,
Moved by the spirit in grooves of rule,

No longer harried, and cropped, and
    fleeced,
Flogged by sheriff and cursed by priest,
But by wiser counsels left at ease
To settle quietly on his lees,
And, self-concentred, to count as done
The work which his fathers scarce begun,
In silent protest of letting alone,
The Quaker kept the way of his own, —
A non-conductor among the wires,
With coat of asbestos proof to fires.
And quite unable to mend his pace
To catch the falling manna of grace,
He hugged the closer his little store
Of faith, and silently prayed for more.
And vague of creed and barren of rite,
But holding, as in his Master's sight,
Act and thought to the inner light,
The round of his simple duties walked,
And strove to live what the others talked.

And who shall marvel if evil went
Step by step with the good intent,
And with love and meekness, side by
    side,
Lust of the flesh and spiritual pride ? —
That passionate longings and fancies
    vain
Set the heart on fire and crazed the
    brain ? —
That over the holy oracles
Folly sported with cap and bells ? —
That goodly women and learned men
Marvelling told with tongue and pen
How unweaned children chirped like
    birds
Texts of Scripture and solemn words,
Like the infant seers of the rocky glens
In the Puy de Dome of wild Cevennes :
Or baby Lamas who pray and preach
From Tartar cradles in Buddha's
    speech ?

In the war which Truth or Freedom
    wages
With impious fraud and the wrong of
    ages,
Hate and malice and self-love mar
The notes of triumph with painful jar,
And the helping angels turn aside
Their sorrowing faces the shame to hide.
Never on custom's oiléd grooves
The world to a higher level moves,
But grates and grinds with friction hard
On granite boulder and flinty shard.
The heart must bleed before it feels,
The pool be troubled before it heals ;

Ever by losses the right must gain,
Every good have its birth of pain ;
The active Virtues blush to find
The Vices wearing their badge behind,
And Graces and Charities feel the fire
Wherein the sins of the age expire :
The fiend still rends as of old he rent
The tortured body from which he went.

But Time tests all. In the over-drift
And flow of the Nile, with its annual
    gift,
Who cares for the Hadji's relics sunk ?
Who thinks of the drowned-out Coptic
    monk?
The tide that loosens the temple's
    stones,
And scatters the sacred ibis-bones,
Drives away from the valley-land
That Arab robber, the wandering sand,
Moistens the fields that know no rain,
Fringes the desert with belts of grain,
And bread to the sower brings again.
So the flood of emotion deep and strong
Troubled the land as it swept along,
But left a result of holier lives,
Tenderer mothers and worthier wives.
The husband and father whose children
    fled
And sad wife wept when his drunken
    tread
Frightened peace from his roof-tree's
    shade,
And a rock of offence his hearthstone
    made,
In a strength that was not his own, be-
    gan
To rise from the brute's to the plane of
    man.
Old friends embraced, long held apart
By evil counsel and pride of heart ;
And penitence saw through misty tears,
In the bow of hope on its cloud of fears,
The promise of Heaven's eternal
    years, —
The peace of God for the world's an-
    noy, —
Beauty for ashes, and oil of joy !

Under the church of Federal Street,
Under the tread of its Sabbath feet,
Walled about by its basement stones,
Lie the marvellous preacher's bones.
No saintly honors to them are shown,
No sign nor miracle have they known ;
But he who passes the ancient church
Stops in the shade of its belfry-porch,
And ponders the wonderful life of him
Who lies at rest in that charnel dim.
Long shall the traveller strain his eye
From the railroad car, as it plunges by,
And the vanishing town behind him
    search
For the slender spire of the Whitefield
    Church ;
And feel for one moment the ghosts of
    trade,
And fashion, and folly, and pleasure
    laid,
By the thought of that life of pure in-
    tent,
That voice of warning yet eloquent,
Of one on the errands of angels sent.
And if where he labored the flood of sin
Like a tide from the harbor-bar sets in,
And over a life of time and sense
The church-spires lift their vain de-
    fence,
As if to scatter the bolts of God
With the points of Calvin's thunder-
    rod, —
Still, as the gem of its civic crown,
Precious beyond the world's renown,
His memory hallows the ancient town !

THE QUAKER ALUMNI.[70]

FROM the well-springs of Hudson, the
    sea-cliffs of Maine,
Grave men, sober matrons, you gather
    again ;
And, with hearts warmer grown as
    your heads grow more cool,
Play over the old game of going to
    school.

All your strifes and vexations, your
    whims and complaints,
(You were not saints yourselves, if the
    children of saints !)
All your petty self-seekings and rival-
    ries done,
Round the dear Alma Mater your hearts
    beat as one !

How widely soe'er you have strayed
    from the fold,
Though your " thee " has grown " you,"
    and your drab blue and gold,
To the old friendly speech and the
    garb's sober form,
Like the heart of Argyle to the tartan,
    you warm.

But, the first greetings over, you glance
    round the hall ;
Your hearts call the roll, but they an-
    swer not all :
Through the turf green above them the
    dead cannot hear ;
Name by name, in the silence, falls sad
    as a tear !

In love, let us trust, they were sum-
    moned so soon
From the morning of life, while we toil
    through its noon ;
They were frail like ourselves, they had
    needs like our own,
And they rest as we rest in God's mercy
    alone.

Unchanged by our changes of spirit and
    frame,
Past, now, and henceforward the Lord
    is the same ;
Though we sink in the darkness, his
    arms break our fall,
And in death as in life, he is Father of
    all !

We are older : our footsteps, so light in
    the play
Of the far-away school-time, move slower
    to-day ; —
Here a beard touched with frost, there a
    bald, shining crown,
And beneath the cap's border gray min-
    gles with brown.

But faith should be cheerful, and trust
    should be glad,
And our follies and sins, not our years,
    make us sad.
Should the heart closer shut as the
    bonnet grows prim,
And the face grow in length as the hat
    grows in brim ?

Life is brief, duty grave ; but, with rain-
    folded wings,
Of yesterday's sunshine the grateful
    heart sings ;
And we, of all others, have reason to
    pay
The tribute of thanks, and rejoice on
    our way ;

For the counsels that turned from the
    follies of youth ;
For the beauty of patience, the white-
    ness of truth ;

For the wounds of rebuke, when love
    tempered its edge ;
For the household's restraint, and the
    discipline's hedge ;

For the lessons of kindness vouchsafed
    to the least
Of the creatures of God, whether human
    or beast,
Bringing hope to the poor, lending
    strength to the frail,
In the lanes of the city, the slave-hut,
    and jail ;

For a womanhood higher and holier, by
    all
Her knowledge of good, than was Eve
    ere her fall, —
Whose task-work of duty moves lightly
    as play,
Serene as the moonlight and warm as
    the day ;

And, yet more, for the faith which em-
    braces the whole,
Of the creeds of the ages the life and the
    soul,
Wherein letter and spirit the same
    channel run,
And man has not severed what God has
    made one !

For a sense of the Goodness revealed
    everywhere,
As sunshine impartial, and free as the
    air ;
For a trust in humanity, Heathen or
    Jew,
And a hope for all darkness The Light
    shineth through.

Who scoffs at our birthright ? — the
    words of the seers,
And the songs of the bards in the twi-
    light of years,
All the foregleams of wisdom in santon
    and sage,
In prophet and priest, are our true
    heritage.

The Word which the reason of Plato
    discerned ;
The truth, as whose symbol the Mithra-
    fire burned ;
The soul of the world which the Stoic
    but guessed,
In the Light Universal the Quaker con-
    fessed !

No honors of war to our worthies belong;
Their plain stem of life never flowered
into song;
But the fountains they opened still gush
by the way,
And the world for their healing is better
to-day.

He who lies where the minster's groined
arches curve down
To the tomb-crowded transept of England's renown,
The glorious essayist, by genius enthroned,
Whose pen as a sceptre the Muses all
owned, —

Who through the world's pantheon
walked in his pride,
Setting new statues up, thrusting old
ones aside,
And in fiction the pencils of history
dipped,
To gild o'er or blacken each saint in his
crypt, —

How vainly he labored to sully with
blame
The white bust of Penn, in the niche of
his fame!
Self-will is self-wounding, perversity
blind:
On himself fell the stain for the Quaker
designed!

For the sake of his true-hearted father
before him;
For the sake of the dear Quaker mother
that bore him;
For the sake of his gifts, and the works
that outlive him,
And his brave words for freedom, we
freely forgive him!

There are those who take note that our
numbers are small, —
New Gibbons who write our decline and
our fall;
But the Lord of the seed-field takes care
of his own,
And the world shall yet reap what our
sowers have sown.

The last of the sect to his fathers may go,
Leaving only his coat for some Barnum
to show;

But the truth will outlive him, and
broaden with years,
Till the false dies away, and the wrong
disappears.

Nothing fails of its end. Out of sight
sinks the stone,
In the deep sea of time, but the circles
sweep on,
Till the low-rippled murmurs along the
shores run,
And the dark and dead waters leap glad
in the sun.

Meanwhile shall we learn, in our ease,
to forget
To the martyrs of Truth and of Freedom
our debt? —
Hide their words out of sight, like the
garb that they wore,
And for Barclay's Apology offer one
more?

Shall we fawn round the priestcraft that
glutted the shears,
And festooned the stocks with our grandfathers' ears? —
Talk of Woolman's unsoundness? — count
Penn heterodox?
And take Cotton Mather in place of
George Fox? —

Make our preachers war-chaplains? —
quote Scripture to take
The hunted slave back, for Onesimus'
sake? —
Go to burning church-candles, and chant-
• ing in choir,
And on the old meeting-house stick up
a spire?

No! the old paths we'll keep until better are shown,
Credit good where we find it, abroad or
our own;
And while "Lo here" and "Lo there"
the multitude call,
Be true to ourselves, and do justice to
all.

The good round about us we need not
refuse,
Nor talk of our Zion as if we were Jews;
But why shirk the badge which our
fathers have worn,
Or beg the world's pardon for having
been born?

We need not pray over the Pharisee's
    prayer,
Nor claim that our wisdom is Benjamin's
    share.
Truth to us and to others is equal and
    one :
Shall we bottle the free air, or hoard up
    the sun ?

Well know we our birthright may serve
    but to show
How the meanest of weeds in the richest
    soil grow ;
But we need not disparage the good
    which we hold ;
Though the vessels be earthen, the treas-
    ure is gold !   .

Enough and too much of the sect and
    the name.
What matters our label, so truth be our
    aim ?
The creed may be wrong, but the life
    may be true,
And hearts beat the same under drab
    coats or blue.

So the man be a man, let him worship,
    at will,
In Jerusalem's courts, or on Gerizim's
    hill.
When she makes up her jewels, what
    cares yon good town
For the Baptist of WAYLAND, the Quaker
    of BROWN ?

And this green, favored island, so fresh
    and sea-blown,
When she counts up the worthies her
    annals have known,
Never waits for the pitiful gaugers of
    sect
To measure her love, and mete out her
    respect.

Three shades at this moment seem walk-
    ing her strand,
Each with head halo-crowned, and with
    palms in his hand, —
Wise Berkeley, grave Hopkins, and, smil-
    ing serene
On prelate and puritan, Channing is
    seen.

One holy name bearing, no longer they
    need
Credentials of party, and pass-words of
    creed :

The new song they sing hath a threefold
    accord,
And they own one baptism, one faith,
    and one Lord !

But the golden sands run out : occasions
    like these
Glide swift into shadow, like sails on
    the seas :
While we sport with the mosses and
    pebbles ashore,
They lessen and fade, and we see them
    no more.

Forgive me, dear friends, if my vagrant
    thoughts seem
Like a school-boy's who idles and plays
    with his theme.
Forgive the light measure whose changes
    display
The sunshine and rain of our brief April
    day.

There are moments in life when the lip
    and the eye
Try the question of whether to smile or
    to cry ;
And scenes and reunions that prompt
    like our own
The tender in feeling, the playful in
    tone.

I, who never sat down with the boys and
    the girls
At the feet of your Slocums, and Cart-
    lands, and Earles, —
By courtesy only permitted to lay
On your festival's altar my poor gift, to-
    day, —

I would joy in your joy : let me have a
    friend's part
In the warmth of your welcome of hand
    and of heart, —
On your play-ground of boyhood unbend
    the brow's care,
And shift the old burdens our shoulders
    must bear.

Long live the good School ! giving out
    year by year
Recruits to true manhood and woman-
    hood dear :
Brave boys, modest maidens, in beauty
    sent forth,
The living epistles and proof of its worth !

In and out let the young life as steadily
  flow
As in broad Narragansett the tides come
  and go ;
And its sons and its daughters in prairie
  and town
Remember its honor, and guard its renown.

Not vainly the gift of its founder was
  made ;
Not prayerless the stones of its corner
  were laid :
The blessing of Him whom in secret they
  sought
Has owned the good work which the
  fathers have wrought.

To Him be the glory forever ! — We bear
To the Lord of the Harvest our wheat
  with the tare.
What we lack in our work may He find
  in our will,
And winnow in mercy our good from the
  ill !

BROWN OF OSSAWATOMIE.

JOHN BROWN OF OSSAWATOMIE spake
  on his dying day :
" I will not have to shrive my soul a
  priest in Slavery's pay.
But let some poor slave-mother whom I
  have striven to free,
With her children, from the gallows-
  stair put up a prayer for me ! "

John Brown of Ossawatomie, they led
  him out to die ;
And lo ! a poor slave-mother with her
  little child pressed nigh.
Then the bold, blue eye grew tender,
  and the old harsh face grew mild,
As he stooped between the jeering ranks
  and kissed the negro's child !

The shadows of his stormy life that moment fell apart ;
And they who blamed the bloody hand
  forgave the loving heart.
That kiss from all its guilty means redeemed the good intent,
And round the grisly fighter's hair the
  martyr's aureole bent !

Perish with him
  through evil
Long live the gener(
  with human
Not the raid of mic
  thought whi
Not the borderer's
  the Christia

Nevermore may y(
  Northern ri(
Nor see the light o
  on the negr(
But let the free-
  their guarde
To teach that right
  and justice 1

So vainly shall Vi
  in array ;
In vain her trampl
  the winter s
She may strike the
  she dares nc
And every gate sh
  open wide t(

FROM 1

" The thing which h
people from the Pope,
— the breaking point 1
has been the encourag
gave to the officer un
the slaughters of Perug
ing point in many hon
to him before." — Har.
ters from Italy."

THE tall, sallow g(
  tails have s(
Flaming out in the
  red ;
And behind go th
  and buff,
And the chamberla
  and ruff ;
Next, in red-legg
  cardinals for
Each a lord of the
  of the earth

What 's this squeal
  batter of dr(
Lo ! the Swiss of
  rugia come,
The militant angel
  home
To the hearts of th
  and abhorre

The good Father's missives, and "Thus
  saith the Lord!"
And lend to his logic the point of the
  sword!

O maids of Etruria, gazing forlorn
O'er dark Thrasymenus, dishevelled and
  torn!
O fathers, who pluck at your gray beards
  for shame!
O mothers, struck dumb by a woe without name!
Well ye know how the Holy Church
  hireling behaves,
And his tender compassion of prisons
  and graves!

There they stand, the hired stabbers,
  the blood-stains yet fresh,
That splashed like red wine from the
  vintage of flesh, —
Grim instruments, careless as pincers
  and rack
How the joints tear apart, and the
  strained sinews crack;
But the hate that glares on them is
  sharp as their swords,
And the sneer and the scowl print the
  air with fierce words!

Off with hats, down with knees, shout
  your vivas like mad!
Here's the Pope in his holiday righteousness clad,
From shorn crown to toe-nail, kiss-worn
  to the quick,
Of sainthood in purple the pattern and
  pick,
Who the *rôle* of the priest and the soldier unites,
And, praying like Aaron, like Joshua
  fights!

Is this Pio Nono the gracious, for whom
We sang our hosannas and lighted all
  Rome;
With whose advent we dreamed the new
  era began
When the priest should be human, the
  monk be a man?
Ah, the wolf's with the sheep, and the
  fox with the fowl,
When freedom we trust to the crozier
  and cowl!

Stand aside, men of Rome! Here's a
  hangman-faced Swiss —

(A blessing for him surely can't go
  amiss) —
Would kneel down the sanctified slipper
  to kiss.
Short shrift will suffice him, — he's
  blest beyond doubt;
But there's blood on his hands which
  would scarcely wash out,
Though Peter himself held the baptismal
  spout!

Make way for the next! Here's another
  sweet son!
What's this mastiff-jawed rascal in epau-
  lets done?
He did, whispers rumor, (its truth God
  forbid!)
At Perugia what Herod at Bethlehem did.
And the mothers? — Don't name them!
  — these humors of war
They who keep him in service must pardon him for.

Hist! here's the arch-knave in a cardinal's hat,
With the heart of a wolf, and the stealth
  of a cat
(As if Judas and Herod together were
  rolled),
Who keeps, all as one, the Pope's conscience and gold,
Mounts guard on the altar, and pilfers
  from thence,
And flatters St. Peter while stealing his
  pence!

Who doubts Antonelli? Have miracles
  ceased
When robbers say mass, and Barabbas is
  priest?
When the Church eats and drinks, at its
  mystical board,
The true flesh and blood carved and
  shed by its sword,
When its martyr, unsinged, claps the
  crown on his head,
And roasts, as his proxy, his neighbor
  instead!

There! the bells jow and jangle the
  same blessed way
That they did when they rang for Bartholomew's day.
Hark! the tallow-faced monsters, nor
  women nor boys,
Vex the air with a shrill, sexless horror
  of noise.

Te Deum laudamus ! — All round without stint
The incense-pot swings with a taint of blood in 't !

And now for the blessing! Of little account,
You know, is the old one they heard on the Mount.
Its giver was landless, his raiment was poor,
No jewelled tiara his fishermen wore ;
No incense, no lackeys, no riches, no home,
No Swiss guards ! — We order things better at Rome.

So bless us the strong hand, and curse us the weak ;
Let Austria's vulture have food for her beak ;
Let the wolf-whelp of Naples play Bomba again,
With his death-cap of silence, and halter, and chain ;
Put reason, and justice, and truth under ban ;
For the sin unforgiven is freedom for man !

FOR AN AUTUMN FESTIVAL.

THE Persian's flowery gifts, the shrine
Of fruitful Ceres, charm no more ;
The woven wreaths of oak and pine
Are dust along the Isthmian shore.

But beauty hath its homage still,
And nature holds us still in debt ;
And woman's grace and household skill,
And manhood's toil, are honored yet.

And we, to-day, amidst our flowers
And fruits, have come to own again
The blessings of the summer hours,
The early and the latter rain ;

To see our Father's hand once more
Reverse for us the plenteous horn
Of autumn, filled and running o'er
With fruit, and flower, and golden corn !

Once more the liberal year laughs out
O'er richer stores than gems or gold ;
Once more with harvest-song and shout
Is Nature's bloodless triumph told.

Our common mother rests and sings,
Like Ruth, among her garnered sheaves ;
Her lap is full of goodly things,
Her brow is bright with autumn leaves.

O favors every year made new !
O gifts with rain and sunshine sent !
The bounty overruns our due,
The fulness shames our discontent.

We shut our eyes, the flowers bloom on ;
We murmur, but the corn-ears fill ;
We choose the shadow, but the sun
That casts it shines behind us still.

God gives us with our rugged soil
The power to make it Eden-fair,
And richer fruits to crown our toil
Than summer-wedded islands bear.

Who murmurs at his lot to-day ?
Who scorns his native fruit and bloom ?
Or sighs for dainties far away,
Beside the bounteous board of home ?

Thank Heaven, instead, that Freedom's arm
Can change a rocky soil to gold, —
That brave and generous lives can warm
A clime with northern ices cold.

And let these altars, wreathed with flowers
And piled with fruits, awake again
Thanksgivings for the golden hours,
The early and the latter rain !

IN WAR TIME.

TO SAMUEL E. SEWALL

AND

HARRIET W. SEWALL,

OF MELROSE.

OLOR ISCANUS queries: "'Why should
    we
Vex at the land's ridiculous miserie?"
So on his Usk banks, in the blood-red
    dawn
Of England's civil strife, did careless
    Vaughan
Bemock his times. O friends of many
    years !
Though faith and trust are stronger
    than our fears,
And the signs promise peace with liberty,
Not thus we trifle with our country's
    tears
And sweat of agony. The future's gain
Is certain as God's truth ; but, mean-
    while, pain
Is bitter and tears are salt : our voices
    take
A sober tone ; our very household songs
Are heavy with a nation's griefs and
    wrongs ;
And innocent mirth is chastened for the
    sake
Of the brave hearts that nevermore shall
    beat,
The eyes that smile no more, the unre-
    turning feet !

THY WILL BE DONE.

WE see not, know not ; all our way
Is night, — with Thee alone is day :
From out the torrent's troubled drift,
Above the storm our prayers we lift,
    Thy will be done !

The flesh may fail, the heart may faint,
But who are we to make complaint,
Or dare to plead, in times like these,
The weakness of our love of ease ?
    Thy will be done !

We take with solemn thankfulness
Our burden up, nor ask it less,
And count it joy that even we
May suffer, serve, or wait for Thee,
    Whose will be done !

Though dim as yet in tint and line,
We trace Thy picture's wise design,
And thank Thee that our age supplies
Its dark relief of sacrifice.
    Thy will be done !

And if, in our unworthiness,
Thy sacrificial wine we press ;
If from Thy ordeal's heated bars
Our feet are seamed with crimson scars,
    Thy will be done !

If, for the age to come, this hour
Of trial hath vicarious power,
And, blest by Thee, our present pain,
Be Liberty's eternal gain,
    Thy will be done !

Strike, Thou the Master, we Thy keys,
The anthem of the destinies !
The minor of Thy loftier strain,
Our hearts shall breathe the old refrain,
    Thy will be done !

A WORD FOR THE HOUR.

THE firmament breaks up. In black
    eclipse
Light after light goes out. One evil
    star,
Luridly glaring through the smoke of
    war,
As in the dream of the Apocalypse,
Drags others down. Let us not weakly
    weep
Nor rashly threaten. Give us grace to
    keep
Our faith and patience ; wherefore
    should we leap
On one hand into fratricidal fight,
Or, on the other, yield eternal right,
Frame lies of law, and good and ill con-
    found ?

What fear we ? Safe on freedom's van-
tage-ground
Our feet are planted : let us there remain
In unrevengeful calm, no means untried
Which truth can sanction, no just claim
denied,
The sad spectators of a suicide !
They break the links of Union : shall
we light
The fires of hell to weld anew the chain
On that red anvil where each blow is
pain ?
Draw we not even now a freer breath,
As from our shoulders falls a load of
death
Loathsome as that the Tuscan's victim
bore
When keen with life to a dead horror
bound ?
Why take we up the accursed thing
again ?
Pity, forgive, but urge them back no
more
Who, drunk with passion, flaunt dis-
union's rag
With its vile reptile-blazon. Let us press
The golden cluster on our brave old flag
In closer union, and, if numbering less,
Brighter shall shine the stars which still
remain.

16th 1st mo., 1861.

"EIN FESTE BURG IST UNSER
GOTT."

(LUTHER'S HYMN.)

WE wait beneath the furnace-blast
  The pangs of transformation ;
Not painlessly doth God recast
  And mould anew the nation.
    Hot burns the fire
    Where wrongs expire ;
    Nor spares the hand
    That from the land
  Uproots the ancient evil.

The hand-breadth cloud the sages feared
  Its bloody rain is dropping ;
The poison plant the fathers spared
  All else is overtopping.
    East, West, South, North,
    It curses the earth ;
    All justice dies,
    And fraud and lies
  Live only in its shadow.

What gives the wheat-field blades of
  steel ?
What points the rebel cannon ?
What sets the roaring rabble's heel
  On the old star-spangled pennon ?
    What breaks the oath
    Of the men o' the South ?
    What whets the knife
    For the Union's life ? —
  Hark to the answer : Slavery !

Then waste no blows on lesser foes
  In strife unworthy freemen.
God lifts to-day the veil, and shows
  The features of the demon !
    O North and South,
    Its victims both,
    Can ye not cry,
    "Let slavery die !" ·
  And union find in freedom !

What though the cast-out spirit tear
  The nation in his going ?
We who have shared the guilt must
  share
  The pang of his o'erthrowing !
    Whate'er the loss,
    Whate'er the cross,
    Shall they complain
    Of present pain
  Who trust in God's hereafter ?

For who that leans on His right arm
  Was ever yet forsaken ?
What righteous cause can suffer harm
  If He its part has taken ?
    Though wild and loud,
    And dark the cloud,
    Behind its folds
    His hand upholds
  The calm sky of to-morrow !

Above the maddening cry for blood,
  Above the wild war-drumming,
Let Freedom's voice be heard, with
  good
  The evil overcoming.
    Give prayer and purse
    To stay the Curse
    Whose wrong we share,
    Whose shame we bear,
  Whose end shall gladden Heaven !

In vain the bells of war shall ring
  Of triumphs and revenges,

While still is spared the evil thing
That severs and estranges.
    But blest the ear
    That yet shall hear
    The jubilant bell
    That rings the knell
Of Slavery forever !

Then let the selfish lip be dumb,
    And hushed the breath of sighing ;
Before the joy of peace must come
    The pains of purifying.
    God give us grace
    Each in his place
    To bear his lot,
    And, murmuring not,
Endure and wait and labor ⊢

TO JOHN C. FREMONT.

THY error, Fremont, simply was to act
A brave man's part, without the states-
        man's tact,
And, taking counsel but of common
        sense,
To strike at cause as well as consequence.
O, never yet since Roland wound his
        horn
At Roncesvalles, has a blast been blown
Far-heard, wide-echoed, startling as
        thine own,
Heard from the van of freedom's hope
        forlorn !
It had been safer, doubtless, for the time,
To flatter treason, and avoid offence
To that Dark Power whose underlying
        crime
Heaves upward its perpetual turbulence.
But if thine be the fate of all who break
The ground for truth's seed, or forerun
        their years
Till lost in distance, or with stout hearts
        make
A lane for freedom through the level
        spears,
Still take thou courage ! God has spoken
        through thee,
Irrevocable, the mighty words, Be free !
The land shakes with them, and the
        slave's dull ear
Turns from the rice-swamp stealthily to
        hear.
Who would recall them now must first
        arrest
The winds that blow down from the free
        Northwest,

Ruffling the Gulf ; or like a scroll roll
        back
The Mississippi to its upper springs.
Such words fulfil their prophecy, and
        lack
But the full time to harden into things.

THE WATCHERS.

BESIDE a stricken field I stood ;
On the torn turf, on grass and wood,
Hung heavily the dew of blood.

Still in their fresh mounds lay the
        slain,
But all the air was quick with pain
And gusty sighs and tearful rain.

Two angels, each with drooping head
And folded wings and noiseless tread,
Watched by that valley of the dead.

The one, with forehead saintly bland
And lips of blessing, not command,
Leaned, weeping, on her olive wand.

The other's brows were scarred and knit,
His restless eyes were watch-fires lit,
His hands for battle-gauntlets fit.

" How long ! " — I knew the voice of
        Peace, —
" Is there no respite ? — no release ? —
When shall the hopeless quarrel cease ?

" O Lord, how long ! — One human soul
Is more than any parchment scroll,
Or any flag thy winds unroll.

" What price was Ellsworth's, young
        and brave ?
How weigh the gift that Lyon gave,
Or count the cost of Winthrop's grave ?

" O brother ! if thine eye can see,
Tell how and when the end shall be,
What hope remains for thee and me."

Then Freedom sternly said : " I shun
No strife nor pang beneath the sun,
When human rights are staked and
        won.   .

" I knelt with Ziska's hunted flock,
I watched in Toussaint's cell of rock,
I walked with Sidney to the block.

"The moor of Marston felt my tread,
Through Jersey snows the march I led,
My voice Magenta's charges sped.

"But now, through weary day and night,
I watch a vague and aimless fight
For leave to strike one blow aright.

"On either side my foe they own :
One guards through love his ghastly
    throne,
And one through fear to reverence
    grown.

"Why wait we longer, mocked, be-
    trayed,
By open foes, or those afraid
To speed thy coming through my aid?

"Why watch to see who win or fall ?—
I shake the dust against them all,
I leave them to their senseless brawl."

"Nay," Peace implored : "yet longer
    wait ;
The doom is near, the stake is great :
God knoweth if it be too late.

"Still wait and watch ; the way prepare
Where I with folded wings of prayer·
May follow, weaponless and bare."

"Too late !" the stern, sad voice re-
    plied,
"Too late !" its mournful echo sighed,
In low lament the answer died.

A rustling as of wings in flight,
An upward gleam of lessening white,
So passed the vision, sound and sight.

But round me, like a silver bell
Rung down the listening sky to tell
Of holy help, a sweet voice fell.

"Still hope and trust," it sang ; "the
    rod
Must fall, the wine-press must be trod,
But all is possible with God !"

TO ENGLISHMEN.

You flung your taunt across the wave ;
    We bore it as became us,
Well knowing that the fettered slave
Left friendly lips no option save
    To pity or to blame us.

You scoffed our plea. "Mere lack of
    will,
    Not lack of power," you told us :
We showed our free-state records ; still
You mocked, confounding good and ill,
    Slave-haters and slaveholders.

We struck at Slavery ; to the verge
    Of power and means we checked it ;
Lo !— presto, change ! its claims you
    urge,
Send greetings to it o'er the surge/
    And comfort and protect it.

But yesterday you scarce could shake,
    In slave-abhorring rigor,
Our Northern palms for conscience' sake :
To-day you clasp the hands that ache
    With "walloping the nigger !" [71]

O Englishmen !— in hope and creed,
    In blood and tongue our brothers !
We too are heirs of Runnymede ;
And Shakespeare's fame and Cromwell's
    . deed
    Are not alone our mother's.

"Thicker than water," in one rill
    Through centuries of story
Our Saxon blood has flowed, and still
We share with you its good and ill,
    The shadow and the glory.

Joint heirs and kinfolk, leagues of wave
    Nor length of years can part us :
Your right is ours to shrine and grave,
The common freehold of the brave,
    The gift of saints and martyrs.

Our very sins and follies teach
    Our kindred frail and human :
We carp at faults with bitter speech,
The while, for one unshared by each,
    We have a score in common.

We bowed the heart, if not the knee,
    To England's Queen, God bless her !
We praised you when your slaves went
    free :
We seek to unchain ours. Will ye
    Join hands with the oppressor ?

And is it Christian England cheers
    The bruiser, not the bruiséd ?
And must she run, despite the tears
And prayers of eighteen hundred years,
    Amuck in Slavery's crusade ?

O black disgrace ! O shame and loss
  Too deep for tongue to phrase on !
Tear from your flag its holy cross,
And in your van of battle toss
  The pirate's skull-bone blazon !

ASTRÆA AT THE CAPITOL.

ABOLITION OF SLAVERY IN THE DIS-
TRICT OF COLUMBIA, 1862.

WHEN first I saw our banner wave
  Above the nation's council-hall,
  I heard beneath its marble wall
The clanking fetters of the slave !

In the foul market-place I stood,
  And saw the Christian mother sold,
  And childhood with its locks of gold,
Blue-eyed and fair with Saxon blood.

I shut my eyes, I held my breath,
  And, smothering down the wrath and
    shame
  That set my Northern blood aflame,
Stood silent, — where to speak was
    death.

Beside me gloomed the prison-cell
  Where wasted one in slow decline
  For uttering simple words of mine,
And loving freedom all too well.

The flag that floated from the dome
  Flapped menace in the morning air;
  I stood a perilled stranger where
The human broker made his home.

For crime was virtue : Gown and Sword
  And Law their threefold sanction gave,
  And to the quarry of the slave
Went hawking with our symbol-bird.

On the oppressor's side was power ;
  And yet I knew that every wrong,
  However old, however strong,
But waited God's avenging hour.

I knew that truth would crush the lie,—
  Somehow, some time, the end would
    be ;
  Yet scarcely dared I hope to see
The triumph with my mortal eye.

But now I see it ! In the sun
  A free flag floats from yonder dome,

And at the nation's hearth and home
  The justice long delayed is done.

Not as we hoped, in calm of prayer,
  The message of deliverance comes,
  But heralded by roll of drums
On waves of battle-troubled air ! —

Midst sounds that madden and appall,
  The song that Bethlehem's shepherds
    knew !
  The harp of David melting through
The demon-agonies of Saul !

Not as we hoped ; — but what are we ?
  Above our broken dreams and plans
  God lays, with wiser hand than man's,
The corner-stones of liberty.

I cavil not with Him : the voice
  That freedom's blessed gospel tells
  Is sweet to me as silver bells,
Rejoicing ! — yea, I will rejoice !

Dear friends still toiling in the sun, —
  Ye dearer ones who, gone before,
  Are watching from the eternal shore
The slow work by your hands begun, —

Rejoice with me ! The chastening rod
  Blossoms with love ; the furnace heat
  Grows cool beneath His blessed feet
Whose form is as the Son of God !

Rejoice ! Our Marah's bitter springs
  Are sweetened ; on our ground of grief
  Rise day by day in strong relief
The prophecies of better things.

Rejoice in hope ! The day and night
  Are one with God, and one with them
  Who see by faith the cloudy hem
Of Judgment fringed with Mercy's light !

THE BATTLE AUTUMN OF 1862.

THE flags of war like storm-birds fly,
  The charging trumpets blow ;
Yet rolls no thunder in the sky,
  No earthquake strives below.

And, calm and patient, Nature keeps
  Her ancient promise well,
Though o'er her bloom and greenness
    sweeps
  The battle's breath of hell.

And still she walks in golden hours
  Through harvest-happy farms,
And still she wears her fruits and flowers
  Like jewels on her arms.

What mean the gladness of the plain,
  This joy of eve and morn,
The mirth that shakes the beard of grain
  And yellow locks of corn ?

Ah ! eyes may well be full of tears,
  And hearts with hate are hot ;
But even-paced come round the years,
  And Nature changes not.

She meets with smiles our bitter grief,
  With songs our groans of pain ;
She mocks with tint of flower and leaf
  The war-field's crimson stain.

Still, in the cannon's pause, we hear
  Her sweet thanksgiving-psalm ;
Too near to God for doubt or fear,
  She shares the eternal calm.

She knows the seed lies safe below
  The fires that blast and burn ;
For all the tears of blood we sow
  She waits the rich return.

She sees with clearer eye than ours
  The good of suffering born, —
The hearts that blossom like her flowers,
  And ripen like her corn.

O, give to us, in times like these,
  The vision of her eyes ;
And make her fields and fruited trees
  Our golden prophecies !

O, give to us her finer ear !
  Above this stormy din,
We too would hear the bells of cheer
  Ring peace and freedom in.

MITHRIDATES AT CHIOS.[72]

Know'st thou, O slave-cursed land !
How, when the Chian's cup of guilt
  Was full to overflow, there came
  God's justice in the sword of flame
That, red with slaughter to its hilt,
Blazed in the Cappadocian victor's hand ?

The heavens are still and far ;
But, not unheard of awful Jove,

The sighing of
Was answered
wave
The keels of Mitl
And the vines shriv
war.

" Robbers of C
The victor cried,
cree !
Pluck your l
vine,
Drain your las
Slaves of your sl
be,
In Colchian mine
dark."

Then rose the
From the hoar se
The priestess
cried,
" Woe ! woe !
less-eyed !"
And, chained and
of slaves,
The lords of Chios

" The gods at
So Hellas sang h
" The fisher in
The Chian hatl
And isle from isle
Took up and sped

Once more the
Bring their aven;
And, more thar
Our wiser lesso
Of slaves uprising
To break, not wie
with their bl

THE PROC

Saint Patrick, sl
herds
Of Ballymena, w
words :
" Arise, and fl
Out from the land
free !"

Glad as a soul in p
heaven
The angels singing

And, wondering, sees
His prison opening to their golden keys,

He rose a man who laid him down a
    slave,
Shook from his locks the ashes of the
    grave,
    And outward trod
Into the glorious liberty of God.

He cast the symbols of his shame away ;
And, passing where the sleeping Milcho
    lay,
    Though back and limb
Smarted with wrong, he prayed, "God
    pardon him !"

So went he forth ; but in God's time he
    came
To light on Uilline's hills a holy flame ;
    And, dying, gave
The land a saint that lost him as a
    slave.

O dark, sad millions, patiently and dumb
Waiting for God, your hour, at last, has
    come,
    And freedom's song
Breaks the long silence of your night of
    wrong !

Arise and flee ! shake off the vile re-
    straint
Of ages ; but, like Ballymena's saint,
    The oppressor spare,
Heap only on his head the coals of
    prayer.

Go forth, like him ! like him return
    again,
To bless the land whereon in bitter pain
    Ye toiled at first,
And heal with freedom what your slav-
    ery cursed.

ANNIVERSARY POEM.

[Read before the Alumni of the Friends' Yearly
Meeting School, at the Annual Meeting at Newport, R. I , 15th 6th mo., 1863.]

ONCE more, dear friends, you meet be-
    neath
    A clouded sky :
Not yet the sword has found its sheath,
And on the sweet spring airs the breath
    Of war floats by.

Yet trouble springs not from the ground,
    Nor pain from chance ;
The Eternal orders circles round,
And wave and storm find mete and
    bound
    In Providence.

Full long our feet the flowery ways
    Of peace have trod,
Content with creed and garb and phrase :
A harder path in earlier days
    Led up to God.

Too cheaply truths, once purchased dear,
    Are made our own ;
Too long the world has smiled to hear
Our boast of full corn in the ear
    By others sown ;

To see us stir the martyr fires
    Of long ago,
And wrap our satisfied desires
In the singed mantles that our sires
    Have dropped below.

But now the cross our worthies bore
    On us is laid ;
Profession's quiet sleep is o'er,
And in the scale of truth once more
    Our faith is weighed.

The cry of innocent blood at last
    Is calling down
An answer in the whirlwind-blast,
The thunder and the shadow cast
    From Heaven's dark frown.

The land is red with judgments. Who
    Stands guiltless forth ?
Have we been faithful as we knew,
To God and to our brother true,
    To Heaven and Earth ?

How faint, through din of merchandise
    And count of gain,
Have seemed to us the captive's cries !
How far away the tears and sighs
    Of souls in pain !

This day the fearful reckoning comes
    To each and all ;
We hear amidst our peaceful homes
The summons of the conscript drums,
    The bugle's call.

Our path is plain ; the war-net draws
    Round us in vain,

While, faithful to the Higher Cause,
We keep our fealty to the laws
    Through patient pain.

The levelled gun, the battle-brand,
    We may not take :
But, calmly loyal, we can stand
And suffer with our suffering land
    For conscience' sake.

Why ask for ease where all is pain ?
    Shall *we* alone
Be left to add our gain to gain,
When over Armageddon's plain
    The trump is blown ?

To suffer well is well to serve ;
    Safe in our Lord
The rigid lines of law shall curve
To spare us ; from our heads shall swerve
    Its smiting sword.

And light is mingled with the gloom,
    And joy with grief ;
Divinest compensations come,
Through thorns of judgment · mercies
        bloom
    In sweet relief.

Thanks for our privilege to bless,
    By word and deed,
The widow in her keen distress,
The childless and the fatherless,
    The hearts that bleed !

For fields of duty, opening wide,
    Where all our powers
Are tasked the eager steps to guide
Of millions on a path untried :
    THE SLAVE IS OURS !

Ours by traditions dear and old,
    Which make the race
Our wards to cherish and uphold,
And cast their freedom in the mould
    Of Christian grace.

And we may tread the sick-bed floors
    Where strong men pine,
And, down the groaning corridors,
Pour freely from our liberal stores
    The oil and wine.

Who murmurs that in these dark days
    His lot is cast ?
God's hand within the shadow lays
The stones whereon His gates of praise
    Shall rise at last.

Turn and o'erturn, O outstretched Hand !
    Nor stint, nor stay ;
The years have never dropped their
        sand
On mortal issue vast and grand
    As ours to-day.

Already, on the sable ground
    Of man's despair
Is Freedom's glorious picture found,
With all its dusky hands unbound
    Upraised in prayer.

O, small shall seem all sacrifice
    And pain and loss,
When God shall wipe the weeping eyes,
For suffering give the victor's prize,
    The crown for cross !

AT PORT ROYAL.

THE tent-lights glimmer on the land,
    The ship-lights on the sea ;
The night-wind smooths with drifting
        sand
    Our track on lone Tybee.

At last our grating keels outslide,
    Our good boats forward swing ;
And while we ride the land-locked tide,
    Our negroes row and sing.

For dear the bondman holds his gifts
    Of music and of song :
The gold that kindly Nature sifts
    Among his sands of wrong ;

The power to make his toiling days
    And poor home-comforts please ;
The quaint relief of mirth that plays
    With sorrow's minor keys.

Another glow than sunset's fire
    Has filled the West with light,
Where field and garner, barn and byre,
    Are blazing through the night.

The land is wild with fear and hate,
    The rout runs mad and fast ;
From hand to hand, from gate to gate
    The flaming brand is passed.

The lurid glow falls strong across
    Dark faces broad with smiles :
Not theirs the terror, hate, and loss
    That fire yon blazing piles.

With oar-strokes timing to their song,
  They weave in simple lays
The pathos of remembered wrong,
  The hope of better days, —

The triumph-note that Miriam sung,
  The joy of uncaged birds :
Softening with Afric's mellow tongue
  Their broken Saxon words.

SONG OF THE NEGRO BOATMEN.

O, praise an' tanks ! De Lord he come
  To set de people free ;
An' massa tink it day ob doom,
  An' we ob jubilee.
De Lord dat heap de Red Sea waves
  He jus' as 'trong as den ;
He say de word : we las' night slaves ;
  To-day, de Lord's freemen.
    De yam will grow, de cotton blow,
      We 'll hab de rice an' corn ;
    O nebber you fear, if nebber you
      hear
    De driver blow his horn !

Ole massa on he trabbels gone ;
  He leaf de land behind :
De Lord's breff blow him furder on,
  Like corn-shuck in de wind.
We own de hoe, we own de plough,
  We own de hands dat hold ;
We sell de pig, we sell de cow,
  But nebber chile be sold.
    De yam will grow, de cotton blow,
      We 'll hab de rice an' corn ;
    O nebber you fear, if nebber you
      hear
    De driver blow his horn !

We pray de Lord : he gib us signs
  Dat some day we be free ;
De norf-wind tell it to de pines,
  De wild-duck to de sea ;
We tink it when de church-bell ring,
  We dream it in de dream ;
De rice-bird mean it when he sing,
  De eagle when he scream.
    De yam will grow, de cotton blow,
      We 'll hab de rice an' corn :
    O nebber you fear, if nebber you
      hear
    De driver blow his horn !

We know de promise nebber fail,
  An' nebber lie de word ;

So like de 'postles in de jail,
  We waited for de Lord :
An' now he open ebery door,
  An' trow away de key ;
He tink we lub him so before,
  We lub him better free.
    De yam will grow, de cotton blow,
      He 'll gib de rice an' corn ;
    O nebber you fear, if nebber you
      hear
    De driver blow his horn !

So sing our dusky gondoliers ;
  And with a secret pain,
And smiles that seem akin to tears,
  We hear the wild refrain.

We dare not share the negro's trust,
  Nor yet his hope deny ;
We only know that God is just,
  And every wrong shall die.

Rude seems the song ; each swarthy face,
  Flame-lighted, ruder still :
We start to think that hapless race
  Must shape our good or ill ;

That laws of changeless justice bind
  Oppressor with oppressed ;
And, close as sin and suffering joined,
  We march to Fate abreast.

Sing on, poor hearts ! your chant shall
    be
  Our sign of blight or bloom, —
The Vala-song of Liberty,
  Or death-rune of our doom !

BARBARA FRIETCHIE.

Up from the meadows rich with corn,
Clear in the cool September morn,

The clustered spires of Frederick stand
Green-walled by the hills of Maryland.

Round about them orchards sweep,
Apple and peach tree fruited deep,

Fair as the garden of the Lord
To the eyes of the famished rebel horde,

On that pleasant morn of the early fall
When Lee marched over the mountain-
    wall, —

Over the mountains winding down,
Horse and foot, into Frederick town.

Forty flags with their silver stars,
Forty flags with their crimson bars,

Flapped in the morning wind : the sun
Of noon looked down, and saw not one.

Up rose old Barbara Frietchie then,
Bowed with her fourscore years and ten ;

Bravest of all in Frederick town,
She took up the flag the men hauled
    down ;

In her attic window the staff she set,
To show that one heart was loyal yet.

Up the street came the rebel tread,
Stonewall Jackson riding ahead.

Under his slouched hat left and right
He glanced : the old flag met his sight.

"Halt !" — the dust-brown ranks stood
    fast.
"Fire !" — out blazed the rifle-blast.

It shivered the window, pane and sash ;
It rent the banner with seam and gash.

Quick, as it fell, from the broken staff
Dame Barbara snatched the silken scarf.

She leaned far out on the window-sill,
And shook it forth with a royal will.

"Shoot, if you must, this old gray head,
But spare your country's flag," she said.

A shade of sadness, a blush of shame,
Over the face of the leader came ;

The nobler nature within him stirred
To life at that woman's deed and word:

"Who touches a hair of yon gray head
Dies like a dog ! March on !" he said.

All day long through Frederick street
Sounded the tread of marching feet :

All day long that free flag tost
Over the heads of the rebel host.

Ever its torn folds rose and fell
On the loyal winds that loved it well ;

And through the hill-gaps sunset light
Shone over it with a warm good-night.

Barbara Frietchie's work is o'er,
And the Rebel rides on his raids no
    more.

Honor to her ! and let a tear
Fall, for her sake, on Stonewall's bier.

Over Barbara Frietchie's grave,
Flag of Freedom and Union, wave !

Peace and order and beauty draw
Round thy symbol of light and law ;

And ever the stars above look down
On thy stars below in Frederick town !

BALLADS.

COBBLER KEEZAR'S VISION.[73]

THE beaver cut his timber
  With patient teeth that day,
The minks were fish-wards, and the
    crows
  Surveyors of highway, —

When Keezar sat on the hillside
  Upon his cobbler's form,
With a pan of coals on either hand
  To keep his waxed-ends warm.

And there, in the golden weather,
  He stitched and hammered and sung ;
In the brook he moistened his leather,
  In the pewter mug his tongue.

Well knew the tough old Teuton
  Who brewed the stoutest ale,
And he paid the goodwife's reckoning
  In the coin of song and tale.

The songs they still are singing
  Who dress the hills of vine,

The tales that haunt the Brocken
  And whisper down the Rhine.

Woodsy and wild and lonesome,
  The swift stream wound away,
Through birches and scarlet maples
  Flashing in foam and spray, —

Down on the sharp-horned ledges
  Plunging in steep cascade,
Tossing its white-maned waters
  Against the hemlock's shade.

Woodsy and wild and lonesome,
  East and west and north and south ;
Only the village of fishers
  Down at the river's mouth ;

Only here and there a clearing,
  With its farm-house rude and new,
And tree-stumps, swart as Indians,
  Where the scanty harvest grew.

No shout of home-bound reapers,
  No vintage-song he heard,
And on the green no dancing feet
  The merry violin stirred.

" Why should folk be glum," said Kee-
    zar,
  " When Nature herself is glad,
And the painted woods are laughing
  At the faces so sour and sad ? "

Small heed had the careless cobbler
  What sorrow of heart was theirs
Who travailed in pain with the births
    of God,
  And planted a state with prayers, —

Hunting of witches and warlocks,
  Smiting the heathen horde, —
One hand on the mason's trowel,
  And one on the soldier's sword !

But give him his ale and cider,
  Give him his pipe and song,
Little he cared for Church or State,
  Or the balance of right and wrong.

" 'T is work, work, work," he mut-
    tered, —
  " And for rest a snuffle of psalms ! "
He smote on his leathern apron
  With his brown and waxen palms.

" O for the purple harvests
  Of the days when I was young !

For the merry grape-stained maidens,
  And the pleasant songs they sung !

" O for the breath of vineyards,
  Of apples and nuts and wine !
For an oar to row and a breeze to blow
  Down the grand old river Rhine ! "

A tear in his blue eye glistened,
  And dropped on his beard so gray.
" Old, old am I," said Keezar,
  " And the Rhine flows far away ! "

But a cunning man was the cobbler ;
  He could call the birds from the trees,
Charm the black snake out of the ledges,
  And bring back the swarming bees.

All the virtues of herbs and metals,
  All the lore of the woods, he knew,
And the arts of the Old World mingled
  With the marvels of the New.

Well he knew the tricks of magic,
  And the lapstone on his knee
Had the gift of the Mormon's goggles
  Or the stone of Doctor Dee.

For the mighty master Agrippa
  Wrought it with spell and rhyme
From a fragment of mystic moonstone
  In the tower of Nettesheim.

To a cobbler Minnesinger
  The marvellous stone gave he, —
And he gave it, in turn, to Keezar,
  Who brought it over the sea.

He held up that mystic lapstone,
  He held it up like a lens,
And he counted the long years coming
  By twenties and by tens.

" One hundred years," quoth Keezar,
  " And fifty have I told :
Now open the new before me,
  And shut me out the old ! "

Like a cloud of mist, the blackness
  Rolled from the magic stone,
And a marvellous picture mingled
  The unknown and the known.

Still ran the stream to the river,
  And river and ocean joined ;
And there were the bluffs and the blue
    sea-line,
  And cold north hills behind.

But the mighty forest was broken
  By many a steepled town,
By many a white-walled farm-house,
  And many a garner brown.

Turning a score of mill-wheels,
  The stream no more ran free ;
White sails on the winding river,
  White sails on the far-off sea.

Below in the noisy village
  The flags were floating gay,
And shone on a thousand faces
  The light of a holiday.

Swiftly the rival ploughmen
  Turned the brown earth from their
    shares ;
Here were the farmer's treasures,
  There were the craftsman's wares.

Golden the goodwife's butter,
  Ruby her currant-wine ;
Grand were the strutting turkeys,
  Fat were the beeves and swine.

Yellow and red were the apples,
  And the ripe pears russet-brown,
And the peaches had stolen blushes
  From the girls who shook them
    down.

And with blooms of hill and wild-
    wood,
  That shame the toil of art,
Mingled the gorgeous blossoms
  Of the garden's tropic heart.

" What is it I see ?" said Keezar :
  " Am I here, or am I there ?
Is it a fête at Bingen ?
  Do I look on Frankfort fair ?

" But where are the clowns and pup-
    pets,
  And imps with horns and tail ?
And where are the Rhenish flagons ?
  And where is the foaming ale ?

" Strange things, I know, will hap-
    pen, —
  Strange things the Lord permits ;
But that droughty folk should be jolly
  Puzzles my poor old wits.

" Here are smiling manly faces,
  And the maiden's step is gay ;

Nor sad by thinking, nor mad by drink-
    ing,
  Nor mopes, nor fools, are they.

" Here's pleasure without regretting,
  And good without abuse,
The holiday and the bridal
  Of beauty and of use.

" Here's a priest and there is a Qua-
    ker, —
  Do the cat and dog agree ?
Have they burned the stocks for oven-
    wood ?
  Have they cut down the gallows-tree ?

" Would the old folk know their chil
    dren ?
  Would they own the graceless town,
With never a ranter to worry
  And never a witch to drown ? "

Loud laughed the cobbler Keezar,
  Laughed like a school-boy gay ;
Tossing his arms above him,
  The lapstone rolled away.

It rolled down the rugged hillside,
  It spun like a wheel bewitched,
It plunged through the leaning willows,
  And into the river pitched.

There, in the deep, dark water,
  The magic stone lies still,
Under the leaning willows
  In the shadow of the hill.

But oft the idle fisher
  Sits on the shadowy bank,
And his dreams make marvellous pic-
    tures
  Where the wizard's lapstone sank.

And still, in the summer twilights,
  When the river seems to run
Out from the inner glory,
  Warm with the melted sun,

The weary mill-girl lingers
  Beside the charméd stream,
And the sky and the golden water
  Shape and color her dream.

Fair wave the sunset gardens,
  The rosy signals fly ;
Her homestead beckons from the cloud,
  And love goes sailing by !

AMY WENTWORTH.

TO W. B.

As they who watch by sick-beds find
relief
Unwittingly from the great stress of
grief
And anxious care in fantasies out-
wrought
From the hearth's embers flickering low,
or caught
From whispering wind, or tread of pass-
ing feet,
Or vagrant memory calling up some
sweet
Snatch of old song or romance, whence
or why
They scarcely know or ask, — so, thou
and I,
Nursed in the faith that Truth alone is
strong
In the endurance which outwearies
Wrong,
With meek persistence baffling brutal
force,
And trusting God against the universe, —
We, doomed to watch a strife we may
not share
With other weapons than the patriot's
prayer,
Yet owning, with full hearts and moist-
ened eyes,
The awful beauty of self-sacrifice,
And wrung by keenest sympathy for all
Who give their loved ones for the living
wall
'Twixt law and treason, — in this evil
day
May haply find, through automatic play
Of pen and pencil, solace to our pain,
And hearten others with the strength we
gain.
I know it has been said our times re-
quire
No play of art, nor dalliance with the
lyre,
No weak essay with Fancy's chloroform
To calm the hot, mad pulses of the
storm,
But the stern war-blast rather, such as
sets
The battle's teeth of serried bayonets,
And pictures grim as Vernet's. Yet
with these
Some softer tints may blend, and milder
keys

18

Relieve the storm-stunned ear. Let us
keep sweet,
If so we may, our hearts, even while we
eat
The bitter harvest of our own device
And half a century's moral cowardice.
As Nürnberg sang while Wittenberg
defied,
And Kranach painted by his Luther's
side,
And through the war-march of the Pu-
ritan
The silver stream of Marvell's music
ran,
So let the household melodies be sung,
The pleasant pictures on the wall be
hung, —
So let us hold against the hosts of night
And slavery all our vantage-ground of
light.
Let Treason boast its savagery, and
shake
From its flag-folds its symbol rattle-
snake,
Nurse its fine arts, lay human skins in
tan,
And carve its pipe-bowls from the bones
of man,
And make the tale of Fijian banquets
dull
By drinking whiskey from a loyal
skull, —
But let us guard, till this sad war shall
cease,
(God grant it soon !) the graceful arts
of peace :
No foes are conquered who the victors
teach
Their vandal manners and barbaric
speech.

And while, with hearts of thankfulness,
we bear
Of the great common burden our full
share,
Let none upbraid us that the waves
entice
Thy sea-dipped pencil, or some quaint
device,
Rhythmic and sweet, beguiles my pen
away
From the sharp strifes and sorrows of
to-day.
Thus, while the east-wind keen from
Labrador
Sings in the leafless elms, and from the
shore

Of the great sea comes the monotonous
    roar
Of the long-breaking surf, and all the
    sky
Is gray with cloud, home-bound and
    dull, I try
To time a simple legend to the sounds
Of winds in the woods, and waves on
    pebbled bounds, —
A song for oars to chime with, such as
    might
Be sung by tired sea-painters, who at
    night
Look from their hemlock camps, by
    quiet cove
Or beach, moon-lighted, on the waves
    they love.
(So hast thou looked, when level sunset
    lay
On the calm bosom of some Eastern
    bay,
And all the spray-moist rocks and waves
    that rolled
Up the white sand-slopes flashed with
    ruddy gold.)
Something it has — a flavor of the
    sea,
And the sea's freedom — which reminds
    of thee.
Its faded picture, dimly smiling down
From the blurred fresco of the ancient
    town,
I have not touched with warmer tints in
    vain,
If, in this dark, sad year, it steals one
    thought from pain.

———

HER fingers shame the ivory keys
    They dance so light along ;
The bloom upon her parted lips
    Is sweeter than the song.

O perfumed suitor, spare thy smiles !
    Her thoughts are not of thee ;
She better loves the salted wind,
    The voices of the sea.

Her heart is like an outbound ship
    That at its anchor swings ;
The murmur of the stranded shell
    Is in the song she sings.

She sings, and, smiling, hears her praise,
    But dreams the while of one
Who watches from his sea-blown deck
    The icebergs in the sun.

She questions all the winds that blow,
    And every fog-wreath dim,
And bids the sea-birds flying north
    Bear messages to him.

She speeds them with the thanks of m
    He perilled life to save,
And grateful prayers like holy oil
    To smooth for him the wave.

Brown Viking of the fishing-smack !
    Fair toast of all the town ! —
The skipper's jerkin ill beseems
    The lady's silken gown !

But ne'er shall Amy Wentworth wear
    For him the blush of shame
Who dares to set his manly gifts
    Against her ancient name.

The stream is brightest at its spring,
    And blood is not like wine ;
Nor honored less than he who heirs
    Is he who founds a line.

Full lightly shall the prize be won,
    If love be Fortune's spur ;
And never maiden stoops to him
    Who lifts himself to her.

Her home is brave in Jaffrey Street,
    With stately stairways worn
By feet of old Colonial knights
    And ladies gentle-born.

Still green about its ample porch
    The English ivy twines,
Trained back to show in English oak
    The herald's carven signs.

And on her, from the wainscot old,
    Ancestral faces frown, —
And this has worn the soldier's sword,
    And that the judge's gown.

But, strong of will and proud as they,
    She walks the gallery floor
As if she trod her sailor's deck
    By stormy Labrador !

The sweetbrier blooms on Kittery-side
    And green are Elliot's bowers ;
Her garden is the pebbled beach,
    The mosses are her flowers.

She looks across the harbor-bar
    To see the white gulls fly ;

His greeting from the Northern sea
Is in their clanging cry.

She hums a song, and dreams that he,
  As in its romance old,
Shall homeward ride with silken sails
  And masts of beaten gold !

O, rank is good, and gold is fair,
  And high and low mate ill ;
But love has never known a law
  Beyond its own sweet will !

       •

THE COUNTESS.

TO E. W.

I KNOW not, Time and Space so inter-
    vene,
Whether, still waiting with a trust se-
    rene,
Thou bearest up thy fourscore years and
    ten,
Or, called at last, art now Heaven's cit-
    izen ;   •
But, here or there, a pleasant thought
    of thee,
Like an old friend, all day has been
    with me.
The shy, still boy, for whom thy kindly
    hand
Smoothed his hard pathway to the won-
    der-land
Of thought and fancy, in gray manhood
    yet
Keeps green the memory of his early
    debt.
To-day, when truth and falsehood speak
    their words
Through hot-lipped cannon and the teeth
    of swords,
Listening with quickened heart and ear
    intent
To each sharp clause of that stern argu-
    ment,
I still can hear at times a softer note
Of the old pastoral music round me float,
While through the hot gleam of our
    civil strife
Looms the green mirage of a simpler
    life.
As, at his alien post, the sentinel
Drops the old bucket in the homestead
    well,
And hears old voices in the winds that
    toss

Above his head the live-oak's beard of
    moss,
So, in our trial-time, and under skies
Shadowed by swords like Islam's para-
    dise,
I wait and watch, and let my fancy
    stray
To milder scenes and youth's Arcadian
    day ;
And howsoe'er the pencil dipped in
    dreams
Shades the brown woods or tints the
    sunset streams,
The country doctor in the foreground
    seems,
Whose ancient sulky down the village
    lanes
Dragged, like a war-car, captive ills and
    pains.
I could not paint the scenery of my
    song,
Mindless of one who looked thereon so
    long ;
Who, night and day, on duty's lonely
    round,
Made friends o' the woods and rocks,
    and knew the sound
Of each small brook, and what the hill-
    side trees
Said to the winds that touched their
    leafy keys ;
Who saw so keenly and so well could
    paint
The village-folk, with all their humors
    quaint, —
The parson ambling on his wall-eyed
    roan,
Grave and erect, with white hair back-
    ward blown ;
The tough old boatman, half amphibious
    grown ;
The muttering witch-wife of the gossip's
    tale,
And the loud straggler levying his black-
    mail, —
Old customs, habits, superstitions, fears,
All that lies buried under fifty years.
To thee, as is most fit, I bring my
    lay,
And, grateful, own the debt I cannot
    pay.

      ————

Over the wooded northern ridge,
  Between its houses brown,
To the dark tunnel of the bridge
  The street comes straggling down.

You catch a glimpse, through birch and
    pine,
Of gable, roof, and porch,
The tavern with its swinging sign,
    The sharp horn of the church.

The river's steel-blue crescent curves
    To meet, in ebb and flow,
The single broken wharf that serves
    For sloop and gundelow.

With salt sea-scents along its shores
    The heavy hay-boats crawl,
The long antennæ of their oars
    In lazy rise and fall.

Along the gray abutment's wall
    The idle shad-net dries;
The toll-man in his cobbler's stall
    Sits smoking with closed eyes.

You hear the pier's low undertone
    Of waves that chafe and gnaw ;
You start, — a skipper's horn is blown
    To raise the creaking draw.

At times a blacksmith's anvil sounds
    With slow and sluggard beat,
Or stage-coach on its dusty rounds
    Wakes up the staring street.

A place for idle eyes and ears,
    A cobwebbed nook of dreams ;
Left by the stream whose waves are
    years
    The stranded village seems.

And there, like other moss and rust,
    The native dweller clings,
And keeps, in uninquiring trust,
    The old, dull round of things.

The fisher drops his patient lines,
    The farmer sows his grain,
Content to hear the murmuring pines
    Instead of railroad-train.

Go where, along the tangled steep
    That slopes against the west,
The hamlet's buried idlers sleep
    In still profounder rest.

Throw back the locust's flowery plume,
    The birch's pale-green scarf,
And break the web of brier and bloom
    From name and epitaph.

A simple muster-roll of death,
    Of pomp and romance shorn,
The dry, old names that common breath
    Has cheapened and outworn.

Yet pause by one low mound, and part
    The wild vines o'er it laced,
And read the words by rustic art
    Upon its headstone traced.

Haply yon white-haired villager
    Of fourscore years can say
What means the noble name of her
    Who sleeps with common clay.

An exile from the Gascon land
    Found refuge here and rest,
And loved, of all the village band,
    Its fairest and its best.

He knelt with her on Sabbath morns,
    He worshipped through her eyes,
And on the pride that doubts and scorns
    Stole in her faith's surprise.

Her simple daily life he saw
    By homeliest duties tried,
In all things by an untaught law
    Of fitness justified.

For her his rank aside he laid ;
    He took the hue and tone
Of lowly life and toil, and made
    Her simple ways his own.

Yet still, in gay and careless ease,
    To harvest-field or dance
He brought the gentle courtesies,
    The nameless grace of France.

And she who taught him love not less
    From him she loved in turn
Caught in her sweet unconsciousness
    What love is quick to learn.

Each grew to each in pleased accord,
    Nor knew the gazing town
If she looked upward to her lord
    Or he to her looked down.

How sweet, when summer's day was o'er,
    His violin's mirth and wail,
The walk on pleasant Newbury's shore,
    The river's moonlit sail !

Ah ! life is brief, though love be long ;
    The altar and the bier,
The burial hymn and bridal song,
    Were both in one short year !

Her rest is quiet on the hill,
  Beneath the locust's bloom :
Far off her lover sleeps as still
  Within his scutcheoned tomb.

The Gascon lord, the village maid,
  In death still clasp their hands ;
The love that levels rank and grade
  Unites their severed lands.

What matter whose the hillside grave,
  Or whose the blazoned stone ?
Forever to her western wave   •
  Shall whisper blue Garonne !

O Love ! — so hallowing every soil
  That gives thy sweet flower room,
Wherever, nursed by ease or toil,
  The human heart takes bloom ! —

Plant of lost Eden, from the sod
  Of sinful earth unriven,
White blossom of the trees of God
  Dropped down to us from heaven ! —

This tangled waste of mound and stone
  Is holy for thy sake ;
A sweetness which is all thy own
  Breathes out from fern and brake.

And while ancestral pride shall twine
  The Gascon's tomb. with flowers,
Fall sweetly here, O song of mine,
  With summer's bloom and showers !

And let the lines that severed seem
  Unite again in thee,
As western wave and Gallic stream
  Are mingled in one sea !

•

OCCASIONAL POEMS

NAPLES.

1860.

INSCRIBED TO ROBERT C. WATERSTON,
OF BOSTON.

I GIVE thee joy ! — I know to thee
The dearest spot on earth must
  be
Where sleeps thy loved one by the summer sea ;

Where, near her sweetest poet's
  tomb,   •
  The land of Virgil gave thee room
To lay thy flower with her perpetual
  bloom.

I know that when the sky shut
  down
  Behind thee on the gleaming town,
On Baiæ's baths and Posilippo's crown ;

And, through thy tears, the mocking day
  Burned Ischia's mountain lines
  away,
And Capri melted in its sunny bay, —

Through thy great farewell sorrow
  shot
  The sharp pang of a bitter thought
That slaves must tread around that holy
  spot.

Thou knewest not the land was
  blest
  In giving thy beloved rest,
Holding the fond hope closer to her
  breast

That every sweet and saintly grave
  Was freedom's prophecy, and gave
The pledge of Heaven to sanctify and
  save.

That pledge is answered. To thy ear
  The unchained city sends its cheer,
And, tuned to joy, the muffled bells of
  fear

Ring Victor in. The land sits free
  And happy by the summer sea,
And Bourbon Naples now is Italy !

She smiles above her broken chain
  The languid smile that follows pain,
Stretching her cramped limbs to the sun
  again.

O, joy for all, who hear her call
  From gray Camaldoli's convent-wall
And Elmo's towers to freedom's carni-
    val !

A new life breathes among her vines
  And olives, like the breath of pines
Blown downward from the breezy Apen-
    nines.

Lean, O, my friend, to meet that
    breath,
  Rejoice as one who witnesseth
Beauty from ashes rise, and life from
    death !

Thy sorrow shall no more be pain,
  Its tears shall fall in sunlit rain,
Writing the grave with flowers : " Arisen
    again ! "

THE SUMMONS.

My ear is full of summer sounds,
  Of summer sights my languid eye ;
Beyond the dusty village bounds
I loiter in my daily rounds,
  And in the noon-time shadows lie.

I hear the wild bee wind his horn,
  The bird swings on the ripened wheat,
The long green lances of the corn
Are tilting in the winds of morn,
  The locust shrills his song of heat.

Another sound my spirit hears,
  A deeper sound that drowns them
    all, —
A voice of pleading choked with tears,
The call of human hopes and fears,
  The Macedonian cry to Paul !

The storm-bell rings, the trumpet blows ;
  I know the word and countersign ;
Wherever Freedom's vanguard goes,
Where stand or fall her friends or foes,
  I know the place that should be mine.

Shamed be the hands that idly fold,
  And lips that woo the reed's accord,
When laggard Time the hour has tolled
For true with false and new with old
  To fight the battles of the Lord !

O brothers ! blest by partial Fate
  With power to match the will and
    deed,

To him your summons comes too late
Who sinks beneath his armor's weight,
  And has no answer but God-speed !

THE WAITING.

I WAIT and watch : before my eyes
  Methinks the night grows thin and
    gray ;
I wait and watch the eastern skies
To see the golden spears uprise
  Beneath the oriflamme of day !

Like one whose limbs are bound in
    trance
  I hear the day-sounds swell and grow,
And see across the twilight glance,
Troop after troop, in swift advance,
  The shining ones with plumes of
    snow !

I know the errand of their feet,
  I know what mighty work is theirs ;
I can but lift up hands unmeet,
The threshing-floors of God to beat,
  And speed them with unworthy
    prayers.

I will not dream in vain despair
  The steps of progress wait for me :
The puny leverage of a hair
The planet's impulse well may spare,
  A drop of dew the tided sea.

The loss, if loss there be, is mine,
  And yet not mine if understood ;
For one shall grasp and one resign,
One drink life's rue, and one its wine,
  And God shall make the balance
    good.

O power to do ! O baffled will !
  O prayer and action ! ye are one.
Who may not strive, may yet fulfil
The harder task of standing still,
  And good but wished with God is
    done !

MOUNTAIN PICTURES.

I.

FRANCONIA FROM THE PEMIGEWASSET.

ONCE more, O Mountains of the North,
    unveil
  Your brows, and lay your cloudy
    mantles by !

And once more, ere the eyes that seek
 ye fail,
Uplift against the blue walls of the sky
Your mighty shapes, and let the sun-
 shine weave
 Its golden net-work in your belting
  woods,
 Smile down in rainbows from your
  falling floods,
And on your kingly brows at morn and eve
 Set crowns of fire ! So shall my soul
  receive
Haply the secret of your calm and
  strength,
 Your unforgotten beauty interfuse
My common life, your glorious shapes
 and hues
 And sun-dropped splendors at my
  bidding come,
 Loom vast through dreams, and
  stretch in billowy length
From the sea-level of my lowland home !

They rise before me ! Last night's
  thunder-gust
Roared not in vain : for where its
  lightnings thrust
 Their tongues of fire, the great peaks
  seem so near,
Burned clean of mist, so starkly bold
 and clear,
I almost pause the wind in the pines to
  hear,
The loose rock's fall, the steps of brows-
  ing deer.
The clouds that shattered on yon slide-
  worn walls
 And splintered on the rocks their
  spears of rain
Have set in play a thousand waterfalls,
Making the dusk and silence of the woods
Glad with the laughter of the chasing
  floods,
And luminous with blown spray and
  silver gleams,
While, in the vales below, the dry-
  lipped streams
 Sing to the freshened meadow-lands
  again.
So, let me hope, the battle-storm that
  beats
 The land with hail and fire may pass
  away
 With its spent thunders at the break of
  day,
Like last night's clouds, and leave, as it
  retreats,

A greener earth and fairer sky be-
  hind,
Blown crystal-clear by Freedom's
  Northern wind !

II.

MONADNOCK FROM WACHUSET.

I WOULD I were a painter, for the sake
 Of a sweet picture, and of her who led,
 A fitting guide, with reverential tread,
Into that mountain mystery. First a
 ' lake
Tinted with sunset ; next the wavy
 lines
 Of far receding hills ; and yet more
 far,
Monadnock lifting from his night of
 pines
 His rosy forehead to the evening star.
Beside us, purple-zoned, Wachuset laid
His head against the West, whose
 warm light made
 His aureole ; and o'er him, sharp
 and clear,
Like a shaft of lightning in mid-launch-
 ing stayed,
A single level cloud-line, shone upon
By the fierce glances of the sunken sun,
 Menaced the darkness with its gold-
 en spear !

So twilight deepened round us. Still
 and black
The great woods climbed the mountain
 at our back ;
And on their skirts, where yet the lingering day
On the shorn greenness of the clearing lay,
 The brown old farm-house like a
 bird's-nest hung.
With home-life sounds the desert air was
 stirred :
The bleat of sheep along the hill we
 heard,
The bucket plashing in the cool, sweet
 well,
The pasture-bars that clattered as they
 fell ;
Dogs barked, fowls fluttered, cattle
 lowed ; the gate
Of the barn-yard creaked beneath the
 merry weight
 Of sun-brown children, listening,
 while they swung,

The welcome sound of supper-call
  to hear;
And down the shadowy lane, in
  tinklings clear,
The pastoral curfew of the cow-bell
  rung.
Thus soothed and pleased, our backward
  path we took,
Praising the farmer's home.   He only
  spake,
Looking into the sunset o'er the lake,
  Like one to whom the far-off is
  most near :
"Yes, most folks think it has a pleasant
  look ;
I love it for my good old mother's sake,
  Who lived and died here in the
  peace of God !"
The lesson of his words we pondered
  o'er,
As silently we turned the eastern flank
Of the mountain, where its shadow
  deepest sank,
Doubling the night along our rugged
  road :
We felt that man was more than his
  abode, —
  The inward life than Nature's rai-
  ment more ;
And the warm sky, the sundown-tinted
  hill,
  The forest and the lake, seemed
  dwarfed and dim
Before the saintly soul, whose human
  will
  Meekly in the Eternal footsteps
  trod,
Making her homely toil and household
  ways
An earthly echo of the song of praise
  Swelling from angel lips and harps of
  seraphim.

OUR RIVER.

FOR A SUMMER FESTIVAL AT "THE
LAURELS" ON THE MERRIMACK.

ONCE more on yonder laurelled height
  The summer flowers have budded ;
Once more with summer's golden light
  The vales of home are flooded ;
And once more, by the grace of Him
  Of every good the Giver,
We sing upon its wooded rim
  The praises of our river :

Its pines above, its waves below,
  The west-wind down it blowing,
As fair as when the young Brissot
  Beheld it seaward flowing, —
And bore its memory o'er the deep,
  To soothe a martyr's sadness,
And fresco, in his troubled sleep,
  His prison-walls with gladness.

We know the world is rich with streams
  Renowned in song and story,
Whose music murmurs through our
  dreams
  Of human love and glory :
We know that Arno's banks are fair,
  And Rhine has castled shadows,
And, poet-tuned, the Doon and Ayr
  Go singing down their meadows.

But while, unpictured and unsung
  By painter or by poet,
Our river waits the tuneful tongue
  And cunning hand to show it, —
We only know the fond skies lean
  Above it, warm with blessing,
And the sweet soul of our Undine
  Awakes to our caressing.

No fickle sun-god holds the flocks
  That graze its shores in keeping ;
No icy kiss of Dian mocks
  The youth beside it sleeping :
Our Christian river loveth most
  The beautiful and human ;
The heathen streams of Naiads boast,
  But ours of man and woman.

The miner in his cabin hears
  The ripple we are hearing ;
It whispers soft to homesick ears
  Around the settler's clearing :
In Sacramento's vales of corn,
  Or Santee's bloom of cotton,
Our river by its valley-born
  Was never yet forgotten.

The drum rolls loud, — the bugle fills
  The summer air with clangor ;
The war-storm shakes the solid hills
  Beneath its tread of anger ;
Young eyes that last year smiled in
  ours
  Now point the rifle's barrel,
And hands then stained with fruits and
  flowers
  Bear redder stains of quarrel.

But blue skies smile, and flowers bloom
  on,
And rivers still keep flowing, —
The dear God still his rain and sun
On good and ill bestowing.
His pine-trees whisper, "Trust and
  wait!"
His flowers are prophesying
That all we dread of change or fall
  His love is underlying.

And thou, O Mountain-born! — no more
  We ask the wise Allotter
Than for the firmness of thy shore,
  The calmness of thy water,
The cheerful lights that overlay
  Thy rugged slopes with beauty,
To match our spirits to our day
  And make a joy of duty.

ANDREW RYKMAN'S PRAYER.

ANDREW RYKMAN's dead and gone;
  You can see his leaning slate
In the graveyard, and thereon
  Read his name and date.

" Trust is truer than our fears,"
  Runs the legend through the moss,
" Gain is not in added years,
  Nor in death is loss."

Still the feet that thither trod,
  All the friendly eyes are dim;
Only Nature, now, and God
  Have a care for him.

There the dews of quiet fall,
  Singing birds and soft winds stray;
Shall the tender Heart of all
  Be less kind than they?

What he was and what he is
  They who ask may haply find,
If they read this prayer of his
  Which he left behind.

———

Pardon, Lord, the lips that dare
Shape in words a mortal's prayer!
Prayer, that, when my day is done,
And I see its setting sun,
Shorn and beamless, cold and dim,
Sink beneath the horizon's rim, —
When this ball of rock and clay
Crumbles from my feet away,

And the solid shores of sense
Melt into the vague immense,
Father! I may come to Thee
Even with the beggar's plea,
As the poorest of Thy poor,
With my needs, and nothing more.

Not as one who seeks his home
With a step assured I come;
Still behind the tread I hear
Of my life-companion, Fear;
Still a shadow deep and vast
From my westering feet is cast,
Wavering, doubtful, undefined,
Never shapen nor outlined :
From myself the fear has grown,
And the shadow is my own.
Yet, O Lord, through all a sense
Of Thy tender providence
Stays my failing heart on Thee,
And confirms the feeble knee;
And, at times, my worn feet press
Spaces of cool quietness,
Lilied whiteness shone upon
Not by light of moon or sun.
Hours there be of inmost calm,
Broken but by grateful psalm,
When I love Thee more than fear Thee,
And Thy blessed Christ seems near me,
With forgiving look, as when
He beheld the Magdalen.
Well I know that all things move
To the spheral rhythm of love, —
That to Thee, O Lord of all!
Nothing can of chance befall :
Child and seraph, mote and star,
Well Thou knowest what we are;
Through Thy vast creative plan
Looking, from the worm to man,
There is pity in Thine eyes,
But no hatred nor surprise.
Not in blind caprice of will,
Not in cunning sleight of skill,
Not for show of power, was wrought
Nature's marvel in Thy thought.
Never careless hand and vain
Smites these chords of joy and pain :
No immortal selfishness
Plays the game of curse and bless :
Heaven and earth are witnesses
That Thy glory goodness is.
Not for sport of mind and force
Hast Thou made Thy universe,
But as atmosphere and zone
Of Thy loving heart alone.
Man, who walketh in a show,
Sees before him, to and fro,

Shadow and illusion go ;
All things flow and fluctuate,
Now contract and now dilate.
In the welter of this sea,
Nothing stable is but Thee ;
In this whirl of swooning trance,
Thou alone art permanence ;
All without Thee only seems,
All beside is choice of dreams.
Never yet in darkest mood
Doubted I that Thou wast good,
Nor mistook my will for fate,
Pain of sin for heavenly hate, —
Never dreamed the gates of pearl
Rise from out the burning marl,
Or that good can only live
Of the bad conservative,
And through counterpoise of hell
Heaven alone be possible.
For myself alone I doubt ;
All is well, I know, without ;
I alone the beauty mar,
I alone the music jar.
Yet, with hands by evil stained,
And an ear by discord pained,
I am groping for the keys
Of the heavenly harmonies ;
Still within my heart I bear
Love for all things good and fair.
Hands of want or souls in pain
Have not sought my door in vain ;
I have kept my fealty good
To the human brotherhood ;
Scarcely have I asked in prayer
That which others might not share.
I, who hear with secret shame
Praise that paineth more than blame,
Rich alone in favors lent,
Virtuous by accident,
Doubtful where I fain would rest,
Frailest where I seem the best,
Only strong for lack of test, —
What am I, that I should press
Special pleas of selfishness,
Coolly mounting into heaven
On my neighbor unforgiven ?
Ne'er to me, howe'er disguised,
Comes a saint unrecognized ;
Never fails my heart to greet
Noble deed with warmer beat ;
Halt and maimed, I own not less
All the grace of holiness ;
Nor, through shame or self-distrust,
Less I love the pure and just.
Lord, forgive these words of mine :
What have I that is not Thine ? —
Whatsoe'er I fain would boast

Needs Thy pitying pardon most.
Thou, O Elder Brother ! who
In Thy flesh our trial knew,
Thou, who hast been touched by these
Our most sad infirmities,
Thou alone the gulf canst span
In the dual heart of man,
And between the soul and sense
Reconcile all difference,
Change the dream of me and mine
For the truth of Thee and Thine,
And, through chaos, doubt, and strife,
Interfuse Thy calm of life.
Haply, thus by Thee renewed,
In Thy borrowed goodness good,
Some sweet morning yet in God's
Dim, æonian periods,
Joyful I shall wake to see
Those I love who rest in Thee,
And to them in Thee allied
Shall my soul be satisfied.

Scarcely Hope hath shaped for me
What the future life may be.
Other lips may well be bold ;
Like the publican of old,
I can only urge the plea,
" Lord, be merciful to me ! "
Nothing of desert I claim,
Unto me belongeth shame.
Not for me the crowns of gold,
Palms, and harpings manifold ;
Not for erring eye and feet
Jasper wall and golden street.
What thou wilt, O Father, give !
All is gain that I receive.
If my voice I may not raise
In the elders' song of praise,
If I may not, sin-defiled,
Claim my birthright as a child,
Suffer it that I to Thee
As an hired servant be ;
Let the lowliest task be mine,
Grateful, so the work be Thine ;
Let me find the humblest place
In the shadow of Thy grace :
Blest to me were any spot
Where temptation whispers not.
If there be some weaker one,
Give me strength to help him on ;
If a blinder soul there be,
Let me guide him nearer Thee.
Make my mortal dreams come true
With the work I fain would do ;
Clothe with life the weak intent,
Let me be the thing I meant ;
Let me find in Thy employ

Peace that dearer is than joy ;
Out of self to love be led
And to heaven acclimated,
Until all things sweet and good
Seem my natural habitude.

So we read the prayer of him
   Who, with John of Labadie,
Trod, of old, the oozy rim
   Of the Zuyder Zee.

Thus did Andrew Rykman pray.
   Are we wiser, better grown,
That we may not, in our day,
   Make his prayer our own ?

THE CRY OF A LOST SOUL.[74]

In that black forest, where, when day is done,
With a snake's stillness glides the Amazon
Darkly from sunset to the rising sun,

A cry, as of the pained heart of the wood,
The long, despairing moan of solitude
And darkness and the absence of all good,

Startles the traveller, with a sound so drear,
So full of hopeless agony and fear,
His heart stands still and listens like his ear.

The guide, as if he heard a dead-bell toll,
Starts, drops his oar against the gunwale's thole,
Crosses himself, and whispers, " A lost soul ! "

" No, Señor, not a bird. I know it well, —
It is the pained soul of some infidel
Or cursed heretic that cries from hell.

" Poor fool ! with hope still mocking his despair,
He wanders, shrieking on the midnight air
For human pity and for Christian prayer.

" Saints strike him dumb ! Our Holy Mother hath
No prayer for him who, sinning unto death,
Burns always in the furnace of God's wrath ! "

Thus to the baptized pagan's cruel lie,
Lending new horror to that mournful cry,
The voyager listens, making no reply.

Dim burns the boat-lamp : shadows deepen round,
From giant trees with snake-like creepers wound,
And the black water glides without a sound.

But in the traveller's heart a secret sense
Of nature plastic to benign intents,
And an eternal good in Providence,

Lifts to the starry calm of heaven his eyes ;
And lo ! rebuking all earth's ominous cries,
The Cross of pardon lights the tropic skies !

" Father of all ! " he urges his strong plea,
" Thou lovest all : thy erring child may be
Lost to himself, but never lost to Thee !

" All souls are Thine ; the wings of morning bear
None from that Presence which is everywhere,
Nor hell itself can hide, for Thou art there.

" Through sins of sense, perversities of will,
Through doubt and pain, through guilt and shame and ill,
Thy pitying eye is on Thy creature still.

" Wilt thou not make, Eternal Source and Goal !
In thy long years, life's broken circle whole,
And change to praise the cry of a lost soul ? "

ITALY.

Across the sea I heard the groans
   Of nations in the intervals
Of wind and wave. Their blood and bones
Cried out in torture, crushed by thrones,
   And sucked by priestly cannibals.

I dreamed of Freedom slowly gained
  By martyr meekness, patience, faith,
And lo ! an athlete grimly stained,
With corded muscles battle-strained,
  Shouting it from the fields of death !

I turn me, awe-struck, from the sight,
  Among the clamoring thousands mute,
I only know that God is right,
And that the children of the light
  Shall tread the darkness under foot.

I know the pent fire heaves its crust,
  That sultry skies the bolt will form
To smite them clear ; that Nature must
The balance of her powers adjust,
  Though with the earthquake and the
    storm.

God reigns, and let the earth rejoice !
  I bow before His sterner plan.
Dumb are the organs of my choice ;
He speaks in battle's stormy voice,
  His praise is in the wrath of man!

Yet, surely as He lives, the day
  Of peace He promised shall be ours,
To fold the flags of war, and lay
Its sword and spear to rust away,
  And sow its ghastly fields with flowers !

THE RIVER PATH.

No bird-song floated down the hill,
The tangled bank below was still ;

No rustle from the birchen stem,
No ripple from the water's hem.

The dusk of twilight round us grew,
We felt the falling of the dew ;

For, from us, ere the day was done,
The wooded hills shut out the sun.

But on the river's farther side
We saw the hill-tops glorified, —

A tender glow, exceeding fair,
A dream of day without its glare.

With us the damp, the chill, the gloom :
With them the sunset's rosy bloom ;

While dark, through willowy vistas seen,
The river rolled in shade between.

From out the darkness where we trod,
We gazed upon those hills of God,

Whose light seemed not of moon or
  sun.
We spake not, but our thought was one.

We paused, as if from that bright shore
Beckoned our dear ones gone before ;

And stilled our beating hearts to hear
The voices lost to mortal ear !

Sudden our pathway turned from night ;
The hills swung open to the light ;

Through their green gates the sunshine
  showed,
A long, slant splendor downward flowed.

Down glade and glen and bank it rolled :
It bridged the shaded stream with gold ;

And, borne on piers of mist, allied
The shadowy with the sunlit side !

" So," prayed we, " when our feet draw
  near
The river dark, with mortal fear,

" And the night cometh chill with dew,
O Father ! let thy light break through !

" So let the hills of doubt divide,
So bridge with faith the sunless tide !

" So let the eyes that fail on earth
On thy eternal hills look forth ;

" And in thy beckoning angels know
The dear ones whom we loved below ! "

A MEMORIAL.

M. A. C.

O, THICKER, deeper, darker growing,
  The solemn vista to the tomb
Must know henceforth another shadow,
  And give another cypress room.

In love surpassing that of brothers,
  We walked, O friend, from childhood's
    day ;
And, looking back o'er fifty summers,
  Our footprints track a common way.

One in our faith, and one our longing
  To make the world within our reach
Somewhat the better for our living,
  And gladder for our human speech.

Thou heard'st with me the far-off voices,
  The old beguiling song of fame,
But life to thee was warm and present,
  And love was better than a name.

To homely joys and loves and friendships
  Thy genial nature fondly clung ;
And so the shadow on the dial
  Ran back and left thee always young.

And who could blame the generous
    weakness
  Which, only to thyself unjust,
So overprized the worth of others,
  And dwarfed thy own with self-dis-
    trust ?

All hearts grew warmer in the presence
  Of one who, seeking not his own,
Gave freely for the love of giving,
  Nor reaped for self the harvest sown.

Thy greeting smile was pledge and prel-
    ude
  Of generous deeds and kindly words ;
In thy large heart were fair guest-cham-
    bers,
  Open to sunrise and the birds !

The task was thine to mould and fashion
  Life's plastic newness into grace :
T' make the boyish heart heroic,
  And light with thought the maiden's
    face.

O'er all the land, in town and prairie,
  With bended heads of mourning,
    stand
The living forms that owe their beauty
  And fitness to thy shaping hand.

Thy call has come in ripened manhood,
  The noonday calm of heart and mind,
While I, who dreamed of thy remaining
  To mourn me, linger still behind :

Live on, to own, with self-upbraiding,
  A debt of love still due from me, —
The vain remembrance of occasions,
  Forever lost, of serving thee.

It was not mine among thy kindred
  To join the silent funeral prayers,

But all that long sad day of summer
  My tears of mourning dropped with
    theirs.

All day the sea-waves sobbed with sor-
    row,
  The birds forgot their merry trills :
All day I heard the pines lamenting
  With thine upon thy homestead hills.

Green be those hillside pines forever,
  And green the meadowy lowlands be,
And green the old memorial beeches,
  Name-carven in the woods of Lee !

Still let them greet thy life companions
  Who thither turn their pilgrim feet,
In every mossy line recalling
  A tender memory sadly sweet.

O friend ! if thought and sense avail not
  To know thee henceforth as thou art,
That all is well with thee forever
  I trust the instincts of my heart.

Thine be the quiet habitations,
  Thine the green pastures, blossom-
    sown,
And smiles of saintly recognition,
  As sweet and tender as thy own.

Thou com'st not from the hush and
    shadow
  To meet us, but to thee we come ;
With thee we never can be strangers,
  And where thou art must still be home.

HYMN,

SUNG AT CHRISTMAS BY THE SCHOL-
ARS OF ST. HELENA'S ISLAND, S. C.

O NONE in all the world before
  Were ever glad as we !
We 're free on Carolina's shore,
  We 're all at home and free.

Thou Friend and Helper of the poor,
  Who suffered for our sake,
To open every prison door,
  And every yoke to break !

Bend low thy pitying face and mild,
  And help us sing and pray ;
The hand that blessed the little child,
  Upon our foreheads lay.

We hear no more the driver's horn,
  No more the whip we fear,
This holy day that saw thee born
  Was never half so dear.

The very oaks are greener clad,
  The waters brighter smile ;
O never shone a day so glad
  On sweet St. Helen's Isle.

We praise thee in our songs to-day,
  To thee in prayer we call,
Make swift the feet and straight the way
  Of freedom unto all.

Come once again, O blessed Lord !
  Come walking on the sea !
And let the mainlands hear the word
  That sets the islands free !

SNOW-BOUND.

A WINTER IDYL.

TO THE MEMORY

OF

THE HOUSEHOLD IT DESCRIBES,

THIS POEM IS DEDICATED BY THE AUTHOR.

" As the Spirits of Darkness be stronger in the dark, so Good Spirits which be Angels of Light are augmented not only by the Divine light of the Sun, but also by our common VVood Fire: and as the Celestial Fire drives away dark spirits, so also this our Fire of VVood doth the same."
—COR. AGRIPPA, *Occult Philosophy,* Book I ch. v.

" Announced by all the trumpets of the sky,
  Arrives the snow ; and, driving o'er the fields,
  Seems nowhere to alight ; the whited air
  Hides hills and woods, the river and the heaven
And veils the farm-house at the garden's end.
The sled and traveller stopped, the courier's feet
Delayed, all friends shut out, the housemates sit
Around the radiant fireplace, enclosed
In a tumultuous privacy of storm."
                      EMERSON.

THE sun that brief December day
Rose cheerless over hills of gray,
And, darkly circled, gave at noon
A sadder light than waning moon.
Slow tracing down the thickening sky
Its mute and ominous prophecy,
A portent seeming less than threat,
It sank from sight before it set.

A chill no coat, however stout,
Of homespun stuff could quite shut out,
A hard, dull bitterness of cold,
  That checked, mid-vein, the circling race
Of life-blood in the sharpened face,
The coming of the snow-storm told.
The wind blew east ; we heard the roar
Of Ocean on his wintry shore,
And felt the strong pulse throbbing there
Beat with low rhythm our inland air.

Meanwhile we did our nightly chores;—
Brought in the wood from out of doors,
Littered the stalls, and from the mows
Raked down the herd's-grass for the cows :
Heard the horse whinnying for his corn ;
And, sharply clashing horn on horn,
Impatient down the stanchion rows
The cattle shake their walnut bows ;
While, peering from his early perch
Upon the scaffold's pole of birch,
The cock his crested helmet bent
And down his querulous challenge sent.

Unwarmed by any sunset light
The gray day darkened into night,
A night made hoary with the swarm,
And whirl-dance of the blinding storm,
As zigzag wavering to and fro
Crossed and recrossed the wingéd snow :
And ere the early bedtime came
The white drift piled the window-frame,
And through the glass the clothes-line
    posts
Looked in like tall and sheeted ghosts.

So all night long the storm roared on :
The morning broke without a sun ;
In tiny spherule traced with lines
Of Nature's geometric signs,
In starry flake, and pellicle,
All day the hoary meteor fell ;
And, when the second morning shone,
We looked upon a world unknown,
On nothing we could call our own.
Around the glistening wonder bent
The blue walls of the firmament,
No cloud above, no earth below, —
A universe of sky and snow !
The old familiar sights of ours
Took marvellous shapes ; strange domes
    and towers
Rose up where sty or corn-crib stood,
Or garden-wall, or belt of wood ; —
A smooth white mound the brush-pile
    showed,
A fenceless drift what once was road ;
The bridle-post an old man sat
With loose-flung coat and high cocked
    hat ;
The well-curb had a Chinese roof ;
And even the long sweep, high aloof,
In its slant splendor, seemed to tell
Of Pisa's leaning miracle.

A prompt, decisive man, no breath
Our father wasted : " Boys, a path ! "
Well pleased, (for when did farmer boy
Count such a summons less than joy ?)
Our buskins on our feet we drew ;
    With mittened hands, and caps drawn
        low,
    To guard our necks and ears from
        snow,
We cut the solid whiteness through.
And, where the drift was deepest, made
A tunnel walled and overlaid
With dazzling crystal : we had read
Of rare Aladdin's wondrous cave,
And to our own his name we gave,
With many a wish the luck were ours

To test his lamp's supernal power.
We reached the barn with merry din,
And roused the prisoned brutes within.
The old horse thrust his long head out,
And grave with wonder gazed about ;
The cock his lusty greeting said,
And forth his speckled harem led ;
The oxen lashed their tails, and hooked,
And mild reproach of hunger looked ;
The hornéd patriarch of the sheep,
Like Egypt's Amun roused from sleep,
Shook his sage head with gesture mute,
And emphasized with stamp of foot.

All day the gusty north-wind bore
The loosening drift its breath before ;
Low circling round its southern zone,
The sun through dazzling snow-mist
    shone.
No church-bell lent its Christian tone
To the savage air, no social smoke
Curled over woods of snow-hung oak.
A solitude made more intense
By dreary-voicéd elements,
The shrieking of the mindless wind,
The moaning tree-boughs swaying b'ind,
And on the glass the unmeaning beat
Of ghostly finger-tips of sleet.
Beyond the circle of our hearth
No welcome sound of toil or mirth
Unbound the spell, and testified
Of human life and thought outside.
We minded that the sharpest ear
The buried brooklet could not hear,
The music of whose liquid lip
Had been to us companionship,
And, in our lonely life, had grown
To have an almost human tone.

As night drew on, and, from the crest
Of wooded knolls that ridged the west,
The sun, a snow-blown traveller, sank
From sight beneath the smothering
    bank,
We piled, with care, our nightly stack
Of wood against the chimney-back, —
The oaken log, green, huge, and thick,
And on its top the stout back-stick ;
The knotty forestick laid apart,
And filled between with curious art
The ragged brush ; then, hovering near,
We watched the first red blaze appear,
Heard the sharp crackle, caught the
    gleam
On whitewashed wall and sagging beam,
Until the old, rude-furnished room
Burst, flower-like, into rosy bloom ;

...th a mimic flame
...kling drift became,
...e bare-boughed lilac-tree
...n hearth seemed blazing

... pendent trammels showed,
The Tur... eads on the andirons glowed;
While childish fancy, prompt to tell
The meaning of the miracle,
Whispered the old rhyme : " *Under the tree,*
When fire outdoors burns merrily,
There the witches are making tea."

The moon above the eastern wood
Shone at its full; the hill-range stood
Transfigured in the silver flood,
Its blown snows flashing cold and keen,
Dead white, save where some sharp ravine
Took shadow, or the sombre green
Of hemlocks turned to pitchy black
Against the whiteness at their back.
For such a world and such a night
Most fitting that unwarming light,
Which only seemed where'er it fell
To make the coldness visible.

Shut in from all the world without,
We sat the clean-winged hearth about,
Content to let the north-wind roar
In baffled rage at pane and door,
While the red logs before us beat
The frost-line back with tropic heat;
And ever, when a louder blast
Shook beam and rafter as it passed,
The merrier up its roaring draught
The great throat of the chimney laughed,
The house-dog on his paws outspread
Laid to the fire his drowsy head,
The cat's dark silhouette on the wall
A couchant tiger's seemed to fall;
And, for the winter fireside meet,
Between the andirons' straddling feet,
The mug of cider simmered slow,
The apples sputtered in a row,
And, close at hand, the basket stood
With nuts from brown October's wood.

What matter how the night behaved?
What matter how the north-wind raved?
Blow high, blow low, not all its snow
Could quench our hearth-fire's ruddy glow.
O Time and Change!— with hair as gray
As was my sire's that winter day,

How strange it seems, with so much gone
Of life and love, to still live on!
Ah, brother! only I and thou
Are left of all that circle now, —
The dear home faces whereupon
That fitful firelight paled and shone.
Henceforward, listen as we will,
The voices of that hearth are still;
Look where we may, the wide earth o'er,
Those lighted faces smile no more.
We tread the paths their feet have worn,
We sit beneath their orchard trees,
We hear, like them, the hum of bees
And rustle of the bladed corn;
We turn the pages that they read,
Their written words we linger o'er,
But in the sun they cast no shade,
No voice is heard, no sign is made,
No step is on the conscious floor!
Yet Love will dream, and Faith will trust,
(Since He who knows our need is just,)
That somehow, somewhere, meet we must.
Alas for him who never sees
The stars shine through his cypress-trees!
Who, hopeless, lays his dead away,
Nor looks to see the breaking day
Across the mournful marbles play!
Who hath not learned, in hours of faith,
The truth to flesh and sense unknown,
That Life is ever lord of Death,
And Love can never lose its own!

We sped the time with stories old,
Wrought puzzles out, and riddles told,
Or stammered from our school-book lore
"The Chief of Gambia's golden shore."
How often since, when all the land
Was clay in Slavery's shaping hand,
As if a trumpet called, I've heard
Dame Mercy Warren's rousing word:
"*Does not the voice of reason cry,*
Claim the first right which Nature gave,
From the red scourge of bondage fly,
Nor deign to live a burdened slave!"
Our father rode again his ride
On Memphremagog's wooded side;
Sat down again to moose and samp
In trapper's hut and Indian camp;
Lived o'er the old idyllic ease
Beneath St. François' hemlock-trees;
Again for him the moonlight shone
On Norman cap and bodiced zone;
Again he heard the violin play

Which led the village dance away,
And mingled in its merry whirl
The grandam and the laughing girl.
Or, nearer home, our steps he led
Where Salisbury's level marshes spread
  Mile-wide as flies the laden bee ;
Where merry mowers, hale and strong,
Swept, scythe on scythe, their swaths
    along
  The low green prairies of the sea.
We shared the fishing off Boar's Head,
  And round the rocky Isles of Shoals
  The hake-broil on the drift-wood
    coals ;
The chowder on the sand-beach made,
Dipped by the hungry, steaming hot,
With spoons of clam-shell from the
    pot.
We heard the tales of witchcraft old,
And dream and sign and marvel told
To sleepy listeners as they lay
Stretched idly on the salted hay,
Adrift along the winding shores,
When favoring breezes deigned to blow
The square sail of the gundelow
And idle lay the useless oars.

Our mother, while she turned her wheel
Or run the new-knit stocking-heel,
Told how the Indian hordes came down
At midnight on Cochecho town,
And how her own great-uncle bore
His cruel scalp-mark to fourscore.
Recalling, in her fitting phrase,
  So rich and picturesque and free,
  (The common unrhymed poetry
Of simple life and country ways,)
The story of her early days, —
She made us welcome to her home ;
Old hearths grew wide to give us room ;
We stole with her a frightened look
At the gray wizard's conjuring-book,
The fame whereof went far and wide
Through all the simple country side ;
We heard the hawks at twilight play,
The boat-horn on Piscataqua,
The loon's weird laughter far away ;
We fished her little trout-brook, knew

Then, haply, with a look more grave,
And soberer tone, some tale she gave
From painful Sewell's ancient tome,
Beloved in every Quaker home,
Of faith fire-winged by martyrdom,
Or Chalkley's Journal, old and quaint, —
Gentlest of skippers, rare sea-saint ! —
Who, when the dreary calms prevailed,
And water-butt and bread-cask failed,
And cruel, hungry eyes pursued
His portly presence mad for food,
With dark hints muttered under breath
Of casting lots for life or death,
Offered, if Heaven withheld supplies,
To be himself the sacrifice.
Then, suddenly, as if to save
The good man from his living grave,
A ripple on the water grew,
A school of porpoise flashed in view.
" Take, eat," he said, " and be content;
These fishes in my stead are sent
By Him who gave the tangled ram
To spare the child of Abraham."

Our uncle, innocent of books,
Was rich in lore of fields and brooks,
The ancient teachers never dumb
Of Nature's unhoused lyceum.
In moons and tides and weather wise,
He read the clouds as prophecies,
And foul or fair could well divine,
By many an occult hint and sign,
Holding the cunning-warded keys
To all the woodcraft mysteries ;
Himself to Nature's heart so near
That all her voices in his ear
Of beast or bird had meanings clear,
Like Apollonius of old,
Who knew the tales the sparrows told,
Or Hermes who interpreted
What the sage cranes of Nilus said ;
A simple, guileless, childlike man,
Content to live where life began ;
Strong only on his native grounds,
The little world of sights and sounds
Whose girdle was the parish bounds,
Whereof his fondly partial pride
The common features magnified.

From ripening corn the pigeons flew,
The partridge drummed i' the wood, the
   mink
Went fishing down the river-brink.
In fields with bean or clover gay,
The woodchuck, like a hermit gray,
  Peered from the doorway of his cell ;
The muskrat plied the mason's trade,
And tier by tier his mud-walls laid ;
And from the shagbark overhead
   The grizzled squirrel dropped his shell.

Next, the dear aunt, whose smile of
   cheer
And voice in dreams I see and hear, —
The sweetest woman ever Fate
Perverse denied a household mate,
Who, lonely, homeless, not the less
Found peace in love's unselfishness,
And welcome wheresoe'er she went,
A calm and gracious element,
Whose presence seemed the sweet in-
   come
And womanly atmosphere of home, —
Called up her girlhood memories,
The huskings and the apple-bees,
The sleigh-rides and the summer sails,
Weaving through all the poor details
And homespun warp of circumstance
A golden woof-thread of romance.
For well she kept her genial mood
And simple faith of maidenhood ;
Before her still a cloud-land lay,
The mirage loomed across her way ;
The morning dew, that dries so soon
With others, glistened at her noon ;
Through years of toil and soil and care,
From glossy tress to thin gray hair,
All unprofaned she held apart
The virgin fancies of the heart.
Be shame to him of woman born
Who hath for such but thought of scorn.

There, too, our elder sister plied
Her evening task the stand beside ;
A full, rich nature, free to trust,
Truthful and almost sternly just,
Impulsive, earnest, prompt to act,
And make her generous thought a
   fact,
Keeping with many a light disguise
The secret of self-sacrifice.
O heart sore-tried ! thou hast the best
That Heaven itself could give thee, —
   rest,
Rest from all bitter thoughts and things !

With thee beneath the low green
   tent
Whose curtain never outward swings !

As one who held herself a part
Of all she saw, and let her heart
  Against the household bosom lean,
Upon the motley-braided mat
Our youngest and our dearest sat,
Lifting her large, sweet, asking eyes,
  Now bathed within the fadeless green
And holy peace of Paradise.
O, looking from some heavenly hill,
  Or from the shade of saintly palms,
  Or silver reach of river calms,
Do those large eyes behold me still ?
With me one little year ago : —
The chill weight of the winter snow
  For months upon her grave has lain
And now, when summer south-wind
   blow
  And brier and harebell bloom again,
I tread the pleasant paths we trod,
I see the violet-sprinkled sod
Whereon she leaned, too frail and weak
The hillside flowers she loved to seek,
Yet following me where'er I went
With dark eyes full of love's content.
The birds are glad ; the brier-rose fills
The air with sweetness ; all the hills
Stretch green to June's unclouded
   sky ;
But still I wait with ear and eye
For something gone which should b
   nigh,
A loss in all familiar things,
In flower that blooms, and bird tha
   sings.
And yet, dear heart ! remembering thee
  Am I not richer than of old ?
Safe in thy immortality,
  What change can reach the wealth
   hold ?
  What chance can mar the pearl an
   gold
Thy love hath left in trust with me ?
And while in life's late afternoon,
  Where cool and long the shadow
   grow,
I walk to meet the night that soon
  Shall shape and shadow overflow,
I cannot feel that thou art far,
Since near at need the angels are ;
And when the sunset gates unbar,
  Shall I not see thee waiting stand,
And, white against the evening star,

Brisk wielder of the birch and rule,
The master of the district school
Held at the fire his favored place,
Its warm glow lit a laughing face
Fresh-hued and fair, where scarce ap-
        peared
The uncertain prophecy of beard.
He teased the mitten-blinded cat,
Played cross-pins on my uncle's hat,
Sang songs, and told us what befalls
In classic Dartmouth's college halls.
Born the wild Northern hills among,
From whence his yeoman father wrung
By patient toil subsistence scant,
Not competence and yet not want,
He early gained the power to pay
His cheerful, self-reliant way ;
Could doff at ease his scholar's gown
To peddle wares from town to town ;
Or through the long vacation's reach
In lonely lowland districts teach,
Where all the droll experience found
At stranger hearths in boarding round,
The moonlit skater's keen delight,
The sleigh - drive through the frosty
        night, .
The rustic party, with its rough
Accompaniment of blind-man's-buff,
And whirling plate, and forfeits paid,
His winter task a pastime made,
Happy the snow-locked homes wherein
He tuned his merry violin,
Or played the athlete in the barn,
Or held the good dame's winding-yarn,
Or mirth-provoking versions told
Of classic legends rare and old,
Wherein the scenes of Greece and Rome
Had all the commonplace of home,
And little seemed at best the odds
'Twixt Yankee pedlers and old gods ;
Where Pindus-born Araxes took
The guise of any grist-mill brook,
And dread Olympus at his will
Became a huckleberry hill.

A careless boy that night he seemed ;
  But at his desk he had the look
And air of one who wisely schemed,
  And hostage from the future took
  In trained thought and lore of book.
Large-brained, clear-eyed, — of such as
        he
Shall Freedom's young apostles be,
Who, following in War's bloody trail,
Shall every lingering wrong assail ;
All chains from limb and spirit strike,
Uplift the black and white alike ;

Scatter before their swift advance
The darkness and the ignorance,
The pride, the lust, the squalid sloth,
Which nurtured Treason's monstrous
        growth,
Made murder pastime, and the hell
Of prison-torture possible ;
The cruel lie of caste refute,
Old forms remould, and substitute
For Slavery's lash the freeman's will,
For blind routine, wise-handed skill ;
A school-house plant on every hill,
Stretching in radiate nerve-lines thence
The quick wires of intelligence ;
Till North and South together brought
Shall own the same electric thought,
In peace a common flag salute,
And, side by side in labor's free
And unresentful rivalry,
Harvest the fields wherein they fought.

Another guest that winter night
Flashed back from lustrous eyes the
        light.
Unmarked by time, and yet not young,
The honeyed music of her tongue
And words of meekness scarcely told
A nature passionate and bold,
Strong, self-concentred, spurning guide,
Its milder features dwarfed beside
Her unbent will's majestic pride.
She sat among us, at the best,
A not unfeared, half-welcome guest,
Rebuking with her cultured phrase
Our homeliness of words and ways.
A certain pard-like, treacherous grace
  Swayed the lithe limbs and dropped
        the lash,
  Lent the white teeth their dazzling
        flash ;
  And under low brows, black with
        night,
  Rayed out at times a dangerous light ;
The sharp heat-lightnings of her face
Presaging ill to him whom Fate
Condemned to share her love or hate.
A woman tropical, intense
In thought and act, in soul and sense,
She blended in a like degree
The vixen and the devotee,
Revealing with each freak or feint
  The temper of Petruchio's Kate,
The raptures of Siena's saint.
Her tapering hand and rounded wrist
Had facile power to form a fist ;
The warm, dark languish of her eyes
Was never safe from wrath's surprise.

Brows saintly calm and lips devout
Knew every change of scowl and pout ;
And the sweet voice had notes more
    high
And shrill for social battle-cry.
Since then what old cathedral town
Has missed her pilgrim staff and gown,
What convent-gate has held its lock
Against the challenge of her knock !
Through Smyrna's plague-hushed thor-
    oughfares,
Up sea-set Malta's rocky stairs,
Gray olive slopes of hills that hem
Thy tombs and shrines, Jerusalem,
Or startling on her desert throne
The crazy Queen of Lebanon
With claims fantastic as her own,
Her tireless feet have held their way ;
And still, unrestful, bowed, and gray,
She watches under Eastern skies,
    With hope each day renewed and
    fresh,
    The Lord's quick coming in the flesh,
Whereof she dreams and prophesies !

Where'er her troubled path may be,
    The Lord's sweet pity with her go !
The outward wayward life we see,
    The hidden springs we may not know.
Nor is it given us to discern
    What threads the fatal sisters spun,
    Through what ancestral years has
    run
The sorrow with the woman born,
What forged her cruel chain of moods,
What set her feet in solitudes,
    And held the love within her mute,
What mingled madness in the blood,
    A life-long discord and annoy,
    Water of tears with oil of joy,
And hid within the folded bud
    Perversities of flower and fruit.
It is not ours to separate
The tangled skein of will and fate,
To show what metes and bounds should
    stand
Upon the soul's debatable land,
And between choice and Providence
Divide the circle of events ;
    But He who knows our frame is just,
Merciful and compassionate,
And full of sweet assurances
And hope for all the language is,
    That He remembereth we are dust !

At last the great logs, crumbling low,
Sent out a dull and duller glow,
The bull's-eye watch that hung in view,
Ticking its weary circuit through,
Pointed with mutely warning sign
Its black hand to the hour of nine.
That sign the pleasant circle broke :
My uncle ceased his pipe to smoke,
Knocked from its bowl the refuse gray,
And laid it tenderly away,
Then roused himself to safely cover
The dull red brands with ashes over.
And while, with care, our mother laid
The work aside, her steps she stayed
One moment, seeking to express
Her grateful sense of happiness
For food and shelter, warmth and
    health,
And love's contentment more than
    wealth,
With simple wishes (not the weak,
Vain prayers which no fulfilment seek,
But such as warm the generous heart,
O'er-prompt to do with Heaven its part)
That none might lack, that bitter night,
For bread and clothing, warmth and
    light.

Within our beds awhile we heard
The wind that round the gables roared,
With now and then a ruder shock,
Which made our very bedsteads rock.
We heard the loosened clapboards tost,
The board-nails snapping in the frost ;
And on us, through the unplastered
    wall,
Felt the light sifted snow-flakes fall.
But sleep stole on, as sleep will do
When hearts are light and life is new ;
Faint and more faint the murmurs grew,
Till in the summer-land of dreams
They softened to the sound of streams,
Low stir of leaves, and dip of oars,
And lapsing waves on quiet shores.

Next morn we wakened with the shout
Of merry voices high and clear ;
And saw the teamsters drawing near
To break the drifted highways out.
Down the long hillside treading slow
We saw the half-buried oxen go,
Shaking the snow from heads uptost,
Their straining nostrils white with frost.
Before our door the straggling train
Drew up, an added team to gain.
The elders threshed their hands a-cold,
    Passed, with the cider-mug, their
    jokes
From lip to lip ; the younger folks

Down the loose snow-banks, wrestling,
   rolled,
Then toiled again the cavalcade
  O'er windy hill, through clogged ra-
   vine,
  And woodland paths that wound be-
   tween
Low drooping pine - boughs winter-
   weighed.
From every barn a team afoot,
At every house a new recruit,
Where, drawn by Nature's subtlest law
Haply the watchful young men saw
Sweet doorway pictures of the curls
And curious eyes of merry girls,
Lifting their hands in mock defence
Against the snow-ball's compliments,
And reading in each missive tost
The charm with Eden never lost.

We heard once more the sleigh-bells'
   sound ;
  And, following where the teamsters
   led,
The wise old Doctor went his round,
Just pausing at our door to say,
In the brief autocratic way
Of one who, prompt at Duty's call,
Was free to urge her claim on all,
That some poor neighbor sick abed
At night our mother's aid would need.
For, one in generous thought and deed,
  What mattered in the sufferer's sight
  The Quaker matron's inward light,
The Doctor's mail of Calvin's creed ?
All hearts confess the saints elect
Who, twain in faith, in love agree,
And melt not in an acid sect
  The Christian pearl of charity !

So days went on : a week had passed
Since the great world was heard from
   last.
The Almanac we studied o'er,
Read and reread our little store,
Of books and pamphlets, scarce a score ;
One harmless novel, mostly hid
From younger eyes, a book forbid,
And poetry, (or good or bad,
A single book was all we had,)
Where Ellwood's meek, drab-skirted
   Muse,
  A stranger to the heathen Nine,
  Sang, with a somewhat nasal whine,
The wars of David and the Jews.
At last the floundering carrier bore
The village paper to our door.

Lo ! broadening outward as we read,
To warmer zones the horizon spread ;
In panoramic length unrolled
We saw the marvels that it told.
Before us passed the painted Creeks,
  And daft McGregor on his raids
  In Costa Rica's everglades.
And up Taygetos winding slow
Rode Ypsilanti's Mainote Greeks,
A Turk's head at each saddle-bow !
Welcome to us its week-old news,
Its corner for the rustic Muse,
  Its monthly gauge of snow and rain,
Its record, mingling in a breath
The wedding knell and dirge of death ;
Jest, anecdote, and love-lorn tale,
The latest culprit sent to jail ;
Its hue and cry of stolen and lost,
Its vendue sales and goods at cost,
  And traffic calling loud for gain.
We felt the stir of hall and street,
The pulse of life that round us beat ;
The chill embargo of the snow
Was melted in the genial glow ;
Wide swung again our ice-locked door,
And all the world was ours once more !

Clasp, Angel of the backward look
  And folded wings of ashen gray
  And voice of echoes far away,
The brazen covers of thy book ;
The weird palimpsest old and vast,
Wherein thou hid'st the spectral past ;
Where, closely mingling, pale and glow
The characters of joy and woe ;
The monographs of outlived years,
Or smile-illumed or dim with tears,
  Green hills of life that slope to death,
And haunts of home, whose vistaed trees
Shade off to mournful cypresses
  With the white amaranths underneath.
Even while I look, I can but heed
  The restless sands' incessant fall,
Importunate hours that hours succeed,
Each clamorous with its own sharp
   need,
  And duty keeping pace with all.
Shut down and clasp the heavy lids ;
I hear again the voice that bids
The dreamer leave his dream midway
For larger hopes and graver fears :
Life greatens in these later years,
The century's aloe flowers to-day !

Yet, haply, in some lull of life,
Some Truce of God which breaks its
   strife,

The worldling's eyes shall gather dew,
  Dreaming in throngful city ways
Of winter joys his boyhood knew;
And dear and early friends — the few
Who yet remain — shall pause to view
  These Flemish pictures of old days;
Sit with me by the homestead hearth,
And stretch the hands of memory forth
  To warm them at the wood-fire's blaze!

And thanks untraced to lips unknown
Shall greet me like the odors blown
From unseen meadows newly mown,
Or lilies floating in some pond,
Wood-fringed, the wayside gaze beyond;
The traveller owns the grateful sense
Of sweetness near, he knows not whence,
And, pausing, takes with forehead bare
The benediction of the air.

THE TENT ON THE BEACH,

AND OTHER POEMS.

I WOULD not sin, in this half-playful
  strain, —
  Too light perhaps for serious years,
  though born
Of the enforced leisure of slow pain, —
  Against the pure ideal which has
  drawn
My feet to follow its far-shining gleam.
A simple plot is mine: legends and
  runes
Of credulous days, old fancies that have
  lain
Silent from boyhood taking voice again,
Warmed into life once more, even as the
  tunes
That, frozen in the fabled hunting-horn,
Thawed into sound: — a winter fireside
  dream
Of dawns and sunsets by the summer
  sea,
Whose sands are traversed by a silent
  throng
Of voyagers from that vaster mystery
Of which it is an emblem; — and the
  dear
Memory of one who might have tuned
  my song
To sweeter music by her delicate ear.

1st mo., 1867.

THE TENT ON THE BEACH.

WHEN heats as of a tropic clime
  Burned all our inland valleys
  through,

Three friends, the guests of summer
  time,
  Pitched their white tent where sea-
  winds blew.
Behind them, marshes, seamed and
  crossed
With narrow creeks, and flower-em-
  bossed,
Stretched to the dark oak wood, whose
  leafy arms
Screened from the stormy East the
  pleasant inland farms.

At full of tide their bolder shore
  Of sun-bleached sand the waters
  beat;
At ebb, a smooth and glistening
  floor
  They touched with light, receding
  feet.
Northward a green bluff broke the
  chain
Of sand-hills; southward stretched a
  plain
Of salt grass, with a river winding
  down,
Sail-whitened, and beyond the steeples
  of the town,

Whence sometimes, when the wind
  was light
  And dull the thunder of the beach,
They heard the bells of morn and
  night
  Swing, miles away, their silver
  speech.

Above low scarp and turf-grown
  wall
They saw the fort-flag rise and fall ;
And, the first star to signal twilight's
  hour,
The lamp-fire glimmer down from the
  tall lighthouse tower.

They rested there, escaped awhile
    From cares that wear the life away,
To eat the lotus of the Nile
    And drink the poppies of Cathay, —
To fling their loads of custom down,
Like drift-weed, on the sand-slopes
  brown,
And in the sea waves drown the restless
  pack
Of duties, claims, and needs that barked
  upon their track.

One, with his beard scarce silvered,
  bore
    A ready credence in his looks,
A lettered magnate, lording o'er
    An ever-widening realm of books.
In him brain - currents, near and
  far,
Converged as in a Leyden jar ;
The old, dead authors thronged him
  round about,
And Elzevir's gray ghosts from leathern
  graves looked out.

He knew each living pundit well,
    Could weigh the gifts of him or
  her,
And well the market value tell
    Of poet and philosopher.
But if he lost, the scenes behind,
Somewhat of reverence vague and
  blind,
Finding the actors human at the best,
No readier lips than his the good he
  saw confessed.

His boyhood fancies not outgrown,
    He loved himself the singer's art;
Tenderly, gently, by his own
    He knew and judged an author's
  heart.
No Rhadamanthine brow of doom
Bowed the dazed pedant from his
  room ;
And bards, whose name is legion, if
  denied,
Bore off alike intact their verses and
  their pride.

Pleasant it was to roam about
    The lettered world as he had done,
And see the lords of song without
    Their singing robes and garlands
  on.
With Wordsworth paddle Rydal
  mere,
Taste rugged Elliott's home-brewed
  beer,
And with the ears of Rogers, at four-
  score,
Hear Garrick's buskined tread and
  Walpole's wit once more.

And one there was, a dreamer born,
    Who, with a mission to fulfil,
Had left the Muses' haunts to turn
    The crank of an opinion-mill,
Making his rustic reed of song
A weapon in the war with wrong,
Yoking his fancy to the breaking-plough
That beam-deep turned the soil for truth
    to spring and grow.

Too quiet seemed the man to ride
    The winged Hippogriff Reform ;
Was his a voice from side to side
    To pierce the tumult of the storm ?
A silent, shy, peace-loving man,
He seemed no fiery partisan
To hold his way against the public
  frown,
The ban of Church and State, the fierce
  mob's hounding down.

For while he wrought with strenuous
  will
    The work his hands had found to
  do,
He heard the fitful music still
    Of winds that out of dream-land
  blew.
The din about him could not drown
What the strange voices whispered
  down ;
Along his task-field weird processions
  swept,
The visionary pomp of stately phantoms
  stepped.

The common air was thick with
  dreams, —
    He told them to the toiling crowd ;
Such music as the woods and streams
    Sang in his ear he sang aloud ;
In still, shut bays, on windy capes,
He heard the call of beckoning shapes,

And, as the gray old shadows prompted
  him,
To homely moulds of rhyme he shaped
  their legends grim.

He rested now his weary hands,
  And lightly moralized and laughed,
As, tracing on the shifting sands
  A burlesque of his paper-craft,
He saw the careless waves o'errun
  His words, as time before had done,
Each day's tide-water washing clean
  away,
Like letters from the sand, the work of
  yesterday.

And one, whose Arab face was tanned
  By tropic sun and boreal frost,
So travelled there was scarce a land
  Or people left him to exhaust,
In idling mood had from him hurled
  The poor squeezed orange of the
  world,
And in the tent-shade, as beneath a
  palm,
Smoked, cross-legged like a Turk, in
  Oriental calm.

The very waves that washed the
  sand
  Below him, he had seen before
Whitening the Scandinavian strand
  And sultry Mauritanian shore.
From ice-rimmed isles, from summer
  seas
Palm-fringed, they bore him messages;
He heard the plaintive Nubian songs
  again,
And mule-bells tinkling down the moun-
  tain-paths of Spain.

His memory round the ransacked
  earth
  On Ariel's girdle slid at ease;
And, instant, to the valley's girth
  Of mountains, spice isles of the
  seas,
Faith flowered in minster stones,
  Art's guess
At truth and beauty, found access ;
Yet loved the while, that free cosmopo-
  lite,
Old friends, old ways, and kept his boy-
  hood's dreams in sight.

Untouched as yet by wealth and pride,
  That virgin innocence of beach :

No shingly monster, hundred-eyed,
  Stared its gray sand-birds out of
  reach ;
Unhoused, save where, at intervals,
  The white tents showed their canvas
  walls,
Where brief sojourners, in the cool,
  soft air,
Forgot their inland heats, hard toil, and
  year-long care.

Sometimes along the wheel-deep sand
  A one-horse wagon slowly crawled,
Deep laden with a youthful band,
  Whose look some homestead old
  recalled ;
Brother perchance, and sisters twain,
  And one whose blue eyes told, more
  plain
Than the free language of her rosy lip,
Of the still dearer claim of love's rela-
  tionship.

With cheeks of russet-orchard tint,
  The light laugh of their native rills,
The perfume of their garden's mint,
  The breezy freedom of the hills,
They bore, in unrestrained delight,
  The motto of the Garter's knight,
Careless as if from every gazing thing
Hid by their innocence, as Gyges by
  his ring.

The clanging sea-fowl came and went,
  The hunter's gun in the marshes
  rang ;
At nightfall from a neighboring tent
  A flute-voiced woman sweetly sang.
Loose-haired, barefooted, hand-in-
  hand,
Young girls went tripping down the
  sand ;
And youths and maidens, sitting in the
  moon,
Dreamed o'er the old fond dream from
  which we wake too soon.

At times their fishing-lines they plied,
  With an old Triton at the oar,
Salt as the sea-wind, tough and dried
  As a lean cusk from Labrador.
Strange tales he told of wreck and
  storm, —
Had seen the sea-snake's awful form,
And heard the ghosts on Haley's Isle
  complain,
Speak him off shore, and beg a passage
  to old Spain !

And there, on breezy morns, they saw
   The fishing-schooners outward run,
Their low-bent sails in tack and flaw
   Turned white or dark to shade and
      sun.
Sometimes, in calms of closing day,
They watched the spectral mirage
      play,
Saw low, far islands looming tall and
      nigh,
And ships, with upturned keels, sail like
   a sea the sky.

Sometimes a cloud, with thunder
      black,
   Stooped low upon the darkening
      main,
Piercing the waves along its track   . .
   With the slant javelins of rain.
And when west-wind and sunshine
      warm
Chased out to sea its wrecks of storm,
They saw the prismy hues in thin spray
      showers
Where the green buds of waves burst
   into white froth flowers.

And when along the line of shore
   The mists crept upward chill and
      damp,
Stretched, careless, on their sandy
      floor
   Beneath the flaring lantern lamp,
They talked of all things old and
      new,
Read, slept, and dreamed as idlers
      do ;
And in the unquestioned freedom of the
    · tent,
Body and o'er-taxed mind to healthful
   ease unbent.

Once, when the sunset splendors died,
   And, trampling up the sloping sand,
In lines outreaching far and wide,
   The white-maned billows swept to
      land,
Dim seen across the gathering shade,
A vast and ghostly cavalcade,
They sat around their lighted kerosene,
Hearing the deep bass roar their every
   pause between.

Then, urged thereto, the Editor
   Within his full portfolio dipped,
Feigning excuse while searching for
   (With secret pride) his manuscript.

His pale face flushed from eye to
      beard,
With nervous cough his throat he
      cleared,
And, in a voice so tremulous it betrayed
The anxious fondness of an author's
      heart, he read :

THE WRECK OF RIVERMOUTH.

Rivermouth Rocks are fair to see,
   By dawn or sunset shone across,
When the ebb of the sea has left them
      free,
   To dry their fringes of gold-green
      moss :
For there the river comes winding down
From salt sea-meadows and uplands
      brown,
And waves on the outer rocks afoam
Shout to its waters, "Welcome home!"

And fair are the sunny isles in view
   East of the grisly Head of the Boar,
And Agamenticus lifts its blue
   Disk of a cloud the woodlands o'er ;
And southerly, when the tide is down,
'Twixt white sea-waves and sand-hills
      brown,
The beach-birds dance and the gray
      gulls wheel
Over a floor of burnished steel.

Once, in the old Colonial days,
   Two hundred years ago and more,
A boat sailed down through the wind-
      ing ways
   Of Hampton River to that low shore,
Full of a goodly company
Sailing out on the summer sea,
Veering to catch the land-breeze light,
With the Boar to left and the Rocks to
      right.

In Hampton meadows, where mowers
      laid
   Their scythes to the swaths of salted
      grass,
"Ah, well-a-day ! our hay must be
      made !"
   A young man sighed, who saw them
      pass.
Loud laughed his fellows to see him
      stand
Whetting his scythe with a listless hand,
Hearing a voice in a far-off song,
Watching a white hand beckoning long.

"Fie on the witch!" cried a merry
    girl,
  As they rounded the point where
    Goody Cole
Sat by her door with her wheel atwirl,
  A bent and blear-eyed poor old soul.
"Oho!" she muttered, "ye 're brave
    to-day!
But I hear the little waves laugh and
    say,
'The broth will be cold that waits at
    home;
For it 's one to go, but another to
    come!'"

"She 's cursed," said the skipper;
    "speak her fair:
I 'm scary always to see her shake
Her wicked head, with its wild gray
    hair,
  And nose like a hawk, and eyes like a
    snake."
But merrily still, with laugh and shout,
From Hampton River the boat sailed
    out,
Till the huts and the flakes on Star
    seemed nigh,
And they lost the scent of the pines of
    Rye.

They dropped their lines in the lazy
    tide,
  Drawing up haddock and mottled
    cod;
They saw not the Shadow that walked
    beside,
  They heard not the feet with silence
    shod.
But thicker and thicker a hot mist
    grew,
Shot by the lightnings through and
    through;
And muffled growls, like the growl of a
    beast,
Ran along the sky from west to east.

Then the skipper looked from the dark-
    ening sea
Up to the dimmed and wading sun;
But he spake like a brave man cheer-
    ily,
  "Yet there is time for our homeward
    run."
Veering and tacking, they backward
    wore;
And just as a breath from the woods
    ashore

Blew out to whispe
  The wrath of the
    last!

The skipper hauled
  "God be our hel₁
As the roaring gal₁
    flail,
  Smote the boat o
The Shoalsmen loo
Dark films of rain-c
Wild rocks lit u₁
    glare,
The strife and torn

Goody Cole looked
  The Isles of Sho₁
    gone,
Scarcely she saw th
  Toss the foam fr₁
She clasped her h
    pain,
The tear on her ch₁
  "They are lost," ;
    and crew!
Lord, forgive me
    true!"

Suddenly seaward ;
  The low sun sn
    rack;
The Shoals stood c
    all
  The trend of th
    black.
But far and wide a
No life was seen u₁
The boat that w₁
    never
Sailed back again i

O mower, lean on t
  Look from the
    low:
The wind of the se₁
  The waves are si:
By silent river, by
Long and vain shal
Never again shall t
Never the white h₁

O Rivermouth Roc
  Ye saw in the
    day!
Dead faces looking
  From sand and
    lay.

The mad old witch-wife wailed and
  wept,
And cursed the tide as it backward
  crept:
"Crawl back, crawl back, blue water-
  snake!
Leave your dead for the hearts that
  break!"

Solemn it was in that old day
  In Hampton town and its log-built
    church,
Where side by side the coffins lay
  And the mourners stood in aisle and
    porch.
In the singing-seats young eyes were
  dim,
The voices faltered that raised the
  hymn,
And Father Dalton, grave and stern,
Sobbed through his prayer and wept in
  turn.

But his ancient colleague did not pray,
  Because of his sin at fourscore years:
He stood apart, with the iron-gray
  Of his strong brows knitted to hide
    his tears.
And a wretched woman, holding her
  breath
In the awful presence of sin and death,
Cowered and shrank, while her neigh-
  bors thronged
To look on the dead her shame had
  wronged.

Apart with them, like them forbid,
  Old Goody Cole looked drearily
    round,
As, two by two, with their faces hid,
  The mourners walked to the burying-
    ground.
She let the staff from her clasped hands
  fall:
"Lord, forgive us! we 're sinners all!"
And the voice of the old man answered
  her:
"Amen!" said Father Bachiler.

So, as I sat upon Appledore
  In the calm of a closing summer day,
And the broken lines of Hampton shore
  In purple mist of cloudland lay,
The Rivermouth Rocks their story told;
And waves aglow with sunset gold,
Rising and breaking in steady chime,
Beat the rhythm and kept the time.

And the sunset paled, and warmed once
  more
  With a softer, tenderer after-glow;
In the east was moon-rise, with boats
  off-shore
  And sails in the distance drifting
    slow.
The beacon glimmered from Ports-
  mouth bar,
The White Isle kindled its great red
  star;
And life and death in my old-time lay
Mingled in peace like the night and
  day!

———

"Well!" said the Man of Books,
  "your story
  Is really not ill told in verse.
As the Celt said of purgatory,
  One might go farther and fare worse."
The Reader smiled; and once again
  With steadier voice took up his
    strain,
While the fair singer from the neighbor-
  ing tent
Drew near, and at his side a graceful
  listener bent.

THE GRAVE BY THE LAKE.

WHERE the Great Lake's sunny smiles
Dimple round its hundred isles,
And the mountain's granite ledge
Cleaves the water like a wedge,
Ringed about with smooth, gray stones,
Rest the giant's mighty bones.

Close beside, in shade and gleam,
Laughs and ripples Melvin stream;
Melvin water, mountain-born,
All fair flowers its banks adorn;
All the woodland's voices meet,
Mingling with its murmurs sweet.

Over lowlands forest-grown,
Over waters island-strown,
Over silver-sanded beach,
Leaf-locked bay and misty reach,
Melvin stream and burial-heap,
Watch and ward the mountains keep.

Who that Titan cromlech fills?
Forest-kaiser, lord o' the hills?
Knight who on the birchen tree
Carved his savage heraldry?

Priest o' the pine-wood temples dim,
Prophet, sage, or wizard grim ?

Rugged type of primal man,
Grim utilitarian,
Loving woods for hunt and prowl,
Lake and hill for fish and fowl,
As the brown bear blind and dull
To the grand and beautiful :

Not for him the lesson drawn
From the mountains smit with dawn.
Star-rise, moon-rise, flowers of May,
Sunset's purple bloom of day, —
Took his life no hue from thence,
Poor amid such affluence ?

Haply unto hill and tree
All too near akin was he:
Unto him who stands afar
Nature's marvels greatest are ;
Who the mountain purple seeks
Must not climb the higher peaks.

Yet who knows in winter tramp,
Or the midnight of the camp,
What revealings faint and far,
Stealing down from moon and star,
Kindled in that human clod
Thought of destiny and God ?

Stateliest forest patriarch,
Grand in robes of skin and bark,
What sepulchral mysteries,
What weird funeral-rites, were his ?
What sharp wail, what drear lament,
Back scared wolf and eagle sent ?

Now, whate'er he may have been,
Low he lies as other men :
On his mound the partridge drums,
There the noisy blue-jay comes ;
Rank nor name nor pomp has he
In the grave's democracy.

Part thy blue lips, Northern lake !
Moss-grown rocks, your silence break !
Tell the tale, thou ancient tree !
Thou, too, slide-worn Ossipee !
Speak, and tell us how and when
Lived and died this king of men !

Wordless moans the ancient pine ;
Lake and mountain give no sign ;
Vain to trace this ring of stones ;
Vain the search of crumbling bones :
Deepest of all mysteries,
And the saddest, silence is.

Nameless, noteless, clay with clay
Mingles slowly day by day ;
But somewhere, for good or ill,
That dark soul is living still ;
Somewhere yet that atom's force
Moves the light-poised universe.

Strange that on his burial-sod
Harebells bloom, and golden-rod,
While the soul's dark horoscope
Holds no starry sign of hope !
Is the Unseen with sight at odds ?
Nature's pity more than God's ?

Thus I mused by Melvin's side,
While the summer eventide
Made the woods and inland sea
And the mountains mystery ;
And the hush of earth and air
Seemed the pause before a prayer, —

Prayer for him, for all who rest,
Mother Earth, upon thy breast, —
Lapped on Christian turf, or hid
In rock-cave or pyramid :
All who sleep, as all who live,
Well may need the prayer, " Forgive !

Desert-smothered caravan,
Knee-deep dust that once was man,
Battle-trenches ghastly piled,
Ocean-floors with white bones tiled,
Crowded tomb and mounded sod,
Dumbly crave that prayer to God.

O the generations old
Over whom no church-bells tolled,
Christless, lifting up blind eyes
To the silence of the skies !
For the innumerable dead
Is my soul disquieted.

Where be now these silent hosts ?
Where the camping-ground of ghosts ?
Where the spectral conscripts led
To the white tents of the dead ?
What strange shore or chartless sea
Holds the awful mystery ?

Then the warm sky stooped to make
Double sunset in the lake ;
While above I saw with it,
Range on range, the mountains lit ;
And the calm and splendor stole
Like an answer to my soul.

Hear'st thou, O of little faith,
What to thee the mountain saith,

What is whispered by the trees ? —
"Cast on God thy care for these ;
Trust him, if thy sight be dim :
Doubt for them is doubt of Him.

" Blind must be their close-shut eyes
Where like night the sunshine lies,
Fiery-linked the self-forged chain
Binding ever sin to pain,
Strong their prison-house of will,
But without He waiteth still.

" Not with hatred's undertow
Doth the Love Eternal flow ;
Every chain that spirits wear
Crumbles in the breath of prayer ;
And the penitent's desire
Opens every gate of fire.

" Still Thy love, O Christ arisen,
Yearns to reach these souls in prison !
Through all depths of sin and loss
Drops the plummet of Thy cross !
Never yet abyss was found
Deeper than that cross could sound !"

Therefore well may Nature keep
Equal faith with all who sleep,
Set her watch of hills around
Christian grave and heathen mound,
And to cairn and kirkyard send
Summer's flowery dividend.

Keep, O pleasant Melvin stream,
Thy sweet laugh in shade and gleam !
On the Indian's grassy tomb
Swing, O flowers, your bells of bloom !
Deep below, as high above,
Sweeps the circle of God's love.

He paused and questioned with his
    eye
The hearers' verdict on his song.
A low voice asked : Is 't well to pry
Into the secrets which belong
Only to God ? — The life to be
Is still the unguessed mystery :
Unscaled, unpierced the cloudy walls
    remain,
We beat with dream and wish the
    soundless doors in vain.

" But faith beyond our sight may go."
He said : " The gracious Fatherhood
Can only know above, below,
    Eternal purposes of good.

From our free heritage of will,
    The bitter springs of pain and ill
Flow only in all worlds. The perfect
    day
Of God is shadowless, and love is love
    alway."

" I know," she said, "the letter kills ;
    That on our arid fields of strife
And heat of clashing texts distils
    The dew of spirit and of life.
But, searching still the written Word,
I fain would find, Thus saith the Lord,
A voucher for the hope I also feel
That sin can give no wound beyond
    love's power to heal."

" Pray," said the Man of Books,
    " give o'er
A theme too vast for time and place.
Go on, Sir Poet, ride once more
    Your hobby at his old free pace.
But let him keep, with step discreet,
    The solid earth beneath his feet.
In the great mystery which around us
    lies,
The wisest is a fool, the fool Heaven-
    helped is wise."

The Traveller said : " If songs have
    creeds,
    Their choice of them let singers
    make ;
But Art no other sanction needs
    Than beauty for its own fair sake.
It grinds not in the mill of use,
Nor asks for leave, nor begs excuse ;
It makes the flexile laws it deigns to
    own,
And gives its atmosphere its color and
    its tone.

" Confess, old friend, your austere
    school
    Has left your fancy little chance ;
You square to reason's rigid rule
    The flowing outlines of romance.
With conscience keen from exercise,
    And chronic fear of compromise,
You check the free play of your rhymes,
    to clap
A moral underneath, and spring it like
    a trap."

The sweet voice answered : " Better so
    Than bolder flights that know no
    check ;

Better to use the bit, than throw
  The reins all loose on fancy's neck.
The liberal range of Art should be
The breadth of Christian liberty,
Restrained alone by challenge and alarm
Where its charmed footsteps tread the
  border land of harm.

" Beyond the poet's sweet dream lives
  The eternal epic of the man.
He wisest is who only gives,
  True to himself, the best he can ;
Who, drifting in the winds of praise,
The inward monitor obeys ;
And, with the boldness that confesses fear,
Takes in the crowded sail, and lets his
  conscience steer.

" Thanks for the fitting word he speaks,
  Nor less for doubtful word unspoken ;
For the false model that he breaks,
As for the moulded grace unbroken ;
For what is missed and what remains,
For losses which are truest gains,
For reverence conscious of the Eternal
  eye,
And truth too fair to need the garnish
  of a lie."

Laughing, the Critic bowed. " I
  yield
  The point without another word ;
Who ever yet a case appealed
  Where beauty's judgment had been
  heard ?
And you, my good friend, owe to me
Your warmest thanks for such a plea,
As true withal as sweet. For my offence
Of cavil, let her words be ample recom-
  pense."

Across the sea one lighthouse star,
  With crimson ray that came and
  went,
Revolving on its tower afar,
  Looked through the doorway of the
  tent.
While outward, over sand-slopes wet,
The lamp flashed down its yellow jet
On the long wash of waves, with red and
  green
Tangles of weltering weed through the
  white foam-wreaths seen.

" ' Sing while we may, — another day
  May bring enough of sorrow ' ; —
  thus

Our Traveller in his own sweet lay,
  His Crimean camp-song, hints to us,"
The lady said. " So let it be ;
Sing us a song," exclaimed all three.
She smiled : " I can but marvel at your
  choice
To hear our poet's words through my
  poor borrowed voice."

Her window opens to the bay,
On glistening light or misty gray,
And there at dawn and set of day
  In prayer she kneels :
" Dear Lord ! " she saith, " to many a
  home
From wind and wave the wanderers
  come ;
I only see the tossing foam
  Of stranger keels.

" Blown out and in by summer gales,
The stately ships, with crowded sails,
And sailors leaning o'er their rails,
  Before me glide ;
They come, they go, but nevermore,
Spice-laden from the Indian shore,
I see his swift-winged Isidore
  The waves divide.

" O Thou ! with whom the night is day
And one the near and far away,
Look out on yon gray waste, and say
  Where lingers he.
Alive, perchance, on some lone beach
Or thirsty isle beyond the reach
Of man, he hears the mocking speech
  Of wind and sea.

" O dread and cruel deep, reveal
The secret which thy waves conceal,
And, ye wild sea-birds, hither wheel
  And tell your tale.
Let winds that tossed his raven hair
A message from my lost one bear, —
Some thought of me, a last fond prayer
  Or dying wail !

" Come, with your dreariest truth shut
  out
The fears that haunt me round about ;
O God ! I cannot bear this doubt
  That stifles breath.
The worst is better than the dread ;
Give me but leave to mourn my dead
Asleep in trust and hope, instead
  Of life in death ! "

It might have been the evening breeze
That whispered in the garden trees,
It might have been the sound of seas
   That rose and fell ;
But, with her heart, if not her ear,
The old loved voice she seemed to hear :
" I wait to meet thee : be of cheer,
   For all is well ! "

———

The sweet voice into silence went,
   A silence which was almost pain
As through it rolled the long lament,
   The cadence of the mournful main.
Glancing his written pages o'er,
   The Reader tried his part once more ;
Leaving the land of hackmatack and
   pine
For Tuscan valleys glad with olive and
   with vine.

THE BROTHER OF MERCY.

PIERO LUCA, known of all the town
As the gray porter by the Pitti wall
Where the noon shadows of the gardens
   fall,
Sick and in dolor, waited to lay down
His last sad burden, and beside his mat
The barefoot monk of La Certosa sat.

Unseen, in square and blossoming
   garden drifted,   .
Soft sunset lights through green Val
   d'Arno sifted ;
Unheard, below the living shuttles
   shifted
Backward and forth, and wove, in love
   or strife,
In mirth or pain, the mottled web of
   life :
But when at last came upward from the
   street
Tinkle of bell and tread of measured feet,
The sick man started, strove to rise in
   vain,
Sinking back heavily with a moan of
   pain.
And the monk said, " 'T is but the
   Brotherhood
Of Mercy going on some errand good :
Their black masks by the palace-wall I
   see."
Piero answered faintly, " Woe is me !
This day for the first time in forty
   years

In vain the bell hath sounded in my
   ears,
Calling me with my brethren of the
   mask,
Beggar and prince alike, to some new
   task
Of love or pity, — haply from the street
To bear a wretch plague-stricken, or,
   with feet
Hushed to the quickened ear and fever-
   ish brain,
To tread the crowded lazaretto's floors,
Down the long twilight of the corridors,
Midst tossing arms and faces full of
   pain.
I loved the work : it was its own reward.
I never counted on it to offset
My sins, which are many, or make less
   my debt
To the free grace and mercy of our Lord ;
But somehow, father, it has come to be
In these long years so much a part of me,
I should not know myself, if lacking
   it,
But with the work the worker too would
   die,
And in my place some other self would
   sit
Joyful or sad, — what matters, if not I ?
And now all 's over. Woe is me ! " —
   " My son,"
The monk said soothingly, " thy work
   is done ;
And no more as a servant, but the guest
Of God thou enterest thy eternal rest.
No toil, no tears, no sorrow for the lost,
Shall mar thy perfect bliss. Thou shalt
   sit down
Clad in white robes, and wear a golden
   crown
Forever and forever." — Piero tossed
On his sick-pillow : " Miserable me !
I am too poor for such grand company ;
The crown would be too heavy for this
   gray
Old head ; and God forgive me if I say
It would be hard to sit there night and
   day,
Like an image in the Tribune, doing
   naught
With these hard hands, that all my life
   have wrought,
Not for bread only, but for pity's sake.
I 'm dull at prayers : I could not keep
   awake,
Counting my beads. Mine 's but a crazy
   head,

Scarce worth the saving, if all else be
    dead.
And if one goes to heaven without a
    heart,
God knows he leaves behind his better
    part.
I love my fellow-men : the worst I know
I would do good to. Will death change
    me so
That I shall sit among the lazy saints,
Turning a deaf ear to the sore complaints
Of souls that suffer ? Why, I never yet
Left a poor dog in the *strada* hard beset,
Or ass o'erladen ! Must I rate man less
Than dog or ass, in holy selfishness ?
Methinks (Lord, pardon, if the thought
    be sin !)
The world of pain were better, if therein
One's heart might still be human, and
    desires
Of natural pity drop upon its fires
Some cooling tears."
        Thereat the pale monk crossed
His brow, and, muttering, "Madman !
    thou art lost !"
Took up his pyx and fled ; and, left alone,
The sick man closed his eyes with a
    great groan
That sank into a prayer, "Thy will be
    done !"

Then was he made aware, by soul or
    ear,
Of somewhat pure and holy bending o'er
    him,
And of a voice like that of her who bore
    him,
Tender and most compassionate : "Never
    fear !
For heaven is love, as God himself is
    love ;
Thy work below shall be thy work
    above."
And when he looked, lo ! in the stern
    monk's place
He saw the shining of an angel's face !

———

The Traveller broke the pause. "I've
    seen
    The Brothers down the long street
    steal,
Black, silent, masked, the crowd be-
    tween,
    And felt to doff my hat and kneel
With heart, if not with knee, in prayer,
For blessings on their pious care."

The Reader wiped his glasses : "Friends
    of mine,
We'll try our home-brewed next, in-
    stead of foreign wine."

THE CHANGELING.

For the fairest maid in Hampton
    They needed not to search,
Who saw young Anna Favor
    Come walking into church, —

Or bringing from the meadows,
    At set of harvest-day,
The frolic of the blackbirds,
    The sweetness of the hay.

Now the weariest of all mothers,
    The saddest two-years bride,
She scowls in the face of her husband,
    And spurns her child aside.

"Rake out the red coals, goodman, —
    For there the child shall lie,
Till the black witch comes to fetch her
    And both up chimney fly.

"It's never my own little daughter,
    It's never my own," she said ;
"The witches have stolen my Anna,
    And left me an imp instead.

"O, fair and sweet was my baby,
    Blue eyes, and hair of gold ;
But this is ugly and wrinkled,
    Cross, and cunning, and old.

"I hate the touch of her fingers,
    I hate the feel of her skin ;
It's not the milk from my bosom,
    But my blood, that she sucks in.

"My face grows sharp with the torment;
    Look ! my arms are skin and bone ! —
Rake open the red coals, goodman,
    And the witch shall have her own.

"She'll come when she hears it crying,
    In the shape of an owl or bat,
And she'll bring us our darling Anna
    In place of her screeching brat."

Then the goodman, Ezra Dalton,
    Laid his hand upon her head :
"Thy sorrow is great, O woman !
    I sorrow with thee," he said.

" The paths to trouble are many,
And never but one sure way
Leads out to the light beyond it:
My poor wife, let us pray."

Then he said to the great All-Father,
"Thy daughter is weak and blind;
Let her sight come back, and clothe her
Once more in her right mind.

" Lead her out of this evil shadow,
Out of these fancies wild ;
Let the holy love of the mother
Turn again to her child.

" Make her lips like the lips of Mary
Kissing her blessed Son ;
Let her hands, like the hands of Jesus,
Rest on her little one.

" Comfort the soul of thy handmaid,
Open her prison-door,
And thine shall be all the glory
And praise forevermore."

Then into the face of its mother
The baby looked up and smiled ;
And the cloud of her soul was lifted,
And she knew her little child.

A beam of the slant west sunshine
Made the wan face almost fair,
Lit the blue eyes' patient wonder,
And the rings of pale gold hair.

She kissed it on lip and forehead,
She kissed it on cheek and chin,
And she bared her snow-white bosom
To the lips so pale and thin.

O, fair on her bridal morning
Was the maid who blushed and smiled,
But fairer to Ezra Dalton
Looked the mother of his child.

With more than a lover's fondness
He stooped to her worn young face,
And the nursing child and the mother
He folded in one embrace.

" Blessed be God !" he murmured.
" Blessed be God !" she said ;
" For I see, who once was blinded, —
I live, who once was dead.

" Now mount and ride, my goodman,
As thou lovest thy own soul !

Woe 's me, if my wicked fancies
Be the death of Goody Cole !'·

His horse he saddled and bridled,
And into the night rode he, —
Now through the great black woodland,
Now by the white-beached sea.

He rode through the silent clearings,
He came to the ferry wide,
And thrice he called to the boatman
Asleep on the other side.

He set his horse to the river,
He swam to Newbury town,
And he called up Justice Sewall
In his nightcap and his gown,

And the grave and worshipful justice
(Upon whose soul be peace !)
Set his name to the jailer's warrant
For Goodwife Cole's release.

Then through the night the hoof-beats
Went sounding like a flail ;
And Goody Cole at cockcrow
Came forth from Ipswich jail.

"Here is a rhyme : — I hardly dare
To venture on its theme worn out ;
What seems so sweet by Doon and
Ayr
Sounds simply silly hereabout ;
And pipes by lips Arcadian blown
Are only tin horns at our own.
Yet still the muse of pastoral walks
with us,
While Hosea Biglow sings, our new
Theocritus."

THE MAIDS OF ATTITASH.

In sky and wave the white clouds swam,
And the blue hills of Nottingham
Through gaps of leafy green
Across the lake were seen, —

When, in the shadow of the ash
That dreams its dream in Attitash,
In the warm summer weather,
Two maidens sat together.

They sat and watched in idle mood
The gleam and shade of lake and
wood, —

The beach the keen light smote,
The white sail of a boat, —

Swan flocks of lilies shoreward lying,
In sweetness, not in music, dying, —
Hardhack, and virgin's-bower,
And white-spiked clethra-flower.

With careless ears they heard the plash
And breezy wash of Attitash,
The wood-bird's plaintive cry,
The locust's sharp reply.

And teased the while, with playful hand,
The shaggy dog of Newfoundland,
Whose uncouth frolic spilled
Their baskets berry-filled.

Then one, the beauty of whose eyes
Was evermore a great surprise,
Tossed back her queenly head,
And, lightly laughing, said, —

" No bridegroom's hand be mine to hold
That is not lined with yellow gold ;
I tread no cottage-floor ;
I own no lover poor.

" My love must come on silken wings,
With bridal lights of diamond rings, —
Not foul with kitchen smirch,
With tallow-dip for torch."

The other, on whose modest head
Was lesser dower of beauty shed,
With look for home-hearths meet,
And voice exceeding sweet,

Answered, — "We will not rivals be ;
Take thou the gold, leave love to me ;
Mine be the cottage small,
And thine the rich man's hall.

" I know, indeed, that wealth is good ;
But lowly roof and simple food,
With love that hath no doubt,
Are more than gold without."

Hard by a farmer hale and young
His cradle in the rye-field swung,
Tracking the yellow plain
With windrows of ripe grain.

And still, whene'er he paused to whet
His scythe, the sidelong glance he met
Of large dark eyes, where strove
False pride and secret love.

Be strong, young mower of the grain ;
That love shall overmatch disdain,
Its instincts soon or late
The heart shall vindicate.

In blouse of gray, with fishing-rod,
Half screened by leaves, a stranger trod
The margin of the pond,
Watching the group beyond.

The supreme hours unnoted come ;
Unfelt the turning tides of doom ;
And so the maids laughed on,
Nor dreamed what Fate had done, —

Nor knew the step was Destiny's
That rustled in the birchen trees,
As, with their lives forecast,
Fisher and mower passed.

Erelong by lake and rivulet side
The summer roses paled and died,
And Autumn's fingers shed
The maple's leaves of red.

Through the long gold-hazed afternoon,
Alone, but for the diving loon,
The partridge in the brake,
The black duck on the lake,

Beneath the shadow of the ash
Sat man and maid by Attitash ;
And earth and air made room
For human hearts to bloom.

Soft spread the carpets of the sod,
And scarlet-oak and golden-rod
With blushes and with smiles
Lit up the forest aisles.

The mellow light the lake aslant,
The pebbled margin's ripple-chant
Attempered and low-toned,
The tender mystery owned.

And through the dream the lovers
        dreamed
Sweet sounds stole in and soft lights
        streamed ;
The sunshine seemed to bless,
The air was a caress.

Not she who lightly laughed is there,
With scornful toss of midnight hair,
Her dark, disdainful eyes,
And proud lip worldly-wise.

Her haughty vow is still unsaid,
But all she dreamed and coveted
Wears, half to her surprise,
The youthful farmer's guise !

With more than all her old-time pride
She walks the rye-field at his side,
Careless of cot or hall,
Since love transfigures all.

Rich beyond dreams, the vantage-ground
Of life is gained ; her hands have found
The talisman of old
That changes all to gold.

While she who could for love dispense
With all its glittering accidents,
And trust her heart alone,
Finds love and gold her own.

What wealth can buy or art can build
Awaits her ; but her cup is filled
Even now unto the brim ;
Her world is love and him !

—————

The while he heard, the Book-man drew
A length of make-believing face,
With smothered mischief laughing through :
"Why, you shall sit in Ramsay's place,
And, with his Gentle Shepherd, keep
On Yankee hills immortal sheep,
While lovelorn swains and maids the seas beyond
Hold dreamy tryst around your huckleberry-pond."

The Traveller laughed ; "Sir Galahad
Singing of love the Trouvere's lay !
How should he know the blindfold lad
From one of Vulcan's forge-boys ?"
— "Nay,
He better sees who stands outside
Than they who in procession ride,"
The Reader answered : "selectmen and squire
Miss, while they make, the show that wayside folks admire.

"Here is a wild tale of the North,
Our travelled friend will own as one
Fit for a Norland Christmas hearth
And lips of Christian Andersen.
They tell it in the valleys green
Of the fair island he has seen,
Low lying off the pleasant Swedish shore,
Washed by the Baltic Sea, and watched by Elsinore."

KALLUNDBORG CHURCH.

"Tie stille, barn min !
Imorgen kommer Fin,
Fa'er di,
Og gi'er dig Esbern Snares öine og hjerte at lege med ! "
Zealand Rhyme.

"BUILD at Kallundborg by the sea
A church as stately as church may be,
And there shalt thou wed my daughter fair,"
Said the Lord of Nesvek to Esbern Snare.

And the Baron laughed. But Esbern said,
"Though I lose my soul, I will Helva wed !"
And off he strode, in his pride of will,
To the Troll who dwelt in Ulshoi hill.

"Build, O Troll, a church for me
At Kallundborg by the mighty sea ;
Build it stately, and build it fair,
Build it quickly," said Esbern Snare.

But the sly Dwarf said, "No work is wrought
By Trolls of the Hills, O man, for naught.
What wilt thou give for thy church so fair ?"
"Set thy own price," quoth Esbern Snare.

"When Kallundborg church is builded well,
Thou must the name of its builder tell,
Or thy heart and thy eyes must be my boon."
"Build," said Esbern, "and build it soon."

By night and by day the Troll wrought on ;
He hewed the timbers, he piled the stone ;

But day by day, as the walls rose fair,
Darker and sadder grew Esbern Snare.

He listened by night, he watched by day,
He sought and thought, but he dared
　　not pray ;
In vain he called on the Elle-maids shy,
And the Neck and the Nis gave no
　　reply.

Of his evil bargain far and wide
A rumor ran through the country-side ;
And Helva of Nesvek, young and fair,
Prayed for the soul of Esbern Snare.

And now the church was wellnigh done ;
One pillar it lacked, and one alone ;
And the grim Troll muttered, "Fool
　　thou art !
To-morrow gives me thy eyes and
　　heart !"

By Kallundborg in black despair,
Through wood and meadow, walked
　　Esbern Snare,
Till, worn and weary, the strong man
　　sank
Under the birches on Ulshoi bank.

At his last day's work he heard the
　　Troll
Hammer and delve in the quarry's hole ;
Before him the church stood large and
　　fair :
"I have builded my tomb," said Esbern
　　Snare.

And he closed his eyes the sight to hide,
When he heard a light step at his side :
"O Esbern Snare !" a sweet voice said,
"Would I might die now in thy stead !"

With a grasp by love and by fear made
　　strong,
He held her fast, and he held her long ;
With the beating heart of a bird afeard,
She hid her face in his flame-red beard.

"O love !" he cried, "let me look to-
　　day
In thine eyes ere mine are plucked away ;
Let me hold thee close, let me feel thy
　　heart
Ere mine by the Troll is torn apart !

"I sinned, O Helva, for love of thee \
Pray that the Lord Christ pardon me !"

But fast as she prayed, and faster still,
Hammered the Troll in Ulshoi hill.

He knew, as he wrought, that a loving
　　heart
Was somehow baffling his evil art ;
For more than spell of Elf or Troll
Is a maiden's prayer for her lover's soul.

And Esbern listened, and caught the
　　sound
Of a Troll-wife singing underground :
"To-morrow comes Fine, father thine :
Lie still and hush thee, baby mine !

"Lie still, my darling ! next sunrise
Thou 'lt play with Esbern Snare's heart
　　and eyes !"
"Ho ! ho !" quoth Esbern, "is that
　　your game ?
Thanks to the Troll-wife, I know his
　　name !"

The Troll he heard him, and hurried on
To Kallundborg church with the lack-
　　ing stone.
"Too late, Gaffer Fine !" cried Esbern
　　Snare ;
And Troll and pillar vanished in air !

That night the harvesters heard the
　　sound
Of a woman sobbing underground,
And the voice of the Hill-Troll loud
　　with blame
Of the careless singer who told his
　　name.

Of the Troll of the Church they sing the
　　rune
By the Northern Sea in the harvest
　　moon ;
And the fishers of Zealand hear him
　　still
Scolding his wife in Ulshoi hill.

And seaward over its groves of birch
Still looks the tower of Kallundborg
　　church,
Where, first at its altar, a wedded pair,
Stood Helva of Nesvek and Esbern
　　Snare !

――――――

"What," asked the Traveller, "would
　　our sires,
　　The old Norse story-tellers, say

Of sun-graved pictures, ocean wires,
  And smoking steamboats of to-day ?
And this, O lady, by your leave,
  Recalls your song of yester eve :
Pray, let us have that Cable-hymn once
    more."
"Hear, hear !" the Book-man cried,
  "the lady has the floor.

"These noisy waves below perhaps
  To such a strain will lend their ear,
With softer voice and lighter lapse
  Come stealing up the sands to hear,
And what they once refused to do
For old King Knut accord to you.
Nay, even the fishes shall your listeners
    be,
As once, the legend runs, they heard
    St. Anthony."

O lonely bay of Trinity,
  O dreary shores, give ear !
Lean down unto the white-lipped sea
  The voice of God to hear !

From world to world his couriers fly,
  Thought-winged and shod with fire ;
The angel of His stormy sky
  Rides down the sunken wire.

What saith the herald of the Lord ?
  "The world's long strife is done ;
Close wedded by that mystic cord,
  Its continents are one.

"And one in heart, as one in blood,
  Shall all her peoples be ;
The hands of human brotherhood
  Are clasped beneath the sea.

"Through Orient seas, o'er Afric's plain
  And Asian mountains borne,
The vigor of the Northern brain
  Shall nerve the world outworn.

"From clime to clime, from shore to
    shore,
  Shall thrill the magic thread ;
The new Prometheus steals once more
  The fire that wakes the dead."

Throb on, strong pulse of thunder !
    beat
  From answering beach to beach ;
Fuse nations in thy kindly heat,
  And melt the chains of each !

Wild terror of the sky above,
  Glide tamed and dumb below !
Bear gently, Ocean's carrier-dove,
  Thy errands to and fro.

Weave on, swift shuttle of the Lord,
  Beneath the deep so far,
The bridal robe of earth's accord,
  The funeral shroud of war !

For lo ! the fall of Ocean's wall
  Space mocked and time outrun ;
And round the world the thought of all
  Is as the thought of one !

The poles unite, the zones agree,
  The tongues of striving cease ;
As on the Sea of Galilee
  The Christ is whispering, Peace !

———

"Glad prophecy ! to this at last,"
  The Reader said, "shall all things
    come.
Forgotten be the bugle's blast,
  And battle-music of the drum.
A little while the world may run
  Its old mad way, with needle-gun
And iron-clad, but truth, at last, shall
    reign :
The cradle-song of Christ was never sung
    in vain ! "

Shifting his scattered papers, "Here,"
  He said, as died the faint applause,
"Is something that I found last year
  Down on the island known as Orr's.
I had it from a fair-haired girl
Who, oddly, bore the name of Pearl,
(As if by some droll freak of circum-
    stance,)
Classic, or wellnigh so, in Harriet
  Stowe's romance."

THE DEAD SHIP OF HARPS-
WELL.

WHAT flecks the outer gray beyond
  The sundown's golden trail ?
The white flash of a sea-bird's wing,
  Or gleam of slanting sail ?
Let young eyes watch from Neck and
    Point,
  And sea-worn elders pray, —
The ghost of what was once a ship
  Is sailing up the bay !

From gray sea-fog, from icy drift,
  From peril and from pain,
The home-bound fisher greets thy lights,
  O hundred-harbored Maine !
But many a keel shall seaward turn,
  And many a sail outstand,
When, tall and white, the Dead Ship
    looms
  Against the dusk of land.

She rounds the headland's bristling
    pines ;
  She threads the isle-set bay ;
No spur of breeze can speed her on,
  Nor ebb of tide delay.
Old men still walk the Isle of Orr
  Who tell her date and name,
Old shipwrights sit in Freeport yards
  Who hewed her oaken frame.

What weary doom of baffled quest,
  Thou sad sea-ghost, is thine ?
What makes thee in the haunts of
    home
  A wonder and a sign ?
No foot is on thy silent deck,
  Upon thy helm no hand ;
No ripple hath the soundless wind
  That smites thee from the land !

For never comes the ship to port,
  Howe'er the breeze may be ;
Just when she nears the waiting shore
  She drifts again to sea.
No tack of sail, nor turn of helm,
  Nor sheer of veering side ;
Stern-fore she drives to sea and night,
  Against the wind and tide.

In vain o'er Harpswell Neck the star
  Of evening guides her in ;
In vain for her the lamps are lit
  Within thy tower, Seguin !
In vain the harbor-boat shall hail,
  In vain the pilot call ;
No hand shall reef her spectral sail,
  Or let her anchor fall.

Shake, brown old wives, with dreary
    joy,
  Your gray-head hints of ill ;
And, over sick-beds whispering low,
  Your prophecies fulfil.
Some home amid yon birchen trees
  Shall drape its door with woe ;
And slowly where the Dead Ship sails,
  The burial boat shall row !

From Wolf Neck and from Flying Point,
  From island and from main,
From sheltered cove and tided creek,
  Shall glide the funeral train.
The dead-boat with the bearers four,
  The mourners at her stern, —
And one shall go the silent way
  Who shall no more return !

And men shall sigh, and women weep,
  Whose dear ones pale and pine,
And sadly over sunset seas
  Await the ghostly sign.
They know not that its sails are filled
  By pity's tender breath,
Nor see the Angel at the helm
  Who steers the Ship of Death !

———

" Chill as a down-east breeze should
    be,"
  The Book-man said. " A ghostly
    touch
The legend has. I 'm glad to see
  Your flying Yankee beat the Dutch."
" Well, here is something of the
    sort
Which one midsummer day I caught
In Narragansett Bay, for lack of fish."
" We wait," the Traveller said ; " serve
  hot or cold your dish."

THE PALATINE.

LEAGUES north, as fly the gull and
    auk,
Point Judith watches with eye of hawk ;
Leagues south, thy beacon flames, Mon-
    tauk !

Lonely and wind-shorn, wood-forsaken,
With never a tree for Spring to waken,
For tryst of lovers or farewells taken,

Circled by waters that never freeze,
Beaten by billow and swept by breeze,
Lieth the island of Manisees,

Set at the mouth of the Sound to hold
The coast lights up on its turret old,
Yellow with moss and sea-fog mould.

Dreary the land when gust and sleet
At its doors and windows howl and
    beat,
And Winter laughs at its fires of peat !

But in summer time, when pool and pond,
Held in the laps of valleys fond,
Are blue as the glimpses of sea beyond ;

When the hills are sweet with the brier-rose,
And, hid in the warm, soft dells, unclose
Flowers the mainland rarely knows ;

When boats to their morning fishing go,
And, held to the wind and slanting low,
Whitening and darkening the small sails show, —

Then is that lonely island fair ;
And the pale health-seeker findeth there
The wine of life in its pleasant air.

No greener valleys the sun invite,
On smoother beaches no sea-birds light,
No blue waves shatter to foam more white !

There, circling ever their narrow range,
Quaint tradition and legend strange
Live on unchallenged, and know no change.

Old wives spinning their webs of tow,
Or rocking weirdly to and fro
In and out of the peat's dull glow,

And old men mending their nets of twine,
Talk together of dream and sign,
Talk of the lost ship Palatine, —

The ship that, a hundred years before,
Freighted deep with its goodly store,
In the gales of the equinox went ashore.

The eager islanders one by one
Counted the shots of her signal gun,
And heard the crash when she drove right on !

Into the teeth of death she sped :
(May God forgive the hands that fed
The false lights over the rocky Head !)

O men and brothers ! what sights were there !
White unturned faces, hands stretched

Down swooped the wreckers, like birds of prey
Tearing the heart of the ship away,
And the dead had never a word to say.

And then, with ghastly shimmer and shine
Over the rocks and the seething brine,
They burned the wreck of the Palatine.

In their cruel hearts, as they homeward sped,
"The sea and the rocks are dumb," they said :
"There 'll be no reckoning with the dead."

But the year went round, and when once more
Along their foam-white curves of shore
They heard the line-storm rave and roar,

Behold ! again, with shimmer and shine,
Over the rocks and the seething brine,
The flaming wreck of the Palatine !

So, haply in fitter words than these,
Mending their nets on their patient knees
They tell the legend of Maniscees.

Nor looks nor tones a doubt betray ;
"It is known to us all," they quietly say ;
"We too have seen it in our day."

Is there, then, no death for a word once spoken ?
Was never a deed but left its token
Written on tables never broken ?

Do the elements subtle reflections give ?
Do pictures of all the ages live
On Nature's infinite negative,

Which, half in sport, in malice half,
She shows at times, with shudder or laugh,
Phantom and shadow in photograph ?

For still, on many a moonless night,
From Kingston Head and from Montauk light
The spectre kindles and burns in sight.

And the wise Sound skippers, though
  skies be fine,
Reef their sails when they see the sign
Of the blazing wreck of the Palatine !

———

"A fitter tale to scream than sing,"
  The Book-man said. "Well, fan-
  cy, then,"
The Reader answered, "on the wing
  The sea-birds shriek it, not for
  men,
But in the ear of wave and breeze !"
The Traveller mused : "Your Mani-
  sees
Is fairy-land : off Narragansett shore
Who ever saw the isle or heard its name
  before ?

"'T is some strange land of Flyaway,
  Whose dreamy shore the ship be-
  guiles,
St. Brandan's in its sea-mist gray,
  Or sunset loom of Fortunate Isles !"
"No ghost, but solid turf and rock
Is the good island known as Block,"
The Reader said. "For beauty and for
  ease
I chose its Indian name, soft-flowing
  Manisees !

"But let it pass ; here is a bit
Of unrhymed story, with a hint
Of the old preaching mood in it,
  The sort of sidelong moral squint
Our friend objects to, which has
  grown,
I fear, a habit of my own.
'T was written when the Asian plague
  drew near,
And the land held its breath and paled
  with sudden fear."

ABRAHAM DAVENPORT.

IN the old days (a custom laid aside
With breeches and cocked hats) the peo-
  ple sent
Their wisest men to make the public
  laws.
And so, from a brown homestead, where
  the Sound
Drinks the small tribute of the Mianas,
Waved over by the woods of Rippowams,
And hallowed by pure lives and tranquil
  deaths,

Stamford sent up t(
  State
Wisdom and grace
  port.

'T was on a Ma
  year
Seventeen hundred
  fell
Over the bloom a(
  Spring,
Over the fresh eart
  noon,
A horror of great
  night
In day of which
  tell, —
The Twilight of t
  hung sky
Was black with o
  where its rin
Was fringed with a
  which climb
The crater's sides f
  low.
Birds ceased to sin
  yard fowls.
Roosted ; the cat
  bars
Lowed, and looked
  leathern win
Flitted abroad ; t
  died ;
Men prayed, and w
  grew sharp
To hear the doom-
  shatter
The black sky, that
  Christ
Might look from th
  he looked
A loving guest at I
As Justice and inex

Meanwhile in tl
  dim as ghost
Sat the lawgivers of
Trembling beneat
  robes.
"It is the Lord's
  adjourn,"
Some said ; and t
  accord,
All eyes were turne(
  port.
He rose, slow clea\
  voice

The intolerable hush. "This well may be
The Day of Judgment which the world awaits;
But be it so or not, I only know
My present duty, and my Lord's command
To occupy till he come. So at the post
Where he hath set me in his providence,
I choose, for one, to meet him face to face, —
No faithless servant frightened from my task,
But ready when the Lord of the harvest calls;
And therefore, with all reverence, I would say,
Let God do his work, we will see to ours.
Bring in the candles." And they brought them in.

Then by the flaring lights the Speaker read,
Albeit with husky voice and shaking hands,
An act to amend an act to regulate
The shad and alewive fisheries. Whereupon
Wisely and well spake Abraham Davenport,
Straight to the question, with no figures of speech
Save the ten Arab signs, yet not without
The shrewd dry humor natural to the man:
His awe-struck colleagues listening all the while,
Between the pauses of his argument,
To hear the thunder of the wrath of God
Break from the hollow trumpet of the cloud.

And there he stands in memory to this day,
Erect, self-poised, a rugged face, half seen
Against the background of unnatural dark,
A witness to the ages as they pass,
That simple duty hath no place for fear.

And, shore-ward, o'er the waters gleamed,
From crest to crest, a line of light,
Such as of old, with solemn awe,
The fishers by Gennesaret saw,
When dry-shod o'er it walked the Son of God,
Tracking the waves with light where'er his sandals trod.

Silently for a space each eye
Upon that sudden glory turned:
Cool from the land the breeze blew by,
The tent-ropes flapped, the long beach churned
Its waves to foam; on either hand
Stretched, far as sight, the hills of sand;
With bays of marsh, and capes of bush and tree,
The wood's black shore-line loomed beyond the meadowy sea.

The lady rose to leave. "One song,
Or hymn," they urged, "before we part."
And she, with lips to which belong
Sweet intuitions of all art,
Gave to the winds of night a strain
Which they who heard would hear again;
And to her voice the solemn ocean lent,
Touching its harp of sand, a deep accompaniment.

The harp at Nature's advent strung
Has never ceased to play;
The song the stars of morning sung
Has never died away.

And prayer is made, and praise is given,
By all things near and far;
The ocean looketh up to heaven,
And mirrors every star.

Its waves are kneeling on the strand,
As kneels the human knee,
Their white locks bowing to the sand,
The priesthood of the sea!

They pour their glittering treasures

The green earth sends her incense up
From many a mountain shrine ;
From folded leaf and dewy cup
She pours her sacred wine.

The mists above the morning rills
Rise white as wings of prayer ;
The altar-curtains of the hills
Are sunset's purple air.

The winds with hymns of praise are loud,
Or low with sobs of pain, —
The thunder-organ of the cloud,
The dropping tears of rain.

With drooping head and branches crossed
The twilight forest grieves,
Or speaks with tongues of Pentecost
From all its sunlit leaves.

The blue sky is the temple's arch,
Its transept earth and air,
The music of its starry march
The chorus of a prayer.

So Nature keeps the reverent frame
With which her years began,

And all her signs and voices shame
The prayerless heart of man.

———

The singer ceased. The moon's white
rays
Fell on the rapt, still face of her.
" *Allah il Allah!* He hath praise
From all things," said the Traveller.
" Oft from the desert's silent nights,
And mountain hymns of sunset lights,
My heart has felt rebuke, as in his tent
The Moslem's prayer has shamed my
Christian knee unbent."

He paused, and lo ! far, faint, and slow
The bells in Newbury's steeples
tolled
The twelve dead hours ; the lamp
burned low ;
The singer sought her canvas fold.
One sadly said, " At break of day
We strike our tent and go our way."
But one made answer cheerily, " Never
fear,
We 'll pitch this tent of ours in type
another year."

———

NATIONAL LYRICS.

THE MANTLE OF ST. JOHN DE MATHA.

A LEGEND OF "THE RED, WHITE, AND
BLUE," A. D. 1154 – 1864.

A STRONG and mighty Angel,
Calm, terrible, and bright,
The cross in blended red and blue
Upon his mantle white !

Two captives by him kneeling,
Each on his broken chain,
Sang praise to God who raiseth
The dead to life again !

Dropping his cross-wrought mantle,
" Wear this," the Angel said ;
' Take thou, O Freedom's priest, its
sign, —
The white, the blue, and red."

Then rose up John de Matha
In the strength the Lord Christ gave,
And begged through all the land of
France
The ransom of the slave.

The gates of tower and castle
Before him open flew,
The drawbridge at his coming fell,
The door-bolt backward drew.

For all men owned his errand,
And paid his righteous tax ;
And the hearts of lord and peasant
Were in his hands as wax.

At last, outbound from Tunis,
His bark her anchor weighed,
Freighted with seven-score Christian
souls
Whose ransom he had paid.

But, torn by Paynim hatred,
  Her sails in tatters hung ;
And on the wild waves, rudderless,
  A shattered hulk she swung.

"God save us !" cried the captain,
  " For naught can man avail ;
O, woe betide the ship that lacks
  Her rudder and her sail !

" Behind us are the Moormen ;
  At sea we sink or strand :
There's death upon the water,
  There's death upon the land !"

Then up spake John de Matha :
  " God's errands never fail !
Take thou the mantle which I wear,
  And make of it a sail."

They raised the cross-wrought mantle,
  The blue, the white, the red ; ·
And straight before the wind off-shore
  The ship of Freedom sped.

"God help us !" cried the seamen,
  " For vain is mortal skill :
The good ship on a stormy sea
  Is drifting at its will."

Then up spake John de Matha :
  " My mariners, never fear !
The Lord whose breath has filled her sail
  May well our vessel steer !"

So on through storm and darkness
  They drove for weary hours ;
And lo ! the third gray morning shone
  On Ostia's friendly towers.

And on the walls the watchers
  The ship of mercy knew, —
They knew far off its holy cross,
  The red, the white, and blue.

And the bells in all the steeples
  Rang out in glad accord,
To welcome home to Christian soil
  The ransomed of the Lord.

So runs the ancient legend
  By bard and painter told ;
And lo ! the cycle rounds again,
  The new is as the old !

With rudder foully broken,
  And sails by traitors torn,

Our country on a midnight sea
  Is waiting for the morn.

Before her, nameless terror ;
  Behind, the pirate foe ;
The clouds are black above her,
  The sea is white below.

The hope of all who suffer,
  The dread of all who wrong,
She drifts in darkness and in storm,
  How long, O Lord ! how long ?

But courage, O my mariners !
  Ye shall not suffer wreck ;
While up to God the freedman's prayers
  Are rising from your deck.

Is not your sail the banner
  Which God hath blest anew,
The mantle that De Matha wore,
  The red, the white, the blue ?

Its hues are all of heaven, —
  The red of sunset's dye,
The whiteness of the moon-lit cloud,
  The blue of morning's sky.

Wait cheerily, then, O mariners,
  For daylight and for land ;
The breath of God is in your sail,
  Your rudder is His hand.

Sail on, sail on, deep-freighted
  With blessings and with hopes ;
The saints of old with shadowy hands
  Are pulling at your ropes.

Behind ye holy martyrs
  Uplift the palm and crown ;
Before ye unborn ages send
  Their benedictions down.

Take heart from John de Matha ! —
  God's errands never fail !
Sweep on through storm and darkness,
  The thunder and the hail !

Sail on ! The morning cometh,
  The port ye yet shall win ;
And all the bells of God shall ring
  The good ship bravely in !

WHAT THE BIRDS SAID.

THE birds against the April wind
  Flew northward, singing as they flew ;

They sang, "The land we leave behind
  Has swords for corn-blades, blood for
    dew."

"O wild-birds, flying from the South,
  What saw and heard ye, gazing down?"
"We saw the mortar's upturned mouth,
  The sickened camp, the blazing town!

"Beneath the bivouac's starry lamps,
  We saw your march-worn children
    die;
In shrouds of moss, in cypress swamps,
  We saw your dead uncoffined lie.

"We heard the starving prisoner's
    sighs,
  And saw, from line and trench, your
    sons
Follow our flight with home-sick eyes
  Beyond the battery's smoking guns."

"And heard and saw ye only wrong
  And pain," I cried, "O wing-worn
    flocks?"
"We heard," they sang, "the freed-
    man's song,
  The crash of Slavery's broken locks!

"We saw from new, uprising States
  The treason-nursing mischief spurned,
As, crowding Freedom's ample gates,
  The long-estranged and lost returned.

"O'er dusky faces, seamed and old,
  And hands horn-hard with unpaid
    toil,
With hope in every rustling fold,
  We saw your star-dropt flag uncoil.

"And struggling up through sounds
    accursed,
  A grateful murmur clomb the air;
A whisper scarcely heard at first,
  It filled the listening heavens with
    prayer.

"And sweet and far, as from a star,
  Replied a voice which shall not cease,
Till, drowning all the noise of war,
  It sings the blessed song of peace!"

So to me, in a doubtful day
  Of chill and slowly greening spring,
Low stooping from the cloudy gray,
  The wild-birds sang or seemed to
    sing.

They vanished in the misty air,
  The song went with them in their
    flight;
But lo! they left the sunset fair,
  And in the evening there was light.

LAUS DEO!

ON HEARING THE BELLS RING ON THE
PASSAGE OF THE CONSTITUTIONAL
AMENDMENT ABOLISHING SLAVERY.

    It is done!
  Clang of bell and roar of gun
  Send the tidings up and down.
  How the belfries rock and reel!
  How the great guns, peal on peal,
  Fling the joy from town to town!

    Ring, O bells!
  Every stroke exulting tells
  Of the burial hour of crime.
  Loud and long, that all may hear,
  Ring for every listening ear
  Of Eternity and Time!

    Let us kneel:
  God's own voice is in that peal,
  And this spot is holy ground.
  Lord, forgive us! What are we,
  That our eyes this glory see,
  That our ears have heard the sound!

    For the Lord
  On the whirlwind is abroad;
  In the earthquake he has spoken;
  He has smitten with his thunder
  The iron walls asunder,
  And the gates of brass are broken!

    Loud and long,
  Lift the old exulting song;
  Sing with Miriam by the sea
  He has cast the mighty down;
  Horse and rider sink and drown;
  "He hath triumphed gloriously!"

    Did we dare,
  In our agony of prayer,
  Ask for more than He has done?
  When was ever his right hand
  Over any time or land
  Stretched as now beneath the sun?

    How they pale,
  Ancient myth and song and tale,

In this wonder of our days,
When the cruel rod of war
Blossoms white with righteous law,
And the wrath of man is praise !

Blotted out !
All within and all about
Shall a fresher life begin ;
Freer breathe the universe
As it rolls its heavy curse
On the dead and buried sin !

It is done !
In the circuit of the sun
Shall the sound thereof go forth.
It shall bid the sad rejoice,
It shall give the dumb a voice,
It shall belt with joy the earth !

Ring and swing,
Bells of joy ! On morning's wing
Send the song of praise abroad !
With a sound of broken chains
Tell the nations that He reigns,
Who alone is Lord and God !

THE PEACE AUTUMN.

WRITTEN FOR THE ESSEX COUNTY
AGRICULTURAL FESTIVAL, 1865.

THANK God for rest, where none molest,
And none can make afraid, —
For Peace that sits as Plenty's guest
Beneath the homestead shade !

Bring pike and gun, the sword's red
scourge,
The negro's broken chains,
And beat them at the blacksmith's
forge
To ploughshares for our plains.

Alike henceforth our hills of snow,
And vales where cotton flowers ;
All streams that flow, all winds that
blow,
Are Freedom's motive-powers.

Henceforth to Labor's chivalry
Be knightly honors paid ;
For nobler than the sword's shall be
The sickle's accolade.

Build up an altar to the Lord,
O grateful hearts of ours !

And shape it of the greenest sward
That ever drank the showers.

Lay all the bloom of gardens there,
And there the orchard fruits ;
Bring golden grain from sun and air,
From earth her goodly roots.

There let our banners droop and flow,
The stars uprise and fall ;
Our roll of martyrs, sad and slow,
Let sighing breezes call.

Their names let hands of horn and tan
And rough-shod feet applaud,
Who died to make the slave a man,
And link with toil reward.

There let the common heart keep time
To such an anthem sung
As never swelled on poet's rhyme,
Or thrilled on singer's tongue.

Song of our burden and relief,
Of peace and long annoy ;
The passion of our mighty grief
And our exceeding joy !

A song of praise to Him who filled
The harvests sown in tears,
And gave each field a double yield
To feed our battle-years !

A song of faith that trusts the end
To match the good begun,
Nor doubts the power of Love to blend
The hearts of men as one !

TO THE THIRTY-NINTH
CONGRESS.

O PEOPLE-CHOSEN ! are ye not
Likewise the chosen of the Lord,
To do his will and speak his word ?

From the loud thunder-storm of war
Not man alone hath called ye forth,
But he, the God of all the earth !

The torch of vengeance in your hands
He quenches ; unto Him belongs
The solemn recompense of wrongs.

Enough of blood the land has seen,
And not by cell or gallows-stair
Shall ye the way of God prepare.

Say to the pardon-seekers, — Keep
  Your manhood, bend no suppliant
    knees,
Nor palter with unworthy pleas.

Above your voices sounds the wail
  Of starving men ; we shut in vain
  Our eyes to Pillow's ghastly stain.

What words can drown that bitter
  cry ?
  What tears wash out that stain of
    death ?
  What oaths confirm your broken faith ?

From you alone the guaranty
  Of union, freedom, peace, we claim ;
  We urge no conqueror's terms of
    shame.

Alas ! no victor's pride is ours ;
  We bend above our triumphs won
  Like David o'er his rebel son.

Be men, not beggars. Cancel all
  By one brave, generous action ; trust
  Your better instincts, and be just !

Make all men peers before the law,
  Take hands from off the negro's throat,
  Give black and white an equal vote.

Keep all your forfeit lives and lands,
  But give the common law's redress
  To labor's utter nakedness.

Revive the old heroic will ;
  Be in the right as brave and strong
  As ye have proved yourselves in wrong.

Defeat shall then be victory,
  Your loss the wealth of full amends,
  And hate be love, and foes be friends.

Then buried be the dreadful past,
  Its common slain be mourned, and let
  All memories soften to regret.

Then shall the Union's mother-heart
  Her lost and wandering ones recall,
  Forgiving and restoring all, —

And Freedom break her marble trance
  Above the Capitolian dome,
  Stretch hands, and bid ye welcome
    home !

OCCASIONAL POEMS.

THE ETERNAL GOODNESS.

O FRIENDS ! with whom my feet have
  trod
  The quiet aisles of prayer,
Glad witness to your zeal for God
  And love of man I bear.

I trace your lines of argument ;
  Your logic linked and strong
I weigh as one who dreads dissent,
  And fears a doubt as wrong.

But still my human hands are weak
  To hold your iron creeds :
Against the words ye bid me speak
  My heart within me pleads.

Who fathoms the Eternal Thought ?
  Who talks of scheme and plan ?

The Lord is God ! He needeth not
  The poor device of man.

I walk with bare, hushed feet the ground
  Ye tread with boldness shod ;
I dare not fix with mete and bound
  The love and power of God.

Ye praise His justice ; even such
  His pitying love I deem :
Ye seek a king ; I fain would touch
  The robe that hath no seam.

Ye see the curse which overbroods
  A world of pain and loss ;
I hear our Lord's beatitudes
  And prayer upon the cross.

More than your schoolmen teach, within
  Myself, alas ! I know :

Too dark ye cannot paint the sin,
   Too small the merit show.

I bow my forehead to the dust,
   I veil mine eyes for shame,
And urge, in trembling self-distrust,
   A prayer without a claim.

I see the wrong that round me lies,
   I feel the guilt within ;
I hear, with groan and travail-cries,
   The world confess its sin.

Yet, in the maddening maze of things,
   And tossed by storm and flood,
To one fixed stake my spirit clings ;
   I know that God is good !

Not mine to look where cherubim
   And seraphs may not see,
But nothing can be good in Him
   Which evil is in me.

The wrong that pains my soul below
   I dare not throne above :
I know not of His hate, — I know
   His goodness and His love.

I dimly guess from blessings known
   Of greater out of sight,
And, with the chastened Psalmist, own
   His judgments too are right.

I long for household voices gone,
   For vanished smiles I long,
But God hath led my dear ones on,
   And He can do no wrong.

I know not what the future hath
   Of marvel or surprise,
Assured alone that life and death
   · His mercy underlies.

And if my heart and flesh are weak
   To bear an untried pain,
The bruised reed He will not break,
   But strengthen and sustain.

No offering of my own I have,
   Nor works my faith to prove ;
I can but give the gifts He gave,
   And plead His love for love.

And so beside the Silent Sea
   I wait the muffled oar ;
No harm from Him can come to me
   On ocean or on shore.

I know not where His islands lift
   Their fronded palms in air ;
I only know I cannot drift
   Beyond His love and care.

O brothers ! if my faith is vain,
   If hopes like these betray,
Pray for me that my feet may gain
   The sure and safer way.

And Thou, O Lord ! by whom are seen
   Thy creatures as they be,
Forgive me if too close I lean
   My human heart on Thee !

OUR MASTER.

IMMORTAL Love, forever full,
   Forever flowing free,
Forever shared, forever whole,
   A never-ebbing sea !

Our outward lips confess the name
   All other names above ;
Love only knoweth whence it came,
   And comprehendeth love.

Blow, winds of God, awake and blow
   The mists of earth away !
Shine out, O Light Divine, and show
   How wide and far we stray !

Hush every lip, close every book,
   The strife of tongues forbear ;
Why forward reach, or backward look,
   For love that clasps like air ?

We may not climb the heavenly steeps
   To bring the Lord Christ down :
In vain we search the lowest deeps,
   For him no depths can drown.

Nor holy bread, nor blood of grape,
   The lineaments restore
Of him we know in outward shape
   And in the flesh no more.

He cometh not a king to reign ;
   The world's long hope is dim ;
The weary centuries watch in vain
   The clouds of heaven for him.

Death comes, life goes ; the asking eye
   And ear are answerless ;
The grave is dumb, the hollow sky
   Is sad with silentness.

The letter fails, and systems fall,
And every symbol wanes ;
The Spirit over-brooding all
Eternal Love remains.

And not for signs in heaven above
Or earth below they look,
Who know with John his smile of
love,
With Peter his rebuke.

In joy of inward peace, or sense
Of sorrow over sin,
He is his own best evidence,
His witness is within.

No fable old, nor mythic lore,
Nor dream of bards and seers,
No dead fact stranded on the shore
Of the oblivious years ; —

But warm, sweet, tender, even yet
A present help is he ;
And faith has still its Olivet,
And love its Galilee.

The healing of his seamless dress
Is by our beds of pain ;
We touch him in life's throng and
press,
And we are whole again.

Through him the first fond prayers are
said
Our lips of childhood frame,
The last low whispers of our dead
Are burdened with his name.

O Lord and Master of us all !
Whate'er our name or sign,
We own thy sway, we hear thy call,
We test our lives by thine.

Thou judgest us ; thy purity
Doth all our lusts condemn ;
The love that draws us nearer thee
Is hot with wrath to them.

Our thoughts lie open to thy sight ;
And, naked to thy glance,
Our secret sins are in the light
Of thy pure countenance.

Thy healing pains, a keen distress
Thy tender light shines in ;
Thy sweetness is the bitterness,
Thy grace the pang of sin.

Yet, weak and blinded though we be,
Thou dost our service own ;
We bring our varying gifts to thee,
And thou rejectest none.

To thee our full humanity,
Its joys and pains, belong ;
The wrong of man to man on thee
Inflicts a deeper wrong.

Who hates, hates thee, who loves be-
comes
Therein to thee allied ;
All sweet accords of hearts and homes
In thee are multiplied.

Deep strike thy roots, O heavenly Vine,
Within our earthly sod,
Most human and yet most divine,
The flower of man and God !

O Love ! O Life ! Our faith and
sight
Thy presence maketh one :
As through transfigured clouds of
white
We trace the noon-day sun.

So, to our mortal eyes subdued,
Flesh-veiled, but not concealed,
We know in thee the fatherhood
And heart of God revealed.

We faintly hear, we dimly see,
In differing phrase we pray ;
But, dim or clear, we own in thee
The Light, the Truth, the Way !

The homage that we render thee
Is still our Father's own ;
Nor jealous claim or rivalry
Divides the Cross and Throne.

To do thy will is more than praise,
As words are less than deeds,
And simple trust can find thy ways
We miss with chart of creeds.

No pride of self thy service hath,
No place for me and mine ;
Our human strength is weakness, death
Our life, apart from thine.

Apart from thee all gain is loss,
All labor vainly done ;
The solemn shadow of thy Cross
Is better than the sun.

Alone, O Love ineffable !
  Thy saving name is given ;
To turn aside from thee is hell,
  To walk with thee is heaven !

How vain, secure in all thou art,
  Our noisy championship ! —
The sighing of the contrite heart
  Is more than flattering lip.

Not thine the bigot's partial plea,
  Nor thine the zealot's ban ;
Thou well canst spare a love of thee
  Which ends in hate of man.

Our Friend, our Brother, and our Lord,
  What may thy service be ? —
Nor name, nor form, nor ritual word,
  But simply following thee.

We bring no ghastly holocaust,
  We pile no graven stone ;
He serves thee best who loveth most
  His brothers and thy own.

Thy litanies, sweet offices
  Of love and gratitude ;
Thy sacramental liturgies,
  The joy of doing good.

In vain shall waves of incense drift
  The vaulted nave around,
In vain the minster turret lift
  Its brazen weights of sound.

The heart must ring thy Christmas bells,
  Thy inward altars raise ;
Its faith and hope thy canticles,
  And its obedience praise !

THE VANISHERS.

Sweetest of all childlike dreams
  In the simple Indian lore
Still to me the legend seems
  Of the shapes who flit before.

Flitting, passing, seen and gone,
  Never reached nor found at rest,
Baffling search, but beckoning on
  To the Sunset of the Blest.

From the clefts of mountain rocks,
  Through the dark of lowland firs,
Flash the eyes and flow the locks
  Of the mystic Vanishers !

And the fisher in his skiff,
  And the hunter on the moss,
Hear their call from cape and cliff,
  See their hands the birch-leaves toss.

Wistful, longing, through the green
  Twilight of the clustered pines,
In their faces rarely seen
  Beauty more than mortal shines.

Fringed with gold their mantles flow
  On the slopes of westering knolls ;
In the wind they whisper low
  Of the Sunset Land of Souls.

Doubt who may, O friend of mine !
  Thou and I have seen them too ;
On before with beck and sign
  Still they glide, and we pursue.

More than clouds of purple trail
  In the gold of setting day ;
More than gleams of wing or sail
  Beckon from the sea-mist gray.

Glimpses of immortal youth,
  Gleams and glories seen and flown,
Far-heard voices sweet with truth,
  Airs from viewless Eden blown, —

Beauty that eludes our grasp,
  Sweetness that transcends our taste,
Loving hands we may not clasp,
  Shining feet that mock our haste, —

Gentle eyes we closed below,
  Tender voices heard once more,
Smile and call us, as they go
  On and onward, still before.

Guided thus, O friend of mine !
  Let us walk our little way,
Knowing by each beckoning sign
  That we are not quite astray.

Chase we still, with baffled feet,
  Smiling eye and waving hand,
Sought and seeker soon shall meet,
  Lost and found, in Sunset Land !

REVISITED.

READ AT THE "LAURELS," ON THE
MERRIMACK, 6TH MONTH, 1865.

THE roll of drums and the bugle's wailing
  Vex the air of our vales no more ;

The spear is beaten to hooks of pruning,
The share is the sword the soldier
    were !

Sing soft, sing low, our lowland river,
Under thy banks of laurel bloom ;
Softly and sweet, as the hour beseemeth,
Sing us the songs of peace and home.

Let all the tenderer voices of nature
    Temper the triumph and chasten
        mirth,
Full of the infinite love and pity
    For fallen martyr and darkened
        hearth.

But to Him who gives us beauty for
        ashes,
    And the oil of joy for mourning long,
Let thy hills give thanks, and all thy
        waters
    Break into jubilant waves of song !

Bring us the airs of hills and forests,
    The sweet aroma of birch and pine,
Give us a waft of the north-wind laden
    With sweetbrier odors and breath of
        kine !

Bring us the purple of mountain sunsets,
    Shadows of clouds that rake the hills,
The green repose of thy Plymouth
        meadows,
    The gleam and ripple of Campton rills.

Lead us away in shadow and sunshine,
    Slaves of fancy, through all thy miles,
The winding ways of Pemigewasset,
    And Winnipesaukee's hundred isles.

Shatter in sunshine over thy ledges,
    Laugh in thy plunges from fall to
        fall ;
Play with thy fringes of elms, and darken
    Under the shade of the mountain wall.

The cradle-song of thy hillside fountains
    Here in thy glory and strength repeat ;
Give us a taste of thy upland music,
    Show us the dance of thy silver feet.

Into thy dutiful life of uses
    Pour the music and weave the flowers ;
With the song of birds and bloom of
        meadows
    Lighten and gladden thy heart and
        ours.

Sing on ! bring do'
    The joy of the
        sea ;
The wealth of th
    mountains,
    The breath of
        with thee.

Here, in the calm
    ley,
    Mirth and labor
Dance of water an
    Both are beauty

Type of the Nor
    glory,
    Pride and ho
        race, —
Freedom lending
    Tints of beauty

Once again, O bea
    Hear our gree
        thanks ;
Hither we come, a
    Throng to the J

For though by
    trodden,
    Though never
        thy waves,
Well for us may 1
    With Christia
        graves.

And well may 1
    token
    Of fairer valle
        these,
Where the rivers o
    And full of sap

THE COMM

Behind us at our
    The gray bird a
Swung downward
    And wiped his 1

He shook his wing
    And set his hea
And, in his sharp,
    Asked, "What

"Fie, silly bird !"
    Your head bene

And go to sleep" ; — but o'er and o'er
He asked the self-same thing.

Then, smiling, to myself I said : —
How like are men and birds !
We all are saying what he says,
In action or in words.

The boy with whip and top and drum,
The girl with hoop and doll,
And men with lands and houses, ask
The question of Poor Poll.

However full, with something more
We fain the bag would cram ;
We sigh above our crowded nets
For fish that never swam.

No bounty of indulgent Heaven
The vague desire can stay ;
Self-love is still a Tartar mill
For grinding prayers alway.

The dear God hears and pities all ; .
He knoweth all our wants ;
And what we blindly ask of him
His love withholds or grants.

And so I sometimes think our prayers
Might well be merged in one ;
And nest and perch and hearth and
church
Repeat, "Thy will be done."

BRYANT ON HIS BIRTHDAY.

WE praise not now the poet's art,
The rounded beauty of his song ;
Who weighs him from his life apart
Must do his nobler nature wrong.

Not for the eye, familiar grown
With charms to common sight de-
nied, —
The marvellous gift he shares alone
With him who walked on Rydal-side ;

Not for rapt hymn nor woodland lay,
Too grave for smiles, too sweet for
tears ;
We speak his praise who wears to-day
The glory of his seventy years.

When Peace brings Freedom in her
train,
Let happy lips his songs rehearse ;

His life is now his noblest strain,
His manhood better than his verse !

Thank God ! his hand on Nature's
keys
Its cunning keeps at life's full
span ;
But, dimmed and dwarfed, in times like
these,
The poet seems beside the man !

So be it ! let the garlands die,
The singer's wreath, the painter's
meed,
Let our names perish, if thereby
Our country may be saved and freed !

HYMN

FOR THE OPENING OF THOMAS STARR
KING'S HOUSE OF WORSHIP, 1864.

AMIDST these glorious works of thine,
The solemn minarets of the pine,
And awful Shasta's icy shrine, —

Where swell thy hymns from wave and
gale,
And organ-thunders never fail,
Behind the cataract's silver veil, —

Our puny walls to Thee we raise,
Our poor reed-music sounds thy praise :
Forgive, O Lord, our childish ways !

For, kneeling on these altar-stairs,
We urge Thee not with selfish prayers,
Nor murmur at our daily cares.

Before Thee, in an evil day,
Our country's bleeding heart we lay,
And dare not ask thy hand to stay ;

But, through the war-cloud, pray to
thee
For union, but a union free,
With peace that comes of purity !

That Thou wilt bare thy arm to
save
And, smiting through this Red Sea
wave,
Make broad a pathway for the slave !

For us, confessing all our need,
We trust nor rite nor word nor deed,
Nor yet the broken staff of creed.

Assured alone that Thou art good
To each, as to the multitude,
Eternal Love and Fatherhood, —

Weak, sinful, blind, to Thee we kneel,
Stretch dumbly forth our hands, and feel
Our weakness is our strong appeal.

So, by these Western gates of Even
We wait to see with thy forgiven
The opening Golden Gate of Heaven !

Suffice it now.   In time to be
Shall holier altars rise to thee, —
Thy Church our broad humanity !

White flowers of love its walls shall
    climb,
Soft bells of peace shall ring its chime,
Its days shall all be holy time.

A sweeter song shall then be heard, —
The music of the world's accord
Confessing Christ, the Inward Word !

That song shall swell from shore to
    shore,
One hope, one faith, one love, restore
The seamless robe that Jesus wore.

THOMAS STARR KING.

THE great work laid upon his twoscore
    years
Is done, and well done.   If we drop our
    tears,
Who loved him as few men were ever
    loved,
We mourn no blighted hope nor bro-
    ken plan
With him whose life stands rounded
    and approved
In the full growth and stature of a man.
Mingle, O bells, along the Western
    slope,
With your deep toll a sound of faith and
    hope !
Wave cheerily still, O banner, half-way
    down,
From thousand-masted bay and stee-
    pled town !
Let the strong organ with its loftiest
    swell
Lift. the proud sorrow of the land, and
    tell
That the brave sower saw his ripened
    grain.
O East and West ! O morn and sunset
    twain
No more forever ! — has he lived in
    vain
Who, priest of Freedom, made ye one,
    and told
Your bridal service from his lips of
    gold !

AMONG THE HILLS,

AND OTHER POEMS.

TO ANNIE FIELDS

THIS LITTLE VOLUME,

DESCRIPTIVE OF SCENES WITH WHICH SHE IS FAMILIAR,

IS GRATEFULLY OFFERED.

PRELUDE.

ALONG the roadside, like the flowers of
    gold
That tawny Incas for their gardens
    wrought,
Heavy with sunshine droops the golden-
    rod,
And the red pennons of the cardinal-
    flowers
Hang motionless upon their upright
    staves.
The sky is hot and hazy, and the wind,
Wing-weary with its long flight from
    the south,
Unfelt ; yet, closely scanned, yon maple
    leaf
With faintest motion, as one stirs in
    dreams,
Confesses it. The locust by the wall
Stabs the noon-silence with his sharp
    alarm.
A single hay-cart down the dusty road
Creaks slowly, with its driver fast asleep
On the load's top. Against the neigh-
    boring hill,
Huddled along the stone wall's shady
    · side,
The sheep show white, as if a snowdrift
    still
Defied the dog-star. Through the open
    door
A drowsy smell of flowers — gray helio-
    trope,
And white sweet clover, and shy migno-
    nette —

Comes faintly in, and silent chorus lends
To the pervading symphony of peace.

No time is this for hands long over-
    worn
To task their strength : and (unto Him
    be praise
Who giveth quietness!) the stress and
    strain
Of years that did the work of centuries
Have ceased, and we can draw our
    breath once more
Freely and full. So, as yon harvesters
Make glad their nooning underneath the
    elms
With tale and riddle and old snatch of
    song,
I lay aside grave themes, and idly turn
The leaves of memory's sketch-book,
    dreaming o'er
Old summer pictures of the quiet hills,
And human life, as quiet, at their feet.

And yet not idly all. A farmer's son,
Proud of field-lore and harvest craft, and
    feeling
All their fine possibilities, how rich
And restful even poverty and toil
Become when beauty, harmony, and love
Sit at their humble hearth as angels sat
At evening in the patriarch's tent, when
    man
Makes labor noble, and his farmer's
    frock
The symbol of a Christian chivalry
Tender and just and generous to her

Who clothes with grace all duty; still,
I know
Too well the picture has another side, —
How wearily the grind of toil goes on
Where love is wanting, how the eye and
ear
And heart are starved amidst the plen-
itude
Of nature, and how hard and colorless
Is life without an atmosphere. I look
Across the lapse of half a century,
And call to mind old homesteads, where
no flower
Told that the spring had come, but evil
weeds,
Nightshade and rough-leaved burdock
in the place
Of the sweet doorway greeting of the
rose
And honeysuckle, where the house
walls seemed
Blistering in sun, without a tree or vine
To cast the tremulous shadow of its
leaves
Across the curtainless windows from
whose panes
Fluttered the signal rags of shiftlessness;
Within, the cluttered kitchen-floor, un-
washed
(Broom-clean I think they called it);
the best room
Stifling with cellar damp, shut from the
air
In hot midsummer, bookless, pictureless
Save the inevitable sampler hung
Over the fireplace, or a mourning piece,
A green-haired woman, peony-cheeked,
beneath
Impossible willows; the wide-throated
hearth
Bristling with faded pine-boughs half
concealing
The piled-up rubbish at the chimney's
back;
And, in sad keeping with all things
about them,
Shrill, querulous women, sour and sullen
men,
Untidy, loveless, old before their time,
With scarce a human interest save their
own
Monotonous round of small economies,
Or the poor scandal of the neighborhood;
Blind to the beauty everywhere re-
vealed,
Treading the May-flowers with regard-
less feet;

For them the song-sparrow and the
bobolink
Sang not, nor winds made music in the
leaves;
For them in vain October's holocaust
Burned, gold and crimson, over all the
hills,
The sacramental mystery of the woods.
Church-goers, fearful of the unseen
Powers,
But grumbling over pulpit-tax and pew-
rent,
Saving, as shrewd economists, their souls
And winter pork with the least possible
outlay
Of salt and sanctity; in daily life
Showing as little actual comprehension
Of Christian charity and love and duty,
As if the Sermon on the Mount had been
Outdated like a last year's almanac:
Rich in broad woodlands and in half-
tilled fields,
And yet so pinched and bare and com-
fortless,
The veriest straggler limping on his
rounds,
The sun and air his sole inheritance,
Laughed at a poverty that paid its taxes,
And hugged his rags in self-compla-
cency!

Not such should be the homesteads of
a land
Where whoso wisely wills and acts may
dwell
As king and lawgiver, in broad-acred
state,
With beauty, art, taste, culture, books,
to make
His hour of leisure richer than a life
Of fourscore to the barons of old time,
Our yeoman should be equal to his home
Set in the fair, green valleys, purple
walled,
A man to match his mountains, not to
creep
Dwarfed and abased below them. I
would fain
In this light way (of which I needs must
own
With the knife-grinder of whom Can-
ning sings,
"Story, God bless you! I have none to
tell you!")
Invite the eye to see and heart to feel
The beauty and the joy within their
reach, —

Home, and home loves, and the beati-
   tudes
Of nature free to all. Haply in years
That wait to take the places of our
   own,
Heard where some breezy balcony looks
   down
On happy homes, or where the lake in
   the moon
Sleeps dreaming of the mountains, fair
   as Ruth,
In the old Hebrew pastoral, at the feet
Of Boaz, even this simple lay of mine
May seem the burden of a prophecy,
Finding its late fulfilment in a change
Slow as the oak's growth, lifting man-
   hood up
Through broader culture, finer manners,
   love,
And reverence, to the level of the hills.

O Golden Age, whose light is of. the
   dawn,
And not of sunset, forward, not behind,
Flood the new heavens and earth, and
   with thee bring
All the old virtues, whatsoever things
Are pure and honest and of good repute,
But add thereto whatever bard has sung
Or seer has told of when in trance and
   dream
They saw the Happy Isles of prophecy !
Let Justice hold her scale, and Truth
   divide
Between the right and wrong; but give
   the heart
The freedom of its fair inheritance;
Let the poor prisoner, cramped and
   starved so long,
At Nature's table feast his ear and eye
With joy and wonder ; let all harmonies
Of sound, form, color, motion, wait
   upon
The princely guest, whether in soft attire
Of leisure clad, or the coarse frock of
   toil,
And, lending life to the dead form of
   faith,
Give human nature reverence for the
   sake
Of One who bore it, making it divine
With the ineffable tenderness of God ;
Let common need, the brotherhood of
   prayer,
The heirship of an unknown destiny,
The unsolved mystery round about us,
   make

A man more precious than the gold of
   Ophir.
Sacred, inviolate, unto whom all things
Should minister, as outward types and
   signs
Of the eternal beauty which fulfils
The one great purpose of creation, Love,
The sole necessity of Earth and Heaven !

AMONG THE HILLS.

For weeks the clouds had raked the
   hills
And vexed the vales with raining,
And all the woods were sad with mist,
   And all the brooks complaining.

At last, a sudden night-storm tore
   The mountain veils asunder,
And swept the valleys clean before
   The besom of the thunder.

Through Sandwich notch the west-wind
   sang
   Good morrow to the cotter ;
And once again Chocorua's horn
   Of shadow pierced the water.

Above his broad lake Ossipee,
   Once more the sunshine wearing,
Stooped, tracing on that silver shield
   His grim armorial bearing.

Clear drawn against the hard blue sky
   The peaks had winter's keenness ;
And, close on autumn's frost, the vales
   Had more than June's fresh green-
   ness.

Again the sodden forest floors
   With golden lights were checkered,
Once more rejoicing leaves in wind
   And sunshine danced and flickered.

It was as if the summer's late
   Atoning for its sadness
Had borrowed every season's charm
   To end its days in gladness.

I call to mind those banded vales
   Of shadow and of shining,
Through which, my hostess at my side,
   I drove in day's declining.

We held our sideling way above
   The river's whitening shallows,

By homesteads old, with wide-flung
    barns
Swept through and through by swal-
    lows, —

By maple orchards, belts of pine
    And larches climbing darkly
The mountain slopes, and, over all,
    The great peaks rising starkly.

You should have seen that long hill-
    range
    With gaps of brightness riven, —
How through each pass and hollow
    streamed
    The purpling lights of heaven, —

Rivers of gold-mist flowing down
    From far celestial fountains, —
The great sun flaming through the
    rifts
Beyond the wall of mountains !

We paused at last where home-bound
    cows
Brought down the pasture's treasure,
And in the barn the rhythmic flails
    Beat out a harvest measure.

We heard the night-hawk's sullen
    plunge,
    The crow his tree-mates calling :
The shadows lengthening down the
    slopes
About our feet were falling.

And through them smote the level sun
    In broken lines of splendor,
Touched the gray rocks and made the
    green
Of the shorn grass more tender.

The maples bending o'er the gate,
    Their arch of leaves just tinted
With yellow warmth, the golden glow
    Of coming autumn hinted.

Keen white between the farm-house
    showed,
    And smiled on porch and trellis,
The fair democracy of flowers
    That equals cot and palace.

And weaving garlands for her dog,
    'Twixt chidings and caresses,
A human flower of childhood shook
    The sunshine from her tresses.

On either hand we saw the signs
    Of fancy and of shrewdness,
Where taste had wound its arms of vines
    Round thrift's uncomely rudeness.

The sun-brown farmer in his frock
    Shook hands, and called to Mary :
Bare-armed, as Juno might, she came,
    White-aproned from her dairy.

Her air, her smile, her motions, told
    Of womanly completeness ;
A music as of household songs
    Was in her voice of sweetness.

Not beautiful in curve and line,
    But something more and better,
The secret charm eluding art,
    Its spirit, not its letter ; —

An inborn grace that nothing lacked
    Of culture or appliance, —
The warmth of genial courtesy,
    The calm of self-reliance.

Before her queenly womanhood
    How dared our hostess utter
The paltry errand of her need
    To buy her fresh-churned butter ?

She led the way with housewife pride,
    Her goodly store disclosing,
Full tenderly the golden balls
    With practised hands disposing.

Then, while along the western hills
    We watched the changeful glory
Of sunset, on our homeward way,
    I heard her simple story.

The early crickets sang ; the stream
    Plashed through my friend's narra-
    tion :
Her rustic patois of the hills
    Lost in my free translation.

"More wise," she said, "than those
    who swarm
Our hills in middle summer,
She came, when June's first roses blow,
    To greet the early comer.

"From school and ball and rout she
    came,
    The city's fair, pale daughter,
To drink the wine of mountain air
    Beside the Bearcamp Water.

" Her step grew firmer on the hills
    That watch our homesteads over ;
On cheek and lip, from summer fields,
    She caught the bloom of clover.

" For health comes sparkling in the
        streams
    From cool Chocorua stealing :
There 's iron in our Northern winds ;
    Our pines are trees of healing.

" She sat beneath the broad - armed
        elms
    That skirt the mowing-meadow,
And watched the gentle west-wind
        weave
    The grass with shine and shadow.

" Beside her, from the summer heat
    To share her grateful screening,
With forehead bared, the farmer stood,
    Upon his pitchfork leaning.

" Framed in its damp, dark locks, his
        face
    Had nothing mean or common, —
Strong, manly, true, the tenderness
    And pride beloved of woman.

" She looked up, glowing with the
        health
    The country air had brought her,
And, laughing, said : ' You lack a
        wife,
    Your mother lacks a daughter.

" ' To mend your frock and bake your
        bread
    You do not need a lady :
Be sure among these brown old homes
    Is some one waiting ready, —

" ' Some fair, sweet girl with skilful
        hand
    And cheerful heart for treasure,
Who never played with ivory keys,
    Or danced the polka's measure.'

" He bent his black brows to a frown,
    He set his white teeth tightly.
' 'T is well,' he said, ' for one like you
    To choose for me so lightly.

" ' You think, because my life is rude
    I take no note of sweetness :
I tell you love has naught to do
    With meetness or unmeetness.

" ' Itself its best excuse, it asks
    No leave of pride or fashion
When silken zone or homespun frock
    It stirs with throbs of passion.

" ' You think me deaf and blind : you
        bring
    Your winning graces hither
As free as if from cradle-time
    We two had played together.

" ' You tempt me with your laughing
        eyes,
    Your cheek of sundown's blushes,
A motion as of waving grain,
    A music as of thrushes.

" ' The plaything of your summer sport,
    The spells you weave around me
You cannot at your will undo,
    Nor leave me as you found me.

" ' You go as lightly as you came,
    Your life is well without me ;
What care you that these hills will close
    Like prison-walls about me ?

" ' No mood is mine to seek a wife,
    Or daughter for my mother :
Who loves you loses in that love
    All power to love another !

" ' I dare your pity or your scorn,
    With pride your own exceeding ;
I fling my heart into your lap
    Without a word of pleading.'

" She looked up in his face of pain
    So archly, yet so tender :
' And if I lend you mine,' she said,
    ' Will you forgive the lender ?

" ' Nor frock nor tan can hide the
        man ;
    And see you not, my farmer,
How weak and fond a woman waits
    Behind this silken armor ?

" ' I love you : on that love alone,
    And not my worth, presuming,
Will you not trust for summer fruit
    The tree in May-day blooming ?'

" Alone the hangbird overhead,
    His hair-swung cradle straining,
Looked down to see love's miracle, —
    The giving that is gaining.

" And so the farmer found a wife,
His mother found a daughter :
There looks no happier home than hers
On pleasant Bearcamp Water.

" Flowers spring to blossom where she
walks
The careful ways of duty ;
Our hard, stiff lines of life with her
Are flowing curves of beauty.

" Our homes are cheerier for her sake,
Our door-yards brighter blooming,
And all about the social air
Is sweeter for her coming.

" Unspoken homilies of peace
Her daily life is preaching ;
The still refreshment of the dew
Is her unconscious teaching.

" And never tenderer hand than hers
Unknits the brow of ailing ;
Her garments to the sick man's ear
Have music in their trailing.

" And when, in pleasant harvest moons,
The youthful huskers gather,
Or sleigh-drives on the mountain ways
Defy the winter weather, —

" In sugar-camps, when south and
warm
The winds of March are blowing,
And sweetly from its thawing veins
The maple's blood is flowing, —

" In summer, where some lilied pond
Its virgin zone is bearing,
Or where the ruddy autumn fire
Lights up the apple-paring, —

" The coarseness of a ruder time
Her finer mirth displaces,
A subtler sense of pleasure fills
Each rustic sport she graces.

" Her presence lends its warmth and
health
To all who come before it.
If woman lost us Eden, such
As she alone restore it.

" For larger life and wiser aims
The farmer is her debtor ;
Who holds to his another's heart
Must needs be worse or better.

" Through her his civic service shows
A purer-toned ambition ;
No double consciousness divides
The man and politician.

" In party's doubtful ways he trusts
Her instincts to determine ;
At the loud polls, the thought of
her
Recalls Christ's Mountain Sermon.

" He owns her logic of the heart,
And wisdom of unreason,
Supplying, while he doubts and weighs,
The needed word in season.

" He sees with pride her richer thought,
Her fancy's freer ranges ;
And love thus deepened to respect
Is proof against all changes.

" And if she walks at ease in ways
His feet are slow to travel,
And if she reads with cultured eyes
What his may scarce unravel,

" Still clearer, for her keener sight
Of beauty and of wonder,
He learns the meaning of the hills
He dwelt from childhood under.

" And higher, warmed with summer
lights,
Or winter-crowned and hoary,
The ridged horizon lifts for him
Its inner veils of glory.

" He has his own free, bookless lore,
The lessons nature taught him,
The wisdom which the woods and
hills
And toiling men have brought him :

" The steady force of will whereby
Her flexile grace seems sweeter ;
The sturdy counterpoise which makes
Her woman's life completer :

" A latent fire of soul which lacks
No breath of love to fan it ;
And wit, that, like his native brooks,
Plays over solid granite.

" How dwarfed against his manliness
She sees the poor pretension,
The wants, the aims, the follies, born
Of fashion and convention !

" How life behind its accidents
Stands strong and self-sustaining,
The human fact transcending all
The losing and the gaining.

"And so, in grateful interchange
Of teacher and of hearer,
Their lives their true distinctness keep
While daily drawing nearer.

" And if the husband or the wife
In home's strong light discovers
Such slight defaults as failed to meet
The blinded eyes of lovers,

" Why need we care to ask ? — who
  dreams
Without their thorns of roses,
Or wonders that the truest steel
The readiest spark discloses ?

" For still in mutual sufferance lies
The secret of true living :
Love scarce is love that never knows
The sweetness of forgiving.

" We send the Squire to General Court,
He takes his young wife thither ;
No prouder man election day
Rides through the sweet June weather.

" He sees with eyes of manly trust
All hearts to her inclining ;
Not less for him his household light
That others share its shining."

Thus, while my hostess spake, there
  grew
Before me, warmer tinted
And outlined with a tenderer grace,
The picture that she hinted.

The sunset smouldered as we drove
Beneath the deep hill-shadows.
Below us wreaths of white fog walked
Like ghosts the haunted meadows.

Sounding the summer night, the stars
  Dropped down their golden plum-
    mets ;
The pale arc of the Northern lights
Rose o'er the mountain summits, —

Until, at last, beneath its bridge,
We heard the Bearcamp flowing,
And saw across the mapled lawn
The welcome home-lights glowing ; —

And, musing on the tale I heard,
'T were well, thought 1, if often
To rugged farm-life came the gift
To harmonize and soften ; —

If more and more we found the troth
Of fact and fancy plighted,
And culture's charm and labor's strength
In rural homes united, —

The simple life, the homely hearth,
With beauty's sphere surrounding,
And blessing toil where toil abounds
With graces more abounding.

MISCELLANEOUS POEMS.

THE CLEAR VISION.

I DID but dream.   I never knew
  What charms our sternest season
    wore.
Was never yet the sky so blue,
  Was never earth so white before.
Till now I never saw the glow
Of sunset on yon hills of snow,
And never learned the bough's designs
Of beauty in its leafless lines.

Did ever such a morning break
  As that my eastern windows see ?

Did ever such a moonlight take
  Weird photographs of shrub and
    tree ?
Rang ever bells so wild and fleet
The music of the winter street ?
Was ever yet a sound by half
So merry as yon school-boy's laugh ?

O Earth ! with gladness overfraught,
  No added charm thy face hath found ;
Within my heart the change is wrought,
  My footsteps make enchanted ground.
From couch of pain and curtained room
Forth to thy light and air I come,

To find in all that meets my eyes
The freshness of a glad surprise.

Fair seem these winter days, and soon
　Shall blow the warm west-winds of
　　spring
To set the unbound rills in tune,
　And hither urge the bluebird's wing.
The vales shall laugh in flowers, the
　　woods
Grow misty green with leafing buds,
And violets and wind-flowers sway,
Against the throbbing heart of May.

Break forth, my lips, in praise, and
　　own
　The wiser love severely kind ;
Since, richer for its chastening grown,
　I see, whereas I once was blind.
The world, O Father ! hath not wronged
With loss the life by thee prolonged ;
But still, with every added year,
More beautiful thy works appear !

As thou hast made thy world without,
　Make thou more fair my world with-
　　in ;
Shine through its lingering clouds of
　　doubt ;
　Rebuke its haunting shapes of sin ;
Fill, brief or long, my granted span
Of life with love to thee and man ;
Strike when thou wilt the hour of rest,
But let my last days be my best !
　　　2d mo , 1868.

THE DOLE OF JARL THORKELL.

THE land was pale with famine
　And racked with fever-pain ;
The frozen fiords were fishless,
　The earth withheld her grain.

Men saw the boding Fylgja
　Before them come and go,
And, through their dreams, the Urdar-
　　moon
　From west to east sailed slow !

Jarl Thorkell of Thevera
　At Yule-time made his vow ;
On Rykdal's holy Doom-stone
He slew to Frey his cow.

To bounteous Frey he slew her ;
　To Skuld, the younger Norn,

Who watches over birth and death,
　He gave her calf unborn.

And his little gold-haired daughter
　Took up the sprinkling-rod,
And smeared with blood the temple
　And the wide lips of the god.

Hoarse below, the winter water
　Ground its ice-blocks o'er and o'er ;
Jets of foam, like ghosts of dead waves,
　Rose and fell along the shore.

The red torch of the Jokul,
　Aloft in icy space,
Shone down on the bloody Horg-stones
　And the statue's carven face.

And closer round and grimmer
　Beneath its baleful light
The Jotun shapes of mountains
　Came crowding through the night.

The gray-haired Hersir trembled
　As a flame by wind is blown ;
A weird power moved his white lips,
　And their voice was not his own !

" The Æsir thirst ! " he muttered ;
" The gods must have more blood
Before the tun shall blossom
　Or fish shall fill the flood.

" The Æsir thirst and hunger,
　And hence our blight and ban ;
The mouths of the strong gods water
　For the flesh and blood of man !

" Whom shall we give the strong ones !
　Not warriors, sword on thigh ;
But let the nursling infant
　And bedrid old man die."

" So be it ! " cried the young men,
　" There needs nor doubt nor parle " ;
But, knitting hard his red brows,
　In silence stood the Jarl.

A sound of woman's weeping
　At the temple door was heard,
But the old men bowed their white
　　heads,
　And answered not a word.

Then the Dream-wife of Thingvalla,
　A Vala young and fair,
Sang softly, stirring with her breath
　The veil of her loose hair.

She sang : "The winds from Alfheim
  Bring never sound of strife ;
The gifts for Frey the meetest
  Are not of death, but life.

" He loves the grass-green meadows,
  The grazing kine's sweet breath ;
He loathes your bloody Horg-stones,
  Your gifts that smell of death.

" No wrong by wrong is righted,
  No pain is cured by pain ;
The blood that smokes from Doom-rings
  Falls back in redder rain.

" The gods are what you make them,
  As earth shall Asgard prove ;
And hate will come of hating,
  And love will come of love.

" Make dole of skyr and black bread
  That old and young may live ;
And look to Frey for favor
  When first like Frey you give.

" Even now o'er Njord's sea-meadows
  The summer dawn begins :
The tun shall have its harvest,
  The fiord its glancing fins."

Then up and swore Jarl Thorkell :
  " By Gimli and by Hel,
O Vala of Thingvalla,
  Thou singest wise and well !

" Too dear the Æsir's favors
  Bought with our children's lives ;
Better die than shame in living
  Our mothers and our wives.

" The full shall give his portion
  To him who hath most need ;
Of curdled skyr and black bread,
  Be daily dole decreed."

He broke from off his neck-chain
  Three links of beaten gold ;
And each man, at his bidding,
  Brought gifts for young and old.

Then mothers nursed their children,
  And daughters fed their sires,
And Health sat down with Plenty
  Before the next Yule fires.

The Horg-stones stand in Rykdal ;
  The Doom-ring still remains ;

But the snows of a thousand winters
  Have washed away the stains.

Christ ruleth now ; the Æsir
  Have found their twilight dim ;
And, wiser than she dreamed, of old
  The Vala sang of Him !

THE TWO RABBIS.

THE Rabbi Nathan, twoscore years and
      ten,
Walked blameless through the evil
      world, and then,
Just as the almond blossomed in his
      hair,
Met a temptation all too strong to bear,
And miserably sinned. So, adding not
Falsehood to guilt, he left his seat, and
      taught
No more among the elders, but went out
From the great congregation girt about
With sackcloth, and with ashes on his
      head,
Making his gray locks grayer. Long he
      prayed,
Smiting his breast ; then, as the Book
      he laid
Open before him for the Bath-Col's
      choice,
Pausing to hear that Daughter of a
      Voice,
Behold the royal preacher's words : " A
      friend
Loveth at all times, yea, unto the end ;
And for the evil day thy brother lives."
Marvelling, he said : " It is the Lord
      who gives
Counsel in need. At Ecbatana dwells
Rabbi Ben Isaac, who all men excels
In righteousness and wisdom, as the
      trees
Of Lebanon the small weeds that the
      bees
Bow with their weight. I will arise,
      and lay
My sins before him."

                    And he went his way
Barefooted, fasting long, with many
      prayers ;
But even as one who, followed una-
      wares,
Suddenly in the darkness feels a hand
Thrill with its touch his own, and his
      cheek fanned

By odors subtly sweet, and whispers near
Of words he loathes, yet cannot choose
    but hear,
So, while the Rabbi journeyed, chanting
    low
The wail of David's penitential woe,
Before him still the old temptation came,
And mocked him with the motion and
    the shame
Of such desires that, shuddering, he ab-
    horred
Himself ; and, crying mightily to the
    Lord
To free his soul and cast the demon out,
Smote with his staff the blankness round
    about.

At length, in the low light of a spent
    day,
The towers of Ecbatana far away
Rose on the desert's rim ; and Nathan,
    faint
And footsore, pausing where for some
    dead saint
The faith of Islam reared a doméd tomb,
Saw some one kneeling in the shadow,
    whom
He greeted kindly : "May the Holy
    One
Answer thy prayers, O stranger!"
    Whereupon
The shape stood up with a loud cry, and
    then,
Clasped in each other's arms, the two
    gray men
Wept, praising Him whose gracious prov-
    idence
Made their paths one. But straightway,
    as the sense
Of his transgression smote him, Nathan
    tore
Himself away : "O friend beloved, no
    more
Worthy am I to touch thee, for I came,
Foul from my sins, to tell thee all my
    shame.
Haply thy prayers, since naught availeth
    mine,
May purge my soul, and make it white
    like thine.
Pity me, O Ben Isaac, I have sinned!"

Awestruck Ben Isaac stood. The des-
    ert wind
Blew his long mantle backward, laying
    bare
The mournful secret of his shirt of hair.

"I too, O friend, if not in act," he said,
"In thought have verily sinned. Hast
    thou not read,
' Better the eye should see than that de-
    sire
Should wander' ? Burning with a hid-
    den fire
That tears and prayers quench not, I
    come to thee
For pity and for help, as thou to me.
Pray for me, O my friend !" But Na-
    than cried,
"Pray thou for me, Ben Isaac !"

                     Side by side
In the low sunshine by the turban stone
They knelt ; each made his brother's woe
    his own,
Forgetting, in the agony and stress
Of pitying love, his claim of selfishness ;
Peace, for his friend besought, his own
    became ;
His prayers were answered in another's
    name ;
And, when at last they rose up to em-
    brace,
Each saw God's pardon in his brother's
    face !

Long after, when his headstone gathered
    moss,
Traced on the targum-marge of Onkelos
In Rabbi Nathan's hand these words
    were read :
"*Hope not the cure of sin till Self is
    dead;*
Forget it in love's service, and the debt
*Thou canst not pay the angels shall for-
    get ;*
*Heaven's gate is shut to him who comes
    alone ;*
*Save thou a soul, and it shall save thy
    own !*"

THE MEETING.

THE elder folks shook hands at last,
Down seat by seat the signal passed.
To simple ways like ours unused,
Half solemnized and half amused,
With long-drawn breath and shrug, my
    guest
His sense of glad relief expressed.
Outside the hills lay warm in sun ;
The cattle in the meadow-run
Stood half-leg deep ; a single bird

The green repose above us stirred.
'What part or lot have you," he said,
" In these dull rites of drowsy-head ?
Is silence worship ? Seek it where
it soothes with dreams the summer air,
Not in this close and rude-benched hall,
But where soft lights and shadows fall,
And all the slow, sleep-walking hours
Glide soundless over grass and flowers !
From time and place and form apart,
its holy ground the human heart,
Nor ritual-bound nor templeward
Walks the free spirit of the Lord !
Our common Master did not pen
His followers up from other men ;
His service liberty indeed,
He built no church, he framed no creed ;
But while the saintly Pharisee
Made broader his phylactery,
As from the synagogue was seen
The dusty-sandalled Nazarene
Through ripening cornfields lead the way
Upon the awful Sabbath day,
His sermons were the healthful talk
That shorter made the mountain-walk,
His wayside texts were flowers and birds,
Where mingled with His gracious words
The rustle of the tamarisk-tree
And ripple-wash of Galilee."

' Thy words are well, O friend," I said ;
' Unmeasured and unlimited,
With noiseless slide of stone to stone,
The mystic Church of God has grown.
Invisible and silent stands
The temple never made with hands,
Unheard the voices still and small
Of its unseen confessional.
He needs no special place of prayer
Whose hearing ear is everywhere ;
He brings not back the childish days
That ringed the earth with stones of praise,
Roofed Karnak's hall of gods, and laid
The plinths of Philæ's colonnade.
Still less He owns the selfish good
And sickly growth of solitude, —
The worthless grace that, out of sight,
Flowers in the desert anchorite ;
Dissevered from the suffering whole,
Love hath no power to save a soul.
Not out of Self, the origin
And native air and soil of sin,
The living waters spring and flow,
The trees with leaves of healing grow.

" Dream not, O friend, because I seek
This quiet shelter twice a week,
I better deem its pine-laid floor
Than breezy hill or sea-sung shore ;
But nature is not solitude :
She crowds us with her thronging wood ;
Her many hands reach out to us,
Her many tongues are garrulous ;
Perpetual riddles of surprise
She offers to our ears and eyes ;
She will not leave our senses still,
But drags them captive at her will :
And, making earth too great for heaven,
She hides the Giver in the given.

" And so, I find it well to come
For deeper rest to this still room,
For here the habit of the soul
Feels less the outer world's control ;
The strength of mutual purpose pleads
More earnestly our common needs ;
And from the silence multiplied
By these still forms on either side,
The world that time and sense have known
Falls off and leaves us God alone.

" Yet rarely through the charmed repose
Unmixed the stream of motive flows,
A flavor of its many springs,
The tints of earth and sky it brings ;
In the still waters needs must be
Some shade of human sympathy ;
And here, in its accustomed place,
I look on memory's dearest face ;
The blind by-sitter guesseth not
What shadow haunts that vacant spot;
No eyes save mine alone can see
The love wherewith it welcomes me !
And still, with those alone my kin,
In doubt and weakness, want and sin,
I bow my head, my heart I bare
As when that face was living there,
And strive (too oft, alas ! in vain)
The peace of simple trust to gain,
Fold fancy's restless wings, and lay
The idols of my heart away.

" Welcome the silence all unbroken,
Nor less the words of fitness spoken, —
Such golden words as hers for whom
Our autumn flowers have just made room ;
Whose hopeful utterance through and through
The freshness of the morning blew ;
Who loved not less the earth that light:

Fell on it from the heavens in sight,
But saw in all fair forms more fair
The Eternal beauty mirrored there.
Whose eighty years but added grace
And saintlier meaning to her face, —
The look of one who bore away
Glad tidings from the hills of day,
While all our hearts went forth to meet
The coming of her beautiful feet !
Or haply hers, whose pilgrim tread
Is in the paths where Jesus led ;
Who dreams her childhood's sabbath
    dream
By Jordan's willow-shaded stream,
And, of the hymns of hope and faith,
Sung by the monks of Nazareth,
Hears pious echoes, in the call
To prayer, from Moslem minarets fall,
Repeating where His works were wrought
The lesson that her Master taught,
Of whom an elder Sibyl gave,
The prophecies of Cumæ's cave !

" I ask no organ's soulless breath
To drone the themes of life and death,
No altar candle-lit by day,
No ornate wordsman's rhetoric-play,
No cool philosophy to teach
Its bland audacities of speech
To double-tasked idolators
Themselves their gods and worshippers,
No pulpit hammered by the fist
Of loud-asserting dogmatist,
Who borrows from the hand of love
The smoking thunderbolts of Jove.
I know how well the fathers taught,
What work the later schoolmen
    wrought ;
I reverence old-time faith and men,
But God is near us now as then ;
His force of love is s ill unspent,
His hate of sin as im ninent ;
And still the measure of our needs
Outgrows the cramping bounds of
    creeds ;
The manna gathered yesterday
Already savors of decay ;
Doubts to the world's child-heart un-
    known
Question us now from star and stone ;
Too little or too much we know,
And sight is swift and faith is slow ;
The power is lost to self-deceive
With shallow forms of make-believe.
We walk at high noon, and the bells
Call to a thousand oracles,
But the sound deafens, and the light

Is stronger than our dazzled sight ;
The letters of the sacred Book
Glimmer and swim beneath our look ;
Still struggles in the Age's breast
With deepening agony of quest
The old entreaty: 'Art thou He,
Or look we for the Christ to be ?'

" God should be most where man is
    least :
So, where is neither church nor priest,
And never rag of form or creed
To clothe the nakedness of need, —
Where farmer-folk in silence meet, —
I turn my bell-unsummoned feet ;
I lay the critic's glass aside,
I tread upon my lettered pride,
And, lowest-seated, testify
To the oneness of humanity ;
Confess the universal want,
And share whatever Heaven may grant.
He findeth not who seeks his own,
The soul is lost that 's saved alone.
Not on one favored forehead fell
Of old the fire-tongued miracle,
But flamed o'er all the thronging host
The baptism of the Holy Ghost ;
Heart answers heart : in one desire
The blending lines of prayer aspire ;
'Where, in my name, meet two or
    . three,'
Our Lord hath said, 'I there will be !'

" So sometimes comes to soul and
    sense
The feeling which is evidence
That very near about us lies
The realm of spiritual mysteries.
The sphere of the supernal powers
Impinges on this world of ours.
The low and dark horizon lifts,
To light the scenic terror shifts ;
The breath of a diviner air
Blows down the answer of a prayer :
That all our sorrow, pain, and doubt
A great compassion clasps about,
And law and goodness, love and force,
Are wedded fast beyond divorce.
Then duty leaves to love its task,
The beggar Self forgets to ask ;
With smile of trust and folded hands,
The passive soul in waiting stands
To feel, as flowers the sun and dew,
The One true Life its own renew.

" So, to the calmly gathered thought
The innermost of truth is taught,

derstood,
re of good,
est trace
holy face;
ly this, —
fishness,
ntal fire,
. desire,
ot the pain
lafing chain;
meaning lies
ifice,
of sense
tence,
edience;
ch and Day are

— for earth, not

holiest ends,
gnant friends;
lwells not afar,
oter star,
ith flattered ear
a selfish fear,
oor and blind,
ng of our kind,
ayers we pray,
es to-day."

WER.

l of reproof,
e weave to-day
warp and woof
;ray.

flesh is weak.
;, that fain would

all some day seek
w way.

hful eye,
king frown;
nes must sigh
down;

raining oar,
mer warmth and

nted shore
alm.

s hour of bloom,
f long desire;
!

This day be mine : be those to come
　As duty shall require.

The deep voice answered to my own,
　Smiting my selfish prayers away;
" To-morrow is with God alone,
　And man hath but to-day.

" Say not, thy fond, vain heart within,
　The Father's arm shall still be wide,
When from these pleasant ways of sin
　Thou turn'st at eventide.

" ' Cast thyself down,' the tempter saith,
　' And angels shall thy feet upbear.'
He bids thee make a lie of faith,
　And blasphemy of prayer.

" Though God be good and free be
　　Heaven,
　No force divine can love compel;
And, though the song of sins forgiven
　May sound through lowest hell,

" The sweet persuasion of His voice
　Respects thy sanctity of will.
He giveth day : thou hast thy choice
　To walk in darkness still;

" As one who, turning from the light,
　Watches his own gray shadow fall,
Doubting, upon his path of night,
　If there be day at all !

" No word of doom may shut thee
　　out,
　No wind of wrath may downward
　　whirl,
No swords of fire keep watch about
　The open gates of pearl;

" A tenderer light than moon or sun,
　Than song of earth a sweeter hymn,
May shine and sound forever on,
　And thou be deaf and dim.

" Forever round the Mercy-seat
　The guiding lights of Love shall
　　burn;
But what if, habit-bound, thy feet
　Shall lack the will to turn ?

" What if thine eye refuse to see,
　Thine ear of Heaven's free welcome
　　fail,
And thou a willing captive be,
　Thyself thy own dark jail ?

"O doom beyond the saddest guess,
As the long years of God unroll
To make thy dreary selfishness
The prison of a soul!

"To doubt the love that fain would break
The fetters from thy self-bound limb;
And dream that God can thee forsake
As thou forsakest him!"

G. L. S.

He has done the work of a true man, —
Crown him, honor him, love him.
Weep over him, tears of woman,
Stoop manliest brows above him!

O dusky mothers and daughters,
Vigils of mourning keep for him!
Up in the mountains, and down by the waters,
Lift up your voices and weep for him!

For the warmest of hearts is frozen,
The freest of hands is still;
And the gap in our picked and chosen
The long years may not fill.

No duty could overtask him,
No need his will outrun;
Or ever our lips could ask him,
His hands the work had done.

He forgot his own soul for others,
Himself to his neighbor lending;
He found the Lord in his suffering brothers,
And not in the clouds descending.

So the bed was sweet to die on,
Whence he saw the doors wide swung
Against whose bolted iron
The strength of his life was flung.

And he saw ere his eye was darkened
The sheaves of the harvest-bringing,
And knew while his ear yet hearkened
The voice of the reapers singing.

Ah, well! — The world is discreet;
There are plenty to pause and wait;
But here was a man who set his feet
Sometimes in advance of fate, —

Plucked off the old bark when the inner
Was slow to renew it,
And put to the Lord's work the sinner
When saints failed to do it.

Never rode to the wrong's redressing
A worthier paladin.
Shall he not hear the blessing,
"Good and faithful, enter in!"

FREEDOM IN BRAZIL.

With clearer light, Cross of the South
shine forth
In blue Brazilian skies;
And thou, O river, cleaving half the earth
From sunset to sunrise,
From the great mountains to the Atlantic waves
Thy joy's long anthem pour.
Yet a few days (God make them less
and slaves
Shall shame thy pride no more.
No fettered feet thy shaded margin
press;
But all men shall walk free
Where thou, the high-priest of the wilderness,
Hast wedded sea to sea.

And thou, great-hearted ruler, through
whose mouth
The word of God is said,
Once more, "Let there be light!" —
Son of the South,
Lift up thy honored head,
Wear unashamed a crown by thy desert
More than by birth thy own,
Careless of watch and ward; thou art
begirt
By grateful hearts alone.
The moated wall and battle-ship may
fail,
But safe shall justice prove;
Stronger than greaves of brass or iron
mail
The panoply of love.

Crowned doubly by man's blessing and
God's grace,
Thy future is secure;
Who frees a people makes his statue's
place
In Time's Valhalla sure.
Lo! from his Neva's banks the Scythian
Czar
Stretches to thee his hand,

Who, with the pencil of the Northern
  star,
Wrote freedom on his land.
And he whose grave is holy by our
  calm
And prairied Sangamon,
From his gaunt hand shall drop the
  martyr's palm
To greet thee with " Well done !"

And thou, O Earth, with smiles thy
  face make sweet,
And let thy wail be stilled,
To hear the Muse of prophecy repeat
  Her promise half fulfilled.
The Voice that spake at Nazareth speaks
  still,
No sound thereof hath died ;
Alike thy hope and Heaven's eternal
  will
Shall yet be satisfied.
The years are slow, the vision tarrieth
  long,
And far the end may be ;
But, one by one, the fiends of ancient
  wrong
Go out and leave thee free.

DIVINE COMPASSION.

Long since, a dream of heaven I had,
  And still the vision haunts me oft ;
I see the saints in white robes clad,
  The martyrs with their palms aloft ;
But hearing still, in middle song,
  The ceaseless dissonance of wrong ;
And shrinking, with hid faces, from the
  strain
Of sad, beseeching eyes, full of remorse
  and pain.

The glad song falters to a wail,
  The harping sinks to low lament ;
Before the still uplifted veil
  I see the crownéd foreheads bent,
Making more sweet the heavenly air,
  With breathings of unselfish prayer ;
And a Voice saith : " O Pity which is
  pain,
O Love that weeps, fill up my sufferings
  which remain !

" Shall souls redeemed by me refuse
  To share my sorrow in their turn ?
Or, sin-forgiven, my gift abuse
  Of peace with selfish unconcern ?

Has saintly ease no pitying care ?
  Has faith no work, and love no prayer ?
While sin remains, and souls in dark-
  ness dwell,
Can heaven itself be heaven, and look
  unmoved on hell ? "

Then through the Gates of Pain, I dream,
  A wind of heaven blows coolly in ;
Fainter the awful discords seem,
  The smoke of torment grows more thin,
Tears quench the burning soil, and
  thence
Spring sweet, pale flowers of penitence ;
And through the dreary realm of man's
  despair,
Star-crowned an angel walks, and lo !
  God's hope is there !

Is it a dream ? Is heaven so high
  That pity cannot breathe its air ?
Its happy eyes forever dry,
  Its holy lips without a prayer !
My God ! my God ! if thither led
  By thy free grace unmerited,
No crown nor palm be mine, but let me
  keep
A heart that still can feel, and eyes that
  still can weep.

LINES ON A FLY-LEAF.

I NEED not ask thee, for my sake,
To read a book which well may make
Its way by native force of wit
Without my manual sign to it.
Its piquant writer needs from me
No gravely masculine guaranty,
And well might laugh her merriest laugh
At broken spears in her behalf ;
Yet, spite of all the critics tell,
I frankly own I like her well.
It may be that she wields a pen
Too sharply nibbed for thin-skinned
  men,
That her keen arrows search and try
The armor joints of dignity,
And, though alone for error meant,
Sing through the air irreverent.
I blame her not, the young athlete
Who plants her woman's tiny feet,
And dares the chances of debate
Where bearded men might hesitate,
Who, deeply earnest, seeing well
The ludicrous and laughable,
Mingling in eloquent excess

Her anger and her tenderness,
And, chiding with a half-caress,
Strives, less for her own sex than ours,
With principalities and powers,
And points us upward to the clear
Sunned heights of her new atmosphere.

Heaven mend her faults ! — I will not
    pause
To weigh and doubt and peck at flaws,
Or waste my pity when some fool
Provokes her measureless ridicule.
Strong-minded is she ? Better so
Than dulness set for sale or show,
A household folly, capped and belled
In fashion's dance of puppets held,
Or poor pretence of womanhood,
Whose formal, flavorless platitude   `
Is warranted from all offence
Of robust meaning's violence.
Give me the wine of thought whose
    bead
Sparkles along the page I read.
Electric words in which I find
The tonic of the northwest wind, —
The wisdom which itself allies
To sweet and pure humanities,
Where scorn of meanness, hate of
    wrong,
Are underlaid by love as strong ;
The genial play of mirth that lights
Grave themes of thought, as, when on
    nights
Of summer-time, the harmless blaze
Of thunderless heat-lightning plays,
And tree and hill-top resting dim
And doubtful on the sky's vague rim,
Touched by that soft and lambent gleam,
Start sharply outlined from their dream.

Talk not to me of woman's sphere,
Nor point with Scripture texts a sneer,
Nor wrong the manliest saint of all
By doubt, if he were here, that Paul
Would own the heroines who have lent
Grace to truth's stern arbitrament,
Foregone the praise to woman sweet,
And cast their crowns at Duty's feet ;
Like her, who by her strong Appeal
Made Fashion weep and Mammon feel,
Who, earliest summoned to withstand
The color-madness of the land,
Counted her life-long losses gain,
And made her own her sisters' pain ;
Or her who, in her greenwood shade,
Heard the sharp call that Freedom
    made,

And, answering, struck from Sappho's
    lyre
Of love the Tyrtæan carmen's fire :
Or that young girl, — Domrémy's maid
Revived a nobler cause to aid, —
Shaking from warning finger-tips
The doom of her apocalypse ;
Or her, who world-wide entrance gave
To the log-cabin of the slave,
Made all his want and sorrow known,
And all earth's languages his own.

HYMN

FOR THE HOUSE OF WORSHIP AT
GEORGETOWN.

ERECTED IN MEMORY OF A MOTHER.

Thou dwellest not, O Lord of all !
    In temples which thy children raise ;
Our work to thine is mean and small,
    And brief to thy eternal days.

Forgive the weakness and the pride,
    If marred thereby our gift may be,
For love, at least, has sanctified
    The altar that we rear to thee.

The heart and not the hand has wrought
    From sunken base to tower above
The image of a tender thought,
    The memory of a deathless love !

And though should never sound of
    speech
    Or organ echo from its wall,
Its stones would pious lessons teach,
    Its shade in benedictions fall.

Here should the dove of peace be found,
    And blessings and not curses given ;
Nor strife profane, nor hatred wound,
    The mingled loves of earth and heaven.

Thou, who didst soothe with dying
    breath
    The dear one watching by thy cross,
Forgetful of the pains of death
    In sorrow for her mighty loss,

In memory of that tender claim,
    O Mother-born, the offering take,
And make it worthy of thy name,
    And bless it for a mother's sake !

MIRIAM,

AND OTHER POEMS.

. P. BARNARD.

ince, in youth and

ik, our horoscope
led with all favor-

s, and faces seamed

ttle, meeting once

y, over dreams so

t it is not in man
t his steps, or plan
of life.   Alike we

nd all our fancies

song.   How since

from the path that

Rich, from lifelong

Academic porch
l of a realm of fact,
nces exact ;
thy hand on Na-

spheral harmonies
v.   I called from
g,
to a strife so long,
he black, abundant

ver-sown and spare
les, now at sunset-

the path of morn-

late I linger where
ased to blow, and

hoice, wilt scarcely

lds his folly with

70.

MIRIAM.

ONE Sabbath day my friend and I
After the meeting, quietly
Passed from the crowded village lanes,
White with dry dust for lack of rains,
And climbed the neighboring slope,
     with feet
Slackened and heavy from the heat,
Although the day was wellnigh done,
And the low angle of the sun
Along the naked hillside cast
Our shadows as of giants vast.
We reached, at length, the topmost
     swell,
Whence, either way, the green turf
     fell
In terraces of nature down
To fruit-hung orchards, and the town
With white, pretenceless houses, tall
Church-steeples, and, o'ershadowing all,
Huge mills whose windows had the
     look
Of eager eyes that ill could brook
The Sabbath rest.   We traced the track
Of the sea-seeking river back
Glistening for miles above its mouth,
Through the long valley to the south,
And, looking eastward, cool to view,
Stretched the illimitable blue
Of ocean, from its curved coast-line ;
Sombred and still, the warm sunshine
Filled with pale gold-dust all the reach
Of slumberous woods from hill to
     beach, —
Slanted on walls of thronged retreats
From city toil and dusty streets,
On grassy bluff, and dune of sand,
And rocky islands miles from land ;
Touched the far-glancing sails, and
     showed
White lines of foam where long waves
     flowed
Dumb in the distance.   In the north,
Dim through their misty hair, looked
     forth
The space-dwarfed mountains to the
     sea,
From mystery to mystery !

So, sitting on that green hill-slope,
We talked of human life, its hope
And fear, and unsolved doubts, and
    what
It might have been, and yet was not.
And, when at last the evening air
Grew sweeter for the bells of prayer
Ringing in steeples far below,
We watched the people churchward go,
Each to his place, as if thereon
The true shekinah only shone ;
And my friend queried how it came
To pass that they who owned the same
Great Master still could not agree
To worship Him in company.
Then, broadening in his thought, he
    ran
Over the whole vast field of man, —
The varying forms of faith and creed
That somehow served the holders'
    need ;
In which, unquestioned, undenied,
Uncounted millions lived and died ;
The bibles of the ancient folk,
Through which the heart of nations
    spoke ;
The old moralities which lent
To home its sweetness and content,
And rendered possible to bear
The life of peoples everywhere :
And asked if we, who boast of light,
Claim not a too exclusive right
To truths which must for all be meant,
Like rain and sunshine freely sent.
In bondage to the letter still,
We give it power to cramp and kill, —
To tax God's fulness with a scheme
Narrower than Peter's house-top dream,
His wisdom and his love with plans
Poor and inadequate as man's.
It must be that He witnesses
Somehow to all men that He is :
That something of His saving grace
Reaches the lowest of the race,
Who, through strange creed and rite,
    may draw
The hints of a diviner law.
We walk in clearer light ; — but then,
Is He not God ? — are they not men ?
Are His responsibilities
For us alone and not for these ?

And I made answer : "Truth is one ;
And, in all lands beneath the sun,
Whoso hath eyes to see may see
The tokens of its unity.
No scroll of creed its fulness wraps,

We trace it not by school-boy maps,
Free as the sun and air it is
Of latitudes and boundaries.
In Vedic verse, in dull Korán,
Are messages of good to man ;
The angels to our Aryan sires
Talked by the earliest household fires ;
The prophets of the elder day,
The slant-eyed sages of Cathay,
Read not the riddle all amiss
Of higher life evolved from this.

"Nor doth it lessen what He taught,
Or make the gospel Jesus brought
Less precious, that His lips retold
Some portion of that truth of old ;
Denying not the proven seers,
The tested wisdom of the years ;
Confirming with his own impress
The common law of righteousness.
We search the world for truth ; we cull
The good, the pure, the beautiful,
From graven stone and written scroll,
From all old flower-fields of the soul ;
And, weary seekers of the best,
We come back laden from our quest,
To find that all the sages said
Is in the Book our mothers read,
And all our treasure of old thought
In His harmonious fulness wrought
Who gathers in one sheaf complete
The scattered blades of God's sown
    wheat,
The common growth that maketh good
His all-embracing Fatherhood.

"Wherever through the ages rise
The altars of self-sacrifice,
Where love its arms has opened wide,
Or man for man has calmly died,
I see the same white wings outspread
That hovered o'er the Master's head !
Up from undated time they come,
The martyr souls of heathendom,
And to His cross and passion bring
Their fellowship of suffering.
I trace His presence in the blind
Pathetic gropings of my kind, —
In prayers from sin and sorrow wrung,
In cradle-hymns of life they sung,
Each, in its measure, but a part
Of the unmeasured Over-Heart ;
And with a stronger faith confess
The greater that it owns the less.
Good cause it is for thankfulness
That the world-blessing of His life
With the long past is not at strife ;

el of His death
nesseth,
ess goodness wakes,
| sequence breaks,
:, rooted is
:s ;
:ring in degree
y,
: others borne,
ring meekly worn,
'or his friend
:he end ;
n nature take,
:r for their sake.

m every source
rimal Force,
self, yet new
t reaches to,
y impulse rolls
man souls ;
d inward word,
the Lord !
t science brings
through   material

sses prove,
ldness move,
3 on worlds that

iverse ;
 Spirit walks
art, and talks
Eden's trees,
;uages.
»me hopeless flaw
f the law,
y day afresh
f the flesh ?
outward signs,
he heart divines ;
of Him we learn,
n we turn,
3 pride to share
ct of a prayer."

/ wont, I told
if old,
:nted books, — in

hint of truth,
ig faiths agree
:harity.
ad golden grown,
' shone ;
he valley swept,
ocean slept,

As time and space I wandered o'er
To tread the Mogul's marble floor,
And see a fairer sunset fall
On Jumna's wave and Agra's wall.

THE good Shah Akbar (peace be his
    alway !)
Came forth from the Divan at close of
    day
Bowed with the burden of his many
    cares,
Worn with the hearing of unnumbered
    prayers, —
Wild cries for justice, the importunate
Appeals of greed and jealousy and hate,
And all the strife of sect and creed and
    rite,
Santon and Gooroo waging holy fight :
For the wise monarch, claiming not to
    be
Allah's avenger, left his people free,
With a faint hope, his Book scarce
    justified,
That all the paths of faith, though sev-
    ered wide,
O'er which the feet of prayerful rever-
    ence passed,
Met at the gate of Paradise at last.

He sought an alcove of his cool
    hareem,
Where, far beneath, he heard the
    Jumna's stream
Lapse soft and low along his palace
    wall,
And all about the cool sound of the fall
Of fountains, and of water circling free
Through marble ducts along the bal-
    cony ;
The voice of women in the distance
    sweet,
And, sweeter still, of one who, at his
    feet,
Soothed his tired ear with songs of a
    far land
Where Tagus shatters on the salt sea-
    sand
The mirror of its cork-grown hills of
    drouth
And vales of vine, at Lisbon's harbor-
    mouth.

The date-palms rustled not ; the
    peepul laid
Its topmost boughs against the balus-
    trade,

Motionless as the mimic leaves and
    vines
That, light and graceful as the shawl-
    designs
Of Delhi or Umritsir, twined in stone ;
And the tired monarch, who aside had
    thrown
The day's hard burden, sat from care
    apart,
And let the quiet steal into his heart
From the still hour. Below him Agra
    slept,
By the long light of sunset overswept :
The river flowing through a level land,
By mango-groves and banks of yellow
    sand,
Skirted with lime and orange, gay
    kiosks,
Fountains at play, tall minarets of
    mosques,
Fair pleasure-gardens, with their flow-
    ering trees
Relieved against the mournful cypresses ;
And, air-poised lightly as the blown
    sea-foam,
The marble wonder of some holy dome
Hung a white moonrise over the still
    wood,
Glassing its beauty in a stiller flood.

    Silent the monarch gazed, until the
        night
Swift-falling hid the city from his
    sight,
Then to the woman at his feet he said :
"Tell me, O Miriam, something thou
    hast read
In childhood of the Master of thy faith,
Whom Islam also owns. Our Prophet
    saith :
' He was a true apostle, yea, — a Word
And Spirit sent before me from the
    Lord.'
Thus the Book witnesseth ; and well I
    know
By what thou art, O dearest, it is so.
As the lute's tone the maker's hand be-
    trays,
The sweet disciple speaks her Master's
    praise."

    Then Miriam, glad of heart, (for in
        some sort
She cherished in the Moslem's liberal
    court
The sweet traditions of a Christian
    child ;

And, through her life of sense, the un-
    defiled
And chaste ideal of the sinless One
Gazed on her with an eye she might not
    shun, —
The sad, reproachful look of pity, born
Of love that hath no part in wrath or
    scorn,)
Began, with low voice and moist eyes,
    to tell
Of the all-loving Christ, and what befell
When the fierce zealots, thirsting for
    her blood,
Dragged to his feet a shame of woman-
    hood,
How, when his searching answer pierced
    within
Each heart, and touched the secret of
    its sin,
And her accusers fled his face before,
He bade the poor one go and sin no
    more.
And Akbar said, after a moment's
    thought,
"Wise is the lesson by thy prophet
    taught ;
Woe unto him who judges and forgets
What hidden evil his own heart besets!
Something of this large charity I find
In all the sects that sever human kind ;
I would to Allah that their lives agreed
More nearly with the lesson of their
    creed !
Those yellow Lamas who at Meerut pray
By wind and water power, and love to
    say :
' He who forgiveth not shall, unfor-
    given,
Fail of the rest of Buddha,' and who
    even
Spare the black gnat that stings them,
    vex my ears
With the poor hates and jealousies and
    fears
Nursed in their human hives. That
    lean, fierce priest
Of thy own people, (be his heart in-
    creased
By Allah's love !) his black robes
    smelling yet
Of Goa's roasted Jews, have I not met
Meek-faced, barefooted, crying in the
    street
The saying of his prophet true and
    sweet, —
' He who is merciful shall mercy
    meet ! ' "

But, next day, so it chanced, as night
  began
To fall, a murmur through the hareem
  ran
That one, recalling in her dusky face
The full-lipped, mild-eyed beauty of a
  race
Known as the blameless Ethiops of
  Greek song,
Plotting to do her royal master wrong,
Watching, reproachful of the lingering
  light,
The evening shadows deepen for her
  flight,
Love-guided, to her home in a far land,
Now waited death at the great Shah's
  command.

Shapely as that dark princess for
  whose smile
A world was bartered, daughter of the
  Nile
Herself, and veiling in her large, soft
  eyes
The passion and the languor of her skies,
The Abyssinian knelt low at the feet
Of her stern lord : "O king, if it be
  meet,
And for thy honor's sake," she said,
  "that I,
Who am the humblest of thy slaves,
  should die,
I will not tax thy mercy to forgive.
Easier it is to die than to outlive
All that life gave me, — him whose
  wrong of thee
Was but the outcome of his love for
  me,
Cherished from childhood, when, be-
  neath the shade
Of templed Axum, side by side we
  played.
Stolen from his arms, my lover followed
  me
Through weary seasons over land and
  sea ;
And two days since, sitting disconso-
  late
Within the shadow of the hareem gate,
Suddenly, as if dropping from the sky,
Down from the lattice of the balcony
Fell the sweet song by Tigre's cow-

This night he waited near
To fly with me. The fault was mine
  alone :
He knew thee not, he did but seek his
  own ;
Who, in the very shadow of thy throne,
Sharing thy bounty, knowing all thou
  art,
Greatest and best of men, and in her
  heart
Grateful to tears for favor undeserved,
Turned ever homeward, nor one mo-
  ment swerved
From her young love. He looked into
  my eyes,
He heard my voice, and could not
  otherwise
Than he hath done ; yet, save one wild
  embrace
When first we stood together face to
  face,
And all that fate had done since last we
  met
Seemed but a dream that left us chil-
  dren yet,
He hath not wronged thee nor thy royal
  bed ;
Spare him, O king ! and slay me in his
  stead ! "

But over Akbar's brows the frown
  hung black,
And, turning to the eunuch at his back,
"Take them," he said, "and let the
  Jumna's waves
Hide both my shame and these accursed
  slaves !"
His loathly length the unsexed bond-
  man bowed :
"On my head be it !"
            Straightway from a cloud
Of dainty shawls and veils of woven
  mist
The Christian Miriam rose, and, stoop-
  ing, kissed
The monarch's hand. Loose down her
  shoulders bare
Swept all the rippled darkness of her
  hair,
Veiling the bosom that, with high, quick
  swell
Of fear and pity, through it rose and fell.

Or thy own prophet's, — 'Whoso doth
  endure
And pardon, of eternal life is sure'?
O great and good! be thy revenge
  alone
Felt in thy mercy to the erring shown;
Let thwarted love and youth their par-
  don plead,
Who sinned but in intent, and not in
  deed!"

One moment the strong frame of Akbar
  shook
With the great storm of passion. Then
  his look
Softened to her uplifted face, that still
Pleaded more strongly than all words,
  until
Its pride and anger seemed like over-
  blown,
Spent clouds of thunder left to tell
  alone
Of strife and overcoming. With bowed
  head,
And smiting on his bosom: "God," he
  said,
"Alone is great, and let His holy name
Be honored, even to His servant's
  shame!
Well spake thy prophet, Miriam, — he
  alone
Who hath not sinned is meet to cast a
  stone
At such as these, who here their doom
  await,
Held like myself in the strong grasp of
  fate.
They sinned through love, as I through
  love forgive;
Take them beyond my realm, but let
  them live!"

And, like a chorus to the words of
  grace,
The ancient Fakir, sitting in his place,
Motionless as an idol and as grim,
In the pavilion Akbar built for him
Under the court-yard trees, (for he was
  wise,
Knew Menu's laws, and through his
  close-shut eyes
Saw things far off, and as an open book
Into the thoughts of other men could
  look,)
Began, half chant, half howling, to re-
  hearse
The fragment of a holy Vedic verse;

And thus it ran:
  forgives
Conquers himself
  and lives
Above the reach
  fear,
Calm as the gods,
  dear."

Two leagues fror
  eller sees
The tomb of Akba
  trees;
And, near at han
  that hide
The Christian Be
  side.
And o'er her vault
  tell
If it be chance alon
The Mission 'ress
  unrolls
The words of Je
  scrolls, —
Tells, in all tongu
  o'er,
And bids the guil
  more!"

—

It now was dew-
The night lay on tl
Down which our
  bent,
And, silent, thr
  went,
Save that the tirele
Their long, monoto
A young moon, at i
Curved sharp aga
  west;
And, momently, th
Slow wheeling o'er
From out the level
One instant and ag
And then my frienc
The thought of be
  see!
Like Islam's symbo
Hints of the light v
Somewhat of goodn
From sun and spiri
All faiths, all wor
  dark
Of ocean shines the
Attests the presenc
Of love and provide

The faith the old Norse heart confessed
In one dear name, — the hopefulest
And tenderest heard from mortal lips
In pangs of birth or death, from ships

Ice-bitten in the winter sea,
Or lisped beside a mother's knee, —
The wiser world hath not outgrown,
And the All-Father is our own !

MISCELLANEOUS POEMS.

NOREMBEGA.

[Norembega, or Norimbegue, is the name given by early French fishermen and explorers to a fabulous country south of Cape Breton, first discovered by Verrazzani in 1524. It was supposed to have a magnificent city of the same name on a great river, probably the Penobscot. The site of this barbaric city is laid down on a map published at Antwerp in 1570. In 1604 Champlain sailed in search of the Northern Eldorado, twenty-two leagues up the Penobscot from the Isle Haute. He supposed the river to be that of Norembega, but wisely came to the conclusion that those travellers who told of the great city had never seen it. He saw no evidences of anything like civilization, but mentions the finding of a cross, very old and mossy, in the woods.]

THE winding way the serpent takes
  The mystic water took,
From where, to count its beaded lakes,
  The forest sped its brook.

A narrow space 'twixt shore and shore,
  For sun or stars to fall,
While evermore, behind, before,
  Closed in the forest wall.

The dim wood hiding underneath
  Wan flowers without a name ;
Life tangled with decay and death,
  League after league the same.

Unbroken over swamp and hill
  The rounding shadow lay,
Save where the river cut at will
  A pathway to the day.

Beside that track of air and light,
  Weak as a child unweaned,
At shut of day a Christian knight
  Upon his henchman leaned.

The embers of the sunset's fires
  Along the clouds burned down ;
" I see," he said, " the domes and spires
  Of Norembega town."

" Alack ! the domes, O master mine,
  Are golden clouds on high ;

Yon spire is but the branchless pine
  That cuts the evening sky."

" O hush and hark ! What sounds are these
  But chants and holy hymns ? "
" Thou hear'st the breeze that stirs the trees
  Through all their leafy limbs."

" Is it a chapel bell that fills
  The air with its low tone ? "
" Thou hear'st the tinkle of the rills,
  The insect's vesper drone."

" The Christ be praised ! — He sets for me
  A blessed cross in sight ! "
" Now, nay, 't is but yon blasted tree
  With two gaunt arms outright ! "

" Be it wind so sad or tree so stark,
  It mattereth not, my knave ;
Methinks to funeral hymns I hark,
  The cross is for my grave !

" My life is sped ; I shall not see
  My home-set sails again ;
The sweetest eyes of Normandie
  Shall watch for me in vain.

" Yet onward still to ear and eye
  The baffling marvel calls ;
I fain would look before I die
  On Norembega's walls.

" So, haply, it shall be thy part
  At Christian feet to lay
The mystery of the desert's heart
  My dead hand plucked away.

" Leave me an hour of rest ; go thou
  And look from yonder heights ;
Perchance the valley even now
  Is starred with city lights."

The henchman climbed the nearest hill,
  He saw nor tower nor town,

But, through the drear woods, lone and
    still,
    The river rolling down.

He heard the stealthy feet of things
    Whose shapes he could not see,
A flutter as of evil wings,
    The fall of a dead tree.

The pines stood black against the moon,
    A sword of fire beyond ;
He heard the wolf howl, and the loon
    Laugh from his reedy pond.

He turned him back : " O master dear,
    We are but men misled ;
And thou hast sought a city here
    To find a grave instead.

" As God shall will ! what matters where
    A true man's cross may stand,
So Heaven be o'er it here as there
    In pleasant Norman land ?

" These woods, perchance, no secret
    hide
    Of lordly tower and hall ;
Yon river in its wanderings wide
    Has washed no city wall ;

" Yet mirrored in the sullen stream
    The holy stars are given :
Is Norembega, then, a dream
    Whose waking is in Heaven ?

" No builded wonder of these lands
    My weary eyes shall see ;
A city never made with hands
    Alone awaiteth me —

" ' Urbs Syon mystica ' ; I see
    Its mansions passing fair,
' Condita cœlo ' ; let me be,
    Dear Lord, a dweller there ! "

Above the dying exile hung
    The vision of the bard,
As faltered on his failing tongue
    The song of good Bernard.

The henchman dug at dawn a grave
    Beneath the hemlocks brown,
And to the desert's keeping gave
    The lord of fief and town.

Years after, when the Sieur Champlain
    Sailed up the unknown stream,

And Norembega proved again
    A shadow and a dream,

He found the Norman's nameless grave
    Within the hemlock's shade,
And, stretching wide its arms to save,
    The sign that God had made,

The cross-boughed tree that marked the
    spot
    And made it holy ground :
He needs the earthly city not
    Who hath the heavenly found.

NAUHAUGHT, THE DEACON.

NAUHAUGHT, the Indian deacon, who
    of old
Dwelt, poor but blameless, where his
    narrowing Cape
Stretches its shrunk arm out to all the
    winds
And the relentless smiting of the waves,
Awoke one morning from a pleasant
    dream
Of a good angel dropping in his hand
A fair, broad gold-piece, in the name of
    God.

He rose and went forth with the early
    day
Far inland, where the voices of the
    waves
Mellowed and mingled with the whis-
    pering leaves,
As, through the tangle of the low, thick
    woods,
He searched his traps. Therein nor
    beast nor bird
He found ; though meanwhile in the
    reedy pools
The otter plashed, and underneath the
    pines
The partridge drummed : and as his
    thoughts went back
To the sick wife and little child at
    home,
What marvel that the poor man felt his
    faith
Too weak to bear its burden, — like a
    rope
That, strand by strand uncoiling, breaks
    above
The hand that grasps it. " Even now,
    O Lord !

Send me," he prayed, "the angel of my
dream!
Nauhaught is very poor; he cannot
wait."

Even as he spake he heard at his bare
feet
A low, metallic clink, and, looking
down,
He saw a dainty purse with disks of
gold
Crowding its silken net. Awhile he
held
The treasure up before his eyes, alone
With his great need, feeling the won-
drous coins
Slide through his eager fingers, one by
one.
So then the dream was true. The angel
brought
One broad piece only; should he take
all these?
Who would be wiser, in the blind, dumb
woods ?
The loser, doubtless rich, would scarcely
miss
This dropped crumb from a table always
full.
Still, while he mused, he seemed to hear
the cry
Of a starved child; the sick face of his
wife
Tempted him. Heart and flesh in fierce
revolt
Urged the wild license of his savage
youth
Against his later scruples. Bitter toil,
Prayer, fasting, dread of blame, and pit-
iless eyes
To watch his halting, — had he lost for
these
The freedom of the woods ; — the hunt-
ing-grounds
Of happy spirits for a walled-in heaven
Of everlasting psalms? One healed the
sick
Very far off thousands of moons ago:
Had he not prayed him night and day to
come
And cure his bed-bound wife? Was
there a hell?
Were all his fathers' people writhing
there —
Like the poor shell-fish set to boil alive—
Forever, dying never? If he kept
This gold, so needed, would the dread-
ful God

Torment him like a stuck
With slow-consuming splinters, the saints
And the white angels dance and laugh
to see him
Burn like a pitch-pine torch ? His
Christian garb
Seemed falling from him; with the fear
and shame
Of Adam naked at the cool of day,
He gazed around. A black snake lay in
coil
On the hot sand, a crow with sidelong
eye
Watched from a dead bough. All his
Indian lore
Of evil blending with a convert's faith
In the supernal terrors of the Book,
He saw the Tempter in the coiling
snake
And ominous, black-winged bird ; and
all the while
The low rebuking of the distant waves
Stole in upon him like the voice of
God
Among the trees of Eden. Girding
up
His soul's loins with a resolute hand, he
thrust
The base thought from him : "Nau-
haught, be a man !
Starve, if need be ; but, while you live,
look out
From honest eyes on all men, un-
ashamed.
God help me! I am deacon of the
church,
A baptized, praying Indian ! Should I
do
This secret meanness, even the barken
knots
Of the old trees would turn to eyes to
see it,
The birds would tell of it, and all the
leaves
Whisper above me : 'Nauhaught is a
thief !'
The sun would know it, and the stars
that hide
Behind his light would watch me, and
at night
Follow me with their sharp, accusing
eyes.
Yea, thou, God, seest me !" Then
Nauhaught drew
Closer his belt of leather, dulling thus

But, through the dr͠͠ ͠ ͠avely still,
The river ͠ ͠ by the
He ͠ ͠ ͠or, cheerily
͠ ͠o-day?"
͠ ͠l," said a voice;
"͠ ͠n a silken purse,
My da͠ ͠work." He looked,
an͠
One stood be͠ ͠him in a coat of frieze,
And the glazed hat of a seafaring man,
Shrewd-faced, broad-shouldered, with no trace of wings.
Marvelling, he dropped within the stranger's hand
The silken web, and turned to go his way.
But the man said: "A tithe at least is yours;
Take it in God's name as an honest man."
And as the deacon's dusky fingers closed
Over the golden gift, "Yea, in God's name
I take it, with a poor man's thanks," he said.

So down the street that, like a river of sand,
Ran, white in sunshine, to the summer sea,
He sought his home, singing and praising God;
And when his neighbors in their careless way
Spoke of the owner of the silken purse —
A Wellfleet skipper, known in every port
That the Cape opens in its sandy wall —
He answered, with a wise smile, to himself:
"I saw the angel where they see a man."

IN SCHOOL-DAYS.

Still sits the school-house by the road,
  A ragged beggar sunning;
Around it still the sumachs grow,
  And blackberry-vines are running.

Within, the master's desk is seen,
  Deep scarred by raps official;
The warping floor, the battered seats,
  The jack-knife's carved initial;

The charcoal frescos on its wall;
  Its door's worn sill, betraying
The feet that, creeping slow to school,
  Went storming out to playing!

Long years ago a winter sun
  Shone over it at setting;
Lit up its western window-panes,
  And low eaves' icy fretting.

It touched the tangled golden curls,
  And brown eyes full of grieving,
Of one who still her steps delayed
  When all the school were leaving.

For near her stood the little boy
  Her childish favor singled:
His cap pulled low upon a face
  Where pride and shame were mingled.

Pushing with restless feet the snow
  To right and left, he lingered; —
As restlessly her tiny hands
  The blue-checked apron fingered.

He saw her lift her eyes; he felt
  The soft hand's light caressing,
And heard the tremble of her voice,
  As if a fault confessing.

"I'm sorry that I spelt the word:
  I hate to go above you,
Because," — the brown eyes lower fell, —
  "Because, you see, I love you!"

Still memory to a gray-haired man
  That sweet child-face is showing.
Dear girl! the grasses on her grave
  Have forty years been growing!

He lives to learn, in life's hard school,
  How few who pass above him
Lament their triumph and his loss,
  Like her, — because they love him.

GARIBALDI.

In trance and dream of old, God's prophet saw
  The casting down of thrones. Thou, watching lone
  The hot Sardinian coast-line, hazy-hilled,

Where, fringing round Caprera's rocky
    zone
With foam, the slow waves gather and
    withdraw,
Behold'st the vision of the seer ful-
    filled,
And hear'st the sea-winds burdened
    with a sound
Of falling chains, as, one by one, un-
    bound,
The nations lift their right hands up
    and swear
Their oath of freedom.   From the
    chalk-white wall
Of England, from the black Carpathian
    range,
    Along the Danube and the Theiss,
        through all
The passes of the Spanish Pyrenees,
And from the Seine's thronged banks,
    a murmur strange
    And glad floats to thee o'er thy sum-
        mer seas
On the salt wind that stirs thy whiten-
    ing hair, —
    The song of freedom's bloodless
        victories!
Rejoice, O Garibaldi!   Though thy
    sword
Failed at Rome's gates, and blood
    seemed vainly poured
Where, in Christ's name, the crownéd
    infidel
Of France wrought murder with the
    arms of hell
    On that sad mountain slope whose
        ghostly dead,
Unmindful of the gray exorcist's ban,
Walk, unappeased, the chambered Vat-
    ican,
    And draw the curtains of Napoleon's
        bed !
God's providence is not blind, but, full
    of eyes,
It searches all the refuges of lies;
And in His time and way, the accursed
    things
    Before whose evil feet thy battle-
        gage
Has clashed defiance from hot youth
    to age
shall perish.   All men shall be priests
    and kings, —
    One royal brotherhood, one church
        made free
By love, which is the law of liberty !
1869.

THE day's sharp strife is ended now,
Our work is done, God knoweth how !
As on the thronged, unrestful town
The patience of the moon looks down,
I wait to hear, beside the wire,
The voices of its tongues of fire.

Slow, doubtful, faint, they seem at first:
Be strong, my heart, to know the worst !
Hark ! — there the Alleghanies spoke ;
That sound from lake and prairie broke,
That sunset-gun of triumph rent
The silence of a continent !

That signal from Nebraska sprung,
This, from Nevada's mountain tongue !
Is that thy answer, strong and free,
O loyal heart of Tennessee ?
What strange, glad voice is that which
    calls
From Wagner's grave and Sumter's
    walls ?

From Mississippi's fountain-head
A sound as of the bison's tread !
There rustled freedom's Charter Oak !
In that wild burst the Ozarks spoke !
Cheer answers cheer from rise to set
Of sun.   We have a country yet !

The praise, O God, be thine alone !
Thou givest not for bread a stone ;
Thou hast not led us through the night
To blind us with returning light ;
Not through the furnace have we passed,
To perish at its mouth at last.

O night of peace, thy flight restrain !
November's moon, be slow to wane !
Shine on the freedman's cabin floor,
On brows of prayer a blessing pour ;
And give, with full assurance blest,
The weary heart of Freedom rest !
1868.

MY TRIUMPH.

THE autumn-time has come ;
On woods that dream of bloom,
And over purpling vines,
The low sun fainter shines.

The aster-flower is failing,
The hazel's gold is paling ;

Yet overhead more near
The eternal stars appear!

And present gratitude
Insures the future's good,
And for the things I see
I trust the things to be;

That in the paths untrod,
And the long days of God,
My feet shall still be led,
My heart be comforted.

O living friends who love me!
O dear ones gone above me!
Careless of other fame,
I leave to you my name.

Hide it from idle praises,
Save it from evil phrases:
Why, when dear lips that spake it
Are dumb, should strangers wake it?

Let the thick curtain fall;
I better know than all
How little I have gained,
How vast the unattained.

Not by the page word-painted
Let life be banned or sainted:
Deeper than written scroll
The colors of the soul.

Sweeter than any sung
My songs that found no tongue;
Nobler than any fact
My wish that failed of act.

Others shall sing the song,
Others shall right the wrong, —
Finish what I begin,
And all I fail of win.

What matter, I or they?
Mine or another's day,
So the right word be said
And life the sweeter made?

Hail to the coming singers!
Hail to the brave light-bringers!
Forward I reach and share
All that they sing and dare.

The airs of heaven blow o'er me;
A glory shines before me
Of what mankind shall be, —
Pure, generous, brave, and free.

A dream of man and woman
Diviner but still human,
Solving the riddle old,
Shaping the Age of Gold!

The love of God and neighbor;
An equal-handed labor;
The richer life, where beauty
Walks hand in hand with duty.

Ring, bells in unreared steeples,
The joy of unborn peoples!
Sound, trumpets far off blown,
Your triumph is my own!

Parcel and part of all,
I keep the festival,
Fore-reach the good to be,
And share the victory.

I feel the earth move sunward,
I join the great march onward,
And take, by faith, while living,
My freehold of thanksgiving.

THE HIVE AT GETTYSBURG.

In the old Hebrew myth the lion's
     frame,
  So terrible alive,
Bleached by the desert's sun and wind,
     became
  The wandering wild bees' hive;
And he who, lone and naked-handed,
     tore
  Those jaws of death apart,
In after time drew forth their honeyed
     store
  To strengthen his strong heart.

Dead seemed the legend: but it only
     slept
  To wake beneath our sky;
Just on the spot whence ravening Trea-
     son crept
  Back to its lair to die,
Bleeding and torn from Freedom's
     mountain bounds,
  A stained and shattered drum
Is now the hive where, on their flowery
     rounds,
  The wild bees go and come.

Unchallenged by a ghostly sentinel,
  They wander wide and far,

Along green hillsides, sown with shot
  and shell,
Through vales once choked with war.
The low reveille of their battle-drum
  Disturbs no morning prayer;
With deeper peace in summer noons
    their hum
Fills all the drowsy air.

And Samson's riddle is our own to-
    day,
  Of sweetness from the strong,
Of union, peace, and freedom plucked
    away
  From the rent jaws of wrong.
From Treason's death we draw a purer
    life,
  As, from the beast he slew,
A sweetness sweeter for his bitter strife
  The old-time athlete drew!

HOWARD AT ATLANTA.

RIGHT in the track where Sherman
  Ploughed his red furrow,
Out of the narrow cabin,
  Up from the cellar's burrow,
Gathered the little black people,
  With freedom newly dowered,
Where, beside their Northern teacher,
  Stood the soldier, Howard.

He listened and heard the children
  Of the poor and long-enslaved
Reading the words of Jesus,
  Singing the songs of David.
Behold! — the dumb lips speaking,
  The blind eyes seeing!
Bones of the Prophet's vision
  Warmed into being!

Transformed he saw them passing
  Their new life's portal!
Almost it seemed the mortal
  Put on the immortal.
No more with the beasts of burden,
  No more with stone and clod,
But crowned with glory and honor
  In the image of God!

There was the human chattel
  Its manhood taking;
There, in each dark, brown statue,
  A soul was waking!
The man of many battles,
  With tears his eyelids pressing,

Stretched over those dusky foreheads
  His one-armed blessing.

And he said: "Who hears can never
  Fear for or doubt you;
What shall I tell the children
  Up North about you?"
Then ran round a whisper, a murmur,
  Some answer devising;
And a little boy stood up: "Massa,
  Tell 'em we're rising!"

O black boy of Atlanta!
  But half was spoken:
The slave's chain and the master's
  Alike are broken.
The one curse of the races
  Held both in tether:
They are rising, — all are rising,
  The black and white together!

O brave men and fair women!
  Ill comes of hate and scorning:
Shall the dark faces only
  Be turned to morning? —
Make Time your sole avenger,
  All-healing, all-redressing;
Meet Fate half-way, and make it
  A joy and blessing!

TO LYDIA MARIA CHILD,

ON READING HER POEM IN "THE
STANDARD."

THE sweet spring day is glad with music,
  But through it sounds a sadder strain;
The worthiest of our narrowing circle
  Sings Loring's dirges o'er again.

O woman greatly loved! I join thee
  In tender memories of our friend;
With thee across the awful spaces
  The greeting of a soul I send!

What cheer hath he? How is it with
    him?
  Where lingers he this weary while?
Over what pleasant fields of Heaven
  Dawns the sweet sunrise of his smile?

Does he not know our feet are treading
  The earth hard down on Slavery's
    grave?
That, in our crowning exultations,
  We miss the charm his presence gave?

Why on this spring air comes no whis-
    per
From him to tell us all is well ?
Why to our flower-time comes no token
Of lily and of asphodel ?

I feel the unutterable longing,
    Thy hunger of the heart is mine ;
I reach and grope for hands in darkness,
    My ear grows sharp for voice or sign.

Still on the lips of all we question
    The finger of God's silence lies ;
Will the lost hands in ours be folded?
    Will the shut eyelids ever rise ?

O friend ! no proof beyond this yearning,
    This outreach of our hearts, we need ;
God will not mock the hope He giveth,
    No love He prompts shall vainly
        plead.

Then let us stretch our hands in dark-
    ness,
    And call our loved ones o'er and o'er ;
Some day their arms shall close about
    us,
    And the old voices speak once more.

No dreary splendors wait our coming
    Where rapt ghost sits from ghost
        apart ;
Homeward we go to Heaven's thanks-
    giving,
    The harvest-gathering of the heart.

THE PRAYER-SEEKER.

ALONG the aisle where prayer was made
A woman, all in black arrayed,
Close-veiled, between the kneeling host,
With gliding motion of a ghost,
Passed to the desk, and laid thereon
A scroll which bore these words alone,
            Pray for me !

Back from the place of worshipping
She glided like a guilty thing :
The rustle of her draperies, stirred
By hurrying feet, alone was heard ;
While, full of awe, the preacher read,
As out into the dark she sped :
        "Pray for me !"

Back to the night from whence she
    came,
To unimagined grief or shame !
Across the threshold of that door
None knew the burden that she bore ;
Alone she left the written scroll,
The legend of a troubled soul, —
            Pray for me !

Glide on, poor ghost of woe or sin !
Thou leav'st a common need within ;
Each bears, like thee, some nameless
    weight,
Some misery inarticulate,
Some secret sin, some shrouded dread,
Some household sorrow all unsaid.
            Pray for us !

Pass on ! The type of all thou art,
Sad witness to the common heart !
With face in veil and seal on lip,
In mute and strange companionship,
Like thee we wander to and fro,
Dumbly imploring as we go :
            Pray for us !

Ah, who shall pray, since he who
    pleads
Our want perchance hath greater needs?
Yet they who make their loss the gain
Of others shall not ask in vain,
And Heaven bends low to hear the
    prayer
Of love from lips of self-despair :
            Pray for us !

In vain remorse and fear and hate
Beat with bruised hands against a fate
Whose walls of iron only move
And open to the touch of love.
He only feels his burdens fall
Who, taught by suffering, pities all.
            Pray for us !

He prayeth best who leaves unguessed
The mystery of another's breast.
Why cheeks grow pale, why eyes o'er-
    flow,
Or heads are white, thou need'st not
    know.
Enough to note by many a sign
That every heart hath needs like thine.
            Pray for us !

A SPIRITUAL MANIFESTATION.

AT THE PRESIDENT'S LEVEE, BROWN
UNIVERSITY, 29TH 6TH MONTH, 1870.

TO-DAY the plant by Williams set
Its summer bloom discloses ;
The wilding sweetbrier of his prayers
Is crowned with cultured roses.

Once more the Island State repeats
The lesson that he taught her,
And binds his pearl of charity
Upon her brown-locked daughter.

Is 't fancy that he watches still
His Providence plantations ?
That still the careful Founder takes
A part on these occasions ?

Methinks I see that reverend form,
Which all of us so well know :
He rises up to speak ; he jogs
The presidential elbow

"Good friends," he says, "you reap a
    field
I sowed in self-denial,
For toleration had its griefs
And charity its trial.

"Great grace, as saith Sir Thomas
    More,
To him must needs be given
Who heareth heresy and leaves
The heretic to Heaven !

"I hear again the snuffled tones,
I see in dreary vision
Dyspeptic dreamers, spiritual bores,
And prophets with a mission.

"Each zealot thrust before my eyes
His Scripture-garbled label ;
All creeds were shouted in my ears
As with the tongues of Babel.

"Scourged at one cart-tail, each de-
    nied
The hope of every other ;
Each martyr shook his branded fist
At the conscience of his brother !

"How cleft the dreary drone of man
The shriller pipe of woman,
As Gorton led his saints elect,
Who held all things in common !

"Their gay robes trailed in ditch and
    swamp,
And torn by thorn and thicket,
The dancing-girls of Merry Mount
Came dragging to my wicket.

"Shrill Anabaptists, shorn of ears ;
Gray witch-wives, hobbling slowly ;
And Antinomians, free of law,
Whose very sins were holy.

"Hoarse ranters, crazed Fifth Mon-
    archists,
Of stripes and bondage braggarts,
Pale Churchmen, with singed rubrics
    snatched
From Puritanic fagots.

"And last, not least, the Quakers came,
With tongues still sore from burning,
The Bay State's dust from off their
    feet
Before my threshold spurning ;

"A motley host, the Lord's *débris*,
Faith's odds and ends together ;
Well might I shrink from guests with
    lungs
Tough as their breeches leather :

"If, when the hangman at their heels
Came, rope in hand to catch them,
I took the hunted outcasts in,
I never sent to fetch them.

"I fed, but spared them not a whit ;
I gave to all who walked in,
Not clams and succotash alone,
But stronger meat of doctrine.

"I proved the prophets false, I pricked
The bubble of perfection,
And clapped upon their inner light
The snuffers of election.

"And, looking backward on my times,
One thing, at least, I 'm proud for ;

I kept each sectary's dish apart,
  And made no spiritual chowder.

"Where now the blending signs of sect
  Would puzzle their assorter,
The dry-shod Quaker kept the land,
  The Baptist held the water.

"A common coat now serves for both,
  The hat's no more a fixture;
And which was wet and which was
    dry,
  Who knows in such a mixture?

"Well! He who fashioned Peter's
    dream
  To bless them all is able;
And bird and beast and creeping thing
  Make clean upon His table!

"I walked by my own light; but when
  The ways of faith divided,
Was I to force unwilling feet
  To tread the path that I did?

"I touched the garment-hem of truth,
  Yet saw not all its splendor;
I knew enough of doubt to feel
  For every conscience tender.

"God left men free of choice, as when
  His Eden-trees were planted;
Because they chose amiss, should I
  Deny the gift He granted?

"So, with a common sense of need,
  Our common weakness feeling,
I left them with myself to God
  And His all-gracious dealing!

"I kept His plan whose rain and sun
  To tare and wheat are given;
And if the ways to hell were free,
  I left them free to heaven!"

Take heart with us, O man of old,
  Soul-freedom's brave confessor,
So love of God and man wax strong,
  Let sect and creed be lesser.

The jarring discords of thy day
  In ours one hymn are swelling;
The wandering feet, the severed paths,
  All seek our Father's dwelling.

And slowly learns the world the truth
  That makes us all thy debtor, —

That holy life is more than rite,
  And spirit more than letter;

That they who differ pole-wide serve
  Perchance the common Master,
And other sheep He hath than they
  Who graze one narrow pasture!

For truth's worst foe is he who claims
  To act as God's avenger,
And deems, beyond his sentry-beat,
  The crystal walls in danger!

Who sets for heresy his traps
  Of verbal quirk and quibble,
And weeds the garden of the Lord
  With Satan's borrowed dibble.

To-day our hearts like organ keys
  One Master's touch are feeling;
The branches of a common Vine
  Have only leaves of healing.

Co-workers, yet from varied fields,
  We share this restful nooning;
The Quaker with the Baptist here
  Believes in close communing.

Forgive, dear saint, the playful tone,
  Too light for thy deserving;
Thanks for thy generous faith in man,
  Thy trust in God unswerving.

Still echo in the hearts of men
  The words that thou hast spoken;
No forge of hell can weld again
  The fetters thou hast broken.

The pilgrim needs a pass no more
  From Roman or Genevan;
Thought-free, no ghostly tollman keeps
  Henceforth the road to Heaven!

"THE LAURELS."

AT THE TWENTIETH AND LAST ANNI-
VERSARY.

FROM these wild rocks I look to-day
  O'er leagues of dancing waves, and
    see
The far, low coast-line stretch away
  To where our river meets the sea.

The light wind blowing off the land
  Is burdened with old voices, through

hut eyes I see how lip and hand
  The greeting of old days renew.

 friends whose hearts still keep their
    prime,
  Whose bright example warms and
    cheers,
e teach us how to smile at Time,
  And set to music all his years !

thank you for sweet summer days,
  For pleasant memories lingering long,
or joyful meetings, fond delays,
  And ties of friendship woven strong.

s for the last time, side by side,
  You tread the paths familiar grown,
reach across the severing tide,
  And blend my farewells with your
    own.

[ake room, O river of our home !
  For other feet in place of ours,
nd in the summers yet to come,
  Make glad another Feast of Flowers !

[old in thy mirror, calm and deep,
  The pleasant pictures thou hast seen ;
orget thy lovers not, but keep
  Our memory like thy laurels green.

ᴸᴱˢ ᴼᶠ ѕʜᴏᴀʟѕ, *7th mo.*, 1870.

HYMN

ᴼʀ ᴛʜᴇ ᴄᴇʟᴇʙʀᴀᴛɪᴏɴ ᴏꜰ ᴇᴍᴀɴᴄɪᴘᴀ-
ᴛɪᴏɴ ᴀᴛ ɴᴇᴡʙᴜʀʏᴘᴏʀᴛ.

ᴏᴛ unto us who did but seek
he word that burned within to speak,
ot unto us this day belong
he triumph and exultant song.

pon us fell in early youth
he burden of unwelcome truth,
nd left us, weak and frail and few,
he censor's painful work to do.

henceforth our life a fight became,
he air we breathed was hot with
    blame ;

For not with gauged and softened tone
We made the bondman's cause our
    own.

We bore, as Freedom's hope forlorn,
The private hate, the public scorn ;
Yet held through all the paths we trod
Our faith in man and trust in God.

We prayed and hoped ; but still, with
    awe,
The coming of the sword we saw ;
We heard the nearing steps of doom,
We saw the shade of things to come

In grief which they alone can feel
Who from a mother's wrong appeal,
With blended lines of fear and hope
We cast our country's horoscope.

For still within her house of life
We marked the lurid sign of strife,
And, poisoning and imbittering all,
We saw the star of Wormwood fall.

Deep as our love for her became
Our hate of all that wrought her shame,
And if, thereby, with tongue and pen
We erred, — we were but mortal men.

We hoped for peace ; our eyes survey
The blood-red dawn of Freedom's day :
We prayed for love to loose the chain ;
'T is shorn by battle's axe in twain !

Nor skill nor strength nor zeal of ours
Has mined and heaved the hostile
    towers ;
Not by our hands is turned the key
That sets the sighing captives free.

A redder sea than Egypt's wave
Is piled and parted for the slave ;
A darker cloud moves on in light ;
A fiercer fire is guide by night !

The praise, O Lord ! is Thine alone,
In Thy own way Thy work is done !
Our poor gifts at Thy feet we cast,
To whom be glory, first and last !
  1865.

THE PENNSYLVANIA PI

AND OTHER POEMS.

FRANCIS DANIEL PASTORIUS.

THE beginning of German emigration to America may be traced to the personal influence of William Penn, who in 1677 visited the Continent, and made the acquaintance of an intelligent and highly cultivated circle of Pietists, or Mystics, who, reviving in the seventeenth century the spiritual faith and worship of Tauler and the " Friends of God " in the fourteenth, gathered about the pastor Spener, and the young and beautiful Eleonora Johanna Von Merlau. In this circle originated the Frankfort Land Company, which bought of William Penn, the Governor of Pennsylvania, a tract of land near the new city of Philadelphia.

The company's agent in the New World was a rising young lawyer, Francis Daniel Pastorius, son of Judge Pastorius, of Windsheim, who, at the age of seventeen, entered the University of Altorf. He studied law at Strasburg, Basle, and Jena, and at Ratisbon, the seat of the Imperial Government, obtained a practical knowledge of international polity. Successful in all his examinations and disputations, he received the degree of Doctor of Law at Nuremberg in 1676. In 1679 he was a law-lecturer at Frankfort, where he became deeply interested in the teachings of Dr. Spener. In 1680–81 he travelled in France, England, Ireland, and Italy with his friend Herr Von Rodeck. " I was," he says, " glad to enjoy again the company of my Christian friends, rather than be with Von Rodeck feasting and dancing." In 1683. in company with a small number of German Friends, he emigrated to America, settling upon the Frankfort Company's tract between the Schuylkill and the Delaware Rivers. The township was divided into four hamlets, namely, Germantown, Krisheim, Crefield, and Sommerhausen. Soon after his arrival he united himself with the Society of Friends, and became one of its most able and devoted members, as well as the recognized head and lawgiver of the settlement. He married, two years after his arrival, Anneke (Anna), daughter of Dr. Klosterman, of Muhlheim.

In the year 1688 he drew up a memorial against slaveholding, which was adopted by the Germantown Friends and sent up to the Monthly Meeting, and thence to the Yearly Meeting at Philadelphia. It is noteworthy as the first protest made by a religious body against Negro Slavery. The original document was discovered in 1844 by the Philadelphia antiquarian, Nathan Kite, and published in " The Friend " (Vol. XVIII. No. 16). It is a bold and direct appeal to the best instincts of the heart. " Have not," he asks, " these negroes as much right to fight for their freedom as you have to keep them slaves? "

Under the wise direction of Pastorius, the Germantown settlement grew and prospered. The inhabitants planted orchards and vineyards, and surrounded themselves with souvenirs of their old home. A large number of them were

linen-weavers, as well
Quakers were the pri
religions were tolerat
harmony. In 1692 Ri
what he called verse, a
vania," in which he al

" The German town of
Which is at least in le
Where lives High Ger
Whose trade in weavir
There grows the flax,
That from the same th
Their trade suits well
We find convenience

Pastorius seems to
terms with William P
Justice Logan, Thoma
men in the Province
ligious society, as also
Mystic of the Wissah
the Swedes' church,
Mennonites. He wro
sylvania, which was p
Leipsic in 1700 and
Saints," etc., written
to Prof. Schurmberg,
lished in 1690. He
published manuscripts
of subjects, most of
huge manuscript folio
Melliotropheum Aluca
remains, containing
about one hundred lin
ley of knowledge and f
and poetry, written in
portion of his poetry i
of gardening, the desc
care of bees. The f
punning Latin is add
ferer : —

" Quisquis in hæc furti
Tangere fallaci poma
Si non obsequeris fa
Cum malis nostris ut

Professor Oswald Se
pers in Der Deutsche
odical the " Penn Mor
am indebted for many
regard to the German p
thus closes his notice o
" No tombstone, not
indicates where his rem
resting-place, and the
ciate the homage due t
with some visible mem
There is no reason to
terred in any other pla
burying-ground in G
fact is not attested by
formation. After all,
last trace of his earthly
of what has overtaken t
sents; that Germantown

saw him live and move, is at present but a quaint idyl of the past, almost a myth, barely remembered and little cared for by the keener race that has succeeded."

The Pilgrims of Plymouth have not lacked historian and poet. Justice has been done to their faith, courage, and self-sacrifice, and to the mighty influence of their endeavors to establish righteousness on the earth. The Quaker pilgrims of Pennsylvania, seeking the same object by different means, have not been equally fortunate. The power of their testimony for truth and holiness, peace and freedom, enforced only by what Milton calls " the unresistible might of meekness," has been felt through two centuries in the amelioration of penal severities, the abolition of slavery, the reform of the erring, the relief of the poor and suffering, — felt, in brief, in every step of human progress. But of the men themselves, with the single exception of William Penn, scarcely anything is known. Contrasted, from the outset, with the stern, aggressive Puritans of New England, they have come to be regarded as " a feeble folk," with a personality as doubtful as their unrecorded graves. They were not soldiers, like Miles Standish ; they had no figure so picturesque as Vane, no leader so rashly brave and haughty as Endicott. No Cotton Mather wrote their Magnalia ; they had no awful drama of supernaturalism in which Satan and his angels were actors ; and the only witch mentioned in their simple annals was a poor old Swedish woman, who, on complaint of her countrywomen, was tried and acquitted of everything but imbecility and folly. Nothing but commonplace offices of civility came to pass between them and the Indians ; indeed, their enemies taunted them with the fact that the savages did not regard them as Christians, but just such men as themselves. Yet it must be apparent to every careful observer of the progress of American civilization that its two principal currents had their sources in the entirely opposite directions of the Puritan and Quaker colonies. To use the words of a late writer : * " The historical forces, with which no others may be compared in their influence on the people, have been those of the Puritan and the Quaker. The strength of the one was in the confession of an invisible Presence, a righteous, eternal Will, which would establish righteousness on earth ; and thence arose the conviction of a direct personal responsibility, which could be tempted by no external splendor and could be shaken by no internal agitation, and could not be evaded or transferred. The strength of the other was the witness in the human spirit to an eternal Word, an Inner Voice which spoke to each alone, while yet it spoke to every man ; a Light which each was to follow, and which yet was the light of the world ; and all other voices were silent before this, and the solitary path whither it led was more sacred than the worn ways of cathedral-aisles."

It will be sufficiently apparent to the reader that, in the poem which follows, I have attempted nothing beyond a study of the life and times of the Pennsylvania colonist, — a simple picture of a noteworthy man and his locality. The colors of my sketch are all very sober, toned down to the quiet and dreamy atmosphere through which its subject is visible. Whether, in the glare and tumult of the present time, such a picture

Mulford's Nation, pp. 207, 208.

will find favor may well be questioned. I only know that it has beguiled for me some hours of weariness, and that, whatever may be its measure of public appreciation, it has been to me its own reward.

J. G. W.

AMESBURY, 5th mo., 1872.

Hail to posterity !
Hail, future men of Germanopolis !
Let the young generations yet to be
Look kindly upon this.
Think how your fathers left their native
      land, —
  Dear   German-land !   O   sacred
      hearths and homes ! —
And, where the wild beast roams,
    In patience planned
New forest-homes beyond the mighty
      sea,
  There undisturbed and free
To live as brothers of one family.
  What pains and cares befell,
  What trials and what fears,
Remember, and wherein we have done
      well
  Follow our footsteps, men of coming
      years !
  Where we have failed to do
    Aright, or wisely live,
Be warned by us, the better way pursue,
And, knowing we were human, even as
      you,
    Pity us and forgive !
  Farewell, Posterity !
  Farewell, dear Germany !
  Forevermore farewell !

From the Latin of FRANCIS DANIEL PASTORIUS *in the Germantown Records.* 1688.

PRELUDE.

I SING the Pilgrim of a softer clime
  And milder speech than those brave
      men's who brought
To the ice and iron of our winter time
  A will as firm, a creed as stern, and
      wrought
  With one mailed hand, and with the
      other fought.
Simply, as fits my theme, in homely
      rhyme
  I sing the blue-eyed German Spener
      taught,

Through whose veiled, mystic faith the
Inward Light,
Steady and still, an easy brightness,
shone,
Transfiguring all things in its radiance
white.
The garland which his meekness never
sought
I bring him ; over fields of harvest
sown
With seeds of blessing, now to ripe-
ness grown,
I bid the sower pass before the reapers'
sight.

THE PENNSYLVANIA PILGRIM.

NEVER in tenderer quiet lapsed the
day
From Pennsylvania's vales of spring
away,
Where, forest-walled, the scattered hamlets lay

Along the wedded rivers.   One long
bar
Of purple cloud, on which the evening
star
Shone like a jewel on a scimitar,

Held the sky's golden gateway. Through
the deep
Hush of the woods a murmur seemed to
creep,
The Schuylkill whispering in a voice of
sleep.

All else was still.   The oxen from their
ploughs
Rested at last, and from their long day's
browse
Came the dun files of Krisheim's home-
bound cows.

And the young city, round whose virgin
zone
The rivers like two mighty arms were
thrown,
Marked by the smoke of evening fires
alone,

Lay in the distance, lovely even then
With its fair women and its stately
men
Gracing the forest court of William
Penn,

Urban yet sylvan; in its rough-hewn
frames
Of oak and pine the dryads held their
claims,
And lent its streets their pleasant woodland names.

Anna Pastorius down the leafy lane
Looked city-ward, then stooped to prune
again
Her vines and simples, with a sigh of pain.

For fast the streaks of ruddy sunset paled
In the oak clearing, and, as daylight
failed,
Slow, overhead, the dusky night-birds
sailed.

Again she looked: between green walls
of shade,
With low-bent head as if with sorrow
weighed,
Daniel Pastorius slowly came and said,

"God's peace be with thee, Anna !"
Then he stood
Silent before her, wrestling with the mood
Of one who sees the evil and not good.

What is it, my Pastorius ?"   As she
spoke,
A slow, faint smile across his features
broke,
Sadder than tears.   "Dear heart," he
said, "our folk

"Are even as others.   Yea, our good-
liest Friends
Are frail ; our elders have their selfish
ends,
And few dare trust the Lord to make
amends

"For duty's loss. So even our feeble word
For the dumb slaves the startled meet-
ing heard
As if a stone its quiet waters stirred;

"And, as the clerk ceased reading, there
began
A ripple of dissent which downward ran
In widening circles, as from man to man.

"Somewhat was said of running before
sent,
Of tender fear that some their guide out-
went,
Troublers of Israel.   I was scarce intent

'On hearing, for behind the reverend row
If gallery Friends, in dumb and piteous show,
saw, methought, dark faces full of woe.

' And, in the spirit, I was taken where
'hey toiled and suffered ; I was made aware
If shame and wrath and anguish and despair !

'And while the meeting smothered our poor plea
Vith cautious phrase, a Voice there seemed to be,
As ye have done to these ye do to me !"

'So it all passed; and the old tithe went on
If anise, mint, and cumin, till the sun
Jet, leaving still the weightier work undone.

' Help, for the good man faileth ! Who is strong,
f these be weak ? Who shall rebuke the wrong,
f these consent ? How long, O Lord ! how long !"

He ceased; and, bound in spirit with the bound,
With folded arms, and eyes that sought the ground,
Walked musingly his little garden round.

About him, beaded with the falling dew,
Rare plants of power and herbs of healing grew,
Juch as Van Helmont and Agrippa knew.

For, by the lore of Gorlitz' gentle sage,
With the mild mystics of his dreamy age
He read the herbal signs of nature's page,

As once he heard in sweet Von Merlau's [75] bowers
Fair as herself, in boyhood's happy hours,
The pious Spener read his creed in flowers.

" The dear Lord give us patience !" said his wife,
Touching with finger-tip an aloe, rife
With leaves sharp-pointed like an Aztec knife

Or Carib spear, a gift to William Penn
From the rare gardens of John Evelyn,
Brought from the Spanish Main by merchantmen.

" See this strange plant its steady purpose hold,
And, year by year, its patient leaves unfold,
Till the young eyes that watched it first are old.

" But some time, thou hast told me, there shall come
A sudden beauty, brightness, and perfume,
The century-moulded bud shall burst in bloom.

" So may the seed which hath been sown to-day
Grow with the years, and, after long delay,
Break into bloom, and God's eternal Yea

" Answer at last the patient prayers of them
Who now, by faith alone, behold its stem
Crowned with the flowers of Freedom's diadem.

" Meanwhile, to feel and suffer, work and wait,
Remains for us. The wrong indeed is great,
But love and patience conquer soon or late."

" Well hast thou said, my Anna !" Tenderer
Than youth's caress upon the head of her
Pastorius laid his hand. "Shall we demur

" Because the vision tarrieth ? In an hour
We dream not of the slow-grown bud may flower,
And what was sown in weakness rise in power !"

Then through the vine-draped door whose legend read,
" PROCUL ESTE PROPHANI !" Anna led
To where their child upon his little bed

Looked up and smiled. "Dear heart,"
she said, "if we
Must bearers of a heavy burden be,
Our boy, God willing, yet the day shall see

"When, from the gallery to the farthest
seat,
Slave and slave-owner shall no longer
meet,
But all sit equal at the Master's feet."

On the stone hearth the blazing walnut
block
Set the low walls a-glimmer, showed the
cock
Rebuking Peter on the Van Wyck clock,

Shone on old tomes of law and physic,
side
By side with Fox and Behmen, played
at hide
And seek with Anna, midst her household pride

Of flaxen webs, and on the table, bare
Of costly cloth or silver cup, but where,
Tasting the fat shads of the Delaware,

The courtly Penn had praised the goodwife's cheer,
And quoted Horace o'er her home-brewed
beer,
Till even grave Pastorius smiled to hear.

In such a home, beside the Schuylkill's
wave,
He dwelt in peace with God and man,
and gave
Food to the poor and shelter to the slave.

For all too soon the New World's scandal shamed
The righteous code by Penn and Sidney
framed,
And men withheld the human rights
they claimed.

And slowly wealth and station sanction
lent,
And hardened avarice, on its gains intent,
Stifled the inward whisper of dissent.

Yet all the while the burden rested sore
On tender hearts. At last Pastorius bore
Their warning message to the Church's
door

In God's name; ɛ
word
Wrought ever af
heard,
And a dead cor
clothes stir

To troubled life,
excuse
Of Hebrew custor
Good in itself if e

Gravely Pastorius
Discerning throu
dress
Of the poor plea i

One Scripture rul
got;
He hid the outca
not;
And, when his p
sought,

He scrupled not, ɪ
And proffered chɛ
ter's stay,
To speed the black

Yet, who shall gu
lends
His life to some
his friends
Shame or betray it

How felt the Mɛ
strove
In childish folly f
And that fond n
love,

Besought him the
throne,
Might sit on eith
own
A stranger oft, co

God's priest and
martyr's pɛ
Is not alone from
chain;
Sharper the pang
train,

His weak disciple
The loud hosanna
And make their e

~mit's cell he found,
:d, drew his hearth
:e upon its neutral

ith battle-bows un-

like those whom

len the world was

y women, lithe and

iend Von Rodeck's

not unpleasing all.

homespun drab and

l on Monthly Meet-

their friendly way.

om the Fatherland,
ck, slow to under-

romise, sought his

'rom his hermit den
ldest of good men,
:hiliast dreams of

where the small

e, the Helmstadt

er arts forbid,

Daniel and of John,
ig-Redness, through

ed to his eyes alone,

lat man ne'er read

i man shall see no

, striding sea and

it, on land or ships,
if the Apocalypse,
us before the dread

Or meek-eyed Mennonist his bearded chin
Leaned o'er the gate; or Ranter, pure
    within,
Aired his perfection in a world of sin.

Or, talking of old home scenes, Op den
    Graaf
Teased the low back-log with his shod-
    den staff,
Till the red embers broke into a laugh

And dance of flame, as if they fain would
    cheer
The rugged face, half tender, half aus-
    tere,
Touched with the pathos of a homesick
    tear !

Or Sluyter,[77] saintly familist, whose word
As law the Brethren of the Manor heard,
Announced the speedy terrors of the
    Lord,

And turned, like Lot at Sodom, from
    his race,
Above a wrecked world with complacent
    face
Riding secure upon his plank of grace !

Haply, from Finland's birchen groves
    exiled,
Manly in thought, in simple ways a
    child,
His white hair floating round his visage
    mild,

The Swedish pastor sought the Quaker's
    door,
Pleased from his neighbor's lips to hear
    once more
His long-disused and half-forgotten lore.

For both could baffle Babel's lingual
    curse,
And speak in Bion's Doric, and rehearse
Cleanthes' hymn or Virgil's sounding
    verse.

And oft Pastorius and the meek old man
Argued as Quaker and as Lutheran,
Ending in Christian love, as they began.

With lettered Lloyd on pleasant morns
    he strayed
Where Sommerhausen over vales of shade
Looked miles away, by every flower
    delayed,

Or song of bird, happy and free with one
Who loved, like him, to let his memory run
Over old fields of learning, and to sun

Himself in Plato's wise philosophies,
And dream with Philo over mysteries
Whereof the dreamer never finds the keys;

To touch all themes of thought, nor weakly stop
For doubt of truth, but let the buckets drop
Deep down and bring the hidden waters up.[78]

For there was freedom in that wakening time
Of tender souls; to differ was not crime;
The varying bells made up the perfect chime.

On lips unlike was laid the altar's coal,
The white, clear light, tradition-colored, stole
Through the stained oriel of each human soul.

Gathered from many sects, the Quaker brought
His old beliefs, adjusting to the thought
That moved his soul the creed his fathers taught.

One faith alone, so broad that all mankind
Within themselves its secret witness find,
The soul's communion with the Eternal Mind,

The Spirit's law, the Inward Rule and Guide,
Scholar and peasant, lord and serf, allied,
The polished Penn and Cromwell's Ironside.

As still in Hemskerck's Quaker Meeting,[79] face
By face in Flemish detail, we may trace
How loose-mouthed boor and fine ancestral grace

Sat in close contrast, — the clipt-headed churl,
Broad market-dame, and simple serving-girl
By skirt of silk and periwig in curl!

For soul touched soul; the spiritual treasure-trove
Made all men equal, none could rise above
Nor sink below that level of God's love.

So, with his rustic neighbors sitting down,
The homespun frock beside the scholar's gown,
Pastorius to the manners of the town

Added the freedom of the woods, and sought
The bookless wisdom by experience taught,
And learned to love his new-found home, while not

Forgetful of the old; the seasons went
Their rounds, and somewhat to his spirit lent
Of their own calm and measureless content.

Glad even to tears, he heard the robin sing
His song of welcome to the Western spring,
And bluebird borrowing from the sky his wing.

And when the miracle of autumn came,
And all the woods with many-colored flame
Of splendor, making summer's greenness tame,

Burned, unconsumed, a voice without a sound
Spake to him from each kindled bush around,
And made the strange, new landscape holy ground!

And when the bitter north-wind, keen and swift,
Swept the white street and piled the dooryard drift,
He exercised, as Friends might say, his gift

Of verse, Dutch, English, Latin, like the hash
Of corn and beans in Indian succotash;
Dull, doubtless, but with here and there a flash

Of wit and fine conceit, — the good man's play
Of quiet fancies, meet to while away
The slow hours measuring off an idle day.

At evening, while his wife put on her look
Of love's endurance, from its niche he took
The written pages of his ponderous book.

And read, in half the languages of man,
His "Rusca Apium," which with bees began,
And through the gamut of creation ran.

Or, now and then, the missive of some friend
In gray Altorf or storied Nürnberg penned
Dropped in upon him like a guest to spend

The night beneath his roof-tree. Mystical
The fair Von Merlau spake as waters fall
And voices sound in dreams, and yet withal

Human and sweet, as if each far, low tone,
Over the roses of her gardens blown
Brought the warm sense of beauty all her own.

Wise Spener questioned what his friend could trace
Of spiritual influx or of saving grace
In the wild natures of the Indian race.

And learned Schurmberg, fain, at times, to look
From Talmud, Koran, Veds, and Pentateuch,
Sought out his pupil in his far-off nook,

To query with him of climatic change,
Of bird, beast, reptile, in his forest range,
Of flowers and fruits and simples new and strange.

And thus the Old and New World reached their hands
Across the water, and the friendly lands
Talked with each other from their severed strands.

Pastorius answered all : while seed and root
Sent from his new home grew to flower and fruit
Along the Rhine and at the Spessart's foot ;

And, in return, the flowers his boyhood knew
Smiled at his door, the same in form and hue,
And on his vines the Rhenish clusters grew.

No idler he ; whoever else might shirk,
He set his hand to every honest work, —
Farmer and teacher, court and meeting clerk.

Still on the town seal his device is found,
Grapes, flax, and thread-spool on a trefoil ground,
With " VINUM, LINUM ET TEXTRINUM " wound.

One house sufficed for gospel and for law,
Where Paul and Grotius, Scripture text and saw,
Assured the good, and held the rest in awe.

Whatever legal maze he wandered through,
He kept the Sermon on the Mount in view,
And justice always into mercy grew.

No whipping-post he needed, stocks, nor jail,
Nor ducking-stool ; the orchard-thief grew pale
At his rebuke, the vixen ceased to rail,

The usurer's grasp released the forfeit land ;
The slanderer faltered at the witness-stand,
And all men took his counsel for command.

Was it caressing air, the brooding love
Of tenderer skies than German land knew of,
Green calm below, blue quietness above,

Still flow of water, deep repose of wood
That, with a sense of loving Fatherhood
And childlike trust in the Eternal Good,

Softened all hearts, and dulled the edge
of hate,
Hushed strife, and taught impatient zeal
to wait
The slow assurance of the better state !

Who knows what goadings in their
sterner way
O'er jagged ice, relieved by granite gray,
Blew round the men of Massachusetts
Bay ?

What hate of heresy the east-wind woke ?
What hints of pitiless power and terror
spoke
In waves that on their iron coast-line
broke ?

Be it as it may : within the Land of Penn
The sectary yielded to the citizen,
And peaceful dwelt the many-creeded
men.

Peace brooded over all. No trumpet
stung
The air to madness, and no steeple flung
Alarums down from bells at midnight
rung.

The lands slept well. The Indian from
his face
Washed all his war-paint off, and in the
place
Of battle-marches sped the peaceful
chase,

Or wrought for wages at the white man's
side, —
Giving to kindness what his native pride
And lazy freedom to all else denied.

And well the curious scholar loved the
old
Traditions that his swarthy neighbors
told
By wigwam-fires when nights were growing cold,

Discerned the fact round which their
fancy drew
Its dreams, and held their childish faith
more true
To God and man than half the creeds he
knew.[80]

The desert blossomed round him; wheat-
fields rolled
Beneath the warm wind waves of green
and gold;
The planted ear returned its hundred-
fold.

Great clusters ripened in a warmer sun
Than that which by the Rhine stream
shines upon
The purpling hillsides with low vines
o'errun.

About each rustic porch the humming-
bird
Tried with light bill, that scarce a petal
stirred,
The Old World flowers to virgin soil
transferred ;

And the first-fruits of pear and apple,
bending
The young boughs down, their gold and
russet blending,
Made glad his heart, familiar odors lending

To the fresh fragrance of the birch and
pine,
Life-everlasting, bay, and eglantine,
And all the subtle scents the woods combine.

Fair First-Day mornings, steeped in
summer calm
Warm, tender, restful, sweet with woodland balm,
Came to him, like some mother-hallowed
psalm

To the tired grinder at the noisy wheel
Of labor, winding off from memory's reel
A golden thread of music. With no peal

Of bells to call them to the house of
praise,
The scattered settlers through green for-
est-ways
Walked meeting-ward. In reverent
amaze

The Indian trapper saw them, from the
dim
Shade of the alders on the rivulet's rim,
Seek the Great Spirit's house to talk
with Him.

There, through the gathered stillness multiplied
And made intense by sympathy, outside
The sparrows sang, and the gold-robin cried,

A-swing upon his elm. A faint perfume
Breathed through the open windows of the room
From locust-trees, heavy with clustered bloom.

Thither, perchance, sore-tried confessors came,
Whose fervor jail nor pillory could tame,
Proud of the cropped ears meant to be their shame,

Men who had eaten slavery's bitter bread
In Indian isles; pale women who had bled
Under the hangman's lash, and bravely said

God's message through their prison's iron bars;
And gray old soldier-converts, seamed with scars
From every stricken field of England's wars

Lowly before the Unseen Presence knelt
Each waiting heart, till haply some one felt
On his moved lips the seal of silence melt.

Or, without spoken words, low breathings stole
Of a diviner life from soul to soul,
Baptizing in one tender thought the whole.

When shaken hands announced the meeting o'er,
The friendly group still lingered at the door,
Greeting, inquiring, sharing all the store

Of weekly tidings. Meanwhile youth and maid
Down the green vistas of the woodland strayed,
Whispered and smiled and oft their feet delayed.

Did the boy's whistle answer back the thrushes?
Did light girl laughter ripple through the bushes,
As brooks make merry over roots and rushes?

Unvexed the sweet air seemed. Without a wound
The ear of silence heard, and every sound
Its place in nature's fine accordance found.

And solemn meeting, summer sky and wood,
Old kindly faces, youth and maidenhood
Seemed, like God's new creation, very good!

And, greeting all with quiet smile and word,
Pastorius went his way. The unscared bird
Sang at his side; scarcely the squirrel stirred

At his hushed footstep on the mossy sod;
And, wheresoe'er the good man looked or trod,
He felt the peace of nature and of God.

His social life wore no ascetic form,
He loved all beauty, without fear of harm,
And in his veins his Teuton blood ran warm.

Strict to himself, of other men no spy,
He made his own no circuit-judge to try
The freer conscience of his neighbors by.

With love rebuking, by his life alone,
Gracious and sweet, the better way was shown,
The joy of one, who, seeking not his own,

And faithful to all scruples, finds at last
The thorns and shards of duty overpast,
And daily life, beyond his hope's forecast,

Pleasant and beautiful with sight and sound,
And flowers upspringing in its narrow round,
And all his days with quiet gladness crowned.

He sang not ; but, if sometimes tempted
   strong,
He hummed what seemed like Altorf's
   Burschen-song,
His good wife smiled, and did not count
   it wrong.

For well he loved his boyhood's brother
   band ;
His Memory, while he trod the New
   World's strand,
A double-ganger walked the Fatherland !

If, when on frosty Christmas eves the
   light
Shone on his quiet hearth, he missed
   the sight
Of Yule-log, Tree, and Christ-child all
   in white ;

And closed his eyes, and listened to the
   sweet
Old wait-songs sounding down his native
   street,
And watched again the dancers' mingling feet ;

Yet not the less, when once the vision
   passed,
He held the plain and sober maxims fast
Of the dear Friends with whom his lot
   was cast.

Still all attuned to nature's melodies,
He loved the bird's song in his dooryard
   trees,
And the low hum of home-returning
   bees ;

The blossomed flax, the tulip-trees in
   bloom
Down the long street, the beauty and
   perfume
Of apple-boughs, the mingling light and
   gloom

Of Sommerhausen's woodlands, woven
   through
With sun-threads; and the music the
   wind drew,
Mournful and sweet, from leaves it over-
   blew.

And evermore, beneath this outward
   sense,
And through the common sequence of
   events,
He felt the guiding hand of Providence

Reach out of space
   his ear,
And lo ! all other
Died at that whis
   clear.

The Light of Life
   by one
The wandering lig
   ing run,
Went out like canc

That Light he fol
   where'er
It led, as in the vi
The wheels moved
   clear

And terrible crys
   their eyes
Watching the livin
Its will their will,

Within himself h
   right,
He walked by fait
   sight,
And read his Bibl

And if sometimes
   rule,
Frozen in their cr
   ter's pool,
Tried the large tc
   school,

His door was free
He welcomed all t
   came,
And no man's fait
   blame.

But best he loved
His own dear Fri
   to knee,
In social converse,

There sometimes
   tell
Who owned it firs
Hushed Anna's bu
   spell

On the black boy
   hearth,
To solemnize his s
Only the old clo
   dearth

f sound ; nor eye was raised nor hand
was stirred
n that soul-sabbath, till at last some
word
f tender counsel or low prayer was
heard.

hen guests, who lingered but farewell
to say
nd take love's message, went their
homeward way;
o passed in peace the guileless Quaker's
day.

Iis was the Christian's unsung Age of
Gold,
truer idyl than the bards have told
f Arno's banks or Arcady of old.

Vhere still the Friends their place of
burial keep,
nd century-rooted mosses o'er it creep,
he Nürnberg scholar and his helpmeet
sleep.

nd Anna's aloe? If it flowered at last
n Bartram's garden, did John Woolman cast
glance upon it as he meekly passed?

nd did a secret sympathy possess
hat tender soul, and for the slave's
redress
end hope, strength, patience? It were
vain to guess.

Nay, were the plant itself but mythical,
Set in the fresco of tradition's wall
Like Jotham's bramble, mattereth not
at all.

Enough to know that, through the
winter's frost
And summer's heat, no seed of truth is
lost,
And every duty pays at last its cost.

For, ere Pastorius left the sun and air,
God sent the answer to his life-long
prayer;
The child was born beside the Delaware,

Who, in the power a holy purpose
lends,
Guided his people unto nobler ends,
And left them worthier of the name of
Friends.

And lo ! the fulness of the time has
come,
And over all the exile's Western home,
From sea to sea the flowers of freedom
bloom !

And joy-bells ring, and silver trumpets
blow ;
But not for thee, Pastorius ! Even
so
The world forgets, but the wise angels
know.

MISCELLANEOUS.

THE PAGEANT.

A SOUND as if from bells of silver,
Or elfin cymbals smitten clear,
Through the frost-pictured panes I
hear.

Where, keen against the walls of sapphire,
The gleaming tree-bolls, ice-em-
bossed,
Hold up their chandeliers of frost.

The flora of the mystic mine-world
Around me lifts on crystal stems
The petals of its clustered gems!

What miracle of weird transforming
In this wild work of frost and
light,
This glimpse of glory infinite!

This foregleam of the Holy City
Like that to him of Patmos given,
The white bride coming down from
heaven!

How flash the ranked and mail-clad alders,
Through what sharp-glancing spears
of reeds
The brook its muffled water leads!

Yon maple, like the bush of Horeb,
Burns unconsumed: a white, cold
fire
Rays out from every grassy spire.

Each slender rush and spike of mullein,
Low laurel shrub and drooping fern,
Transfigured, blaze where'er I turn.

How yonder Ethiopian hemlock
Crowned with his glistening circlet
stands!
What jewels light his swarthy
hands!

Here, where the forest opens southward,
Between its hospitable pines,
As through a door, the warm sun
shines.

The jewels loosen on the branches,
And lightly, as the soft winds
blow,
Fall, tinkling, on the ice below.

And through the clashing of their cym-
bals
I hear the old familiar fall
Of water down the rocky wall,

Where, from its wintry prison breaking,
In dark and silence hidden long,
The brook repeats its summer song.

I hear the rabbit li
The foolish sc
The chopper's

The clamor of son
yard,
The lazy cock'
Or cattle-tram

And, as in some ei
The lost knigl
sing,
And, near at
ring,

So welcome I thes
These airs 1
blown,
This life that

For the white glor
The crystal to
Of Chebar's v:

Rebuke me not, O
Thou stainle:
me.
Thy keen rep

If, in this august
I sigh for
gloom
And warm ai
bloom!

Let the strange
crumble,
And let the
swing,
Till all their !

Shine warmly dow
time,
On this chil
move
The winter's !

And, soft and lo
blowing,
Breathe throi
haze
Thy prophecy

THE SINGER.

YEARS since (but names to me before),
Two sisters sought at eve my door ;
Two song-birds wandering from their
    nest,
A gray old farm-house in the West.

How fresh of life the younger one,
Half smiles, half tears, like rain in
    sun !
Her gravest mood could scarce displace
The dimples of her nut-brown face.

Wit sparkled on her lips not less
For quick and tremulous tenderness ;
And, following close her merriest glance,
Dreamed through her eyes the heart's
    romance.

Timid and still, the elder had
Even then a smile too sweetly sad ;
The crown of pain that all must wear
Too early pressed her midnight hair.

Yet ere the summer eve grew long,
Her modest lips were sweet with song ;
A memory haunted all her words
Of clover-fields and singing birds.

Her dark, dilating eyes expressed
The broad horizons of the west ;
Her speech dropped prairie flowers ; the
    gold
Of harvest wheat about her rolled.

Fore-doomed to song she seemed to
    me :
I queried not with destiny :
I knew the trial and the need,
Yet, all the more, I said, God speed !

What could I other than I did ?
Could I a singing-bird forbid ?
Deny the wind-stirred leaf ? Rebuke
The music of the forest brook ?

She went with morning from my door,
But left me richer than before ;
Thenceforth I knew her voice of cheer,
The welcome of her partial ear.

Years passed : through all the land her
    name
A pleasant household word became :
All felt behind the singer stood
A sweet and gracious womanhood.

Her life was earnest work, not play ;
Her tired feet climbed a weary way ;
And even through her lightest strain
We heard an undertone of pain.

Unseen of her her fair fame grew,
The good she did she rarely knew,
Unguessed of her in life the love
That rained its tears her grave above.

When last I saw her, full of peace,
She waited for her great release ;
And that old friend so sage and bland,
Our later Franklin, held her hand.

For all that patriot bosoms stirs
Had moved that woman's heart of
    hers,
And men who toiled in storm and sun
Found her their meet companion.

Our converse, from her suffering bed
To healthful themes of life she led :
The out-door world of bud and bloom
And light and sweetness filled her
    room.

Yet evermore an underthought
Of loss to come within us wrought,
And all the while we felt the strain
Of the strong will that conquered pain.

God giveth quietness at last !
The common way that all have passed
She went, with mortal yearnings fond,
To fuller life and love beyond.

Fold the rapt soul in your embrace,
My dear ones ! Give the singer place
To you, to her, — I know not where, —
I lift the silence of a prayer.

For only thus our own we find ;
The gone before, the left behind,
All mortal voices die between ;
The unheard reaches the unseen.

Again the blackbirds sing ; the streams
Wake, laughing, from their winter
    dreams,
And tremble in the April showers
The tassels of the maple flowers.

But not for her has spring renewed
The sweet surprises of the wood ;
And bird and flower are lost to her
Who was their best interpreter !

What to shut eyes has God revealed ?
What hear the ears that death has sealed ?
What undreamed beauty passing show
Requites the loss of all we know ?

O silent land, to which we move,
Enough if there alone be love,
And mortal need can ne'er outgrow
What it is waiting to bestow !

O white soul ! from that far-off shore
Float some sweet song the waters o'er,
Our faith confirm, our fears dispel,
With the old voice we loved so well !

How instant rose, to take thy part,
The angel in the human heart !

Ah ! not in vain the flames that tossed
Above thy dreadful holocaust ;
The Christ again has preached through
    thee
The Gospel of Humanity !

Then lift once more thy towers on
    high,
And fret with spires the western sky,
To tell that God is yet with us,
And love is still miraculous !

CHICAGO.

MEN said at vespers : " All is well ! "
In one wild night the city fell ;
Fell shrines of prayer and marts of gain
Before the fiery hurricane.

On threescore spires had sunset shone,
Where ghastly sunrise looked on none.
Men clasped each other's hands, and said :
"The City of the West is dead ! "

Brave hearts who fought, in slow retreat,
The fiends of fire from street to street,
Turned, powerless, to the blinding glare,
The dumb defiance of despair.

A sudden impulse thrilled each wire
That signalled round that sea of fire ;
Swift words of cheer, warm heart-throbs
    came ;
In tears of pity died the flame !

From East, from West, from South and
    North,
The messages of hope shot forth,
And, underneath the severing wave,
The world, full-handed, reached to save.

Fair seemed the old ; but fairer still
The new, the dreary void shall fill
With dearer homes than those o'erthrown,
For love shall lay each corner-stone.

Rise, stricken city ! — from thee throw
The ashen sackcloth of thy woe ;
And build, as to Amphion's strain,
To songs of cheer thy walls again !

How shrivelled in thy hot distress
The primal sin of selfishness !

MY BIRTHDAY.

BENEATH the moonlight and the snow
    Lies dead my latest year ;
The winter winds are wailing low
    Its dirges in my ear.

I grieve not with the moaning wind
    As if a loss befell ;
Before me, even as behind,
    God is, and all is well !

His light shines on me from above,
    His low voice speaks within, —
The patience of immortal love
    Outwearying mortal sin.

Not mindless of the growing years
    Of care and loss and pain,
My eyes are wet with thankful tears
    For blessings which remain.

If dim the gold of life has grown,
    I will not count it dross,
Nor turn from treasures still my own
    To sigh for lack and loss.

The years no charm from Nature take ;
    As sweet her voices call,
As beautiful her mornings break,
    As fair her evenings fall.

Love watches o'er my quiet ways,
    Kind voices speak my name,
And lips that find it hard to praise
    Are slow, at least, to blame.

How softly ebb the tides of will !
    How fields, once lost or won,
Now lie behind me green and still
    Beneath a level sun !

How hushed the hiss of party hate,
  The clamor of the throng !
How old, harsh voices of debate
  Flow into rhythmic song !

Methinks the spirit's temper grows
  Too soft in this still air ;
Somewhat the restful heart foregoes
  Of needed watch and prayer.

The bark by tempest vainly tossed
  May founder in the calm,
And he who braved the polar frost
  Faint by the isles of balm.

Better than self-indulgent years
  The outflung heart of youth,
Than pleasant songs in idle years
  The tumult of the truth.

Rest for the weary hands is good,
  And love for hearts that pine,
But let the manly habitude
  Of upright souls be mine.

Let winds that blow from heaven refresh,
  Dear Lord, the languid air ;
And let the weakness of the flesh
  Thy strength of spirit share.

And, if the eye must fail of light,
  The ear forget to hear,
Make clearer still the spirit's sight,
  More fine the inward ear !

Be near me in mine hours of need
  To soothe, or cheer, or warn,
And down these slopes of sunset lead
  As up the hills of morn !

THE BREWING OF SOMA.

"These libations mixed with milk have been prepared for Indra : offer Soma to the drinker of Soma." — VASHISTA, Trans. by MAX MÜLLER.

THE fagots blazed, the caldron's smoke
  Up through the green wood curled ;
" Bring honey from the hollow oak,
Bring milky sap," the brewers spoke,
  In the childhood of the world.

And brewed they well or brewed they ill,
  The priests thrust in their rods.

They drank, and lo ! in heart and roar
  A new, glad life began ;   · shore.
The gray of hair grew young again,
The sick man laughed away his pain, ·.
  The cripple leaped and ran.

" Drink, mortals, what the gods have
  sent,
  Forget your long annoy."
So sang the priests. From tent to tent
The Soma's sacred madness went,
  A storm of drunken joy.

Then knew each rapt inebriate
  A winged and glorious birth,
Soared upward, with strange joy elate,
Beat, with dazed head, Varuna's gate,
  And, sobered, sank to earth.

The land with Soma's praises rang ;
  On Gihon's banks of shade
Its hymns the dusky maidens sang ;
In joy of life or mortal pang
  All men to Soma prayed.

The morning twilight of the race
  Sends down these matin psalms ;
And still with wondering eyes we trace
The simple prayers to Soma's grace,
  That Vedic verse embalms.

As in that child-world's early year,
  Each after age has striven
By music, incense, vigils drear,
And trance, to bring the skies more near,
  Or lift men up to heaven ! —

Some fever of the blood and brain,
  Some self-exalting spell,
The scourger's keen delight of pain,
The Dervish dance, the Orphic strain,
  The wild-haired Bacchant's yell, —

The desert's hair-grown hermit sunk
  The saner brute below ;
The naked Santon, hashish-drunk,
The cloister madness of the monk,
  The fakir's torture-show !

And yet the past comes round again,
  And new doth old fulfil ;
In sensual transports wild as vain
We brew in many a Christian fane
  The heathen Soma still !

What to [...] ightful mind,
What [...] nd brain [...] rvice find,
Wh [...] 373 [...] ce, praise.
[...] theirs who heard
[...] sea
The gracious ca[...]g of the Lord,
Let us, like them, without a word,
Rise up and follow thee.

O Sabbath rest by Galilee !
O calm of hills above,
Where Jesus knelt to share with thee
The silence of eternity
Interpreted by love !

With that deep hush subduing all
Our words and works that drown
The tender whisper of thy call,
As noiseless let thy blessing fall
As fell thy manna down.

Drop thy still dews of quietness,
Till all our strivings cease ;
Take from our souls the strain and stress,
And let our ordered lives confess
The beauty of thy peace.

Breathe through the heats of our desire
Thy coolness and thy balm ;
Let sense be dumb, let flesh retire ;
Speak through the earthquake, wind, and fire,
O still, small voice of calm !

A WOMAN.

O, DWARFED and wronged, and stained
with ill,
Behold ! thou art a woman still !
And, by that sacred name and dear,
I bid thy better self appear.
Still, through thy foul disguise, I see
The rudimental purity,
That, spite of change and loss, makes
good
Thy birthright-claim of womanhood ;
An inward loathing, deep, intense ;
A shame that is half innocence.
Cast off the grave-clothes of thy sin !
Rise from the dust thou liest in,
As Mary rose at Jesus' word,
Redeemed and white before the Lord !
Reclaim thy lost soul ! In His name,
Rise up, and break thy bonds of
shame.

Art weak ? He 's strong. Art fearful ?
Hear
The world's O'ercomer : " Be of cheer !"
What lip shall judge when He approves ?
Who dare to scorn the child he loves ?

DISARMAMENT.

" PUT up the sword ! " The voice of
Christ once more
Speaks, in the pauses of the cannon's
roar,
O'er fields of corn by fiery sickles reaped
And left dry ashes ; over trenches heaped
With nameless dead ; o'er cities starving
slow
Under a rain of fire ; through wards of
woe
Down which a groaning diapason runs
From tortured brothers, husbands,
lovers, sons
Of desolate women in their far-off homes,
Waiting to hear the step that never
comes !
O men and brothers ! let that voice be
heard.
War fails, try peace ; put up the useless
sword !

Fear not the end. There is a story told
In Eastern tents, when autumn nights
grow cold,
And round the fire the Mongol shepherds
sit
With grave responses listening unto it :
Once, on the errands of his mercy bent,
Buddha, the holy and benevolent,
Met a fell monster, huge and fierce of
look,
Whose awful voice the hills and forests
shook.
" O son of peace ! " the giant cried,
" thy fate
Is sealed at last, and love shall yield to
hate."
The unarmed Buddha looking, with no
trace
Of fear or anger, in the monster's face,
In pity said : " Poor fiend, even thee I
love."
Lo ! as he spake the sky-tall terror sank
To hand-breadth size ; the huge abhor-
rence shrank
Into the form and fashion of a dove ;
And where the thunder of its rage was
heard.

Circling above him sweetly sang the
    bird :
"Hate hath no harm for love," so ran
    the song;
"And peace unweaponed conquers every
    wrong!"

THE ROBIN.

My old Welch neighbor over the way
    Crept slowly out in the sun of spring,
Pushed from her ears the locks of gray,
    And listened to hear the robin sing.

Her grandson, playing at marbles,
    stopped,
    And, cruel in sport as boys will be,
Tossed a stone at the bird, who hopped
    From bough to bough in the apple-tree.

"Nay !" said the grandmother ; "have
    you not heard,
My poor, bad boy ! of the fiery pit,
And how, drop by drop, this merciful
    bird
Carries the water that quenches it ?

"He brings cool dew in his little bill,
    And lets it fall on the souls of sin :
You can see the mark on his red breast
    still
Of fires that scorch as he drops it in.

"My poor Bron rhuddyn ! my breast-
    burned bird,
Singing so sweetly from limb to limb,
Very dear to the heart of Our Lord
    Is he who pities the lost like Him !"

"Amen !" I said to the beautiful myth ;
    "Sing, bird of God, in my heart as
    well ;
Each good thought is a drop wherewith
    To cool and lessen the fires of hell.

"Prayers of love like rain-drops fall,
    Tears of pity are cooling dew,
And dear to the heart of Our Lord are all
    Who suffer like Him in the good they
    do !"

THE SISTERS.

Annie and Rhoda, sisters twain,
Woke in the night to the sound of rain,

The rush of wind,
Of great waves clin

Annie rose up in h
And looked out into

"Hush, and hearke
"Hearest thou not

"I hear the sea, an
And roar of the noi

"Get thee back to
No good comes of

"What is it to the
That waves are ro
    blow ?

"No lover of thin
The harbor-lights o

"But I heard a vo
Up from the sea on

"Twice and thrice
And the voice is
    Hall !"

On her pillow the
"Hall of the Hero

"In the tautest sc
He rides at anchor

"And, if in peril f
Or lee shore rock
    thee ?"

But the girl heard
    tide,
And wringing her
    cried :

"O sister Rhoda
    wrong ;
I hear it again, so

"'Annie ! Annie !
And the voice is
    Hall !"

Up sprang the elde
"Thou liest ! He
    name !

"If he did, I woul
    sea
To keep him foreve

Then out of the sea blew a dreadful blast;
Like the cry of a dying man it passed.

The young girl hushed on her lips a
　　groan,
But through her tears a strange light
　　shone, —

The solemn joy of her heart's release
To own and cherish its love in peace.

"Dearest!" she whispered, under breath,
"Life was a lie, but true is death.

"The love I hid from myself away
Shall crown me now in the light of day.

"My ears shall never to wooer list,
Never by lover my lips be kissed.

"Sacred to thee am I henceforth,
Thou in heaven and I on earth!"

She came and stood by her sister's bed:
"Hall of the Heron is dead!" she said.

"The wind and the waves their work
　　have done,
We shall see him no more beneath the sun.

"Little will reck that heart of thine,
It loved him not with a love like mine.

"I, for his sake, were he but here,
Could hem and 'broider thy bridal gear,

"Though hands should tremble and eyes
　　be wet,
And stitch for stitch in my heart be set.

"But now my soul with his soul I wed;
Thine the living, and mine the dead!"

MARGUERITE.

THE robins sang in the orchard, the buds
　　into blossoms grew;
Little of human sorrow the buds and the
　　robins knew!

Sick, in an alien household, the poor
　　French neutral lay;
Into her lonesome garret fell the light of
　　the April day.

Through the dusty window, curtained
　　by the spider's warp and woof,
On the loose-laid floor of hemlock, on
　　oaken ribs of roof.

The bedquilt's faded patchwork, the tea-
　　cups on the stand,
The wheel with flaxen tangle, as it
　　dropped from her sick hand!

What to her was the song of the robin,
　　or warm morning light,
As she lay in the trance of the dying,
　　heedless of sound or sight?

Done was the work of her hands, she
　　had eaten her bitter bread;
The world of the alien people lay behind
　　her dim and dead.

But her soul went back to its child-time;
　　she saw the sun o'erflow
With gold the basin of Minas, and set
　　over Gasperau;

The low, bare flats at ebb-tide, the rush
　　of the sea at flood,
Through inlet and creek and river, from
　　dike to upland wood;

The gulls in the red of morning, the
　　fish-hawk's rise and fall,
The drift of the fog in moonshine, over
　　the dark coast-wall.

She saw the face of her mother, she
　　heard the song she sang;
And far off, faintly, slowly, the bell for
　　vespers rang!

By her bed the hard-faced mistress sat,
　　smoothing the wrinkled sheet,
Peering into the face, so helpless, and
　　feeling the ice-cold feet.

With a vague remorse atoning for her
　　greed and long abuse,
By care no longer heeded and pity too
　　late for use.

Up the stairs of the garret softly the son
　　of the mistress stepped,
Leaned over the head-board, covering
　　his face with his hands, and wept.

Outspake the mother, who watched him
　　sharply, with brow a-frown:
"What! love you the Papist, the beg-
　　gar, the charge of the town?"

"Be she Papist or beggar who lies here,
    I know and God knows
I love her, and fain would go with her
    wherever she goes !

"O mother ! that sweet face came plead-
    ing, for love so athirst.
You saw but the town-charge ; I knew
    her God's angel at first."

Shaking her gray head, the mistress
    hushed down a bitter cry ;
And awed by the silence and shadow of
    death drawing nigh,

She murmured a psalm of the Bible ; but
    closer the young girl pressed,
With the last of her life in her fingers,
    the cross to her breast.

"My son, come away," cried the mother,
    her voice cruel grown.
"She is joined to her idols, like Eph-
    raim ; let her alone ! "

But he knelt with his hand on her fore-
    head, his lips to her ear,
And he called back the soul that was pass-
    ing : "Marguerite, do you hear ?"

She paused on the threshold of Heaven ;
    love, pity, surprise,
Wistful, tender, lit up for an instant the
    cloud of her eyes.

With his heart on his lips he kissed her,
    but never her cheek grew red,
And the words the living long for he
    spake in the ear of the dead.

And the robins sang in the orchard,
    where buds to blossoms grew ;
Of the folded hands and the still face
    never the robins knew !

KING VOLMER AND ELSIE.

AFTER THE DANISH OF CHRISTIAN
WINTER.

WHERE, over heathen doom-rings and
    gray stones of the Horg,
In its little Christian city stands the
    church of Vordingborg,

In merry mood King Volmer sat, for-
    getful of his power,
As idle as the Goose of Gold that brooded
    on his tower.

Out spake the King to Henrik, his young
    and faithful squire :
"Dar'st trust thy little Elsie, the maid
    of thy desire ?"
"Of all the men in Denmark she loveth
    only me :
As true to me is Elsie as thy Lily is to
    thee."

Loud laughed the king : "To-morrow
    shall bring another day, *
When I myself will test her ; she will
    not say me nay."
Thereat the lords and gallants, that
    round about him stood,
Wagged all their heads in concert and
    smiled as courtiers should.

The gray lark sings o'er Vordingborg,
    and on the ancient town
From the tall tower of Valdemar the
    Golden Goose looks down :
The yellow grain is waving in the pleas-
    ant wind of morn,
The wood resounds with cry of hounds
    and blare of hunter's horn.

In the garden of her father little Elsie
    sits and spins,
And, singing with the early birds, her
    daily task begins.
Gay tulips bloom and sweet mint curls
    around her garden-bower,
But she is sweeter than the mint and
    fairer than the flower.

About her form her kirtle blue clings
    lovingly, and, white
As snow, her loose sleeves only leave
    her small, round wrists in sight ;
Below the modest petticoat can only half
    conceal
The motion of the lightest foot that ever
    turned a wheel.

The cat sits purring at her side, bees
    hum in sunshine warm ;
But, look ! she starts, she lifts her face,
    she shades it with her arm.

* A common saying of Valdemar; hence his
sobriquet *Atterday*.

And, hark ! a train of horsemen, with
    sound of dog and horn,
Come leaping o'er the ditches, come
    trampling down the corn !

Merrily rang the bridle-reins, and scarf
    and plume streamed gay,
As fast beside her father's gate the riders
    held their way ;
And one was brave in scarlet cloak, with
    golden spur on heel,
And, as he checked his foaming steed,
    the maiden checked her wheel.

" All hail among thy roses, the fairest
    rose to me !
For weary months in secret my heart
    has longed for thee ! "
What noble knight was this? What
    words for modest maiden's ear?
She dropped a lowly courtesy of bashful-
    ness and fear.

She lifted up her spinning-wheel; she
    fain would seek the door,
Trembling in every limb, her cheek with
    blushes crimsoned o'er.
" Nay, fear me not," the rider said, " I
    offer heart and hand,
Bear witness these good Danish knights
    who round about me stand.

" I grant you time to think of this, to
    answer as you may,
For to-morrow, little Elsie, shall bring
    another day."
He spake the old phrase slyly as, glan-
    cing round his train,
He saw his merry followers seek to hide
    their smiles in vain.

" The snow of pearls I 'll scatter in your
    curls of golden hair,
I 'll line with furs the velvet of the kirtle
    that you wear;
All precious gems shall twine your neck ;
    and in a chariot gay
You shall ride, my little Elsie, behind
    four steeds of gray.

" And harps shall sound, and flutes shall
    play, and brazen lamps shall glow;
On marble floors your feet shall weave
    the dances to and fro.
At frosty eventide for us the blazing
    hearth shall shine,
While, at our ease, we play at draughts,
    and drink the blood-red wine."

Then Elsie raised h
    wooer face t⸱
A roguish smile sh⸱
    her lip foun⸱
Back from her lo⸱
    curls of gold
And lifted up her ⸱
    clear and bl⸱

" I am a lowly pe⸱
    lant knight⸱
I will not trust a
    cool and tur⸱
If you would wed
    peasant, not
I bid you hang up⸱
    and trusty s⸱

" To please you, ⸱
    Dynadel aw⸱
And in its place ⸱
    and mow yo⸱
" Nay, but your
    my eyes can
A Vadmal coat, so
    that you mu⸱

" Well, Vadmal ⸱
    the rider ga⸱
" And on the Lord
    my scarlet c⸱
" But mark," she s⸱
    my peasant⸱
A yoke of steers b⸱
    that he mus⸱

The knight looked
    " Well, let ⸱
No other man mus
    has been ba⸱
Henceforth I 'll tre
    my oxen tal⸱
If only little Elsie⸱
    walk."

" You must take
    cask of wine
The homely mead⸱
    a peasant-m⸱
" Most willingly,⸱
    that mead of
And leave my min⸱
    to drain my

" Now break your
    shatter sign
Unmeet for peasan⸱
    knightly kn⸱

And pull me down your castle from top
    to basement wall,
And let your plough trace furrows in the
    ruins of your hall!"

Then smiled he with a lofty pride;
    right well at last he knew
The maiden of the spinning-wheel was
    to her troth-plight true.
"Ah, roguish little Elsie! you act your
    part full well:
You know that I must bear my shield
    and in my castle dwell!

"The lions ramping on that shield be-
    tween the hearts aflame
Keep watch o'er Denmark's honor, and
    guard her ancient name.
For know that I am Volmer; I dwell in
    yonder towers,
Who ploughs them ploughs up Denmark,
    this goodly home of ours!

"I tempt no more, fair Elsie! your heart
    I know is true;
Would God that all our maidens were
    good and pure as you!
Well have you pleased your monarch,
    and he shall well repay;
God's peace! Farewell! To-morrow will
    bring another day!"

He lifted up his bridle hand, he spurred
    his good steed then,
And like a whirl-blast swept away with
    all his gallant men.
The steel hoofs beat the rocky path;
    again on winds of morn
The wood resounds with cry of hounds
    and blare of hunter's horn.

"Thou true and ever faithful!" the
    listening Henrik cried;
And, leaping o'er the green hedge, he
    stood by Elsie's side.
None saw the fond embracing, save,
    shining from afar,
The Golden Goose that watched them
    from the tower of Valdemar.

O darling girls of Denmark! of all the
    flowers that throng
Her vales of spring the fairest, I sing for
    you my song

No praise as yours so bravely rewards
    the singer's skill;
Thank God! of maids like Elsie the land
    has plenty still!

THE THREE BELLS.

BENEATH the low-hung night cloud
    That raked her splintering mast
The good ship settled slowly,
    The cruel leak gained fast.

Over the awful ocean
    Her signal guns pealed out.
Dear God! was that thy answer
    From the horror round about?

A voice came down the wild wind,
    "Ho! ship ahoy!" its cry:
"Our stout Three Bells of Glasgow
    Shall lay till daylight by!"

Hour after hour crept slowly,
    Yet on the heaving swells
Tossed up and down the ship-lights,
    The lights of the Three Bells!

And ship to ship made signals,
    Man answered back to man,
While oft, to cheer and hearten,
    The Three Bells nearer ran;

And the captain from her taffrail
    Sent down his hopeful cry.
"Take heart! Hold on!" he shouted,
    "The Three Bells shall lay by!'

All night across the waters
    The tossing lights shone clear;
All night from reeling taffrail
    The Three Bells sent her cheer.

And when the dreary watches
    Of storm and darkness passed,
Just as the wreck lurched under,
    All souls were saved at last.

Sail on, Three Bells, forever,
    In grateful memory sail!
Ring on, Three Bells of rescue,
    Above the wave and gale!

Type of the Love eternal,
    Repeat the Master's cry,
As tossing through our darkness
    The lights of God draw nigh!

HAZEL BLOSSOMS.

NOTE. — I have ventured, in compliance with the desire of dear friends of my beloved sister ELIZABETH H. WHITTIER, to add to this little volume the few poetical pieces which she left behind her. As she was very distrustful of her own powers, and altogether without ambition for literary distinction, she shunned everything like publicity, and found far greater happiness in generous appreciation of the gifts of her friends than in the cultivation of her own. Yet it has always seemed to me, that had her health, sense of duty and fitness, and her extreme self-distrust permitted, she might have taken a high place among lyrical singers. These poems, with perhaps two or three exceptions, afford but slight indications of the inward life of the writer, who had an almost morbid dread of spiritual and intellectual egotism, or of her tenderness of sympathy, chastened mirthfulness, and pleasant play of thought and fancy, when her shy, beautiful soul opened like a flower in the warmth of social communion. In the lines on Dr. Kane her friends will see something of her fine individuality, — the rare mingling of delicacy and intensity of feeling which made her dear to them. This little poem reached Cuba while the great explorer lay on his death-bed, and we are told that he listened with grateful tears while it was read to him by his mother.

I am tempted to say more, but I write as under the eye of her who, while with us, shrank with painful deprecation from the praise or mention of performances which seemed so far below her ideal of excellence. To those who best knew her, the beloved circle of her intimate friends, I dedicate this slight memorial.

J. G. W.

AMESBURY, 9th mo., 1874.

THE summer warmth has left the sky,
The summer songs have died away;
And, withered, in the footpaths lie
The fallen leaves, but yesterday
With ruby and with topaz gay.

The grass is browning on the hills;
No pale, belated flowers recall
The astral fringes of the rills,
And drearily the dead vines fall,
Frost-blackened, from the roadside wall.

Yet through the gray and sombre wood,
Against the dusk of fir and pine,
Last of their floral sisterhood,
The hazel's yellow blossoms shine,
The tawny gold of Afric's mine!

Small beauty hath my unsung flower,
For spring to own or summer hail;
But, in the season's saddest hour,
To skies that weep and winds that wail
Its glad surprisals never fail.

O days grown cold! O life grown old!
No rose of June may bloom again;
But, like the hazel's twisted gold,

Through early frost and latter rain
Shall hints of summer-time remain.

And as within the hazel's bough
A gift of mystic virtue dwells,
That points to golden ores below,
And in dry desert places tells
Where flow unseen the cool, sweet wells,

So, in the wise Diviner's hand,
Be mine the hazel's grateful part
To feel, beneath a thirsty land,
The living waters thrill and start,
The beating of the rivulet's heart!

Sufficeth me the gift to light
With latest bloom the dark, cold days;
To call some hidden spring to sight
That, in these dry and dusty ways,
Shall sing its pleasant song of praise.

O Love! the hazel-wand may fail,
But thou canst lend the surer spell,
That, passing over Baca's vale,
Repeats the old-time miracle,
And makes the desert-land a well.

SUMNER.

"I am not one who has disgraced beauty of sentiment by deformity of conduct, or the maxims of a freeman by the actions of a slave; but, by the grace of God, I have kept my life unsullied." — MILTON's *Defence of the People of England.*

O MOTHER STATE! — the winds of March
  Blew chill o'er Auburn's Field of God,
Where, slow, beneath a leaden arch
  Of sky, thy mourning children trod.

And now, with all thy woods in leaf,
  Thy fields in flower, beside thy dead
Thou sittest, in thy robes of grief,
  A Rachel yet uncomforted!

And once again the organ swells,
  Once more the flag is half-way hung,
And yet again the mournful bells
  In all thy steeple-towers are rung.

And I, obedient to thy will,
  Have come a simple wreath to lay,
Superfluous, on a grave that still
  Is sweet with all the flowers of May.

I take, with awe, the task assigned;
  It may be that my friend might miss,
In his new sphere of heart and mind,
  Some token from my hand in this.

By many a tender memory moved,
  Along the past my thought I send;
The record of the cause he loved
  Is the best record of its friend.

No trumpet sounded in his ear,
  He saw not Sinai's cloud and flame,
But never yet to Hebrew seer
  A clearer voice of duty came.

God said: "Break thou these yokes; undo
  These heavy burdens. I ordain
A work to last thy whole life through,
  A ministry of strife and pain.

"Forego thy dreams of lettered ease,
  Put thou the scholar's promise by,
The rights of man are more than these."
  He heard, and answered: "Here am I!"

He set his face against the blast,
  His feet against the flinty shard,

Till the hard service grew, at last,
  Its own exceeding great reward.

Lifted like Saul's above the crowd,
  Upon his kingly forehead fell
The first, sharp bolt of Slavery's cloud,
  Launched at the truth he urged so well.

Ah! never yet, at rack or stake,
  Was sorer loss made Freedom's gain,
Than his, who suffered for her sake
  The beak-torn Titan's lingering pain!

The fixed star of his faith, through all
  Loss, doubt, and peril, shone the same;
As through a night of storm, some tall,
  Strong lighthouse lifts its steady flame.

Beyond the dust and smoke he saw
  The sheaves of freedom's large in-
    crease,
The holy fanes of equal law,
  The New Jerusalem of peace.

The weak might fear, the worldling
  mock,
  The faint and blind of heart regret;
All knew at last th' eternal rock
  On which his forward feet were set.

The subtlest scheme of compromise
  Was folly to his purpose bold;
The strongest mesh of party lies
  Weak to the simplest truth he told.

One language held his heart and lip,
  Straight onward to his goal he trod,
And proved the highest statesmanship
  Obedience to the voice of God.

No wail was in his voice, — none heard,
  When treason's storm-cloud blackest
    grew,
The weakness of a doubtful word;
  His duty, and the end, he knew.

The first to smite, the first to spare;
  When once the hostile ensigns fell,

He stretched out hands of generous care
　To lift the foe he fought so well.

For there was nothing base or small
　Or craven in his soul's broad plan ;
Forgiving all things personal,
　He hated only wrong to man.

The old traditions of his State,
　The memories of her great and good,
Took from his life a fresher date,
　And in himself embodied stood.

How felt the greed of gold and place,
　The venal crew that schemed and
　　planned,
The fine scorn of that haughty face,
　The spurning of that bribeless hand !

If than Rome's tribunes statelier
　He wore his senatorial robe,
His lofty port was all for her,
　The one dear spot on all the globe.

If to the master's plea he gave
　The vast contempt his manhood felt,
He saw a brother in the slave, —
　With man as equal man he dealt.

Proud was he ?　If his presence kept
　Its grandeur wheresoe'er he trod,
As if from Plutarch's gallery stepped
　The hero and the demigod,

None failed, at least, to reach his ear,
　Nor want nor woe appealed in vain ;
The homesick soldier knew his cheer,
　And blessed him from his ward of
　　pain.

Safely his dearest friends may own
　The slight defects he never hid,
The surface-blemish in the stone
　Of the tall, stately pyramid.

Suffice it that he never brought
　His conscience to the public mart ;
But lived himself the truth he taught,
　White-souled, clean-handed, pure of
　　heart.

What if he felt the natural pride
　Of power in noble use, too true
With thin humilities to hide
　The work he did, the lore he knew ?

Was he not just ?　Was any wronged
　By that assured self-estimate ?

He took but what
　Unenvious of an

Well might he hee
　And scan with c
Through which he
　　wake
The hearts of in

Ah ! who shall bla
　He solaced thus
Should not the o'e
　And hold to ligh

No sense of humor
　On the hard wa_
Small play of fanc
　He spake alone

He loved his book
　A beauty veiled
The graver's line,
　The chisel's sha

He cherished, void
　The social court
And sweeten life,
　With most unw

But still his tired
　The glad relief b
Her mountain rang
　His current of p

The sea rolled cho
　Three-banked li
　　reme,
With laboring oa
　　beach
　Were Forum and

The sensuous joy f
　His strenuous be
And left from yout
　Few hours for pl

For all his life was
　O Nature, make
Train all thy flowe
　And make th_
　　friends !

Revive again, thou
　The broken turf
Breathe, summer
　　strain
　Of low, sweet m_

With calm and beauty symbolize
  The peace which follows long annoy,
And lend our earth-bent, mourning eyes
  Some hint of his diviner joy.

For safe with right and truth he is,
  As God lives he must live alway ;
There is no end for souls like his,
  No night for children of the day !

Nor cant nor poor solicitudes
  Made weak his life's great argument ;
Small leisure his for frames and moods
  Who followed Duty where she went.

The broad, fair fields of God he saw
  Beyond the bigot's narrow bound ;
The truths he moulded into law
  In Christ's beatitudes he found.

His State-craft was the Golden Rule,
  His right of vote a sacred trust ;
Clear, over threat and ridicule,
  All heard his challenge : "Is it just ?"

And when the hour supreme had come,
  Not for himself a thought he gave ;
In that last pang of martyrdom,
  His care was for the half-freed slave.

Not vainly dusky hands upbore,
  In prayer, the passing soul to heaven

Whose mercy to His suffering poor
  Was service to the Master given.

Long shall the good State's annals tell,
  Her children's children long be taught,
How, praised or blamed, he guarded well
  The trust he neither shunned nor
    sought.

If for one moment turned thy face,
  O Mother, from thy son, not long
He waited calmly in his place
  The sure remorse which follows wrong.

Forgiven be the State he loved
  The one brief lapse, the single blot ;
Forgotten be the stain removed,
  Her righted record shows it not !

The lifted sword above her shield
  With jealous care shall guard his fame ;
The pine-tree on her ancient field
  To all the winds shall speak his name.

The marble image of her son
  Her loving hands shall yearly crown,
And from her pictured Pantheon
  His grand, majestic face look down.

O State so passing rich before,
  Who now shall doubt thy highest claim ?
The world that counts thy jewels o'er
  Shall longest pause at SUMNER's name !

HAZEL BLOSSOMS.

THE PRAYER OF AGASSIZ.

ON the isle of Penikese,
Ringed about by sapphire seas,
Fanned by breezes salt and cool,
Stood the Master with his school.
Over sails that not in vain
Wooed the west-wind's steady strain,
Line of coast that low and far
Stretched its undulating bar,
Wings aslant along the rim
Of the waves they stooped to skim,
Rock and isle and glistening bay,
Fell the beautiful white day.
Said the Master to the youth :
"We have come in search of truth,

Trying with uncertain key
Door by door of mystery ;
We are reaching, through His laws,
To the garment-hem of Cause,
Him, the endless, unbegun,
The Unnamable, the One
Light of all our light the Source,
Life of life, and Force of force.
As with fingers of the blind,
We are groping here to find
What the hieroglyphics mean
Of the Unseen in the seen,
What the Thought which underlies
Nature's masking and disguise,
What it is that hides beneath
Blight and bloom and birth and death.

By past efforts unavailing,
Doubt and error, loss and failing,
Of our weakness made aware,
On the threshold of our task
Let us light and guidance ask,
Let us pause in silent prayer!"

Then the Master in his place
Bowed his head a little space,
And the leaves by soft airs stirred,
Lapse of wave and cry of bird
Left the solemn hush unbroken
Of that wordless prayer unspoken,
While its wish, on earth unsaid,
Rose to heaven interpreted.
As, in life's best hours, we hear
By the spirit's finer ear
His low voice within us, thus
The All-Father heareth us ;
And his holy ear we pain
With our noisy words and vain.
Not for Him our violence
Storming at the gates of sense,
His the primal language, his
The eternal silences !

Even the careless heart was moved,
And the doubting gave assent,
With a gesture reverent,
To the Master well-beloved.
As thin mists are glorified
By the light they cannot hide,
All who gazed upon him saw,
Through its veil of tender awe,
How his face was still uplit
By the old sweet look of it,
Hopeful, trustful, full of cheer,
And the love that casts out fear.
Who the secret may declare
Of that brief, unuttered prayer?
Did the shade before him come
Of th' inevitable doom,
Of the end of earth so near,
And Eternity's new year ?

In the lap of sheltering seas
Rests the isle of Penikese ;
But the lord of the domain
Comes not to his own again :
Where the eyes that follow fail,
On a vaster sea his sail
Drifts beyond our beck and hail.
Other lips within its bound
Shall the laws of life expound ;
Other eyes from rock and shell
Read the world's old riddles well :
But when breezes light and bland

Blow from Summer's blossomed land,
When the air is glad with wings,
And the blithe song-sparrow sings,
Many an eye with his still face
Shall the living ones displace,
Many an ear the word shall seek
He alone could fitly speak.
And one name forevermore
Shall be uttered o'er and o'er
By the waves that kiss the shore,
By the curlew's whistle sent
Down the cool, sea-scented air;
In all voices known to her,
Nature owns her worshipper,
Half in triumph, half lament.
Thither Love shall tearful turn,
Friendship pause uncovered there,
And the wisest reverence learn
From the Master's silent prayer.

THE FRIEND'S BURIAL.

My thoughts are all in yonder town,
  Where, wept by many tears,
To-day my mother's friend lays down
  The burden of her years.

True as in life, no poor disguise
  Of death with her is seen,
And on her simple casket lies
  No wreath of bloom and green.

O, not for her the florist's art,
  The mocking weeds of woe,
Dear memories in each mourner's heart
  Like heaven's white lilies blow.

And all about the softening air
  Of new-born sweetness tells,
And the ungathered May-flowers wear
  The tints of ocean shells.

The old, assuring miracle
  Is fresh as heretofore ;
And earth takes up its parable
  Of life from death once more.

Here organ-swell and church-bell toll
  Methinks but discord were, —
The prayerful silence of the soul
  Is best befitting her.

No sound should break the quietude
  Alike of earth and sky ; —
O wandering wind in Seabrook wood,
  Breathe but a half-heard sigh !

Sing softly, spring-bird, for her sake ;
  And thou not distant sea,
Lapse lightly as if Jesus spake,
  And thou wert Galilee !

For all her quiet life flowed on
  As meadow streamlets flow,
Where fresher green reveals alone
  The noiseless ways they go.

From her loved place of prayer I see
  The plain-robed mourners pass,
With slow feet treading reverently
  The graveyard's springing grass.

Make room, O mourning ones, for me,
  Where, like the friends of Paul,
That you no more her face shall see
  You sorrow most of all.

Her path shall brighten more and more
  Unto the perfect day ;
She cannot fail of peace who bore
  Such peace with her away.

O sweet, calm face that seemed to wear
  The look of sins forgiven !
O voice of prayer that seemed to bear
  Our own needs up to heaven !

How reverent in our midst she stood,
  Or knelt in grateful praise !
What grace of Christian womanhood
  Was in her household ways !

For still her holy living meant
  No duty left undone ;
The heavenly and the human blent
  Their kindred loves in one.

And if her life small leisure found
  For feasting ear and eye,
And Pleasure, on her daily round,
  She passed unpausing by,

Yet with her went a secret sense
  Of all things sweet and fair,
And Beauty's gracious providence
  Refreshed her unaware.

She kept her line of rectitude
  With love's unconscious ease ;
Her kindly instincts understood
  All gentle courtesies.

An inborn charm of graciousness
  Made sweet her smile and tone,

And glorified her farm-wife dress
  With beauty not its own.

The dear Lord's best interpreters
  Are humble human souls ;
The Gospel of a life like hers
  Is more than books or scrolls.

From scheme and creed the light goes
    out,
  The saintly fact survives ;
The blessed Master none can doubt
  Revealed in holy lives.

JOHN UNDERHILL.

A SCORE of years had come and gone
Since the Pilgrims landed on Plymouth
    stone,
When Captain Underhill, bearing scars
From Indian ambush and Flemish wars,
Left three-hilled Boston and wandered
    down,
East by north, to Cocheco town.

With Vane the younger, in counsel
    sweet
He had sat at Anna Hutchinson's feet,
And, when the bolt of banishment fell
On the head of his saintly oracle,
He had shared her ill as her good report,
And braved the wrath of the General
    Court.

He shook from his feet as he rode away
The dust of the Massachusetts Bay.
The world might bless and the world
    might ban,
What did it matter the perfect man,
To whom the freedom of earth was
    given,
Proof against sin, and sure of heaven ?

He cheered his heart as he rode along
With screed of Scripture and holy song,
Or thought how he rode with his lances
    free
By the Lower Rhine and the Zuyder-
    Zee,
Till his wood-path grew to a trodden
    road,
And Hilton Point in the distance
    showed.

He saw the church with the block-
house nigh,
The two fair rivers, the flakes thereby,
And, tacking to windward, low and
crank,
The little shallop from Strawberry
Bank;
And he rose in his stirrups and looked
abroad
Over land and water, and praised the
Lord.

Goodly and stately and grave to see,
Into the clearing's space rode he,
With the sun on the hilt of his sword
in sheath,
And his silver buckles and spurs be-
neath,
And the settlers welcomed him, one and
all,
From swift Quampeagan to Gonic Fall.

And he said to the elders: " Lo, I come
As the way seemed open to seek a home.
Somewhat the Lord hath wrought by
my hands
In the Narragansett and Netherlands,
And if here ye have work for a Chris-
tian man,
I will tarry, and serve ye as best I can.

"I boast not of gifts, but fain would
own
The wonderful favor God hath shown,
The special mercy vouchsafed one day
On the shore of Narragansett Bay,
As I sat, with my pipe, from the camp
aside,
And mused like Isaac at eventide.

" A sudden sweetness of peace I found,
A garment of gladness wrapped me
round;
I felt from the law of works released,
The strife of the flesh and spirit ceased,
My faith to a full assurance grew,
And all I had hoped for myself I knew.

"Now, as God appointeth, I keep my
way,
I shall not stumble, I shall not stray;
He hath taken away my fig-leaf dress,
I wear the robe of his righteousness;
And the shafts of Satan no more avail
Than Pequot arrows on Christian mail."

"Tarry with us," t
"Thou man of G
guide."
And Captain Unde
"The will of the L
And the morrow be
In the ruler's seat

And he judged tl
should;
His words were w
good;
He coveted not his
From the holding
hand;
And through the
ran
A wholesome fear

But the heart is de
saith,
And life hath over
Through hymns of
calls,
And whoso thinke
Alas! ere their rou
There was grief in
man.

The tempter's arro
Had found the joint
And men took not
The shame in his
prayer,
The signs of a batt
The pain of a soul

Then a whisper o
name
With broken vows
And the people loo
As he walked an
grim,
Ill at ease, and bit
And prompt of q
sword.

None knew how, w
still,
He strove in the b
But he shook hi
length,
And girded anew l
And bade the crier
And call together

Jeer and murmur and shaking of head
Ceased as he rose in his place and said :
"Men, brethren, and fathers, well ye
    know
How I came among you a year ago,
Strong in the faith that my soul was
    freed
From sin of feeling, or thought, or deed.

"I have sinned, I own it with grief and
    shame,
But not with a lie on my lips I came.
In my blindness I verily thought my
    heart
Swept and garnished in every part.
He chargeth His angels with folly; He
    sees
The heavens unclean. Was I more than
    these ?

"I urge no plea. At your feet I lay
The trust you gave me, and go my way.
Hate me or pity me, as you will,
The Lord will have mercy on sinners
    still ;
And I, who am chiefest, say to all,
Watch and pray, lest ye also fall."

No voice made answer : a sob so low
That only his quickened ear could know
Smote his heart with a bitter pain,
As into the forest he rode again,
And the veil of its oaken leaves shut
    down
On his latest glimpse of Cocheco town.

Crystal-clear on the man of sin
The streams flashed up, and the sky
    shone in ;
On his cheek of fever the cool wind blew,
The leaves dropped on him their tears
    of dew,
And angels of God, in the pure, sweet
    guise
Of flowers, looked on him with sad sur-
    prise.

Was his ear at fault that brook and
    breeze
Sang in their saddest of minor keys ?
What was it the mournful wood-thrush
    said ?
What whispered the pine-trees overhead ?
Did he hear the Voice on his lonely way
That Adam heard in the cool of day ?

Into the desert alone rode he,
Alone with the Infinite Purity ;

And, bowing his soul to its tender rebuke,
As Peter did to the Master's look,
He measured his path with prayers of
    pain
For peace with God and nature again.

And in after years to Cocheco came
The bruit of a once familiar name ;
How among the Dutch of New Nether-
    lands,
From wild Danskamer to Haarlem sands,
A penitent soldier preached the Word,
And smote the heathen with Gideon's
    sword !

And the heart of Boston was glad to hear
How he harried the foe on the long
    frontier,
And heaped on the land against him
    barred
The coals of his generous watch and ward.
Frailest and bravest ! the Bay State still
Counts with her worthies John Underhill.

IN QUEST.

HAVE I not voyaged, friend beloved,
    with thee
On the great waters of the unsounded
    sea,
Momently listening with suspended oar
For the low rote of waves upon a shore
Changeless as heaven, where never fog-
    cloud drifts
Over its windless woods, nor mirage lifts
The steadfast hills; where never birds
    of doubt
Sing to mislead, and every dream dies
    out,
And the dark riddles which perplex us
    here
In the sharp solvent of its light are clear ?
Thou knowest how vain our quest ; how,
    soon or late,
The baffling tides and circles of debate
Swept back our bark unto its starting-
    place,
Where, looking forth upon the blank,
    gray space,
And roundabout us seeing, with sad eyes,
The same old difficult hills and cloud-
    cold skies,
We said : "This outward search availeth
    not

To find Him.   He is farther than we
  thought,
Or, haply, nearer.   To this very spot
Whereon we wait, this commonplace of
  home,
As to the well of Jacob, He may come
And tell us all things."   As I listened
  there,
Through the expectant silences of prayer,
Somewhat I seemed to hear, which hath
  to me
Been hope, strength, comfort, and I give
  it thee.

"The riddle of the world is understood
Only by him who feels that God is good,
As only he can feel who makes his love
The ladder of his faith, and climbs above
On th' rounds of his best instincts;
  draws no line
Between mere human goodness and di-
  vine,
But, judging God by what in him is best,
With a child's trust leans on a Father's
  breast,
And hears unmoved the old creeds bab-
  ble still
Of kingly power and dread caprice of
  will,
Chary of blessing, prodigal of curse,
The pitiless doomsman of the universe.
Can Hatred ask for love?   Can Selfish-
  ness
Invite to self-denial?   Is He less
Than man in kindly dealing?   Can He
  break
His own great law of fatherhood, forsake
And curse His children?   Not for earth
  and heaven
Can separate tables of the law be given.
No rule can bind which He himself de-
  nies;
The truths of time are not eternal lies."

So heard I; and the chaos round me
  spread
To light and order grew; and, "Lord,"
  I said,
"Our sins are our tormentors, worst of
  all
Felt in distrustful shame that dares not
  call
Upon Thee as our Father.   We have set
A strange god up, but Thou remainest
  yet.
All that I feel of pity Thou hast known
Before I was; my best is all Thy own.

From Thy great heart of goodness mine
  but drew
Wishes and prayers; but Thou, O Lord,
  wilt do,
In Thy own time, by ways I cannot see,
All that I feel when I am nearest Thee!"

A SEA DREAM.

WE saw the slow tides go and come,
  The curving surf-lines lightly drawn,
The gray rocks touched with tender
    bloom
  Beneath the fresh-blown rose of dawn.

We saw in richer sunsets lost
  The sombre pomp of showery noons;
And signalled spectral sails that crossed
  The weird, low light of rising moons.

On stormy eves from cliff and head
  We saw the white spray tossed and
    spurned;
While over all, in gold and red,
  Its face of fire the lighthouse turned.

The rail-car brought its daily crowds,
  Half curious, half indifferent,
Like passing sails or floating clouds,
  We saw them as they came and went.

But, one calm morning, as we lay
  And watched the mirage-lifted wall
Of coast, across the dreamy bay,
  And heard afar the curlew call,

And nearer voices, wild or tame,
  Of airy flock and childish throng,
Up from the water's edge there came
  Faint snatches of familiar song.

Careless we heard the singer's choice
  Of old and common airs; at last
The tender pathos of his voice
  In one low chanson held us fast.

A song that mingled joy and pain,
  And memories old and sadly sweet;
While, timing to its minor strain,
  The waves in lapsing cadence beat.

_____

The waves are glad in breeze and sun;
  The rocks are fringed with foam;

I walk once more a haunted shore,
  A stranger, yet at home, —
  A land of dreams I roam.

Is this the wind, the soft sea-wind
  That stirred thy locks of brown ?
Are these the rocks whose mosses knew
  The trail of thy light gown,
  Where boy and girl sat down ?

I see the gray fort's broken wall,
  The boats that rock below ;
And, out at sea, the passing sails
  We saw so long ago
  Rose-red in morning's glow.

The freshness of the early time
  On every breeze is blown ;
As glad the sea, as blue the sky, —
  The change is ours alone ;
  The saddest is my own.

A stranger now, a world-worn man,
  Is he who bears my name ;
But thou, methinks, whose mortal life
  Immortal youth became,
  Art evermore the same.

Thou art not here, thou art not there,
  Thy place I cannot see ;
I only know that where thou art
  The blessed angels be,
  And heaven is glad for thee.

Forgive me if the evil years
  Have left on me their sign ;
Wash out, O soul so beautiful,
  The many stains of mine
  In tears of love divine !

I could not look on thee and live,
  If thou wert by my side ;
The vision of a shining one,
  The white and heavenly bride,
  Is well to me denied.

But turn to me thy dear girl-face
  Without the angel's crown,
The wedded roses of thy lips,
  Thy loose hair rippling down
  In waves of golden brown.

Look forth once more through space and
    time,
  And let thy sweet shade fall
In tenderest grace of soul and form

On memory's frescoed wall.
  A shadow, and yet all !

Draw near, more near, forever dear !
  Where'er I rest or roam,
Or in the city's crowded streets,
  Or by the blown sea foam,
  The thought of thee is home !

At breakfast hour the singer read
  The city news, with comment wise,
Like one who felt the pulse of trade
  Beneath his finger fall and rise.

His look, his air, his curt speech, told
  The man of action, not of books,
To whom the corners made in gold
  And stocks were more than seaside
    nooks.

Of life beneath the life confessed
  His song had hinted unawares ;
Of flowers in traffic's ledgers pressed,
  Of human hearts in bulls and bears.

But eyes in vain were turned to watch
  That face so hard and shrewd and
    strong ;
And ears in vain grew sharp to catch
  The meaning of that morning song.

In vain some sweet-voiced querist sought
  To sound him, leaving as she came ;
Her baited album only caught
  A common, unromantic name.

No word betrayed the mystery fine,
  That trembled on the singer's tongue ;
He came and went, and left no sign
  Behind him save the song he sung.

A MYSTERY.

The river hemmed with leaning trees
  Wound through its meadows green ;
A low, blue line of mountains showed
  The open pines between.

One sharp, tall peak above them all
  Clear into sunlight sprang :
I saw the river of my dreams,
  The mountains that I sang !

No clew of memory led me on,
But well the ways I knew;
A feeling of familiar things
With every footstep grew.

Not otherwise above its crag
Could lean the blasted pine;
Not otherwise the maple hold
Aloft its red ensign.

So up the long and shorn foot-hills
The mountain road should creep;
So, green and low, the meadow fold
Its red-haired kine asleep.

The river wound as it should wind;
Their place the mountains took;
The white torn fringes of their clouds
Wore no unwonted look.

Yet ne'er before that river's rim
Was pressed by feet of mine,
Never before mine eyes had crossed
That broken mountain line.

A presence, strange at once and known,
Walked with me as my guide;
The skirts of some forgotten life
Trailed noiseless at my side.

Was it a dim-remembered dream?
Or glimpse through æons old?
The secret which the mountains kept
The river never told.

But from the vision ere it passed
A tender hope I drew,
And, pleasant as a dawn of spring,
The thought within me grew,

That love would temper every change,
And soften all surprise,
And, misty with the dreams of earth,
The hills of Heaven arise.

CONDUCTOR BRADLEY.

CONDUCTOR BRADLEY, (always may his
name
Be said with reverence!) as the swift
doom came,
Smitten to death, a crushed and mangled
frame,

Sank, with the brake he grasped just
where he stood
To do the utmost that a brave man
could,
And die, if needful, as a true man should.

Men stooped above him; women dropped
their tears
On that poor wreck beyond all hopes or
fears,
Lost in the strength and glory of his
years.

What heard they? Lo! the ghastly lips
of pain,
Dead to all thought save duty's, moved
again:
"Put out the signals for the other
train!"

No nobler utterance since the world
began
From lips of saint or martyr ever ran,
Electric, through the sympathies of man.

Ah me! how poor and noteless seem to
this
The sick-bed dramas of self-conscious-
ness,
Our sensual fears of pain and hopes of
bliss!

O, grand, supreme endeavor! Not in
vain
That last brave act of failing tongue and
brain!
Freighted with life the downward rushing train,

Following the wrecked one, as wave follows wave,
Obeyed the warning which the dead lips
gave.
Others he saved, himself he could not
save.

Nay, the lost life *was* saved. He is not
dead
Who in his record still the earth shall
tread
With God's clear aureole shining round
his head.

We bow as in the dust, with all our pride
Of virtue dwarfed the noble deed beside.
God give us grace to live as Bradley died!

CHILD-SONGS.

STILL linger in our noon of time
And on our Saxon tongue
The echoes of the home-born hymns
The Aryan mothers sung.

And childhood had its litanies
In every age and clime ;
The earliest cradles of the race
Were rocked to poet's rhyme.

Nor sky, nor wave, nor tree, nor flower,
Nor green earth's virgin sod,
So moved the singer's heart of old
As these small ones of God.

The mystery of unfolding life
Was more than dawning morn,
Than opening flower or crescent moon
The human soul new-born !

And still to childhood's sweet appeal
The heart of genius turns,
And more than all the sages teach
From lisping voices learns, —

The voices loved of him who sang,
Where Tweed and Teviot glide,
That sound to-day on all the winds
That blow from Rydal-side, —

Heard in the Teuton's household songs,
And folk-lore of the Finn,
Where'er to holy Christmas hearths
The Christ-child enters in !

Before life's sweetest mystery still
The heart in reverence kneels ;
The wonder of the primal birth
The latest mother feels.

We need love's tender lessons taught
As only weakness can ;
God hath his small interpreters ;
The child must teach the man.

We wander wide through evil years,
Our eyes of faith grow dim ;
But he is freshest from His hands
And nearest unto Him !

And haply, pleading long with Him
For sin-sick hearts and cold,
The angels of our childhood still
The Father's face behold.

Of such the kingdom ! — Teach thou us,
O Master most divine,
To feel the deep significance
Of these wise words of thine !

The haughty eye shall seek in vain
What innocence beholds ;
No cunning finds the key of heaven,
No strength its gate unfolds.

Alone to guilelessness and love
That gate shall open fall ;
The mind of pride is nothingness,
The childlike heart is all !

THE GOLDEN WEDDING OF LONGWOOD.

WITH fifty years between you and your
well-kept wedding vow,
The Golden Age, old friends of mine, is
not a fable now.

And, sweet as has life's vintage been
through all your pleasant past,
Still, as at Cana's marriage-feast, the
best wine is the last !

Again before me, with your names, fair
Chester's landscape comes,
Its meadows, woods, and ample barns,
and quaint, stone-builded homes.

The smooth-shorn vales, the wheaten
slopes, the boscage green and soft,
Of which their poet sings so well from
towered Cedarcroft.

And lo ! from all the country-side come
neighbors, kith and kin ;
From city, hamlet, farm-house old, the
wedding guests come in.

And they who, without scrip or purse,
mob-hunted, travel-worn,
In Freedom's age of martyrs came, as
victors now return.

Older and slower, yet the same, files in
the long array,
And hearts are light and eyes are glad,
though heads are badger-gray.

The fire-tried men of Thirty-eight who
saw with me the fall,
Midst roaring flames and shouting mob,
of Pennsylvania Hall ;

And they of Lancaster who turned the
  cheeks of tyrants pale,
Singing of freedom through the grates
  of Moyamensing jail !

And haply with them, all unseen, old
  comrades, gone before,
Pass, silently as shadows pass, within
  your open door, —

The eagle face of Lindley Coates, brave
  Garrett's daring zeal,
The Christian grace of Pennock, the
  steadfast heart of Neal.

Ah me ! beyond all power to name, the
  worthies tried and true,
Grave men, fair women, youth and maid,
  pass by in hushed review.

Of varying faiths, a common cause fused
  all their hearts in one.
God give them now, whate'er their
  names, the peace of duty done !

How gladly would I tread again the old-
  remembered places,
Sit down beside your hearth once more
  and look in the dear old faces !

And thank you for the lessons your fifty
  years are teaching,
For honest lives that louder speak than
  half our noisy preaching ;

For your steady faith and courage in
  that dark and evil time,
When the Golden Rule was treason, and
  to feed the hungry, crime ;

For the poor slave's house of refuge when
  the hounds were on his track,
And saint and sinner, church and state,
  joined hands to send him back.

Blessings upon you ! — What you did
  for each sad, suffering one,
So homeless, faint, and naked, unto our
  Lord was done !

Fair fall on Kennett's pleasant vales and
  Longwood's bowery ways
The mellow sunset of your lives, friends
  of my early days.

May many more of quiet years be added
  to your sum,
And, late at last, in tenderest love, the
  beckoning angel come.

Dear hearts are here, dear hearts are
  there, alike below, above ;
Our friends are now in either world, and
  love is sure of love.

KINSMAN.

DIED AT THE ISLAND OF PANAY (PHI-
LIPPINE GROUP), AGED 19 YEARS.

WHERE ceaseless Spring her garland
  twines,
  As sweetly shall the loved one rest,
As if beneath the whispering pines
  And maple shadows of the West.

Ye mourn, O hearts of home ! for him,
  But, haply, mourn ye not alone ;
For him shall far-off eyes be dim,
  And pity speak in tongues unknown.

There needs no graven line to give
  The story of his blameless youth ;
All hearts shall throb intuitive,
  And nature guess the simple truth.

The very meaning of his name
  Shall many a tender tribute win ;
The stranger own his sacred claim,
  And all the world shall be his kin.

And there, as here, on main and isle,
  The dews of holy peace shall fall,
The same sweet heavens above him
  smile,
  And God's dear love be over all !

VESTA.

O CHRIST of God ! whose life and death
  Our own have reconciled,
Most quietly, most tenderly
  Take home thy star-named child !

Thy grace is in her patient eyes,
  Thy words are on her tongue ;
The very silence round her seems
  As if the angels sung.

Her smile is as a listening child's
  Who hears its mother call;
The lilies of Thy perfect peace
  About her pillow fall.

She leans from out our clinging arms
  To rest herself in Thine;
Alone to Thee, dear Lord, can we
  Our well-beloved resign!

O, less for her than for ourselves
  We bow our heads and pray;
Her setting star, like Bethlehem's,
  To Thee shall point the way!

THE HEALER.

TO A YOUNG PHYSICIAN, WITH DORÉ'S
PICTURE OF CHRIST HEALING THE
SICK.

So stood of old the holy Christ
  Amidst the suffering throng;
With whom his lightest touch sufficed
  To make the weakest strong.

That healing gift he lends to them
  Who use it in his name;
The power that filled his garment's hem
  Is evermore the same.

For lo! in human hearts unseen
  The Healer dwelleth still,
And they who make his temples clean
  The best subserve his will.

The holiest task by Heaven decreed,
  An errand all divine,
The burden of our common need
  To render less is thine.

The paths of pain are thine. Go forth
  With patience, trust, and hope;
The sufferings of a sin-sick earth
  Shall give thee ample scope.

Beside the unveiled mysteries
  Of life and death go stand,
With guarded lips and reverent eyes
  And pure of heart and hand.

So shalt thou be with power endued
  From Him who went about
The Syrian hillsides doing good,
  And casting demons out.

That Good Physician liveth yet
  Thy friend and guide to be;
The Healer by Gennesaret
  Shall walk the rounds with thee.

A CHRISTMAS CARMEN.

I.

SOUND over all waters, reach out from
  all lands,
The chorus of voices, the clasping of
  hands;
Sing hymns that were sung by the stars
  of the morn,
Sing songs of the angels when Jesus was
  born!
  With glad jubilations
  Bring hope to the nations!
The dark night is ending and dawn has
  begun:
Rise, hope of the ages, arise like the sun,
  All speech flow to music, all hearts
  beat as one!

II.

Sing the bridal of nations! with chorals
  of love
Sing out the war-vulture and sing in the
  dove,
Till the hearts of the peoples keep time
  in accord,
And the voice of the world is the voice
  of the Lord!
  Clasp hands of the nations
  In strong gratulations:
The dark night is ending and dawn has
  begun;
Rise, hope of the ages, arise like the sun,
  All speech flow to music, all hearts
  beat as one!

III.

Blow, bugles of battle, the marches of
  peace;
East, west, north, and south let the long
  quarrel cease:
Sing the song of great joy that the
  angels began,
Sing of glory to God and of good-will to
  man!
  Hark! joining in chorus
  The heavens bend o'er us!
The dark night is ending and dawn has
  begun;

Rise, hope of the ages, arise like the
  sun,
All speech flow to music, all hearts
  beat as one!

HYMN

FOR THE OPENING OF PLYMOUTH
CHURCH, ST. PAUL, MINNESOTA.

ALL things are Thine: no gift have we,
Lord of all gifts! to offer Thee ;
And hence with grateful hearts to-day,
Thy own before Thy feet we lay.

Thy will was in the builders' thought ;
Thy hand unseen amidst us wrought;

Through mortal motive, scheme and plan,
Thy wise eternal purpose ran.

No lack Thy perfect fulness knew ;
For human needs and longings grew
This house of prayer, this home of rest,
In the fair garden of the West.

In weakness and in want we call
On Thee for whom the heavens are small ;
Thy glory is Thy children's good,
Thy joy Thy tender Fatherhood.

O Father! deign these walls to bless .
Fill with Thy love their emptiness .
And let their door a gateway be
To lead us from ourselves to Thee !

POEMS BY ELIZABETH H. WHITTIER.

THE DREAM OF ARGYLE.

EARTHLY arms no more uphold him
  On his prison's stony floor ;
Waiting death in his last slumber,
  Lies the doomed MacCallum More.

And he dreams a dream of boyhood ;
  Rise again his heathery hills,
Sound again the hound's long baying,
  Cry of moor-fowl, laugh of rills.

Now he stands amidst his clansmen
  In the low, long banquet-hall,
Over grim, ancestral armor
  Sees the ruddy firelight fall.

Once again, with pulses beating,
  Hears the wandering minstrel tell
How Montrose on Inverary
  Thief-like from his mountains fell.

Down the glen, beyond the castle,
  Where the linn's swift waters shine,
Round the youthful heir of Argyle
  Shy feet glide and white arms twine.

Fairest of the rustic dancers,
  Blue-eyed Effie smiles once more,
Bends to him her snooded tresses,
  Treads with him the grassy floor.

Now he hears the pipes lamenting,
  Harpers for his mother mourn,
Slow, with sable plume and pennon,
  To her cairn of burial borne.

Then anon his dreams are darker,
  Sounds of battle fill his ears,
And the pibroch's mournful wailing
  For his father's fall he hears.

Wild Lochaber's mountain echoes
  Wail in concert for the dead,
And Loch Awe's deep waters murmur
  For the Campbell's glory fled !

Fierce and strong the godless tyrants
  Trample the apostate land,
While her poor and faithful remnant
  Wait for the Avenger's hand.

Once again at Inverary,
  Years of weary exile o'er,
Armed to lead his scattered clansmen,
  Stands the bold MacCallum More.

Once again to battle calling
  Sound the war-pipes through the glen
And the court-yard of Dunstaffnage
  Rings with tread of arméd men.

All is lost! The godless triumph,
  And the faithful ones and true
From the scaffold and the prison
  Covenant with God anew.

On the darkness of his dreaming
  Great and sudden glory shone;
Over bonds and death victorious
  Stands he by the Father's throne!

From the radiant ranks of martyrs
  Notes of joy and praise he hears,
Songs of his poor land's deliverance
  Sounding from the future years.

Lo, he wakes! but airs celestial
  Bathe him in immortal rest, .
And he sees with unsealed vision
  Scotland's cause with victory blest.

Shining hosts attend and guard him
  As he leaves his prison door;
And to death as to a triumph
  Walks the great MacCallum More!

LINES

WRITTEN ON THE DEPARTURE OF
JOSEPH STURGE, AFTER HIS VISIT
TO THE ABOLITIONISTS OF THE
UNITED STATES.

FAIR islands of the sunny sea! midst
    all rejoicing things,
No more the wailing of the slave a wild
    discordance brings;
On the lifted brows of freemen the tropic
    breezes blow,
The mildew of the bondman's toil the
    land no more shall know.

How swells from those green islands,
    where bird and leaf and flower
Are praising in their own sweet way the
    dawn of freedom's hour,
The glorious resurrection song from
    hearts rejoicing poured,
Thanksgiving for the priceless gift, —
    man's regal crown restored!

How beautiful through all the green and
    tranquil summer land,
Uplifted, as by miracle, the solemn
    churches stand!

The grass is trodden from the paths
    where waiting freemen throng,
Athirst and fainting for the cup of life
    denied so long.

O, blessed were the feet of him whose
    generous errand here
Was to unloose the captive's chain and
    dry the mourner's tear;
To lift again the fallen ones a brother's
    robber hand
Had left in pain and wretchedness by the
    waysides of the land.

The islands of the sea rejoice; the har-
    vest anthems rise;
The sower of the seed must own 't is
    marvellous in his eyes;
The old waste places are rebuilt, — the
    broken walls restored, —
And the wilderness is blooming like the
    garden of the Lord!

Thanksgiving for the holy fruit! should
    not the laborer rest,
His earnest faith and works of love have
    been so richly blest?
The pride of all fair England shall her
    ocean islands be,
And their peasantry with joyful hearts
    keep ceaseless jubilee.

Rest, never! while his countrymen have
    trampled hearts to bleed,
The stifled murmur of their wrongs his
    listening ear shall heed,
Where England's far dependencies her
    might, not *mercy*, know,
To all the crushed and suffering there
    his pitying love shall flow.

The friend of freedom everywhere, how
    mourns he for our land,
The brand of whose hypocrisy burns on
    her guilty hand!
Her thrift a theft, the robber's greed and
    cunning in her eye,
Her glory shame, her flaunting flag on
    all the winds a lie!

For us with steady strength of heart and
    zeal forever true,
The champion of the island slave the
    conflict doth renew,
His labor here hath been to point the
    Pharisaic eye
Away from empty creed and form to
    where the wounded lie.

How beautiful to us should seem the
coming feet of such !
Their garments of self-sacrifice have healing in their touch ;
Their gospel mission none may doubt,
for they heed the Master's call,
Who here walked with the multitude,
and sat at meat with all !

JOHN QUINCY ADAMS.

HE rests with the immortals ; his journey has been long :
For him no wail of sorrow, but a pæan
full and strong!
So well and bravely has he done the
work he found to do,
To justice, freedom, duty, God, and man
forever true.

Strong to the end, a man of men, from
out the strife he passed ;
The grandest hour of all his life was that
of earth the last.
Now midst his snowy hills of home to
the grave they bear him down,
The glory of his fourscore years resting
on him like a crown.

The mourning of the many bells, the
drooping flags, all seem
Like some dim, unreal pageant passing
onward in a dream ;
And following with the living to his last
and narrow bed,
Methinks I see a shadowy band, a train
of noble dead.

'T is a strange and weird procession that
is slowly moving on,
The phantom patriots gathered to the
funeral of their son !
In shadowy guise they move along, brave
Otis with hushed tread,
And Warren walking reverently by the
father of the dead.

Gliding foremost in the misty band a
gentle form is there,
In the white robes of the angels and
their glory round her hair.
She hovers near and bends above her
world-wide honored child,
And the joy that heaven alone can know
beams on her features mild.

And so they bear him to his grave in
the fulness of his years,
True sage and prophet, leaving us in a
time of many fears.
Nevermore amid the darkness of our
wild and evil day
Shall his voice be heard to cheer us,
shall his finger point the way.

DR. KANE IN CUBA.

A NOBLE life is in thy care,
A sacred trust to thee is given ;
Bright Island ! let thy healing air
Be to him as the breath of Heaven.

The marvel of his daring life —
The self-forgetting leader bold —
Stirs, like the trumpet's call to strife,
A million hearts of meaner mould.

Eyes that shall never meet his own
Look dim with tears across the sea,
Where from the dark and icy zone,
Sweet Isle of Flowers ! he comes to thee.

Fold him in rest, O pitying clime !
Give back his wasted strength again ;
Soothe, with thy endless summer time,
His winter-wearied heart and brain.

Sing soft and low, thou tropic bird,
From out the fragrant, flowery tree, —
The ear that hears thee now has heard
The ice-break of the winter sea.

Through his long watch of awful night,
He saw the Bear in Northern skies ;
Now, to the Southern Cross of light
He lifts in hope his weary eyes.

Prayers from the hearts that watched in
fear,
When the dark North no answer gave,
Rise, trembling, to the Father's ear,
That still His love may help and save.

LADY FRANKLIN.

FOLD thy hands, thy work is over ;
Cool thy watching eyes with tears ;
Let thy poor heart, over-wearied,
Rest alike from hopes and fears. —

Hopes, that saw with sleepless vision
  One sad picture fading slow ;
Fears, that followed, vague and name-
    less,
  Lifting back the veils of snow.

For thy brave one, for thy lost one,
  Truest heart of woman, weep !
Owning still the love that granted
  Unto thy beloved sleep.

Not for him that hour of terror
  When, the long ice-battle o'er,
In the sunless day his comrades
  Deathward trod the Polar shore.

Spared the cruel cold and famine,
  Spared the fainting heart's despair,
What but that could mercy grant him ?
  What but that has been thy prayer ?

Dear to thee that last memorial
  From the cairn beside the sea ;
Evermore the month of roses
  Shall be sacred time to thee.

Sad it is the mournful yew-tree
  O'er his slumbers may not wave ;
Sad it is the English daisy
  May not blossom on his grave.

But his tomb shall storm and winter
  Shape and fashion year by year,
Pile his mighty mausoleum,
  Block by block, and tier on tier.

Guardian of its gleaming portal
  Shall his stainless honor be,
While thy love, a sweet immortal,
  Hovers o'er the winter sea.

NIGHT AND DEATH.

The storm-wind is howling
  Through old pines afar ;
The drear night is falling
  Without moon or star.

The roused sea is lashing
  The bold shore behind,
And the moan of its ebbing
  Keeps time with the wind.

On, on through the darkness,

Where, like moaning of broken hearts,
  Surges the grass !

I see her lone head-stone, —
  'T is white as a shroud ;
Like a pall, hangs above it
  The low drooping cloud.

Who speaks through the dark night
  And lull of the wind ?
'T is the sound of the pine-leaves
  And sea-waves behind.

The dead girl is silent, —
  I stand by her now ;
And her pulse beats no quicker,
  Nor crimsons her brow.

The small hand that trembled,
  When last in my own,
Lies patient and folded,
  And colder than stone.

Like the white blossoms falling
  To-night in the gale,
So she in her beauty
  Sank mournful and pale.

Yet I loved her ! I utter
  Such words by her grave,
As I would not have spoken
  Her last breath to save.

Of *her* love the angels
  In heaven might tell,
While mine would be whispered
  With shudders in hell !

'T was well that the white ones
  Who bore her to bliss
Shut out from her new life
  The vision of this.

Else, sure as I stand here,
  And speak of my love,
She would leave for my darkness
  Her glory above.

THE MEETING WATERS.

Close beside the meeting waters,
  Long I stood as in a dream,
Watching how the little river

Calm and still the mingled current
　Glided to the waiting sea ;
On its breast serenely pictured
　Floating cloud and skirting tree.

And I thought, " O human spirit !
　Strong and deep and pure and blest,
Let the stream of my existence
　Blend with thine, and find its rest ! "

I could die as dies the river,
　In that current deep and wide ;
I would live as live its waters,
　Flashing from a stronger tide !

THE WEDDING VEIL.

DEAR Anna, when I brought her veil,
　Her white veil, on her wedding night,
Threw o'er my thin brown hair its folds,
　And, laughing, turned me to the light.

"See, Bessie, see ! you wear at last
　The bridal veil, forsworn for years ! "
She saw my face, — her laugh was
　　hushed,
　Her happy eyes were filled with tears.

With kindly haste and trembling hand
　She drew away the gauzy mist ;
" Forgive, dear heart ! " her sweet voice
　　said :
　Her loving lips my forehead kissed.

We passed from out the searching light ;
　The summer night was calm and fair :
I did not see her pitying eyes,
　I felt her soft hand smooth my hair.

Her tender love unlocked my heart ;
　Mid falling tears, at last I said,
" Forsworn indeed to me that veil
　Because I only love the dead ! "

She stood one moment statue-still,
　And, musing, spake in undertone,
" The living love may colder grow ;
　The dead is safe with God alone ! "

CHARITY.

THE pilgrim and stranger who through
　　the day
Holds over the desert his trackless way,
Where the terrible sands no shade have
　　known,
No sound of life save his camel's moan,
Hears, at last, through the mercy of
　　Allah to all,
From his tent-door at evening the Be-
　　douin's call :
" *Whoever thou art whose need is great,*
In the name of God, the Compassionate
And Merciful One, for thee I wait ! "

For gifts in His name of food and rest
The tents of Islam of God are blest,
Thou who hast faith in the Christ above,
Shall the Koran teach thee the Law of
　　Love ? —
O Christian ! — open thy heart and door,
Cry east and west to the wandering poor :
" *Whoever thou art whose need is great,*
In the name of Christ, the Compassionate
And Merciful One, for thee I wait ! "

NOTES.

NOTE 1, page 1

MOGG MEGONE, or Hegone, was a leader among the Saco Indians, in the bloody war of 1677. He attacked and captured the garrison at Black Point, October 12th of that year; and cut off, at the same time, a party of Englishmen near Saco River. From a deed signed by this Indian in 1664, and from other circumstances, it seems that, previous to the war, he had mingled much with the colonists. On this account, he was probably selected by the principal sachems as their agent in the treaty signed in November, 1676.

NOTE 2, page 1.

Baron de St. Castine came to Canada in 1644. Leaving his civilized companions, he plunged into the great wilderness and settled among the Penobscot Indians, near the mouth of their noble river. He here took for his wives the daughters of the great Modocawando, — the most powerful sachem of the East. His castle was plundered by Governor Andros, during his reckless administration; and the enraged Baron is supposed to have excited the Indians into open hostility to the English.

NOTE 3, page 2.

The owner and commander of the garrison at Black Point, which Mogg attacked and plundered. He was an old man at the period to which the tale relates.

NOTE 4, page 2.

Major Phillips, one of the principal men of the Colony. His garrison sustained a long and terrible siege by the savages. As a magistrate and a gentleman, he exacted of his plebeian neighbors a remarkable degree of deference. The Court Records of the settlement inform us that an individual was fined for the heinous offence of saying that "Major Phillips's mare was as lean as an Indian dog."

NOTE 5, [

Captain Harmon, o York, was, for many ye Eastern Indians. In or up the Kennebec Rive party of rangers, he di the savages asleep by tiously creeping towa was certain of his aim, to single out their obj charge killed or mor whole number of the u

NOTE 6, [

Wood Island, near Saco. It was visited Monts and Champlain, lowing extract, from latter, relates to it : Kennebec, we ran alo westward, and cast an island, near the mainl twenty or more natives island, beautifully cl growth of forest trees, oak and walnut ; and vines, that, in their sea lent grapes. We nam Bacchus."— *Les Voya; plain*, Liv. 2, c. 8.

NOTE 7, [

John Bonython was Bonython, Gent., one c and able magistrates of proved to be "a dege 1635, we find, by the C for some offence, he i 1640, he was fined fo Gibson, the minister, Soon after he was fined duct in the house of hi the "Great and Genera John Bonython outlawe any of his Majesty's la him a rebel." (Court R ince, 1645.) In 1651, he bade defiance to the laws of Massachusetts, and was again outlawed. He acted independently of all law and authority ; and hence, doubtless, his burlesque title of "The Sagamore of Saco," which has come down to the present generation in the following epitaph : —

"Here lies Bonython ; the Sagamore of Saco,
He lived a rogue, and died a knave, and went
to Hobomoko."

By some means or other, he obtained a large estate. In this poem, I have taken some liberties with him, not strictly warranted by historical facts, although the conduct imputed to him is in keeping with his general character. Over the last years of his life lingers a deep obscurity. Even the manner of his death is uncertain. He was supposed to have been killed by the Indians ; but this is doubted by the able and indefatigable author of the History of Saco and Biddeford. — Part I. p. 115.

NOTE 8, page 2.

Foxwell's Brook flows from a marsh or bog, called the "Heath," in Saco, containing thirteen hundred acres. On this brook, and surrounded by wild and romantic scenery, is a beautiful waterfall, of more than sixty feet.

NOTE 9, page 3.

Hiacoomes, the first Christian preacher on Martha's Vineyard ; for a biography of whom the reader is referred to Increase Mayhew's account of the Praying Indians, 1726. The following is related of him : "One Lord's day, after meeting, where Hiacoomes had been preaching, there came in a Powwaw very angry, and said, 'I know all the meeting Indians are liars. You say you don't care for the Powwaws' ; — then calling two or three of them by name, he railed at them, and told them they were deceived, for the Powwaws could kill all the meeting Indians, if they set about it. But Hiacoomes told him that he would be in the midst of all the Powwaws in the island, and they should do the utmost they could against him ; and when they should do their worst by their witchcraft to kill him, he would without fear set himself against them, by remembering Jehovah. He told them also he did put all the Powwaws under his heel. Such was the faith of this good man. Nor were these Powwaws ever able to do these Christian Indians any hurt, though others were frequently hurt and killed by them." — *Mayhew*, pp. 6, 7, c. I.

NOTE 10, page 4.

"The tooth-ache," says Roger Williams in his observations upon the language and customs of the New England tribes, "is the only paine which will force their stoute hearts to cry." He afterwards remarks that even the Indian women never cry as he has heard "some of their men in this paine."

NOTE 11, page 5.

Wuttamuttata, "Let us drink." *Weekan*, "It is sweet." *Vide* Roger Williams's Key to the Indian Language, "in that parte of America called New England." London, 1643, p. 35.

NOTE 12, page 6.

Wetuomanit, — a house god, or demon. "They — the Indians — have given me the names of thirty-seven gods which I have, all which in their solemne Worships they invoke !" R. Williams's Briefe Observations of the Customs, Manners, Worships, &c., of the Natives, in Peace and Warre, in Life and Death : on all which is added Spiritual Observations, General and Particular, of Chiefe and Special use — upon all occasions — to all the English inhabiting these parts ; yet Pleasant and Profitable to the view of all Mene. — p. 110, c. 21.

NOTE 13, page 7

Mt. Desert Island, the Bald Mountain upon which overlooks Frenchman's and Penobscot Bay. It was upon this island that the Jesuits made their earliest settlement.

NOTE 14, page 8.

Father Hennepin, a missionary among the Iroquois, mentions that the Indians believed him to be a conjurer, and that they were particularly afraid of a bright silver chalice which he had in his possession. "The Indians," says Père Jerome Lallamant, "fear us as the greatest sorcerers on earth."

NOTE 15, page 8.

Bomazeen is spoken of by Penhallow, as "the famous warrior and chieftain of Norridgewock." He was killed in the attack of the English upon Norridgewock, in 1724.

NOTE 16, page 9.

Père Ralle, or Rasles, was one of the most zealous and indefatigable of that band of Jesuit missionaries who, at the beginning of the seventeenth century, penetrated the forests of America, with the avowed object of converting the heathen. The

of the Jesuits, to the · exhortation, for the purpose of inspiring
ierica, was in 1611. them with horror at those vices to which
s for the conversion they are most addicted, or to confirm them
Catholic faith knew in the practice of some particular virtue."
, they plunged into *Vide Lettres Edifiantes et Cur.*, Vol. VI.
lderness ; habituated p. 127.
hardships and priva-
uffered cold, hunger,

NOTE 17, page 12.

ith itself, by the ex- The character of Ralle has probably
'ère Brebeuf, after never been correctly delineated. By his
e of his mission for brethren of the Romish Church, he has
with his companion, been nearly apotheosized. On the other
burned alive. To hand, our Puritan historians have repre-
the names of those sented him as a demon in human form.
it to death by the He was undoubtedly sincere in his devotion
arnier, Buteaux, La to the interests of his church, and not over-
onstantin, and Lie- scrupulous as to the means of advancing
says Father Lalla- those interests. "The French," says the
de ce qui s'est dans author of the History of Saco and Bidde-
640, c. 3, "we have ford, "after the peace of 1713, secretly
le piece of bark of a promised to supply the Indians with arms
:, a handful or two and ammunition, if they would renew hos-
or soaked in water, tilities. Their principal agent was the
es our hunger ; and celebrated Ralle, the French Jesuit." — p.
g to perform even the 215.
igion, without being
rs." Their success

NOTE 18, page 13.

wever, by no means Hertel de Rouville was an active and
ns. Père Lallamant unsparing enemy of the English. He was
to adult persons, in the leader of the combined French and
little apparent suc- Indian forces which destroyed Deerfield
there have been noth- and massacred its inhabitants, in 1703.
vhirlwinds from that He was afterwards killed in the attack
upon Haverhill. Tradition says that, on
examining his dead body, his head and face
stablished himself, were found to be perfectly smooth, without
year 1670, at Nor- the slightest appearance of hair or beard.
ontinued more than
accused, and perhaps

NOTE 19, page 13.

exciting his praying
English, whom he *Cowesass ? — tawhich wessaseen ?* Are
emies not only of his you afraid ? — why fear you ?
atholic religion. He

NOTE 20, page 15.

lish, in 1724, at the
h his own hands had Winnepurkit, otherwise called George,
church was broken Sachem of Saugus, married a daughter of
ither killed outright Passaconaway, the great Pennacook chieftain, in 1662. The wedding took place at
y Ralle to his nephew Pennacook (now Concord, N. H.), and the
ing account of his ceremonies closed with a great feast. Ac-
labors : "All my cording to the usages of the chiefs, Passa-
he church regularly conaway ordered a select number of his men
t, very early in the to accompany the newly-married couple
ass, and again in the to the dwelling of the husband, where in
he prayers at sunset. turn there was another great feast. Some
x the imagination of time after, the wife of Winnepurkit ex-
ntion is easily dis- pressing a desire to visit her father's house,
osed prayers, calcu- was permitted to go, accompanied by a
with just sentiments brave escort of her husband's chief men.
: of our altars : they But when she wished to return, her father
e them aloud, during sent a messenger to Saugus, informing her
ling to them on Sun- husband, and asking him to come and take
I seldom let a work- her away. He returned for answer that
t making a concise

ne had escorted his wife to her father's house in a style that became a chief, and that now if she wished to return, her father must send her back in the same way. This Passaconaway refused to do, and it is said that here terminated the connection of his daughter with the Saugus chief. — *Vide Morton's New Canaan.*

NOTE 21, page 18.

This was the name which the Indians of New England gave to two or three of their principal chiefs, to whom all their inferior sagamores acknowledged allegiance. Passaconaway seems to have been one of these chiefs. His residence was at Pennacook. (Mass. Hist. Coll., Vol. III. pp. 21, 22.) " He was regarded," says Hubbard, " as a great sorcerer, and his fame was widely spread. It was said of him that he could cause a green leaf to grow in winter, trees to dance, water to burn, &c. He was, undoubtedly, one of those shrewd and powerful men whose achievements are always regarded by a barbarous people as the result of supernatural aid. The Indians gave to such the names of Powahs or Panisees." " The Panisees are men of great courage and wisdom, and to these the Devill appeareth more familiarly than to others." — *Winslow's Relation.*

NOTE 22, page 20.

" The Indians," says Roger Williams, " have a god whom they call Wetuomauit, who presides over the household."

NOTE 23, page 22.

There are rocks in the river at the Falls of Amoskeag, in the cavities of which, tradition says, the Indians formerly stored and concealed their corn.

NOTE 24, page 23.

The Spring God. — See *Roger Williams's Key,* &c.

NOTE 25, page 25.

" Mat wonck kunna-monee." We shall see thee or her no more. — *Vide Roger Williams's Key to the Indian Language.*

NOTE 26, page 26.

" The Great South West God." — See *Roger Williams's Observations,* &c.

NOTE 27, page 26.

The celebrated Captain Smith. after resigning the government of the Colony in Virginia, in his capacity of " Admiral of New England," made a careful survey of the coast from Penobscot to Cape Cod, in the summer of 1614.

NOTE 28, page 26.

Lake Winnipiseogee, — *The Smile of the Great Spirit,* — the source of one of the branches of the Merrimack.

NOTE 29, page 26.

Captain Smith gave to the promontory, now called Cape Ann, the name of Tragabizanda, in memory of his young and beautiful mistress of that name, who, while he was a captive at Constantinople, like Desdemona, " loved him for the dangers he had passed."

NOTE 30, page 27.

Some three or four years since, a fragment of a statue, rudely chiselled from dark gray stone, was found in the town of Bradford, on the Merrimack. Its origin must be left entirely to conjecture. The fact that the ancient Northmen visited New England, some centuries before the discoveries of Columbus, is now very generally admitted.

NOTE 31, page 36.

De Soto, in the sixteenth century, penetrated into the wilds of the new world in search of gold and the fountain of perpetual youth.

NOTE 32, page 41.

TOUSSAINT L'OUVERTURE, the black chieftain of Hayti, was a slave on the plantation " de Libertas," belonging to M. BAYOU. When the rising of the negroes took place, in 1791, TOUSSAINT refused to join them until he had aided M. BAYOU and his family to escape to Baltimore. The white man had discovered in Toussaint many noble qualities, and had instructed him in some of the first branches of education ; and the preservation of his life was owing to the negro's gratitude for this kindness.

In 1797, Toussaint L'Ouverture was appointed, by the French government, General-in-Chief of the armies of St. Domingo, and, as such, signed the Convention with General Maitland for the evacuation of the island by the British. From this period, until 1801, the island, under the government of Toussaint, was happy, tranquil, and prosperous. The miserable attempt of Napoleon to re-establish slavery in St. Domingo, although it failed of its intended object, proved fatal to the negro chieftain. Treacherously seized by Leclerc, he was hurried on board a vessel by night, and conveyed to France, where he was confined in a cold subterranean dungeon, at Besançon, where, in April, 1803, he died. The treatment of Toussaint finds a parallel only in the murder of the Duke D'Enghien. It was the remark of Godwin, in his Lectures, that the West India Islands, since their first discovery by Columbus, could not boast of a single name which deserves comparison with that of Toussaint L'Ouverture.

Note 33, page 43.

The reader may, perhaps, call to mind the beautiful sonnet of William Wordsworth, addressed to Toussaint L'Ouverture, during his confinement in France.

" Toussaint! — thou most unhappy man of men!
Whether the whistling rustic tends his plough
Within thy hearing, or thou liest now
Buried in some deep dungeon's earless den ;
O miserable chieftain! — where and when
Wilt thou find patience? — Yet, die not, do
      thou
Wear rather in thy bonds a cheerful brow ;
Though fallen thyself, never to rise again,
Live and take comfort. Thou hast left behind
Powers that will work for thee ; air, earth, and
      skies, —
There 's not a breathing of the common wind
That will forget thee : thou hast great allies.
Thy friends are exultations, agonies,
And love, and man's unconquerable mind."

Note 34, page 43.

The French ship LE RODEUR, with a crew of twenty-two men, and with one hundred and sixty negro slaves, sailed from Bonny, in Africa, April, 1819. On approaching the line, a terrible malady broke out, — an obstinate disease of the eyes, — contagious, and altogether beyond the resources of medicine. It was aggravated by the scarcity of water among the slaves (only half a wineglass per day being allowed to an individual), and by the extreme impurity of the air in which they breathed. By the advice of the physician, they were brought upon deck occasionally ; but some of the poor wretches, locking themselves in each other's arms, leaped overboard, in the hope, which so universally prevails among them, of being swiftly transported to their own homes in Africa. To check this, the captain ordered several who were stopped in the attempt to be shot, or hanged, before their companions. The disease extended to the crew ; and one after another were smitten with it, until only *one* remained unaffected. Yet even this dreadful condition did not preclude calculation : to save the expense of supporting slaves rendered unsalable, and to obtain grounds for a claim against the underwriters, *thirty-six of the negroes, having become blind, were thrown into the sea and drowned !*

In the midst of their dreadful fears lest the solitary individual, whose sight remained unaffected, should also be seized with the malady, a sail was discovered. It was the Spanish slaver, Leon. The same disease had been there ; and, horrible to tell, all the crew had become blind ! Unable to assist each other, the vessels parted. The Spanish ship has never since been heard of. The Rodeur reached Guadaloupe on the 21st of June ; the only man who had escaped the disease, and had thus been enabled to steer the slaver into port, caught it in three days after its arrival.— *Speech of M. Benjamin Constant, in the French Chamber of Deputies,* June 17, 1820.

Note 35, page 61.

The Northern author of the Congressional rule against receiving petitions of the people on the subject of Slavery.

Note 36, page 70.

Dr. Thacher, surgeon in Scammel's regiment, in his description of the siege of Yorktown, says : " The labor on the Virginia plantations is performed altogether by a species of the human race cruelly wrested from their native country, and doomed to perpetual bondage, while their masters are manfully contending for freedom and the natural rights of man. Such is the inconsistency of human nature." Eighteen hundred slaves were found at Yorktown, after its surrender, and restored to their masters. Well was it said by Dr. Barnes, in his late work on Slavery : " No slave was any nearer his freedom after the surrender of Yorktown than when Patrick Henry first taught the notes of liberty to echo among the hills and vales of Virginia."

Note 37, page 76.

• The rights and liberties affirmed by MAGNA CHARTA were deemed of such importance, in the thirteenth century, that the Bishops, twice a year, with tapers burning, and in their pontifical robes, pronounced, in the presence of the king and the representatives of the estates of England, the greater excommunication against the infringer of that instrument. The imposing ceremony took place in the great Hall of Westminster. A copy of the curse, as pronounced in 1253, declares that, " by the authority of Almighty God, and the blessed Apostles and Martyrs, and all the saints in heaven, all those who violate the English liberties, and secretly or openly, by deed, word, or counsel, do make statutes, *or observe them being made,* against said liberties, are accursed and sequestered from the company of heaven and the sacraments of the Holy Church."

WILLIAM PENN, in his admirable political pamphlet, "England's Present Interest considered," alluding to the curse of the Charter-breakers, says : "I am no Roman Catholic, and little value their other curses ; yet I declare I would not for the world incur this curse, as every man deservedly doth, who offers violence to the fundamental freedom thereby repeated and confirmed."

NOTE 38, page 91.

"The manner in which the Waldenses and heretics disseminated their principles among the Catholic gentry, was by carrying with them a box of trinkets, or articles of dress. Having entered the houses of the gentry and disposed of some of their goods, they cautiously intimated that they had commodities far more valuable than these, — inestimable jewels, which they would show if they could be protected from the clergy. They would then give their purchasers a Bible or Testament ; and thereby many were deluded into heresy."— *R. Saccho.*

NOTE 39, page 107.

Chalkley Hall, near Frankford, Pa., the residence of THOMAS CHALKLEY, an eminent minister of the Friends' denomination. He was one of the early settlers of the Colony, and his Journal, which was published in 1749, presents a quaint but beautiful picture of a life of unostentatious and simple goodness. He was the master of a merchant vessel, and, in his visits to the West Indies and Great Britain, omitted no opportunity to labor for the highest interests of his fellow-men. During a temporary residence in Philadelphia, in the summer of 1838, the quiet and beautiful scenery around the ancient village of Frankford frequently attracted me from the heat and bustle of the city.

NOTE 40, page 110.

August. Soliloq. cap. xxxi. " Interrogavi Terram," &c.

NOTE 41, page 112.

For the idea of this line, I am indebted to Emerson, in his inimitable sonnet to the Rhodora, —

"If eyes were made for seeing,
Then Beauty is its own excuse for being."

NOTE 42, page 121.

Among the earliest converts to the doctrines of Friends in Scotland was Barclay of Ury, an old and distinguished soldier, who had fought under Gustavus Adolphus, in Germany. As a Quaker, he became the object of persecution and abuse at the hands of the magistrates and the populace. None bore the indignities of the mob with greater patience and nobleness of soul than this once proud gentleman and soldier. One of his friends, on an occasion of uncommon rudeness, lamented that he should be treated so harshly in his old age who had been so honored before. "I find more satisfaction," said Barclay, "as well as honor, in being thus insulted for my religious principles, than when, a few years ago, it was usual for the magistrates, as I passed the city of Aberdeen, to meet me on the road and conduct me to public entertainment in their hall, and then escort me out again, to gain my favor."

NOTE 43, page 131.

Lucy Hooper died at Brooklyn, L. I., on the 1st of 8th mo., 1841, aged 24 years.

NOTE 44, page 132.

The last time I saw Dr. Channing was in the summer of 1841, when, in company with my English friend, Joseph Sturge, so well known for his philanthropic labors and liberal political opinions, I visited him in his summer residence in Rhode Island. In recalling the impressions of that visit, it can scarcely be necessary to say, that I have no reference to the peculiar religious opinions of a man whose life, beautifully and truly manifested above the atmosphere of sect, is now the world's common legacy.

NOTE 45, page 135.

"O vine of Sibmah ! I will weep for thee with the weeping of Jazer !" — *Jeremiah* xlviii. 32.

NOTE 46, page 138.

Sophia Sturge, sister of Joseph Sturge, of Birmingham, the President of the British Complete Suffrage Association, died in the 6th month, 1845. She was the colleague, counsellor, and ever-ready helpmate of her brother in all his vast designs of beneficence. The Birmingham Pilot says of her : "Never, perhaps, were the active and passive virtues of the human character more harmoniously and beautifully blended than in this excellent woman."

NOTE 47, page 139.

Winnipiseogee : "Smile of the Great Spirit."

NOTE 48, page 142.

This legend is the subject of a celebrated picture by Tintoretto, of which Mr. Rogers possesses the original sketch. The slave

NOTES.

405

lies on the ground, amid a crowd of spectators, who look on, animated by all the various emotions of sympathy, rage, terror; a woman, in front, with a child in her arms, has always been admired for the lifelike vivacity of her attitude and expression. The executioner holds up the broken implements ; St. Mark, with a headlong movement, seems to rush down from heaven in haste to save his worshipper. The dramatic grouping in this picture is wonderful ; the coloring, in its gorgeous depth and harmony, is, in Mr. Rogers's sketch, finer than in the picture.—*Mrs. Jamieson's Poetry of Sacred and Legendary Art*, Vol. I. p. 121.

NOTE 49, page 143.

Pennant, in his "Voyage to the Hebrides," describes the holy well of Loch Maree, the waters of which were supposed to effect a miraculous cure of melancholy, trouble, and insanity.

NOTE 50, page 145.

The writer of these lines is no enemy of Catholics. He has, on more than one occasion, exposed himself to the censures of his Protestant brethren, by his strenuous endeavors to procure indemnification for the owners of the convent destroyed near Boston. He defended the cause of the Irish patriots long before it had become popular in this country ; and he was one of the first to urge the most liberal aid to the suffering and starving population of the Catholic island. The severity of his language finds its ample apology in the reluctant confession of one of the most eminent Romish priests, the eloquent and devoted Father Ventura.

NOTE 51, page 146.

Ebenezer Elliott, the intelligence of whose death has recently reached us, was, to the artisans of England, what Burns was to the peasantry of Scotland. His "Corn-law Rhymes" contributed not a little to that overwhelming tide of popular opinion and feeling which resulted in the repeal of the tax on bread. Well has the eloquent author of "The Reforms and Reformers of Great Britain" said of him. "Not com-

of Clarkson and Romilly, cannot fail to admire his simple and beautiful record of a tour through Europe, in the years 1818 and 1819, in the company of his American friend, Stephen Grellett.

NOTE 53, page 154.

" Thou 'mind'st n e of a story told
In rare Bernardin's leaves of gold."

The incident here referred to is related in a note to Bernardin Henri Saint Pierre's *Etudes de la Nature.*

" We arrived at the habitation of the Hermits a little before they sat down to their table, and while they were still at church. J. J. Rousseau proposed to me to offer up our devotions. The hermits were reciting the Litanies of Providence, which are remarkably beautiful. After we had addressed our prayers to God, and the hermits were proceeding to the refectory, Rousseau said to me, with his heart overflowing, ' At this moment I experience what is said in the gospel : *Where two or three are gathered together in my name, there am I in the midst of them.* There is here a feeling of peace and happiness which penetrates the soul.' I said, ' If Fenelon had lived, you would have been a Catholic.' He exclaimed, with tears in his eyes, ' O, if Fenelon were alive, I would struggle to get into his service, even as a lackey ! '"

In my sketch of Saint Pierre, it will be seen that I have somewhat antedated the period of his old age. At that time he was not probably more than fifty. In describing him, I have by no means exaggerated his own history of his mental condition at the period of the story. In the fragmentary Sequel to his Studies of Nature, he thus speaks of himself : " The ingratitude of those of whom I had deserved kindness, unexpected family misfortunes, the total loss of my small patrimony through enterprises solely undertaken for the benefit of my country, the debts under which I lay oppressed, the blasting of all my hopes, —these combined calamities made dreadful inroads upon my health and reason. . . . . I found it impossible to continue in a room where there was company, especially if the doors were shut. I could not even cross an alley in a public garden, if mind and body to the counsels of his friend, J. J. Rousseau. "I renounced," says he, "my books. I threw my eyes upon the works of nature, which spake to all my senses a language which neither time nor nations have it in their power to alter. Thenceforth my histories and my journals were the herbage of the fields and meadows. My thoughts did not go forth painfully after them, as in the case of human systems ; but their thoughts, under a thousand engaging forms, quietly sought me. In these I studied, without effort, the laws of that Universal Wisdom which had surrounded me from the cradle, but on which heretofore I had bestowed little attention."

Speaking of Rousseau, he says : "I derived inexpressible satisfaction from his society. What I prized still more than his genius, was his probity. He was one of the few literary characters, tried in the furnace of affliction, to whom you could, with perfect security, confide your most secret thoughts. . . . . Even when he deviated, and became the victim of himself or of others, he could forget his own misery in devotion to the welfare of mankind. He was uniformly the advocate of the miserable. There might be inscribed on his tomb these affecting words from that Book of which he carried always about him some select passages, during the last years of his life : *His sins, which are many, are forgiven, for he loved much.*"

NOTE 54, page 155.

"Like that the gray-haired sea-king passed."

Dr. Hooker, who accompanied Sir James Ross in his expedition of 1841, thus describes the appearance of that unknown land of frost and fire which was seen in latitude 77° south, — a stupendous chain of mountains, the whole mass of which, from its highest point to the ocean, was covered with everlasting snow and ice : —

"The water and the sky were both as blue, or rather more intensely blue, than I have ever seen them in the tropics, and all the coast was one mass of dazzlingly beautiful peaks of snow, which, when the sun approached the horizon, reflected the most brilliant tints of golden yellow and scarlet ; and then, to see the dark cloud of smoke, tinged with flame, rising from the volcano in a perfect unbroken column, one side jet-black, the other giving back the colors of the sun, sometimes turning off at a right angle by some current of wind, and stretching many miles to leeward ! This was a sight so surpassing everything that can be imagined, and so heightened by the consciousness that we had penetrated, un-der the guidance of our commander, into regions far beyond what was ever deemed practicable, that it caused a feeling of awe to steal over us at the consideration of our own comparative insignificance and helplessness, and at the same time an indescribable feeling of the greatness of the Creator in the works of his hand."

NOTE 55, page 161.

The election of Charles Sumner to the U. S. Senate "followed hard upon" the rendition of the fugitive Sims by the U. S. officials and the armed police of Boston.

NOTE 56, page 164.

The storming of the city of Derne, in 1805, by General Eaton, at the head of nine Americans, forty Greeks, and a motley array of Turks and Arabs, was one of those feats of hardihood and daring which have in all ages attracted the admiration of the multitude. The higher and holier heroism of Christian self-denial and sacrifice, in the humble walks of private duty, is seldom so well appreciated.

NOTE 57, page 167.

It is proper to say that these lines are the joint impromptus of my sister and myself. They are inserted here as an expression of our admiration of the gifted stranger whom we have since learned to love as a friend.

NOTE 58, page 171.

This ballad was originally published in a prose work of the author's, as the song of a wandering Milesian schoolmaster.

In the seventeenth century, slavery in the New World was by no means confined to the natives of Africa. Political offenders and criminals were transported by the British government to the plantations of Barbadoes and Virginia, where they were sold like cattle in the market. Kidnapping of free and innocent white persons was practised to a considerable extent in the seaports of the United Kingdom.

NOTE 59, page 172.

It can scarcely be necessary to say that there are elements in the character and passages in the history of the great Hungarian statesman and orator, which necessarily command the admiration of those, even, who believe that no political revolution was ever worth the price of human blood.

NOTE 60, page 175.

"Homilies from Oldbug hear."

Dr. W——, author of "The Puritan," under the name of Jonathan Oldbug.

Note 61, page 187.

William Forster, of Norwich, England, died in East Tennessee, in the 1st month, 1854, while engaged in presenting to the governors of the States of this Union the address of his religious society on the evils of slavery. He was the relative and coadjutor of the Buxtons, Gurneys, and Frys; and his whole life, extending almost to threescore and ten years, was a pure and beautiful example of Christian benevolence. He had travelled over Europe, and visited most of its sovereigns, to plead against the slave-trade and slavery; and had twice before made visits to this country, under impressions of religious duty.

Note 62, page 188.

No more fitting inscription could be placed on the tombstone of Robert Rantoul than this : " He died at his post in Congress, and his last words were a protest in the name of Democracy against the Fugitive-Slave Law."

Note 63, page 200.

"*Sebah, Oasis of Fezzan, 10th March,* 1846. — This evening the female slaves were unusually excited in singing, and I had the curiosity to ask my negro servant, Said, what they were singing about. As many of them were natives of his own country, he had no difficulty in translating the Mandara or Bornou language. I had often asked the Moors to translate their songs for me, but got no satisfactory account from them. Said at first said, ' O, they sing of *Rubee* ' (God). ' What do you mean ? ' I replied, impatiently. ' O, don't you know ? ' he continued, ' they asked God to give them their *Atka* ! ' (certificate of freedom.) I inquired, ' Is that all ? Said : ' No ; they say, " Where are we going ? The world is large. *O God ! Where are we going ? O God !* " ' I inquired, ' What else ? ' Said : ' They remember their country, Bornou, and say, "*Bornou was a pleasant country, full of all good things ; but this is a bad country, and we are miserable !* " ' ' Do they say anything else ? ' Said : ' No ; they repeat these words over and over again, and add, " O God ! give us our *Atka, and let us return again to our dear home.*" '

" I am not surprised I got little satisfaction when I asked the Moors about the songs of their slaves. Who will say that the above words are not a very appropriate song ? What could have been more congenially adapted to their then woful condition ? It is not to be wondered at that these poor bondwomen cheer up their hearts, in their long, lonely, and painful wanderings over the desert, with words and sentiments like these ; but I have often observed that their fatigue and sufferings were too great for them to strike up this melancholy dirge, and many days their plaintive strains never broke over the silence of the desert." — *Richardson's Journal.*

Note 64, page 201.

One of the latest and most interesting items of Eastern news is the statement that Slavery has been formally and totally abolished in Egypt.

Note 65, page 213.

A letter from England, in the *Friends' Review,* says : "Joseph Sturge, with a companion, Thomas Harvey, has been visiting the shores of Finland, to ascertain the amount of mischief and loss to poor and peaceable sufferers, occasioned by the gunboats of the Allied squadrons in the late war, with a view to obtaining relief for them."

Note 66, page 226.

A remarkable custom, brought from the Old Country, formerly prevailed in the rural districts of New England. On the death of a member of the family, the bees were at once informed of the event, and their hives dressed in mourning. This ceremonial was supposed to be necessary to prevent the swarms from leaving their hives and seeking a new home.

Note 67, page 235.

" Too late I loved Thee, O Beauty of ancient days, yet ever new ! And lo ! Thou wert within, and I abroad searching for thee. Thou wert with me, but I was not with Thee." — *August. Soliloq.*, Book X.

Note 68, page 235.

" And I saw that there was an Ocean of Darkness and Death : but an infinite Ocean of Light and Love flowed over the Ocean of Darkness : And in that I saw the infinite Love of God." — *George Fox's Journal.*

Note 69, page 243.

The massacre of unarmed and unoffending men, in Southern Kansas, took place near the Marais du Cygne of the French *voyageurs.*

Note 70, page 254.

Read at the Friends' School Anniversary, Providence, R. I., 6th mo., 1860.

Note 71, page 264.

See English caricatures of America:

Slaveholder and cowhide, with the motto,
"Have n't I a right to wallop my nigger?"

Note 72, page 266.

It is recorded that the Chians, when subjugated by Mithridates of Cappadocia, were delivered up to their own slaves, to be carried away captive to Colchis. Athenæus considers this a just punishment for their wickedness in first introducing the slave-trade into Greece. From this ancient villany of the Chians the proverb arose, "The Chian hath bought himself a master."

Note 73, page 270.

This ballad was written on the occasion of a Horticultural Festival. Cobbler Keezar was a noted character among the first settlers in the valley of the Merrimack.

Note 74, page 283.

Lieutenant Herndon's Report of the Exploration of the Amazon has a striking description of the peculiar and melancholy notes of a bird heard by night on the shores of the river. The Indian guides called it "The Cry of a Lost Soul"!

Note 75, page 361.

Eleonora Johanna Von Merlau, or, as Sewall the Quaker Historian gives it, Von Merlane, a noble young lady of Frankfort, seems to have held among the Mystics of that city very much such a position as Annia Maria Schurmaus did among the Labadists of Holland. William Penn appears to have shared the admiration of her own immediate circle for this accomplished and gifted lady.

Note 76, page 363.

Magister Johann Kelpius, a graduate of the University of Helmstadt, came to Pennsylvania in 1694, with a company of German Mystics. They made their home in the woods on the Wissahickon, a little west of the Quaker settlement of Germantown. Kelpius was a believer in the near approach of the Millennium, and was a devout student of the Book of Revelation, and the *Morgen-Rothe* of Jacob Behmen. He called his settlement "The Woman in the Wilderness" (*Das Weib in der Wueste*). He was only twenty-four years of age when he came to America, but his gravity, learning, and devotion placed him at the head of the settlement. He disliked the Quakers, because he thought they were too exclusive in the matter of ministers. He was, like most of the Mystics, opposed to the severe doctrinal views of Calvin and even Luther, declaring "that he could as little agree with the *Damnamus* of the

Augsburg Confession
of the Council of Tre
He died in 1704, sit
surrounded by his gr
vious to his death it
his famous "Stone c
river, where that n
times of Van Helm
Agrippa has lain ovei

Note 77,

Peter Sluyter, or
Wesel, united hims
Labadists, who beliei
mission of John D
Catholic priest conve
enthusiastic, eloque
cere in his special c
separate the true an
the Church of Chris
and hypocrisy of the
Keith and Robert E
Amsterdam and after
ties of Herford and V
ing to Gerard Croes,
them on some points
take him into the So
offer, if it was reall)
tainly doubtful, w
Friends at least,
Herford in Westp
daughter of the E
Labadie and his foll
santly, and succeedc
enthusiasm among t
lected their business
citements and strang
women, it was said,
drank and danced t
marriages, or spiritua
Labadie died in 1674
mark, maintaining h
last. "Nothing rem
"except to go to
merely ascending frc
rower chamber to om
In 1679, Peter Slu
kers were sent to An
nity at the Castle
journal, translated
edited by Henry C.
recently published
Historical Society.
verts, and among the
of Hermanns, the prc
of land at the head
known as Bohemia
tained a grant of this
upon it a communit
time a hundred souls
statements are on
headship of this spiri
pline of which seems

than monastic severity. Certain it is that he bought and sold slaves, and manifested more interest in the world's goods than became a believer in the near Millennium. He evinces in his journal an overweening spiritual pride, and speaks contemptuously of other professors, especially the Quakers whom he met in his travels. The latter, on the contrary, seem to have looked favorably upon the Labadists, and uniformly speak of them courteously and kindly. His journal shows him to have been destitute of common gratitude and Christian charity. He threw himself upon the generous hospitality of the Friends wherever he went, and repaid their kindness by the coarsest abuse and misrepresentation.

NOTE 78, page 364.

Among the pioneer Friends were many men of learning and broad and liberal views. Penn was conversant with every department of literature and philosophy. Thomas Lloyd was a ripe and rare scholar. The great Loganian Library of Philadelphia bears witness to the varied learning and classical taste of its donor, James Logan. Thomas Story, member of the Council of State, Master of the Rolls, and Commissioner of Claims under William Penn, and an able minister of his Society, took a deep interest in scientific questions, and in a letter to his friend Logan, written while on a religious visit to Great Britain, seems to have anticipated the conclusion of modern geologists. "I spent," he says, "some months, especially at Scarborough, during the season attending meetings, at whose high cliffs and the variety of strata therein and their several positions I further learned and was confirmed in some things, — that the earth is of much older date as to the beginning of it than the time assigned in the Holy Scriptures as commonly understood, which is suited to the common capacities of mankind, as to six days of progressive work, by which I understand certain long and competent periods of time, and not natural days." It was sometimes made a matter of reproach by the Anabaptists and other sects, that the Quakers read profane writings and philosophies, and that they quoted heathen moralists in support of their views. Sluyter and Dankers, in their journal of American travels, visiting a Quaker preacher's house at Burlington, on the Delaware, found "a volume of Virgil lying on the window, as if it were a common hand-book ; also Helmont's book on Medicine (*Ortus Medicinæ, id est Initia Physica inaudita progressus medecinæ novus in morborum ultionam ad vitam longam*), whom, in an introduction they have made to it, they make to pass for one of their own sect, although in his lifetime he did not know anything about Quakers." It would appear from this that the half-mystical, half-scientific writings of the alchemist and philosopher of Vilverdo had not escaped the notice of Friends, and that they had included him in their broad eclecticism.

NOTE 79, page 364.

"The Quaker's Meeting," a painting by E. Hemskerck (supposed to be Egbert Hemskerck the younger, son of Egbert Hemskerck the old), in which William Penn and others — among them Charles II., or the Duke of York — are represented along with the rudest and most stolid class of the British rural population at that period. Hemskerck came to London from Holland with King William in 1689. He delighted in wild, grotesque subjects, such as the nocturnal intercourse of witches and the temptation of St. Anthony. Whatever was strange and uncommon attracted his free pencil. Judging from the portrait of Penn, he must have drawn his faces, figures, and costumes from life, although there may be something of caricature in the convulsed attitudes of two or three of the figures.

NOTE 80, page 366.

In one of his letters addressed to his friends in Germany he says : "These wild men, who never in their life heard Christ's teachings about temperance and contentment, herein far surpass the Christians. They live far more contented and unconcerned for the morrow. They do not overreach in trade. They know nothing of our everlasting pomp and stylishness. They neither curse nor swear, are temperate in food and drink, and if any of them get drunk, the mouth-Christians are at fault, who, for the sake of accursed lucre, sell them strong drink."

Again he wrote in 1698 to his father that he finds the Indians reasonable people, willing to accept good teaching and manners, evincing an inward piety toward God, and more eager, in fact, to understand things divine than many among you who in the pulpit teach Christ in word, but by ungodly life deny him.

"It is evident," says Professor Seidenstecker, "Pastorius holds up the Indian as Nature's unspoiled child to the eyes of the 'European Babel,' somewhat after the same manner in which Tacitus used the barbarian *Germani* to shame his degenerate countrymen."

As believers in the universality of the Saving Light, the outlook of early Friends upon the heathen was a very cheerful and hopeful one. God was as near to them as to Jew or Anglo-Saxon ; as accessible at Timbuctoo as at Rome or Geneva. Not the letter of Scripture, but the spirit which dictated it, was of saving efficacy. Robert Barclay is nowhere more powerful than in his argument for the salvation of the heathen, who live according to their light, without knowing even the name of Christ. William Penn thought Socrates as good a Christian as Richard Baxter. Early Fathers of the Church, as Origen and Justin Martyr, held broader views on this point than modern Evangelicals. Even Augustine, from whom Calvin borrowed his theology, admits that he has no controversy with the admirable philosophers, Plato and Plotinus. " Nor do I think," he says in *De Civ. Dei.*, lib. xviii., cap. 47, "that the Jews dare affirm that none belonged unto God but the Israelites."

INDEX.

412   INDEX.